I AM ROME

A NOVEL OF

Julius Caesar

I AM ROME

SANTIAGO POSTEGUILLO

Translated by
FRANCES RIDDLE

BALLANTINE BOOKS

NEW YORK

Translation copyright © 2024 by
Penguin Random House Editorial SAU

Published in the United States by Ballantine Books,
an imprint of Random House,
a division of Penguin Random House LLC, New York.

BALLANTINE is a registered trademark and the colophon
is a trademark of Penguin Random House LLC.

Originally published in Spain as *Roma Soy Yo* by B,
an imprint of Penguin Random House Grupo Editorial,
Madrid, Spain, in 2022. Copyright © 2022 by Santiago Posteguillo.
Represented by Agencia Literaria Carmen Balcells, S.A.

Hardback ISBN 978-0-593-59804-7
Ebook ISBN 978-0-593-59805-4
Printed in Canada on acid-free paper
randomhousebooks.com

2 4 6 8 9 7 5 3 1
FIRST EDITION
Book design by Barbara M. Bachman

To my daughter Elsa,
who is my day and my night,
and to Alba,
my new dawn

Cowards die many times before their deaths.
The valiant never taste of death but once.

—WILLIAM SHAKESPEARE,
Julius Caesar, ACT I SCENE II

I AM ROME

Principium

THE WOMAN SPOKE QUIETLY TO HER BABY AS SHE ROCKED him. "Always remember your ancestors," she said. "I, your mother, descend from an ancient lineage, the *gens* Aurelia, heralds of the cult of the sun. In you, my bloodline converges with your father's, and he is of the gens Julia, a noble family that refuses to amass wealth through corruption and violence like so many others. The gens Julia holds the most special birthright in all of Rome: the goddess Venus lay with the shepherd Anchises and from them Aeneas was born. As a young man, Aeneas fled the city of Troy as it burned to the ground, escaping with his father, his wife Creusa, and their son Ascanius, who in Rome we call Julus. Years later, the beautiful princess Rhea Silvia of Alba Longa, direct descendant of Julus, would be possessed by the god Mars himself, and from that union Romulus and Remus were born. Romulus founded Rome, and here we are today. You are a direct descendant of Julus, from whom the gens Julia takes its name.

"This world that you have yet to take your first steps into is ruled by patrician families like your own. Many powerful senators have built immense fortunes in Rome's recent years of growth, and because of this they believe themselves to be chosen and special, favored by the gods, granted the right to do as they please. They feel superior to other citizens and to the *socii*, our allies in broader Italy. These vile senators call themselves the optimates, the best. But remember, my son: Your family descends directly from Julus, son of Aeneas; you share the blood of Venus and of Mars. You are uniquely special. You alone, my little one. You alone. And I pray to Venus and to Mars that they may protect you and guide you in times of peace as well as in times of war. Because you will see war, my son. That is your destiny. I can only hope that in those times of war you will be as strong as Mars, as victorious as Venus. Remember this always, my son: You are Rome."

Aurelia repeated the story over and over to her infant son like a prayer. And, although he did not understand her words, they filtered into his mind and settled in his memory, forever etched onto his brain, as if carved in stone, forging Julius Caesar's destiny.

Prooemium

Rome's growth is unstoppable.

Since the fall of the Carthaginian Empire, Rome has become the dominant power in the Western Mediterranean region. Already controlling Hispania, Sicily, Sardinia, Italy, and parts of northern Africa, it has begun to set its sights farther, on Cisalpine Gaul, the Celtic lands north of Italy, and Greece and Macedonia to the east.

Rome's expansion has filled the republic's coffers to the brim, but the distribution of wealth and conquered lands is far from equal. A small group of aristocratic senators accumulates ever more territory, ever more riches, while the vast majority of those governed by Rome remain deeply impoverished. All confiscated lands, gold, silver, and slaves are controlled by a few landowning senators from patrician families.

Such blatant inequality leads to conflict: the Assembly of the Roman People demands a more equal allotment of wealth and power. A few bold men speak out in favor of redistribution. Tiberius Sempronius Gracchus is among them. Son of famed Roman mother Cornelia and grandson of the great statesman Scipio Africanus, he is chosen as plebeian tribune, the people's highest representative, and sponsors a law of land redistribution in the year 133 B.C. But the Senate ambushes him on one of the city's main thoroughfares, beating him to death in broad daylight and tossing his body into the Tiber, without a proper burial. His brother, Gaius Sempronius Gracchus, is later elected plebeian tribune and attempts to further Tiberius's reforms. In response, the Senate passes an unprecedented decree granting the Roman consuls, top leaders of the Senate, the authority to detain and execute Gaius Gracchus or any other plebeian tribune who supports the redistribution of lands. In 121 B.C., finding himself surrounded by the Senate's assassins, Gaius Gracchus asks a slave to kill him so that he does not fall into his enemies' hands.

Supporters of the Gracchi brothers and their thwarted attempts at reform join forces to create a group that calls itself the *populares,* "in defense of the people." The more conservative senators, in turn, form the party of the optimates, meaning "the best," since they consider themselves to be superior and favored by the gods. Rome is officially divided into two opposing political factions when a third group emerges. The socii, inhabitants of Rome's allied cities in broader Italy, demand Roman citizenship and the right to vote so that they might take part in decisions that affect them directly.

The Assembly of the Roman People, time and again, elects new plebeian tribunes who, over and over, try to pass reforms like those initiated by the Gracchi years prior. All of them are systematically killed by the optimate senators. Finally, a young Roman appears, patrician by birth but sympathetic to the demands of the populares and the socii. He understands that a fourth group has entered the fray: the inhabitants of the new Roman provinces that have been annexed from Hispania to Greece and Macedonia, from the Alps to Africa.

This young man believes that it is time for things to change once and for all, but he is only twenty-three years old, with few supporters. In fact, hardly anyone in Rome has even taken notice of him. That is, until a trial in the year 77 B.C. when this man, despite his youth, agrees to prosecute a powerful senator.

The defendant, accused of corruption during his term as governor of Macedonia, is none other than optimate senator Gnaeus Cornelius Dolabella, who amassed unthinkable wealth and power as a close ally to the tyrannical Lucius Cornelius Sulla, former dictator of Rome.

Sulla, during his dictatorship, decreed that senators could only be tried by a jury of their peers: other senators. This means that the tribunal set to hear Dolabella's case is composed entirely of optimates and is expected to fully exonerate Dolabella, who has also hired the two best defense attorneys in Rome: Hortensius and Aurelius Cotta. Seeing the case as a lost cause, no Roman lawyer will agree to prosecute Dolabella. Only a madman or a fool would bring charges against such a powerful senator under such disadvantageous circumstances.

Until one man finally steps forward. Dolabella laughs when they tell him who has agreed to serve as prosecutor in the trial against him. He continues his endless series of parties and banquets, secure in the notion that his case has already been won.

The name of the inexperienced young lawyer who agrees to prosecute him is Gaius Julius Caesar.

The Trial

I

PETITIO

During the petitio period of a Roman trial, any free person may formally seek a lawyer to serve as either defense attorney or prosecutor for a given case. Should a non-Roman citizen wish to bring a Roman citizen to trial, they must find another Roman citizen willing to serve as prosecutor and present charges for the alleged crimes.

CAESAR'S DECISION

Julia family domus
The Suburra neighborhood, Rome
77 B.C.

"EVERYONE WHO HAS ATTEMPTED SOMETHING LIKE THIS has been killed. You should not, cannot, accept their proposal. It will only lead to ruin. It's suicide." Titus Labienus spoke vehemently with the passion of someone trying to keep a friend from committing the biggest mistake of his life. "You can't change the world, Gaius, and this trial aims to do just that. Do I need to remind you of everyone who has died trying to challenge the optimates? They have always been in control and they always will be. Opposing them only spells death. And you know it."

Caesar listened intently to his childhood friend's heartfelt advice but for the moment remained silent.

Cornelia, Caesar's young wife of nineteen, stood watching the scene from the center of the domus atrium. He paced around her, weighing Labienus's words and contemplating the response he would give the Macedonian men who had come seeking his help. The three Macedonians themselves sat nearby, looking on uncomfortably as Labienus made his case.

As Labienus watched Caesar circle Cornelia—the action symbolic of how central she was to him—he appealed to his friend's wife. "Cornelia, by Hercules, you love Gaius. Tell him that for your sake, for his mother's sake, for the sake of his family, he has to reject this insane proposal. Dolabella is untouchable. Your husband already escaped a death sentence once before, for defying Sulla. If he takes on Sulla's favorite crony now, in this trial, he's as good as dead. By all the gods, help me reason with him!"

Cornelia blinked as she stood listening to Labienus. Just then, the sound of crying filled the air. Little Julia, Caesar and Cornelia's daughter, barely five years old, appeared in the atrium with her nursemaid close at her heels.

"I'm sorry, *domina,* so sorry," the nursemaid apologized. "The girl is so quick."

"Mama, Mama . . ." Julia shouted, clinging to her mother's legs.

Little Julia's interruption saved Cornelia from having to give the response Labienus demanded. "I'll be right back," she said, taking her daughter by the hand.

Caesar, wearing a serious expression, nodded to his wife.

"Goodbye, Papa," the child said as she passed him.

Gaius Julius Caesar smiled at the girl as Cornelia led her out of the atrium, followed by the nursemaid.

Labienus continued to press his case, ignoring the presence of the three Macedonians who wanted to hire Julius Caesar as their lawyer. Perdiccas, Archelaus, and Aeropus were made uncomfortable by Titus Labienus's words, but they didn't dare interrupt the discussion between the two Roman men.

"Listen to me, Gaius," Labienus continued, disregarding the Macedonians' hostile stares. "If you accept, you will most likely be defeated in trial and then murdered, either on some dark corner or perhaps even in the forum, in broad daylight. It wouldn't be the first time it's happened. The optimates think they are more powerful than ever. They *are* more powerful than ever. And even in the unlikely event that the tribunal determines in your favor, it would mean going up against Cotta, your own uncle, who Dolabella has hired for his defense. Is that really what you want? To force your mother to choose sides between her brother and her son?"

At those words Julius Caesar raised his hands slightly, as if begging his friend to be silent. He looked down and seemed to study the cracked tile floor of the family home. The gens Julia was of the patrician order, but money was not as abundant as it had once been. With the death of Caesar's paternal uncle, the great Gaius Marius, Sulla had confiscated many of the Julia family's assets as punishment for supporting the popular political faction. They couldn't even afford to repair that cursed tile. But Caesar had more pressing concerns at the moment.

"That's the crux of it," he said.

Cornelia reappeared and discreetly took her place beside her husband in the center of the atrium. Julia was back in the care of the servants. The girl was fussy. She had been sick but seemed to be on the mend. Cornelia knew that the child could feel the tension in the air and was affected by it. It was said that children could sense impending doom. She wondered if it was true. Her thoughts were interrupted by her husband's calm, firm voice.

"Is Julia all right?"

"She's fine. The fever is down. Don't worry," Cornelia responded succinctly. She always tried to be supportive of her husband and this was no time to concern him unnecessarily. He had more important things to worry about than a little girl's temper tantrums.

Labienus steered the conversation back to the issue at hand. "What's the crux of it?" he asked. He'd trotted out so many arguments in his attempt to convince Caesar that he had no idea which one his friend was referring to.

"My mother. Aurelia." He pronounced her name slowly, as if charging each syllable with the woman's great authority. "What would she think best? Should I agree to prosecute a case in which my uncle Cotta serves as the defense and, as you rightly say, cause a rift in the family? Or should I refuse to get involved, even though my blood boils? Dolabella was one of the despicable Sulla's closest allies. If only half of what they say about him is true," he said, gesturing toward the Macedonians, "he's committed unspeakable crimes. Felonies made all the more atrocious by the fact that he is a senator, someone who should set an example with his behavior. How can I let him walk free when I have the chance to submit him to public trial? After all the damage he's done to us, profiting from Sulla's confiscations of our property."

"You're not experienced enough to go up against your uncle Cotta and Hortensius, two of the most seasoned defense lawyers in all of Rome. And the judges will be bought and bribed, you can be certain," Labienus said, appealing to common sense.

The buying of judges was common practice in Rome, especially when the accused was a rich and powerful senator. And it had become even more customary now that, through Sulla's judicial reform, the tribunals that heard cases against senators were made up entirely of other senators. Dolabella had served as consul, Rome's highest political office; he had received a triumph for defeating the Thracians; and he had amassed a great fortune in the shadows of Sulla's dictatorship. And, according to the Macedonian representatives, he had increased his immense wealth even further by embezzling public funds and forcing the inhabitants of that wealthy Roman province to pay fictitious taxes. Money always won out in Roman trials, and Dolabella was too wealthy for the other senators to ever dare charge him, no matter how horrific his crimes.

"Cornelia, by all the gods, by everything you hold dear, help me convince your husband to stay out of this. It's insanity," Labienus said.

This time no child burst in to keep Cornelia from speaking her mind. Labienus knew that despite her youth, Cornelia's opinion was important to Caesar. She lowered her gaze to the scar on Labienus's left calf. The wound was a constant reminder of his debt to her husband, one more reason for his infinite loyalty to Caesar. She didn't want to contradict Labienus, but Caesar's judgment, in the end, would always win out.

"Whatever my husband decides . . ." she began, "his choice will be the correct one. I stand with him. Always." She met Caesar's eyes. "Just as he has always stood with me."

The two men understood what Cornelia was referring to. It was an event of the recent past when Caesar's love for his wife was cruelly tested and he had shown what he was truly made of.

"Whatever you decide," she repeated. Then she fixed her gaze on the floor. She didn't plan on intervening any further.

Caesar felt thankful that Cornelia wasn't going to make things harder by trying to convince him one way or another. Her neutrality permitted him to act freely. It was clear that after what had happened with Sulla she did not need any further proof of his love.

His friend's logic, however, was flawless: accepting the Macedonians' proposal was suicide and it would also spark conflict within the family. He sighed.

"Let's call your mother in," said Labienus, seeing that his friend was beginning to have doubts.

"No!" Caesar responded. "If there's one thing I'm certain of, it's that my mother wants me to make up my own mind, just as Cornelia does. My mother . . . has always taught me to be independent, no matter how much I respect her and value her advice."

Labienus shook his head, although deep down, well versed in the dynamics of his friend's family, he knew that this was exactly what the highly revered Aurelia would say if they called her into the atrium at that moment. Just like Cornelia, she would want Caesar to decide for himself. It was as if the matriarch had aimed to forge in her young son a natural leader who would defer to no one. And his wife had accepted that characteristic as something inherent to her husband's nature. But, as far as Labienus was concerned, it would only lead to disaster.

Julius Caesar looked to the Macedonians. "Why me?" he asked.

The representatives of the eastern province exchanged glances. Finally, Aeropus, the eldest of the three, spoke up: "We know that the young Julius Caesar defied the terrible dictator Sulla when so many others cowered in the face of his atrocities. We believe that you alone can stand up to Dolabella, who we accuse of stealing money from our compatriots, among other, even more abject offenses . . ." Here Aeropus had to stop and swallow his rage, not wishing to again recount the crimes against his daughter Myrtale. "Offenses . . . that we have already described. Dolabella was a friend to the reviled dictator Sulla. It has been said that he was Sulla's right hand in the civil war and in the oppression of his detractors in Rome. Only someone who was not afraid of Sulla in the past could be brave enough to now confront Dolabella, despite his wealth, his crookedness, and his cruelty. That is why we have come to plead with the young Julius Caesar, to ask that he, and no other man, should be our lawyer, our prosecutor. According to your law, only a Roman citizen can bring another Roman citizen to trial. And I don't think we'll find many Roman citizens bold enough to challenge the former governor and former consul Gnaeus Cornelius Dolabella—"

"I'll admit it, Gaius," Labienus said, interrupting the Macedonian man. "He is correct on a few points, the most dreadful ones: Dolabella is cruel. He's crooked. He has a lot of money and he'll readily use it to buy off the tribunal or hire assassins to murder anyone who becomes too much of a nuisance. And yes, it is true that you stood up to Sulla, but it is also true that it almost cost you your life. The goddess Fortuna was with you then, but I don't think it prudent to push your luck to the limits once more. I know you believe that Venus and Mars are your protectors, but I beg you, don't put them to the test."

Gaius Julius Caesar nodded several times. He looked between his friend Labienus and the Macedonian emissaries. He took a deep breath and put his hands on his hips. He nodded again and eyed the floor. Then he raised his eyes and fixed them on the Macedonians: "I agree to act as your lawyer. I will serve as prosecutor in this trial."

Labienus shook his head in disappointment.

Cornelia closed her eyes and silently begged the gods to protect her husband.

The Macedonians bowed in a gesture of appreciation and politely took their leave, not before depositing on the table a heavy bag of coins as the first payment for the prosecutor's services. Then they left the two men and the young woman alone, eager to depart before the Roman citizen had a chance to reconsider his audacious promise. Like everyone else in that great city by the Tiber, they knew full well that the trial could not be won. But at least an attempt at vengeance had been set in motion. If that failed, they had a backup plan. Dolabella, one way or another, would die for what he'd done to them. They did not care how many others might be lost in the process—all of them, perhaps, including this brave young prosecutor. It mattered little. The Macedonians were out for blood. And in their thirst for revenge they underestimated the strength of their enemy.

In the atrium of the Julia family domus in the center of the Suburra, Labienus heaved a sigh of defeat.

Julius Caesar studied the mosaic floor. The decision had been made, but he wondered how his mother would react. This was his only concern at the moment. He recalled the tales his mother had told him of the turbulent events that had taken place in Rome shortly after his birth. Would history repeat itself? Would he be just another victim of the eternal conflict between the optimates and the populares? Would he share the same fate as the rest?

He then felt the soft arms of his wife encircling him.

Caesar closed his eyes and welcomed her embrace.

MEMORIA

PRIMA*

———

AURELIA

—

CAESAR'S MOTHER

SENTENCED TO DEATH

Julia family domus
99 B.C.
Twenty-two years before Dolabella's trial

I T WAS A TIME OF ELECTIONS; IT WAS, THEREFORE, A TIME OF violence.

Brutality, death, and chaos always seemed to reach a crescendo whenever it came time to elect the men who would occupy the most important offices in the Roman Republic: consuls, plebeian tribunes, and praetors.*

Aurelia tried to calm Gaius Julius Caesar, her infant son, only a few months old. The boy had been taking his afternoon nap when he was awoken by shouting from the atrium. He started to cry, which infuriated Aurelia. It was hard to get her little one to sleep since he was a very active baby, and the young mother was convinced he needed more rest. Aurelia knew about the elections and the unchecked political tensions in Rome, but her baby took priority.

"Take him," Aurelia said as she carefully handed her baby to the

---

* Consul: the Roman Republic's highest elected position. A chief magistrate with extensive administrative, legislative, and judicial powers. Also commander in chief in times of war.

Plebeian tribune: elected leader of the Plebeian Assembly. Tribunes uniquely held the power of *intercessio*, the right to veto actions taken by magistrates, giving them the important role of acting as a check on other branches of government and protecting citizens from unfair actions.

Praetor: a powerful magistrate charged with authority over the judiciary, who could also serve as highest military commander in the consul's stead. In terms of military and administrative authority, a praetor was always below a Roman consul.

nursemaid. "Try to soothe him. I'll shut those men up, or at least get them to stop shouting like maniacs."

Aurelia strode through the halls of the Julia family domus, the home she'd managed efficiently ever since marrying Gaius Julius Caesar Sr. a few years prior. She had planned to burst into the atrium calling to the gods and scolding her husband and his friends for shouting. But then she heard the loud, clear voice of her brother-in-law Gaius Marius.

She paused.

Marius had been consul six times, including five consecutive terms, something unprecedented and normally prohibited under Roman law. Aurelia was struck by the fact that Marius sounded . . . fearful. For a six-time consul, a brave general who'd led troops to victory in dozens of battles against the barbarians, to speak with fear in his voice, something very serious must be happening.

Frozen in place beside the door to the atrium, she strained her ears.

"Saturninus and Glaucia have lost their minds," the veteran consul said.

Aurelia pressed her lips together. Saturninus and Glaucia were the current plebeian tribune and praetor. She nodded to herself. Ambitious populares always ended up clashing with the Senate, leading to revolts, disturbances, and blood in the streets of Rome.

She took a deep breath and entered the atrium.

Still wanting to express her anger, she broke with polite custom and did not greet the men gathered there. But she did not call to the gods or raise her voice, either. After all, the idea was that everyone should try to speak more calmly.

"Why do you say that Saturninus and Glaucia have lost their minds?" she asked Marius directly as she stopped beside her husband and clasped his arm. "You men have woken the baby with all your shouting. I hope it's something very serious indeed to warrant disturbing my son's rest."

"It's not a debate, Aurelia," her husband answered with a certain air of disapproval over her failure to greet their guest with the respect he deserved.

"Gaius Marius knows that he is always welcome here," she said in response to her husband's expression. "And as the practical military man he is, I am sure he doesn't mind that I've dispensed with the long-winded formalities. Is that not so, *clarissime vir** and consul?" she added with a demure smile.

Marius did, in fact, always prefer directness. The pragmatic general who had won victories over Jugurtha in Africa and the Cimbri and Teutons in the North admired the outspoken woman his brother-in-law had married. Aurelia was attractive and intelligent and would've made an outstanding legatus of the Roman legions had she not been born a woman.

"Yes, you needn't worry about your wife's candidness, Gaius. We are all friends here," the consul said, and then turned to address Aurelia. "But this is more than just another tiresome debate: Saturninus and Glaucia have hired assassins to murder Memmius, the optimates' candidate for consul."

"Violence always begets violence," Aurelia said as she lay down on a *triclinium* and gestured for Marius and her husband to do the same.

When the men had followed her example, she gestured for the atriense to bring out food and wine for their guest. Aurelia knew that with the men reclining for a meal, their moods would lighten and their voices would soften.

"Violence begets violence, yes, but the Senate is always stronger when it comes to a show of force," Gaius Marius said.

"Well then Saturninus and Glaucia should be worried, shouldn't they?" Aurelia said before inviting Marius to drink the wine that had been brought in.

Aurelia was a generous but authoritative domina, making sure she and her guests were always well attended to and that all members of the household carried out their tasks with due diligence.

Marius took a long sip of wine and sighed deeply. He had so much to do and so little time. There was an urgent life-or-death decision

---

* Common term of respect given to senators. Literally "most illustrious man." Equivalent to "Your Excellency."

to be made, which is why he'd come to talk things over with his brother-in-law. Gaius Julius Caesar Sr. was a discreet, unambitious man, something quite infrequent in Rome. He knew how to listen and always gave unexpected advice. And Caesar's wife, Aurelia, made sure Marius felt comfortable in the Julia domus. In these times of constant political treachery, finding a place where he could speak freely and feel supported was something Marius prized. He set his cup down and took in Aurelia's questioning expression.

"As you know, my victories in the North over the Cimbri and the Teutons, in addition to my triumph in Africa, have made me quite popular with the people. And this intimidates the optimates," he said, deciding to bring Aurelia up to speed so she could join in the conversation. "They have long wanted to remove me from power, which is why I allied myself with Saturninus and Glaucia, who, as populares, were also being harassed by the Senate. We made a pact to help one another obtain key political positions, and that's how Glaucia was chosen as praetor, Saturninus as plebeian tribune, and I as consul for the sixth time. Saturninus and Glaucia helped me pass the agrarian law that granted farmland to the veterans of my legions in compensation for their service. Some received land north of the Po, and others in Africa. This caused resentment among the socii of our allied cities in Italy, who felt that those lands north of the Po should go to them since they'd lived there before the Cimbri and Teuton invasions. So Saturninus, Glaucia, and I together made concessions to the Italic people and allowed them to move into the new colonies of Sicily and Macedonia. That in turn upset many Romans, who believed that access to those colonies should be their unique right as citizens, so to placate the Roman people, we agreed to distribute wheat at a subsidized price to all Roman citizens.

"And so I have rewarded my veterans, who bravely defended Rome from barbaric attacks. I have appeased the Roman masses as well as the Italic people, the socii. We've finally achieved a delicate balance where everyone is satisfied."

"Everyone except the optimates in the Senate," Aurelia pointed out.

Marius nodded, pleased but not surprised at how well his sister-in-law was able to interpret Roman politics. "Everyone except the optimates, that's right," the consul agreed. "The optimates see only a redistribution of wealth, whether it be lands, wheat, or rights, and any such redistribution makes the senators greatly uncomfortable. With the Roman people and the Italic tribes on our side, they have been hesitant to retaliate against us. But Saturninus and Glaucia have confused the Senate's inaction with weakness, and with the elections for consul coming up, they wanted Memmius out of the way . . ."

"So they killed the optimates' candidate," Aurelia said.

Marius nodded. "And the Senate could not let this violence go unanswered. They have ordered a *senatus consultum ultimum.** Every paid assassin in Rome is out looking for Saturninus and Glaucia."

A silence fell over the room. Julius Caesar Sr. wore a concerned expression and had not so much as touched the food. Marius, on the other hand, took advantage of the pause in conversation to pick up a piece of bread and a hunk of cheese. He wasn't sure when he'd have time to eat again for the next several hours, and he knew from experience that it was never good to enter into battle on an empty stomach.

"This is just how they murdered Gaius Gracchus when he confronted the optimates," Aurelia said.

"That's right," said Caesar Sr. as Marius continued eating.

"So with this new decree, the Senate means to . . . murder Glaucia and Saturninus?"

"That's right," Caesar Sr. said again.

Marius was still eating.

"And who has the Senate appointed to carry out their order?" she asked.

This time her husband just looked at his brother-in-law.

Gaius Marius stopped chewing. He quickly swallowed the bread and cheese. "Yes, they've appointed me, in my capacity as consul, to carry out the order of execution."

---

*   Literally, "ultimate decree of the Senate." An order authorizing magistrates to take measures outside the law's normal boundaries to defend the republic from its "enemies." Essentially gives legal permission to kill those mentioned in the decree.

"They mean to eliminate all your political allies," Aurelia commented, just loudly enough to be heard in the hushed atrium.

"Glaucia and Saturninus *were* my allies," Marius said, "but they failed to consult with me on their plan to assassinate Memmius."

"True, such an important decision should've been agreed upon between the three of you," Aurelia said. "They didn't confer with you because you would have been opposed."

"Without a doubt," Marius replied. "Beyond the moral issue of murder, there's also a fatal error in judgment: Saturninus and Glaucia think that the optimates are defeated, but I believe they are simply biding their time, calculating how and when to take back control. They aim to put men they can trust in the positions of plebeian tribune and praetor before dealing me the final blow. Rome tonight is crawling with the Senate's hired daggermen. I can only move around with my guards because the Senate has ordered them not to lay a hand on me as they wait to see which band I'll join—whether I'll try to protect Saturninus and Glaucia or side with the optimates and agree to carry out their senatus consultum ultimum. So that's why I'm here, because what I decide will affect my entire family, including you. If I refuse to carry out the Senate's orders, their assassins will come for me and perhaps for my friends and relatives . . . and I don't have enough men to protect us all."

A new, tense silence fell between them.

"It's Sulla," Marius said, gazing down at the atrium floor as if talking to himself. "He's a skillful manipulator. I never thought he'd go so far, but now I see it clearly: he wants to emerge as the leader of the optimates, and he has to prove his worth to Metellus and the rest who admire any man bold enough to stand up to me."

"But Sulla fought alongside you," Aurelia said, "in Africa, as *quaestor,* if I remember correctly. And then under your command against the barbarians in the North as well, didn't he?"

"You have a good memory. He was a competent soldier and very skilled at reading the enemy. But then he tried to take full credit for our victory and made himself quite disagreeable to many of my men. To me as well, which is why I backed Glaucia over him for the position of praetor. Ever since then, Sulla has been stirring up trouble for me in the Senate. But I never thought any of them would go as far as this."

"Saturninus's and Glaucia's arrogance has provoked their ire," Aurelia commented.

"Perhaps. Sulla is extremely calculating, but such a brutal response is unlike him ..." Marius sat for a moment, silently organizing his thoughts. "By Jupiter!" the consul at last exclaimed. "It's that young Dolabella. It's all becoming clear."

"Dolabella?" Aurelia and her husband asked at once. The name was new to them.

"You wouldn't know him," Marius said. "Gnaeus Cornelius Dolabella has done nothing of relevance. His father was well-known, but the son has yet to make a name for himself. His political career is hardly worth mentioning. He's never excelled at anything or occupied any important position. But he has many friends in the Senate, where he delivers long-winded diatribes that whip the optimates into a fervor. I've often seen him sitting beside Sulla, talking into his ear. That must be it: Dolabella is feeding Sulla's ego, urging him to take bold actions that may help him become a leader among the optimates. The Metelli have dominated the conservative party for the last several years, but they're old and tired, and many feel they are incapable of standing up to me. So Sulla put forth the senatus consultum ultimum as a way to place me in this complicated position, to get back at me. I knew that he'd eventually try to take me down, but I didn't think it would happen so soon."

Marius went silent again.

Gaius Julius Caesar Sr. didn't say a word, unsure what advice to give.

"So ... have you made your decision?" Aurelia asked, but then quickly corrected herself: "You have made your decision. That's why you're here. You've come to warn us."

"You're right," Marius confirmed, nodding his head several times. "I am going to arrest Saturninus and Glaucia. I have no choice, thanks to the senatus consultum ultimum and the seriousness of their crime, murdering a candidate for consul. But I will not execute them. I will arrest them and have them guarded by my men while I negotiate a trial. I still don't know how it will all work out. Tumultuous times are upon us: you should remain on alert. I'll leave men posted outside your home for as long as I can."

He stood.

"Thank you, Marius," said Gaius Julius Caesar Sr., "for thinking of us."

"Be careful," the consul responded as his hosts walked him to the door. "It was under my command that Sulla's runaway ambitions grew out of hand, and so it is my duty to now stop him. Dolabella . . . he's younger, of another generation, only just emerging as a threat. I wonder who will be there to stand up to him when Sulla and I are no longer among the living."

At that moment they heard a cry.

"Your nephew," Aurelia said. "Gaius Julius Caesar. I'll see to him."

Marius simply smiled. At the time, no one made the connection.

THE
PLEBEIAN TRIBUNE

Capitoline Hill, Rome
99 B.C.
Later that night

"TRAITOR!" SHOUTED LUCIUS APPULEIUS SATURNINUS AS HE found himself surrounded by Marius's men, veteran warriors the consul had brought to carry out the Senate's order.

Marius could have used the city's Night Guard for this task; they had pledged loyalty to him in his capacity as consul, after all. But in these times of shifting loyalties, he trusted only his own men. Also, his seasoned soldiers were better prepared to face the brutalities of the Roman night.

Marius's men, hardened in dozens of battles against the Numidians, the Cimbri, the Teutons, and other fierce, warring peoples, easily overpowered the guards that Saturninus had posted on the streets leading to the temple of Jupiter, where he had taken refuge. Saturninus's daggermen might be able to beat an unarmed senator to death on a dark street, as they'd done to Memmius, but they didn't stand a chance against the consul's battle-hardened soldiers.

"I am not a traitor, I am a survivor, Lucius, and, by Castor and Pollux, I can see things for what they are, unlike you and Glaucia," Gaius Marius responded, grabbing Saturninus by the arm to place him under arrest outside the temple.

"I helped you obtain the lands you wanted for your soldiers, your guard dogs," Saturninus practically spat. "This is how you repay me?"

"You helped me, and I, in turn, helped you and Glaucia achieve

your own political aims," Marius argued. "All three of us have benefitted from the alliance. But killing the optimates' candidate for consul was uncalled for, and too blatant a challenge to their power. It was
never part of our plan."

"You're just like the rest of them," Saturninus said angrily.

Gaius Marius had been insulted many times. In his attempts to
strike balance between the interests of the populares and the optimates, one side or the other always ended up blaming him for all the
evils of Rome. He'd prefer any battlefield—be it the parched deserts
of Africa or the dense forests of the North—to the ruthless political
conflicts in Rome, where Marius, more soldier than statesman, had
never felt fully comfortable.

They left the Capitoline Hill, strewn with the bodies of the plebeian tribune's guards, and began their descent to the forum. As they
drew nearer to the political heart of Rome, the men could feel more
and more eyes peering out at them from the shadows. The Senate's
hired assassins lurked in the darkest corners of the city. Without a
single torch to light the streets, Rome at night was more dangerous
than the blackest German forest.

"If I hadn't arrested you, they would've sent someone much less
sympathetic to your cause," Marius said quietly to the tribune, keeping a rapid pace. "Without me, you'd already be dead at the hands of
one of the assassins hired to do the Senate's dirty work. I, on the
other hand, will see that you have a fair trial."

"A fair trial? In Rome?" Saturninus laughed sarcastically.

"You're right, by Hercules," Marius said. "There's no such thing.
But while the trial is being arranged, we can buy some time to negotiate a way out for you."

Saturninus shook his head. "You've never understood politics.
The Senate must either be made to submit, or they will take everything they can. There's no middle ground. I was wrong to think them
so weak but, clarissime vir, the optimates in the Senate do not negotiate; they will never negotiate. They will continue to stamp out all
opposition, as they've been doing since the time of the Gracchi. Do
you honestly believe that you're safe just because you've carried out
their order to arrest me? They'll get rid of me first, then Glaucia, and

then you'll be next, you can count on that. They want a Senate composed entirely of optimates all equally unwilling to hear the people's
demands. They want to root out the populares in the Curia so they
can have it all for themselves. All the slaves, all the lands, all the
power."

Saturninus's argument was more solid than Marius expected from
a man in such a desperate position. They walked in silence for a few
tense minutes that felt endless, both men fearful of being ambushed
before they reached the forum.

Marius's veterans were skilled fighters, but he knew that the optimates' assassins, former gladiators or soldiers whose loyalty had been
purchased by senators such as Metellus, Sulla, or even Dolabella,
would be more difficult to defeat than Saturninus's guards.

"Where are you taking me?" Saturninus asked. "Are you going to
push me off the Tarpeian Rock? Or throw me into the Tullianum and
leave me to rot in the dungeons? Am I your new Jugurtha?"

Saturninus was referring to the African king whom Marius had
defeated and dragged through the streets of Rome before locking
him away in the prison near the forum. He clearly did not trust Marius to give him a shot at surviving.

"I'm taking you to the Curia Hostilia," he replied. "Not the Tullianum."

"The house of the Senate. That's clever, I'll admit," Saturninus
said with a tragic smile; maybe Marius really did want to help him.
"But I doubt that will stop them. They're capable of burning the
building to the ground with me inside it. I am the most antagonistic
plebeian tribune since Gaius Gracchus. The optimates will do anything to get rid of me."

"No, I don't think they'll set fire to the Senate," Marius argued.
"It's too important to them. There is only one Curia, and burning
down their own house would be a bad omen, a desperate act that
would make them seem weak and fearful. I think they'd be willing to
burn you out of anywhere else, even a temple, except maybe the temple of Vesta. Yes, the Curia Hostilia is the only safe place for you tonight."

They stopped in front of the sturdy bronze doors of the Senate building. In the dim light of the torches his men held, Marius contemplated the immense mural covering a wall of the Comitium outside the Curia Hostilia. It showed scenes of the legendary Valerius Maximus Messalla's victory against the Carthaginians and Hiero II in Sicily during the First Punic War. A massive display of power to the world, all while Rome decayed from within like a lustrous piece of fruit that, on the inside, was rotten.

Marius sighed and shook his head. "Open the doors!" he ordered, and his men obeyed. "Stay here, by Hercules!" he said to Saturninus. "My soldiers will protect you. I'll make sure you and Glaucia see a trial and that the senatus consultum ultimum is annulled so that your lives may be spared."

"You have nothing to negotiate with," the plebeian tribune argued, feeling utterly hopeless. "It's fight or die, and if you—"

"We have Metellus," Marius interrupted.

"No, never!" Saturninus howled, filled with rage. "Never, by Jupiter!"

"Shut him in!" Marius shouted in response. His soldiers pushed closed the heavy bronze doors.

Still clamoring for the gods and cursing Marius, Saturninus found himself locked inside the Senate building, the illustrious Curia Hostilia transformed into a makeshift prison in the heart of Rome. Alone in the weak light of the few torches the consul's men had lit, the plebeian tribune found it ironic that the very room in which his death sentence had been decreed was now the only safe place for him in all of Rome.

IV

AN IMPOSSIBLE
NEGOTIATION

Julia family domus, Rome
99 B.C.
That same night

GAIUS MARIUS WORE A GRAVE EXPRESSION.

He was welcomed back into the atrium of the Julia family domus by Julius Caesar Sr. and his wife Aurelia, as well as Aurelius Cotta, Aurelia's brother, who had gathered with them that turbulent night.

"What happened?" Caesar Sr. asked as he invited Marius to make himself comfortable on a triclinium.

Marius shook his head. "There's no time for drinking or rest; not tonight. I've only come to tell you how things stand and to warn you to bar your windows and doors. No one should go out tonight. Blood will run. I will try to keep it from becoming an all-out massacre, but I'm not sure I'll be able."

"There's no stopping it," Cotta said with a certain air of superiority, as if he'd warned everyone that this would happen and now that disaster had struck he delighted in the pleasure of saying *I told you so.*

Marius ignored Cotta and laid out his plan. "I have Saturninus detained in the Curia Hostilia, with Sertorius, my bravest, most loyal man, assuring that he's well guarded. Some more of my men are still out looking for Glaucia; the idiot must believe he's safer in hiding than under my custody. I will demand that they both see trial for ordering Memmius's assassination. But I will try to negotiate their death sentences down to exile. The trial will allow me to stall for time."

Aurelia could see that her brother was about to speak again, and she didn't like the tone he'd used with Marius. The man was a six-time consul who had defended Rome's borders from Jugurtha, the Cimbri, and the Teutons, all while ensuring that his soldiers were well paid and that grain was distributed to the people. And all that besides, he was her brother-in-law, and he had taken the trouble to come warn them of the machinations at work tonight. He deserved respect, even if he'd had to align himself with questionable characters such as Saturninus and Glaucia to achieve his aims. The optimate senators were much worse, lacking all scruples entirely.

So Aurelia spoke up to ask the question she knew was on her brother's mind, hoping that, coming from her, in a more careful tone, it would not seem as offensive. "What can you offer them that might tempt them to negotiate? The optimates, I mean," she said gently as she handed Marius a cup of wine she'd poured as he was speaking.

Marius accepted it and drank. "Thank you," he said, emptying it and handing it back.

Aurelia set the cup on a low table beside her and a slave immediately whisked it away before retreating into the shadows cast by the torchlight.

"I will allow the leader of the optimates, Quintus Caecilius Metellus Numidicus, to return from exile. I'm on my way to speak with his son now. His father's reinstatement is something he will want to consider."

Caesar Sr. nodded. Cotta remained silent.

Gaius Marius stood and bid them farewell, then disappeared into the black streets of Rome, escorted by his regiment of veteran warriors.

"He will not be successful," Cotta declared once Marius and his men had gone.

"Perhaps not," his sister conceded. "But I'd appreciate if you'd behave as a guest in my husband's home and, as such, abstain from making other guests feel unwelcome. I love and respect you, brother. I know you are wise and that Marius, who is great on the battlefield, might not be quite as great a statesman. But he's trying. And trying is, in itself, an achievement."

Aurelius Cotta paused a moment, then looked at his brother-in-law. "I'm sorry if I have offended you, Gaius Julius Caesar. As my sister points out, I can sometimes speak too bluntly."

"There's nothing to apologize for. But, by Hercules, I agree with Aurelia that we should be respectful of Marius. He has always kept us close."

"That's precisely my concern," Cotta said. "Being close to him may now prove dangerous. The Senate is trying to recover all the power and influence it has lost because of Marius, Saturninus, and Glaucia. The optimates are on the counterattack and they will try to grab everything they can. They've been waiting for an excuse— Memmius's assassination has provided it. Nothing will stop them now. Not even Marius, no matter how many times he's been consul."

A silence fell over the room.

Uncomfortable.

Tense.

"I should go," Cotta finally said, feeling that his hard truths were unwelcome there.

"We'll have none of that, brother," Aurelia responded. "I only ask that you be more courteous to our guests. Even if you disagree with Marius on almost everything, you have to know he is correct when he says that the city is extremely dangerous tonight."

Cotta nodded.

"So you must stay here until daylight," Aurelia said, looking to her husband.

"Yes, that would be the safest thing," Julius Caesar Sr. agreed.

"I'll have some food brought in," Aurelia said. "All we can do now, with Rome in such tumult, is stick together. I won't abide any conflict within the heart of the family."

Another domus in the Suburra, Rome

"No! Damn them! No!" Glaucia wailed as the Senate's hired assassins dragged him out of the domus where he had taken refuge as soon as he received news of the Senate's order. His first impulse had been to flee the city, but there were already hundreds of the Senate's men watching the streets. By the time he learned of the Senate's ruling, escape was already impossible.

So he hunkered down in the home of a friend, where he thought he'd be safe.

He was wrong.

The friend opened his doors to him and left, taking his family. But unbeknownst to Glaucia, the friend had in fact betrayed him immediately thereafter, revealing his location in an attempt to safeguard himself from the Senate's vengeance.

A strong pine board barred the thick wooden door, but it did little good against the huge logs used as battering rams by the Senate's henchmen. The door split open with a loud crack.

"No! Curse you all!" Glaucia screamed.

The men, brandishing sharp daggers, surrounded their victim and looked back, awaiting orders. Lucius Cornelius Sulla entered the atrium, eager to get at his prey. Metellus had divided up the night's hunt: Sulla was responsible for Glaucia, while Dolabella would see to Saturninus.

Sulla aimed to carry out his orders with lethal efficacy and earn the respect of the leading optimates. He'd proven his abilities on the battlefield; he now wanted to prove himself skilled in Roman politics as well.

"Kill him," said Sulla in a low voice, almost a whisper.

The execution order, dictated so quietly, sounded all the more sinister in its cold premeditation, devoid of rage or hatred.

"No! Please! No! By all the gods . . ." Glaucia shouted even as the daggers punctured his flesh.

Dozens of times.

Painstakingly.

Patiently.

With the calm composure of well-paid assassins.

Metellus Jr.'s domus

Quintus Caecilius Metellus Jr.* reluctantly admitted Marius into his home that black and red night in Rome.

"Wh-what do you want? Wh-why do you darken our doorway, enemy of the Metelli?" he snapped.

Metellus Pius stuttered not out of nervousness, but because of a speech impediment he'd had since childhood. It was a weakness he'd never been able to overcome, which kept him from giving public speeches and severely limited his political life. But being the son of Metellus Numidicus, the great leader of the optimates, now forced into exile, afforded him a prestigious position among the conservatives despite his clumsy manner of speaking.

They were standing in an atrium crowded with armed guards. Although Marius had been admitted with six of his own men, Metellus Jr. had so much force on his side that a half-dozen veteran warriors posed no threat.

But Marius had not come to fight, only to negotiate. An impossible negotiation, as Aurelius Cotta had said. Was he correct? He would soon find out.

"Let's set aside our old differences, Metellus," Marius said. He and the Metelli had a long-standing rivalry, its origins tracing to the war in Africa. The Metelli had taken that military campaign as something personal, their family's nontransferable legacy. Marius had not only won lead command over the Roman troops in Africa, but also achieved total victory, bringing the African king Jugurtha back to Rome and parading him through the streets in chains. Marius's blazing triumph was hard for the Metelli to swallow. They still believed that that victory, that shackled king, that triumph, should've belonged to Quintus Caecilius Metellus Numidicus.

"If I h-h-had been thinking of our p-p-past disputes, Consul, I w-wouldn't have let you through the d-door," Metellus Jr. replied with an icy glare.

---

* Later known in history as Quintus Caecilius Metellus Pius.

Marius looked around. Dozens of armed men stood in the ring of torchlight and many more loomed in the shadows, beyond the reach of the flickering flames.

"Saturninus and Glaucia have gone too far. Let's stop before Rome becomes a sea of blood."

"S-sometimes blood can be p-purifying," Metellus said, then added a phrase in Greek that Marius didn't understand: "λως εἰ τό τῶν ἡμέτερων ἐχθρῶν αἷμα ἐστίν."*

Several of Metellus's men laughed at their commander's comment.

It was not the first time that one of the Metelli had ridiculed Marius for his limited understanding of Greek. The family considered the general to be dim-witted, uncultured, and clumsy, although fortunate in combat. But their claims that he was victorious by luck and not by design were absurd: he'd accumulated too many victories against the Africans, Cimbri, and Teutons for anyone to believe it could all be attributed to the favor of the goddess Fortuna. He might not speak Greek, but he knew how to employ the Roman legions on a battlefield. The mockery irritated him, but he ignored the comment and went directly to the point. "I offer you the return of your father from exile in exchange for a pact that will ensure the lives of Saturninus and Glaucia," Marius said.

The laughter stopped.

The atrium was silent as all looked to Metellus Jr. His father, Quintus Caecilius Metellus Sr., known as Numidicus, had chosen exile over voting in favor of the laws proposed by Saturninus in the Senate. The populares had taken advantage of his departure to strip away many of his lands, formally expulse him from the Senate, and even revoke his Roman citizenship.

"The return of my f-f-father . . ." Metellus Jr. said. "With the recovery of our l-l-lands, reinstatement in the C-c-curia, and the restoration of his c-citizenship with all its r-r-rights?"

"With all rights restored," Marius agreed.

* "Especially if it's the blood of our enemies."

Another silence fell over the crowded atrium cast in dim torch-light and deep shadow. Silence in a deserted space may be peaceful, but silence among a large group of tense, armed men is terrifying.

Metellus laughed loudly, forcedly, and then stopped.

"You are not in the p-p-p-position to negotiate anything, C-c-consul. A *senatus c-c-consultum ultimum* has been issued, and the only thing you can do is ob-bey. Also . . ."

But Metellus did not finish the sentence.

"Also?" Marius asked, surprised by Metellus Jr.'s unwillingness to reach an agreement. He had been certain that the promise of his father's return, with the restoration of lost lands, rights, and citizenship, would entice him, and yet . . ."

"Also, you are too late. Glaucia and Saturninus will be executed. B-b-by your own hand, if you want to save your p-p-position, or by our men, if not. Then we, the optimates, will take control of Rome and the Senate will ap-p-prove the r-r-restoration of my father's citizenship, his p-p-properties, and his p-place in the Curia. I don't need anything from you. In f-fact . . ." he craned his neck to look over Marius's shoulder. "I believe Glaucia might already be d-dead. Is that right, Lucius?"

Gaius Marius turned around to see Lucius Cornelius Sulla wearing a bloodstained tunic. Sulla had served under Marius in Africa, helping to trap king Jugurtha. But since returning to Rome, all his efforts had gone toward impressing the Metelli and the other optimates. This sight now confirmed for Marius that Sulla, his former ally, had sided fully with his enemies.

"It's true," Sulla confirmed, throwing Marius a defiant look. "Glaucia is history." He tugged at his toga as if trying to shake the bloodstains from it.

"I knew you were involved in all of this," Marius said scornfully, "but I never imagined you'd do the dirty work yourself."

"Oh no, by Jupiter," Sulla protested laughingly. "I'd never tarnish my blade with the blood of someone as lowly as Glaucia. But unfortunately, he resisted. It got messy. A shame about the stains, but the spectacle was worth it."

Marius was about to reply, but Metellus spoke up again. "And Saturninus? By Hercules, he's the w-w-worst of the two. What's the news of him?"

"Dolabella will take care of him," Sulla said.

Marius knew nothing of Dolabella beyond his ambition. He didn't consider the man capable of anything relevant, neither good nor bad, in peace or in war. Dolabella may have encouraged Sulla to defect from Marius's ranks, but he wasn't capable of much more than poisoned speech. And he would not be able to touch Saturninus, Marius knew. They had made fun of his limited understanding of Greek, his supposed inability to negotiate; decreed that he was no longer worthy of admiration, respect, or fear. But he would have the last laugh.

"Ha! By Jupiter Optimus Maximus!" Marius said. "Yes, Saturninus is the one you most want to see dead. But he is alive and there will be a trial, and in that trial everything will come out: the crimes committed by Saturninus, yes, but also the crimes and excesses of the Senate. We'll see then if you have enough men to control Rome, with my soldiers and the people against you. Saturninus is under arrest in the Curia, and you wouldn't dare set fire to the house of the Senate. He is guarded by my top officer, Sertorius, and all my best men. So are you still so certain you don't wish to negotiate?"

Metellus looked at Sulla, his eyes filled with rage. A public trial, no matter how much they might manipulate it, was not in their best interest. Just as Marius had said, the process would reveal too many of the Senate's dirty secrets and incite the masses. The situation could easily get out of hand. No, they had to execute Glaucia and Saturninus that night, forcing Marius to take part. Once that triple alliance was destroyed, the populares would be decapitated. There would be no one left to oppose them, and, little by little, the optimates would take back total power. But with Saturninus inside the Senate, guarded by Marius's men . . .

Sulla and Marius stood sizing each other up. Marius: fifty-eight years old, six-time consul and triumphant general. Sulla: aged thirty-nine, hardly any recognized merits, defeated in the last elections for praetor thanks to the alliance between Marius, Saturninus, and Glaucia. Sulla sat watching the seasons change as his *cursus honorum,* the sequence of political offices he aspired to, remained stagnated, blocked by Marius, who detested him. Would the old man once again come out on top? No. Not this time. The consul was making a grave mistake: he underestimated Dolabella's natural talent for sowing terror. Up to now, Dolabella had only shown flashes of his truly perverse nature. Sulla understood that they had reached a turning point. He, Sulla, would now start to ascend, while the older man, Marius, began his steady decline. He turned away from Marius and looked Metellus in the eye. He spoke confidently, leaving no room for doubt.

"Dolabella will take care of Saturninus. He is"—he searched for the right word—"yes, Dolabella is . . . motivated."

Metellus immediately understood Sulla's meaning: Dolabella's father had been killed mere months prior in a clash with Saturninus's men. Without a doubt, Dolabella would be highly motivated to execute the man who had caused his father's death.

"But he won't b-b-burn the Senate to the ground, will he?" Metellus asked.

"No," Sulla answered. "Dolabella will find some other solution."

Gaius Marius looked down. He understood Dolabella's personal motivations and knew they would add fuel to his rage. He needed to get to the forum to help Sertorius defend the Curia Hostilia.

Metellus fixed his gaze on the veteran consul. He considered ordering his death then and there, but the Senate had not approved it and many still respected Marius. His legendary victory in Aquae Sextiae against the Teutons, which saved Rome from an invasion perhaps as terrible as Hannibal's, lived on in the memory of many *patres conscripti*. It was always better to remain within the law when possible. Marius would soon see his last night. They would erode his prestige a little more each day, and he'd fall from the tree of ambition like overripe fruit, as so many others had done. Glaucia was already dead. Saturninus was not likely to see the dawn. Marius's time would come . . . soon.

"I th-th-think it's time the pro-c-consul take his leave," Metellus said, and then added: "*Arx Tarpeia Capitolii proxima.*"*

---

* Possible origin of the expression "The bigger they are, the harder they fall."

Gaius Marius understood the threat clearly. "The Tarpeian Rock is near the capitol" alluded to the fact that even at the height of power, represented by the temple of Jupiter at the top of Capitoline Hill, one could easily be thrown from the Tarpeian Rock, the cliff beside the capitol used as an execution site.

The consul did not respond and he did not bid the men farewell. He simply turned and, flanked by his guards, left Metellus's home. All he could think about was getting to the Senate as quickly as possible. He still had faith in Sertorius's ability to protect Saturninus, but Sulla's rabid, feline gaze had held such assuredness over Dolabella's success. Doubts began to creep into Marius's mind as he rushed to the forum for the second time that night. He couldn't shake the feeling that disaster was about to strike.

V

STONE-COLD
JUSTICE

Roman Forum, around the Senate building
99 B.C.
That same night

GNAEUS CORNELIUS DOLABELLA, FOLLOWED BY MORE THAN a hundred of the optimates' hired daggermen, marched toward the Curia Hostilia. He was serious and silent. The men watched him. They all knew that Saturninus was behind those bronze doors, that the Senate had ordered his arrest and immediate execution, but that for Dolabella it was more than a simple legal matter—it was also something personal. And they loved a tale of vengeance.

Dolabella reached the Senate building and stopped a few paces from Sertorius, the man in charge. Sulla had spoken often of Marius's top officer, known for his bravery and efficiency. Gaius Marius had been wise to leave him in charge of securing the forum.

Dolabella didn't say a word.

For now.

He carefully weighed his options.

He knew that revenge was not something to be rushed but should be carried out with premeditation and patience, ensuring that the single, true blow was delivered in the precise moment. Not a second too soon, not a second too late.

Outside the bronze doors of the Curia Hostilia

Quintus Sertorius watched the men arrive by the dozens. The mob of assassins hired and armed by the Senate rushed like a torrent of water down the old Via Sacra and stopped when they came to the Curia Hostilia. Their leader, the young senator Gnaeus Cornelius Dolabella, stood right in front of him.

Just a few paces.

Dolabella moved closer.

He was five steps away, then four, three, two.

"Enough." Sertorius moved his right hand to the hilt of his *gladius* and gestured to unsheathe it.

Dolabella stopped. He smiled.

For a few seconds no one said a word.

Dolabella held Sertorius's hard stare.

"Leave, you and your men," Dolabella said. "Spare their blood."

"I have orders to stay here until Consul Marius returns," Sertorius replied. "And I always fulfill my orders."

"Very well," said Dolabella, still smiling. After a tense pause he rejoined the ranks of his men.

Sertorius had served in several military campaigns under Gaius Marius. No threat, whether silent or verbalized, could intimidate him. He did a quick calculation: there were a hundred of the Senate's men, all armed. On his side, he had thirty former legionaries, all well-trained veteran warriors, blocking the doors. Enough to put up a good fight and maybe even win, depending on the assassins' tenacity or how well they'd been paid.

Tucked under his tunic was the old command whistle that he'd used in many a campaign. He'd reached the rank of military tribune and even legatus, with an entire legion under his command, but the whistle reminded him of his times as a centurion. He remembered his youth fondly.

He raised the whistle to his mouth and permitted himself a faint smile. He blew with all his might.

Julia family domus

"I can't believe you really think it was a mistake for Marius to have addressed Rome's inequalities." Aurelia held her son, Caesar, on her lap as she spoke.

Cotta sighed. "No, sister, of course I don't think that. Of course I agree that more land needs to be distributed to the citizens of Rome, that we need to listen to the socii's demands and many other things . . . but now is not the time. The optimates are still strong, too strong. In fact . . . they are invincible. No one who has ever opposed them has survived for long. Not even Marius will be able to defeat them."

Caesar Sr. did not interrupt. In spite of himself, he shared his brother-in-law's pessimistic view of the situation.

Cotta shook his head. "There's not a man alive who could take on those senators . . . and win."

Aurelia did not respond. She simply kept rocking her son Caesar.

The streets of Rome

Gaius Marius left the Metellus residence newly aware that everything was much more complicated than it had seemed. Just as Cotta had warned him, the Metelli were unwilling to negotiate even with the return of Numidicus on the table. This showed that they believed themselves to be much stronger than the populares and planned to fight them to the end. Glaucia was already dead. He had Saturninus in the Senate building with Sertorius, his best man, leading the defense of the Curia Hostilia, but he could be outnumbered by the Senate's army of assassins.

Marius increased his pace.

Julia family domus

The nursemaid came to put the baby to bed, and the slaves brought in dinner. Stewed meat with Eastern spices purchased in the *tabernae,* aged goat cheeses, and abundant wine with dried fruit and nuts for dessert. A tasty, hearty meal without any luxuries, which they could not afford.

"If you think, brother, that the optimates are too strong now," said Aurelia, returning to the topic they had been discussing since before dinner, "when do you expect them to weaken? Will that ever happen?"

Julius Caesar Sr. shook his head and sighed. He was exhausted by his wife's insistence on talking politics, but his brother-in-law seemed authentically interested in the conversation.

"In some years, perhaps. By the time your young son comes of age, Rome may be ready to accept change." Cotta did not sound convincing, only hopeful. His statement, however, caused both Julius Caesar Sr. and Aurelia to pause their eating and drinking.

Roman Forum

Sertorius's command whistle screamed out across the forum.

At his call, from all sides of the Curia building, forty veteran warriors rushed to join the thirty already stationed before the bronze doors. Now there were seventy armed legionaries ready for combat against the hundred hitmen sent by the optimates.

The smile faded from Dolabella's face. The odds were no longer so clearly in his favor. Sertorius's men had fought in campaigns against the Numidians in Africa and against the Teutons in the North. Seasoned in battle, they would not be intimidated and would never surrender, no matter how unbalanced the odds. Dolabella had seen a bit of combat and he relished violence, but he knew that the majority of the men with him that night were petty criminals who used darkness and surprise to overpower innocents. They didn't stand a chance in hand-to-hand combat against these hardened fighters. He took a few steps back.

Dolabella examined his enemies' organized defense: a frontal attack would be a waste of time . . . or would it?

"What do we do?" asked one of the hitmen.

"He's failed to guard his flanks," Dolabella said to no one in particular. "He's crowded all his men in front of the door because it's the only way into the Curia Hostilia. The building has no accessible windows; it's impenetrable. The light comes in through the doors, when they're open, and from a few skylights."

"We could try to climb in through those skylights," the man suggested.

"No, we can't," Dolabella responded, "because the Senate installed thick iron bars after the last disturbances, ensuring that the building would be impregnable."

"The roof beams are made of wood. We could shoot flaming arrows to set it on fire," another one of the men proposed, eager to avoid direct combat.

Dolabella tilted his head. "Better not," he said. "For one thing, they wouldn't like it if we burned down a building with such symbolic value, and for another, the wooden beams are covered by clay tiles. The arrows would burn out before they caused much damage . . ." And there he stopped.

"So what do we do then?" asked another man. None of them wished to enter into battle with the legionaries and were eager for a different plan.

"Tiles . . ." Dolabella muttered.

Suddenly he saw what to do and he grinned. He gestured to several of his trusted guards and they gathered around to listen to his instructions. Dolabella spoke quietly. He finished transmitting his orders, and a few of the men raced from the forum down Via Sacra. The rest took up positions in front of the opposing troops.

Sertorius understood that confrontation was inevitable. Imminent.

He shrugged his shoulders.

One more battle in his life mattered little.

"Shields up, by Hercules! Unsheathe your *gladii*!" he howled.

The Senate's hired assassins, seeing the legionaries move in perfect coordination, instinctively took a few steps back.

"Stop!" Dolabella ordered.

He could see that the men were frightened of the experienced troops, but he knew that Marius's soldiers could not move from the door of the Senate. Remaining there in front of them, at a prudent distance, would be enough to distract Sertorius and his seventy men from what was happening right above their heads.

Inside the Curia

Lucius Appuleius Saturninus paced back and forth across the wide room, dimly lit by a few torches. The long and wavering shadows swept over the floor like *lemures,* the specters of the many souls condemned to death in that very room. Men like himself, who had tried to challenge the status quo, reduce the power of the patres conscripti, and expand the rights of the people.

"May the gods curse them all," Saturninus muttered to himself as he walked between the shadows.

Just then he heard a command whistle and the shouting of voices: Marius's soldiers were defending the Senate against the killers sent to murder him.

"I'm not scared of you," he hissed, facing the bronze doors.

Then he looked down.

Marius was delusional: even if the optimates agreed to negotiate, they'd never let him and Glaucia walk away from this confrontation with their lives. He had to escape. Yes, that's what he had to do. If Marius somehow managed to arrange a trial, he'd have to take advantage of any opportunity that presented itself. He had many friends in the city. Some of them might come to the trial. If he could create a distraction, he might be able to slip away. He had to at least try. He and Glaucia had already been sentenced to death. Even if the optimates agreed to a public trial, it would be a farce, like so many others.

Another sound. A strange noise, from above.

Saturninus looked up to the dark ceiling of the Curia.

More sounds, like footfalls.

Someone was walking on the roof.

Roman Forum, outside the Curia building

Sertorius was calm. Attentive to the enemy's movements, but secure in the notion that he had the situation under control. He'd been afraid they'd try to rally more men, but for the moment, there was no sign of reinforcements arriving, and the group gathered there didn't dare to come any closer . . .

"Tribune!"

Sertorius turned to the legionary who had addressed him using his former military rank. He saw that many of his men were staring at the roof of the building. In the darkness, he couldn't see exactly what was happening, but after squinting for a moment in the dim torchlight, Sertorius managed to make out some shadows moving across the tiled roof of the Curia.

"By Hercules! What are they playing at?" he exclaimed.

Roof of the Curia Hostilia

Dolabella was thirty years old and several pounds overweight. He was not agile, but he'd managed to climb up to the roof using a rope ladder his men had secured for him. He moved tentatively over the slanted surface, eager to survey the scene from above. He didn't trust anyone; no one else was as determined to do away with Saturninus as he was. From on high, he confirmed that Sertorius, just as he'd suspected, had left the other walls of the Curia unguarded in order to concentrate all of his legionaries at the door. It was logical, but it left an opportunity for someone with a bit of imagination. An opportunity that he was not about to pass up. He'd ordered his men to gather maces, ropes, and saws. They'd been perplexed but in a short time had collected everything. Many of them already carried rope, which often came in handy, especially on a night like this one, where multiple altercations were taking place across the city. They also carried maces, which were useful for so many things: breaking walls, doors, or skulls. The saws were easily stolen from a shop in the tabernae.

From his spot on the roof of the Curia, Dolabella continued giving instructions.

"Remove the tiles!" he shouted.

And his men began tossing the roof tiles to the streets below.

"No, you imbeciles!" Dolabella yelled, irate. "Take them off and pile them up on the other side! Then saw through the beams of the roof's wooden understructure! We need a good hole!"

None of them fully understood what the point of all that was, but they knew that the man they were after, the plebeian tribune, was inside the Curia and that a hole in the roof would bring them closer to their target.

Inside the Curia

Saturninus heard heavy blows against the ceiling. Some of the Senate's hired goons must've climbed the wall and were now trying to break through the roof. Suddenly, several chunks of plaster and broken brick crashed against the large mosaic tiles of the Curia floor, shattering the tesserae.

Everything happened quickly after that.

What started as a crack in the ceiling became a large hole in a matter of seconds. Saturninus expected the men to scale down with a rope tied to one of the large crossbeams, but that would leave them nowhere to run if the legionaries opened the doors and rushed in to save him. He couldn't understand exactly what they planned to do until a roof tile crashed at his feet. And then another.

He hadn't been hit, but there was nowhere to take cover. He thought about trying to climb to the stands farthest from the center, but they were also the highest up, and therefore closest to the roof, which would make him an easier target for his enemies.

He rushed around the room, not knowing what to do.

More tiles crashed down around him.

On the roof of the Curia

"By Jupiter! It's hard to aim between the beams!" one of the men shouted.

"Get the saws," said Dolabella without hesitation.

In an instant, the men were attacking the beams. They might've been decent assassins, but they did not make for good construction workers. One of them had stupidly placed himself in the center of a beam that was being sawed by his companions while he continued trying to hit the plebeian tribune with the broken roof tiles.

"Aaah!" he wailed as he felt the rafter give way beneath him and he slipped downward. The enormous beam tumbled to the mosaic floor below along with the man, dead on impact, his blood splattering the surrounding tiles.

"Imbeciles!" Dolabella said again. "Don't stand on the beams we're cutting!"

They all moved to the side.

A short while later, a second beam fell down into the Curia. They had created an enormous hole, much easier to aim through.

"Now!" Dolabella ordered.

They had a mountain of roof tiles on hand. The bombardment could now commence.

Inside the Curia

Saturninus had not yet recovered from the shock and horror of seeing one of his attackers fall to his death when, shortly thereafter, a second beam broke away and a tile exploded at his feet.

He screamed in pain as another crashed against his right shoulder. "Damn you! You miserable wretches!"

Before he had time to move, tiles began raining down all around him. He raced across the room toward the bronze doors and began to pound on them. "Open up! Open up before these madman kill me!" he wailed.

Tiles clanged loudly against the bronze doors and shattered into a thousand pieces.

On the roof of the Curia

Dolabella heard the plebeian tribune shouting for Marius's men to open the doors and let him out. He'd planned for this eventuality.

"Tell them to attack now," he ordered. The message was quickly transmitted from the edge of the roof, shouted down to the many hired hitmen still gathered on the street below.

One of them rushed to the front of the crowd with the order.

Outside the bronze doors

Sertorius frowned when he heard Saturninus's shouts from inside.

"They're going to stone him to death!" he said to one of the legionaries. "I think they're throwing roof tiles at him!"

Sertorius was about to instruct his men to open the door when a shout came from one of the men gathered before them.

"Attack now!"

Sertorius looked back at the forum. The Senate's men were charging. The veteran officer did not have time to order that the doors be opened as all of his men turned their attention to fending off the attack launched at them. He knew it was meant as a distraction, but if he did not deflect that frontal attack, they would all lose their lives.

Inside the Curia

Crack.

It was a dull thud, different from the sound of the tiles pinging the metal doors. It was quieter, with no echo, a softer blow, but an exacting one.

Saturninus's vision went cloudy. A roof tile had split open the back of his head.

He didn't lose consciousness but fell gently to the floor, his nails scraping at the bronze doors of the Senate house, which had become his prison cell, his very own Tarpeian Rock, the site of his execution. That same Senate he'd rebelled against, just as the brothers Gracchi and many other plebeian tribunes before him, all of them wiped out one by one. Saturninus, already a corpse, was nothing more than another tribune murdered by the Senate, dead within those walls, in that dragon's lair.

Clang, clang, clang.

More tiles crashed against the metal doors, falling all around him.

And then the muffled blows of the tiles that landed on his back, his head, his shoulders, his legs, his hands, as he lay motionless on the floor.

An incessant shower of deadly projectiles.

A true stoning.

Unending.

Merciless.

Stone cold.

On the roof of the Curia

"That's it," said one of the men. "That's enough. Let's get out of here, by Jupiter. Quickly."

Dolabella glared at him and everyone froze. The senator who paid them should be the one to give the orders. It seemed to everyone that the plebeian tribune was good and dead, but no one moved as they waited for their leader's response.

"I'll decide when it's been enough," Dolabella said, staring down the hired goon who'd dared to declare the mission complete.

The man lowered his head in a sign of submission.

"What should we do, clarissime vir?" one of the other men asked.

"Dump the rest of it on him."

The men hurriedly carried out the order, tossing the broken tiles down onto the inert body of the plebeian tribune until his corpse was no longer visible, completely buried under a mound of hard clay shards.

"Enough," said Dolabella. "Our message to Rome is now clear."

Roman Forum

"Attack! Attack! Attack!" Sertorius shouted.

His men, inflamed by his fury and hatred for their attackers, thrust their gladii from behind their shields with beastly power, seeking human flesh to rip into.

Several of the hired assassins fell wounded, some dead, from the force of the veteran warriors' initial push. The Senate's men quickly lost their courage and began to flee, abandoning the wounded to their fate.

"Stay! By Hercules, do not chase them!" Sertorius shouted to keep his legionaries from abandoning the door.

He knew that they longed to pursue their attackers, to complete the slaughter, but their duty was to guard the Curia, to preserve the life of . . .

He suddenly realized how long he had been distracted by the attack.

"Open the doors! Quickly!"

His men stepped away from the entrance and a dozen or so set down their shields, sheathed their swords, and rushed to open the doors.

Sertorius waited anxiously. With the Senate's men in retreat, the forum was quiet. And there were no sounds of shouting from inside the Curia. That was not a good sign.

As they pushed open the heavy doors and got their first glimpse inside, they immediately saw the bloodied arm of Lucius Appuleius Saturninus, his body buried under a true mountain of tiles. A trail of blood trickled out from beneath the improvised tomb.

Just then Gaius Marius, who had rushed down the Via Sacro to the forum, appeared at Sertorius's side. The scene did not require any explanation and he did not ask for one. The cursed Metellus had been right: he was too late.

Then, from around the side of the Curia Hostilia, Marius saw Gnaeus Cornelius Dolabella moving toward them, surrounded by men, his hard face lit by torches.

Marius and Dolabella locked eyes.

It was a challenge.

Marius suddenly felt old and tired. Dolabella had bested him. Some other man would have to take him down. But who? And when?

VI

THE BLOOD
OF AENEAS

Julia family domus
99 B.C.
That same night

"I'M SURPRISED TO HEAR THAT YOU BELIEVE THINGS CAN change in Rome," Aurelia said to her brother with a hard stare. "Gaius Marius aims to save Saturninus and Glaucia, and you've told him that his negotiation is doomed to fail. So what makes you think that something will weaken the optimates in a few years?"

"It will be some outside force," Cotta clarified.

"What? Or who?" Aurelia insisted, unwilling to accept that ambiguous response.

"The socii," Cotta answered, taking a sip of his wine before continuing. "Everyone, always, ever since the Gracchi, has focused on the inequities between the people and the Senate. But it will be the allied cities that ultimately destabilize everything, tip the balance one way or the other. If the people and the socii could join forces against the Senate, they'd surely win. But they have to be the ones to make the first move, once they get fed up. War will come—all we have to do is wait for it. Marius knows this, deep down, which is why he insisted on concessions to the allied cities. But our pacts with them need to go further. The extension of Roman citizenship beyond the walls of Rome is key."

Julius Caesar Sr. raised his eyebrows.

Aurelia frowned as a slave refilled her wine.

Knocks at the door.

The voice of Gaius Marius, calling to them.

It had been a few hours since he'd left.

At Julius Caesar Sr.'s request, the slaves opened the doors and the veteran consul entered, but he did not step into the atrium. He simply stood in the vestibule and spoke: "The Metelli have made a mockery of me. Cotta was right: they assassinated Glaucia and then stoned Saturninus to death with roof tiles in the Curia. I was attacked in the street. Only Sertorius and a few of my men managed to survive. Barricade yourselves inside; don't go out tonight. Dolabella is leading the hunt. Don't go out tonight!" he repeated before turning back into the dark, bloody, murderous streets of Rome.

Aurelia didn't say a word in the midst of the chaos that then ensued. She simply rushed to the small room where her son slept, leaving her husband and brother to supervise the barricading of the doors and windows.

"Give me the boy," she said to the nursemaid as she entered the room. The nurse carefully handed him over and rushed out.

Aurelia sat on a *solium* lined with pillows and began to rock Gaius Julius Caesar Jr. as she whispered the story she'd told him countless times. "Always remember where you come from, your roots, the origin of your family, the gens Julia, the most special and noble gens in all of Rome. The goddess Venus laid with the shepherd Anchises and from there begot Aeneas. The son of Aeneas was called Julus. You are a direct descendant of the heroes of Troy . . ."

The Trial

II

DIVINATIO

In the divinatio portion of a Roman trial,
the jury hears arguments from all lawyers
who would like to try the case and chooses
one of them as lead prosecutor.

VII

AN UNEXPECTED
OPPONENT

Via Sacra, Roman Forum
77 B.C.

Caesar and Labienus walked swiftly over the stone slabs of the city's main avenue.

Caesar was lost in thought, his eyes fixed on the ground. His mother had proved supportive of his choice to prosecute the despicable senator Dolabella on behalf of the Macedonians.

A boy with a frightened look on his face approached the two men and spoke into Labienus's ear. Caesar's friend had spread the word that he was willing to pay for useful information gathered in taverns or other gossip mills, where news often circulated well before it became public knowledge in the forum.

"I want to know anything you hear related to the case against Dolabella," he'd told his informants.

"Anything?" asked one of the young men who moved among the rabble.

"Anything at all," Labienus had said categorically as he handed the boy several silver *denarii*.

Titus Labienus wanted to help his friend Caesar, to whom he was eternally indebted.

Now, as they neared the Basilica Sempronia, a look of shock spread across Labienus's face.

"What's going on?" Caesar asked, noticing Labienus's tense, bitter expression.

Labienus knew it would be better not to dance around the issue, so he got straight to the point: "In the taverns around the port they're saying that Cicero is planning to compete for the role of lead prosecutor."

"Cicero?" Caesar said without slowing his pace. "Marcus Tullius Cicero?"

"The very same."

Caesar couldn't help letting out a nervous laugh. "By all the gods. And we were worried about Dolabella's lawyers, Hortensius and my uncle Aurelius Cotta. Don't you see the tragic comedy in it? Now I probably won't even get to prosecute the case that I myself brought before the tribunal. Cicero has won several trials, brilliantly, I might add. He's young, but older than me. What is he, thirty? I'm only twenty-three. He has experience, and his public speaking skills are lauded by everyone. I'm finished before I've even begun." Caesar laughed again.

But Labienus knew that his friend would not give up so easily. He watched closely as Caesar stopped his nervous laughter and his eyes narrowed into that feline glare that Labienus knew well. The same look he'd had as they charged into combat outside the walls of Mytilene. Labienus's slight limp would always remind him of that moment when he'd thought all hope was lost . . . He brought his mind back to the matter at hand. He was confused as to why Cicero would want to involve himself in this trial at all.

"I don't think it's Dolabella's doing," Caesar said, as if reading his friend's mind. "Cicero wants fame, prestige, like everyone. He's won several cases already and this would be his biggest one yet. He knows that successfully charging Dolabella for corruption would win him the respect of both the optimates and the populares."

"But it's a lost cause, everyone says so," Labienus argued, unconvinced.

"They think it's a lost cause with someone as inexperienced as me as prosecutor. But with a skilled lawyer like Cicero, who knows? He wants respect, prestige; he's out to make a name for himself," Caesar said. "Or perhaps he could pull out before the end of the trial or bring a weak prosecution to see Dolabella acquitted. Not many men have dared to truly challenge the optimates, after all."

"So then . . . the tribunal might choose him as prosecutor, hoping he will deliberately bring the weaker case. Or that he'll be willing to negotiate a lesser charge, as you certainly would not."

Caesar was silent for a few seconds. "Probably," the young lawyer said. "Unless . . ." But he did not finish the thought. They had arrived at the Basilica Sempronia.

"You're the one who brought this case to trial," Labienus reminded him as they entered the building. "You will speak first."

Caesar nodded. "I will speak first."

Basilica Sempronia, Rome

And, in fact, Gaius Julius Caesar spoke first.

Everything seemed to unfold very quickly, and Labienus, along with many others in attendance, was left perplexed. To the judges on the tribunal, however, Caesar's argument was exactly as expected.

A murmur went through the crowd when Caesar finished his speech. There was no applause.

Labienus placed his hand on his friend's shoulder as he took his seat. "You did well."

"No, by Hercules, I did not do well," Caesar replied. "You're a bad liar, Titus—a good friend, but a bad liar."

"You covered the things we talked about and you didn't leave anything out," Labienus said.

It was true that Caesar had been less than fully convincing, and he'd seemed to lose his train of thought a few times, but he had indeed touched on all the arguments he'd prepared the night before.

"Don't try to console me," Caesar said glumly as he searched for his mother among the crowd that filled the Basilica Sempronia.

Dolabella's trial had garnered the attention of everyone in Rome. The late dictator Sulla's right-hand man's being openly accused of corruption was all the city could talk about, to such an extent that the populist uprising in Hispania was barely discussed in the taverns. But now, Quintus Caecilius Metellus Pius, the optimate leader sent to end that rebellion and defeat its populist leader, Sertorius, was being spoken of. The fifty-three-year-old senator, returned to Rome to attend his aged mother's funeral, had been named president of the tribunal in the case against Dolabella.

Being a man who liked to have everything under control, Dolabella had begged Metellus to remain in Rome so that he might preside over the tribunal. Metellus had agreed to delay his return to Hispania for Dolabella, who had earned the Senate's respect after his stoning of that cursed plebeian tribune so many years ago. He'd all but forgotten the name of the man who'd been murdered that night; any tribune who defied the Senate did not bear remembering, to Metellus's cold, hard mind.

In allowing Metellus, one of Sulla's close allies, to preside over the trial of his fellow crony Dolabella, the Senate had shown beyond a doubt that it did not want the prosecution to stand a chance—regardless of which lawyer ended up leading it.

Caesar located his mother's penetrating gaze from the right corner of the basilica. He could read the disappointment on her face: her only son's first public speech, despite all the faith she'd placed in him, had been a total disaster.

Her expression pained him. He never wanted to let his mother down. But, on the other hand, if even his own mother had not understood what he was truly doing, then surely the tribunal had not realized it either.

Caesar continued scanning the crowd: his wife, Cornelia, just behind his mother, had lowered her gaze, clearly worried. Sitting to his left was his unexpected rival, Marcus Tullius Cicero, and beside him, the old Greek Archias, Cicero's mentor. They were going to destroy him. Without a doubt, he'd need Mars and Venus, and even Minerva, with all her ingenuity, to survive this trial with any shred of a political career intact. To survive, period.

Dolabella. Caesar looked around and found him seated comfortably in a wide *cathedra* right behind Cicero. Only the sturdiest of chairs could hold Dolabella's immense frame. Almost nothing remained of that young senator who had climbed the roof of the Curia Hostilia to stone Saturninus to death that violent night that his uncle Marius and his mother had told him of so many times. Dolabella now sat, obese, self-satisfied, smiling, chuckling with his friends over the clumsy speech that the would-be prosecutor had just delivered.

Caesar looked down. He knew that even Gaius Marius, from the underworld, would be disappointed by his stumbling argument. He had only proven to them all how green and inexperienced he was. He looked back to Dolabella. The aging senator was intentionally ignoring his presence, indifference being the greatest insult one could show toward another man.

Caesar smiled to himself. No one suspected that things were going just as he had planned.

The president of the tribunal, Quintus Caecilius Metellus Pius, looked to the other prosecutor: it was Cicero's turn. Metellus did not need to speak, a fact he was grateful for since he disliked exhibiting his stutter in public.

Marcus Tullius Cicero stood and, with a calculated slowness as he waited for the crowd to fall quiet, walked to the center of the basilica. He situated himself squarely in front of the president of the tribunal and the fifty-two judges.

Finally, the well-modulated voice of Cicero, thirty years old, at the height of his powers, flooded the large room, spellbinding his listeners, making his mentor Archias proud. He spoke without a moment of hesitation, without a single mispronounced word, without a hint of doubt in any of his well-elaborated arguments. The exact opposite of his rival, Julius Caesar.

"Respected patres conscripti, *iudices,* I thank you for the opportunity to present myself to this tribunal of men known for their great wisdom and *experience,*" he said, this last word pronounced slowly to emphasize it. "I thank you for allowing me to illustrate why a case like this one should be left to an *experienced*"—that word again—"prosecutor, and not in the hands of a rash, impulsive young lawyer"—here he turned to Caesar—"who although is no doubt well-intentioned, is nonetheless very young and totally inexperienced."

Julius Caesar held his opponent's gaze without blinking, without moving a muscle. Labienus, beside him, had the urge to march across the basilica and punch Cicero in the face, but he knew that such an action would do nothing to help his friend.

Everyone gathered there was shocked to learn that Cicero wished
to prosecute Dolabella. But Cicero, for some time now, had longed to
establish himself as a famed jurist and orator. Winning a corruption
case against the former dictator Sulla's right-hand man would be a
huge step toward that fame. Assuming, of course, that the case could
be won. Whatever his reasons, there he was, and he had the floor.
And it had to be said that he was very skilled with his words: "He is
totally inexperienced. Yes, this is an irrefutable fact, not open for interpretation or debate, not one of the half-truths or outright lies we
hear so often here in our hall of justice. Because how many public
trials, I ask you, esteemed iudices, has the young Gaius Julius Caesar
participated in?"

He paused.

"He keeps saying *young* like it's an insult," Labienus whispered.

"I know," Caesar muttered in response, without taking his eyes off
Cicero. Caesar was not allowed to object during the divinatio, so all
he could do was listen . . . and learn.

"I'll tell you," Cicero continued. "None. Our young and impetuous colleague Julius Caesar has never taken part in a single trial before today, and yet he puts himself forth as prosecutor without
consideration for the complexity of this case. I do not mean to suggest that Julius Caesar has ill intentions—merely a lack of awareness,
due, I have no doubt, to his youth." He turned again to Caesar, who
remained silent, seated in his *sella curulis,* taking in Cicero's claims.
"Perhaps some desperate desire to achieve notoriety is what has
driven this naïve lawyer to wade in too deep. In over his head. Lost at
sea. Where, undoubtedly, the Macedonians' charges will inevitably
flounder." He glanced briefly at Perdiccas, Archelaus, Aeropus, and
the other Macedonians present, but then immediately turned back to
the judges. "What is absolutely certain is that Gaius Julius Caesar has
never participated in any public trial, whereas I, Marcus Tullius Cicero, on the other hand, have systematically won three cases, in defense of Publius Quinctius, Roscio of Amerio, and Quintus Roscius.
All extremely complex, for diverse reasons. So my multiple victories
should give this tribunal faith in my ability to successfully argue the
finer points of the law, insightfully, impartially, and efficiently, since,

in each and every case I have tried, the iudices sided with me and not the opposing lawyer."

Cicero paused for a moment. He put his hands on his hips and looked down.

Caesar watched him carefully: his rival commanded the room, using only his words, his movements, his measured silences, his gaze. In the unlikely event that he was chosen as prosecutor over Cicero, he'd have to go up against his uncle Aurelius Cotta and the very skilled Hortensius, who were together defending Dolabella. Caesar looked at them, seated behind their client, giving Cicero their full attention. Their concentrated expressions were a sharp contrast to the mocking grins they'd worn as they listened to Caesar's clumsy argument. His uncle had shown restraint, clearly reluctant to humiliate his nephew, but Hortensius had laughed out loud when Caesar confused a legal term or stumbled over the names of the witnesses he had already secured for the trial. But his rival went on . . .

Cicero looked up and fixed his gaze on the Macedonians, who would be present for the entirety of the trial. Cicero had made the point of his rival's inexperience, but Caesar had put forth an argument that might have weight in the minds of the judges. This was the issue Cicero now wanted to address. He'd initially planned to leave it until the end, but he'd just conceived of a much more damning close to his speech. Now he'd turn to the issue of the Macedonians, the aggrieved parties.

Cicero faced the tribunal.

"The Macedonians, it is true, have appealed to the young Caesar and not to me. They have asked that Caesar, and no other Roman citizen, act as prosecutor. And it seems reasonable that we consider the wishes of these men who have accused Gnaeus Cornelius Dolabella of crimes against the people of their province during his time as governor there. They have chosen the young Caesar, this young lawyer, to be their lead prosecutor."

"I wish he would shut up about how *young* you are," Labienus murmured to his friend.

"Me too. But hold on, I want to listen," Caesar replied quietly. "I want to see if he finds a way to twist the fact that the Macedonians asked me to be their prosecutor. He just admitted it's something the tribunal should take into consideration."

"The only convincing argument he's made so far," Labienus agreed. "I bet he'll change the subject now . . ."

Cicero looked to the tribunal, his head tilted slightly, as he resumed his speech: "The Macedonians, it is true, asked the young Caesar to be their prosecutor. But I wonder: Do the Macedonians understand our legal system in all its complexity? The only thing that they know for certain is that, as noncitizens, they lack the right to bring formal charges against a Roman citizen and so must apply to another Roman citizen to do so. They know they cannot themselves directly bring the senator and former governor Dolabella to trial. So they have turned to young Caesar, the first person they met who was willing to listen to their accusations and take the case. But the very fact that the Macedonians do not understand the subtleties of our laws means, to me, that they need to have the most experienced lawyer possible argue their case in this basilica. And, I'd venture to say, they did not realize that there might be other Roman citizens much better prepared to serve them. So here we encounter a true moral dilemma. What should a tribunal do under such circumstances: accept the wishes of the aggrieved party and favor the prosecutor they have chosen to represent them? Or should the judges of this *quaestio perpetua,* this specialized tribunal, instead rectify the Macedonians' clear error in judgment upon hastily selecting the first person who agreed to argue their case? Would it not be more correct for the tribunal, with all their experience and wisdom, to choose the lawyer they know to be best equipped to defend the rights of the Macedonians? Yes, that is the moral dilemma that I leave for the consideration of the fifty-two wise iudices and the president magistrate who, I have no doubt, will know how to act and do not require anyone else's opinion on the matter."

Cicero paused.

He relaxed his shoulders and walked back to the center of the basilica as he continued his speech. "But there is an even bigger issue, something that concerns me greatly and which I feel obligated to call to the attention of all the members of this tribunal. I've already alluded to the intricacy of our judicial system, but this case holds a further complexity that concerns me even more. The case at hand has social and political ramifications that could lead to strong reactions from people right here in the courtroom, outside in the forum, or across the entire city. The man on trial is not some unknown citizen. No, on trial is the clarissime vir Gnaeus Cornelius Dolabella, powerful senator and close ally to the late dictator Sulla. For these reasons alone, many members of the plebeian tribune and among the general public are biased against him. And my fear is that if our more conservative senators are forced to listen to manipulative tactics by an inexperienced prosecutor instead of facts, evidence, and credible testimonies, we could see a violent reaction from some of these optimates. By the same token, if the good people of Rome perceive that the prosecution is being bungled by a clumsy, unskilled prosecutor who has not done his due diligence, we might see tumult and unrest in the streets of Rome.

"I see surprise on the faces of some of those among us, including my rival prosecutor and even some members of the tribunal. But I don't think that anyone here needs to be reminded of our recent years of political unrest, in which violence, murder, and even war have frequently caused blood to run through the streets of Rome. The war against the Marsi, one of our allied tribes in Italy who demanded Roman citizenship, is still fresh in our memory, as are the assassinations of certain optimate senators and plebeian tribunes. And it is my fear that the complex case we have at hand could light the fuse of a dormant violence in our society that, to be certain, no one wishes to revive. The defendant in this trial, who has the right to select the lawyers for his defense, has chosen Aurelius Cotta and Hortensius, two of the best jurists in our great city. Two formidable rivals that will be hard to defeat even with the best of arguments, evidence, and testimonies. We may rest assured that, from the defense, all these considerations will be taken into account." He turned now to look at Caesar. "But now that we have finally learned to coexist with relative peace, would it be prudent to leave a case that has the capacity to incite chaos and senseless violence in the inexperienced hands of Gaius Julius Caesar?"

A sarcastic smile spread across Cicero's face and he turned back to the tribunal. "I give you, as an example of what to expect, should you choose young Caesar as prosecutor, the fact that he has already revealed his main witnesses. He claims to have secured testimonies from a priest of the temple of Aphrodite in Thessaloniki and from a prestigious Roman engineer. Nothing wrong with that, except for the small detail that these witnesses have been revealed prematurely, during the divinatio, whereas the exposition of witnesses is meant to take place during the prima actio, the first session of the trial. Young Caesar has jumped ahead, galloping along as if this were a chariot race in the Circus Maximus and not a carefully structured process." Cicero walked toward the public, raising his arms. "Perhaps our young prosecutor would have more success in the carceres at the hippodrome, where he could throw some of his youthful energy into the chariot races." His arms dropped and he let out a loud laugh. The majority of those present, the audience, senators, and even judges, joined in.

Caesar swallowed Cicero's insult, recalling the advice his uncle Marius had given him when he told the story of the battle of Aquae Sextiae and how the Teutons had humiliated and taunted him. But Marius knew that he had to wait for the precise moment to attack, and in the end had been victorious. Caesar held that example in mind and did not speak. Cicero was attempting to destroy his character, but the only thing that mattered was being chosen as prosecutor. And everything was going according to his plan . . . his silent, furtive plan.

"Yes, the situation is not without its comic value," Cicero continued as if he were making an effort to suppress a laugh. "If it weren't for the fact that this haste, this rush to present his witnesses, were a sign of our young Caesar's desperate eagerness to bring this trial to a conclusion that has been predetermined by him. Because this case, to Caesar, for personal reasons I will explain in detail, is not a mere collection of evidence and testimonies.

"Lastly, I return to Gaius Julius Caesar's haste. He seems to want to rush to the end of a trial that has not yet even begun, and this haste stems from a marked lack of impartiality. And impartiality, we all know, is paramount in any judicial trial. So important is impartiality to us, as Roman citizens, that part of our judiciary process includes the reiectio, where the lawyers on either side can ask any member of the tribunal suspected to be incapable of impartiality, for whatever reason, to step down. The reiectio, another phase of the trial that comes before the exposition of witnesses, a fact of which the young Caesar seems to be unaware. I, you can be certain, will follow the order of a Roman trial to the letter.

"Speaking of the recusal process: a judge may be asked to recuse himself when he is deemed unable to rule impartially against the accused, whether due to a familial bond or a shared economic interest. Similarly, it is the tribunal's task at this stage in the judicial process to make certain that the prosecutor assigned to the case has no personal connection to the accused. I for one have no ties to Gnaeus Cornelius Dolabella beyond the fact that we are both Roman citizens. But can the same be said of young Caesar?"

Marcus Tullius Cicero paused before launching his final attack, the final blow. "Gaius Julius Caesar could never be objective or impartial in this trial. Our young lawyer is the nephew of Gaius Marius, longtime leader of the populares, whereas Dolabella, the defendant, was closely allied with Sulla, leader of the optimates. And if this clear underlying political conflict isn't enough to disqualify Julius Caesar from acting as prosecutor for this case"—here he at last left out the adjective *young*, as if it were no longer necessary to highlight his inexperience in the face of the powerful new arguments he was trotting out—"if that weren't enough, may we recall that Julius Caesar is married to Cornelia, daughter of Cinna, Gaius Marius's brutal guard dog. Sulla, Dolabella's close ally, persecuted Julius Caesar for this marriage, even going as far as to sentence him to . . ." He swept the air with his hand. "But I don't want to rehash events we are already familiar with, which will only bore the tribunal. The fact is that Julius Caesar is here not because he wants to serve as prosecutor to the Macedonians in a trial over misappropriation and extortion. Julius Caesar appears here before us today in search of revenge."

Silence.

Cicero sighed deeply. "A trial in a Roman basilica before such a worthy tribunal with an esteemed quaestio perpetua at the head is no place for personal vendettas. Gaius Julius Caesar should not be, cannot be, named prosecutor for this trial. His inexperience, the mistakes he has already made in this procedure, his familial ties, and his political leanings should bar him from consideration. He is, simply put, a hired daggerman sent by the more radical factions to draw even more blood over political differences. And our hall of justice is no place for revenge. No place for blood. It is a place for legality, legitimacy, and justice. Nothing more."

Cicero lowered his arms and fell silent, exhausted from the vehemence of his final words. Thunderous applause burst forth from every corner of the basilica.

It was clear who had won the divinatio. And who had lost.

VIII

AN UNEXPECTED
CHOICE

Basílica Sempronia, Rome
77 B.C.
Later that afternoon

THE DECISION WAS CLEAR TO ALL THOSE IN ATTENDANCE, but it was ultimately up to the tribunal. And the tribunal's decision was . . . unexpected.

The fifty-two judges announced their unanimous decision and promptly exited the great hall of the basilica, laughing and joking with each other as they went. The judges were satisfied, secure in the notion that they'd saved themselves a lot of headache by selecting the young and inexperienced Julius Caesar as lead prosecutor. The people, however, were confused: Cicero had constructed a much more solid argument and would undoubtedly do a better job prosecuting the corrupt and widely despised Dolabella. But they knew their opinions wouldn't make a bit of difference in a trial. The more intelligent among them understood that it was a calculated decision on the part of the senators. They had chosen the clumsy young lawyer to help assure that the trial would go the way they wanted without any surprises. But many were utterly bewildered by the selection. All they could do was hope that Caesar might truly be Marius's worthy successor. At least he had mentioned he had witnesses willing to testify against Dolabella. That was somewhat encouraging.

Cicero took the tribunal's decision with dignity, showing no signs of anger or disappointment as he quickly gathered his notes.

Caesar was not in such a hurry to leave. "No, Titus," he said. "Put the scrolls with the notes against Dolabella in this basket, and the scrolls with the arguments we expect from the defense in this other one."

After his disastrous first public appearance in court, he wanted to make sure everything was systematic and orderly going forward. The judges' decision had cheered him up enormously. His secret strategy had been successful.

"We didn't do so bad," he said with a slight smile.

"We?" Titus Labienus asked, puzzled to have been given any credit for the outcome.

"Without your help, I'd never have convinced them to choose me as lead prosecutor," Caesar said.

"It's the least I can do; I've hardly begun to repay my debt to you."

Caesar knew that Labienus was referring to what had happened at the siege of Mytilene. "There are no debts among friends," he replied as they continued organizing the many scrolls spread out across the table.

Labienus knew his friend was being sincere, but he still felt the weight of his debt. "One day I will make it up to you, you'll see, but it will take a lot more than helping you organize notes or come up with arguments against the vile Dolabella," Labienus said.

Caesar was about to respond when Cicero, on his way out of the basilica, paused and turned to them: "I hope you work to improve your oratory skills before the reiectio and the other phases of the trial. But to be honest, I don't think you stand even half a chance against Hortensius and Cotta. I suppose you understand why the tribunal has selected you as lead prosecutor over me."

Julius Caesar let a few seconds pass. He knew better than anyone that his arguments had been weaker, but Cicero's insulting tone put him on the defensive. "You may have expressed yourself better, but I put forth a stronger argument and I have already secured two witnesses," he replied. "You made a joke of it, but revealing my witnesses early was no mistake. It was a wise strategic move that showed the tribunal I'm further along with the case."

Now it was Cicero who smiled, cynically, as he shook his head. "So you don't know, then. You don't have a clue why the tribunal has se-

lected you. By Hercules! Hortensius and Cotta are going to have it
even easier than I thought. And to be certain, your cursus honorum,
your political career, should you aspire to political influence, will be
over the day the trial begins. The shortest trial ever held, due to your
utter incompetence."

Labienus lurched toward Cicero, causing him to take a step back.
His assistants moved in front of him. Julius Caesar put out an arm to
restrain his friend.

But just because he rejected violence didn't mean he would allow
Cicero to insult him in the middle of the Basilica Sempronia. "They
have chosen me because they saw that I have gathered more evidence
and witnesses against Dolabella. It's as simple as that," he said. "You
merely went on and on about politics and family connections."

Cicero gestured for his assistants to move out of the way and
stepped in front of Caesar. "You've made a grave mistake by telling
the jury everything you have," he said calmly. "I hope those witnesses
of yours make it to the trial alive."

"What do you mean by that?" Caesar asked.

"I know you're young, but I didn't expect you to be so naïve," Cicero said. "I mean exactly what I said: I hope you manage to present
that engineer and that priest before the tribunal, alive. Do I have to
spell it out for you? Haven't you experienced the cruelty of Sulla's
men firsthand? Don't you know how far Dolabella and senators like
him will go to defend their interests?"

Julius Caesar remained silent. Maybe it had been unwise to reveal
the names of his main witnesses so early, but he'd had so little to
argue with, and mentioning those witnesses had seemed like a good
way to assure everyone that he was diligently preparing for the trial.

Cicero took a step closer to Julius Caesar. "They chose you because you are, by far, the lesser man, the lesser orator. Because you
don't know what to say or when to say it. You're predictable and inexperienced. They've selected you, Gaius Julius Caesar, because
you're the worst possible prosecutor."

Silence hung around them like a dense cloud.

The basilica was empty except for Caesar, Labienus, Cicero, and
his assistants.

"You're wise to stay silent," Cicero said. "And, by all the gods, there's still hope." He took a deep breath before continuing: "I'll give you one piece of advice. Only because I don't like the Dolabellas of the world. Because I think we have to root out the corruption eroding the Roman Republic from the inside out, threatening to destroy it. If you're smart, you might be able to interpret my words, and maybe, with the help of the goddess Fortuna, Minerva, and the other deities, against all odds, you might be able to make Dolabella's defense nervous."

"We don't need any advice from the loser of the divinatio," said Labienus, who couldn't stand the belittling tone Cicero used with his friend.

But Caesar raised a hand to silence him. "What's your advice?" he asked.

Cicero looked first at Labienus: "This is not the advice of a loser. It's the advice of a lawyer who has won all of his trials." He then turned to Caesar: "Don't be the prosecutor. No one likes the prosecutor. You have to be the defense." And with that seemingly contradictory advice, Marcus Tullius Cicero turned and left, followed closely by his assistants.

"That's absurd," said Labienus. "Hortensius and Cotta are the defense in this case and you're the prosecutor. Do you understand what he meant? He's mocking us, that's all it is."

"No, I don't know what he meant," Caesar admitted. "But I don't think he was mocking us."

"But the prosecutor can't be the defense," Labienus insisted. "It's impossible. It's—"

"It's like a riddle," Caesar interrupted, his gaze fixed on the marble floor of the basilica as he spoke quietly: "Maybe I have to, somehow, be the prosecution and the defense . . ."

"Both at the same time?"

"Both at the same time," Caesar nodded, finally lifting his gaze.

"And how do you do that?"

"I have no idea."

Julia family domus
That night

———————

They were in their room.

Locked in embrace.

Julius Caesar lay on his back, propped against a pile of pillows. Cornelia was curled up beside him, her thin arms around her husband's neck. She ran her soft hands over his skin.

"The judges chose me as prosecutor because I'm the worst," said Julius Caesar.

"No, they chose you because they *think* you're the worst," Cornelia corrected him, kissing her husband's bare chest. "I disagree."

He smiled. "You always know just what to say to cheer me up. I'd risk my life for you all over again in a heartbeat."

"I'm glad you don't regret it," she said with her cheek on his chest. "Those months were so hard. Things would've been so much easier for you if you'd . . ." Cicero hadn't gone into detail at the trial, and she didn't want to rehash it now, either. "It would've been so much easier if you'd just done . . . what Sulla wanted you to. But you never . . . abandoned me. The least I can do is try to be a supportive wife." She swept her bare legs over the unmade bed. "The judges think you're worse than Cicero, but that's just their opinion. It's up to you to prove them wrong. I know they're wrong. In fact, I know that you're hiding something from them."

Caesar looked at her, intrigued. "What?"

She sat up and looked him in the eye. "You're not as clumsy as you pretended to be. You never stumble over your words," she said knowingly. "You faked it."

Caesar did not respond. Cornelia remained silent as well. She knew she'd touched a nerve, uncovering her husband's secret scheme. She was afraid he might be annoyed with her for having figured out his strategy, or for pointing it out.

"Yes, I pretended to be a worse orator than I am," he at last admitted. "Do you think anyone else could tell?"

"Your mother suspects it, but she wouldn't say anything, of course.

Your sisters didn't notice a thing. They were disappointed by your lack of oratory skill but happy that you were chosen in spite of it. I don't think your uncle realized what you were up to: Cotta underestimates you. And you fooled the judges completely."

Caesar listened carefully. Cornelia had just given a detailed analysis of all the relevant reactions. He knew his wife was intelligent, but he was still surprised sometimes by her perceptiveness.

She continued: "You can show them. You will show them: they're expecting the worst from you, but that's not what they'll get. I know you'll prepare your arguments carefully; I know you'll make them nervous. And that scares me, because . . ." Cornelia looked down and curled her small body even tighter against her husband's muscular torso.

"Why does it scare you that I might make them nervous? That would be a good thing."

She shook her head ever so slightly and Caesar felt the gesture against his chest.

"Because if you make the wrong person nervous enough, you might have a new death sentence hanging over your head," she said. "And this time it might not come with a warning. It won't be a legal order for execution—they'll simply send one of their hitmen to kill you on some dark street."

Caesar was quiet.

They lay in silence for a long time in a tight embrace, feeling each other's beating hearts. Caesar shook his head. It was true that everyone who had tried to change things, as Labienus had said, were all dead. It was true that prosecuting any optimate senator usually ended badly for the lawyer who did his job well. Dolabella represented the old order, where a few extremely rich senators controlled everyone and everything—the impoverished Roman people, the Italic tribes who had seen their lands stripped away from them, the inhabitants of the provinces who watched, time and again, as Roman justice ruled in favor of the corrupt governors who exploited them. But all that was about to change. If Rome wanted to survive, it would have to restructure. And corruption would have to be rooted out.

"Do you really think I'll be able to prove them wrong?"

"Yes," she muttered, as if she now regretted having encouraged him.

They said nothing for another long while.

"Is there any other way I might serve my husband tonight?" Cornelia finally asked, trying to distract him from thinking of how he would challenge his rivals. She knew that the conflict ahead was dangerous. In fact, it would be better for her husband to lose the trial. It was likely the key to his survival.

"Again?"

"Yes," she said, forgetting her fears over the future and that cursed case.

Caesar ran his hands over Cornelia's silky skin, starting with her feet. Unhurried. Just feeling her softness against his fingertips. He moved up her legs and she closed her eyes. Caesar rubbed her thighs and smiled: not even Cornelia had figured him out completely. He gently massaged her. Caesar remembered the words of his uncle Marius, years prior, around the table of a tavern after a fight with some other boys on the Campus Martius: "You can pretend to be a coward although you are brave, you can pretend to be clumsy when in fact you are agile. The final victory is all that matters. Never enter a battle you don't believe you can win, even if it makes you look cowardly. Because later, in time, the winner is the only one who will be remembered. Everything that happened before will be forgotten. Remember that, boy, and never enter a battle you can't win."

He'd followed that advice and it had worked. He'd held back.

His hands slipped between his wife's thighs. Cornelia trembled as she gave herself over to him, trustingly.

His uncle's words made perfect sense to him, but he did not understand Cicero's advice at the end of the divinatio: How could he be the defense for a case in which he'd been assigned as prosecutor?

But his member was erect. His wife panting.

He had other matters to attend to.

Caesar positioned himself carefully over Cornelia's beautiful body.

Gnaeus Cornelius Dolabella domus
At that same moment

The two slave girls sat at his feet. Perfectly still. They were afraid their master would lash them again. For a while now, that had seemed to be the only way he derived pleasure. One of them had a bloody gash on her back and was choking back a sob of pain.

Dolabella lay with his gigantic belly pointing up at the ceiling. He wasn't asleep but simply catching his breath, small exertions becoming harder and harder for him. Even the whippings wore him out. But he was happy. The divinatio had gone very well. His lawyers would eat that idiot Julius Caesar alive. The question was what to do with Gaius Marius's impertinent nephew after the trial. Sulla had always wanted to see the boy dead, and maybe he could finally carry out the late dictator's wishes.

He smiled. He liked the idea.

But a doubt crept into his mind: What if Sulla's many warnings about the young Julius Caesar proved correct? What if the boy was in fact truly a threat? He had no experience in court, but he had shown boldness in the past, on more than one occasion. No, on second thought, he didn't feel content with the result of the divinatio. He felt uneasy. He needed to vent his frustrations. Again.

He sat up.

The slaves trembled.

Julia family domus
Half an hour later

Julius Caesar, arched over his wife, gave a sigh of ecstasy. Cornelia hugged his body to hers as she felt him erupt inside her. She tried to whisper in his ear, but pleasure overcame her, leaving her mute. After a few seconds, still clutching him, she spoke: "One thing I'm sure of, you're the best. In here," she said, gesturing to the bed, "and in the basilica as well. The best."

He gently pulled out of her and lay on his back beside her. He closed his eyes.

Their breathing began to slow. It was the *prima vigilia* of the night, the time when darkness blanketed the sprawling city of Rome as the slaves lit the torches in the corridor and the shadows trembled in the light of the flames.

Caesar's eyes shot open. "Of course! By Jupiter!" he whispered, as if wanting to make sure that Cornelia alone could hear him. "I understand what Cicero meant." He turned toward her, but Cornelia did not reply. She was sleeping peacefully, exhausted by passion, contented by the love they'd shared.

Caesar smiled and kissed her tenderly on the cheek before sitting up, pulling the sheets over both of their bodies and lying back down beside her in an embrace.

"I'll be the defense, Cornelia, not the prosecutor," he continued in a whisper, aware that she could not hear him, but feeling the need to tell her anyway. "And it makes perfect sense. Cicero is smart. I have to combine his advice with the words of Gaius Marius."

Caesar closed his eyes.

Gaius Marius. His uncle. His memory.

Caesar slept.

GAIUS MARIUS

Caesar's uncle
Seven-time consul

IX

MARIUS'S RETURN

Campus Martius
90 B.C.
Thirteen years before Dolabella's trial

"COME ON, GET UP, COWARD!" THEY SHOUTED AT THE BOY curled up on the ground bleeding from his face and arm.

"Coward! Traitor!" others jeered as an ever-larger crowd gathered on one side of the Campus Martius.

It was the field where the noble boys of Rome met for military training exercises and to learn about combat, horseback riding, and the use of arms. The fight that had broken out did not garner the attention of the patrols of urban militia since it simply looked like a practice skirmish.

But it wasn't.

The boy lying on the ground was barely nine years old.

He received a kick to the liver.

"Come on, Julius Caesar, stand up and fight! Didn't you descend from the gods?"

The boys laughed and continued calling him a traitor. He'd done nothing, but they hated him because he was . . .

New kicks to the side and face clouded his thoughts.

"Leave him alone, you miserable wretches!" Titus Labienus shouted, jumping in to defend the boy. Not yet ten himself, he couldn't stand injustice or cruelty of any kind. He did not belong to a noble family and had few friends on the training field. And friends were what Caesar needed most at the moment.

The attackers were dumbfounded that anyone would be so stupid as to stick up for Julius Caesar, so greatly outnumbered. The conflict had been started by three boys, but some fifty more had now joined in.

Titus Labienus, without thinking, punched one of the three ringleaders in the face, then quickly dealt another one a punch to the gut. The others hesitated. But the third boy who had attacked Caesar knew that most of the others gathered around thought similarly to him: Caesar belonged to a family of traitors to the Senate, to Rome. A new war had broken out, the city was in danger, and those boys, sons of optimate senators, had heard any number of comments about the Julia family, whose loyalty to Rome was in question. It was only a matter of time before they turned against the Julia boy who trained alongside them.

"We'll give you what you've got coming too, by Jupiter," the third boy said to Titus Labienus.

"He's not even one of us," another of the boys said with venom, alluding to the fact that Titus Labienus was a member of the equestrian order, which, from the perspective of the conservative optimates who controlled Rome, was beneath them.

Labienus swallowed.

He clenched his fists and prepared to defend himself.

Just then, Julius Caesar, one cut on his forehead and another on his arm, stood up beside him.

"Thank you," he said quietly.

There was no time for conversation as the boys were thrown into a whirlwind of kicks and punches.

"What's going on here?"

The booming voice of an adult. A seasoned warrior.

A person born with authority never has to repeat a question.

The boys immediately separated. Some examined their wounds, others checked to make sure all their parts were still in the right places. Caesar pressed a hand to his side, which was where he hurt the most, although he could feel blood running down his face as well. Labienus massaged his wounded shoulder: he was certain someone had bitten him, but they had not broken the skin.

Gaius Marius waited for an answer.

The heavyset frame of the six-time consul, flanked by his personal guard of veteran soldiers, loomed gigantic against the midday sky.

All the boys recognized Marius immediately: Despite the fact that he was reviled by the optimates, there were still many statues of the popular leader across Rome. His enemies would've liked to tear them down but hadn't dared. Not even during his long absence from the city—not yet.

Caesar, for his part, walked past a marble bust bearing his uncle's likeness on a daily basis in the atrium of his own home. And he found it curious that Gaius Marius was even more imposing in flesh and blood, whether due to his size, his stern expression, or his thunderous voice. Or perhaps it was his armed escort of veteran warriors. Or all of the above.

It was the first time Caesar could remember seeing his uncle in person. For Julius's entire childhood, Marius had been in exile, forced out of Rome by the optimates after the violent events of almost ten years prior when the populares had assassinated Memmius and the optimates had responded by executing Glaucia and stoning Saturninus to death. That brutal night, Gaius Marius had fled Rome as power fell squarely into the hands of the most conservative senators.

But Marius had now returned.

In fact, this was the true reason behind the brawl. Marius was all anyone could talk about in Rome. That, and the treachery of the allied states.

"We got into a fight, clarissime vir," Julius Caesar said, in answer to his uncle's question not adding any details about how or why it had occurred.

Gaius Marius slowly scanned the circle of boys. They lowered their heads as the eyes of the heroic ex-consul fell upon them.

Marius could tell that he inspired a combination of contempt and fear. More the latter than the former. In all of them, that is, except the boy who had answered his question and the other boy who had fought to defend him. Having been absent from the city for so many years, he wasn't sure if his nephew was among the boys gathered there, though they all looked to be the right age. The one who had answered him reminded Marius of his sister-in-law, but the boy's face was so bloodied that he couldn't be sure.

"Is the young Gaius Julius Caesar here?"

A brief silence.

Caesar processed the fact that his uncle, whose face he knew so well, had not seen him since he was a baby and did not recognize him.

"I am Julius Caesar, clarissime vir," the boy finally said.

Marius scanned the group of boys who had tried to lynch his nephew. He sighed. The reason for the fight was now clear. He had been wise to stop by the Campus Martius on his way into the city.

"Come with me," he said.

The boy turned briefly to Titus Labienus. He knew his name and had seen him training at the Campus Martius, but they'd never exchanged more than a few words. "Thank you," he said.

Labienus was about to respond when Gaius Marius's deep voice rang out: "You, what's your name? You'd better come along as well, or else these idiots might take their frustrations out on you."

The sons of the optimates were forced to swallow the insult without a word.

Titus looked from Caesar to the former consul, then nodded and obeyed without a word.

In an instant, the two boys were surrounded by an escort of armed guards, following in the wake of Gaius Marius.

X

THE ONLY VICTORY
THAT MATTERS

The streets of Rome
90 B.C.
That same day

THEY WALKED QUICKLY AND SOON ARRIVED AT THE FORUM
Boarium then turned toward the river.

Neither Caesar nor Labienus knew where they were going.

The former consul led the way.

They reached the taverns that lined Rome's river port and Gaius
Marius burst into the largest and busiest of them all, his men making
way through the crowd of drinkers.

Marius stopped at a table under a large window with a view of the
ships setting sail for Ostia. It was the best spot in the house to enjoy
a cup of nice wine, but it was occupied by a group of sailors waiting to
board their ship. As soon as they recognized the former consul and
his escort of ex-legionaries, they quickly stood, bowing their heads,
and vacated the table.

"Sit down," Marius said to his nephew and Labienus.

The innkeeper approached them. "Praise the gods! What an
honor on my house!" he exclaimed, genuinely happy.

Like many of the Roman people, he adored Gaius Marius, who
had saved the city time and again. And now that Rome was once
again in peril, Marius, the great victor of the wars in Africa and in the
North, had once again returned to make sure that everything would
be all right.

"Fewer words, innkeeper," Marius said, not angrily. Then, "More food and drink. You know what I want."

"Yes, of course, of course . . ." He hesitated upon seeing the two boys. "Wine and cheese for everyone?"

Marius understood the question and, looking to the boys, he said in a loud voice: "The innkeeper wants to know if you two are boys or men."

Caesar and Labienus exchanged a glance: neither of them had yet donned the *toga viril* worn by all male Roman citizens, but they turned to the former consul and responded, quietly, hesitantly, in unison: "Men, clarissime vir."

They swallowed.

The veteran consul could see that the boys wore *bullae,* the amulet indicating that a Roman boy was still a child. He pounded the table, threw back his head, and let out a loud laugh that his guards, the innkeeper, and several others in the tavern joined in on.

The former consul cut his laugh short and stared at the men seated nearby. "Are you mocking my nephew?" he asked.

Everyone went silent.

Marius turned back to Caesar and Labienus. "Today you fought like men. Like stupid men, but like men. Your bloody wounds can attest to that." He turned to the innkeeper: "You heard the boys, they're men. Wine and cheese for the three of us. And for my guards as well."

The innkeeper nodded and went to fetch his best food and drink.

Marius gestured to one of his men without taking his eyes off the boys. The guard leaned forward. "Call a doctor to come right away," Marius ordered.

The soldier raised his fist to his chest in salute. "Yes, clarissime vir," he said before quickly leaving to carry out the orders.

"These wounds need to be treated," Marius said, examining his nephew's face. "I can't let your mother see you in this state. Aurelia angry is worse than any horde of savage Teutons armed to the teeth, my boy, and all the legions of Rome wouldn't be able to save me from her wrath. Your mother enraged is capable of anything."

It sounded like a joke but Gaius Marius didn't laugh.

Caesar didn't either. His mother was very sweet when she wanted to be, but she had an iron will.

"We're not stupid," Caesar said in response to his uncle's earlier insult, attributing their bravery to a lack of intelligence.

"Well, by Hercules," exclaimed Marius. "It would seem that my nephew has inherited his mother's boldness. Are you saying I'm a liar or that I don't know what I'm talking about?"

"No . . ." Caesar felt his throat go dry.

The innkeeper returned carrying a plate of aged cheese and a pitcher of wine with three cups made of *terra sigillata,* the best drink-ware he had, reserved for his most special customers. He made a move to serve them, but the former consul gestured for him to stop, so the innkeeper turned and quickly left.

Gaius Marius filled the cups to the brim.

"Drink," he said to his nephew. "Maybe it will loosen your tongue."

Caesar brought the wine to his lips and took a few sips. He felt the burn of the alcohol on his throat, but his mouth was still dry with anxiety.

"Let's see," Gaius Marius said, leaning over the table: "Two against . . . how many? Twenty? There were more than that, but I think the ones actually attacking you numbered about twenty. Those odds are idiotic. How many battles do you think I could've won with that strategy?" He sat back, emptied his cup in one long gulp, and slammed it back down onto the table. He looked each boy in the eye. "Never enter into battle if the enemy outnumbers you tenfold. Even the cretins you fought this morning know that."

"They were insulting you," Caesar explained.

"I imagined. Most of those boys are sons of the optimates, my enemies."

"What should we have done, then?" his nephew asked, indignant.

Gaius Marius leaned over his young listeners, resting his powerful arms on the table. "You should've retreated and waited for a better time to launch your attack." He sat back and served himself more wine.

The boys still had full cups.

"At least . . ." Caesar hesitated before going on. "At least . . . now they know I'm brave."

Marius paused with his cup in midair and looked at his nephew: "Yes, my boy, your enemies now know that you are brave—brave and stupid. And your friend, too. Why did you get involved in that fight? And what's your name?"

"My name is Titus, Titus Labienus, clarissime vir. And I joined in because . . . because it was unfair for so many of them to pick on him like that."

"Oh I see, another brave, stupid boy. Makes sense that you'd be friends."

Caesar was red with rage over his uncle's disrespect. He opened his mouth to defend his wounded pride, but his uncle raised a hand to stop him. Marius took another long drink but did not empty the cup.

"I've been called a coward before. By hundreds—no, more . . . thousands of legionaries under my command. But I did not let it force me into combat under conditions in which we'd have surely been defeated. I knew how to swallow my pride." He looked at each boy in turn, leaning over the table, and said, "I knew how to wait for the right moment to win the decisive victory. Because, listen well, there is only one victory that matters in war: the final one."

The boys looked at him in shock. Everyone in Rome knew that Marius had won not one, but two wars, and many pitched battles. Not only that—he'd completely restructured the Roman army and modernized the legions. The boys couldn't believe any legionary would ever think that Gaius Marius, six-time consul of Rome, was a coward.

Marius seemed to read their minds. "Sertorius!" he boomed.

One of the guards approached the table.

"Tell these two boys about the time everyone, you included, thought I was cowardly."

Sertorius cleared his throat. The moment when, in fact, all of Marius's men had doubted his courage was not something they had ever talked about.

"Come on, Sertorius," Marius insisted. "I'm trying to teach my nephew an important lesson and I don't have much time. There's another war starting and I've been called to the front lines, in case you've forgotten. So speak, by Jupiter!"

Sertorius took a deep breath and prayed to the gods that his answer would be the correct one: "It was before the battle of Aquae Sextiae, clarissime vir."

The tavern went silent. Everyone was listening intently.

"That's right," Gaius Marius agreed, "before Aquae Sextiae. For days, my boy, all my men thought that I, your uncle Gaius Marius, was a coward. And you know what?"

Caesar shook his head. He and Labienus were transfixed by the veteran general and Roman politician, the only man who had ever been named consul six times. They were sitting across from a living legend.

Gaius Marius leaned back over the table and whispered to Caesar: "It doesn't matter what they think of you, do you understand?" He looked at Labienus as well. "Do you boys understand? Just because someone thinks you are a coward does not make you one. Cowardice is something you carry inside you. I've never been a coward. On the battlefield I have always been . . . strategic." He sighed and leaned back in his chair. "In politics, less so. But that's another story. For now I'll just tell you about the time my men called me a coward behind my back. They would never have dared to say it to my face, but they thought it. And in the end I won another great victory for Rome. Because I am a leader, and a leader has to know when to swallow their pride, when to do what's best for the Republic, and when to focus on the only thing that matters: the final victory. I'll tell you boys about the battle of Aquae Sextiae."

XI

Memoria in Memoria

THE WRATH OF
THE GODS

Rome, 105 B.C.
Twenty-eight years before Dolabella's trial
Five years before Caesar's birth

THEY WERE GOING TO BE BURIED.

Alive.

"No! Noooo!" the men howled.

"Have mercy on us! Have mercy!" the women begged as they were dragged around the Forum Boarium among the stalls selling livestock.

It was two pairs of slaves, one of Gallic origin and the other Greek. The four miserable wretches were being guided to a pit in the very center of the market. To be buried alive. Whenever a vestal virgin broke her sacred vow of chastity she was buried alive to appease the wrath of the gods. And it had always seemed to work, but the priestesses of Vesta had been very well behaved of late. No, the crushing defeats at Noreia, Burdigala, and Arausio couldn't be attributed to sacrilege on the part of the maidens who tended the sacred flames of Vesta. Yet Rome hung on the brink of disaster. The Ambrones, the Cimbri, and especially the fearsome Teutons did as they pleased in southern Gaul, sacking territories that were allied with Rome. The consular armies had been defeated, one after another, in three brutal battles. The Republic hadn't seen such a prolonged series of setbacks since Hannibal had tried to take Rome, destroying the legions in Ticino, Trebia, and Trasimeno and, finally, the atrocity at Cannae. At that time, after Hannibal had annihilated several entire legions, the

Romans resorted, *in extremis,* desperate, panicked, to human sacrifice. It had not occurred again since. But then came the losses in Noreia, Burdigala, and Arausia, which saw the defeat of a Roman army that, counting the allies and auxiliary troops, was equivalent to almost ten legions. They were terrified, with no buffer between the city of Rome and the barbaric hordes of the North. Additionally, much of their military force had been deployed to Africa in an attempt to end the long war against Jugurtha.

The four slaves continued to struggle, begging for their lives.

But the Romans' fear made them merciless.

The slaves were tossed into the pit without any of the considerations given to the vestal virgins, who were permitted to climb down a ladder to the depths of what would become their tomb. The Gallic and Greek slaves were unceremoniously pushed from the top of the black pit in the center of the Forum Boarium.

Their screams rose as they fell. Both men broke several bones; the Gallic woman's skull was cracked open, blood pouring down her face as she rushed to crouch in a corner of the open grave. The other woman, unharmed except for a few bruises, paced the perimeter of that rectangle dug into the entrails of Rome, desperately feeling the walls for some foothold that might allow her to climb out.

"Nooo! By all the gods!" the Gallic man wailed, clutching his right leg and feeling his splintered bones.

The slaves had been chosen at random through a sinister lottery system that made no concessions for behavior, religion, or origin.

They heard the ominous sound of a gigantic slab being dragged across the ground above. The sky darkened.

The four slaves, wounded and terrified, were thrown into shadow. And then pitch darkness. The black hole swallowed them up, echoing the sounds of their sobs back to them. They were buried alive. To appease the wrath of the gods.

XII

Memoria in Memoria

A NEW SCIPIO?

Disputed territories controlled by the Cimbri and the Teutons
Southern Gaul
105—103 B.C.

IT SEEMED THAT THE ROMAN GODS HAD TAKEN PITY ON THE city by the Tiber.

Were they appeased by the brutal sacrifice?

It was hard to know. But in any case, the Cimbri, the Teutons, and the rest of the barbaric northern peoples did not march directly on Rome after Arausio. Instead, they busied themselves with the plundering of southern Gaul and even made some incursions into Hispania. This bought the Romans precious time, which the Senate used—as they always did when circumstances pushed Rome to its limit—to seek out the best possible commander for their legions. To defeat Hannibal, Rome had called upon Scipio Africanus. They now needed a new Scipio.

Gaius Marius was Rome's most accomplished general at the time. He'd ended the long war in Africa against Jugurtha and was called back home, where he was named consul with the order to recruit a new army and march northward to secure the border with Gaul. He'd been trained in battle at Numantia under Scipio Aemilianus, Scipio Africanus's adopted grandson. Marius was no Scipio, but he was the closest thing they had.

And he was up to the task. He promptly gathered a consular army of two legions that totaled six thousand regular legionaries plus two *alae* units of conscripts from among the socii. He also recruited thousands more auxiliary troops from among Rome's poor. This was a highly unorthodox practice since, traditionally, a Roman soldier was required by law to be a landowner and to fund his own campaign of battle, weapons included. But there simply weren't enough men in Rome who, after seven years of war in Africa, could afford all the swords, shields, breastplates, and combat gear, not to mention the dishes and other items needed for daily life in the military camp. If it was men they needed, however, the poorer classes of Rome had many. Thousands of men who had nothing and, therefore, nothing to lose, everything to gain in battle. Marius provided them with the tools needed for combat, along with something truly revolutionary: paid wages, called a *salarium,* since the legionaries were often paid in salt, highly valued for its ability to conserve food. They also received cold hard cash. The legionaries and the auxiliaries alike were paid a regular wage on top of any possible war spoils taken in the case of victory. It was an unprecedented opportunity and many men answered consul Gaius Marius's recruitment call. He quickly gathered thirty-five thousand soldiers, armed them, and marched them northward.

The Senate watched with unease as Marius skirted laws to integrate the common people of Rome into his army. But desperate times called for desperate measures. All that mattered was that an army be placed between Rome and the barbaric tribes spread out across southern Gaul. The optimates let Marius do as he pleased, but assigned Sulla, one of the more conservative young senators, as legatus. He would keep an eye on the leader of the first professional army Rome had ever seen. They could never have imagined where it would all lead.

The mutual dislike between Marius and Sulla was immediately apparent to all. The consul surrounded himself with his veteran officers from Africa, men like Sertorius whom he trusted completely, as he marched his unconventional army northward.

Marius subjected his soldiers to rigorous training, aiming to instill discipline in them, just as Scipio Aemilianus had done in the siege of Numantia. Through the long war in Africa, he'd learned that preparation was key. So he reduced the number of *calones,* slaves or servants that the legionaries were allowed to have, meaning every soldier was forced to carry dozens of pounds on their back, as Marius loaded them down with war equipment, tools for carpentry and ironworking, cooking utensils, and other items. Soon, it was said in Rome that Marius didn't have soldiers, but pack mules, and the optimates laughed, calling the new army "Marius's mules." Others, such as Metellus Numidicus and his son, Metellus Pius, observed the consul's actions with increasing distrust.

The consul was unconcerned by any outside opinions. His men received their regular salary and lived in austere conditions as they all worked to build and secure the fort established in Gaul. Marius was trying to make authentic war machines out of his legionaries, and total victory was his only concern.

They built their fortress at the mouth of the Rhône.

The Cimbri and the Teutons did not attack.

An entire year went by without a single major battle.

The Senate grudgingly agreed to extend Marius's consulship for the year 104 B.C.

Everyone waited for Marius to order the advance of his troops. But Marius gave no such order. He was still fortifying his base on the southern bank of the Rhône, where he'd ordered his soldiers to dig a canal deep enough for the boats carrying provisions from Rome to navigate. This trench, called the Fossa Mariana, was a massive undertaking that required backbreaking labor, which kept the legionaries in top physical condition while also providing a quick, consistent supply line with Rome that the Cimbri and the Teutons, lacking a fleet, could not block.

Another year passed and the barbarians did not attack Marius's fortress. The consul did not order any major incursion into the territories controlled by the Cimbri and the Teutons. The barbarians watched and waited, as did the senators back in Rome. And no one could understand Marius's unwavering patience.

Some soldiers began to wonder if their leader wished to see war at all. His veterans from Africa, however, trusted their general. They knew he must have his reasons for the long wait.

The year 103 arrived.

The situation remained unchanged, and the Senate through gritted teeth, extended Marius's consulship for a third consecutive term. Sulla stayed on in Marius's army, watching and reporting back to the optimates, but Marius had reduced his responsibilities, demoting him from legatus to tribune. He did not trust Sulla, who openly declared that the entire operation in the North was doomed to failure. When a third year passed with no major battles, Sulla returned to Rome, saying that he wanted no part in what he was certain would be a huge military fiasco.

Many soldiers began to doubt Marius.

The year 102 arrived.

Faced with the legionaries' growing misgivings about their leader, Sertorius shared their mounting doubts with Marius.

"Scipio Aemilianus took more than a year to conquer the city of Numantia. A single city. And no one questioned his strategy. We are now up against the gigantic armies of several barbaric peoples who threaten the very existence of Rome. It seems perfectly reasonable to take all the time necessary, years even, to do away with them."

He didn't say anything else.

Sertorius accepted his explanation.

But . . . how were things viewed in the Roman Senate?

Roman Senate

102 B.C.

Sulla stood before the Curia. Dolabella stood beside him, watching admiringly. The Metelli, father and son, gave him their full attention. They were debating whether or not Marius's consulship should be renewed for the fourth time.

"Patres conscripti, friends, senators: the situation in the North is a delicate one. It would be unprecedented to allow any man to serve even a second term as consul, much less a fourth, but I ask myself: What do we have to gain by changing this leader? We are all fed up with his inaction, but the barbarians will eventually force his hand. I believe that the Cimbri and the Teutons will soon march toward Rome, pushing Marius into action whether he likes it or not. He will have no choice but to respond to the enemy's advance. Within the coming year, I have no doubt that we will see an end to the wait. I suggest we do not oblige anyone else to assume control of a fortification that they are not familiar with, with troops trained by another man, in an inhospitable region. Marius is the commander who has planned the defense of our northern border, for better or for worse. Which is why I'd like to put forth a motion to renew Gaius Marius's tenure as consul for another year."

The senators voted in favor of the motion.

"Do you really think this is for the best?" the elder Metellus asked when the meeting had concluded.

"It's the best thing for *us*. For the optimates," Sulla answered, shadowed by Dolabella, his right-hand man.

"What do you mean by that, boy? Don't speak in riddles," said Metellus the elder, leader of the conservatives.

"The legionaries have lost their faith in Marius," Sulla said in a grave tone. "So when the barbarians make their move, when they attack, the legionaries, distrusting of their leader, will undoubtedly be slaughtered, Marius along with them. It's the ideal situation for us: The barbarians will do the dirty work of eliminating Marius and his army of beggars. We'll have to recruit a new army, but we can recall some of our troops from Africa and Hispania to do so. It won't be easy but it can be done. Once the populares have lost their leader, we will be the ones to dictate the laws of Rome with scant opposition from the people, too terrified by the advance of the Cimbri and the Teutons to speak up as we pass new measures—measures in defense of the city, to be certain, but also in defense of our interests, the only interests that matter."

Everyone accepted Sulla's assessment of the situation.

It was the first and last time Sulla would underestimate Marius.

General Gaius Marius's encampment
beside the Fossa Mariana
Mouth of the Rhône River 102 B.C.

Marius had just received news that his tenure as consul had been renewed for another year. He knew it would be the last extension he'd

see if there was no notable advance in the war. But he was still unhurried.

More messengers arrived.

Sertorius entered the consul's *praetorium.*

"The barbarians are on the move, clarissime vir."

"The Cimbri or the Teutons?" asked Marius, seated in the commander's tent behind a table crowded with maps and empty cups of
wine.

Sertorius swallowed before giving the details. "The Cimbri still
seem to be holding their position, Consul, but the Ambrones and the
Teutons are marching in this direction. The patrols have just returned with reports that thousands of barbarians, tens of thousands,
will soon be upon us."

Gaius Marius nodded without looking up from the map he was
studying. Finally he lifted his gaze. "As soon as they are visible from
the wall of the encampment, let me know. Until then, let no one interrupt me."

He served himself some wine from a pitcher on a small table. Sertorius watched him slowly pour his drink. That was the moment he
began to worry that perhaps the legionaries were right—that the
consul was no longer the man he'd been in Africa, the fearless commander who had defeated Jugurtha. They claimed that, at fifty-five,
the consul was too old, too weak, and too cowardly. That he was not,
by any means, the new Scipio.

XIII

Memoria in Memoria

THE BARBARIC
GIANTS

Καὶ Κίμβροις μὲν ἐγίνετο πλείων ἡ διατριβὴ καὶ μέλλησις, Τεύτονες
δὲ καὶ Ἄμβρωνες ἄραντες εὐθὺς καὶ διελθόντες τὴν ἐν μέσῳ χώραν,
ἐφαίνοντο πλήθει τ᾽ἄπειροι καὶ δυσπρόσοπτοι τὰ εἴδη φθόγγον τε
καὶ θόρυβον οὐχ ἑτέροις ὅμοιοι. Περιβαλόμενοι δὲ τοῦ πεδίου μέγα
καὶ στρατοπεδεύσαντες, προύκαλοῦντο τὸν Μάριον εἰς μάχην.

On the part of the Cimbri there was considerable delay and loss of time, but the
Teutones and Ambrones set out at once, passed through the intervening country,
and made their appearance before Marius. Their numbers were limitless, they
were hideous in their aspect, and their speech and cries were unlike those of other
peoples. They covered a large part of the plain, and after pitching their camp,
challenged Marius to battle.

—PLUTARCH OF CHAERONEA, *Parallel Lives,* MARIUS, XV

Roman camp beside the Fossa Mariana
Mouth of the Rhône River
Spring, 102 B.C.

THE IMMENSE PLAIN THAT SPREAD OUT BEFORE THE MAIN
Roman encampment was choked with armed Ambrones and Teutons as far as the eye could see.

Marius took in the scene from atop the *vallum.* The barbarians
marched defiantly across the land they believed belonged to them,

seemingly undaunted by that great Roman fortification. These same men had defeated the Roman armies on three occasions, sometimes with the help of other barbaric peoples. The repeated military defeats—in Noreia, Burdigala, and especially Arausio—had caused a rumor to spread among the legionaries. They whispered that these barbarians were unlike other enemies, that they were somehow more formidable, that they were gigantic, indestructible beasts, other-worldly, of colossal size and invincible might, who would vanquish any army that dared to challenge them.

He knew that a rumor could be more powerful than an entire army. So he had to destroy that lie before he launched his legions against the warriors fanned out on the other side of the Rhône.

He climbed down from the wall, giving orders to Sertorius and the other officers. "I want everyone to come up here and see them," said Marius.

The tribunes exchanged glances.

"Who is everyone, clarissime vir?" Sertorius asked. "And you want them to see . . . what, exactly, consul?"

They'd reached the base of the tall wall erected by the Roman legions to protect their fortress.

Gaius Marius merely pointed to the sea of tents before them. "Everyone is everyone," he said, then clarified, "I want each and every legionary and auxiliary soldier to climb the vallum and see with their own eyes that there is not a single giant among these cursed barbarians, not a single mythical cyclops. I want each and every warrior under my command to understand that we are up against ordinary men: armed, but disorganized and undisciplined. That's what I meant by *everyone,* and that's what I want them to see."

The tribunes nodded, understanding that Marius aimed to put an end to the rumors of their enemy's superhuman strength. And they thought it was a brilliant idea.

Sertorius watched the consul walk away flanked by his guards. Perhaps Gaius Marius was getting older and weaker, and perhaps he would never be the new Scipio, but he was still clever. There was hope for victory yet.

XIV

A DOCTOR FOR
YOUNG CAESAR

Tavern beside the Tiber, Rome
90 B.C.

"AND SO, BOYS, THAT'S HOW I MANAGED TO BANISH MY men's fears of the supposedly gigantic barbarians," Gaius Marius explained with a broad smile on his face as he poured more wine for himself, his nephew, and Labienus. "When the legionaries saw for themselves that our enemies were merely ordinary humans, their attitudes changed..." He paused, lost in thought. "Perhaps too much..."

"The doctor has arrived, clarissime vir," Sertorius said, taking advantage of the break in the former consul's story.

"Who?" asked Marius, still distracted. Sertorius was about to repeat the message when Marius shook his head and returned to the present. "Oh yes, the doctor. Is he a good one? I won't have my nephew treated by just anyone. I want a real Greek who knows how to heal wounds, not some quack trying to pass themselves off as a medic."

"It's the doctor from the *valetudinarium* who treated the legions in Africa and then in the North, in the very campaign clarissime vir was describing for his nephew."

"Aaah!" exclaimed Marius, sounding almost pleased. "The good doctor Anaxagoras is still alive?"

"Still kicking, clarissime vir," said an old man with a wise, aged face, as the guards stepped aside to make way for him.

Marius did not stand, since a six-time consul does not stand for anyone, but he nodded in appreciation and recognition, which, coming from him, was a lot.

"It's good to know you're still with us."

"The tribune knew where to find me, clarissime vir."

"Valerius Flaccus is always efficient."

The man referenced stood straighter. It was rare for the former consul to flatter anyone.

"My nephew has taken a good beating . . . his friend as well."

"I see, clarissime vir." The old man leaned over the boys and took each one by the chin, turning their heads to get a good look at the bruises and cuts on their faces.

"I suppose they'll survive it, but I'd prefer to have my nephew cleaned up a bit before I return him to his mother. The idiot got himself into a battle he couldn't win."

The young Caesar frowned and was about to protest, but Anaxagoras turned his face again to examine a bruise more closely.

"Yes, my boy," his uncle continued, "you were foolish and clumsy today. When it's only your own neck you're risking we can call it that: stupidity. But if you enter into a battle you can't win with thirty thousand men under your command, you're more than an idiot—you're a murderer . . . of your own people. And you do want to command legions one day, don't you?"

The doctor moved the cups aside and spread his medical utensils out on the table. He asked the innkeeper for hot water and clean cloths. A few of the cuts needed sewing up.

"I do," confirmed Caesar, who dreamed of following in his uncle's footsteps. He knew it was an impossible ambition, but he could at least try, even if he was only named consul for one year, which was the norm. Commanding an army and doing so victoriously was, for every young man in Rome, the ultimate goal, the dream. Very few made it to consul.

"Well then, you need to learn to swallow your pride and bide your time until you're in the position to return a humiliation. I'm not suggesting you should ignore an insult; no, my boy, you keep it inside you and hold onto it. For days, weeks, months, or even years if necessary. So that it doesn't get diluted over time, so that it always hurts like the first day they said it. You wait until you can repay them not with another insult, but with blood, with the mortal blow that hits its mark, annihilating your enemy."

Everyone was silent. The only sound was the doctor's damp cloth wiping Caesar's bruised skin and the boy's suppressed whimpers as he tried not to show his pain before his uncle and the group of seasoned warriors.

XV

Memoria in Memoria

—

TEUTOBOD

Mouth of the Rhône River
Spring, 102 B.C.

THE BARBARIANS SET UP CAMP ON THE PLAIN WITH THE armed fighters at the head of the group, closest to the Roman base. Behind them were thousands of women and children and carts packed with all manners of provisions and supplies for their long southward journey. Along the way, they planned to wipe out anything and everyone that stood in their path.

They could've simply continued on into Italy. Nothing was forcing them to march so close to that Roman encampment, much less stop there. In fact, many of Teutobod's officers wondered why their king had decided to camp immediately outside the Roman fortification.

"They have the river on one side," said a member of the royal council in the central tent of the immense camp. "They haven't come out to harass us. We can continue advancing straight past them."

Several men nodded their assent but looked to the king, awaiting his comment. Teutobod had won their admiration through his defeats of the Romans, and he had led them around all of Gaul for several years now without anyone or anything stopping them. They always deferred to his decisions, even when they didn't understand them.

"We won't get far with a well-equipped armed enemy at our backs," said the king from his wide seat in the center of the tent. Everyone remained silent. "What if, for example, we were to encounter, upon reaching Rome, another army there? We'd be trapped between two enemy forces. No. It is better to first destroy the opponent here and then continue onward. Also, a new defeat, which will be the fourth for Rome within a few years, will sow panic among their soldiers. I doubt they'd be able to find many men brave enough to confront us again. If we vanquish this Roman army here and now, our march on Rome will be a victory parade."

One officer nodded. And then another. Within seconds, everyone had sided with the king.

"But . . ." one of the nobles ventured, then stopped short.

"Speak, your king is listening," said Teutobod.

The man bowed his head in a sign of deference, then finished what he'd started to say: "What can we do, Your Majesty, to force them into combat? We've been here for two days now and they haven't made any move to leave their fortress and engage in battle."

Teutobod nodded. "We will have to provoke them," he responded.

He'd been able to lure other Roman consuls into battle. Why should this new Roman leader be any different?

Roman fortification beside the Fossa Mariana
Atop the vallum

The legionaries had seen with their own eyes that the Teutons and the other barbarians were no giants. The rumor had been dispelled. But the Roman troops, no longer wary of confronting that enemy, were now eager to enter into combat with them. What had they been training for nonstop the past two years if not battle? And wasn't their army the single obstacle standing between the Teutons and the city of Rome? Wasn't it their mission to stop the barbarian advance? They weren't giants. That was now clear. So why not get the war over with and vanquish this threat to Rome?

Gaius Marius observed from atop the vallum as the Teutons began to charge at the Roman encampment.

"That doesn't seem like a very effective tactic," Sertorius said, standing with the consul and a group of tribunes gathered to observe the enemy's movements.

"No, it is doomed to failure," Marius agreed. "We have too many obstructions in place. Most of those barbarians will fall into our *lilia* or be impaled by our *sudes* before they even reach the vallum. And they know it. They can't take the time to uncover our traps or dig through our embankments, because our archers would riddle them with arrows. No, their king has another aim . . ."

And he was right. As they approached the vallum, the Teutons and the Ambrones fell into the traps lined with spikes or were run through by the many sudes, long sharpened stakes spread out along the field, impeding their advance and causing a great many injuries. The barbarians struggled to reach the wall as they dodged the hidden holes in that sea of lethal thorns.

Any enemy who somehow managed to approach the vallum was met with punishing arrows or *pila,* depending on the consul's orders, launched furiously from the Roman fortification. The legions easily repelled all attempts to reach the main wall of their encampment.

"So . . ." Sertorius said hesitantly.

"So?" Gaius Marius repeated, inviting his trusted officer to express his thoughts.

"So . . . the Teuton king is sacrificing his men . . . for nothing?"

Marius remained silent for a moment as they watched the Teutons repeatedly fall victim to their traps.

"Not for nothing," the consul said. "He's trying to get a reaction out of us."

And to be certain, the longer the Roman troops warded off the Teuton attack, the more impatient they became for combat. They were roused and eager to fight. His officers suggested it would be wise to take advantage of the legionaries' thirst for battle and march out to attack the enemy.

"No," was Marius's categorical response each time a tribune made a suggestion to that effect.

An entire day passed.

Gaius Marius tried to dampen the ardent enthusiasm for battle.

By the following morning, the Teutons seemed to have tired of losing men without eliciting the desired response. They began instead to display some of their fiercest warriors, challenging the Romans to send out their best men for individual contests of strength.

Several centurions appeared before the consul asking to be sent up against the strongest Teuton warrior. But Gaius Marius was once again categorical in his refusal.

"No. I will not waste a single officer to a senseless duel that will solve nothing."

The military tribunes closest to the consul kept their opinions to themselves. Winning a battle wasn't everything, they felt. There was also the matter of the troops' honor to consider. But maybe they were wrong. Maybe Gaius Marius understood things better than they did.

Whatever the case, he did not allow any man to leave the camp for a duel with the Teutons.

Desperate to elicit some response, the barbarians began to jeer at the Romans and even went as far as to get some of their Latin-speaking slaves to teach them how to pronounce the gravest insults they could think of. They bellowed that the Romans were "cowards," "yellow-bellied," or simply "women." But, from behind their fortified wall, the furious Roman troops could only obey their consul's orders and swallow their humiliation.

The Teutons, howling with laughter, showed their bare butts to the Romans. Gaius Marius simply looked on, impassive. He would not let the enemy force his hand.

"Perhaps a small attack, just a few cohorts, to show that we won't accept such ridicule," Sertorius suggested. "That would at least appease our men."

"No. Either we all attack or none of us attack," the consul decreed. "A smaller contingent would be substantially outnumbered and easily annihilated. And I will not fight with the river at my back. It's a death trap. That's exactly what happened at Arausio, where the barbarians wiped out several legions."

Silence.

More jeers, mockery, and laughter from the enemy lines.

*"Romani, quid uestris mulieribus mittere uultis? Quoniam illae nostrae mox erunt!"** several Teuton warriors chanted loudly.

Those words were especially infuriating for the legionaries, but

---

* "Romans, do you want to start sending over some of your women? Because soon they will be ours."

Marius remained inflexible. He would not risk a single cohort in a futile attack. It would only be a senseless loss of men.

Night fell.

The officers dispersed.

Marius walked back to his tent.

"With all due respect, *vir eminentissimus,*" Sertorius began.

"Go ahead, tribune."

"If . . . if this isn't a good position from which to attack, why did we set up camp here?"

It was a valid question.

"Because this was and is a good position from which to receive provisions from Rome by sea. Here, the Teutons are not able to interrupt our supply chain," the consul explained. "But this is not our combat position. Our troops were ambushed by barbarians in Noreia and Burdigala. And in Arausio they were forced into battle with the river at their backs. I won't repeat the same mistakes made by other consuls. And I won't permit any dissent among my ranks. The disagreements between the two consuls in command in Arausio only further complicated matters, which is why I asked the Senate for total control of this army. We will engage in battle when and where I say."

"Yes, clarissime vir."

Ἐπορεύοντο δ'ἐγγύς, πυνθανόμενοι τῶν Ῥωμαίων μετὰ γέλωτος, εἴ
τι πρὸς τὰς γυναῖκας ἐπιστέλλοιεν· αὐτοὶ γὰρ ἔσεσθαι ταχέως
παρ'αὐταῖς.

And they marched close to the camp, inquiring whether the Romans had any
messages for their wives; "For," said they, "we shall soon be with them."

—PLUTARCH OF CHAERONEA, *Parallel Lives*, MARIUS, XVIII, 2

XVI

Memoria in Memoria

THE KING'S
CHALLENGE

Roman camp beside the Fossa Mariana
102 B.C.

I T WAS THE THIRD DAY OF TEUTON PROVOCATIONS OUTSIDE
the Roman camp.

The consul was awoken at dawn.

The Teutons had presented the ultimate challenge.

"What is it this time?" Gaius Marius asked the military calones
who had come in to tighten the strings of his armor.

But neither Sertorius nor any of the other tribunes dared to give
him a precise explanation.

"They are insisting . . . with the individual battles, clarissime vir,"
Sertorius said, and the vagueness of his response led Marius to think
that there was something more.

He didn't ask any further. It was clear that his most trusted tribune wanted Marius himself to evaluate the situation from the top of
the wall.

When they neared the vallum, Marius saw hundreds of legionaries leaning over the top, looking out onto the plain. He thought to
himself with a smile that perhaps the Teutons had rolled out a giant
wooden horse, and in that case, all they'd have to do was burn the
horse with the Teutons inside. But as he reached the top of the wall,
the consul forgot about *The Iliad* and his smile faded. Out in front of
the huge barbarian army stood a single warrior in silver armor that
glimmered in the morning sun. He was gripping a long sword and

brandishing a green, oval-shaped shield with golden rivets that shone even brighter than his breastplate. Only a high-ranking barbarian would flaunt such ostentatious weapons and defensive armor.

"Who is that?" the consul asked without taking his eyes off the fierce, imposing man.

"He claims to be . . . their king," Sertorius responded.

Gaius Marius nodded. He could see where this was going, and he didn't like it. He considered ordering all his men except the sentinels down from the wall. A few days prior he had invited his legionaries to lean over the vallum and see the enemy for themselves. But now he wished more than anything for them to look away from the enemy. The man who claimed to be the Teuton king shouted his challenge, and the consul wished that his men were unable to hear the enemy as well. But it was too late for that. It was obvious that Sertorius and the other officers had roused him because the Teuton king had already proclaimed his challenge several times, in Latin, with a strong Germanic accent, but fully comprehensible to all the legionaries.

*"Ego, Teutobod, Teutonorum rex, deposco romanum consulem Caium Marium ad singularem pugnam! Si uirtutem habet et socors non est!"**

All the legionaries atop the wall had heard it loud and clear and were already repeating it to their comrades craning up from the foot of the vallum. Soon, the entire Roman army had heard about the Teuton king's challenge for their consul, their leader. Would the clarissime vir, chief commander of the Roman legions deployed to the North, remain impassive in the face of such a direct challenge?

Gaius Marius was as still and silent as a marble statue.

The Teuton king repeated his challenge once again. He didn't want the Roman consul to be able to claim he hadn't heard or understood him. When he pronounced his new challenge, Teutobod looked to the Roman slave who had translated for him. The slave nodded, confirming for the Germanic king that he'd correctly pronounced the Latin phrase he'd memorized the night before.

Teutobod scanned the Roman troops as they observed him from

---

* "I, Teutobod, king of the Teutons, challenge the Roman consul Gaius Marius to individual combat. If he has the courage and is not a coward."

their protected position behind the defensive wall. He could see that the legionaries' heads were all turned toward a specific point on the vallum where a corpulent figure, without a helmet but with a gleaming breastplate and gray hair, stood surrounded by several officers, staring down at him. The Germanic king was certain that this was the enemy consul.

Though outwardly calm, Gaius Marius's mind raced.

And his blood boiled. Why deny it? He had a blazing urge to go out and fight, the same desire that had been consuming his men for days. Noreia, Burdigala, Arausio. Three brutal defeats. Tens of thousands of legionaries dead. Rome had been shaken to the core, humiliated, almost annihilated. Every fiber of his being screamed out for revenge.

Upon identifying Gaius Marius's position, the Teuton king took several steps to situate himself directly in front of the consul, yet still too far for the enemy arrows to reach him.

From there he decried his challenge one last time, now looking directly at the immutable Roman leader.

"Ego, Teutobod, Teutonorum rex, deposco romanum consulem Caium Marium ad singularem pugnam! Si uirtutem habet et socors non est!"

Gaius Marius could feel his officers, his legionaries, the slaves, everyone, all looking to him. He knew that he had to do something, and he knew what his gut was telling him to do. But he was also very conscious of what his calculated military mind, the mind of an astute commander, was telling him. Discipline, in the truest sense, begins with the self. If that event had occurred fifteen years earlier, he would've put on his helmet, tightened his breastplate, and unsheathed his sword. But time had taken its toll. He was fifty-five, with infinite experience, but his strength and reflexes weren't what they'd once been. He carefully scrutinized the Teuton king: How old was that monarch from the North—thirty, at most? He looked young, strong, virile, quick, and agile, with muscular arms and a powerful torso. A man at the height of his physical potency. Gaius Marius swallowed: the duel, if he chose to accept it, was as good as lost for him. He didn't have to be a genius to see that. But he had to do something. He couldn't let this challenge go unanswered.

"Sertorius," he finally said.

"Yes, clarissime vir," the man quickly replied, welcoming anything besides silence from his leader.

"Call Ahenobarbus," Marius ordered.

Sertorius didn't understand. "Ahenobarbus?" he asked, confused. "The military trainer?"

Gaius Marius wasn't accustomed to giving explanations, only orders. He turned slowly and, with a look, conveyed his irritation at the question. He didn't need to say anything more.

Sertorius bowed and took off quickly in search of Ahenobarbus, the fierce centurion, *primus pilus,* who, at thirty-four years old, had been awarded many medals of valor for his various feats in battle. He was, by far, their best warrior in hand-to-hand combat and the head trainer of the consular army at Fossa Mariana.

Moments later, Ahenobarbus was seen making his way down a path through the crowd of legionaries, Sertorius at his heels. He reached the wall and ascended the steps to present himself before the consul.

"Breastplate, helmet, sword, and shield. Arm yourself well, Ahenobarbus," the consul ordered. "You will answer the Teuton king's challenge in my stead."

There was a deathly silence among the officers gathered around. But no one dared to say a word.

The trainer nodded, turned around, and went to fetch his weapons and armor. Shortly thereafter, the main door of the wall opened and Ahenobarbus, sword at the ready, shield held high, left the Roman fortification prepared to battle the enemy king to the death.

Teutobod observed the armed Roman officer, strong, mature, like him, but not old, and surely his equal in individual combat. But this was not the consul; this was not the leader of the enemy army.

Ahenobarbus walked briskly, almost at a run, and stopped a few paces from the Germanic monarch.

Teutobod looked from the Roman fighter to the top of the wall from where the consul stood observing the scene.

The Teuton king shook his head several times, spit in the dirt, and threw his sword and shield against the soil of Gaul with a loud clang.

He shouted an insult in Latin. It was not a phrase he'd learned from an interpreter; it was the term that the Teutons often used to refer to the Roman soldiers: "*Socors! Socors! Socors!*"* he barked, staring up at the vallum.

He turned around and rejoined the ranks of his warriors, raising his arms in a gesture of victory, shouting that insult over and over: "*Socors! Socors! Socors!*"

The king's slaves picked up his weapons and rushed after him.

Ahenobarbus, now alone and confused, looked up at the wall, where the consul stood immobile. The fierce warrior had no one to fight, so he simply returned to the safety of the Roman fortification.

There would be no individual combat between the Teuton king and the Roman consul.

That night, as the legionaries sat cooking their dinner over the bonfires, they heard, in an almost imperceptible but constant murmur: *socors, socors, socors . . .*

Inside his tent, Gaius Marius sat alone sipping wine. It seemed to leave the sour taste of cowardice in his mouth. But then again, maybe it was the bittersweet tang of wisdom.

Sertorius entered the tent to get the new password for the sentinels and night patrols.

"Victory," said Gaius Marius.

Sertorius couldn't suppress a half smile that he turned his head in an attempt to hide, but the consul noticed anyway.

"You think I'm a coward too, don't you?"

Sertorius did not respond.

"Your silence is telling, tribune," Marius decreed. "Leave me to sit alone, since alone is how I feel."

Sertorius left the tent but stopped short outside. He felt as if he had betrayed his superior. But he shook his head and walked off to communicate the password to the officers on the night watch.

Inside his tent, Gaius Marius served himself a second cup of wine, which tasted more bitter than the first: even his most loyal officer believed him to be a coward. How quickly they'd forgotten his victo-

---

*   "Coward! Coward! Coward!"

ries of the recent past; what a short memory the legionaries, centurions, and tribunes had. Yes, they all thought he was a coward: his men,
but also the Teutons—in particular, the enemy king. From that day
forward, Teutobod would always underestimate him, that much was
certain.

That meant that Teutobod would underestimate his ability to
achieve victory.

But all in due time.

Gaius Marius smiled as he poured himself a third cup of wine.

One day very soon, he would surprise the Teuton monarch. But
not yet. First the barbarians would attack.

The veteran Roman consul sipped his wine. It tasted much
sweeter.

XVII

Memoria in Memoria

THE
TEUTON ATTACK

Mouth of the Rhône River
Southern Gaul
102 B.C.

Plains beyond the Roman encampment

Just as the Roman consul had predicted, Teutobod soon unleashed his full fury. The very next day, the Teutons began to charge at the Roman fortification with all their might. It wasn't a particularly well-planned attack. The enormous confidence they'd built over the past several days insulting and humiliating their cowardly enemy had lulled the northern king into a false sense of security. Not only did he believe this Roman army to be just as weak as the ones he'd already defeated in Noreia, Burdigala, and Arausio, but it was plainly obvious that their commander was a coward.

Roman camp

Gaius Marius returned to the vallum to supervise the defense.

"It's not just another provocation," Sertorius commented quietly. "They're giving it everything they've got. He doesn't care if we come out or not—he's trying to break through the defenses and destroy us, clarissime vir."

"Yes, that's his aim. He's truly coming for us now," Marius agreed, calm and impassive despite the tens of thousands of Teutons and their thousands of allies advancing on the wall.

But the Romans had spent many months strengthening their defenses under the consul's orders: digging trenches and pits to the point of exhaustion, lining the bottoms with sharpened stakes, and covering the openings with dry brush. They'd fortified the wall and built watchtowers, now crowded with auxiliary archers, to reinforce any point more vulnerable to attack. And all along the vallum, the legionaries had thousands of pila ready to be launched at the consul's command. The men were still angry and disappointed with their leader, but the barbarians were now attacking in full force and it was their job to follow orders. The consul couldn't simply sit still anymore. He'd have to fight, launching arrows and javelins and everything they had at the enemy. And, by all the gods, each and every one of the legionaries burned with the desire to slaughter those cursed barbarians who had taunted and humiliated them. They could only kill from a distance for now, but the Roman soldiers held out hope that, faced with the enemy's brutal charge, their consul might finally order them to march out and enter into hand-to-hand combat.

Teuton army

The Teutons advanced, fierce yet disorganized, toward the wall of the Roman fortification.

And they began to die. Many fell into the trenches and pits hidden by brush; their screams of pain reached the ears of the legionaries armed to the teeth atop the wall.

Teutobod, never on the front line but near the head of his huge invading army, looked on as more and more of his fighters fell into the Romans' traps. The deaths tallied up. He'd expected to see losses, having known about those fatal pits from their previous attacks, but he was willing to lose as many men as necessary to force the cowardly Romans into battle. His pride had been wounded by the enemy consul's refusal to accept his challenge. He was now out for vengeance and would stop at nothing short of razing that fortification to the ground before marching onward to Rome. He had thousands and thousands of warriors, many more than the Romans. He could afford to lose some. But he himself kept a prudent distance from the vallum, not prepared to risk his own life. Individual combat with the enemy leader was one thing, but he would not see himself senselessly impaled by an arrow thrown from on high.

The Teutons fell by the dozens, then by the hundreds. But, once their comrades had exposed most of the traps, they managed to reach the wall.

Roman camp

Marius observed the scene and finally spoke.

"Launch your pila! Do not stop! By all the gods!" he shouted from atop the wall.

Sertorius and the other officers felt the consul's order like a soothing balm; for a moment they'd thought their leader might keep his mouth shut for the entire battle.

The Roman auxiliary forces began firing their arrows from the towers, and the legionaries launched hundreds of javelins at the front lines of Teutons approaching the base of the wall.

Soon there were too many enemy corpses to count.

Sertorius looked at the consul without a word. Admiration was finally beginning to replace the disappointment of recent days—the consul's self-control had clearly shaken the Teuton king to such an extent that he was incited to attack at a clear disadvantage.

Teuton army

Despite the great many losses on his side, Teutobod refused to cease his brutal attack. He'd breached other Roman fortifications in the past and, in hand-to-hand combat, his men had always proven superior to the Romans. It was just a matter of reaching the top of that wall. From there, his victory was assured.

Roman camp

The first Teutons began to scale the vallum on ropes cast upward from the base of the wall. The legionaries tried to cut down these makeshift ladders, but the Teutons clustered at the base of the wall with so many men and so many ropes that many of them managed to climb up despite the rain of Roman arrows and javelins.

"The slingsmen," Gaius Marius said calmly, even as the Teutons began to ascend the wall directly beneath him and his officers unsheathed their gladiī.

At the base of the vallum, on the Roman side, the slingsmen now replaced the archers and javelin throwers who had been forced into hand-to-hand combat. The terrifying whistle of their *glans plumbea* sling bullets filled the air as the legionaries flung the deadly lead balls over their comrades atop the wall, ensuring that a mortal rain of lead and iron fell ceaselessly upon the enemy's head.

Teuton army

Teutobod watched from his privileged position, safely removed from the enemy projectiles. Many of his men had fallen in their attempt to reach the Roman fortification, but many had made it and were now fighting atop the wall.

Roman camp

"Perhaps the consul should retreat to a more secure position," Sertorius suggested as the first Teutons reached the top of the wall very near them.

Marius gave him a scornful look.

The tribune bowed, brought his fist to his chest, unsheathed his sword, and stood at the ready beside the consul.

The struggle for control of the vallum was ruthless, with neither side showing a hint of mercy. In past battles, the Teutons had always managed to win out. But Marius had been preparing his men for a long time. He'd trained them to be beastly warriors, forcing them to fight one another for hours on end with the best military trainers available. His legionaries were not your average Roman soldiers, and the Teutons were surprised by their strength as the majority of their men were forcefully thrown from the wall. All the while, the Roman archers shot their arrows from the towers in an endless stream and the slingsmen tirelessly launched their large leaden bullets.

The Teuton death toll continued to mount.

Many legionaries fell wounded or even dead atop the wall, but in numbers incomparably lower than the enemy losses.

The few Teutons who managed to get past the wall found themselves immediately surrounded by Roman centuries and were massacred indiscriminately. The legionaries had received orders to take no prisoners; Marius was not interested in accumulating possible future slaves. His only concern was to eliminate the threat of the Teutons entirely. He knew that many leaders became bogged down with the superfluous and were unable to see what was most essential. And losing sight of the main objective often led to failure. At that moment, defeating the Teutons once and for all was the only thing that mattered.

Teuton army

The Germanic king spat on the ground. He looked back: two-thirds of his army was still intact and, if he ordered a retreat now, he could save many of the men who were fighting on the wall. He'd lost a number of great warriors but not enough to halt his plans to invade Italy. Not yet. But this fruitless attack was producing too many losses among his troops. It was beginning to seem absurd.

Shrewdness won out over rage.

"Order the retreat," he said to his officers.

He turned around and began walking back to his own camp.

Roman camp

Sertorius's *spatha* sliced through a Teuton warrior who had come too near the consul. Gaius Marius's heart pounded, but he maintained his composure. He'd had his hand on the handle of his own gladius and was about to unsheathe it when, in that precise instant, the Celtic horns announced that the Teuton king had ordered a retreat. Sertorius ran his blade through one last Teuton who'd been distracted by his king's horns, stabbing him repeatedly in quick succession before pushing him off the top of the wall. The other officers took care of the rest of the Teuton stragglers who had reached the top of the vallum only to find themselves abandoned by their comrades, already in retreat.

Everything was over as quickly as it had begun.

Marius, from his position, saw the ocean of barbarian corpses left behind by the Teutons in their failed attack. They'd collected their wounded but abandoned their dead. The consul could feel his officers' eyes on him. He knew they thought he should order an immediate attack to take advantage of the legionaries' eagerness for more combat after successfully repelling the enemy's savage charge. But Gaius Marius simply gave orders to increase the number of guards in all the towers and to distribute abundant water and a double ration of food at dinner. No wine that night for anyone. He didn't want them drunk in the case of a second attack by the Teutons.

He retired to his tent.

There was not another attack.

Sertorius, atop one of the watchtowers, looked for a few seconds at the Teuton army in retreat, then fixed his gaze on the consul's tent. Many of the legionaries were disappointed with Marius for not having launched an immediate counterattack. But the tribune had the feeling that he was learning a great deal, not only about how to win a battle, but about how to win a war.

XVIII

Memoria in Memoria

OUT FOR ROME

Mouth of the Rhône River
102 B.C.

Teuton camp

The king's tent was the scene of a heated debate among the royal council: some argued in favor of a new attack on the Roman defenses at dawn, while others spoke of trying to burn down the wall. The king thought differently.

"We march," said Teutobod, staring at the ground, his brow creased. He looked up and read the uncertainty on his officers' faces as he continued. "Leaving a powerful Roman army led by a brave consul behind us as we advanced on Rome would've been foolish. But I have no fear of this cowardly leader and his frightened troops. They don't dare leave their hideout. All they know how to do is launch projectiles from behind a fence. We march. At dawn."

The officers nodded.

Their king's words made sense: if all that Roman consul could do was defend his fortress, they didn't need to be worried. Nothing would stop them from taking Rome.

Roman camp

Once again Marius was called at dawn to observe the Teutons' movements.

"They're leaving," Sertorius commented, once Marius had ascended the vallum. "For good. They're taking their supplies and all their carts."

He was right. The barbarians were moving eastward away from the Fossa Mariana at the mouth of the Rhône River, parallel to the coast of the Mare Internum, toward Italy, toward Rome. The seemingly infinite line of troops and mules was advancing at a good pace, with the majority of the warriors at the head and the carts of food and military supplies behind them. Lastly, closing the ranks of that unending serpent of Teutons were the carts carrying their women and children, escorted by a few units of fighters.

It was not unexpected—Marius knew they'd either attack again or leave. The Teutons were not interested in a prolonged siege. Or, more accurately, the only siege they were interested in was the siege of Rome itself. There, they would be willing to stay for however many weeks or months it took.

Marius was silent, as usual. Once again, the tribunes wished he would order an attack, taking advantage of the fact that the enemy were moving not only their warriors, but also their women and children, which made them more vulnerable.

But the consul did not say a word.

Some of the Teuton warriors passing closest to the Roman vallum made obscene gestures or shouted insults in their language, which the Romans did not understand but could intuit the meanings of. By order of King Teutobod, some of the warriors approached the watchtowers where the Roman sentinels stood and shouted the most insulting and perverse Latin phrases they knew, then ran away laughing.

And the legionaries spat on the ground, swallowed their rage, and looked to their consul who, as always, remained impassive and unmoved.

Which is why, accustomed as they were to the consul's inaction, the legionaries and officials alike were shocked by the orders that Gaius Marius now gave: "Let the legionaries gather only what is strictly necessary for several days' march," he ordered as he climbed down the wooden stairs. "Armor, shields, and tools for digging. We leave in . . ." Marius looked at the sun: it was still early. He didn't want

the Teutons to see them abandoning the camp, not yet, but he had to
make sure the enemy column didn't get too far ahead of them, either.
"We leave in two hours," he decreed.

The tribunes couldn't believe it.

Finally, the consul was making a move. After so many months,
they were now springing into action.

"You, to my tent," he said to Sertorius.

The tribune followed the consul to the praetorium.

As soon as they entered, Marius unrolled a map of southern Gaul
across the table and pointed to a specific spot: the city-state of Mas-
salia, some sixty miles east.

"They will march through here, but I want to head them off," the
consul explained. "This is where we will block their way: Aquae Sextiae. They may or may not attack this village, but I want to arrive
there before them and establish a camp on one of the surrounding
hillsides. We will be far from the river, far from water, which will
cause some supply issues. It's a bad site for a long siege, no place to
hold out for weeks as we've done here, but I don't plan on doing that.
We're going to attack. The Teutons, the Ambrones, and their allies
will be forced to travel the central route through the region, and
there are so many of them that they'll fill it entirely." He continued
speaking and pointing at the map as Sertorius stood taking in the
plan his consul had surely been devising for months now. "We'll take
a shortcut to get ahead of the enemy columns either through the
countryside or along the coast. It will be a difficult march. Do you
think the legionaries are up to the task?"

"They will be able to do it," Sertorius affirmed. "You've kept them
in good shape digging trenches and pits all these months. They are
strong and they are eager for battle. If we tell them that we're deviat-
ing from the central route, the most comfortable one, to head off our
enemies and block their path, their sandals will fly over the soil of
Gaul, I am certain."

"Well then, let the legionaries know that this is our goal, since, by
Jupiter, as you rightly say, it will undoubtedly motivate them."

With that, Gaius Marius sighed deeply and sat down.

Sertorius understood that the consul did not require his presence any longer and so he went to transmit the orders to the other officers. The old Marius, who had defeated entire armies in Africa, was back.

Teuton camp, nightfall

The Teuton patrols reported to their king. There was no doubt about it: the Romans, against all predictions, had left their camp and were following them.

"I'm not worried about them," Teutobod said to his royal council. "Whenever we've faced them in open battlefield we've defeated them. If they attack, we'll turn around and confront their army. I want the patrols to keep me informed of their movements. The only place the Romans have ever been able to resist us was back at that cursed fort at the mouth of the river. Only because they barricaded themselves inside. That they have finally come out from behind their wall is good news for us. They have become desperate upon seeing that we are marching on Rome. Perhaps reminding them of what we'll do to their women had its desired effect." He threw his head back and laughed.

All his councilmen and officers joined in his mockery of the Roman army, which had been an endless source of amusement for the Teutons in recent years.

Southern Gaul
Roman army, en route to Massalia

Marius's soldiers advanced *magnis itineribus,* on a strenuous march, as if they really were pack mules, each soldier carrying his armor, supplies for everyday use, and even tools they would need to build their defenses. The arduous training the consul had subjected them to for recent years, intensified in the past few months, was paying off. They very quickly caught up with the almost infinite column of Teutons and Ambron warriors with their women, children, supplies, carts, and animals of all kinds. The gigantic cloud of dust kicked up by the enemy caravan made it easy to spot them for miles in the distance.

On the second day of the march, the consul addressed his officers: "We'll now turn in to open countryside. All of us. We're taking a shortcut. We're going to get ahead of them."

Upon leaving the road taken by the Teutons, the easier route, the Roman advance became even more grueling. But the legionaries were spurred on by the consul's plan to block the Teutons' path to Rome and his promise that, this time, they would at last be able to fight, not simply remain barricaded *sine die* behind their wall.

Hungry for battle and desperate to let the enemy know they were anything but *socors,* the Roman legionaries quickly overtook the Teuton army.

XIX

A MEETING OF
THE SENATE

Tavern beside the Tiber River, Rome
90 B.C.

"**H**ERE IS WHERE IT GETS INTERESTING, BOYS," SAID GAIUS
Marius with a wide smile of satisfaction: he was getting to his favorite
part of the story.

The former consul was so immersed in his narration, in fact, that
his men had not dared to interrupt him, even though several messengers from the Curia had entered the tavern.

Sertorius finally decided to speak up. "Clarissime vir," the tribune
said, bending over the table where Marius sat.

Gaius Marius seemed as if he would go right on recounting the
events leading up to the battle of Aquae Sextiae without a thought
for anyone besides Caesar and Labienus, their eyes lit up by his excit-
ing tales of war.

"Clarissime vir!" Sertorius said again, raising his voice.

Marius stopped speaking and turned to his most loyal officer with
a look of irritation.

"I'm sorry, clarissime vir," Sertorius said in a more controlled tone,
"but several messengers have come from the forum. The Senate is
ready to meet, and they are all waiting on Gaius Marius. Metellus
himself has signed one of the messages and the others are from Sulla
and Dolabella."

"And in his message, did Metellus write the words out correctly,
or does he break them into pieces like when he speaks?" Marius
laughed. Metellus had always mocked his inability to speak Greek,

so he felt justified in making fun of the conservative senator's stutter.

Instinctively, Sertorius began to scan the messages in search of the one from Metellus.

"Oh, it doesn't matter how he writes!" Marius said angrily, without looking back at the tribune. "They can wait! Especially the cursed Metellus and his minions Sulla and Dolabella! Can't you see I'm doing something important here? Can't you see I'm trying to teach my nephew a valuable lesson? Can't you see I'm trying to instill in him some common sense and, while we're at it, a bit of military strategy? The boy is too impulsive, with his head in the clouds and his heart ablaze with a hatred of injustice."

A hush fell over the tavern.

Sertorius closed his mouth, stood at attention, and bowed his head.

Marius took a long, deep breath as he leaned back in his seat. Caesar and Labienus remained perfectly still.

Marius placed his palms on the table and slowly let the air out of his lungs in an attempt to calm himself. "Sertorius," he said, his back to the tribune. "You are my best man. I shouldn't have raised my voice to you like that. The message is important and it's your obligation to transmit it. That's done. I'm going to finish this story, then we'll take my nephew home and go to the forum. The Senate can wait a little while for the only one among them who has been consul six times. Six for now," he said, finally turning to Sertorius. "They need me. It pains them to admit it, but they need me just as they did when the Teutons threatened Rome and we stopped them at Aquae Sextiae."

"Yes, clarissime vir," Sertorius said. "They will wait, without doubt."

"Good. Let's see then . . . Where were we?" Marius said, furrowing his brow, turning back to the boys, then staring down into his empty cup.

"Your army had just overtaken the Teutons," Caesar quickly reminded him.

"That's right, my boy," his uncle nodded. "Very good. You're paying attention. That's right. We overtook that endless column of Teutons and Ambrones. Only the gods know how many thousands of them there were . . ."

XX

Memoria in Memoria

AQUAE SEXTIAE

Near the Roman colony of Aquae Sextiae
Summer, 102 B.C.

Roman camp

THE LEGIONARIES NUMBERED SOME THIRTY THOUSAND BE-tween the regular and auxiliary troops. And yet, despite the many barbarian losses in their futile attack against the fort at Fossa Mariana, the Romans were outnumbered threefold by the enormous Teuton army marching steadily toward Rome.

Hundreds of legionaries were hauling tree trunks to build a new defensive wall atop the hill where Gaius Marius had ordered his men to set up camp. From this elevated vantage point, the commander could see the gigantic horde of enemies on the horizon. The sun was getting low in the sky and, just like his men were doing, the Teutons were pitching tents for the night. They didn't seem particularly worried about building walls to protect themselves, placing faith in their greater numbers and in the fact that he, Marius, did not seem predisposed to attack.

Marius sighed. The Teutons had good reason to feel secure: a nighttime attack might take them by surprise, but it would only serve to wear down the troops of both armies, and Marius had too few men to allow them to become exhausted. The Teuton king had permitted himself the luxury of losing a couple thousand men in the offensive against the Roman camp at the mouth of the Rhône. And he could afford to lose another one, two, or even three thousand more in an overnight battle that was not likely to end the war. But for Marius, losing three thousand legionaries could only happen in the key, decisive battle—in that case only, under those circumstances.

"Water!" the consul shouted.

Immediately, one of the army's calones handed him a cup of water poured from a half-empty wineskin. The fact that the flask was almost empty did not go unnoticed by the leader of the Roman army. He handed the cup back to the slave and regarded Sertorius, who wore a grave expression.

"I know," said Marius. "We're far from the river, far from any water source, and we don't have much left. We have to send water bearers into the valley to fill all the wineskins we've got. Tell them to set out immediately."

Sertorius conveyed the consul's orders, then returned to his superior and spoke to him quietly, with that tinge of worry in his voice that Gaius Marius had learned to detect: "The officers, the legionaries . . . Everyone is asking why we've camped so far from the water, clarissime vir."

The consul responded without looking at his subordinate, his eyes, instead, fixed on the Teuton camp below. "I like to see," he said. "From here atop the hill, I can see."

Teuton camp

The Teutons were camped in the middle of the plain beside the river that ran through the valley. The colony of Aquae Sextiae was only a few miles away. Teutobod had promised his men that they could plunder the village, but he'd been reflecting on what had happened at the mouth of the Rhône: he'd lost warriors without managing to defeat the enemy. He might have succeeded in intimidating the Romans and bolstering his own men's courage, but the Teuton king would not tally more losses in unnecessary attacks. He wanted to reach Italy with the bulk of his army intact and, once on the Italic peninsula, they would pillage and plunder every town they passed, sowing terror in their wake so that their brutality would reach the ears of everyone in Rome.

For that moment, however, he wasn't thinking about pillaging. Teutobod looked at the Roman camp on the top of that hill, perplexed. "Why there?" he asked his councilors. "Why has he positioned his troops so far from the water?"

No one could provide the king a logical explanation.

They all turned their eyes toward the Roman camp. Soon they could see the units of water bearers moving from the top of the hill to the valley, the river, below.

"They're getting water now, my king," said one of the officers.

Teutobod sniffled. He had a hard time adjusting to that unusual climate: hot during the day, always sweating, with a chill that set in at night. He had an incessantly runny nose.

"Maybe we could stop the Romans from getting the water they need," another Teuton officer suggested.

Teutobod nodded his head: that might be a good idea, but he didn't want to send any of his warriors. He looked beyond the main Teuton camp to where their allies had settled for the night with their women and children.

"Let the Ambrones go," the king decreed. "They didn't help much at the Rhône. Let them prove themselves useful now. Let them do something more than eat, drink, and fornicate."

Teutobod watched as his officers set out for the Ambron encampment to transmit the order.

"Yes, let the Romans go thirsty," he added with a broad smile.

River in the central valley of Aquae Sextiae

The Roman water bearers were filling hundreds of wineskins from the river, only the first of several trips they'd have to make to fill the flasks for an entire army. The idea was to have enough fresh water for several days, since, if a battle broke out, it would be impossible to gather any more water from their position atop the hill. The Teutons, on the other hand, were camped beside a clear, wide stream,

and the water bearers, like the rest of the legionaries, did not understand why the consul had chosen that hill of all places to set up camp.
The fact that it was a good position from which to observe the valley
didn't seem like sufficient justification.

They were all having the same thought when they saw a column of
enemy warriors approaching from the far end of the Teuton camp. It
was a very large regiment of Ambrones, the barbaric tribe traveling
with the Teutons in search of new lands to conquer.

"Call for reinforcements!" one of the water bearers shouted.

The message was quickly sent back to the main camp atop the
cursed hill where the consul had taken up position.

Column of Ambrones

They plodded across the valley floor. They had just finished a huge
feast to celebrate the welcome respite from so many long days of
marching en route to Rome. They were happy to take a break from
the dust of the road that cut through that flat plain with its hot climate and abundant water.

The Ambrones had not only stuffed their faces, they'd also drunk
to excess. The proximity of the Roman cowards did not worry them
in the least. They'd already seen that this Roman army could only
fight from behind a wall, barricading themselves in for days, weeks,
months. That's why, when they received the order from the Teuton
king to attack the cowardly army's water bearers, they didn't hesitate.
Their bellies full and heads light, they picked up their swords, shields,
and spears and began marching to the river. The Romans might've
been able to resist from behind their cursed wall at the Rhône, but
they'd never shown any skill on the open battlefield. This would be a
walk in the park.

Center of the valley

The few legionaries who had accompanied the water bearers stepped
into the Ambrones' path, ready to defend their comrades who were
still filling wineskins.

The Ambrones let out loud, savage shrieks as they began to charge. But their pace soon slowed from a sprint to a trot as they clutched their swollen bellies.

"Pila! Now, by Jupiter!" several centurions ordered in unison as soon as the enemies had reached an appropriate distance.

A broadside of javelins flew across the valley and fell heavily onto the Ambrones, who were surprised by the quick reaction of the scant Roman soldiers guarding the water bearers. Scant but alert, efficient, well trained, and disciplined.

"Aaah!"

Several dozen Ambrones fell wounded, some dead, pierced by enemy spears.

But the setback did not stop the Ambron advance and in fact only served to rouse them. Up to that point, their advance had been almost a parade, a jaunt along the river to terrorize the few Roman cowards spread out along the bank. Now, with the blood of their brothers spilled on the valley floor, it was suddenly personal. The Ambrones were no longer simply following the Teuton king's orders. Now, they were avenging their dead and injured comrades.

The two sides met in an explosive clash. The Romans received the Ambrones in perfect formation—shields firm, gladii held aloft between their defensive armor—but it wasn't enough.

There were too few of them.

The Ambrones, much greater in number, made way through the Romans on the sheer force of their rage and numerical superiority, swinging swords and battle axes anywhere they saw a crack in the line of enemy shields.

"Retreat!" the centurions ordered, understanding that it was impossible to maintain their formation.

The consul had taught them to withdraw when they were in the position to lose.

But just then several cohorts of reinforcements arrived from the top of the hill. The retreat, then, was not a disorderly stampede, but a replacement of the first line of soldiers, an exchange of overwhelmed troops for fresh, strong soldiers eager to enter that unexpected battle.

The centurions reorganized the front line of combat as an officer turned to the water bearers: "Take the water up to camp and return with more wineskins! Don't halt your task under any circumstances!"

He was transmitting the orders he'd received from the tribune Sertorius who, in turn, communicated the consul's instructions.

Roman camp

From a defensive tower erected at the entrance to the camp, Gaius Marius watched his men battle the horde of Ambrones.

"The battle is equally matched," Sertorius said, "but if we send even more reinforcements, we could completely destroy that column of Ambrones and have them fleeing back to their camp. We could even set fire to their carts, if everything goes well."

Marius evaluated the situation. He knew that this was not a decisive battle, not while the Teutons, who made up the bulk of the enemy army, were still outside the fight. But the Ambron camp was a good distance from the Teutons' encampment, and King Teutobod, for the moment, didn't seem prepared to involve his men, busy setting up their tents, cooking, or even resting, as if the skirmish on the riverbank had nothing to do with them.

"Send five more cohorts," Marius said. That was half a legion, a lot to risk in that battle, all while the Teutons remained securely in their camp. "If Teutobod gives any sign of intervening, everyone retreats back here, to the hill." He looked his subordinate in the eye. "Are my instructions clear?"

"Yes, clarissime vir, but . . ." Sertorius began.

"But?"

"If the Ambrones flee, do we have permission to surround their camp?"

Marius sighed deeply. "Only their camp," he said, nodding, "without going near the Teutons. Understood?"

"Understood," Sertorius confirmed.

"Good. I want you to personally lead these cohorts. I don't trust anyone else to order a retreat if the Teutons become involved. Many of the tribunes are too quick to anger; they don't use their heads. You, on the other hand, have a cold, calculating mind."

It was the highest compliment the consul had ever paid him. Sertorius brought his fist to his chest and set off to lead the troops down to the river. He would never again doubt the consul. Just because they didn't understand his logic didn't mean that it wasn't solid.

Center of the valley

The Ambrones fought viciously. Their bellies were overfull and some were clumsy from too much wine, but their rage over their fallen comrades caused them to fiercely fend off the Roman replacements, who were now showing signs of exhaustion. The Ambrones noticed that the legionaries were flagging, and they threw themselves into the battle with increased vigor. But then more Romans began to appear, almost out of nowhere, since the Ambrones could hardly see beyond that first line of combat.

The two sides were now equally matched.

Once all the cohorts under his command had reached the base of the hill, Sertorius organized the ranks of soldiers and implemented a systematic rotation of the front line. This ensured that no legionary would spend too much time in direct combat with the enemy and that new legionaries were ceaselessly cycled through the point on the battlefield where the violence was at its worst. The Ambrones fought with vigor, but they did so unthinkingly, so disorganized that after a short while, almost without realizing it, they found themselves in retreat. The Romans thrust forward with their shields, gaining ground, pushing the Ambrones away from the river.

With the battle now at a safe distance, the Roman water bearers were able to safely fill the wineskins.

Sertorius moved alongside the front line, constantly shouting instructions. The military tribune's presence inspired courage and temperance in the centurions, officers, and troops.

The Ambrones retreated, many of them wounded by the legionaries' gladiī.

In a short while, the retreat had become a desperate escape.

It was the moment of truth.

Sertorius looked up the hillside to the watchtower, where he knew the consul stood observing the scene. He saw no gesture indicating that they should withdraw and he had received Marius's consent to pursue the enemy as long as they stayed away from the Teutons.

He gazed down into the valley: the Ambrones were running straight back to their own camp.

"After them!" Sertorius shouted.

The order took some of the legionaries by surprise, accustomed as they were to merely defending their positions, rather than attacking, much less pursuing an enemy in retreat. But they were not wanting for motivation. Some of the centurions glanced over their shoulders. The consul was there, in the watchtower, but he made no signal or gesture. The *buccinators'* horns had not sounded, meaning no withdrawal had been ordered. The trumpeters' silence was the consul's silence, lending Sertorius's order legitimacy.

The Roman troops chased the Ambrones back to their camp, where the barbarians didn't even put up a fight. Instead, leaving their women, children, and carts unprotected, they continued retreating, some toward the Teuton king's camp, others into the nearby woods.

Sertorius was about to order his men to stop the cowardly Ambrones from fleeing into the trees when they found themselves blocked by the Ambron women, prepared to defend their camp against the Romans using anything they had on hand, from cooking utensils to farm tools to their own sheer strength. The children stood right alongside them. Some cried, others bit and scratched any Roman who came near. The legionaries showed no mercy as the women put up a fierce resistance. It was an unequal battle, but the barbarians' recent insults and mockery were still fresh, and the soldiers were angry. They had not forgotten how the enemy had vowed to rape their own daughters, wives, and mothers as soon as they reached the city by the Tiber. All Sertorius could do was attempt to curb the massacre. He had orders not to pursue the Ambrones who had taken refuge in the Teuton camp, and chasing the other men into the forest did not seem wise.

"Set fire to the carts!" he ordered.

In a matter of minutes, the Ambron camp was nothing more than fuel for the glowing flames, consuming everything in sight as the brave women continued fighting till their last breath.

Sertorius then noticed some of the men dragging the tough barbarian women toward a dip in the plain, with clear intentions. The tribune studied the forest where the supposed warriors had chosen to flee instead of staying to defend their families. Some of the children, their mothers captured by the Roman troops, cried as they watched the scene.

"Let the women go," Sertorius said without raising his voice. The same way he'd observed the consul give orders. In a calm, even tone. Never repeating himself.

The legionaries did not wish to release the wives of these barbarians who had mocked and humiliated them, but, seeing the tribune's icy gaze, they loosened their grips and the women rushed away.

The camp was in flames.

Utterly destroyed, in a matter of minutes.

"We withdraw," said Sertorius.

And the men obeyed.

Teuton camp

"We're not going to respond?" a member of the Germanic king's royal council asked upon learning that the Romans had set fire to the Ambron camp.

Teutobod looked around: the men were all pitching their tents or sitting down to eat. They were not prepared for combat. The Ambrones themselves had hastily rushed into battle against the Romans and it had been a disaster. He could order his army to attack, but that would doubtlessly end in either a quick Roman retreat or in all of the enemy troops joining in a pitched battle he had not planned for. He couldn't make up his mind.

"We're not going to aid the Ambrones, my king?" another member of his council asked.

Teutobod had acted impetuously in sending the Ambrones to impede the Roman water bearers, and this was the result. He would not make any more rash decisions.

"Men who won't even fight to defend their women and children don't deserve our help," the Germanic king finally decreed.

He took a sip of water. From that same river, the same water that the Ambrones had all died for. The monarch poured out the rest of what was left in his cup, then cleared his throat, spit in the dirt, and turned his back on the blazing carts, on the dead bodies of the Ambron men, women, and children.

He looked to the watchtower from where the Roman consul surely surveyed the scene. Although he could not see him at that distance, he was certain that the Roman commander was up there staring down at him.

Roman camp

Sertorius, still panting, his brow beaded with sweat and his uniform stained with blood, presented himself before the consul atop the watchtower.

"We set fire to the camp," he explained, "but I didn't think it prudent to chase the Ambrones into the woods, nor, of course, into the Teuton camp."

"You did well," Gaius Marius said, always sparing with his praise, turning to look back out over the sea of tents being pitched on the plain below. In the distance, he could see the Germanic king walking away from the blaze that had once been the Ambron encampment.

"We should have wine for the legionaries who have participated in this victory," one of the tribunes suggested.

Several officers agreed, but Sertorius did not say a word. He remained silent, still catching his breath.

"Better yet, wine for all the legionaries, to further boost morale," said another.

Gaius Marius followed the Teuton king's movements. Everyone respected the consul's silence as they waited for his response.

"It is not a time for celebration," he finally said without looking at the officers. "We were lucky that the Ambrones sent their drunk soldiers to fight and not their women. If they'd simply handed their weapons to their wives, from what I saw, things might've been a lot more difficult for us."

The tribunes blinked. None of them had ever considered something as absurd as a woman fighting. But it was true that they had shown more bravery than their men.

Gaius Marius turned around and began to climb down from the tower as he gave his orders to the officers: "No wine. Dinner and rest. Up at dawn, breakfast, and then reinforcement of all the fortifications."

Marius reached the base of the tower and began walking through the lines of tents to his own praetorium.

"You heard our commander," Sertorius said to the other tribunes, who immediately dispersed to transmit the orders they'd received. Sertorius caught up with the consul and posed a question: "The key battle, the final one, is what we're waiting for, isn't it, clarissime vir?"

"That's right," Marius replied without slowing his pace.

Sertorius could tell that his superior had no interest in conversation, so he stopped short and stood watching as the consul walked away, alone, straight-backed, then disappeared among the legionaries, who all stood at attention as he passed.

XXI

Memoria in Memoria

THE PEOPLE'S
LEGIONS

Valley of Aquae Sextiae, southern Gaul
102 B.C.

TEUTOBOD WAS ONCE AGAIN AIMING TO PROVOKE AND DIS-
orient the Romans. At the Fossa Mariana he'd had his men insult the
legions; this time the Teuton warriors circled the Roman camp at
night, banging their swords and shields loudly to disrupt the enemies' sleep.

Gaius Marius responded with the same tactic, sending the Roman
night guard to ensure that no Teuton fighter could get a peaceful
night's rest.

It seemed like they might be destined for another long, slow wait.
Until events began to unfold very quickly.

Roman camp

The consul had summoned all the tribunes to the praetorium on the
top of the hill.

He was direct. He was concise. He was succinct.

"Tonight, a hearty dinner, but no excesses and no wine. Tomorrow, breakfast before dawn, and make sure all the soldiers drink milk
or water. No man should be thirsty by the time the sun comes up." He
unrolled a papyrus showing a rough map of the hill, the river, and the
Roman and Teuton camps. Leaning over the map, he began to explain the plan he'd spent the past several days devising. "Tonight, I
want double the number of guards making noise around the Teuton

camp. And you, Claudius Marcellus," he said, looking to one of his most veteran tribunes, "I want you to take three thousand legionaries and position yourselves here, in this nearby oak grove." He pointed to a spot on one side of the hill. "You'll take pack mules and almost all of the calones. I'd prefer for you to take even more men, but we'll need the bulk of the troops here on the hill. You'll stay hidden away until the middle of the battle, when the Teutons have begun their retreat. You'll have to try to make it look like you have far more than three thousand men. That's why you'll take the animals and the slaves with you. Spread them out among your troops. That will give the appearance of a much larger force. Understood?"

Claudius Marcellus nodded as he tried to process this unexpected order. Like the majority of the officers, he couldn't believe what he was hearing: the consul was presenting a plan for an all-out battle. Finally.

To Sertorius, however, it came as no surprise. Ever since Marius's response to the Ambrones, he'd been certain that the consul was merely biding his time to launch an attack.

"Good, by all the gods," Gaius Marius continued. "Tomorrow at dawn, all the troops except Claudius Marcellus's men will be ready to stand in *triplex acies* on the hillside."

The consul knew that his men understood the classic triplex acies formation, a huge checkerboard of military units staggered at alternating intervals that allowed for a seamless renewal of the troops in combat.

This would be the decisive battle in their long war with the Teutons, and everything had to go exactly according to the plan he'd been devising for the last . . . days? weeks? months? No, years. Marius had been dreaming of this battle ever since he first began studying the great defeats of the other consular armies in Noreia, Burdigala, and Arausio.

"At dawn," he continued, "with the first rays of light, our troops will already be in formation on the hillside and our *turmae* cavalry will charge the enemy camp. The riders will provoke the Teutons until their king orders his men to pursue them. Then the Teutons will have to cross the river and climb the hillside to face our legions, who will make way for the cavalry to situate themselves at the rear. And then the battle will begin." The consul paused. He looked at the map. "Any questions?" he asked.

Everything seemed perfectly clear to the officers, who were mentally reviewing the plan.

It was Claudius Marcellus who dared to voice the concern that everyone, in one way or another, was feeling: "The Teutons outnumber us," he pointed out. "Even with our annihilation of the Ambrones, there are still a great many more of them."

The consul nodded, but his response was unequivocal: "That's why we'll fight from the position on the top of the hill. That's why the river will remain at their back and not ours. That's why you, Marcellus, will charge forth to ambush them in the middle of the battle. No one said it would be easy. Isn't this what you've been waiting for all these months? A fight? Well, the time has come."

Teuton camp, the next morning at dawn

Teutobod had slept badly because the Roman troops had been unexpectedly bothersome. But the dawn brought an even greater shock.

"They are here, my king!" exclaimed one of his councilors.

Teutobod looked up to see the entire Roman army spread out along the slope outside their camp in perfect combat formation. And, what was more, the enemy cavalry was galloping toward them, ready to attack.

Teutobod looked around: many of his warriors were still having breakfast. None of them had expected any provocation from the Romans, but here was the enemy cavalry, quickly drawing nearer. There weren't very many of them, but they'd have to fend them off.

"Ready the troops," the king ordered.

Soon, the guards Teutobod had placed outside the camp were joined by the rest of the soldiers brandishing shields, swords, axes, and spears. Many had not had the chance to eat; they were hungry and, like their king, had not slept as well as they would've liked, thanks to the raucous Roman night patrols that had seemed even more eager than usual to disturb them.

Roman camp

The cavalry turmae galloped back toward the tight Roman lines. They'd fought the Teutons until the bulk of the Germans joined the battle. The riders knew they were too greatly outnumbered and had instructions from the tribunes to simply harass the enemy into pursuing them. So, as the immense Teuton army finally gathered in its full numbers, the *decurions* of the Roman cavalry ordered a retreat, galloping across the river and up the slope to where the legions stood in formation.

As soon as he saw the cavalry returning to camp, with the huge Teuton army in pursuit, Gaius Marius climbed down from the watchtower. This surprised his officers, who had expected him to command the battle from his raised vantage point. The consul, moving quickly and trailed by Sertorius and the rest of the military tribunes, left the safety of the camp's defensive wall and marched through the lines of the Roman army spread out on the broad hillside.

"Make way!" Marius ordered.

The tribunes and centurions echoed the command.

The cohorts were staggered in such a way that wide corridors could easily be opened up between each unit, and the consul now moved through the center of the troops toward the vanguard forces as the cavalry units simultaneously galloped up the side corridors to take their positions in the rearguard, where they would wait for the Roman leader to call them back into action.

In no time, Gaius Marius had positioned himself in the front line of combat—to everyone's shock. It was unusual, almost unheard of, for a commander to fight alongside his men, something that had not happened since the time of Scipio.

The consul looked toward the enemy: their approach was slow, almost languid. He had time and he would use it to whip his men into a fervor.

Gaius Marius began to pace in front of the vanguard cohorts: "Close your ranks!" he ordered.

The military units moved back into their battle positions like pieces on a *ludus latrunculorum* board. There wasn't a single crack in their perfect formation; only a colossal force could break their ranks. But anything was possible—it had happened. In Arausio, for example. And it could happen again.

The Teutons were advancing over the plain.

"Legionaries of Rome!" Marius raised his arms to get his men's attention.

His voice thundered over the hillside, which formed a kind of natural amphitheater, allowing the middle and rearguard soldiers to see their leader and amplifying the consul's words across the entire slope.

Sertorius watched from behind Marius, surprised, still not fully understanding what the consul had in mind. Maybe he would simply whip up the legionaries and then return to command the battle from a safer position . . .

"Legionaries of Rome!" the consul said again to make sure that everyone was listening. "I'd like to be able to tell you that you're cherished, beloved by the Senate, adored by every member of our great republic! Yes, I'd like to be able to tell you that. But I would be lying."

He paused for a moment.

The thirty thousand legionaries remained silent, listening to the footfalls of the sixty thousand Teutons echoing across the hillside like the drumbeat of that imminent, inexorable, unstoppable battle. A battle in which the odds were not in their favor. They were outnumbered, and previous Roman armies had been defeated by this same enemy three times. They were eager for combat, but also suddenly . . . frightened.

"No, you are not considered the best of Rome!" the consul continued. "In fact, you are not even thought to be average or mediocre. No, no, it's much worse than that. You are widely considered to be the scum of Rome! The lowest of the low!"

Sertorius furrowed his brow, as did the other tribunes.

The legionaries did not understand where their commander was going with this. They'd imagined that he would try to embolden them for battle and they expected some speech to that effect. They had not expected to be insulted. Sertorius looked down and shook his head. This was no way to motivate soldiers who would have to fight until their last drop of blood. Had the consul lost all sense?

"Yes, you are considered the scum of Rome, the poorest and most miserable, perpetually overlooked. Your votes never count for the Senate, and they never even wanted you here. They think only wealthy landowners are fit to carry combat weapons and participate in war! You are the ones who have always been excluded from defending Rome and, therefore, from the glory and riches of triumph! The Senate would have you remain in poverty, because to them, you are worth nothing; you don't even exist! They expect only defeat and failure from you and, as we speak, they are already planning to recruit a new army like the ones before, made up of wealthy landowners! To the powerful men in Rome, you don't count, and you never will! To the powerful men in Rome, you're finished before you've even started!"

Now all the legionaries were choking back rage and hatred. The Teutons had humiliated them at the Fossa Mariana, and now came these insulting words from their leader, which cut deep. As painful as it was for the men to admit, he was correct. It was the first time in over a century, since the times of Hannibal, that Rome had allowed the poor to join an army.

Gaius Marius raised his arms again.

The legionaries were furious at everything and everyone, and they didn't want to give their lives for a Rome that didn't appreciate them. But they listened, eager to hear what he had to say.

"No, the Senate has no faith in you!" Marius continued. "But do you know who does have faith in you? Do you know who does see your strength, your fortitude, your years of ceaseless training? Do you know who is ready to fight alongside you, to die alongside you, to win alongside you?"

The consul once again paused, now silently pacing in front of his army's vanguard lines.

Sertorius, focused on his superior's speech but also on the enemy's movements, approached the consul and said into his ear: "The enemy has reached the river."

Marius nodded without looking at him, his attention focused on the legionaries.

"Who has faith in us?" one of the Roman soldiers finally asked.

Marius nodded again, this time more emphatically, showing satisfaction at that question put forth from the ranks of his men.

"I do!" he howled. "I, Gaius Marius, Roman consul, victor of the war in Africa, defeater of Jugurtha! I have faith in you and in your strength and fortitude! I, Gaius Marius, decreed that the Senate should arm you all, give you all the same weapons, creating a unified army of equal force! I, Gaius Marius, place all my trust in you! You may say, If you have so much faith in us, why have you never allowed us to fight the Teutons, the very enemy who now approaches, who taunted us at the mouth of the Rhône? I'll tell you why: because that fortification was a good place to receive supplies and train and watch the enemy's movements, but that was not the location of the final battle. This is the location of the final battle!" He spread his arms wide as if encompassing the entire hillside sloping down to dense forest. "Here, the enemy cannot surround us, so it does not matter that they double us in number. The front line of battle is the same for both armies! If we'd fought at the Rhône, the river would've been at our back, as happened with our troops in Arausio, but now it will be at the backs of our enemies. Are you thirsty? Would you like some water? Well then today we will push the barbarians down the hillside, force them back across the river, and then drink from the cool stream that runs red with their blood! We will massacre the Teutons once and for all. Why didn't I let you fight at the Rhône? Not because I didn't think you capable of victory, not because I doubted your courage, your strength. I merely doubted that any victory was possible there. Because, I will be honest with you, the wealthy senators of Rome will not give you a second chance. They see you as scum; they look away from you on the streets as they make their way to the forum or the market. And they will not give you a second chance if you fail. You, Rome's poor and downtrodden, have only one chance. And this is it. This slope of this hill beside this river, these cliffs surrounding us, these weapons you carry, these years of ceaseless training, this is your one chance!"

Gaius Marius paused for an instant to catch his breath. He was inflamed, speaking from his heart, from his gut. He went on: "And you might be wondering, Why should I fight for a city that rejects me? I'll tell you why! Because all of Rome does not reject you. The Senate has little faith in you, it's true; the great majority of the patres conscripti look down on you. Especially the ones who call themselves the optimates, convinced that they are the best! But you have wives and children back in Rome. And if the Teutons are allowed to have their way, your wives and children will be raped and murdered by the barbarians, as they've vowed a thousand times in their attempts to lure us out of our camp on the Rhône. The Senate may recruit a new army of wealthy soldiers. But I have no faith, none at all, in any army recruited by the senators! Because they will be soft, untrained, lacking the strength, the fortitude, the rage needed to massacre these savages who advance toward us and who, tomorrow, if we fail, will march unimpeded on Rome, where your families wait, unprotected."

Marius was sweating from so much shouting in the huge natural amphitheater of that hillside crowded with legionaries.

Sertorius, who now understood the aim of the consul's speech, was still concerned with the enemy's advance. "The Teutons have crossed the river and are beginning to climb the slope, clarissime vir," he said quietly.

Marius nodded again.

"Tighten my breastplate," he said. "The cords are loose."

Sertorius gestured to a calon who came over to retie the strings on the back of the consul's breastplate so that it would not move out of place when he entered combat.

With this gesture, the tribune now understood that the consul was on the front line not only to give a speech, but to fight. He could see the legionaries' eyes gleaming, emboldened by their leader's words.

"Let me know when they're a thousand paces away," Gaius Marius added, still without looking at the tribune, facing the legionaries.

He took a few steps closer to the vanguard cohorts. He scanned the crowd of military units under his command—the ones nearest him, but also the ones farther back, at the top of the hill. And to all of them he spoke his final words before the start of the battle: "Are you prepared to fight for your wives and children, for your brothers, for the people of Rome, for all of those overlooked by the Senate, your friends and loved ones who *do* believe in you, who *do* have faith in you? Are you willing to stand and fight with me, alongside me? I have armed you, trained you, and I now offer you this one chance. So my question is: Are you ready for this battle? Are you ready to defeat the barbarians? Are you ready to change the history of Rome?" The consul thundered on. "Will you show these spineless barbarians, those spineless senators in Rome, that our legions, the true legions of the Roman people, are stronger, more powerful, more indestructible than any other army we've ever dreamed of? Will you fight, and win, and revel in the glory of victory? Answer me! I am prepared to fight alongside you, to die alongside you, to triumph alongside you! Are you ready, damn it? By all the gods, answer meeeeeeee!" The consul let out a savage shriek with his last word. A howl that could not go unanswered.

"Yes, we are! Yes, we are! Yes, we are!" the vanguard legions shouted, and soon all the cohorts had joined the deafening cry of thirty thousand voices sweeping down the slope to the ears of the approaching Teutons.

It was a battle cry that would forever change the history of Rome.

XXII

Memoria in Memoria

THE FINAL BATTLE

Valley of Aquae Sextiae, southern Gaul
102 B.C.

At the vanguard of the Teuton army

King Teutobod was not on the front line. He was situated squarely in the center of his troops as he marched with his huge army up the hill. Even so far back, he could hear the roaring of the Roman legions.

The officers near the king were surprised at the fury of the enemy's voices. Teutobod detected a hint of hesitation in his men.

"We double them in number," he said. "And we've already defeated them on multiple occasions. They're going to wear themselves out with all that screaming, and we know they need all the strength they can get . . ."

He let out a loud cackle and his laughter spread first to his council, then, gradually, to every one of his warriors, serving to lighten their mood. It was much needed, since for a moment, the legionaries' battle cry had indeed intimidated them.

At the Roman vanguard

The enemies' mocking laughter reached the Roman legionaries, and they quieted. It was like a pitcher of cold water bringing them back to reality after the passion they'd felt while listening to the consul's words.

Gaius Marius had already said what he had to say, and he knew that his men were too inflamed to let their blaze be snuffed out by a few chuckles from the approaching enemy. But still, perhaps a few final words . . .

"A thousand paces," said Sertorius.

"Good," the consul said quietly, and then once again addressed his men in a voice that boomed across the hillside: "Yes, they laugh at you. Just like the senators of Rome have spent years laughing at you. But today, legionaries, is the day we will put an end to their mockery! Today is a day for new beginnings, the birthday of the new legions of Rome. Today is your day! For your women and children! For your friends and families and for the people of Rome. For the gods!" He unsheathed his sword and raised it high into the sky. "For yourselves! Victory or death! Victory or death!"

And the Roman legions howled in unison: "Victory or death! Victory or death!"

Now, finally, the consul turned and faced the Teutons, who were ascending the slope, slowly but steadily, planning to put an end to the battle before the sun reached the peak of its journey across the sky.

Marius spoke to his most trusted tribune. "If the Teutons surround us, surround me, and there's no possibility of escape, kill me. Do you understand? Run me through with your own sword and give me death. A Roman consul may die in combat, but he must never be taken prisoner. A true consul, never. Is that understood, tribune?"

Sertorius nodded. "Yes, understood, clarissime vir. If they surround us, I will assist the consul in his *devotio*," the tribune assured his commander, agreeing that suicide was the most noble path for a top-ranking Roman general in the case of defeat.

"Very good. Then let's go after those cursed Teutons," Marius said.

It had been a long while since he'd seen direct combat. The last time would've been in Africa, but at that moment, his memory flashed much further back, to the years of his youth. He recalled his time under the command of Scipio Aemilianus at the siege of Numantia. "This is going to be like in Iberia," he muttered to himself. "Very difficult, arduous, a colossal battle."

Gaius Marius paced menacingly before the cohorts at the vanguard. "Hold your advance!" he shouted, and the centurions repeated his orders.

"They're six hundred paces out, clarissime vir," said Sertorius, always beside his consul, looking between the Teuton troops and the Roman cohorts.

"Let them get closer. The closer they get, the steeper the slope. It is in our interest to battle from the higher position."

Sertorius nodded, his heart pounding in his ears. Never before had he witnessed the unstoppable approach of such a large horde of barbarians. "Yes, clarissime vir," the tribune agreed, and immediately added, "They are five hundred fifty paces away."

"Prepare the pila!" the consul then howled.

The legionaries raised their javelins.

"Five hundred paces, clarissime vir."

"I already know I'm senator and consul, as much as those miserable optimates hate it. You don't have to remind me of my rank every second. Just give me the paces. You're better at calculating them. You have better eyesight than I do."

Sertorius was about to respond but merely nodded.

The Teutons were releasing guttural cries like beasts from the underworld. Their aim was to frighten the Romans. And it was working.

"Four hundred paces," said the tribune.

Gaius Marius turned to the cohorts at the vanguard. "Wait for my signal! Anyone who throws out a single *pilum* ahead of time will see me personally after the battle!" he decreed before adding between gritted teeth, "if we're still alive."

"Three hundred paces."

Marius turned back to face the Teutons, who were continuing their inexorable march up the slope toward the Roman legions.

"Two hundred paces!" Sertorius wailed to make himself heard over the enemy war cries. "One hundred fifty paces!" He ran his hand over his sweaty chin.

Gaius Marius raised his arms.

Everything would happen very quickly, almost all at once, but the closer the barbarians got, the more of them would fall. The charge had to be perfectly calculated so that the legionaries would have time to plant themselves firmly in their positions with their shields up to resist the push of the enemy who was now almost upon them.

"One hundred paces, clarissime vir!" Sertorius shouted at the top of his lungs, automatically adding the honorific his superior had asked him to drop. His words sounded pleading, as if begging the consul to give the order.

Gaius Marius lowered both arms at the same time.

Thousands of javelins flew through the air as the sky became a dark cloud of iron and wood.

Crack, crack, crack, crack . . .

The Roman javelins landed on the first lines of Teuton soldiers like a violent hail storm. Dozens died instantly; hundreds more fell wounded. They paused their ascent for an instant, a mere thirty paces away. In the enemies' brief confusion, the legionaries positioned their shields to receive the press of the Teuton advance.

"Swords at the ready! Swords at the ready! By all the gods!" Gaius Marius shouted, taking a few steps back, shadowed by Sertorius, and he fell into the first line of men at the vanguard.

The Teutons stepped over the bodies of their dead and wounded, trampling them if necessary to continue their advance up the hill. That first shower of pila had caused losses, many, but now they were like a wild wounded animal, desperate to attack, to destroy, to annihilate.

They threw themselves fiercely against the Roman shields.

"Attack! Attack! Attack!" the consul, tribunes, and centurions cried as one. And the legionaries thrust their gladii through the gaps between their shields, willing the tips of their blades to puncture the chests, arms, legs, and if possible, hearts and guts of their enemies.

The Teutons were ferocious, yes, but they had marched several miles from their camp, crossed the river, and made the long climb up the slope all without stopping to rest, and many had no food in their stomachs. Their stamina was already waning and the Roman front line, although it had suffered some losses, soon gained ground. The slope was in the Romans' favor since it was much easier to move downhill than to climb upward, as the tired Teutons were forced to do. The strength of each legionary was increased by the hillside, whereas each Teuton's force was diminished.

Nevertheless, Marius wanted the front line of combat to be as strong as possible. "First replacement!" he ordered.

The legionaries in the first line halted, took a few steps back, and were quickly replaced by the comrades immediately behind them, who could battle with more vigor.

Marius found himself beside Sertorius, with no enemy to stab or fend off. The Teutons had been pushed back by the Romans' sheer might and military discipline. His spatha, a bit longer than a legionary's gladius, was dripping with blood. Gaius Marius was fighting on the front line like any other soldier, and his legionaries, witnessing this, were further emboldened. Their consul was fighting alongside them, shoulder to shoulder. Literally.

Suddenly, Gaius Marius felt dampness on his temple.

"The consul has a cut on his forehead," said Sertorius. "Call the *medicus!*"

"I want a quick rotation of troops. We need to continue advancing down the hillside all the way to the bottom," Marius said, ignoring his wound.

"Yes, clarissime vir."

"And water brought for all the legionaries as they come off the front line so they can drink as much as they need. It doesn't matter if we use all of it today. Today is the only day that matters. Do you understand? Today we risk everything."

The officers nodded and took off in different directions to communicate the orders.

The Romans, with the rapid and tightly coordinated rotation of troops they had perfected over many hours of training, kept fresh, skilled fighters on the front line. And despite the numerous losses at the hands of the virulent Teutons, they were in fact pushing the barbarians down the slope to the river. Little by little, with great difficulty, but consistently. And that progress down the hill gave them hope for victory. They might be the supposed scum of Rome, but they would be victorious. They would change history and no one would be able to laugh at them ever again.

The consul's words still echoed in their ears as they continued to push the Teutons farther and farther down the slope toward the river.

Oak grove, halfway between the
Roman and Teuton camps

Hidden between the trees with his men, Marcellus had seen the entire Teuton army march past. They did not attempt to impede them. They had other orders to follow.

He could now see that the barbarians were gradually retreating, pushed back by the Roman troops, with the consul personally leading the charge.

"They're still too far," Marcellus said to his officers, "but ready the men and the beasts. It will soon be our time."

Center of the Teuton army

Teutobod watched as his warriors failed to defeat the Roman cohorts. He didn't like the way things were going, but he still believed that, in the end, his greater numbers would prevail. He refused to consider any other option. He had many men and could afford to lose several thousand, but it might not be a bad idea to pull back to the plain. The Romans had a clear advantage there on the hillside because of the slope and because the cliffs on two sides kept him from using his superior numbers to surround the enemy. It had taken him too long to figure it out, but there was still time to correct that error. Yes, giving up some ground might be a good strategy. He understood that he'd taken the bait when he responded to the Roman cavalry's attack at dawn. He'd let himself be lured into the mouth of the wolf, but he'd get his men out of there now, in an orderly fashion. Once on the plain, they'd reorganize, surround the Romans as soon as they crossed the river, and, once the water was at the legionaries' backs, they would massacre them on three fronts, pushing them into the river as they'd done in Arausio. That little stream down there was no Rhône, but it was still uncomfortable to fight with it at your back. Victory would be theirs. Once again. It would only take a little more effort. They would still win.

"By Odin! Continue retreating, quickly but controlled!"

Vanguard of the Roman army

"He's figured it out," said Gaius Marius, observing the Teuton withdrawal. "The barbarian king understands that he's marched into a trap."

"What do we do, clarissime vir?" Sertorius asked.

"We continue with the plan."

"Do we cross the river?"

"Everything according to plan," the consul insisted. "He wants out of the trap. But he's not out yet. Today, we are the hunters and he is our prey. And when Gaius Marius goes on the hunt, Gaius Marius returns with his prize."

On the plain

Heat.

The sun was inching higher over southern Gaul, beating down on the plains. The Teutons, unaccustomed to the humid Mediterranean climate, were dripping with sweat and losing stamina. Their withdrawal, which should've been calm and organized, was at times a desperate stampede as they tried to reach the river as quickly as possible. They wanted to cool off in the water, to take a drink, and to escape the Roman legions bearing down on them.

Teutobod had lost his voice in his attempts to control his men's retreat. Things weren't going well, but as his men descended the slope, he was encouraged by the thought that, on the plains, once the Romans came out from between the cliffs and the enemy's flanks were exposed, he would be able to surround them, and his greater numbers would ultimately win out. That was his plan—a proven, winning formula.

Many of his men had already crossed the river, and Teutobod was repositioning his troops to create a front line that was much wider than the one presented by the legions. This would allow them to overwhelm the Roman cohorts from all sides. But suddenly . . .

"What is that?" several Germanic officers shouted.

Teutobod looked past the rearguard and saw that a second enemy force, both cavalry and infantry, was emerging from a grove of oak trees, charging at his men as they regrouped on the plain.

"It's another army!" the Teuton soldiers shouted. "The Romans have called in a second army!"

As the unexpected forces approached from behind and the consul's troops were already crossing the river and charging toward them from the other side, the Teutons found themselves surrounded by two enemy armies. They were demoralized by their failed attack on the hillside, and they were tired, thirsty, and disorganized. They did not stop to scrutinize this supposed second army. They began to flee in panic. Total chaos ensued.

Teutobod took a better look at those new troops and realized there weren't as many soldiers as there seemed to be, and many were poorly outfitted—some strange combination of cavalry and foot soldiers, but not regular legionaries, maybe auxiliaries. It almost looked as if they'd simply armed some slaves. And there were many animals without any riders at all.

"It's a ruse, that's all," he said. Then shouted: "Stop them, by Odin, it's not a second army!"

But fear had taken root in the hearts of the barbarians. First the Romans had massacred the Ambrones, then they'd forced them from the hillside, and now they were attacking with a second army they'd known nothing about. It was too much; there were too many surprises. Escape seemed like the best option.

Roman army

"Attack the ones who are still climbing out of the river," Gaius Marius ordered. "And let the cavalry hunt down anyone who tries to escape. Tell them to help Marcellus and his men."

"Yes, clarissime vir," Sertorius said, and quickly communicated the instructions.

On the plain

Teutobod was desperate. He tried to regain control of the situation, but half his army was retreating in a massive stampede, pursued by the Roman cavalry and the military unit that had ambushed them from the woods. There weren't that many Romans chasing them, but his warriors, fleeing without looking back, were easy prey. They fell, massacred by the hundreds.

The Teuton king looked toward the river. The situation was no better there: his men, disheartened, barely showed resistance to the well-disciplined Roman troops who continued advancing, killing left and right. Some even threw down their weapons and begged for mercy. Seeing this angered the king to such an extent that he placed himself, for the first time since the start of the battle, in the front line of combat. But his gesture of honor came too late. His presence made some of his men, those closest to him, pick their weapons back up out of shame and stand with their monarch against the Roman cohorts. But the legions ceaselessly rotated their front line, continuously throwing fresh soldiers into combat. The Teuton king was left with fewer and fewer men until he was eventually surrounded by only the wounded and dead. Finally, he found himself alone against the Roman legions' entire front line.

He couldn't resist this army. This was nothing like the Roman troops he'd defeated in the past. Teutobod understood that there was something different about these legions. They were more spirited. And he had been abandoned.

He howled in pain as first one gladius penetrated his body, then another.

Just then a centurion recognized the enemy king's armor and ordered the legionaries to halt their attack and guard the wounded monarch, fallen and defeated, until their consul determined what should be done with him.

In the meantime, the massacre continued all around them: in the river, where the Roman legionaries were either killing the Teutons or taking them as prisoners, and on the plain, where the cavalry, along with Marcellus's troops, were hunting the barbarians down like frightened bunnies. The Teutons were accustomed to waging battles in which victory was all but assured from the outset. They were not prepared, mentally or physically, for combat that felt like a lost cause from start to finish.

The bodies piled up.

The massacre was brutal.

Several cohorts reached the enemy camp and found, as had been the case with the Ambrones, that the women were prepared to fight for their lives, brave but weaponless, desperate to save their children. Many were murdered and many more captured as slaves.

The Teuton defeat was absolute.

"It's a resounding victory, clarissime vir," said Sertorius as they approached the Teuton king, wounded on the ground and surrounded by hundreds of legionaries proudly taking in the scene.

"A great victory it is," Gaius Marius said to the crowd of tribunes, officers, and legionaries as he crouched beside the defeated king. "Tell me, king of the Teutons, who is the coward now?"

Teutobod let out a muffled grunt of pain and heartfelt rage, blood gushing from his mouth.

Gaius Marius smiled briefly.

Then he stood up and took a few steps away from the dying king.

"Should we kill him?" Sertorius asked.

Marius turned toward the Teutobod. He was bleeding slowly; it would take hours yet for him to die if they did not execute him.

"No, we won't kill him," he responded. "He laughed at us for years; we can laugh at him for a few hours."

Sertorius nodded, satisfied.

"Wine for all the legionaries as soon as they finish capturing the last few cowards who attempt to flee!" the consul shouted for all his men to hear. "Today is a day for celebration and drinking! And those who like can toast with the defeated enemy king!"

Cheers from all around. Gaius Marius then walked toward a rise in the land from where he could better take in the entire scene. Sertorius followed him in case there were any further instructions that needed to be communicated to the other officers. From that vantage point, they could see the Teutons surrendering as their fleeing comrades were hunted down.

"Tell Marcellus not to follow anyone into the forest," the consul ordered. "I don't want to lose any men in an ambush by the cowards who manage to escape."

Sertorius looked to the other officers but did not need to repeat the instructions, as several of them took off to transmit the message.

Gaius Marius gazed toward the river. It was red with the blood of thousands of Teuton warriors impaled by Roman gladii and pila.

"Do you know what the name *Teuton* means, according to the Gauls?" he asked Sertorius.

"No, I don't know, clarissime vir."

"*Teut* means 'tribe' and *on,* 'water.' For the Gallic, the Teutons are the tribe of the waters, because they come from across faraway seas in the uncharted north. Doesn't it seem curious to you?"

Sertorius didn't understand what the consul was getting at.

"The Teutons, the tribe of the waters," Gaius Marius said, pointing to the river tinged red with blood, "have perished in the waters. They came on the waters, and on the waters they have succumbed."

In that moment, an officer reached the top of the rise—he brought news.

"Marcellus has been informed," said the officer. "And the Teuton king . . . no longer breathes."

Gaius Marius gave a slight nod. He had just annihilated Teutobod, Rome's most formidable foe, on track to becoming the next Hannibal. But for the veteran consul, the news of that death only merited a small nod. His humility in this moment of great triumph over his mortal enemy would be recounted for generations to come, garnering Marius legendary status among his admiring legions.

"*Imperator! Imperator! Imperator!*" the Roman soldiers chanted.

They'd once believed their commander to be a coward, but now they hailed him as *imperator,* their maximum leader.

News of the resounding victory soon reached the Senate.

As did the news of Marius's men's boundless adoration for him, their cheers of *imperator,* placing Gaius Marius above all others.

XXIII

A NEW WAR

A tavern near the Tiber, Rome
90 B.C.

"SOMETIMES, MY BOY," GAIUS MARIUS SAID, LOOKING HIS nephew in the eye, "it takes more than combat to win a war. Not allowing your enemies to provoke you into fighting on their terms, when those terms are not favorable to you, can be more decisive than a key battle. Do you understand?"

Caesar nodded, hanging on his uncle's every word.

"And it doesn't matter if they insult you. You can pretend to be a coward although you are brave, you can pretend to be clumsy when in fact you are agile. The final victory is all that matters. Never enter a battle you don't believe you can win, even if it makes you look cowardly. Because later, in time, the winner is the only one who will be remembered. Everything that happened before will be forgotten. Remember that, boy, and never enter a battle you can't win."

"Yes . . ." Caesar answered, and was going to add *sir,* but instead said tentatively, "Uncle?"

Sertorius's eyes widened and the rest of the officers seemed to freeze, as if holding their breath.

The words Marius said next seemed to echo through the silence that had fallen over the tavern: "Did you just call me Uncle?" the former consul asked, then, turning to his men, repeated it in a louder voice, in case they hadn't heard: "He called me Uncle."

Caesar swallowed.

Marius turned back to his nephew, who was pale and looked as if he might faint. Caesar felt the wine rush to his head.

Then Gaius Marius started laughing. A loud, clean, joyful laugh.

Caesar relaxed, as did Labienus, Sertorius, and the other guards.

Marius leaned over the table. "You can call me Uncle," he said to Caesar. He then looked to Labienus. "Not you, but you helped my nephew, so I like you."

Titus Labienus nodded his head. "Thank you . . . clarissime vir," he murmured.

Gaius Marius leaned back in his chair and sighed.

He looked into his empty cup of wine as he started speaking again, quietly. It wasn't clear if he was talking to his nephew, to everyone present, or to no one in particular, as if he were merely voicing his thoughts aloud. "That's the story of the Teutons. I could tell the tale of the Cimbri and the battle of Vercellae, but the Senate is waiting. And there's also Numantia. I learned so much there: twenty years of war and some four hundred sieges. Hard to defeat were those Numantians. The Senate," he repeated, paused for an instant, and finally continued, still lost in thought, "the Senate have called me now to a new war. The optimates only summon me when they're afraid. First to Africa, then to defeat the Teutons and the Cimbri, now it's the allied cities. If they'd have listened to Glaucia, Saturninus, and me ten years ago, if they'd conferred some rights to the socii, to our allied cities in Italy, such as citizenship and the right to vote, at least in matters that affect them directly, this Marsi uprising would never have happened. Or if they'd listened to Druso, who tried to negotiate with them. But the optimates murdered Glaucia and Saturninus, forced me into exile, and have now killed Druso. The Marsi and the rest of the socii have no alternatives besides war."

"Are you going to fight with the optimates against the socii?" Caesar asked, bewildered and disappointed.

"No, my boy, I'm going to defend Rome. After that we can focus on changing things to make a Rome that belongs not only to the optimates and the populares but also to the people, and to the socii. But first we have to defend it. A grave crisis is no time for political disputes. Only an idiot puts politics first in times of war. That's what happened in Athens with that deadly plague . . ." Here he stopped and seemed to fall into a trance. He quickly snapped out of it and looked back to his nephew. "They laugh at me, the optimates, because I don't speak Greek, it is true, but I can read it, my boy. Do you know what Thucydides said of the war between Sparta and Athens and the terrible plague that laid waste to so many?"

Caesar had read many Greek texts, but mostly plays, which were more entertaining than the dense scrolls on ancient history.

"I don't know," he responded.

Marius leaned over the table again. Sertorius was unable to repress a sigh of impatience. He didn't think it prudent to make the Senate wait so long, considering how tense the mood was in Rome. He'd lived through other waves of unchecked violence before, like when he was unable to stop Saturninus from being stoned to death inside the Senate.

Marius noticed Sertorius's anxiousness and raised his left hand to stop him from speaking. He wanted to finish this last story. "Athens was at war with Sparta, a terrible war," he began. "And in the midst of that conflict, a horrifying illness broke out, a true epidemic that ripped through Athens, crowded with people who had taken refuge from the Spartans behind the city walls. The leader of the Athenians at the time was Pericles. Have you heard of him, my boy?"

"Yes I have," Caesar said, "but I don't know very much about him."

"A great general and statesman. A better statesman than your uncle, to be certain," he chuckled. "He knew the plague had to be stopped first and foremost, but he himself died from that illness, which, they say, came to Athens from across the sea. On some boat. But more importantly, because it relates to what's now happening in Rome, is that Pericles was replaced by politicians who were infinitely inferior, clumsy, unintelligent, underprepared. Instead of ruling with the good of the public in mind, the good of the city and its inhabitants, first ending the plague and then putting an end to the war, they chased power and popularity. And what did that lack of vision lead to? Athens lost a third of its population to the epidemic, fell to Sparta, and was never again the great city it had once been. It's a pattern that has been repeated many times throughout history, my boy. Cyclically. There's no avoiding it."

"What's the cycle?" asked Caesar, struggling to process so much information.

"Selfish, corrupt, and unintelligent politicians will take advantage of a crisis, whether it be a war or a widespread illness, and seek to exploit the terrible circumstances to gain advantage, or to stay in power, without consideration for the consequences that their personal ambitions might have on the people they govern," said Gaius Marius somberly. "Some will even play at trying to draw a crisis out for longer than necessary if they believe it could benefit them. Here, in Rome now, it's as if history were repeating itself. The optimates think more about how to hold on to their power than about the public well-being. But I for one place the common good over my own self interests. If I thought like them, like the optimates, I'd just sit back with my arms crossed and do nothing as the Marsi and the other Italic people rise up in arms against us. I'd wait until the senators desperately needed me and then make off with all the power in Rome. But I'm not like the optimates. I will put an end to this crisis as soon as possible and thereby reduce the number of victims. I will march into the Senate, that den of selfishness and greed, and consent to helping Rome and its people. I will fight for Rome. Always the people of Rome and their interests over the interests of the senators or myself. That's the difference between your uncle and the optimates, and that, my boy, must always be the difference between you and them as well. The Senate has summoned me because they know that I am the best at winning a war, even if it pains them to admit it. And I will agree to fight on their side in this conflict, not for them, but for the good of Rome. Do you understand?"

"I understand," Caesar said. "But why do they hate you so much? Because of your victories?"

"No, it's not only that, my boy. It's because I proved that the people of Rome, armed and trained, are invincible. That's why they hate me; that's why they fear me. I proved it in Aquae Sextiae, and they came for me after my victories against the Teutons, the Ambrones, and the Cimbri. So I allied myself with Saturninus and Glaucia. Both of them dead. But your mother must've already told you about the turmoil of the days shortly after your birth. I survived. And they hate that I keep on surviving. As soon as the war against the Marsi and the other socii is over, the optimates, like always, will turn against me."

Much to Sertorius's relief, Marius finally stood and bid his nephew goodbye. Then the former consul turned to his most trusted tribune. "A dozen men shall escort my nephew and his friend to their homes."

Sertorius nodded.

Gaius Marius turned back to the boys who, out of respect, had stood up.

"I'm very sorry, so sorry," he said to Caesar with an almost pained expression on his face.

"For what?" the boy asked, confused.

"That you have the misfortune of being my nephew," Marius responded gravely.

"Why would you say that?" Caesar asked, still not understanding. "I'm very proud to be your nephew."

Marius sighed, knowing it might be the last time he spoke to the young Caesar for a while. He rested his hands on the table and spoke quietly, so that only his nephew and Labienus could hear. "You don't understand the problem you're up against, my boy. Your enemies, my enemies, will forgive you anything except one thing: Sulla and Dolabella, his hound, will never forgive you for being my nephew. I'm sorry, my boy, you'll have to live with it. You'll have to try to survive under these unfavorable conditions." He went silent for a moment and looked at Labienus, then back to his nephew. "But today you've won an important victory."

"A victory? Me?"

"Today you made a friend. Today you met the person who might be the Gaius Laelius to your Scipio." He looked at Labienus, whose eyes were wide, unblinking. "I consider myself a good judge of character, and I say this friend of yours will never betray you. I must go now. Remember: you will have to always remain vigilant of the optimates, my boy. Sulla and Dolabella are especially cruel; you must avoid drawing their attention. Grow up quickly. Become strong quickly, boy. You don't have a second to lose."

Gaius Marius stepped back from the table, turned, and walked out of the tavern, followed by Sertorius and his other guards in perfect step, like a military cohort headed into battle. Caesar and Labienus were left alone with the innkeeper and the twelve guards who would escort them home.

"I'll never be as great as him," Caesar muttered. "Never."

Οἱ δὲ ταῦτά τε πάντα ἐς τοὐναντίον ἔπραξαν καὶ ἄλλα ἔξω τοῦ πολέμου δοκοῦντα εἶναι κατὰ τὰς ἰδίας φιλοτιμίας καὶ ἴδια κέρδη κακῶς ἔς τε σφᾶς αὐτοὺς καὶ τοὺς ξυμμάχους ἐπολίτευσαν, ἃ κατορθούμενα μὲν τοῖς ἰδιώταις τιμὴ καὶ ὠφελία μᾶλλον ἦν, σφαλέντα δὲ τῇ πόλει ἐς τὸν ὄλεμον βλάβη καθίστατο.

What they did was the very contrary, allowing private ambitions and private interests, in matters apparently quite foreign to the war, to lead them into projects unjust both to themselves and to their allies—projects whose success would only conduce to the honor and advantage of private persons, and whose failure entailed certain disaster on the country in the war.

—Thucydides, *History of the Peloponnesian War* II, 65, 7
   (About the rulers of Athens after the death of Pericles
   in the middle of a typhoid fever epidemic during
   the war with Sparta)

The Trial

III

INQUISITIO

The inquisitio is the period granted to
both the prosecution and the defense of
a trial to gather evidence and witnesses.

XXIV

THE WITNESSES

Julia family domus
77 B.C.

"**I** UNDERSTAND WHAT CICERO MEANT AT THE END OF THE divinatio," Caesar said. Labienus had arrived wearing a grave expression, but Caesar, in his excitement over the discovery, had not yet noticed. "I have to be the defense. No one likes the *accusator,* the prosecutor. He is always unpopular, like the annoying child who tattles on the other kids. By accusing a senator like Dolabella, we're aiming to put an end to his political career, push him out of public life for good, to humiliate him and strip away his prestige."

Labienus, caught up in Caesar's fervor, momentarily forgot the bad news he came to deliver. "But Dolabella is a corrupt senator who should be stripped of his prestige, who should be exposed for what he is, and whose political career needs to be put to an end. Before he becomes the new Sulla. Only worse."

"I agree, of course, my friend," Caesar said. "And Cicero must take that view as well, but I think he was referring to how to achieve that objective without being hated. Accusing someone makes you unpopular; defending the weaker side in a trial, however, is seen as heroic. We know that Dolabella is anything but weak; he is strong and powerful, and he controls the tribunal of optimate senators who are just as corrupt as him. They have granted us four months for the inquisitio, not because they want to make it easier for us to gather evidence against Dolabella, but simply because they want to give their leader, Metellus, time to take care of his family matters so he can serve as president of the tribunal. At Dolabella's request, to be sure. He won't leave a single loose end.

"They've selected me as accusator over Cicero because they're sure that I'm infinitely inferior to him and, of course, less experienced, whereas Dolabella has hired the best lawyers in Rome. But to the eyes of the people, in the basilica, he's still the reus, the accused. So it's as if he were weak and I, his accuser, were tattling on him, defaming him. If I let them paint me into that role, I will never be popular with the people. I can't let that happen, by Jupiter. I have to prove that I am the defender of a just and noble cause."

"Exposing a corrupt senator and removing him from power is certainly a just and noble cause."

"Yes, but I'm still the prosecutor. So I have to present myself in the basilica as defender of the Macedonians, honorable people who respect Roman authority, who, despite having an unjust governor, have not rebelled against Rome, even with more than enough reason to do so. They have instead decided to accept Roman law as their own. And they deserve, therefore, a fair defense. I'll be their defender. I will rip Dolabella to shreds in the trial, but I will do so in defense of those people who have been so badly mistreated by him. Do you see what I mean?"

Labienus nodded as he paced the atrium of the Julia family domus. "Yes, I see. It makes perfect sense," he agreed, but then his face clouded over. "It's a shame you'll have fewer witnesses than expected for your defense," he added gravely.

"What do you mean by that? And why do you have that dire look on your face?"

Labienus stopped pacing and looked his friend in the eye. "I come as the bearer of very bad news."

"Tell me," Caesar said, taking a seat on a solium.

"Vetus, the engineer who was set to testify in our favor, the man Dolabella claims he hired to repair the Via Egnatia, and who was going to tell everyone how he never received any payment even though Dolabella collected taxes specifically to fund the road works—"

"Because Dolabella kept all the money for himself, yes," Caesar interrupted impatiently. "His testimony is key for us. What happened to him?"

"He was found dead today in his home," Labienus said, delivering the news without preamble.

"How?"

"Stabbed," Labienus said, pulling a thin knife with a red-and-black handle from beneath his toga. He set it on the table. The blade was stained with blood. "He was murdered with this."

Caesar's face twisted into a livid grin. "By Jupiter! They didn't even bother to make it look like an accident."

"They didn't even bother," Labienus agreed. "But there's more. I've received a message from the Macedonians via Perdiccas, who came to me while you were absent from Rome at your country villa. The priest of the temple of Aphrodite in Thessaloniki, who agreed to travel here to testify in the trial, was also found dead a few days ago, inside the temple itself."

"In Macedonia?"

"In Macedonia."

"Dolabella's agents reach that far . . ." Caesar muttered between gritted teeth. He was shocked, but he needed to know more. "Stabbed as well?"

"Yes. It's a curious coincidence, isn't it? Your two most important witnesses, the most credible ones, both murdered right after you announced their names in the divinatio."

Caesar pondered this for a moment, thankful that he hadn't revealed all his witnesses.

"Announcing their names was a grave mistake," he murmured. "I did it intentionally to appear foolish, just like I pretended to be a clumsy orator. I assumed they'd use that information against us, but I have to admit I thought they'd simply ask around about the engineer and the priest to better prepare their interrogations, or bring in witnesses of their own to poke holes in the testimonies. I never thought they'd sink as low as murder."

There was a long silence.

"It's serious," Labienus finally said.

"It's very serious," Caesar agreed, recalling how his uncle Marius had warned of Dolabella's cruelty and the danger in drawing his attention. Now, suddenly, those words seemed to echo through his mind.

The two friends were quiet for a moment, lost in thought, trying to come up with some solution.

They were both devastated.

"What are you going to do now?" Labienus asked.

"Well, we still have one witness I didn't mention in the divinatio."

"That won't be enough," his friend answered frankly. "She's a woman. Hortensius and Cotta will destroy her. She's very young; I doubt she'll be able to withstand the pressure. And even if she does, their interrogation will surely make light of what Dolabella did to her."

"I know," Caesar agreed. "But Myrtale's story is powerful. She's not some slave girl; she's the daughter of an aristocratic Thessaloniki family. She'll appeal to their consciences. But it won't be enough. We have to protect her, and also to find witnesses to replace the men murdered by Dolabella. Are the Macedonians still guarding Myrtale?"

"The girl never leaves the domus," answered Labienus, "and the Macedonians are armed to the teeth. They'd have to kill them all before they could even lay a finger on her."

"Good. Then we'll focus on the other issue. They've given us four months for our inquisitio," Caesar continued, recovering his composure. "They've given us four months and I plan to take full advantage of that time. They've made a grave mistake."

"In giving you so much time?"

"In giving me this time and in murdering the engineer and the priest so soon. If they'd waited to kill them at the end of this investigation period, we'd have been left without any witnesses and with no time to find new ones."

"It would've been smarter for them to wait," Labienus agreed.

"Exactly, by Hercules, but now we have time to gather new witnesses."

"Who?"

"That's the question." Caesar looked at his friend, eyes ablaze. "Do you want to take a journey with me?"

"Where do you want to go?"

Caesar knew exactly where: "To Macedonia."

XXV

THE
VIA EGNATIA

Italic peninsula, en route to Macedonia
77 B.C.

FOUR MONTHS WAS ENOUGH TIME, JUST BARELY, TO GET TO Thessaloniki and back before the next phase of the trial: the reiectio. Caesar and Labienus set out on horseback the following morning, headed south down the Via Apia to the port of Brundisium. They wanted to get there as quickly as possible. They took with them several slaves and a group of former gladiators as hired guards since traveling was always dangerous. They were also accompanied by an experienced Roman engineer by the name of Marcus.

"Why is the engineer coming with us?" Labienus asked as they set off at first light.

"He will replace the man Dolabella hired to repair the Via Egnatia," Caesar answered. "We need an engineer to certify that the current state of the road proves that no money, not a single *sestertius,* has been invested to maintain it for years."

Labienus nodded. "But how did you persuade him to get involved in this insanity? He must have heard what happened to the previous engineer who agreed to testify."

"Sulla's proscriptions, when he confiscated the property of his political enemies with Dolabella's help, left their main contractors out of work. Since then, everything has been miserable for Marcus. So we could say he's motivated to deal a blow to Dolabella. And he doesn't have much left to lose."

Labienus could see the gleam in his young friend's eyes. The jury had been bought off, and the president of the tribunal had been hand-picked by the defendant, who also had the best lawyers defending him. Yet Caesar, somehow, still thought he could win. As impossible as the odds seemed, his enthusiasm was contagious.

They reached Brundisium and hired the first trireme they found willing to take them to the port of Dyrrhachium* on the Macedonian coast, across the Mare Superum.†

"Are you planning to recuse any of the judges?" Labienus asked as they sailed northward, the sea breeze stinging their faces. The reiectio would allow both the prosecution and defense to ask any member of the tribunal with a possible conflict of interest to recuse themselves from the trial. "Have you given it any thought?"

"There's only one judge I'd like to recuse," Caesar answered. "All the senators on the tribunal are sympathetic to Dolabella's cause, but the strongest, the most powerful, the one they all look to, is the judge I most want to see gone."

"Metellus?" Labienus asked, shocked. "The president of the tribunal?"

"Metellus, yes," Caesar replied, unblinking.

"And how do you plan on achieving that?"

"I don't know. I'll have to talk to someone first."

"To who?"

"To my mother. She's the most intelligent person I know in Rome. I want her advice on how to approach the reiectio."

Labienus was not surprised by that response. He knew how much Caesar admired his mother, and he well knew of Aurelia's good judgment and wisdom. Labienus thought that his friend placed too much importance on the advice of a single woman, but he chose to keep that opinion to himself. The two men fell silent as they surveyed the horizon where the Macedonian coastline would soon appear.

When the sun set, they went down into the cabin to rest. At dawn their slaves came to wake them.

"The coast is in sight, my master," one of them said to Caesar.

---

*   Modern-day Durrës in what is now Albania.

†   The Adriatic Sea.

They disembarked in Dyrrhachium, the bustling port city that was the starting point for the Via Egnatia. They would ride eastward to Claudiana, a small military encampment* where they could stay the night under the protection of the Roman troops stationed there.

The following day they continued advancing to Mansio Scampa and then on to Lychnidos,† where they ate at a tavern on the shores of the transparent lake that gave the city its name, from the Greek word *lychnitis.*‡ As clear as those waters was the fact that the Via Egnatia was in an atrocious state of disrepair. The paving stones, in many cases, were either broken or completely missing, possibly stolen to use in the construction of nearby villas. And even worse was the total lack of pavement for large stretches. The road was riddled with potholes and it was not uncommon to come across abandoned carts with broken wheels, which further slowed the transportation of merchandise through the province. The best way to travel that long and utterly neglected road was by foot or on horseback. The bridges were in especially poor condition, and landslides in the mountainous zones had made the road practically impassable in places.

Marcus took careful notes of the many imperfections he found along the way, all evidence for use against Dolabella.

They continued on, always eastward.

Heraclea Lyncestis, Florina, Edessa, and Pella§ were the next stops. Everywhere they went, the road's disrepair was evident, making their march to the capital arduous and slow. Originally well built, the Via Egnatia had truly been allowed to deteriorate in the recent years under Dolabella's governorship. They passed through village after village without stopping except to supply themselves with food and water until they came to Pella. Here, Caesar wanted to spend an entire day visiting the ghost town that had once been the glorious

---

* Modern-day Pekin, Albania.

† Mansio Scampa is modern-day Elbasan, Albania; Lychnidos is modern-day Ohrid (Northern Macedonia).

‡ In Greek: Λυχνίτις.

§ Heraclea Lyncestis is modern-day Bitola in Northern Macedonia. The three other cities have retained their original names in modern-day Greece.

capital of Ancient Macedonia under King Phillip II, father of Alexander the Great.

Caesar took Labienus on a tour of the ruins of the immense city that the Romans had razed in their wars against the Macedonians and Greeks a century prior. It had never been rebuilt, as if Rome feared a possible resurrection of that ancient and powerful capital. Like the legendary Carthage, Pella had been destroyed and left uninhabited for many decades. But such an imposing city retains its grandeur even in abandonment and ruin.

"Euripides, near the end of his life, put on his plays in this city," Caesar explained as they walked past once opulent mansions now covered in vines, with cracked, crumbling walls. He was reminded of a line from *Helena:* " 'You are fools, who try to win a reputation for virtue through war and marshalled lines of spears, senselessly putting an end to mortal troubles; for if a bloody quarrel is to decide it, strife will never leave off in the towns of men.'* That's what Euripides said about human conflicts and war, my friend. We cannot and should not resolve everything through force and weapons; that's why justice, trials like the one we have at hand, are so important." Caesar could tell that Euripides's plays weren't of much interest to his friend, so he moved on to other facts about Pella. "It was also here in Pella that Aristotle gave classes. And here, in this very city, Alexander the Great was born."

The names of the playwrights and ancient philosophers meant little to Labienus, but Caesar's mention of Alexander the Great made him see the destroyed city with new eyes. "Alexander the Great was born here?" he asked admiringly.

They entered crumbling palaces with magnificent mosaics on the walls: tiles of every color depicting mythological scenes. The city seemed to them not dead, only dormant, as if it were simply lying in wait for the right moment to reawaken.

---

*   Ἄφρονες ὅσοι τὰς ἀρετὰς πολέμῳ κτᾶσθε δορὸς ἀλκαίου λόγχαισιν καταπαυόμενοι πόνους θνατῶν

   ἀμαθῶς. Εἰ γὰρ ἄμιλλα κρινεῖ νιν αἵματος, οὔποτ'ἔρις λείψει κατ'ἀνθρώπων πόλεις." From *Helen,* play by Euripides, lines 1,151–1,157.

"Sooner or later, this city should be rebuilt,"* Caesar added as they returned to the Via Egnatia.

The next day, they continued their journey east.

Finally, they reached Thessaloniki.

It was true that the long journey was proving worthwhile, as they accumulated more and more evidence of Dolabella's poor steward-ship. Yet still, Caesar began to feel anxious. If they ran into any bad weather, their return would be even slower than their arrival to the capital of Macedonia, and he still had two important things to do. For one, he needed to find a prestigious witness, some respected local aristocrat, if possible, who would be willing to testify against Dola-bella in Rome. He also wanted to continue along the Via Egnatia beyond Thessaloniki toward Byzantium to confirm more of what they'd seen up to that point about the horrible state of the road.

"Our journey here down that cursed road was too slow. We don't have enough time, by Hercules," Caesar said, furious.

He was beginning to regret having permitted himself a full day in Pella, letting his curiosity get the better of him and losing sight, mo-mentarily, of his objective.

"Do you trust Marcus?" Labienus asked.

"Up to a point, yes."

"Then let him travel the rest of the Via Egnatia to gather infor-mation on the state of the road while you and I stay here in Thessa-loniki and try to find a witness willing to testify against Dolabella. Specifically, someone who saw him pillage the temple of Aphrodite. Or someone who can attest to his horrific treatment of that young noblewoman."

Caesar sat down on a solium and rested his elbow on a table. They had been invited to stay as guests in a domus belonging to friends of Aeropus and Perdiccas, who had sent them with letters informing the local aristocracy that Caesar was the Roman prosecutor in the trial against Dolabella. The Macedonians had welcomed them with a

---

*   Emperor Augustus, Caesar's great-nephew and successor, would order the rebuilding of the city during his rule.

certain cold skepticism, but Caesar had also detected a glimmer of hope in the eyes of some of the locals he'd had the opportunity to speak with. The Macedonians were instinctively distrustful of all Romans, but they desperately wished to see Dolabella held accountable for his heinous crimes. If that had to come at the hands of a Roman, so be it.

"I'd feel more confident if you accompanied the engineer to gather facts for the trial," said Caesar. "They've received us reasonably well here and I don't expect to have any trouble. I just need time to persuade some citizen of note to travel back to Rome with us and testify. Some old priest perhaps. A priest's testimony is always treated with more respect."

"That's why Dolabella murdered the priest who was going to come to Rome to testify," said Labienus.

"Exactly."

"I almost forgot, just this morning we received the dagger used to murder that priest. I left it for you in the vestibule. It's the same thin knife with the same handle as the one that was used against the engineer in Rome."

Caesar sighed and nodded. Thinking of those daggers, he could almost feel Dolabella's hot breath on the back of his neck.

"Well," Labienus said, sitting beside him and returning to the previous topic of conversation. "If you want me to go with the engineer, I will."

Caesar smiled and placed his hand on his friend's forearm.

"Yes, my friend. I think it's best. I want you to go as far as Cypsela* in the province of Thrace. It's not necessary to go all the way to Byzantium and there's not enough time, it would delay us too greatly. The important thing is to verify that the Via Egnatia continues to be in poor condition beyond Thessaloniki and, this interests me especially, to observe whether, upon crossing the limit of Dolabella's jurisdiction, the state of the road improves. That would be very revealing. Can you do this for me, my friend?"

---

*   Corresponding to the city of Ipsala in modern-day Turkey.

"We'll set out tomorrow at dawn," Labienus agreed.

"Perfect." Caesar stood up and looked to the slaves, who interpreted his intentions and quickly brought in food and wine. "But first we have time to enjoy a decent meal after so many days on one of the worst roads I've ever seen."

XXVI

THE SAD EYES
OF ORESTES

Home of the elderly Orestes in the
acropolis of Thessaloniki, Macedonia
77 B.C.

ALL THE RESPECTABLE CITIZENS OF THESSALONIKI TOLD
Caesar to speak with the same man: the elderly Orestes, who seemed
to inspire the utmost admiration from wealthy aristocrats and humble citizens alike. So Caesar decided to pay him a visit.

His home was not the most luxurious, but it had an air of peace
and calm about it.

"I am Orestes," the old man said, introducing himself without
making his Roman visitor wait.

"And I, Gaius Julius Caesar," he responded, not adding his titles in
an attempt to be as discreet as his host. Besides, all of Thessaloniki
already knew who he was and what he was doing there.

"Can I offer you some water? Or perhaps wine?" the old man
asked as he gestured for his guest to take a seat in the sparse but clean
and tranquil courtyard.

"Water is fine," Caesar said, wanting to present himself as a serious man of moderate habits.

Orestes turned to one of the servants. "Water and wine, cups for
both." He sat down across from Caesar. "I'll have a bit of wine, and I
invite you to join me if you enjoy the good drink of Dionysus. I live
an austere life, but I allow myself a few indulgences. At my age, with
the pleasures of the flesh long behind me, that boils down to not
much more than the occasional libation."

"I'll gladly accompany you."

The cups were served.

They drank.

"It's an excellent wine," Caesar said, sipping from his cup.

"It is," Orestes agreed. He set his cup on a table that the servants had placed beside him. Then his expression turned serious. "What brings you to my home, however, is not at all excellent."

"No," Caesar admitted, not sure exactly how to interpret his host's words.

"No, it is not excellent by any means. On one hand, the crimes you're investigating are clearly despicable, from rape to the plundering of a sacred temple, to the illegal appropriation of funds stolen from us through a series of made-up taxes. And your youth betrays the fact that my compatriots were not able to find a prosecutor known for his excellence. I've heard that this is your very first trial in Rome."

Caesar stopped drinking.

Slowly, he set his cup on another small table.

"It is my first trial, you are well-informed," he admitted. "I aim to make up for my lack of experience with hard work and dedication, as well as the strength and fortitude that I bring to everything. I'm looking for the best witnesses so that Dolabella may pay for the vile crimes he perpetrated against the good people of this province."

"The fact that you have traveled here proves your dedication to the trial, without a doubt," Orestes commented, "but tell me more about this nobility of spirit you refer to."

Caesar blinked. The conversation had taken an unexpected turn. He'd come prepared to question the old man about the temple that had been illegally looted by Dolabella, and to ask him to travel to Rome and testify to that crime. It was a long journey down a terrible road, and therefore, an exhausting and complicated trip for someone of Orestes's age. But his host was now interrogating him, questioning his skill as a lawyer, before Caesar had had the opportunity to ask any questions of his own.

He would have to give the old man the explanation he demanded, since he sensed that only with a foundation of mutual trust would the man agree to testify. And everyone he'd spoken to had praised the former priest's honor and exemplary reputation in both his private and public lives. Orestes, however, knew hardly anything about him.

"By 'nobility of spirit' I refer to my determination to seek justice," Caesar explained. "Justice for everyone, equally: the powerful and the powerless alike, Romans as well as non-Romans subject to the laws of Rome. To me, Dolabella has shown anything but nobility of spirit. As governor of this province, he abused his power to extort and rob the people and even went as far as to rape a young noblewoman. He is without remorse for his crimes, which were motivated only by his desperate thirst for power, riches, and personal pleasure. I believe in a just Rome. Just for everyone. And if that implies taking down corrupt senators like Dolabella, my pulse does not quicken at the prospect and I do not cower at the difficulty of the task."

"I admire your nobility. Your naïvety, however, is disappointing. If you can manage to maintain that nobility of spirit as you age, you will achieve great things, I am certain. But noble spirits often fade, or . . ." He searched for words that would not sound too brutal. "Or are stamped out. In fact, if I had to venture a guess as to whether you'll make it to old age, I'd say it seems to me highly unlikely."

"Why do you think that?" Caesar asked.

Orestes leaned forward in his chair and brought a hand to his ear.

"Why do you think that about me," he asked again, raising his voice so that the elderly man could hear him.

"Don't you realize that you were doomed from the moment you agreed to prosecute this trial? Whether you win or lose."

Caesar furrowed his brow. "Whether I win or lose?"

Orestes felt like Aristotle illuminating the mind of a young student. The boy had the ambitions of Alexander the Great but he overestimated his ability to defeat an enemy who was clearly superior in power and resources.

"If you lose, young Gaius Julius Caesar, your political career in Rome will come to an end, as surely many of your friends and relatives will have already warned you."

"Yes, but if I win—"

"But if you win," Orestes interrupted, his voice like an oracle predicting the future, "if you win, then your enemies will see that you are a true threat. And they will kill you. As soon as they can."

There was a long silence.

The slanted afternoon sunlight threw beautiful shadows across the courtyard. Caesar sat mulling over Orestes's words, his eyes fixed on the white walls lit up by the last breath of the day.

"The sunset is beautiful here," he said.

The old man looked around and sighed. "I fear that, in the sunset of my life, my tired eyes miss much of the beauty still left in this world."

Ignoring Orestes's allusion to his loss of sight, Caesar finally decided to ask the key question: "So, am I to understand that you will not come to Rome to testify against Dolabella?"

Another silence.

Orestes seemed distracted, as if his mind were elsewhere.

"Haven't I already answered that question?" he asked.

"No, you haven't."

"Oh, I thought we'd already talked about that," Orestes said, as if waking from a trance. "I'm old and I don't have much life left to lose. It pains me to think you will meet an untimely death. But if you must take on that scoundrel Dolabella, then yes, I will go to Rome."

"Thank you," said Caesar, relieved. "We leave in one week, if that is possible for you."

"One week," Orestes agreed, and stood up.

The old Macedonian walked his guest to the door and bid him a silent farewell with a sad look that made Caesar suddenly doubt everything.

He returned with his escort of armed guards to the residence of the family that had agreed to host him. He sat in his room anxious and pensive.

Seven days later, Labienus and Marcus returned from their journey to the border between Macedonia and Thrace having gathered the promised intelligence on the state of the Via Egnatia beyond Thessaloniki.

"The road remains in terrible condition all the way to Thrace," Labienus said. "Once across the border, it improves remarkably."

"Different governor, different level of respect for public services," Caesar said.

"It would seem so."

"So this confirms that Dolabella let the road fall into disrepair across the entire province, and we can then conclude that he must've kept the tax money for his own personal enrichment."

"Yes," Labienus agreed.

"Well, by Jupiter, this is excellent news." Caesar was exultant.

Labienus did not fully share his friend's enthusiasm; he did not believe that the optimates who sat on the tribunal in Rome would be easily convinced. "Have you found another witness?" he asked.

Caesar told him about his meeting with the elderly Orestes and Labienus looked concerned. "He's very old," he said. "He could die on the journey to Rome."

Caesar sighed. "It's a risk, but on the other hand, his age will inspire respect from the tribunal," he argued.

"Possibly."

"Definitely," Caesar countered. Then, hoping to cheer his friend up, he invited him to drink some wine and relax over a nice dinner.

Night fell and Labienus went to bed, tired from his arduous journey.

In the solitude of his room, Caesar thought about his witnesses: Marcus the engineer, the venerable Orestes, and he could not forget young Myrtale, closely guarded by the Macedonians in Rome. Still, no one believed he could win this trial. Not old Orestes, not his friend Labienus, not anyone.

A thought then came into his mind.

And he permitted himself a smile.

His young wife, Cornelia. She had faith in him.

He leaned back in his chair.

"Cornelia," he said aloud to the shadows projected by the torchlight.

He missed her.

He missed her unshakable confidence in him. And, he had to admit, he missed her beautiful body as well.

CORNELIA

Caesar's wife

XXVII

A PACT FOR POWER

Julia family domus, Rome
88 B.C.
Eleven years before Dolabella's trial

THE WAR WITH THE MARSI AND THE OTHER ITALIC PEOPLES
who had rebelled against Rome came to an end. The socii—the various populations of Italy normally allied with Rome who had risen up to demand Roman citizenship, first through negotiation, then by force—had been defeated. And the end of the war also brought an end to the unspoken truce between the optimates and the populares.

Marius had known this would happen. Years ago, he had seen just such a pact dissolve into chaos and violence, when his allies Glaucia and Saturninus were assassinated and he had been forced to flee the city. The optimates had grudgingly accepted his return from that exile because they needed his military genius to restore order across Italy. But once the rebellion had effectively been stamped out, the differences between the optimates and the populares once again came to the forefront. There were still some pockets of resistance against Rome on the Italic peninsula, specifically among the Samnites, but this was a minor threat to the eyes of the Senate, who were once again focused on the eternal conflict between the wealthy conservatives and those who wanted to make Roman society more equitable.

Rome faced a new military threat, as dangerous or more so than the one posed by Jugurtha in Africa or the Cimbri and Teutons in the North: Mithridates VI Eupator, King of Pontus. The despot had already attacked several Roman protectorates in Asia and was positioning himself to move into Greece. Someone had to stop him. But Mithridates was not, like the Teuton king or even Jugurtha, simply another tribal leader accustomed to warring and combat. Mithridates was the powerful king of a bellicose state with an experienced army and a large naval fleet that could easily take control of the entire eastern Mediterranean. He was a new Hannibal and they would surely see epic battles as they had in the legendary days of the Punic wars. The Senate built a new professional army like the one Marius had created through reforms for his campaign against the Teutons, arming Rome's poor. He had proven in Aquae Sextiae that, once trained, these men could combat with tremendous efficiency. They had recruited no fewer than six legions, and this new army would march eastward to confront Mithridates's seasoned troops.

Marius knew that whoever commanded these legions, after defeating Mithridates, would have control of Rome. No existing military force could oppose an army of that size. He had to be named consul or proconsul with *imperium* over that army that would travel to the East and later, most importantly, return to Rome victorious. But Marius feared that the senatorial Curia would grant control of the new army to Sulla, who had risen to become one of the most prominent members of the optimates.

Aware of Sulla's schemes to take control of that army from within the Senate, Marius decided to make his move and to do so quickly. The Senate was ruled by the optimates; he had no chance there. So he looked for support from the institution that was most resistant to the power of the Senate: the Plebeian Council. But his long exile meant he was disconnected from the populares. Lucius Cornelius Cinna was now the leader of that party and so Marius requested a meeting with him.

Cinna agreed. He was secure in his position as the leader of the populares, but Gaius Marius was a legend among all those who opposed the optimates. Perhaps he was more a part of the past than the present, but his was a past so glorious, so legendary, that the mere mention of his name could inspire a powerful rallying around the popular cause. Cinna now felt that there was hope for a change in the structure of Rome and a greater distribution of wealth, land, and rights. He was prepared to listen to whatever Marius had to say and to make any pact necessary. He only asked that the meeting take place on neutral ground: neither Gaius Marius's home nor his own domus.

Marius proposed the home of Gaius Julius Caesar Sr. in the center of the Suburra. Cinna arrived at the meeting accompanied by Sulpicius Rufus, the plebeian tribune, and by a little girl of eight years old: his daughter Cornelia, who also had a part to play in the plan he had in mind. He knew that, in certain situations, a woman could prove more useful than a man.

Julius Caesar Sr. attended the meeting in his capacity as host. His political career had been of little note, since as a member of the populares it was hard to prosper in a Rome that had been dominated for so long by the optimates. For such prominent politicians as Marius and Cinna to choose his domus as their meeting place conferred him with an importance that, for the moment, it would've been impossible for him or anyone in his family to achieve through the habitual sequence of the cursus honorum. His wife, Aurelia, enjoyed the chance to serve as hostess.

"Since we're never going to cross over to the optimates' side, we might as well make friends with the most powerful members of the populares," her young son Caesar heard her say to his father when asked over dinner whether they should agree to host the meeting.

Sulpicius Rufus and Lucius Cornelius Cinna entered the central atrium of the Julia family domus, where Julius Caesar Sr. and Gaius Marius were already waiting. Aurelia—off to the side, as this was a meeting for men only—noticed that Cinna was accompanied by his young daughter. She could guess where this was going, but she was not opposed to the notion, and so she turned to her twelve-year-old son, who was also present.

"Gaius, why don't you take our guest's daughter out into the garden in the back atrium and show her around while the men here debate the future of Rome?"

Caesar blinked several times. His mother didn't usually give him such specific instructions.

The boy looked at the little girl. The girl looked to her father. Cinna nodded.

"This way," he said, motioning to her.

She followed.

Caesar and Cornelia left the central atrium. Another boy his age might have been bothered by the presence of a little girl, but Caesar, accustomed as he was to his mother and two sisters, was more than comfortable around females.

"Do you have any brothers or sisters?" he asked to break the ice.

"A brother," she responded, staring at the ground as she trailed behind him. She felt shy around this older boy.

"I have two sisters. I get along with them pretty well, but I would have liked to have a brother. At least I have my friend Labienus. He's my same age and we do everything together. Do you have friends?"

"No." She shook her head emphatically. "I'm never allowed to leave the house. Today is special," she ventured, feeling bolder.

Caesar understood. Young girls were rarely allowed to leave home except occasionally to help with the shopping. So it was strange that Cinna had brought his daughter and not his son, unless the boy was very young.

"Are you older than your brother?"

"No," she answered. "My brother is the same age as you."

"Oh. Well then it is very special that your father brought you instead of him."

They'd reached the domus's back atrium.

"My mother calls it the garden," Caesar said, changing the subject, "but as you can see, it's really just a few flowerpots she likes to water."

Cornelia walked among the plants.

"It's pretty," she commented, trying to be cordial. She'd been taught to always be pleasant and polite when speaking to friends of the family, and she assumed Caesar fell into that category.

As a boy, Caesar was sometimes slow to pick up on certain things. He had an inkling as to why the girl was here. But for him, an inkling was never good enough. He always preferred to be certain, to have all the information. His mother had assigned him the task of entertaining this little girl, which meant . . .

"Have you met the Luperci?" he asked her.

This was a very direct question. During the festival of Lupercalia, the Luperci ran around Rome with strips of goatskin turned into whips called *februa,* which they used to slap the hands of young women who presented themselves as being of childbearing age. The festival took place in the second month of the year, called February after the goatskin whips. Being whipped by the Luperci was believed to grant young women future fertility.

A girl never received one of the Luperci's playful slaps until she had officially become a woman and had begun to menstruate. Cornelia was confused. "No, I haven't been hit by the Luperci," she answered, lowering her head as if ashamed by her youth. "I'm too little. I have a birthday soon but I'll only be . . . nine."

"That's what I thought. I just meant have you seen them in the streets, hitting the older girls with their februa and that funny shout they make. I didn't mean to embarrass you."

"Oh." Cornelia nodded, but she didn't dare to look up as she spoke. "I've seen them; they once whipped one of my cousins."

He felt bad for making her feel uncomfortable, but he was curious as to why she might be there. Maybe he was wrong, but he couldn't help looking her up and down. She was still a little girl, but she was pretty and nice and polite. He didn't know much about her except that she seemed very shy, as was to be expected in such a situation, with a boy she didn't know in a house that was not her own.

"Do you want to hear what your father and my father and Gaius Marius and Sulpicius Rufus are talking about?" he asked.

Cornelia looked up and studied the boy's face, which she thought was very handsome. He was tall and strong and he was being nice to her. She hadn't spoken very much but she felt comfortable in his presence.

"But can we? Listen without their permission?"

He smiled and brought a finger to his lips as he leaned over and whispered, "Follow me."

He took her by the hand.

She quivered. She'd never held a boy's hand before, not even her brother's. Once past the initial shock of it, she liked his strong yet gentle grip, which made her feel safe.

Caesar led her down several hallways until they reached a kind of small library full of scrolls.

"My father's *tablinum*," he explained in a whisper. "It has two entrances. We've come in from the back atrium, but it also opens onto the main one. If we sit close to that door, which is only covered by a curtain, we can hear everything they say. My uncle Marius always speaks very loudly."

"My father does as well," Cornelia said, excited by the adventure this boy was leading her on.

"That's good for us. Follow me, stay right beside me, but don't say anything, no matter what you hear, all right?"

"All right," she whispered.

He was still holding her hand as he led her to the tablinum. The men's voices became ever louder as they crossed the library.

Caesar then dropped her hand.

She wished he hadn't, but she didn't say anything as they crouched beside the curtain, careful not to touch it. They both sat listening intently.

Julia family domus, main atrium

"If Sulla seizes command of the army stationed at Nola, it will be the end of our hopes for legislative change of any kind," Gaius Marius said, his booming voice exuding authority with every syllable. "Also, with the new conscripts, this army numbers six legions. Six. That, counting the auxiliaries, is sixty thousand men. In Sulla's hands, that will be the end of us; the optimates will be able to blatantly rule as they wish. They'll do away with us, literally. They'll annihilate us."

"There's nothing we can do about it," Sulpicius Rufus argued. "They've had control of the Senate ever since they put an end to the reforms you and Saturninus tried to impose all those years ago. They joined forces with us against the Marsi and the rest of the socii in the rebellion, but now that they have been defeated, as you say, Sulla and the rest of the optimates, with their rule in the Senate, will give the consulships to one of their own. They'll do whatever they can to win the elections and give command of that army to Sulla."

"The Plebeian Council can oppose them," Marius countered.

"How?" asked Cinna, a man of few words who always liked to get straight to the point.

"The Council can pass a law granting themselves the power to name the commander of the army at Nola. And the Council can decide that I, Gaius Marius, should be granted the command of the army that will be sent to defeat Mithridates."

Everyone fell silent.

"Sulpicius, could you convince the Council to openly defy the Senate that way?" asked Cinna.

The plebeian tribune thought carefully before answering. The army in question would be sent beyond the borders of Rome, to the East, to fight Mithridates, and that made it an issue of foreign policy, placing it under the Senate's specific authority. "With any other commander it wouldn't be so easy," began Sulpicius Rufus, "but if we nominate Marius, who saved us from Jugurtha, from the Cimbri and the Teutons in the North, something the people still remember and feel grateful for, then yes. Especially if I emphasize the fact that Mithridates could be the new Hannibal, that there could be yet another invasion from Italy even after everything we've gone through with the rebellion of the Marsi and the other socii. Yes, that would convince the Council to vote in favor of Marius. There's no doubt that the people trust him more than they do Sulla."

"It is no lie," added Marius. "Mithridates is threatening to cross the Hellespont and attack Greece. If we don't confront him there, he won't think twice about marching straight on Rome itself. He is extremely ambitious. But we have to act quickly: the Senate is meeting this very week and they'll surely nominate Sulla as commander."

"The Council can meet this week as well," Sulpicius Rufus offered.

"That would be perfect," Marius said.

It seemed like the matter had been resolved, but Cinna had his own private agenda. "I want you to have command of that army, but in doing so, you will go off to the East and leave us here in Rome to deal with the optimates, who will be furious if Sulla loses command of those legions."

Marius had expected this response. No one in Rome offered their support without asking for something in return. "I'm listening, Cinna." He lay back on a triclinium and extended his arm so a slave could refill his wine.

"You obtain command of that army, as *privatus.** But . . ." Cinna thought for an instant. He was asking a lot, but he could tell that Marius was eager to lead those troops. He finally made up his mind. "But once you have command of that army, with the optimates on the defensive, I'd like to nominate myself as consul, with your support, and Sulpicius as praetor. And your men across all of Rome will support us in these endeavors."

Marius didn't have to think too much about it. A consulship and praetorship seemed like a reasonable price for control of an army that would be the key to ruling Rome.

"So be it. We are in agreement," he said.

"A toast to this pact," said Julius Caesar Sr., who had prudently refrained from speaking in the presence of Marius, Cinna, and Sulpicius, rulers of the entire popular faction of Rome between them.

Aurelia, who had stayed in the background, spoke to the slaves: "Wine for everyone and food. In abundance," she ordered. And then, in a friendly tone, looking at Marius, Cinna, and Sulpicius, she said, "Would you do us the honor of sharing a meal in our home? I pray to the gods that your duties will permit you this small respite."

The men accepted the invitation.

Everything seemed to have been settled, but Cinna still wanted something more. "I'm a man who believes that pacts, more than being toasted to, should also be sealed with some type of union," he said.

Aurelia took a deep breath. She'd seen this coming ever since Cinna entered her domus accompanied by his daughter.

---

*   Meaning "private citizen," as opposed to a government official or member of the military. The idea here is that, like Scipio Africanus before him, Marius would be made *privatus cum imperio*—a private citizen invested with the power of command, despite not holding a formal rank or title.

"What kind of union?" asked Marius, his mind swirling with ideas on how to supply the six legions it would take to defeat Mithridates.

"I have a son, and Gaius Marius does as well," began Cinna. "But Marius's son is married, to Licinia, and our admired leader, six-time consul, has no daughters. We won't get very far that way." He let out a chuckle that the others met with a smile, before continuing. "But I also have a young daughter, Cornelia. And Julius Caesar and"—he looked politely at Aurelia— "and our hostess have a young son, Julius Caesar Jr., Gaius Marius's nephew. If my daughter and Gaius Marius's nephew were joined by matrimony that would seal our pact and guarantee that our alliance endures. Difficult times are upon us. I'd like to have the assurance that we are all . . . family. Such a union would make us all stronger."

Cinna fell silent. He was unaccustomed to speaking so many words at once. Sulpicius was the orator among them, which was why they were counting on him to convince the Council they should defy the Senate and grant command of the new army to Gaius Marius.

Cinna took a sip from his cup as he waited for everyone to process this additional request.

Marius met eyes with Julius Caesar Sr., who in turn looked to Aurelia. She nodded slightly, but Julius Caesar Sr. could tell that she had some reservations. They hadn't expected their son to become embroiled in the agreement between Marius and Cinna.

"It's a proposal that both pleases and honors us, Cinna," Caesar Sr. began, "but your daughter is still a girl, is she not?"

"She is not yet a woman, if that's what you mean, but she soon will be. I'm not suggesting the wedding take place tomorrow. I'm just saying we should agree to it today."

Marius remained silent. He didn't want anything to get in the way of his commanding this new army. The Senate would never grant him control of six legions; the Council was his only possible hope. That meant he had to satisfy whatever requests Sulpicius and Cinna made. Especially the latter, who truly controlled the popular faction of Rome.

Caesar Sr. could sense the anxiety in Marius's gaze. He ran the back of his hand over his mouth.

"The wedding shall take place in due course, when the time is right," he decreed. "Once the daughter of Lucius Cornelius Cinna has grown, once she has become a woman."

Julia family domus, tablinum

Julius Caesar and Cornelia locked eyes in the dim light of the library.

They didn't say a word.

He held her hand, as he'd done before, and led her out of the library, then down the halls to the back atrium.

Once there he dropped her hand.

Cornelia sat in silence, studying a flower in Aurelia's garden.

Caesar examined her face.

"I'm sorry," Cornelia said, barely a whisper, as if they were still hiding in the library.

"What is it you're sorry about?" he asked, confused.

"That they're making you marry me."

"Well, they're making both of us. You too."

"Yes, but I'm used to everyone telling me what I have to do. Maybe you're not."

"You're right," he agreed.

They both fell silent.

"I was scared, you know?" she said after a few seconds.

"Scared of what?"

"Of who they would make me marry."

"And are you still scared?"

"No . . . You're nice. And . . . handsome. And you're not too much older than me."

"No, no one is ever scared of me," he said with a sarcastic, almost sad smile. "But I'm scared."

"Of me?" she asked, surprised.

"No." He smiled again, then added sincerely, "I'm not scared of you. You're nice and you're young, very." He laughed. "And pretty," he added once they'd stopped giggling.

"So what are you afraid of then? The gods? I'm scared of them, too," Cornelia admitted.

"I'm not afraid of the gods. I descend from Venus. Or my family does, on the Julus side, via Aeneas," he declared categorically, an inarguable fact. "What I'm afraid of is not being able to do what they all expect of me. My uncle has been consul six times, and everyone in this house wants me to be like him. They don't say it, but I can see it in my parents' eyes. I don't have any brothers. It has to be me. How could I possibly measure up to the victor of the war in Africa, the hero who saved us from the Teutons, the man who transformed our legions into the most powerful army in the world?"

"It won't be easy," Cornelia agreed.

He looked at her again. He liked that she didn't say stupid things like "don't worry" or "you'll figure it out." It wouldn't be easy and that was the truth.

"In fact," the girl added, "it's impossible." She giggled and her laughter was infectious.

The somber mood that had descended on them seemed to lighten. Their laughter subsided and they both fell quiet for a moment.

"Do you know how to read?" he asked.

"Of course," she answered, her pride somewhat wounded. "Do you think I'm stupid?" But she quickly changed her tone and added, "Well, I can read Latin. Not Greek. I'd like to learn, but my father says that Greek and public speaking are not proper things for women to study. He says that my job is to give my husband children."

Caesar looked at her, suddenly realizing that this little girl would be the mother of his children. "I like to read," he commented. He thought of the authors he liked. There was Euripides, but he was Greek. "Have you ever read anything by Plautus?"

"I've heard of him, but I haven't read anything by him or gone to the theatre to see any of his plays."

"Wait here," Caesar said, rushing out of the atrium and leaving the girl to wait among the flowers.

Aurelia entered the atrium. "Cornelia, your father wishes for you to join us for dinner." The woman glanced around the courtyard looking for her son. "Were you alone here this entire time?" she asked with clear disapproval in her voice.

"No, no. Caesar was with me. He only just left to get something for me," she quickly explained.

Caesar soon reappeared, greeted his mother, then turned to Cornelia with a roll of papyrus in his hand. "It's Plautus's *Asinaria*. His first play. It's funny."

"It's your favorite," Aurelia commented, bemused that her son would give his most cherished scroll to a girl he'd only just met.

"I can't accept it," said Cornelia, looking at the ground.

"Please," he insisted. "That way we can talk about it."

Aurelia looked on, perplexed by the conversation. It was obvious the two children shared a connection: they liked each other. That was a good sign. Everything would be so much easier if they liked each other.

Cornelia accepted the scroll and they both followed Aurelia back to the main atrium, where they joined the meal already in progress.

When the guests had all left, Aurelia turned to her son: "What did you think of Cinna's daughter? She's nice, isn't she?"

"Yes," he said. Then he gave his mother a kiss on the cheek and went to bed.

"They know," Aurelia declared as soon as she was alone with her husband.

"What?" he asked, drowsy from the wine.

He looked tired. He had been worried when Cinna began with his requests. As had she. For a few moments, they had both been afraid that the meeting would end in disaster. Her husband needed sleep. "Nothing, husband, nothing important. I think it best that we go to bed."

They stood up and made their way to their bedroom. The slaves began to clean up, trying not to make too much noise as they gathered the plates and cups and cutlery spread across the table.

Out in the street, closely guarded, Cinna and his daughter walked back to their residence, the torches held up by their slaves slicing through the darkness of the Roman night.

"Grow up quickly, little girl," Cinna said out of nowhere.

Cornelia nodded without saying a word. Her father didn't expect any response besides obedience and she knew it.

XXVIII

CAESAR'S
APPRENTICESHIP

Julia family domus, Rome
88 B.C.

AURELIA ENTERED THE TABLINUM TO FIND HER SON, AS expected, writing diligently under the attentive gaze of Marcus Antonius Gnipho, his incredibly knowledgeable tutor. Gnipho was Gallic by birth but had studied in the most important academies of the Greek world, making him a curious mixture of eastern erudition and barbaric origin. More than once she'd overheard the old tutor diverge from Aristotle, Euripides, or Menander to focus instead on the history of Gaul and its people. She considered it a waste of time, but Caesar seemed fascinated by the tales of the barbaric Celts, and it helped him understand his tutor's roots. The legends of the brave Gallic warriors also served to break up the long hours reciting Greek and Latin.

"Your uncle Marius is here, son," Aurelia said.

The boy hurriedly finished what he was writing and jumped out of his seat, but his mother's stern expression stopped him in his tracks. The fact that Caesar's tutor was a freedman made no difference to Aurelia, who wanted her son to always show respect for knowledge.

Caesar turned to his tutor. "Can I continue working on the text later, if that's all right, Gnipho?" he asked.

The tutor nodded and Caesar rushed past his mother to greet his uncle.

Gnipho picked up the text that Caesar had been writing a moment prior.

"What is it?" asked Aurelia.

"He's titled it *Laudes Herculis*," Gnipho replied, and went on without taking his eyes off his student's text. "A poem of praise to Hercules for his many valiant feats. Very well written, of course." He stopped reading and raised his eyes. "He just needs to finish it."

"Hercules . . ." she repeated. "A great hero. Interesting topic."

"I believe the boy has great aspirations."

Aurelia replied categorically, "Greatness is his destiny."

"You think he shall turn out to be a legendary hero like Hercules?" Gnipho asked, as if he found the mother's declaration excessive.

"A great hero like Hercules, yes," she replied without hesitation, then turned toward the atrium, where son and brother-in-law waited.

"But Hercules dies in the end, victim of treachery," Gnipho commented.

Aurelia froze and turned back toward the Greek tutor for a moment. "That is true," she agreed. "Just as it is true that all of us mortals must one day perish. But Hercules was transformed into a god."

Gnipho nodded and bowed to his student's mother.

Atrium of the Julia family domus

Aurelia found Gaius Marius and Caesar engaged in lively conversation. "I've come to take the boy to Campus Martius," Marius said to Aurelia as she entered. "I want to see if he's improved in combat."

"Of course. His father isn't here and I'm sure Gaius would love to go with you." Aurelia was pleased at the prospect of her son training with the legendary general.

The young Caesar excitedly prepared to leave, anxious to show his uncle the progress he'd made with the use of a gladius, in his fighting abilities, his resistance, and agility.

Campus Martius

The field used for military training on the outskirts of Rome was crowded with young men, some still boys, practicing in the art of

hand-to-hand combat or archery, or learning to gallop a horse without stirrups, in the Roman style. As soon as Gaius Marius appeared,
escorted by Sertorius and several other veteran warriors, the crowd
parted to make way for the former consul.

"This looks like a good place," Marius said, eager to see how his
nephew's military training was coming along.

Marius had other nephews and a son of his own, whom he loved
dearly and had shaped into a great man, but at only twelve, young
Caesar already showed a strength and determination that made him
Marius's particular favorite. In that young boy, Marius perceived
something he didn't know how to define: a fortitude of spirit combined with brilliant intelligence. But all that would be worth nothing
if the boy was a clumsy combatant and was taken down in his first
skirmish, whether in the wilds of the North or on the battlefield
against the armies of Mithridates or another king from some remote
region of the world.

"Give him a training gladius," Marius ordered, and one of his men
immediately handed the boy a wooden sword; his uncle took up
something similar.

Caesar was still weighing the sword, as if trying to verify that it
was the same as the others he'd trained with, when his uncle, without
saying a word, hit him on the shoulder with the flat part of the practice blade. It was a hard blow that caused the boy to lose his balance,
and he fell to the ground. He looked at Marius with surprise and
anger.

"You think the enemy is going to warn you, my boy?" Marius
snapped. "You think the Gauls or Mithridates's soldiers will ask politely for permission before attacking? Get up, by Hercules, and stay
on your guard!"

Caesar picked himself up and raised his weapon, ready to lunge at
his uncle. But Marius spoke again.

"Wait, boy. If this is going to be a true training lesson, you should
go up against someone in better physical condition. I'm not nearly as
agile as a twelve-year-old."

Gaius Marius was now sixty-nine and slow with a gladius. He

considered himself the best man to command an army against Mithridates, but perhaps not the best choice to train an angry young buck eager to show what he was made of.

The veteran consul looked at Sertorius, who nodded and accepted the wooden weapon that his superior handed him.

Caesar swallowed. Quintus Sertorius, lieutenant of his uncle's armies for years, was in his mid-thirties and appeared to be in top physical form.

A circle of curious onlookers formed around Marius and his guards.

"Why don't you attack, boy?" Marius asked from a comfortable distance.

Caesar was sweating. He didn't dare rush at the hulking officer, seasoned in a thousand battles. He ran his hand over his damp face, the midday sun falling like lead upon him. He tried to charge at his opponent from the side, but as soon as he made any move, Sertorius shifted, prepared to fend off the attack. Charging the man directly was not an option.

"Not long ago, you told me that I should never enter a battle I couldn't win, Uncle," Caesar said loudly. "I don't stand a chance against Sertorius, and you know it."

Marius nodded. He seemed pleased by his nephew's response, but he wanted to test the boy. "I'm glad to hear you remember my lessons. You're right, you cannot and should not attack Sertorius. But what if he attacks you? Will you defend yourself?" The former consul made a gesture to indicate that his lieutenant should charge at his nephew.

Quintus Sertorius moved forward. Not swiftly, but decidedly. Caesar tried to dodge, but the tight circle of onlookers did not leave him much range of motion. Before he had time to react, Sertorius landed a blow on his shoulder.

"Ouch!" the boy cried.

And then the other.

"By Jupiter!" Caesar exclaimed.

He stepped back and blandished his gladius, trying to block any more hits, but Sertorius, with great skill, continued to land blow after blow: on one side of Caesar's torso, then the other, again on the shoulder, then crashing against a forearm the boy held up as an improvised shield.

Marius looked on, attentive but unspeaking. He knew he was pushing his nephew to the limit. He wanted to see how he would react under such pressure. What would he do? Beg? Kneel? Order Sertorius to stop? Or ask him, Marius, to order him to stop?

But Caesar did none of those things. He merely took the blows. He was dripping with sweat, and bruises had begun to appear on his arms and legs, as well as trails of blood from a few cuts. The dull wooden swords were rough and crude and the occasional scrape was not uncommon during a day of training.

Sertorius halted his attack and looked to the former consul.

Caesar took advantage of his opponent's distraction to lean on his sword and catch his breath. His whole body hurt. He was being made to look ridiculous and he didn't know what to do. If he attacked, Sertorius would come at him even harder. If he kept his distance, he'd suffer less harm but a greater blow to his pride.

Sertorius was still looking to Marius. Marius was looking at his nephew. Caesar stared at the ground.

"Keep going!" Marius ordered. "I didn't give you the order to stop."

Sertorius sighed. He didn't understand what the former consul was after. He could infer that he wanted to teach his nephew some kind of lesson, but this was beginning to feel less like a training session than a harsh punishment.

Sertorius once again raised his gladius high.

Caesar, who had heard his uncle's orders, held up his arms to cushion the next round of blows, knowing he was incapable of stopping them.

Sertorius landed a hard thwack to Caesar's thigh with the flat part of the gladius. The boy bent to the ground in pain. Sertorius then landed the definitive blow, directly to the boy's face. He didn't act out of cruelty. It was an automatic reaction in a combat situation combined with a desire to end the boy's misery. He thought it would be better to defeat him quickly than to drag it out.

But perhaps Sertorius hadn't expected his blow to land so hard. Or perhaps he hadn't expected that Caesar would fail to shield himself. Whatever the reason, the gladius connected with Caesar's unprotected face with a sickening crack. The young Gaius Julius Caesar, twelve years old, fell to the ground of the Campus Martius like dead weight. He lay there, unmoving.

A shocked silence fell over the crowd.

Marius was petrified.

Sertorius immediately threw down his wooden sword and rushed over to the boy. He'd gone too far. He feared the worst. He leaned over Caesar's body and was about to touch him to see if he responded, when Caesar suddenly sat up and, swinging his gladius with all the strength he had left, bashed it against Sertorius's testicles like Vulcan wielding his hammer.

"Aaah!" Sertorius fell to the ground, doubled over with his hands on his crotch, panting with pain. Julius Caesar stood up and raised his wooden sword, ready to continue fighting.

One cheek sliced open and bleeding, his arms covered in bruises and scratches, Caesar stood firm, ready to defend himself. Quintus Sertorius, still huffing, struggled to his feet.

"Enough!" Gaius Marius shouted.

Sertorius nodded and, with a hand on his inflamed testicles, stepped aside.

Marius approached his nephew.

"You may have fooled Sertorius, my boy, but take note of one thing: you can only fool an intelligent opponent once. That trick you used will never work on him again. Do you understand?"

"I understand," Caesar nodded, "but it worked this time."

Marius nodded. "Let's get you home. We need to clean up that cut. Your mother is going to kill me for letting your face get hurt," he said, laughing.

As Marius and Caesar walked away, a messenger approached Sertorius. Meanwhile, the crowd of curious onlookers dispersed, humming with talk of how this boy of only twelve had been clever enough to defeat the great general's most trusted officer. Marius placed his hand on his nephew's shoulder, and the gentle contact pained Caesar, but he didn't flinch, because he liked what the gesture implied: affection, maybe even pride.

"You have learned that you should never enter battle without a plan for a possible victory. You've shown that you're clever in defending yourself, and you've taken note that you can only fool an intelligent enemy once. But my boy, do you know the most important thing in this cursed conflict between the populares and the optimates, so eternal that you will surely find yourself embroiled in it some day?"

Caesar furrowed his brow, thoughtful.

Just at that moment, Sertorius approached them and spoke quietly to his superior. "The Senate, in its next session, will grant Sulla command of the six legions recruited to fight Mithridates," he informed Marius.

"We need to speak with Cinna and have him call a meeting of the Plebeian Council," Marius replied decisively.

They all continued walking back to the center of Rome.

"Intelligence," Caesar said suddenly. "Intelligence is the key in this conflict, isn't it, Uncle?"

"Intelligence is important, certainly, my boy, but it doesn't do you any good unless you use it, like I'm doing now, to win command of an army. Command of an army: that is and always will be the most important thing."

Blood trickling down his cheek, his entire body in pain from the beating he'd received and the weight of his uncle's hand on his shoulder, Julius Caesar stored Gaius Marius's wise words in the deepest recesses of his mind so that he would never forget them.

XXIX

ROME IS MINE

Nola, Italic Peninsula
88 B.C.
Six weeks later

THE SENATE NAMED SULLA CONSUL AND HANDED HIM CONtrol of the army at Nola so that he could march eastward and stop Mithridates from expanding across the entire Mediterranean region.

At the same time, the Plebeian Council, acting of their own accord, granted themselves the right to give control of the army to whomever they deemed fit. Through an impassioned speech, Sulpicius Rufus, the plebeian tribune, convinced the people of Rome to entrust command to Gaius Marius.

The stage was set for conflict.

But Sulla had anticipated this struggle and was the quicker of the two contenders for control of the legions. He knew he had to assume control of the army as swiftly as possible, so he left for Nola before anyone else, traveling alone with only a few of his most trusted men, Dolabella among them. They rode almost without rest to get ahead of Marius's power grab, which they knew would come.

Marius, exercising more caution, took his time gathering a large group of veteran warriors from Africa and the North. His prudence had often yielded excellent results—for example, in Aquae Sextiae—but it now caused him to lose the upper hand in this clash with the much bolder Sulla. Only time would tell which of the two men had been the wiser.

Sulla reached Nola at dawn and immediately called a meeting of the tribunes. He would present them with the Senate's mandate appointing him as consul and assume effective control of that immense army, precisely according to plan. But Marius, Sulpicius, and Cinna were not inexperienced in political matters and had sent messengers announcing that the Plebeian Council had named Marius commander of the army. And although Marius himself was still organizing things in Rome, his messengers reached Nola at the same time as Sulla, who found the tribunes doubtful over whether to accept the Senate's nomination. If the Plebeian Council had put forth any other man, the officers wouldn't have thought twice, but Marius was a legend. Sulla had gained his fair share of prestige, but Gaius Marius's victory against the Teutons, specifically the Battle of Aquae Sextiae, was a military milestone like no other in the history of Rome, not since the times of Scipio's victory over Hannibal.

The meeting with the tribunes was not going well. Dolabella could see that Sulla was frustrated and he understood that he was worried, but not yet defeated. Sulla realized that he was not up against another man, a leader of the opposing faction. He was up against a living legend.

"I'd like to propose a solution," Sulla said to the tribunes. "Summon all your officers, centurions, *optiones,* and the rest to a meeting in the center of the camp. There, before everyone, we'll have the Plebeian Council's messengers explain their reasons for nominating Marius as commander. Then I'll lay out all the reasons that the Senate has named me as your leader instead. Once you've heard both sides, you can decide for yourselves who you consider to be the best leader."

The tribunes exchanged glances: they all thought it sounded reasonable.

They agreed.

Sulla and Dolabella were left alone in the praetorium. The tent was reserved for the army's highest commander, although they did not yet know whom that would be.

"I saw the faces of the officers when the Council's messengers told them that the people had chosen Marius," said Dolabella, nervous. "I don't see how you'll be able to persuade them to accept the Senate's nomination over the Council's. And the legal formalities, the fact that the legions are meant to fight outside of Italy and foreign policy pertains to the Senate, is not going to matter to them. Military men have no interest in such subtleties."

There was a pitcher of wine and cups on the table in the center of the tent. Sulla, pensive, poured a drink for each of them and handed a cup to Dolabella.

They both drank, Sulla quickly emptying his cup.

"No, there's no doubt that the Roman legionaries have no interest in the subtleties of foreign policy," he agreed, "but I know what does interest these new legions, who have been recruited from among the city's most depraved." He flashed his enigmatic smile. "We have Marius himself to thank for that, after he allowed any poor beggar to become a legionary. Don't forget, Dolabella, that's whom we're dealing with: a mob of miserable, starving wretches."

One of the tribunes returned to the tent.

"The officers will be ready soon and the Council's messengers are already waiting."

Sulla nodded to the tribune, who saluted and left.

"Neither these soldiers nor the populares realize how much is at stake here today," Sulla said to Dolabella. "First of all, Mithridates. The King of Pontus is not just another enemy, not an aging leader on his way out. He's a monarch at the height of his power, hungry for expansion. And he has lofty ambitions. Mere months ago he kidnapped Ptolemy, the eleventh of his name to reign over Egypt, now held hostage at Pontus. Mithridates has granted himself the power to decide who will rule Egypt, as his control extends to all of Asia, affecting our interests there. Meanwhile, he is preparing to cross the sea and invade Greece. That's just the start. The populares don't even see. Maybe Marius. The rest only think about the game of politics in Rome. And it's true that whoever commands this army shall control Rome. We must first win the game in Rome and then make sure, at all costs, we win the larger game against Mithridates. All that, my friend, is at stake today."

Dolabella hurried to empty his wine as he listened to Sulla's explanations. He set his cup on the table and looked his friend in the eye. "But first we have to persuade the officers to accept you as leader over Marius," he said, still unsure how Sulla planned to achieve this objective.

"Exactly," he agreed, standing up. "Watch . . . and learn. I'll give you a lesson in human nature."

Center of the Roman camp at Nola

The Samnites, the latest socii to rebel against Rome, were still resisting the Romans at Nola, but the terrible siege they were being submitted to had left them exhausted. Their only hope was that division within Rome itself, the conflict between the optimates and the populares, might in some way relieve the situation. Maybe the Romans would abandon the siege completely if a civil war broke out.

Sulla, like the besieged Samnites, also thought of civil war as he listened to the Plebeian Council's messengers explaining why command of the army should be given to Gaius Marius. They said nothing new or surprising, simply reminding everyone once again of Marius's great victory at Aquae Sextiae against the Teutons, who had threatened the very safety of Rome. To them, only Marius could free Italy from the growing threat posed by the King of Pontus and his ceaseless expansion across the Mediterranean region.

When the men sent by the Council had finished, the officers all turned their gaze to Sulla. He nodded and stepped onto the wooden platform that served as a stage.

He stretched his stiff neck, having hardly slept on his nonstop gallop from Rome. He had been eager to reach this precise place, at this precise moment. He cleared his throat a few times. Then he began his speech: "Marius is a great legatus, an excellent military leader," Sulla began. Dolabella was taken aback, and there was confusion among the officers, who had expected a fierce attack against the Council's candidate. "We all remember his past actions, his successful campaigns. What can I say? That his victories were easy, simple? That Marius did not defeat powerful enemies? No, I did not come all this way to lie to you. I won't deny the truth, especially not to those of you gathered here today, men who bravely fight to ensure the safety of Rome. We have one last rebellion among the Marsi to bring to an end, and I am told your siege of the Samnites will soon come to a successful conclusion. But meanwhile, in the East, Mithridates of Pontus, a formidable enemy, gains strength, threatening now not only Egypt, Asia, and Greece, but all of Italy, as the Council's messengers have explained. So this is no time for lies or falsehoods. No, not in this crucial moment when we must decide how to do away with this new enemy before he grows too powerful to be stopped." Sulla paused for a few seconds.

He knew everyone was listening intently. His praise of Marius had left them curious as to where he aimed to go with his words. He placed his hands on his hips. "But even though Marius is a good legatus," he continued, "I have also proven my intelligence, efficiency, and leadership ability, commanding cohorts and legions in Africa and in the North, where I accompanied Marius during his successful campaigns. I don't have to remind you that, for example, the capture of the rebel king Jugurtha was to a large extent possible thanks to me personally. And, in the recent war against the rebellious socii, I once again proved my military prowess."

He sighed. He now had to criticize himself, something necessary if he was to compare himself to Marius. "I know what you're all thinking: that even if everything I've said is true, even if I'm a good military leader, Gaius Marius is still better."

He paused. He looked at his audience. The tribunes in the first rows were nodding.

"I could try to refute that notion, to argue against that opinion," Sulla continued, "but honestly, I don't want to start that senseless argument. Because—and this is key—not only is the command of this army up for debate. Also up for debate is which army will actually do the fighting."

Sulla watched as the tribunes and centurions exchanged confused glances.

"Yes, by Jupiter. The Council's messengers have told you that you should accept Marius as commander of the army that will fight Mithridates, but they have not confirmed that your army will be the one sent eastward to wage this war. They want you to agree to let Marius make all the decisions about this next military campaign, one that will bring immense wealth to the legionaries who fight it, riches much greater than any war in recent memory, since the East holds treasures, gold and silver, in quantities infinitely superior to what you might obtain plundering cities in Africa or Cisalpine Gaul. In Asia, where many cities have already joined the side of Mithridates, or in Greece, where we may have to fight the King of Pontus, the spoils that await will be immeasurably larger, more precious, more coveted. And Marius knows this. Marius wants those spoils. But, my friends— if you'll allow me to count you as friends since we have fought shoulder to shoulder in this war against the rebel socii—Gaius Marius does not plan to use your strength and experience to go east and destroy Mithridates."

Sulla gave them a few seconds to process what they'd just heard and, after a brief pause, he resumed his speech. "No, my friends. I am here, standing before you, with the Senate's nomination. But don't you wonder why Marius is not here as well? Why not, if he claims to have the Council's nomination for commander? Have you stopped to think about that?"

Another brief pause.

The officers sat in silence with furrowed brows as murky thoughts clouded their minds and they began to feel uneasy.

"I'll give you the answer, by Jupiter! I'm here and he's not because I have nothing to hide from you and he does: Gaius Marius is not here because he's busy gathering his veteran warriors from Africa and the North. He plans to march those troops east and fight Mithridates, then divide the lavish spoils among fewer men. That is the reason Gaius Marius is not standing here today before you!"

Sulla saw first shock, then rage, on the faces of many of the centurions and tribunes. The Council's messengers blinked, confused. They couldn't confirm the claims the senator was making, but they knew that Marius was gathering a group of men to serve as his guards, and it was possible that his intention was to recruit an entire army of his trusted veterans as Lucius Cornelius Sulla had just indicated.

Dolabella looked at his admired mentor. Sulla's lies had been fully convincing, and not only that: his falsehoods were so clever, so astute . . .

Sulla could see the seed of doubt germinating in the Council's messengers and the discord and anger already in full bloom among the tribunes and centurions of the army at Nola. They wanted those eastern spoils for themselves.

Sulla looked somberly out onto the sea of faces. These were the kinds of "subtleties" that interested the legions of Rome: money. Marius had professionalized the Roman army, and that regular wage paid to them was of the utmost importance. Sulla understood this better than any other Roman leader. Better, even, than Marius himself.

"So, my friends, you have two options," Sulla went on. "You can accept me as your supreme leader, or you can wait for Marius to gather his veterans, stop to give you a few words of encouragement as you continue this endless siege, and take off with that other army, his own army, to amass an enormous fortune that, by order of the Roman Senate, rightfully belongs to you. I know you will do what you think best. But there is one more thing I should warn you of before you make your decision."

He could see that the tribunes and centurions were now primed to accept him as commander, but he wanted to make sure that their decision would be unshakable, irreversible.

"I have to warn you, by Hercules, that if we leave from here directly to the East, it's very likely that Marius, Cinna, Sulpicius, and the other populares of Rome will manipulate the laws to ensure the spoils, the riches born through your own efforts, which rightfully belong to you, will be confiscated and divided among them. If you truly want to march east, to defeat Mithridates and return wealthy to a comfortable future for your families, you must do so under my command. But first, we must all march together . . . ." He paused. He took a deep breath. And said it: ". . . on Rome!"

Dolabella, up to that moment, had listened to Sulla with a sly smile on his face. His mouth now fell open. No one had ever marched Roman legions against Rome itself. The very notion was unheard of, absurd, impossible. Or was it?

Sulla understood that what he'd just suggested was unthinkable, but he also understood the desperate thirst for money felt most urgently by men who had never tasted it—men like these soldiers at Nola. And he knew this thirst was powerful enough to make the unthinkable happen.

"Only if we go first to Rome and make it perfectly clear that the Senate's decision outweighs the Plebeian Council's attempt to manipulate our laws," he went on, "only if we are there to ensure that the Senate's order is upheld over the illegitimate ruling of the plebeian tribune Sulpicius, who impertinently dares to dictate command of the Roman legions, only then can we march east confident in the notion that all the many spoils obtained will be, in fact, yours. So your choice is: submit to the will of a corrupt Council, ruled by the populares, and watch as Marius and his men make off with everything; or accept me as commander, as decreed by the Senate, and march with me on Rome to declare that the eastern campaign rightfully, lawfully, with all the spoils implied, belongs to you and you alone. What say you, officers of the mighty legions of Rome? Will you remain here locked in this pointless, endless siege? Or will you march with me to Rome to uphold the Senate's decree that the eastern campaign should remain in your hands? Will you wait and watch as your dreams vanish, or march with me today?"

Here Sulla threw up his arms as he finished his speech and stood waiting for the officers' response.

"March on Rome!" one tribune finally responded. Immediately dozens, then hundreds, of officers began to chant those words over and over in unison: "March on Rome! March on Rome! March on Rome!"

Sulla stepped down from the platform.

Dolabella rushed over to him.

"You can't turn against Rome," he said, still shocked.

"I'm not turning against Rome," Sulla said. Then, looking into Dolabella's still incredulous eyes, he went on, "Rome is mine."

XXX

CORNELIA'S
APPRENTICESHIP

Julia family domus, Rome
88 B.C.

CAESAR'S MOTHER HAD INVITED CORNELIA TO SPEND THE
morning with her. Cinna, who normally didn't allow his daughter to
leave the house even to go shopping with the slaves at the Forum
Boarium, made an exception, adding that the girl should speak little,
be humble, and try not to embarrass him.

Cinna did not find it odd that the mother of the young Caesar
would want to get to know the girl who would grow up to marry her
only male child. He thought it needless, since the marriage had already been agreed upon, but he knew that women often entertained
themselves with such things. Beyond keeping the marriage agreement intact, he cared little about the interpersonal relationships between the two families.

Cornelia arrived at the Julia residence in the Suburra escorted by
a group of slaves and clutching the scroll of Plautus's first play.

"Did you read it?" Aurelia asked as the girl returned *Asinaria* to
her.

"Yes," she replied, trying to remain sparing with her words per her
father's advice.

"Did you like it?" her hostess pressed as she gestured for the girl to
take a seat on a solium across from her in the central atrium. The
empty triclinia indicated that it was not yet time to eat.

Cornelia didn't know what to say.

"Did you like the play?" Aurelia asked again.

"It was funny."

"It is funny. The male protagonist is made to look like an idiot. Men can be so stupid sometimes, don't you agree?"

Cornelia was silent, her mouth hanging open.

Now she really didn't know how to respond.

Aurelia decided to drop the interrogation. The girl was not yet even nine years old and had hardly set foot outside her father's home.

"Why do you think I've asked you to come?"

"I don't know," she lied.

"Yes you do. Let's not start out being dishonest with each other so soon."

Cornelia imagined that Aurelia wanted to find out what she thought of young Caesar, whom she would wed as soon as she came of age. But saying this would reveal that she knew of the betrothal, which would mean admitting that she and Caesar had eavesdropped on the adults from the tablinum. Worse still: if she spoke up, she'd be showing Caesar's mother that she was prepared to betray young Caesar the first chance she got.

Cornelia was struck mute. She could lie and say that her father had told her about the arranged marriage. But everyone knew that Cinna barely acknowledged his daughter.

"You're aware that we've arranged for you and my son to marry," Aurelia said. "Caesar has been listening in on our conversations from the tablinum since around the time he learned to walk. He thinks I don't know, but I do. I asked you if you know why I called you here."

Cornelia swallowed. It was not going to be easy to follow her father's order to remain silent. "To talk about Caesar, the domina's son, I suppose."

"What foolishness, by all the gods," Aurelia replied. "What interest would I have in discussing a subject I already know everything about? No, I haven't called you here to talk about my son. You're here to talk about yourself."

"About me?" Cornelia couldn't believe it. "But I'm not important."

"Surely not, at least not to your father, except to the extent that your union with my son, that is to say, Gaius Marius's nephew, might bring him closer to being the leader of the populares. I've seen how he ignores you. But I am not in the habit of ignoring people. So tell me about yourself. What do you like to do?"

Cornelia looked down, confused. She didn't know where to start. "I like sewing and learning how to manage a household and knitting—"

"I don't want you to give me the answer you think I expect from you," Aurelia interrupted. "I want you to tell me what it is you truly enjoy doing."

Cornelia looked up and pressed her lips together. "I truly enjoy knitting; it's fun. Giving orders is necessary to running a household, but I never know how to do it. I guess I'll learn. But what I really like to do is read."

"Read what?"

"Anything. There aren't very many scrolls at my house. Not like here." She looked toward the tablinum but blushed and looked back down, embarrassed as she remembered that she'd hidden there to eavesdrop.

"I can lend you more works by Plautus. Do you read Greek?"

Cornelia sighed. That question again. "No. My father doesn't think it practical to educate me beyond the tasks that will fall to me as a wife and mother."

"I see."

A brief silence.

"Would you like to learn to read Greek so that you can understand, for example, stories like the one about Thalestris, queen of the Amazonian warrior women, or about lovely Helen, who sparked the Trojan War? Do you know those stories?"

"No I don't. And I'd love to be able to read them, but my father—"

"Do me a favor, my child, and stop worrying about your father. You're talking to me here, Aurelia."

Cornelia nodded several times.

"Do you want me to teach you to read Greek?"

The girl felt tears spring to her eyes. "Yes, I'd like that very much, domina."

Caesar and Labienus burst into the atrium.

"Sulla is marching on Rome!" Caesar announced. "With the six legions from Nola."

Aurelia stared at the boys in bewilderment.

"Do you know what you're saying, son? That's impossible. No Roman senator would ever turn the legions against Rome."

Just then Caesar's father entered the atrium. "Well, the impossible has just occurred," he confirmed, having heard Aurelia's last words. "It's all anyone can talk about in the forum." He was covered in sweat, having run all the way from the center of the city to bring her the news.

"Water!" she commanded, glancing sharply at the atriense. The slave jumped up and rushed off to comply. Aurelia looked to Cornelia. "That is how you give an order."

The girl nodded quickly without opening her mouth.

"He's not bringing the entire six legions," Caesar Sr. went on. "It would appear that he's left a large contingent of troops to maintain the siege of Nola against the Samnites, but he is marching several legions on Rome. Nothing and no one will be able to stand in his way. Marius will have to return to exile—I've just spoken with him. He doesn't have enough men to go up against an army of that size. And there's no convincing those legionaries to change loyalties, since it seems Sulla has promised them all the spoils from the war against Mithridates. There's nothing better anyone could offer those men. Sulla, as much as we might hate to admit it, is very clever and has won their absolute loyalty. Marius will have to leave, just as he did after that disaster with Saturninus and Glaucia the night of that cursed senatus consultum ultimum. He'll have to take refuge in Africa. Cinna . . ." And here he seemed to notice little Cornelia for the first time, although he had no idea what the girl was doing in his home. "Cinna will stay in Rome. Sulla's animosity toward him is not as strong as his hatred of Marius. Cinna has assured me that he will reach some kind of an agreement to avoid blood being spilled. But it's not going to be easy."

The water was brought in.

Caesar Sr. took a long drink.

He sat down.

"Not easy at all," he repeated.

Lucius Cornelius Cinna's domus
That same night

Cornelia returned home. Her father was agitated, as she'd imagined he would be after everything she'd heard at the Julia domus.

"What are you going to do, Father?" Cinna's son asked.

The *pater familias* was mired in a tense silence.

Cornelia looked on without saying a word, knowing it was better to remain silent and out of sight when her father was in one of those moods.

"We will wait," Cinna finally said. "We will accept all the conditions that Sulla wishes to impose. But once he leaves Rome with his army to confront Mithridates, we will act. That will be our moment. We will take advantage of that moment to prepare."

Cinna's son accepted the explanation, but Cornelia didn't fully understand his meaning. If her mother had been a more determined woman, more like Aurelia, she might've joined the conversation, but Annia was by nature very passive and she never questioned her husband on anything. This was in part because she'd been taught to be submissive and in part because Cinna was not as tolerant a man as Julius Caesar Sr.

To everyone's surprise, it was Cornelia who dared to challenge her father's vague response: "What is it that you'll have to prepare for, Father?"

Cinna looked up, annoyed at having to explain something so obvious. "Sulla will take power now but then he'll be forced to leave. We will prepare for his return. Of course, you couldn't possibly understand such a matter, being a girl," he responded scornfully.

Cornelia decided not to ask any more questions. The truth was that she felt more comfortable and more appreciated in the Julia home than in her own. She didn't hate her father, but he was impossible to please. And her mother was all silence.

XXXI

THE CULT OF
SULLA

Rome, 87 B.C.

J UST AS JULIUS CAESAR SR. HAD PREDICTED, THERE WERE NOT
enough men left in Rome to resist Sulla and his legions. The citizens
were forced to look on, shocked and stupefied, as Sulla took control
of the city and all its political institutions. The Senate was with him,
so he focused his ire on the Plebeian Council. Sulpicius Rufus, in his
capacity as plebeian tribune, was the one who had appointed Marius
as commander of the army at Nola. He had also passed new legislation ceding Roman citizenship to the socii. This, even though the
war with the allied tribes was still very recent and, in the case of the
Samnites in Nola, not even officially over. But extending Roman citizenship was what allowed them to modify the census by adding new
members to the Plebeian Council and to pass the vote for Marius as
chief commander.

Sulla painstakingly pulled apart the entirety of Sulpicius's new
legislation. He abolished all reforms, voided the new census, and revoked the socii's citizenship. He also ordered the arrest of Gaius
Marius and Sulpicius Rufus. Marius, with his escort of veteran fighters, had already sailed to Africa. But Sulpicius didn't have the means
to do the same. Before Sulla's march on Rome, the Senate had at-
tempted to remove Sulpicius from his post as plebeian tribune but
was forced to annul the *justitium* when confronted by Marius's army
of veterans. With Marius now gone and Sulla's legions flooding the
city, Sulpicius had no choice but to flee.

He was caught in Laurentum, just a few miles outside of Rome.

And executed.

Sulla seemed satisfied and relaxed as he paced before a crowd of senators and other citizens of the city by the Tiber. Before him, mounted on a spike in the center of the forum, was the decapitated head of Sulpicius Rufus, still dripping blood. Marius might have escaped, but this would serve as warning for the rest of the popular leaders.

"Should we go after them all?" asked Dolabella, referring to Cinna and other prominent members of the popular faction who remained in the city.

Sulla paused before answering. "No," he said. "We'll come to an agreement. Our laws in exchange for their lives."

"And why not our laws without sparing their lives?" asked Dolabella. Standing here with Sulpicius's severed head on proud display made him begin to think that they could do away with the populares entirely. And Dolabella had always enjoyed watching others suffer.

"A large-scale purge would require the legions to remain in Rome for months. And there are two problems with keeping the troops in the city."

"Two problems? By Hercules! What problems?" Dolabella couldn't see why they shouldn't take advantage of the opportunity to wipe out all opposition in the popular faction once and for all. Annihilate them. Massacre them.

Sulla sighed. "I've promised these legions huge spoils and we don't have enough gold and silver here in Rome to satisfy the appetites of six legions. Not without pillaging our temples or emptying the state's coffers. And Mithridates is still a very real threat. The best thing would be to leave and take the legions with me. And without military might, we can't rule the city. Not for now at least. We'll have to come to an agreement with Cinna. In Marius's absence, he's the voice of the populares."

"That's why you haven't killed him," said Dolabella, suddenly understanding.

"Yes. I need a popular leader capable of controlling the plebes. I'll make sure he agrees to the annulment of the laws passed by Sulpicius." Sulla turned toward the bloody spike and permitted himself a malevolent smile. "I think the head of the plebeian tribune will serve as a nice reminder to anyone who would try to manipulate the electoral census again. Now that I have revoked the voting rights unlawfully conceded to our enemies, the election will easily go in the Senate's favor. I'll offer to make Cinna consul. He is ambitious; he will accept. And after that, you and I, my friend, will march on Mithridates."

Sulla, hands on hips, paced around the forum, circling the gruesome spike.

Lucius Cornelius Sulla was pleased with himself. He knew that many people in the city at that very moment were praying to the gods, making sacrifices, and begging the deities to have mercy on Rome, lest a civil war break out. But he had his own religion. He was his own god. His desires were his pantheon, the legionaries his priests. A new religion for a new world: his world.

XXXII

CINNAMUM TEMPUS·

Rome, 87 B.C.

E VERYONE IN ROME, EVEN IN SULLA'S ABSENCE, ACTED AC-
cording to Sulla's will. At first.

Cinna was named consul as representative of the popular faction,
and Gnaeus Octavius† was chosen as the second consul to represent
the optimates. All was going according to Sulla's plan. Not long after
his departure, however, Cinna reinstated the legislative changes that
had been put forth by Sulpicius before he was decapitated, expanding
the Roman electoral census by extending Roman citizenship to the
Marsi tribe. Octavius tried to negotiate, but Cinna would accept
nothing less than the incorporation of thirty-five Italic tribes into
the census. This was unacceptable to the optimates, who controlled
the Senate, and they removed Cinna from his position as consul and
ordered him expulsed from Rome, naming Merula in his place.

Cinna left the city, taking his family, Cornelia included, with him.
But the Senate had made a mistake. Sulla had warned them not to go
against Cinna without the army there to support them. "Even if he
breaks the pact," Sulla had said, "don't turn on him. Await my return."
But they did not heed the order and Cinna was indeed prepared to
do anything to stay in power, even go to war. He freed slaves and en-

---

* "The time of Cinna," the name given to the period in which Rome was controlled by the
popular leader. The period was also referred to by other authors as *Cinnae dominatio,* or "Cinna's
dominion."

† Not to be confused with Octavius Augustus, the first emperor of Rome. The former had
not been born at the time.

listed socii to an improvised army in Italy, where the allied tribes were hungry for revenge over their defeat in the recent wars. Then Cinna marched his troops on Rome just as Sulla had done a few months prior. Sulla had left some of his legionaries behind and they were placed under the command of Metellus Pius, the city's most experienced general. But the stuttering Metellus could see that he did not have enough men to fend off Cinna's imminent attack and so, as Marius had done when faced with Sulla's advance, he chose to flee Rome rather than face down Cinna and his fierce army.

The better part of Gnaeus Octavius's troops defected and the consul took refuge in the temple of Janus, west of the Tiber, beyond the city walls.

In no time, Cinna was restored to power and the populares once again ruled the capital of the republic. As Sulla began his war against Mithridates on Greek soil, Gnaeus Octavius was caught and executed. The former consul's head was mounted on a spike in the same spot where Sulla had exhibited Sulpicius's. Cinna thought it only fair that an optimate consul be decapitated in retribution for Sulla's cruel treatment of the plebeian tribune. Many populares felt the same way, but not all; some believed they should reach some kind of agreement with the optimates, lest the bloodshed go on endlessly. Cinna decided then to call Gaius Marius back to Rome along with his son, so that their presence might further strengthen his control of the populares. Marius agreed, marching through southern Italy back to the city by the Tiber with his son and a small army of veterans. Once there, he immediately held a meeting with Cinna on neutral ground in the Julia family home. They planned to completely reorganize the republic in Sulla's absence.

Julia family domus
That night

Once again, Cornelia and Caesar found themselves together in the back atrium of the Julia family's Suburra residence.

"Are you all right?" he asked. "I worried when I heard that the Senate had banished your father and he was taking you with him."

"I'm fine," Cornelia responded, touched by his concern. "My father didn't want them to be able to take my brother or me as hostages."

"Your father cares about you, about your safety."

She shook her head. "No, my father only cares about himself," Cornelia said. She looked up to meet Caesar's gaze. "I only matter because I can be used to join our family to yours, to Marius's. That is the only thing that matters to him."

The young man stayed quiet.

"I don't care that he doesn't love me," Cornelia continued. "I'm used to it. My father has always said he would use me to further his political interests. I thank Fortuna that it is you he has chosen. You treat me well. And your parents, too. Your mother especially."

"She's teaching you Greek," he said. "She told me."

"Yes. I'm very grateful to her. I know she's doing it for you. She wants me to be a worthy wife. She didn't say it, but I know that's the reason."

"You might be right," Caesar admitted, "but I can assure you that if she didn't like you, she wouldn't do it."

"Do what?" she asked.

"Teach you Greek," he clarified. "My mother always says that she's too old to suffer fools. If she didn't think you were smart, she wouldn't spend her afternoons teaching you anything. Also, she says you're a quick learner."

"Your mother is very smart," she replied, surprised at how easy she found it to talk to Caesar. He had experience speaking with girls thanks to his two sisters. "Your mother knows everything that's happening, even though she pretends not to. And . . ." She left the sentence hanging in the air.

"And?"

Cornelia didn't dare to say what she was thinking out loud, so she whispered it: "Your mother has ideas about everything. Even politics."

Caesar burst out laughing and Cornelia joined him. She liked seeing him so relaxed around her.

"It's true," he agreed. "My mother certainly has opinions of her own."

They fell silent.

He considered asking her what she was reading now, but there was something else that had him even more curious. "Should we go listen?" he suggested, looking toward the tablinum.

She whispered again, "Your mother knows that you listen . . . that we listened."

"I guessed as much," he replied without a hint of surprise. "But did she tell you not to do it again?"

She furrowed her brow. "No, she didn't say that."

He offered her his hand.

She took it.

"Then let's go."

Once again, Caesar led Cornelia down the long hallway into the tablinum that opened onto the central atrium where Cinna, Marius, their two sons, Sertorius, Caesar Sr., and Aurelia were conversing.

Julia family domus, central atrium

Cinna and Marius were shouting over each other.

Their sons looked concerned. They'd never seen their fathers so angry with each other.

Caesar Sr. for his part was trying to calm them. "Hold on, you're both right," their host said. "By all the gods, you have each done what you thought best and you both want to implement changes to the republic in a way that may actually stick for once. You have to leave here with some kind of an agreement. Sulla will return, as you both well know, and unless we are strongly united, he will take back control."

Marius and Cinna seemed to calm slightly.

Aurelia remained silent, glancing from time to time toward the door of the tablinum.

"Decapitating Gnaeus Octavius was a mistake," Marius insisted. "Blood only brings more blood."

"Fear is the only thing that will keep the optimates in check," Cinna argued. "They understand nothing else. They used it against the Gracchi, against Saturninus, Drusus, and now Sulpicius."

"That may be the case, but Sulla will not be cowed by a simple decapitation. He is strong, very strong," said Marius.

"Everything hinges on this war with Mithridates," Cinna said. "The King of Pontus may get rid of Sulla for us. For now, thanks to my actions here in Rome, Metellus has fled, and you have been able to return."

Marius sighed. "That's true, just as it is certain that this campaign against Mithridates is crucial," he admitted in a conciliatory tone.

"By the gods!" Caesar Sr. exclaimed. "Finally, something we can all agree on. Wine!" he shouted to the atriense.

The slave rushed away.

The cups were served.

The drink of Bacchus soon lightened the mood.

"What's done is done," Marius said, "but I would make two suggestions."

"I'm listening," Cinna responded.

"Rein in the slaves you freed and armed to help you take control of Rome; they are out of control, sowing terror in the streets. I won't even get into whether I think it was an excessive response to the optimates and their hired daggermen, but Rome, under our governance, should be synonymous with order. My veterans know how to keep the peace. They can assure our control of the city without unchecked violence."

"I can order the armed slaves to clear the streets," Cinna agreed. "What other suggestion do you have?"

"If we want the people's unconditional support," Marius continued, "we have to enact the legal reforms that our side has always defended. I don't mean simply granting citizenship to the allied tribes to manipulate the census. I'm talking about a true distribution of land and grain."

There was a tense pause.

"I concur," Cinna said quietly.

"Then we are in agreement?" Marius insisted. He wanted Cinna's response to be unequivocal.

"We are in agreement," Cinna said in a more convincing tone.

"So be it."

"Good!" Caesar Sr. said cheerfully before ordering more wine and food to be served.

Aurelia stood, and for the first time, spoke. "I shall call the children to join us now."

Caesar Sr. and Cinna nodded and she walked slowly to the back of the domus, giving Caesar and Cornelia time to reach the rear atrium.

Marius turned in his chair and spoke quietly to Sertorius, who was standing behind him. "I want our men to take control of the streets," he said, his words masked by the sound of the slaves serving platters of food and the other guests commenting on the impressive banquet. "If they have to kill some of those miscreants Cinna has unleashed on the city, then so be it."

Sertorius merely nodded.

"Good." Marius raised his empty cup to be refilled. Everything seemed to be settled, but there was still something that concerned him. His son was grown and could already lead legions if called to. But Caesar was still too young to fight, and he worried for the safety of his favorite nephew should the tides of power change again. He had spoken with the boy's father about how best to protect him in the event that their plans went awry and Sulla took power yet again. "There's one more matter I'd like to discuss," Marius said, looking at Cinna.

Just then Caesar Jr. entered the atrium followed by Cornelia, and Aurelia gestured for them to share a triclinium.

"What is it?" Cinna asked.

"The charge of *flamen Dialis,* the high priest of Jupiter, remains vacant," Marius said.

This was no surprise: it was the highest religious office in Rome but subject to a series of limitations for the person who held the charge—limitations that were at the very least inconvenient, if not completely impossible, to fulfil. The flamen Dialis, for example, could not spend more than one night at a time outside Rome and was never allowed to sleep anywhere but his own bed for more than three consecutive nights; he could not undress in public, which impeded him from using the public baths so important to Romans of all orders. He could not wear rings that encircled a finger completely or so much as touch certain plants that grew profusely in humid Rome, such as grapevines or ivy. He was forbidden from riding on horseback, viewing weapons, or witnessing military action, along with an endless list of other restrictions. Few men were willing to take on such a charge, even if it implied notable privileges, among them the right to attend sessions of the Senate, to sit in a sella—a seat signifying authority previously reserved only for Roman kings, and now only used by consuls—and the constant presence of a *lictor,* an armed bodyguard.

"Yes, that position is vacant," Cinna said. "What of it?"

"In the spirit of sealing this renewed alliance," Marius said, "I'd like you to name my nephew, Gaius Julius Caesar Jr., flamen Dialis."

Cinna was thoughtful as he drank his wine.

Caesar Sr. and Aurelia anxiously awaited his reply.

Young Caesar was so startled by the announcement that he choked on his food. He took a sip of water to calm his fit of coughing. No one had warned him of this. Just as they had not consulted him regarding his betrothal to Cornelia. He knew about the flamen Dialis and its advantages as well as its many drawbacks, and he was overwhelmed by the prospect, but he remained silent, as was expected of him.

Cornelia rested her hand lightly on Caesar's arm, something uncommon during a meal.

Cinna took a sip of wine. "To be named flamen Dialis a man must first be married," he said. "We can twist many laws, but breaking any rule that involves the gods will make us very unpopular."

"I am not suggesting you grant him the charge today," Marius commented. "My nephew shall marry your daughter when she comes of age and then Caesar can be named flamen Dialis of Rome."

Cinna liked that this arrangement would guarantee an early marriage for the young couple. "So be it," he said, raising his cup to toast the new agreement between himself and Marius.

The slaves finished arranging the decadent trays of food before them.

Caesar Jr. didn't take a single bite.

"Are you all right?" Cornelia asked quietly.

"I seem to have lost my appetite," the boy replied.

XXXIII

THE TEMPLES
OF GREECE

Delphi, Greece
87 B.C.

SULLA ENTERED GREECE THROUGH EPIRUS, AND WHEN HIS army reached the famous oracle at Delphi, he ordered the legions to diverge from the route that would lead them directly to Mithridates.

"I want to consult the Pythonesses," he said as justification for the detour.

Dolabella found his leader's sudden religious streak highly inconvenient; slowing the legions' advance would only give Mithridates more time to consolidate his position in Greece. But he chose not to argue and simply transmitted the orders to the tribunes.

The temple of Delphi had been in decline for some time, but many still made the pilgrimage, not only from within Greece, but from such far-flung places as Asia or Gaul, crowding around the temple of the sacred oracle, where the three Pythonesses emitted their famous predictions.

The pilgrims moved aside as Sulla, accompanied by Dolabella and several well-armed centurions, made his way up the steep mountainside trail leading to that sacred place. Sulla had already sacked Olympia, and many thought the Roman commander might be capable of another similar atrocity. But no one believed he'd sink so low as to pillage Delphi, which was extremely sacred in their religion. The temple had seen highs and lows over its many centuries in existence, periods of splendor and decline, like at present, but it had never been widely plundered. No one dared, fearing the wrath of Apollo, to whom the temple had been consecrated hundreds of years prior. Since time immemorial, in fact, kings and leaders from all over the Grecian world made extravagant gifts to the oracle in appreciation for predictions that had either come true or helped them to determine the fates of their people in times of peace—or especially in times of war. An earthquake had destroyed part of the site, but it had been rebuilt. The Foci had once sacked the main temple to pay Phillip II of Macedonia, Alexander the Great's father, for their defeat. But Phillip himself had forced the Foci to return everything they had stolen and restore the temple to its former splendor. Since then, few had dared to rob Delphi of so much as a small statue.

"Will we see the Pythonesses?" Dolabella asked Sulla as they continued their climb to the sanctuary.

"It's possible," Sulla responded, seemingly distracted, continuously looking from side to side on that path that snaked in a steady ascent to the temple.

"I thought that the Pythonesses could only be consulted on certain dates."

"Nine times a year. Between the months of February and October, once a month."

Sulla's reply surprised Dolabella, who had not imagined the fierce commander to be so well versed in the cult of Delphi. "I've always wondered why the priestesses who predict the future in Delphi were called pythonesses. Seems like a strange name. Reminds me of the snake."

Sulla sighed. Dolabella's utter lack of culture was embarrassing. It was one thing to hate your enemies, like the Greeks, or to lack true faith in the gods and oracles, but it was entirely unacceptable to be completely ignorant of history. "The temple was originally dedicated to Gaia," Sulla explained, "and it was guarded by her daughter, a huge serpent named Python. They say that Apollo killed the snake, giving him his nickname Apollo Pythian. He then entrusted the site to his priestesses, calling them 'Pythonesses' or 'Pythia' in memory of the reptile he destroyed."

Dolabella was again perplexed. "I didn't know you felt such devotion to this oracle."

"I feel no devotion," Sulla clarified, "but I've studied history and, therefore, I know we'll find more treasures here than in all of Greece. Statues of silver and gold, chests full of coins and all kinds of offerings to the oracle, all accumulated in the temple—which is poorly guarded because no one would dare to take them for fear of Apollo's revenge. Most of the gifts will be piled up in the main sanctuary, but I'm sure all these little temples we see along the road are filled with riches as well. Every Greek city, every kingdom that venerates the oracle, has placed shrines along this path with offerings."

"You plan to plunder the oracle of Delphi?" Dolabella asked, eyes wide.

"Do you see any army trying to stop me?"

"No."

"Well, we do have an army, and it needs to see some gold and silver soon. I promised these men they would obtain great wealth on this campaign. They will fight harder against Mithridates's troops if they believe that being in my service will truly benefit them, don't you agree?"

From a purely strategic point of view, Sulla's plan was perfect, but Dolabella still had his doubts, whether out of religiosity or pure superstition. "But Delphi . . . Delphi is the center of the world."

"The center of the world, yes, I see that you've heard that legend, at least," Sulla commented, amused at his lieutenant's sudden scruples.

"Zeus unleashed two eagles, didn't he?" Dolabella asked. "One from the most eastern point of the world and another from the most western point. They met here, marking Delphi as the *ónfalos,* the belly button of the world."

"So they say," Sulla agreed, never slowing his pace and always looking around, as if making sure there were only pilgrims climbing the trail, no armed men.

They reached the ramp ascending directly to the temple and found only a few guards.

Sulla looked to one of the tribunes, who knew what to do. The guards were surrounded by the few men Sulla had brought with him and were quickly forced to give up their swords and spears.

But there were still too many pilgrims mulling about for Sulla's liking. He turned to another of his military tribunes. "Bring an entire legion, here, to the temple. And clear everyone out. By force if necessary. I don't want a single pilgrim left at Delphi in under an hour."

The tribune saluted with a closed fist to his chest and left with several centurions to carry out the assigned task.

Sulla, along with Dolabella and a healthy cohort of armed legionaries, began ascending the ramp.

The Pythonesses were nowhere to be seen.

"Perhaps they do know how to read the future after all, and they've taken off into the hills," Sulla said with a hint of respect in his voice. "Those priestesses are clever."

Dolabella didn't say a word. He was not religious, but he was superstitious, very, and he didn't like to trivialize anything related to gods or goddesses, priests or priestesses.

"Of course, I've counted twenty-seven," Sulla added.

"Twenty-seven what?" Dolabella asked.

"Twenty-seven shrines on the path leading to the main temple. That's twenty-seven structures built to hold gifts for the oracle. Even more than I imagined. And some of those buildings are outright temples."

Dolabella was silent.

They entered the temple and heard the rush of the Castalia Spring, supposedly magical, as it splashed into a small pool with a statue of a lion suspended over one edge. In a prominent position in the center of the temple stood the famous sphynx. Carved below it was an old adage attributed to the Seven Sages of the ancient Greek world: Γνῶθι σεαυτὸν. "Know thyself."

"Good advice," Sulla said. "Now spread out and search all the rooms. I want gold and silver and coins and every object of value piled up here, in the center, quickly. Then enter every shrine along the path and remove everything of value. We'll need the carts to transport it all. We'll melt down the gold and silver later, to be distributed among the troops."

And so began the most brutal and sacrilegious pillaging that Delphi had seen in its many centuries of existence.

The legionaries began piling up silver and gold statues, chests full of precious stones, gold coins, and all kinds of valuable objects, from goblets to elaborately bejeweled weapons. The entire temple smelled of laurel, which the Pythonesses used to reach the transcendental state and connect to the deities of Mount Olympus, communicating the will of the gods to those seeking advice.

Dolabella approached Sulla, who had an exultant gleam in his eyes. "Do you truly not fear the gods? Do you not fear Apollo's wrath?" Dolabella asked.

Sulla looked surprised at the question. "No. My only fear was not being able to pay the army. But that's been solved today, with this very lucrative pilgrimage to Delphi. Tomorrow we march to Athens."

Sulla felt satisfied as the day came to an end. Everything was going according to plan: he had a well-trained army that, now, thanks to the gold and silver of Delphi, would be completely loyal to him. He had a military campaign against a complicated enemy ahead, but he was in high spirits and felt invincible as he retired to his tent. He was about to get into bed when Dolabella entered the praetorium.

"Apollo has spoken: Cinna has taken control of Rome. Gnaeus Octavius has been executed and Marius has returned to the city," he said, giving a quick devastating summary.

Sulla sat down and nodded several times, staring at the ground. "Apollo has done nothing," he replied without looking up. "I knew Cinna would break the pact as soon as he could. He was quicker and more methodical than I expected, I have to give him that."

A suffocating silence followed. "What do we do?" Dolabella asked.

Sulla slowly expelled all the air from his lungs. He looked up to the roof of the tent, stretching his neck to ease his tension: "We will march on Athens and then defeat Mithridates. After that, we will return to Rome as a strong, united army. And we will show our enemies no mercy."

Dolabella nodded. His mentor seemed to have considered everything, and he had nothing to add.

"I'm going to sleep," Sulla said in an even tone, as if Cinna's assault on power, the death of the consul Octavius, and Marius's return to Rome were merely small irritations that would not disturb his slumber.

XXXIV

THE EAGLE
AT REST

Gaius Marius's residence, Rome
January of 86 B.C.

EVEN THE STRONGEST EAGLE, THE ONE WHO SOARS THE HIGH-est, will one day find his wings in need of rest.

The newly appointed consuls for that year were Cinna, for a second time, and Gaius Marius, for the seventh. A seven-time consul was something that had never been seen before and would never be seen again in the Roman Republic. But the man who had won the wars in Africa and the North, who had changed the symbol of the Roman legions to the eagle of his family crest, and who had transformed the very nature of the Roman army, fell ill only a few days after assuming his seventh consulship.

Marius had been in bed for a week.

He was over seventy years old.

He was weak.

He raved wildly.

His illness clouded his thoughts and whipped him into a confused frenzy for hours on end as he dreamed that it was him, not Sulla, commanding the legions against Mithridates.

But he had moments of lucidity as well, when he would ask to speak with his son, Cinna, and other important popular leaders. Sertorius now led the hundreds of veterans loyal to Marius, responsible for guarding the home of the seven-time consul and for safeguarding all of Rome as well.

"Are we alone?" Marius asked Sertorius.

"Yes, my consul," he said, then, noticing Marius seemed agitated, continued: "Cinna left hours ago. Only your son and young Caesar remain in the atrium. You said you wanted to speak with both of them. And with me."

"Yes . . . good," the consul said, struggling to speak. "Cinna is foolish . . . he will only bring trouble . . . to the popular cause . . . he is too radical . . . it will not end well . . ."

"Everything hinges on the campaign against Mithridates, doesn't it?" Sertorius said, trying to anticipate the veteran consul's words, which he struggled to pronounce.

"You have learned much," Marius replied, appreciative.

"If Sulla defeats Mithridates and obtains great spoils of war to distribute among his legions, he'll have a fiercely loyal army that we will never be able to defeat," Sertorius continued. "I don't think Cinna fully understands that."

"Cinna . . . underestimates Sulla."

"If Sulla achieves victory in Asia and begins a triumphant return to Rome, I've thought that we should withdraw from the city, but not to Africa this time."

"Do not speak in the plural, my friend . . . I will not be here."

Sertorius swallowed back tears, deeply touched by the fact that the consul had referred to him as his friend.

"Where . . . would you go if Sulla takes total control?" Marius asked.

"To Hispania," Sertorius responded. "It is rich in resources. With our men, along with support, I should be able to rally there. I could go into the mountains and try to keep the popular cause alive. Then, later, from a position of strength, I could renegotiate the situation. That is my plan."

Gaius Marius sighed. He was slow to respond, needing more time than usual to process information, but he finally spoke up. "That . . . is a magnificent plan," the old consul declared.

The two shared a long silence.

There were many things they could have said to each other. Sertorius had served under Marius on numerous military campaigns and had always proven to be thoroughly loyal. And loyalty, whether during peacetime or in war, through the eternal conflict between the optimates and the populares, was a scarce resource in Rome, as valuable as the most extravagant jewels imaginable, or more so.

But neither of the two men, seasoned in combat, brilliant with strategy, and loyal to the end, said a word. They simply shared a long silence. A silence of farewell.

"I want to speak for a moment to my nephew," Marius said.

Sertorius stood, saluted, and, without breaking that silence, wanting to carry it with him, turned and left the room.

Once in the atrium, he spoke to young Caesar, who sat with his father and Marius's son.

"The consul wishes to see you."

Gaius Julius Caesar looked at his father, who nodded. He then looked to Marius's son, who also nodded, and said, "He's fine right now. When the fever abates a bit he's able to speak. But be brief, my boy."

The young Caesar walked down the corridor lined with armed men posted to safeguard the home of the ailing consul, a man so great he had been nicknamed the third founder of Rome.

"Come closer . . . Gaius," Marius mumbled, his voice ever weaker.

Caesar walked to the bed and sat beside it.

"I don't have much strength . . ." Marius began. "So I'll get . . . to the point . . . I've warned you many times of Sulla . . . I shall do so again now. Cinna is in control of the city and he believes he will always have control . . . but Sulla will return . . . Mithridates is no match for him. And Cinna . . . I'm not sure . . . You are to marry his daughter . . . He will keep his promise to name you flamen Dialis . . . I know it's a nuisance to you, boy, but I asked him to do it for your own protection: no one has ever ordered the execution of a flamen Dialis. The office . . . will protect you . . . give you time . . . to think . . . if everything goes wrong . . ." Marius paused. He did not have the strength to continue.

"Accept the charge as flamen Dialis and be wary of Sulla," Caesar said, summarizing his uncle's words of advice to show that he had understood.

"That's it, my boy . . . Very good . . . And now . . . call in my son . . . This eagle has only one flight left in him . . . the flight to Hades."

Caesar stood and was walking to the door when Marius, in an almost inaudible whisper, spoke again: "And Dolabella . . . Watch out for him . . . He's just as dangerous as Sulla . . ."

Young Caesar nodded.

Marius closed his eyes.

Caesar left the room and Marius Jr. promptly entered, eager to be near his father in his final moments.

"What did he say to you?" Caesar Sr. quietly asked his son as they sat waiting in the atrium, since it would've been inappropriate to leave without bidding a proper farewell to the man who would soon become pater familias of the gens Maria.

"He said that I should marry Cornelia, become high priest of Jupiter, and be careful of Sulla and Dolabella," Caesar Jr. answered.

"That marriage, under the current circumstances, benefits us all and I will insist on your appointment as priest, you can be sure of that," his father commented. "As for Sulla and Dolabella, may the gods protect us. I don't know if Cinna and Marius Jr. will be able to stop them, but we must have faith."

Sertorius, overhearing the hushed father-son conversation, kept his pessimistic thoughts about the future of Cinna's rule to himself. He now had the consul's approval for his own plan: Hispania.

Gaius Marius's bedroom

Marius Jr. sat waiting for his father to speak but the man only writhed in his bed. He put his hand on his father's forehead. It was boiling.

"Jugurtha!" Marius howled. "Where is that bastard?"

"He's dead, father. He was taken prisoner by your troops and executed right here in Rome, don't you remember?"

Gaius Marius nodded, but he remained agitated. "And Teutobod? What is the news of him? He has an immense army . . . we have to avoid a direct attack . . . we have to wait . . ."

"Teutobod fell in combat, father, in Aquae Sextiae. You defeated his army just as you defeated the armies of the Cimbri and the Ambrones and everyone else you've gone up against. You have always been victorious, Father."

Gaius Marius seemed calmed. He was still as he spoke again: "Then we have to stop . . . Mithridates . . . You will be in charge of the left flank . . . Sertorius will take the right . . . I'll command the center . . . We have to surround him . . . with the cavalry . . . like in Aquae Sextiae . . . do you understand?"

"I understand, Father. That's what we'll do," he said, not wanting to contradict him again.

Gaius Marius turned to his son and stared at him for an instant: "I've won all the wars, haven't I?"

"All of them, Father."

Gaius Marius, seven-time consul, seemed to relax at those words and, as he'd done during his conversation with Caesar, he closed his eyes.

It was only a moment.

The sheets stopped moving up and down. The bed was still.

Gaius Marius Jr. pulled a gold coin from underneath his toga. He carefully opened his father's mouth and placed it inside. The funeral rites would soon begin, but first he wanted to make sure that Charon would guide his father safely across the River Styx. They had just lost the man he believed would always be the greatest, most intelligent, most skillful Roman military leader of all time. Marius's son believed this, of course, because he could not see the future.

Atrium of Gaius Marius's residence

Marius Jr. appeared in the atrium. He made the announcement without fanfare, like a messenger stating the facts and nothing more, as Marius would've liked him to: "My father . . . has died."

Roman Forum
January of 86 B.C.

One day after the death of Gaius Marius

Caesar's family was returning from the forum after attending Marius's cremation.

"Marius's death is such a great loss," Aurelia said to her husband as they walked back to the Suburra, flanked by their slaves and a few of Marius's men who continued to protect the Julia family out of friendship and loyalty. "I only hope that his dream for peace in Rome will be fulfilled."

Just then they crossed paths with a large group of armed men, led by a relatively young man in his late twenties.

"That's Fimbria," Caesar Sr. said, increasing his pace and urging his wife, son, and daughters to speed up as well. "Let's get home."

"Who is Fimbria?" asked Caesar Jr.

"He's Cinna's right-hand man, and Cinna, my son, is the *de facto* ruler of Rome, now that the Senate has been suppressed and the Plebeian Council is under his command," his father replied before glancing at Aurelia. "And with Fimbria controlling the streets, I would not count on peace in Rome. He is the most violent of Cinna's men. We might share the popular cause, but neither Marius nor I agree with—agreed with—Fimbria and Cinna's methods."

Athens

March, 86 B.C.

Sulla ascended to the top of the Acropolis in Athens to take in the scene. It was a catastrophe for the Greeks, a lesson. The entire city was fuel for the fire. And, wherever the all-consuming flames had not yet reached, the Roman soldiers wreaked havoc, raping, pillaging, and plundering.

Dolabella was a man of few scruples, but seeing that legendary city made beautiful by the sculptor Phidias and governed in times past by the brilliant Pericles reduced to rubble and ashes made him feel uneasy. Sulla was out of control. First he'd marched on Rome with the legions, something unheard of, outrageous. Then he'd pillaged the sacred temple of Delphi, and now he'd set fire to Athens with the excuse that the city had been too submissive when Mithridates advanced through Greece in hopes that the King of Pontus would free the Hellenic people from the Roman yoke.

"Was all this really necessary?" Dolabella asked, while smoke and flames raged as far as the eye could see.

"From a strictly military standpoint, no," Sulla admitted, "but from a strategic perspective, in the context of this war in which cities must decide whether to remain loyal to Rome or align themselves with Mithridates, yes, it was necessary. I think my message will be heard loud and clear throughout the entire Greek world: you're either with us, or our flames will consume your homes. There's no middle ground. Come, let's climb down from here before the fire surrounds us completely and blocks our way."

Dolabella trailed behind Sulla, processing his leader's cruel and merciless intelligence.

Julia family domus, Rome
Autumn, 86 B.C.

Cinna appeared unannounced at the Julia family residence, where as always he was welcomed as a guest of honor. And as always, he was accompanied by his daughter.

The girl, now ten, was comfortable in this home, where the domina treated her like one of her own daughters. Aurelia was still regularly giving her lessons in Greek and was always kind to her.

Caesar and Cornelia, without having to be told by their parents, immediately went off together to the back atrium of the domus to let the adults talk politics and other serious matters. And once in the back atrium, without a word, Caesar took Cornelia by the hand and they went directly to the tablinum, where they could listen in on that adult conversation.

"We are all greatly saddened to lose Marius but I am glad to see you are doing a fine job ruling the city on your own," Caesar Sr. began in a friendly tone. "Appointing Lucius Valerius Flaccus to replace Marius as consul was a good idea. He's a prudent man and will know how to appease the more hostile conservatives in the Senate." He avoided mention of the violent Fimbria, to whom Cinna had conceded broad powers.

"Yes, that's why I appointed him," Cinna responded as he served himself wine. "Flaccus is prudent, to be certain. Sometimes I think he may be too prudent."

Caesar Sr. let the comment go unanswered. He knew that Cinna was in favor of more radical actions and violence to keep control of power, which was why he had supported the cruel Fimbria's ascent.

"I'm going to send a new army to Greece," Cinna announced. "I don't want the war against Mithridates to stay in Sulla's hands alone."

"He's won several victories," Caesar Sr. pointed out cautiously. "In Chaeronea and Orchomenus, if my information is correct. Perhaps . . . too many victories?"

Cinna smiled. "The wise Caesar has always remained on the margins of Roman politics," he said, watching Caesar Sr. attentively and noting his reactions and expressions. "Many believe it is because you are a poor politician. But I think differently: I think you've seen too many men die after getting close to power. I think you're more intelligent than you let on. Gaius Marius regularly visited your home. He valued your advice, and so do I. Caesar, do you think it's a good idea to send a second army?"

Caesar Sr. drank from his cup and quickly considered his response. It didn't make sense to deny his reasons for remaining discreet and distant from politics. Cinna had figured it out. He knew that his family's safety was at stake.

"Yes. I'd say that sending a second army to keep Sulla from taking full credit for the imminent victory against Mithridates seems like a good idea," Caesar finally said.

"I knew it! By Hercules!" Cinna exclaimed. "The fact that you support this move tells me that it's even more necessary. I'll send Flaccus to lead that army. That will appease the Senate, the optimates, I mean."

"Flaccus is a good choice," Caesar Sr. agreed.

"Good," Cinna continued. "If your son was older, I'd suggest he join this new army. It would be a good opportunity for him to begin to make a name for himself. But I suppose he's still too young, isn't he?"

"He is only fourteen. Too young for this campaign."

"Still too young for war, but not too young to marry."

Caesar Sr. and Aurelia had been expecting a comment such as this.

"Remember that we have an agreement, my friend," Cinna went on, still smiling.

"I haven't forgotten, my friend and consul," Caesar Sr. responded. "My son and your daughter shall marry. But your little girl is not yet a woman. She is only . . ."

"Ten years old," Cinna answered with a certain air of annoyance, as if the girl were somehow guilty of growing up too slowly. "But she will soon reach *viri potens* and be able to grow a strong male heir in her womb."

His words sounded more like a threat than a declaration of fact.

Aurelia looked down. No one noticed. She was beginning to harbor doubts about the marriage between her son and the young Cornelia. Marius had served as a counterweight to Cinna's unchecked ambition. With him gone, an alliance with the popular leader seemed less and less advantageous every day. For now, the only things standing in the way of this marriage were her husband's cleverness and the fact that the girl had not yet menstruated.

"Shall we eat?" Aurelia suggested, forcing a smile.

"Please," said Cinna.

A short while later, without anyone calling them in, Caesar Jr. and Cornelia appeared in the central atrium to join the meal.

Aurelia noticed that the children were quite content in each other's company and decided not to make any rash decisions. The natural course of events would determine their destiny.

Caesar's sisters, Julia Major and Julia Minor, joined the informal gathering and, as everyone chatted amicably, Aurelia forgot her underlying concerns about Cinna's haste to accelerate the marriage. The dinner ended, and Cinna and his daughter bid their hosts a warm farewell.

That night, alone in their bedroom, seated on the edge of the bed, Caesar Sr. surprised his wife with an unexpected comment: "I'm going to accept the marriage proposals our daughters have received."

"From Pinarius and Balbus?" she asked, referring to the two men who had recently asked to marry their daughters.

The first, who wanted to marry Julia Major, was of the patrician order, and the second, who wanted to wed Julia Minor, was of plebeian birth. Neither man came from a prominent family, but, in those uncertain times, it seemed wiser, safer, to wed their daughters to men of little public importance.

"I'll say yes to both of them," Caesar Sr. declared.

Aurelia nodded: "So we'll only have one worrisome match to deal with."

"Exactly," her husband replied.

"The most delicate, the most important."

"The most delicate, the most important," he sighed. "I'm tired."

The comment was odd and perturbed Aurelia; her husband never complained.

Lucius Cornelius Cinna's domus
That same night

Fimbria arrived past midnight. He was armed and accompanied by a large group of men who loved violence as much as he did, all of them answering to him.

"You have summoned me, Consul?" he said.

"I have summoned you," Cinna confirmed, then took the man by the arm and led him into the tablinum. "I'm going to move forward with my plan to send a second army to the East against Mithridates."

"Very good," said Fimbria, unclear how the news affected him.

"Valerius Flaccus will be at the command of that army."

"Flaccus? But Flaccus is a coward. As a politician he might be all right, as consul, here in Rome. But he's so . . . weak."

"I know. That is precisely why the Senate will accept him in this role. The conservatives in particular will not see him as a threat to Sulla, knowing that someone like Flaccus could never prevail in the war against Mithridates. So we'll be able to get them to agree without any difficulty."

Fimbria could understand the logic, but he didn't see what good it would do to send someone like Flaccus to battle a wolf like Sulla.

"I know, I know," Cinna continued, as if reading the thoughts of his most trusted man. "Flaccus is easy prey for Sulla. That's why you will accompany him on this military campaign to the East. You will do so in the capacity of legatus at the head of a legion. That's why I've called you here tonight."

Fimbria nodded, slowly. "The consul could have told me this in the morning at the forum or in the Curia Hostilia or—"

Cinna interrupted him. "Of course. I've summoned you in the middle of the night not merely to tell you this, but to inform you that you'll have two missions on this campaign. Missions that I can't speak of in the forum, surrounded by senators from one faction or another."

Fimbria remained very still. "Two missions?"

Cinna liked the fact that Fimbria was hanging on his every word. "I would've liked to name you consul, or proconsul with imperium over that second army in the East, but you are too young, not yet thirty. And, as we've said, Flaccus will be readily accepted. Your first mission will be to assassinate him and take control of the army. I don't care how you do it, but do it. The army must be under your control before you reach Asia."

"Agreed. I can do it," Fimbria said. He liked the idea of an entire army under his command. He had risen rapidly to power, and he didn't mind killing to reach new heights. Even if the man he had to kill was a Roman consul. In any case, he was a weak consul. "You said I'll have two missions."

"Yes, two," Cinna said, then paused, as if the second mission were so difficult it was hard to say it aloud. He sat on a solium.

Fimbria remained standing. He thought he knew the consul's second objective. "The second mission is to defeat Mithridates myself, isn't it?"

Cinna slowly ran his fingers through his beard. He swallowed. He looked down, then raised his eyes to meet Fimbria's as he spoke methodically, in a low voice that nonetheless rang out cold and clear as day: "No. Mithridates doesn't matter. He is secondary. We shall eliminate him in due time. Your second mission will be to assassinate Sulla."

XXXV

THE DEATH OF
JULIUS CAESAR

Julia family domus, Rome
85 B.C.

T HEY HAD JUST CREMATED CAESAR'S FATHER.
Within weeks, the tiredness Caesar Sr. had mentioned to Aurelia evolved into pain, the pain to illness, the illness to death.

Caesar sat at one end of a triclinium curled in on himself with his hands over his ears, as if he didn't want to hear anyone or anything.

He'd just become pater familias at the tender age of fifteen. The great general Scipio had also been forced into that responsibility at a young age, but not that young. And he didn't feel at all like Scipio. He felt like nothing.

The young Caesar was overwhelmed. Frightened. His father had wrapped up some important matters, such as his sisters' marriages, which had provided him with his last moments of happiness. Before dying, Caesar Sr. had gotten to meet his granddaughter Acia,* daughter of Julia Minor and Balbus.

Caesar, in the center of the atrium, his eyes closed, intuited someone's presence and sat up as he lowered his hands and opened his eyes.

Cornelia was standing there.

"I'm sorry," she said.

Caesar looked at her in silence. At only eleven years old, the girl was already starting to look like a woman. A calm, attractive woman.

---

* Future mother of the Emperor Augustus.

Cornelia was growing up quickly, even if it wasn't quick enough for her father.

"Thank you," Caesar said, and he gestured for her to take a seat on a comfortable cathedra beside him.

The Senate, now controlled by the populares, had named Cinna consul for the third time. Gnaeus Papirius Carbo, more moderate, was the other maximum leader for that year, but everyone knew that Papirius was a straw man and Cinna the true ruler.

She sat down beside him. She didn't know the correct thing to do or say, but she hated seeing Caesar so sad.

"I feel so alone," Caesar said. "Without my uncle and my father, I'm nothing."

"You're not nothing," she quickly replied. "You're brave."

He smiled sadly. "Right. I'm brave enough to eavesdrop behind the curtain of the tablinum. So brave. I can already see Sulla trembling before me."

Cornelia, undaunted, replied calmly, "You won't have to hide behind a curtain anymore. You're the pater familias. Now, whoever comes into this house has to address you directly, has to talk to you, let you be the one to decide."

Caesar suddenly saw her through new eyes: she was not just a little girl, but someone he could turn to. He no longer felt so alone or so overwhelmed. And . . . there was something else. He looked at her and she at him. They stared into each other's eyes intensely. And out of nowhere he felt desire for her, a strong desire. He moved his hand closer to hers, but she remained perfectly still.

They'd held hands before, when he led her to the tablinum to listen in on their fathers' conversations, but those had been the hands of a little boy and a little girl. Now, as Caesar rested his hand on Cornelia's, she trembled. These were not the hands of two children rushing off to spy on the grown-ups. The longing he felt, her quivering response, were anything but childish. And he imagined taking her face in his hands and kissing her. He imagined many things in that moment. He sensed that she'd sit there and let him kiss her without moving away. But they shouldn't. And so Caesar, wanting to do only what was best for her, simply held her hand.

Aurelia entered the atrium, calm and collected as always despite her husband's recent death. She could not afford to let herself be overcome with sadness, even though, on the inside, she was tormented by grief. Without her husband, she now had to remain extra vigilant of everything and everyone.

"Would you like to stay and dine with us today?" she asked the girl.

Cornelia shook her head as if snapping out of a daze and then looked at Caesar. "Would you like me to stay?" she asked before answering Aurelia.

Aurelia did not find Cornelia's reaction inappropriate. The girl was merely recognizing Caesar's authority as pater familias.

Caesar nodded.

Aurelia ordered the atriense to bring in another triclinium.

"Is your father coming too?" Caesar asked.

Cornelia shrugged, still flustered by the moment they'd just shared. "My father barely speaks to me, you know that."

"He is coming," Aurelia said. "Cinna will be here shortly. He comes to speak with you, Gaius. You can be certain of that."

Aurelia did not say any more, but, like everyone in Rome, she knew that Cinna had sent a second army to the East under the command of Valerius Flaccus to reduce Sulla's power in the campaign against Mithridates. It was clearly a political move aimed at putting an end to the populares' greatest fears: Sulla and, in particular, his victorious return from the East. If Cinna's plan worked, her son's match to Cornelia remained advantageous. If Sulla managed to foil Cinna's plot, however, the union could be just the opposite: a danger, a connection that marked Caesar as an enemy. And Aurelia was certain that Sulla would show Cinna's son-in-law little mercy.

Aurelia invited Cornelia to recline beside Caesar for the meal. The girl's father was still the ruler of Rome, for now. Aurelia could also tell that Caesar and Cornelia were looking at each other . . . differently.

XXXVI

FIMBRIA VS. SULLA

Nicomedia, Kingdom of Bithynia, Asia
85 B.C.

VALERIUS FLACCUS COULD RUN NO FARTHER.
Fimbria's men captured the Roman consul in Nicomedia.

It had all started in Byzantium, before the army even made the crossing into Asia: Valerius Flaccus had proven to be very harsh and strict with the troops in his attempt to prepare them for the war against Mithridates. Fimbria took advantage of the soldiers' discontent to stage a mutiny and seize control from Flaccus. But Valerius Flaccus managed to escape. Fimbria knew he could not allow a Roman consul to remain on the loose in Asia, where he could recruit troops or make allies with local kings. So he pursued him relentlessly until finally capturing him in Bithynia.

Valerius Flaccus was held tightly by two legionaries as Gaius Flavius Fimbria thrust his sword into the runaway consul's guts.

"By Jupiter!" Flaccus wailed as Fimbria's weapon twisted in his entrails. "You're insane—you and Cinna both . . ." he fell to his knees in agony, blood spouting from his mouth, his face twisted by pain.

Fimbria, purely out of curiosity, knelt beside the dying consul. "Insane? Why would you say that?" he asked. "Do you really think that Cinna and I are incapable of defeating Mithridates? That we are no match for him?"

Valerius Flaccus fell over onto his side. He was bleeding profusely, but in his pain and rage, he began to laugh wildly, in fits and starts, as he continued spitting blood: his murderer was so utterly stupid that it was comical. Knowing that the person who had betrayed him was, like him, a dead man, made his agony less bitter. "No, not Mithridates..." Flaccus could barely speak. He contorted his face in an attempt to take more air in through his nose and mouth, but he inhaled only blood. He was suffocating.

Fimbria furrowed his brow and bent down to hear Flaccus's last words: "You are... no match... for Sulla," the consul said.

And he died.

Flaccus lay on his side, hands on his guts, in a puddle of blood, eyes open wide, his face a mask of suffering and surprise. Unresolved emotions he'd have to take with him to Hades.

Fimbria stood up, a serious expression on his face.

Behind him, his officers awaited his orders.

He turned to them: "We march on Mithridates."

Roman fleet on the Aegean Sea
85 B.C.

Sulla, Dolabella, and Lucullus stood around a table strewn with maps in the captain's cabin. No war against Mithridates would be successful without adequate naval support, since the King of Pontus's fleet dominated the eastern Mediterranean. Sulla had tasked Lucius Licinius Lucullus, one of the optimates' most trusted men, to appeal to supporters of Rome along the coast of northern Africa, Egypt, and other eastern kingdoms, and Lucullus had managed to piece together an impressive fleet to aid Sulla's attack on Athens. But now there was a new player in this war: Fimbria.

"He executed Valerius Flaccus in Nicomedia without thinking twice. Fimbria seems to have whipped his troops into a brutal fury. They say they're as savage as he is," Lucullus said, summarizing the latest news from Asia. "He has defeated the King of Pontus's troops in Pitane, and Mithridates has taken refuge in Mytilene, on the isle of Lesbos."

Lucullus didn't dare to suggest any type of action against Mithridates or, much less, Fimbria. When it came to Sulla, he preferred to maintain a prudent silence and await his orders.

Dolabella, however, saw so clearly what should be done that he proposed it immediately: "We can sail the fleet to Lesbos and surround the island. Our troops combined with Fimbria's can easily capture Mithridates and put an end to his ambitions once and for all."

"We could . . ." Sulla agreed, then paused as he looked at the map spread over the table. After a moment he casually added, "But we won't."

He remained silent, eyes fixed on the map depicting the contours of the eastern Mediterranean and the borders of the major kingdoms. Fimbria was in Asia, Mithridates in Lesbos but with troops in Asia as well. Sulla himself had his fleet and troops stationed in Asia. It was a complex situation. Or yet, perhaps, it was actually a very simple one.

"What will we do, then?" Dolabella asked.

Sulla looked up from the map. He took a deep breath and then finally spoke, his voice almost bored: "We will offer Mithridates a peace treaty, a favorable one, and we'll aid him in his return to his kingdom along the coasts of the Pontus Euxinus."* Seeing the surprise not only on Dolabella's face but on Lucullus's as well, he felt obliged to explain what to him seemed so obvious. "Mithridates isn't important now. Fimbria is the one who matters."

"But total victory is within our reach," Dolabella replied, exasperated.

"That's not the victory I seek," Sulla said. "I won't allow this second army, commanded by a popular legatus, to aid the defeat of Mithridates in any way."

"What is the victory you seek, then?"

"Victory in Rome. And that starts with wiping Fimbria off the map. The populares have taken back power. Marius is dead, but Cinna is in control and has once again changed the census to incorporate the socii, going against our agreement. That will only be the beginning of his reforms. He sent Fimbria into this war to keep me from taking credit for the imminent victory and returning to Rome

---

*   The Black Sea.

triumphant, with euphoric legions parading through the streets in celebration. He thinks himself quite clever, but this will lead to a new war. So we'll start it here and now, by eliminating Fimbria."

Dolabella shook his head. Lucullus didn't fully agree with Sulla either, but he didn't dare to speak up.

"But if we offer Mithridates peace, he won't have to pay for our war expenses. We need that money to keep our men happy, especially, as you say, if there's about to be a second war," Dolabella said. "Without money, none of that can happen."

"You're right about that," Sulla agreed, and then smiled. "Without a doubt, someone will have to pay for this war, as well as for the battle against Fimbria. And while we're at it, we might as well raise funds for the war we'll have to wage with Cinna once we return to Italy."

Mytilene, Lesbos
85 B.C.

───────────

The King of Pontus read and reread the letter sent by Lucius Cornelius Sulla, who, in his capacity as proconsul of Rome, was extending a peace treaty. It was a quite favorable agreement: he wouldn't be required to pay any war expenses, not even a single tribute in compensation. The only stipulation, in fact, was that he return to his kingdom and respect the borders as they were before the conflict. Surrounded as he was by two Roman armies, his fleet greatly debilitated by the constant attacks from Rome's naval fleet, Mithridates received the treaty like a gift from the gods. He didn't understand the reasoning behind it, but he decided not to overthink it.

"Tell the proconsul that I accept," Mithridates VI said to the Roman officer awaiting his reply.

Julia family domus, Rome
85 B.C.

───────────

Cinna got directly to the point. He first gave young Caesar, only fifteen, his condolences over the tragic death of his father. Then, immediately, he reminded the boy that he had agreed to a wedding and said he wanted to set the date.

His future father-in-law held total control of Rome. Despite his youth, Caesar was wise enough to know that he could not and should not oppose Cinna. He also liked Cornelia very much and considered himself fortunate that she was to be his wife. In a world where marriages were negotiated like contracts, he'd gotten lucky.

"As soon as she becomes a woman," Caesar answered.

"Right," Cinna commented. "That's what we agreed. I'm glad to see that you plan to honor your father's word . . ."

Suddenly, a sweaty messenger entered the Julia family atrium, asking loudly for Cinna. The consul stepped forward and the legionary spoke: "I bring news from Asia, Consul."

Cinna, standing in the center of the atrium as if he owned the domus, turned up his hands. "And?" he demanded. The messenger hesitated. "By all the gods, soldier, speak! The consul is among friends here! Isn't that so?" he said, turning for an instant toward Caesar.

The boy nodded.

Also present were Aurelia, Cotta, Cornelia, and Caesar's sisters. A mostly female audience, which doubtlessly made the legionary less than comfortable delivering news of a sensitive military nature. But, yielding to Cinna's pressure, he explained: "Fimbria has died, my consul. Sulla offered peace to Mithridates, who accepted, and retreated to Pontus. Then Sulla turned on Fimbria as if he were a mortal enemy, cornering him in Thyatira, between Sardis and Pergamon. Fimbria ordered his troops to attack Sulla, saying he had made the peace agreement without consulting the Senate, but Sulla had already bribed Fimbria's army with large sums of money. They refused to stand with him and Fimbria was forced to flee to Pergamon. But Sulla pursued him and surrounded him in the temple of Asclepius, where Fimbria ended up taking his own life. Sulla now has control of both armies in Asia and, since he no longer has Mithridates to defeat, should be back in Rome in a matter of weeks."

Cinna was silent, as was everyone else in the atrium.

As Roman consul and leader of the populares, Cinna controlled the city, but he had no army with which to resist Sulla.

"Where did he get enough money to bribe two armies?" Cinna asked. "If he offered a peace treaty to Mithridates, he wouldn't have received any funds from him. So how did he pay the troops? More plundering?"

No one dared to answer those questions and Cinna didn't expect them to. He was once again lost in thought. His plan to defeat Sulla in Asia had failed. Worse still: Sulla had been strengthened in the process. It was clear now that he had to take care of all important matters himself. He'd delegated power to Fimbria and it had ended in disaster.

Cinna looked again to Caesar. "The wedding will take place. I have to take care of some things." Turning to leave and without looking at his daughter, he shouted, "Cornelia, come!"

"Yes, Father," the girl said obediently. As she left, she glanced back at Caesar. Her future husband responded with a faint smile.

Father and daughter left the atrium of the Julia family domus.

Aurelia immediately understood that the marriage between her son and Cornelia, which mere moments ago had seemed to be a good alliance, could soon become a heavy burden. She didn't know how to broach the subject with Cinna. But how could she let the betrothal stand as Sulla grew ever stronger and his return to Rome ever closer? Sulla would surely continue his rampage here in Rome, wiping out all his enemies, the young man married to Cinna's daughter among them.

Aurelia swallowed; her brow creased with worry.

XXXVII

CAESAR'S WEDDING

Rome, 84 B.C.

CORNELIA HAD FINALLY BECOME A WOMAN.

She was only thirteen, still half girl, but she could now technically bear children. And her father was impatient. Preparations for the wedding between Caesar and Cornelia were immediately set in motion as they looked at the calendar to set the date. No easy feat, since the Romans divided the days between *dies fasti,* appropriate for celebrating weddings or starting any new endeavors, and *dies nefasti,* in which no marriages or important undertakings should commence. Both parties were eager to seal the marriage pact, but the Romans were very superstitious, and the times uncertain, which made finding a portentous date of the utmost importance. The day was finally set.

The two families first met for the *sponsalia,* where the betrothal was made official. The two parties agreed on the terms of the dowry and that the marriage would be *cum manu,* not *sine manu,* meaning that Caesar, not Cinna, would be bestowed with the power to make all decisions for Cornelia. Caesar requested this condition specifically and although Cinna did not like the idea of losing control of his daughter, he thought it more important to seal the union with Gaius Marius's family than to get into a tedious debate on the terms of the marriage.

The contract was signed.

Caesar placed an iron band on the ring finger of Cornelia's left hand, which the Romans believed communicated directly with the heart through a nerve. He planned to replace it, in the near future, with a gold ring, as was customary. From here, the wedding would take place in a matter of months. A maximum of two years.

The sponsalia concluded with an extravagant banquet as the two families exchanged wishes of happiness and prosperity for the new couple. It was an island of goodwill in the political storm that had besieged Rome.

Asia, 84 B.C.

Sulla had spent all his reserves of gold and silver, gained through the plunder of Greece, to bribe Fimbria's army. In military and political terms, the operation had been a resounding success, but now he needed money, great sums of *sesterce,* denarii, or *talents;* the currency was irrelevant. He had not one but two armies to pay, and the coffers of the Roman state were controlled by Cinna, his mortal enemy. To avoid wearing out his troops in a long war against Mithridates, he'd permitted the King of Pontus to exit the conflict through a treaty that did not require him to reimburse Rome for war costs. This was highly unusual, especially since Mithridates had both initiated and lost the war. Rome was not known for being so merciful with its defeated enemies. But this treaty had allowed Sulla to gain total control of both Roman armies in the East and restore the borders to where they'd been before the conflict, without losing any more legionaries. And Sulla needed all the armed men he could get, since he was going to march on Rome. For a second time.

Dolabella never stopped reminding him that they needed money. There was still some gold and silver left over from the pillaging of Delphi and Athens, but it wouldn't be enough to fund a war against Cinna in Rome. Not with these troops used to earning a regular salary.

Sulla, nevertheless, did not seem worried. Before proposing peace to Mithridates, he'd conceived of a way to finance the next military campaign: he'd impose a huge tribute on all the cities and kingdoms that had been previously allied to Rome and then moved over to Mithridates's side. He would make them pay as punishment for their treachery. These Eastern cities, kingdoms, and provinces would fund

Sulla's armies. It would be a generalized plundering of Asia, one without pillaging or sacking, but with the threat of such action for those who did not deliver the required sums. The burning of Athens served as a very recent example of Sulla's wrath, ensuring that everyone was motivated to pay.

Sulla now had legions, money, and a thirst for blood.

Rome, 84 B.C.

Cinna knew that it had to be him, in person, who went out to meet Sulla when he disembarked in Italy. The marriage connection between his daughter and Marius's nephew strengthened his claim to leadership of the populares, which, he calculated, would help keep the treachery at bay in his absence from the city by the Tiber.

Betrayal from behind his back in Rome was his biggest concern.

He was looking in the wrong direction.

Eastern Mediterranean, 84 B.C.

Sulla sailed now to Rome. He would stop in Greece to collect the troops he stationed there on his march to Athens, then immediately continue to Brundisium, from where he hoped to launch his second military campaign for control of the empire. The final battle.

From the prow of the ship, he studied the horizon. Dolabella approached him. Sulla sensed his presence and spoke without turning around, always looking to the sea, to Rome.

"Did all the messengers leave before we set sail?"

"Yes."

"Messengers to Crassus in Hispania, Metellus Pius in Africa, and Pompey in Italy?" Sulla asked.

He'd written to the most important optimate senators in exile, calling for a general regrouping of the conservative forces. His legions had gained much combat experience through the naval battles commanded by Lucullus and their land victories over Mithridates in Greece and Asia. But Cinna, he was totally certain, was going to recruit a huge army to confront him. Any additional support from Metellus, Crassus, or Pompey could only help. If they joined this new war in Italy, it could tip the balance in his favor.

"Messengers were sent to all three, Proconsul," Dolabella assured him.

"Good," said Sulla, still looking to the sea, to Rome.

Lucius Cornelius Cinna's domus, Rome
84 B.C.

"*Ubi tu Gaius, ego Gaia,*" Cornelia said, voicing her consent to the marriage. It was a more intimate ceremony than Cinna would have liked, but all his energies were being put toward recruiting an enormous army to stop Sulla as soon as he disembarked onto the Italic peninsula. He was enlisting hundreds, thousands, of Romans, but also many socii, who had benefitted from the extension of Roman citizenship. In fact, he found more support and enthusiasm from their Italic allies than from among the Roman people, which should've come as no surprise. Cinna had extended Roman citizenship to inhabitants outside the city, but he had neglected the historic demands of the populares in Rome itself. The people of the *urbe* saw no redistribution of lands or wheat. Cinna had never championed that cause; it was Marius who had insisted on passing those reforms that had been talked about for decades, first by the Gracchi, then by Drusus, Saturninus, and other plebeian tribunes. All killed by the optimates. But Cinna liked power too much to start redistributing things. Also, slowing those reforms had decreased hostilities from the city's remaining conservatives and helped secure Cinna's position. Now, with Sulla's return so imminent, it was too late for him to start distributing lands and grains. That would take too much time. He'd thought, in fact, that he could ignore the demands of his popular bases indefinitely but he now saw that he would eventually have to make some concessions. If not, his support—in particular in the Council—would soon wane.

These thoughts occupied Cinna's mind as the wedding ceremony concluded and Cornelia threw herself into her mother's arms, begging not to be ripped away from her family, wailing as if being led to the home of her new husband was the most abominable fate she could suffer. This was a common Roman wedding ritual that recalled the legendary kidnapping of the Sabine women. The bride was expected to play her part convincingly so that the *lares,* the gods of her family home, would not think that she was leaving them willingly and become vengeful.

Annia, Cornelia's mother, also acted as if she were grief-stricken over the forced sequestering of her daughter, but hers was a more subdued performance, in line with her preference to always pass unnoticed.

After the scene was over, the group began the long *deductio* march to the home of the groom. The nuptial parade was led by three children, followed by relatives, friends, musicians playing pipes, and men bearing torches. Cinna, his wife, Annia, and Aurelia, representing both herself as mother as well as the deceased father of the groom, carried hawthorn torches, a spindle, and a spinning wheel, symbols of the new life that Cornelia would lead from that moment onward in the Julia family domus.

"*Thalassio!* Thalassio!" hundreds of people shouted along the sides of the streets as the wedding party made its way through the Suburra. The term was used to applaud the groom's good fortune in successfully kidnapping the loveliest of brides.

Young Caesar, Marius's nephew, embodied the hopes of Rome's most disadvantaged. Here was someone who, maybe, someday, might take on the most powerful senators and finally help distribute lands, grain, and other wealth more equally. These reforms had been so often promised, most recently by Cinna, but never delivered. Back when the conservative optimates controlled the Senate, they had pushed to further oppress the already downtrodden people. But now that the Senate was at last controlled by the popular faction, the people were simply ignored. Caesar was getting married, growing up, and with him, among some circles, grew a tentative optimism: Could Marius's nephew be the future leader who would bring about lasting change?

Some in Rome considered the notion. But only a few. The majority were merely enjoying the spectacle, invoking the god of weddings, son of Venus and Bacchus: "*Hymenaeus!* Hymenaeus!" the people shouted as the couple passed.

Cinna, for his part, reached several conclusions during that long nuptial march. As soon as the wedding was over, he'd order a new purge of the optimate senators and their families. Blood would once again run through the streets of Rome. Later, after defeating Sulla, he would confiscate the lands that had belonged to those optimates, outlaws and assassins every one of them, and redistribute them to the benefit of the people. That would appease the masses and make it easier to stay in power for longer . . . forever?

They'd reached the home of the Julia family, where neighbors were waiting to meet the bride and groom, throwing walnuts to the three children who headed the procession to bestow fertility on the new couple. Caesar then took a strip of wool and some oil and offered it to his new wife, who accepted it. Cornelia, in turn, gave Caesar several coins, one for him to keep and the rest as an offering to the lares, the guardian deities of her new home.

Caesar and Cornelia stood before the door of the Julia domus in the center of the Suburra.

Caesar lifted his new bride into his arms. Still almost a girl, she was light, and he, already becoming a man, was strong. Cornelia liked the feel of her husband's embrace.

Caesar carried Cornelia across the threshold, taking great care since tripping as he passed through the door would've been a bad omen. He did not falter. This meant that the union was blessed by the gods and there would be happiness and fertility.

Cinna left the Julia family residence, left the Suburra, left Rome. He took his huge army and marched to Brundisium, where Sulla would soon disembark.

The new bride and groom were left alone, finally, in the atrium of the gens Julia residence.

The world around them was preparing for yet another war.

But they were newlyweds.

XXXVIII

CINNA CONFRONTS
SULLA

Eastern coast of Greece
84 B.C.

SULLA'S TROOPS WOULD SOON BOARD THEIR SHIPS ON THE
Grecian coast and return to Italy. "What is your strategy?" Dolabella
asked, wanting to know how his commander planned to defeat Cinna's army there.

"The same one we used with Fimbria," Sulla replied categorically.

That very night, a group of legionaries set off for Ancona prepared to infiltrate the legions Cinna had gathered there. They would
plant a rumor among those soldiers and they knew from experience
that the word would spread quickly.

Rome, 84 B.C.

Caesar stared at Cornelia.

He led her by the hand through the house, just as he'd done the
afternoon they first met, when he'd guided her from the back atrium
into the tablinum to listen to what their fathers had to say about
Rome and about them. The marriage their families had arranged all
those years ago had finally taken place.

They were husband and wife.

The house was lit by gentle candlelight.

The night was theirs and no one would interrupt them. They
were legally wed.

Caesar led Cornelia to the bedroom that would be theirs forever after. Now that her son was pater familias, Aurelia had given up the room she'd occupied with Caesar Sr., changing out the furniture, since a marriage bed could only be used by the woman it was originally gifted to.

So Aurelia had a new *lectus genialis* placed in the room and consecrated with a small statue of the god of fertility, who would bestow its blessings on the new matrimony. Cornelia, undaunted by the statuette with its enormous phallus, disproportionately large in comparison to the rest of its body, climbed on the bed and sat on top of it. She did not place its phallus inside her, but merely pressed its erect member against her vulva. That was as far as she'd been instructed, and she had no idea what was supposed to happen next.

The couple made love that night, with the statue beside them, and they would do so many more nights, now with the statue in a corner of the room, but always near the bed.

Caesar thought Cornelia was beautiful.

She felt safe with him.

The first time hurt, but only a little. He was very gentle with her. He was surprised to find that it was so different from what he'd experienced when he'd lain with the prostitutes of the Suburra. It was much more satisfying to lie with a woman who was not being paid to do it. He had no idea, at the time, to what extent the pursuit of that gratification would influence his life and the history of Rome. The history of the world.

Caesar simply lay with Cornelia, slept peacefully beside her, loved her.

They lived entirely removed from the violence between Cinna and Sulla, as if they were an island that had broken off and drifted away from the known world. And the two of them, in secret, without confessing it even to each other, silently wished, as they inhaled each other's breath, that they could truly live on a deserted island far removed from the harsh world and the bloody war that loomed on the horizon.

Main camp of Cinna's troops, Ancona, northern Italy
84 B.C.

Sulla's men easily infiltrated the ranks of Cinna's troops. The group had been sent by boat from Greece with the mission to start a rumor in the massive main camp in Ancona.

Preparations were under way for a huge battle outside Italy, in Thessaly, on Greek soil, as Cinna planned to keep the war as far away from Rome as possible. But Sulla's envoys began to spread the word that their commander would pardon the men of the new army at Ancona and that, in addition, he'd pay them very handsomely for deserting. Sulla's soldiers backed their words with gold and silver coins that they flashed and even handed over to any man interested in hearing more.

"And Sulla has much more where that came from: sesterce, denarii, and talents," they said to every soldier who would listen.

Cinna, meanwhile, had yet to even pay his legions. It was his fourth consulship, his fourth consecutive term as maximum leader of Rome, and he had not redistributed any lands or grains. He was beginning to earn a reputation as a man of great promises but little action.

Some of the soldiers, the ones recruited from the lower classes of Rome, were tempted by Sulla's offer. The socii, however, were still loyal to Cinna, who had at least granted them Roman citizenship. But then another rumor began to spread through the camp: Sulla's allies—Pompey, Metellus, and Crassus—had reached Italy. These were three of the most brutal *legati* in the war against the socii, who well remembered their names and their cruelty. The Italic tribes began to lose confidence in Cinna, who had little military experience. A combination of fears, concerns, and temptations began to erode the loyalty of Cinna's legions at Ancona.

The combination proved lethal.

For Cinna.

Rome, 84 B.C.

Caesar was named flamen Dialis, the highest religious office in Rome. The fifteen *flamines* consisted of the *maiores* priests, devoted to the major gods, such as Jupiter, Mars, and Quirinus, and the *minores,* priests of gods of lesser importance, such as Vulcan, Volturnus, Flora, Ceres, and others. Among them all, the high priest of Jupiter was the most important. But the many restrictions that the post brought with it, greatly limiting freedom of movement inside and outside the city, were a nuisance to Caesar.

And Sulla was on his way back to Italy, which made him uneasy, as it did all members of the populares.

Cornelia tried to cheer him up.

She wanted to do something more than merely lie naked on her back with her legs spread. Something that would excite him beyond the usual kisses and make him forget all his woes. So she offered to do something she'd seen engraved on a series of coins called *spintriae,* which an Egyptian slave had shown her a few weeks prior. The slave had told her that the coins were pieces of an erotic game: each one depicted a pair of lovers in sexual positions that Cornelia had never even imagined. One of them, the one that stood out most in her memory, showed a woman kneeling before a man, introducing his erect member into her mouth.

"And men like that?" Cornelia had asked the slave.

"A lot," she replied, before adding an important note: "But a Roman *matrona* should never do it."

"Why?"

"I do not know, domina. Where I come from, in Egypt, it is a commonplace practice. But here, the other slaves born in Rome tell me that a Roman matrona should never do those types of things."

With that conversation in mind, Cornelia began to kiss Caesar's bare chest. She did so lovingly and sweetly as she'd done on many other nights. But this time she continued moving down his body until she reached his stomach. And then lower. Her full lips slid over her husband's skin to the base of his erection. She then parted her lips and moved to kiss his engorged member. But before Cornelia could go any further, Caesar gently pushed her away.

"No," he said.

"You don't like it?" she asked.

"That's neither here nor there." Caesar pulled her up to sit beside him. "You should not do that."

"Why?"

"Because the mouth is sacred. It is the organ we use to speak, and our words are what permit us to communicate, to debate, to sway minds with our persuasive speeches. The mouth is sacred. The mouth of a Roman citizen or matrona should never be profaned in that way."

Cornelia caressed her husband's chest.

"But have you ever been kissed or ... anything else ... down there?"

"You ask too many questions," he said, pressing his lips to hers to ensure that the only sounds from her mouth would be moans of pleasure.

When their own erotic game finally concluded, the lovers lay on the bed, watching the quivering shadows in the corners of the room. The candlelight was dim, the silence total. Everyone in the domus slept except them.

"Why is it that in Egypt, women can do such things?" Cornelia asked.

"Things like kiss a man's penis?" he asked.

"Yes. The Egyptian slave girl told me it was a normal sexual practice there."

Caesar lay on his side and, as he caressed his wife's naked body, he spoke to her in a low voice. "They say that the Egyptian god Osiris ruled alongside his sister Isis, to whom he was wed. But the god Set, envious of Osiris's power, killed him. To assure that his victim could never be resurrected, he cut Osiris's body into pieces and scattered them across the land. But his wife Isis, with the help of other deities, recovered his body parts and put him back together. Only she was missing one part, the penis. They say that Isis made a member out of clay and, once the body was complete, she magically brought Osiris back to life. Some say that she revived him by flapping her magical wings, others say she did it by blowing or sucking on the clay penis. Maybe that's why in Egypt it's not considered wrong for a woman and man to do that."

"Where did you hear that story?" she asked.

"Ha! It's not what you think. Herodotus tells it in his second book of *Histories.* There are many scrolls in my father's library. I've read them all."

"Have you ever been with an Egyptian slave? Or any Egyptian . . . woman?" Cornelia was avoiding the word *prostitute* as her husband continued caressing her. Whether he had lain with other women before her was something they had never discussed.

"I've never been with any Egyptian woman." He leaned over to kiss Cornelia on the cheek as he rubbed her belly. "And I don't expect I ever will."

They both laughed.

He lay on his back.

"But Egypt is an important land," Caesar commented.

"Why?"

"It's crucial for control of the East. In fact, it's one of the reasons we went to war with Mithridates. The King of Pontus wasn't just threatening our eastern provinces and Greece. He also wanted to take possession of Egypt. The kingdom of the pharaohs is a very rich land."

"Do they have gold, like in Hispania?" Cornelia asked.

"No. Even better, they have grain."

She looked confused; gold seemed much more important than grain.

"Rome is growing quickly," he explained, "and people have to eat. So we need more and more grain. That's why Egypt is so important. It's the key to keeping Rome fed and key for control of the East, if Rome is ever to truly conquer that part of the world."

Caesar was still talking in his calm, soothing voice. "Just like Gaul is crucial to the North. We've always been attacked from the north. In the times of Scipio, Hannibal came from the North, just like the

Cimbri and the Teutons in the days of my uncle Marius. If we could
truly control Gaul, Rome would be safer. The sheer number of Gallic
tribes makes ruling that territory nearly impossible, but one day
someone should try to tame them once and for all. I know a lot about
Gaul because Marcus Antonius Gnipho, my boyhood tutor, was Gallic. He'd studied in Alexandria, but he came from Gaul and had done
much research on his birthplace. He told me so many stories that I
could recite the names of all the tribes in Gaul, their customs, where
they lived, where they came from. Gnipho was a good tutor. He now
teaches at a school he's opened himself . . ." Caesar lay down beside
Cornelia. She had fallen asleep.

He looked up at the ceiling and kept thinking.
About Gaul.
And about Egypt.

Cinna's main camp, Ancona, northern Italy
84 B.C.

Cinna had called a meeting of his officers in the center of the military camp. He'd received news that his men feared confronting
Sulla, whom they believed to be invincible. That enraged him: Sulla
hadn't even properly defeated Mithridates. Instead he'd negotiated
peace with the tyrant through a treaty that was shamefully disadvantageous to Rome. It was true that Sulla had achieved some victories in Greece and had years ago proven instrumental in the capture
of Jugurtha in Africa, but that was it. He'd done nothing in the
war against the Teutons, where, indisputably, all the credit should
go to Marius. Cinna was far from awed by Sulla, but he knew that
he couldn't send a huge army into battle without first guarantee-
ing their loyalty. So he would promise them an additional payment
after they successfully defeated Sulla in Greece. And he would also
pay them their initial salary immediately to motivate them as they
charged into battle.

Focused as he was on the political issues in Rome, Cinna wasn't
aware that Sulla had already bribed his army. He was offering too
little too late.

Without so much as a bodyguard beyond his symbolic escort of lictores, Cinna made his way to the front of the crowd of officers. Suddenly a soldier stood in his path, blocking his way, demanding payment of his salary. One of the consul's lictores pushed him aside, but that only further enraged the legionaries who had spontaneously gathered, without being summoned, to join the meeting of officers in the center of the camp.

In his haste to reach the elevated platform from which he could address his officers, Cinna ordered his lictores to quickly clear the way.

"Make way for the Consul of Rome!" he shouted.

But the legionaries would not step aside, shouting insults at the popular leader and demanding payment.

Cinna was furious.

"Imbeciles," he said, through gritted teeth. "If you only knew that your salary is exactly what I'm here to talk about."

He was unable to see that the army at Ancona had already slipped from his control and no words or promises could bring it back under his command. Sulla had sent money, real silver and gold, to the legionaries. And the jingle of coins was the only sound the men would answer to.

Stones began to rain down before Cinna had even made it to the platform. One of his lictores tried to shield him, but the situation was already out of control. The legionaries were livid over the delayed payment of their salary, fearful of going to war against the merciless Sulla and assured by the promise of pardon if they abandoned the popular cause. Most of all, Sulla had already placed real coins in their pockets, which was more than they could say for Cinna. They unsheathed their gladiī.

Blood began to flow.

Cinna's lictores were easily overwhelmed by the mob of furious legionaries. The officers, centurions, and tribunes looked on in silence. No one gave a single order.

Cinna was surrounded by angry, armed soldiers.

The first sword was thrust into his back.

The second into his side.

The rest, a half dozen more, came from everywhere at once.

Cinna was dead in an instant.

He fell like all tyrants fall: suddenly, and with a look of surprise on his face.

Sulla's bribery scheme had once again paid off.

XXXIX

AURELIA'S
DECISION

Rome, 84 B.C.

SULLA'S RETURN TO ROME WAS NOW INEVITABLE. IT WAS ONLY a matter of time.

News of Cinna's death reached the Julia family residence.

Caesar hugged his wife, who immediately burst into tears. She was saddened not so much over the death of a father who'd never loved her, but because the consul's fall foretold the collapse of the popular regime. News of Crassus, Pompey, and Metellus had also reached Rome. Sulla's allies had recruited men throughout all of Hispania and Italy to join the victorious commander on his homeward march.

Everyone in Caesar's household understood that the situation was dire. Would Papirius Carbo, the other popular consul, the only leader they had left now that Cinna was dead, be capable of recruiting an army powerful enough, and more important, loyal enough, to confront Sulla and his optimate allies?

"I'm going out," Aurelia said.

Caesar thought it peculiar that his mother should leave the domus in those tense circumstances.

"I want to stock the larder with enough food to last a few weeks in case things get difficult," she explained. "If Sulla attacks Rome, it could become hard to find supplies."

Caesar nodded. His mother was always so cautious.

"Take as many slaves as you need, Mother," he said. "Don't skimp on security."

Cornelia was still sobbing in Caesar's arms as her two sisters-in-law attempted to console her.

Aurelia was about to leave when Cornelia sat up and wiped her face. "I should do something to help," she said. "I'm going to go out with your mother."

The woman froze. "No!" she replied harshly, then went on in a softer tone. "You have suffered a heavy blow and you need rest . . ." She looked at her daughters, who seemed to think they should join her as well. "I'd prefer you girls to stay home and take stock of the pantry. If there's something I haven't thought of, you can go out and get the rest of the things we need."

And, without giving anyone a chance to join her besides the slaves who would serve as escorts, Aurelia stepped into the street.

Caesar's mother hurried down the narrow lanes of the Suburra. The slaves assumed they would be going straight to the Forum Boarium, one of the city's largest markets, to acquire the supplies the domina had mentioned, but she seemed to be going first to the shops of tabernae *veteres* in the city center.

Aurelia's face was tense as she thought about her son's wife, a girl who no longer linked them to power in any way. All benefits that union had previously afforded would very soon begin to work against them. Nothing and no one could stop Sulla, and any resistance from the populares would only drag their suffering out for longer. Cornelia was dead weight. A burden that could prove dangerous.

"I will enter alone," she said to the atriense, stopping outside a spice shop.

The slave nodded and stood in the doorway to block it while her mistress was inside.

Aurelia entered and greeted the owner. Then, in a low voice, she asked, "Is your wife here? I requested a very rare spice a few days ago and I hoped she might have it by now."

The man didn't say a word, but simply nodded before turning to the back of the shop. When someone asked specifically for his wife, he preferred not to know anything more.

A middle-aged woman with a pretty face calmly stepped out from the back of the shop to attend to the domina.

"Do you have it, Mucia?" Aurelia asked, addressing the woman by her first name as a sign of trust.

"I do. But the domina should be warned again of its dangers."

"All poisons are dangerous; the question is whether it is quick. I have a serious problem to solve, but I don't want to cause unnecessary suffering. Death is already sad enough."

"It is very quick," Mucia assured her. "But it was very hard to get . . ."

Aurelia smiled slightly. She had expected this. She took out a bag of coins and placed it on the table crowded with spices.

The woman went into the back of the shop and returned a few seconds later holding a small vial.

"Is this enough to be lethal?" Aurelia asked as she carefully picked up the tiny vessel.

"A few drops will kill the most strapping of legionaries," the woman explained. "It comes from a plant called sardonia, named for the island from which it hails,* and it is highly lethal. It works quickly and painlessly to leave only a strange smile on the face of its victim."†

Aurelia nodded once, turned around, and hurriedly left the shop. She still had food to buy at the Forum Boarium, then dinner to prepare, and a dead weight to cut loose. And she felt terrible. She cared for Cornelia. But with Cinna dead, everything had changed. Above all else, she had to protect her son, free him from the chains that bound him to that collapsing regime. Sulla would soon enter the city, and he would be ruthless with anyone who had ties to the deposed Cinna. Aurelia was saddened, her stomach in knots, her heart pounding. But she was resolute in her decision.

Rome was no place for the sentimental, only for the practical.

And the speedy.

* Sardinia.

† A sardonic smile.

XL

SULLA'S ADVANCE

Italy 83–82 B.C.

SULLA ADVANCED TOWARD ROME AS HIS ALLIES BEGAN TO move through Italy. Campania fell under Sulla's control. The consul Norbanus, appointed by the populares as replacement for Cinna, was defeated, and the troops of the other consul, Scipio—too great a name for such an inefficient leader—switched over to Sulla's side as soon as the unstoppable general reached their camp at Teanum.

In the North, in Picenum, Metellus and Pompey vanquished the troops led by the new popular consul Papirius Carbo, who had replaced the unfortunate Norbanus.

Then, in a desperate attempt to put the most charismatic leader possible up against Sulla, the populares chose Gaius Marius Jr. as consul. He rose to the challenge with an army improvised in extremis and marched to Sacriportus to wage war with Sulla and Dolabella's troops.

"What do we do?" Sulla's tribunes wanted to know.

"We attack," Sulla said without hesitation.

He'd had a dream in which Marius Sr. had told his son not to fight on that day, and he thought it a good omen. Dolabella, however, was of another mind. "The troops have been marching for days. They need rest. It would be better to wait—"

Dolabella was interrupted by several soldiers who came running from the other side of the camp: "The enemy is attacking! They're attacking!"

Unaware of Sulla's portentous dream, Gaius Marius Jr. had decided to ambush his enemy *oppugnatio repentina,* without warning, without giving anyone time to rest, neither Sulla's troops nor his own.

"Then we have no choice," Dolabella said. "We have to defend ourselves."

Sulla simply nodded, concluding the meeting as the tribunes rushed to take their combat positions.

The battle lasted hours.

Rome, 82 B.C.

Aurelia was not able to carry out her plan. She simply didn't have the guts.

Her stomach churned with worry. She put it off for months, day after day, until over a year had passed. She maintained the hope, weakly flickering inside her, that the forces the populares had managed to gather under the command of different popular consuls would somehow manage to stop Sulla.

But, through victory after victory, Sulla circled ever closer to Rome. Aurelia's hopes in Marius Jr.'s ability to stop Sulla were waning. The boy was brave, but he lacked his father's influence and intelligence. Aurelia was convinced that the spirit of the great Marius had passed to his nephew, young Caesar. But he was precisely that: young. At only eighteen, there was nothing he could do.

"What do you think will happen?" Cornelia asked her mother-in-law one afternoon.

"Caesar has gone to the forum. He'll bring news," she responded calmly, but she could sense that total defeat was inevitable. The return of Metellus and Pompey, combined with Sulla's experience and Marius Jr.'s lack thereof, could only end one way.

That's why Aurelia had finally made up her mind.

She offered her young daughter-in-law a cup of hot broth.

"Drink this, dear, it will be good for you," she said. "The weather has been so cold and damp lately and we have enough worries as it is without anyone falling ill, don't you agree?"

Cornelia took the cup in her hands.

"Careful," Aurelia warned her. "It's very hot."

The heat made it easier to dilute the poison and also better masked its taste.

Cornelia blew several times into the cup. Then, slowly, taking care not to spill any of the broth, she brought the edge of the cup to her lips.

"Ow!" the girl cried. "By Jupiter, it is hot! I'll wait a little while." She set the cup very carefully on the table in front of her.

Aurelia stared at it.

"I would like to tell you something," Cornelia then said.

"Tell me, dear," Aurelia said calmly, without taking her eyes off the steaming cup.

"I wanted to thank you for everything you've done for me, the way you've accepted me into your home," the girl began. "My father died and my mother has always been very distant. My brother is not strong and intelligent like Caesar. Without my beloved husband and you and your daughters, I'd be . . . lost. I would feel so alone. And terrified. Well, I am scared. Everyone, I think, is afraid that Sulla will achieve victory, but I don't feel alone. You have treated me so warmheartedly, as if I were one of your own daughters. From the beginning. You taught me Greek and have always had kind words for me. Becoming Caesar's wife was the greatest moment of my life. But having you as my mother-in-law is the next best thing that could've ever happened to me."

Aurelia nodded without saying a word, her eyes fixed on the cup. She didn't have the nerve to look the girl in the face. Not after what she'd just said.

Cornelia carefully picked up the steaming broth but continued speaking: "I just wanted you to know that I will always remain loyal to the Julia family and I'll stand by my husband no matter the circumstances. I'll do whatever is necessary, whatever is asked of me, whatever Caesar wishes, whatever the Julia family decides is best. You have my utmost loyalty."

Aurelia looked down.

Cornelia brought the cup to her lips, slowly, so as not to spill the broth. She paused. It was still steaming.

Sitting there waiting for the broth to cool, alone with her mother-in-law . . . Cornelia hadn't planned to announce it yet, but the girl suddenly felt it was the right moment to share her news. "There's something else I've been wanting to tell you, and especially Caesar," she began, cradling the warm cup in her hands.

"What is it, dear," Aurelia asked with a sigh. The girl was not making this easy. Aurelia was consumed with doubt as Cornelia spoke so sweetly, but the greater good of protecting her son from what was now a dangerous alliance kept her firm in her decision, as cruel as it was.

"I am with child," Cornelia said. And, after making that announcement, so small yet so monumental, she brought the cup back to her lips.

"Wait!" Aurelia shouted, jumping up.

Startled, the girl dropped the cup, and it shattered against the mosaic floor. The liquid spread over the tiles and seeped down into the cracks.

"By Hercules! I'm so sorry!" the girl cried, embarrassed. "I'm terribly clumsy."

"No, it's my fault," Aurelia assured her. "I thought I saw . . . a stain . . . on the cup . . . and the wife of my son should never drink from a dirty cup. We'll ask for another one."

"But you prepared that broth for me yourself . . . I'm so sorry . . ."

"It's only broth, Cornelia. It's of no consequence. And a pregnant woman has the right to break all the cups in the world. Bring more broth," Aurelia said to the atriense. "Two cups, one for each of us. I wish to drink something hot as well. And, by all the gods, clean up this mess."

"Would the domina like to prepare this one?" the slave asked quietly, unsure how to proceed since the lady of the house had insisted on serving the previous cup herself.

"No, you do it," Aurelia said. "Forget about the spilled broth," she then said to Cornelia. "Caesar will be back from the forum soon and he will have news. That's what's important. And more important still is what you've just told me. How long have you known?"

"It's been three months since I last bled," the girl answered.

Aurelia stood up, walked over to her daughter-in-law, and embraced her lovingly.

"Next time tell me right away."

"Yes, Aurelia . . . Can I call you Aurelia?"

"Yes, dear, you can," replied Caesar's mother, closing her eyes.

Cornelia nodded. She was still flushed and embarrassed at her clumsiness, but she was reassured of her mother-in-law's infinite kindness. Even though the entire popular faction of Rome seemed to be on the verge of collapse, she felt fortunate to be part of a family that cared so much for her.

XLI

MARIUS'S ASHES

Julia family domus, Rome
82 B.C.

CAESAR RECEIVED THE NEWS OF CORNELIA'S PREGNANCY with the surprise and emotion typical of a young husband and first-time father. He spent his days going to the forum and returning home with news of Sulla's advance through Italy. Privately, he feared that the world was growing ever darker for the new life Cornelia carried inside her. He was powerless to reverse the course of events that, to his horror, threatened the safety of his entire family.

One night he arrived home with especially bad news. Marius Jr. had launched a surprise attack on Sulla's troops, but Sulla, more experienced in war and aided by the other optimates, had managed to turn the battle around and achieve final victory. Marius Jr. had taken refuge in Praeneste. And that wasn't all: the popular consul Norbanus had been defeated and his replacement, Carbo, had fled to Africa. Metellus, Pompey, and Crassus were now moving through Italy destroying any and all cells of popular resistance.

"It's only a matter of time before they converge with Sulla on Rome to take total control," Caesar concluded.

No one said a word. It was Cornelia who finally broke the silence. "I'm tired . . . I'm going to retire to our room," she said, standing up cautiously, since the pregnancy was now advanced and she could not move with her habitual agility.

"I'll join you," Caesar said, always very attentive to Cornelia.

Night was falling on the atrium of the Julia family domus.

Night was falling on Rome.

Night was falling on all the Romans who had believed that the people's cause could somehow prevail in the city by the Tiber.

Roman Forum

Crassus was the first of the optimates to reach Rome as reinforcement for Sulla's conservative cause. Metellus and Pompey advanced more systematically, taking time to vanquish all resistance from the socii, who refused to see their dreams of Roman citizenship dashed by Sulla and the restrictive policies he would surely put in place.

Sulla finally entered the city of Rome.

He was met with no resistance. Nothing could stand in his way. Differing political opinions were not enough to stop an army. The populares had no troops, and Sulla's legions seized total control.

But it was not enough for him. Sulla desired something beyond complete domination. He wanted revenge.

"Where is he?" he asked the senators who greeted him in the forum outside the Curia building.

The patres conscripti didn't understand. Not even Crassus. Only Dolabella knew how to interpret his mentor's desires.

"Marius," Dolabella clarified. "Where is he buried?"

The senators nodded and led Sulla and his guards to the tomb where the popular leader's ashes had been laid to rest. The mausoleum had been hastily constructed beside the Via Apia when the efforts to stop Sulla had caused the populares to set aside their initial plans to give their great leader a more fitting tomb, a grandiose monument that would honor Marius's peerless successes in politics and in war.

Sulla stopped before the shrine where his enemy's remains were housed.

No, it was not a grand funerary monument fit for a seven-time consul of Rome. But still, he couldn't stand to see the old leader of the populares rest in peace.

"They cremated him?" Sulla asked.

"Yes," several senators confirmed.

"Remove his ashes," Sulla ordered.

The legionaries beat down the doors of the shrine and in moments presented Sulla with a small metal urn containing the remains of the legendary Gaius Marius.

"Follow me," said Sulla as he began to walk away.

Dolabella fell in step beside his mentor to voice the question nobody else dared to ask: "Where are we going?"

"Outside the city, far," he responded vaguely.

The march was, in fact, several miles long. They left Rome behind and followed the course of the Tiber to where it joined the Aniene River. It was there that Sulla ultimately stopped.

"This seems far enough," he said. He looked to the soldier carrying Marius's remains. "Dump them here."

The soldiers' faces showed hesitation.

This was the legendary general who had saved the city on numerous occasions, most notably from the deadly advance of the Teutons, who would've destroyed Rome and massacred all its people. Scattering Marius's ashes into the river would prevent him from resting eternally in Hades. And the man had been a great hero, no matter how much Sulla and the optimates hated to admit it.

But Sulla's expression left no room for doubt.

The legionaries swallowed their reluctance and waded into the river. They then opened the urn, dumping Marius's earthly remains into the rushing current.

"Good!" Sulla exclaimed.

He stood there for a while, watching the ashes swirl, enjoying that post mortem victory over Marius, his most detested enemy, now defeated, dead, and deprived of eternal peace. A complete, total victory.

Julia family domus
That afternoon

When Caesar found out what Sulla had done with the ashes of his beloved uncle Gaius Marius, he didn't say a word. Labienus respected his friend's silence, leaving him alone with Cornelia. He'd been the one to communicate the devastating message, begging his friend to forgive him for being the bearer of such terrible news.

Cornelia entered the vestibule where Caesar's friend waited.

"I think it would be best if you left," the young woman said. "I've never seen him like this. He needs time to ... to accept what happened."

Labienus bid her farewell and took his leave.

Cornelia returned to the atrium, where her husband was still sitting on a sella beside the *impluvium* in total silence, staring into the rectangular pool.

Aurelia had gone out to the market and the two of them were alone. Cornelia sat beside Caesar and wrapped her arms around him.

"I don't know how. I don't know when," Caesar said calmly, coldly, quietly, "but someday I will stand up to Sulla. Someday I will stand up to all of them, each and every one."

"Them?" she asked softly.

"The optimates."

"But it was only Sulla who profaned the tomb," Cornelia pointed out, frightened by the notion of Caesar taking on all the corrupt senators at once.

"Sulla committed this latest insult," Caesar agreed. "But Pompey, Crassus, Dolabella, none of the others tried to stop his sacrilege. They're all complicit. They all deserve my eternal hatred." He looked into his wife's sweet face. "I can understand their desire to get wealthy through corruption, Cornelia; I can understand their rage toward those of us who want to change things, and I can understand that they will fight to protect their many privileges. I can even understand how they could go as far as to kill for it. But profaning the grave of one of the greatest generals Rome has ever seen, purely out of vile revenge, is beyond me. No one has the right to do such a thing. They've crossed the line today. And one day, I'll cross the line as well. I will get revenge, in blood, for the atrocity they've perpetrated today. I swear it ... by Jupiter."

This wasn't merely an empty promise. It was a solemn vow delivered by the flamen Dialis, the high priest of Jupiter.

A roll of thunder boomed across the sky as a torrential downpour was unleashed on the city of Rome.

"Let's go inside," Cornelia said gently, as she took her husband's hand and led him out of the open atrium.

XLII

THE
LONGEST NIGHT

Rome
October 31, 82 B.C.
In the morning, HORA TERTIA*

IT WAS ALL OVER FOR THE POPULARES.

Sulla was set to begin a long series of Senate sessions where he planned to abolish, one by one, all the laws that had been passed first by Marius, then by Cinna. There would soon be nothing left of the old regime. Not a trace.

Yes, everything seemed to be over for the populares when something unexpected happened. A twist of fate that would go down in history: the Samnites and the Lucanians, two Italic tribes who had never surrendered or called an end to the long social war,† had armed themselves with everything they had and marched on Rome, determined to massacre Sulla. They knew that the leader of the conservative faction would never take their demands into consideration and so had decided to attack the city by the Tiber before the other senators, Pompey and Metellus, could join their forces with Sulla and Crassus's troops.

---

* Literally, "third hour." In the Roman timekeeping system, daylight hours began at sunrise, and since the day was divided into twelve hours, the term here means "three hours after sunrise," or something roughly equivalent to 7, 8, or 9 A.M. depending on time of year. In October, around 8 A.M.

† The term *social war* originates from the Latin *bellum sociale* (literally "the war of the allies," since *sociale* comes from *socii,* which means *allies*). This was a war fought between the Roman Republic and allied tribes mostly from 91 to 87 B.C., although some territories extended the conflict for a longer period.

Sulla received the news of the Samnites' advance on Rome as he was entering the Senate, just as he was about to begin the first session to abolish the laws passed by the populares in his absence.

He stopped.

He looked down at the floor.

He put his hands on his hips.

Dolabella and Crassus watched him closely.

Without a word, Lucius Cornelius Sulla slowly turned around. The Senate sessions would have to wait.

Julia family domus

That same day, HORA TERTIA

Labienus was buoyed by hope as he entered the home of his friend Julius Caesar. "The Samnites are marching on Rome! And they've come by the thousands! Sulla is going to have a hard time fending them off, even with his huge army! It's a generalized socii uprising. The Lucanians have already joined in as well."

Caesar perked up at the news. "Maybe Sulla and his men were too quick to declare victory."

"It would appear so," Labienus continued. "With Cinna in power, the socii's rights and demands for citizenship were at least heard, but they know that Sulla will strip them of everything they've gained."

"They have every reason to be furious. I hope the Samnites tear that miserable Sulla limb from limb," Caesar snapped, unable to contain his rage. Sulla's desecration of Marius's tomb was still fresh in his memory. He wished Sulla a slow, painful death. Just then, he heard a heartrending cry.

The two men looked toward the bedrooms.

Aurelia was exiting her daughter-in-law's room. She walked into the atrium. "Cornelia has begun her labors!" she exclaimed. Her voice was calm yet somehow transmitted a clear sense of urgency. "She is very young; one midwife might not be enough. By Jupiter, my son, go in search of the old Greek doctor."

Aurelia had given birth three times, and something in her tone led Caesar to understand that the labor was not going well.

The walls of Rome

HORA SEXTA

Sulla had spent several hours checking Rome's fortifications, and his face showed neither calm nor confidence: the walls would not resist a siege, and he knew it. After so many years of domination over the Italic peninsula, the city hadn't bothered to maintain the ancient battlements, built in distant times when an attack could occur at any moment.

Not even in the darkest days of the recent social war or when the Teutons advanced toward Rome had anyone made efforts to reconstruct the broken sectors of the wall and create a solid defense against a large-scale attack. They'd always expected Rome's enemies to be stopped before reaching their doorstep. This was in fact one reason why it had been so easy for Sulla and his troops to take control of the city both times he'd marched on Rome. But the very thing that had favored him in the past was now working against him.

"We'll have to fight them outside the city, beyond the walls," Sulla said to the conclave of his most loyal officers gathered in the hastily erected praetorium near the *Porta Collina,* one of Rome's main access points.

"The walls won't withstand a siege, but they provide a good vantage point for the archers . . ." Here Sulla paused. "We have to prepare for combat. Reports indicate that the Samnites are advancing fast and will arrive by nightfall."

"That means they won't attack until dawn," Crassus pointed out.

Sulla shook his head. "I wouldn't be so sure of that. I want to ready the men for an overnight battle, just in case; I won't leave anything to chance. There are many of them and they're coming for everything."

Julia family domus

HORA SEPTIMA

Cornelia wailed relentlessly.

The doctor finally left the room, where the girl was being assisted by Aurelia, the midwife, and a few slaves.

"How is she?" Caesar asked. He was no expert in childbirth, but Cornelia's wails of pain seemed to go beyond a woman's typical suffering in these circumstances.

"By Asclepius, things are not going well," the doctor said. "The baby is breech, the mother is very young, and this is her first child. I have to tell you, honestly . . . I think you should be prepared for the worst."

Aurelia had followed the doctor out into the atrium and heard his words. "If she dies, doctor . . . is there any chance you would be able to save the baby?" she asked, ever pragmatic.

The doctor recoiled slightly at her crude question but responded honestly: "If the worst happens, I could perform a post-mortem cesarean and we could try to save the baby. For now, everything depends on what happens in the next few hours."

"Hours?" Caesar asked in a worried tone. "Cornelia can't go on like that for hours!"

"She is suffering greatly, yes," the doctor said, "but in my experience, in cases like this, labor tends to be long. It's not going to be easy on her, and we need to be prepared for any eventuality. Right now, what I need is more hot water and clean rags. I'd pray to all the gods if I were you," he added as he turned and went back into the room where Cornelia lay in agony.

Caesar paced the atrium with his hands on his head.

Labienus watched his friend, unsure of what to say.

Aurelia was lost in thought. Perhaps this horrible labor would take poor Cornelia's life and free Caesar of the burdensome ties to Cinna's regime. She was still desperate to keep her son from being noticed by Sulla, who doubtlessly planned to eliminate all prominent populares as soon as his power was consolidated. On the other hand . . . would Sulla in fact secure control of Rome? How would the Samnite rebellion end? Would these socii be able to stop the man neither Cinna nor Marius had been able to contain? The legions were vulnerable to bribes, but the Samnites were not Romans. They were fighting for their own rights and their rebellion was not for sale. Sulla would have to do battle, as he'd done in Greece. And in combat, anything could happen.

"Is there any news of the Samnites?" Aurelia asked.

"We've heard that they're approaching Rome more quickly than expected," Caesar answered. "That's all we know."

"Well, you're not doing anyone any good sitting around here. Go out and try to gather more information," she said, eager to return to the doctor's aid.

"Let's go," said Labienus. "We'll find out what's going on beyond the walls."

Caesar would have preferred to remain nearby while Cornelia was in labor, but he grudgingly followed his friend out of the domus and into the streets of Rome.

Beyond the walls of Rome

HORA OCTAVA

Sulla marched through the gates of Rome with two-thirds of his legions, taking his most trusted warriors from the campaign against Mithridates as well as part of Cinna's army whose loyalty he had purchased. A third of his troops remained inside the city to assure that the populares could not rise up in arms, which would have created a second battlefront at his back and made control of Rome all but impossible.

He positioned the troops chosen for battle along the outside of the wall, where they expected the imminent arrival of the Samnite army, along with the Lucanians and other Italic tribes who had joined them in that last, desperate attempt to obtain Roman rights.

Sulla gave Crassus command of the more veteran troops; com-

mand of the less experienced legions fell to Dolabella. He then positioned himself at the Porta Collina to observe the scene.

The sun was beginning to set on the horizon.

"Here they come!" one of the sentinels announced.

First they saw a huge cloud of dust in the distance; then, little by
little, they began to make out the first units of armed Samnite warriors advancing quickly, almost at a run, toward the place where the
Romans stood.

Sulla swallowed.

It would soon be nightfall.

"Bring the torches, by Jupiter!" he ordered. "I want all the torches
in Rome!"

If they were going to be fighting all night, he'd need to be able to
see what was happening on the battlefield.

Julia family domus

HORA NONA

Caesar and Labienus were unable to leave the Suburra. Sulla's troops
blocked all the access points to the forum or any main avenue, as
their leader had given express orders for the Suburra to be locked
down. It was a neighborhood favored by populares, and therefore
one where he feared an internal uprising might begin. Any rebellion
there could spark a generalized revolt in Rome.

"Let's go home," Caesar said.

Labienus nodded. Military action against Sulla from inside the
city was impossible. They would never even make it past the troops
positioned on every corner.

They returned to the Julia family domus.

Aurelia was in the atrium dabbing her forehead and neck with a
damp cloth.

Cornelia was still howling in pain.

"Is there any news?" she asked as soon as she saw them.

"Sulla has the Suburra surrounded," her son answered. "There's
no way to get to the walls."

Cornelia wailed again.

"By all the gods!" Caesar exclaimed. "Can't they do anything for her?"

Aurelia didn't respond. Cornelia's situation was not improving and she had nothing new to add to what the doctor had already said.

Atop the walls of Rome

HORA DECIMA

Sulla watched his legions spread out beyond the wall in combat position. The troops were well organized, but there were other factors at play.

Several tribunes stood awaiting his orders; Dolabella and Crassus were already at the command of the legions they'd been assigned.

Sulla turned to the officers: "I want two-thirds of the torches you collect to be distributed equally among Dolabella's and Crassus's troops. Place the other third here, along the wall. And all available archers here, atop the wall."

Julia family domus

HORA UNDECIMAL

Cornelia had stopped screaming.

On one hand, it was a relief, but on the other, if she lost consciousness and couldn't push, the baby would never be born. In that case, both the boy and the young mother might die. Caesar was convinced that it was a boy.

He sat—no, collapsed—onto a triclinium: his world was falling to pieces. First the populares had lost control of the city when Sulla returned. And now it looked like he might lose his wife and child as well.

"Maybe the Samnites will be able to do what we weren't able to," Labienus said, trying to distract Caesar from what was happening in Cornelia's room.

"Do what?" he asked, hardly paying attention.

"Defeat Sulla," his friend said.

Atop the walls of Rome
HORA DUODECIMA

The Samnite army advanced to a thousand paces from the legions.

The last rays of sunlight faded.

Everything went dark, and in that sea of shadows, the Samnite army disappeared from view.

Sulla was scrutinizing the scene below. A tribune approached to transmit a message, but he held up a hand to silence him. He was listening carefully to the sounds of the night.

The Samnites began to light their torches.

Hundreds, thousands, of glowing flames spread out like a blazing mosaic as far as the eye could see.

Dolabella and Crassus gave the order for their soldiers to follow suit, and the Roman legions were soon lit up as well.

Sulla, for the moment, did not need more light, and he knew it would be a mistake to burn down all their torches too soon. They couldn't know how many the enemy had, but he knew how many he had.

"Tell Crassus and Dolabella to use only a quarter of the torches now and save the next fourth for the *secunda vigilia,* and so on," he ordered the tribunes, who hurried off to transmit his instructions.

Light was crucial to a nighttime battle.

Sulla stalked the shadows atop the old walls of Rome. He could see the enemy, but they could not see him.

The Samnites began their attack.

Julia family domus
November 1, *PRIMA VIGILIA**

Caesar could hear the roar of the battle from the uncovered atrium of his home. By the sound of it, the conflict seemed as colossal as it

---

* "First vigil." Roman timekeeping split the nighttime hours into four vigils, or "watches." So in context this denotes the first few hours after the sun has set.

was brutal. Beyond that, nothing was certain. Rumors raced from house to house that the Samnites were making their way through the tight ranks of the Roman cohorts. But . . . was that truly happening?

Caesar paced desperately. Labienus looked on, helpless. Cornelia had paused her heartrending cries, but neither the doctor nor Aurelia emerged to offer any news on how the labor was advancing.

Beyond the walls of Rome

SECUNDA VIGILIA

Dolabella watched as the legions under his command, inexperienced and unmotivated, quickly lost ground, even though he ordered constant rotations of the first line of combat. He was shouting nonstop, trying to maintain their position, always careful to keep his distance from the front line where the fighting was most fierce. The Samnites were brutally battling for their freedoms and rights, their anger making them more fierce and powerful than the bribed legionaries. Soon chaos spread through the Roman ranks.

Dolabella, slowly but decidedly, began to retreat with his entourage. Sacrificing himself in battle was not something he was prepared to do.

Crassus, commanding the more veteran troops, soldiers who had fought in Greece and Asia, held his position. The Samnites didn't seem to be gaining any notable ground against him.

From atop the wall, Sulla noticed the disorganization of Dolabella's troops.

"Light your torches!" he ordered, and soon the walls of Rome showed hundreds of archers ready to shoot.

The Samnites were getting closer, pushing Dolabella's men back against the walls. Some of the legionaries turned around and began to run toward the Porta Collina and other gates that remained open so Sulla could send out reinforcements or allow replacements.

The archers were waiting for the order to fire on the Samnites, who were still too far away, when Sulla had another idea: "Aim for the cowardly legionaries who would seek refuge within the walls of Rome!"

The tribunes looked at their commander.

But no one said a word.

The archers looked at the tribunes and other officers. The only order came from Sulla: "Shoot any legionaries who would flee! By all the gods! Now!"

The archers, who had been aiming over the heads of the legionaries in battle, calculating whether they could hit the Samnites, now aimed at the base of the wall as they had been instructed.

"Now, by Jupiter!" Sulla roared.

A rain of steel fell upon the legionaries in retreat.

More than a hundred Romans were shot down in that first broadside. Killed by Roman arrows. It was a brutal punishment for deserting combat, but, as if in a state of shock, the other legionaries stopped fleeing.

Dolabella, seeing what had just happened, stopped his own retreat and ordered his men to return to combat.

Sulla turned to his officers, still atop the wall. "All legionaries who come too close to the walls of Rome shall be shot! All officers who retreat shall be shot! By Jupiter, shoot me dead if I try to flee!"

And that said, leaving everyone around him stupefied, he quickly descended from atop the walls of Rome and down the avenue that led to the Porta Collina. Every time he passed an open gate in the wall, he gave a loud, clear order: "Close it!"

In his wake came the sound of the iron bars falling into place, sealing each and every one of Rome's access points.

Sulla reached the Porta Collina.

"As soon as I leave, close this one too!" he instructed.

Surrounded by a group of loyal men, he marched directly to the legions commanded by Dolabella.

Sulla had bent laws and pressured senators to obtain command of the war against Mithridates. He'd battled his way across Greece and Asia and all the way back across the Italic peninsula. Now, with Rome finally under his control, he damned well wasn't going to lose it all to a cursed Samnite rebellion.

"Victory or death!" he howled at the top of his lungs. Hundreds of men around him answered his cry: "Victory or death! Victory or death! Victory or death!"

Lucius Cornelius Sulla was a selfish, social-climbing senator, a shrewd military strategist, a pillager of sacred temples. He was willing to purchase loyalties, break promises, and betray anyone to achieve his aims. He was a miserable, corrupt politician who would stop at nothing to satisfy his personal ambitions. But there was one thing Sulla was not: he was not a coward.

Julia family domus

TERTIA VIGILIA

The birth was a slow agony.

It seemed that Cornelia was dying, and with her, the life she carried inside.

Caesar then did something inappropriate for a man to do. He committed a transgression, he crossed a line, but it would not be the most surprising border he'd breach in his life: the young husband entered the room where Cornelia, lying in bed, was struggling to give birth.

As soon as they saw him, the slaves jumped back from the bed. The doctor looked at him but did not say a word, his mind focused on the task at hand.

Aurelia seemed less surprised than anyone else. She'd taught her son never to give up anything as impossible, that he could do anything if he set his mind to it. She wasn't going to start telling him what he should and shouldn't do now; he was the pater familias after all.

Caesar saw a seat beside Cornelia, where the slave who had been cooling her head with damp cloths had been sitting seconds prior.

"If she can't keep pushing, there's nothing to be done," the doctor said.

Caesar leaned over Cornelia. The bottom half of the bed was soaked in blood. His wife was sweating profusely and her eyes were closed. Aurelia approached her with a bowl of water.

"Gaius is here," Caesar's mother said.

Cornelia opened her eyes and feebly took a drink.

There were tearstains on the young woman's cheeks. Tears of pain, sadness, helplessness. She was too weak to utter a single word.

"You have to push again," Caesar implored her. "You have to do it for yourself, for me, for the little one. You can do it. I know you can."

Cornelia nodded and strained with all her might, but once again, her efforts seemed to be in vain.

"It's best that the father leave the room," the doctor said.

Caesar looked at his mother and Aurelia nodded in agreement. Caesar obeyed their wishes.

For what seemed like hours, he and Labienus sat outside in the atrium listening to Cornelia's suffering.

Finally, when Caesar had lost all hope of anything going well that cursed night, a voice rang out across the atrium: "It's a girl."

Beyond the walls of Rome

QUARTA VIGILIA

Whatever the reason, whether it was Sulla's ceaseless orders repeated by Dolabella and the other officers, or because of the threat of being riddled with arrows if they neared the walls, the majority of the legionaries continued to battle the Samnites.

Both sides suffered countless losses, but the socii did not desist in their attack, and for a moment it looked as if they would defeat the weaker legions commanded by Dolabella.

Then a tribune arrived at Sulla's side carrying a message. "Crassus has destroyed the Samnites on his side and he wants to surround them and attack from the rear."

Sulla nodded. "Let Crassus surround them," he said. "Victory is ours, my friend," he declared confidently, looking at Dolabella.

The long night was coming to an end.

The battle would soon be over.

The first rays of sunlight fell onto the sea of dead Samnites and

Romans that had piled up during the cruel overnight battle. Crassus's legions waded through the Samnite corpses, advancing slowly but inexorably, systematically killing everyone in their path. Like a perfectly oiled machine, grinding the flesh of the socii who, exhausted, began to comprehend the true scale of their defeat.

Lucius Cornelius Sulla watched the sun rise over Rome. "This is not merely a new dawn, Dolabella," he said. "This is the start of a new era."

Just then, Crassus reached him, flanked by a group of legionaries. "I have destroyed them. It was easy," he said. "In a matter of hours, not a single one of them will remain alive. Fortunately I've done better than Dolabella," he said, smiling.

Sulla could see the fury in Dolabella's eyes. It was true that Crassus had achieved what Dolabella had not, but it was also true that Crassus had commanded the more veteran legions, whereas Dolabella led the inexperienced men, for whom that battle had been a trial by fire. Sulla saw many things clearly that dawn. He saw that Crassus was as ambitious as he was petty, and that he gave himself too much credit, something that, in the long run, would prove to be the death of him. He saw that Dolabella now, forever after, would hate Crassus. And his final premonition that dawn: now he, Sulla, would have everything his heart desired.

And there was so much he desired.

Julia family domus

HORA PRIMA

"It's a girl," the doctor said again.

For many men, the news would've been disappointing, but to Caesar, in that moment, having a male heir did not seem at all urgent or important. There would be time to think about that later. The only thing that mattered now was the well-being of his family—the newborn baby's health and, above all, Cornelia's recovery.

"She's lost consciousness," said Aurelia, looking at the young mother.

The doctor handed the baby girl to a slave to wash and dry as he placed a hand on Cornelia's forehead. She did not react. More than weak and unconscious, she looked dead.

The doctor shook his head, pressing his lips together with a sad look on his face.

Caesar knelt beside his wife and took her hand.

He spoke quietly into her ear: "Don't leave me, Cornelia . . . Don't leave me . . ."

The Trial

IV

REIECTIO

During the reiectio, lawyers for both
the prosecution and the defense may recuse
any judge whose association with the accused
places their impartiality in doubt.

XLIII

AURELIA'S ADVICE

Julia family domus, Rome
77 B.C.

FIVE YEARS HAD PASSED SINCE THAT DIFFICULT BIRTH, AND
the members of the Julia family now found themselves absorbed with
the trial against Dolabella.

Caesar's home in the Suburra was a true conclave of women that
evening, as his wife, Cornelia, Aurelia, his sisters, and his niece Acia
gathered for dinner in the central atrium to welcome him home from
his journey east. His father and his uncle Marius were both dead, and
his other uncle, Aurelius Cotta, would not visit while the trial against
Dolabella lasted, since, as defense attorney for the accused, he was
Caesar's rival. So the young pater familias of the gens Julia had no
older, experienced man to turn to for advice. His brothers-in-law,
Pinarius and Balbus, did not frequent the Julia residence, as if prefer-
ring to keep a prudent distance from the young man who had dared
to take on the all-powerful Dolabella. Labienus, his closest confidant,
was just as inexperienced as he was. The logical, expected thing
would've been for Caesar to seek out some respected senator or politician in the Plebeian Council sympathetic to the popular cause. But
Caesar, who often did the unexpected, sought advice elsewhere. As
Labienus had predicted during their trip to Macedonia, it was his
mother, Aurelia, to whom he turned.

"The reiectio is a few days away, Mother," said Caesar. This next
phase of the trial had occupied his mind all the way home from Thessaloniki. "The trip east has turned up new witnesses and evidence

that will support my claims, but the tribunal is packed with optimates who are planning to exonerate Dolabella no matter the arguments I lay out in the basilica. So I have to take full advantage of the opportunity presented by the reiectio."

"You can't recuse all the judges," Aurelia said, understanding that her son had a specific question for her.

"No, I can't, and in any case, they'd only replace them with other optimates favorable to Dolabella. No, I don't want to waste time or energy on a tedious, exhausting debate that would barely improve my situation in the trial. I've been thinking about a different way to approach it."

"What way?" his mother asked.

"I want to recuse a single person: Quintus Caecilius Metellus," he announced solemnly.

"The president of the tribunal, no less," Aurelia said.

"Yes, the president of the tribunal. Metellus is the leader of the optimates, the most respected. With Sulla dead and Dolabella distracted, Metellus is the brains of the party now. A mere gesture from him, a frown, a single syllable, and they all heel to him like trained dogs. I can't change the tribunal, but I can cut off its head. I have to get Metellus out somehow, but . . ."

"But?" Aurelia inquired.

Caesar took a few seconds to respond. "I don't know how," he said, unashamed to admit that he had not been able to come up with a solution even after four months of constant thought. He knew what he had to do, but he didn't know how to do it. He looked Aurelia in the eye. "That's why I'm turning to you, Mother. You're the most intelligent woman I know, and I trust you completely. I could ask Cicero or his oratory master, old Archias. I could seek out some veteran lawyer from the forum, some senator or councilman, but no one will give me their honest opinion, not in this case. They're all too scared of Dolabella and Metellus to give me useful advice. I know you don't have any experience in trial, Mother, but I also know how good you are at sizing people up. What is Metellus's weak spot? Where can I attack him?"

No one spoke. Cornelia, Caesar's sisters, and Caesar himself all remained respectfully silent as Aurelia sat with a calm, somber expression, thinking.

"It's fairly simple," his mother began. "Metellus wants to emulate his father, to live up to his name. Quintus Caecilius Metellus Numidicus was consul. Metellus Pius, president of the tribunal in the case against Dolabella, has also achieved this."

"Yes, appointed by Sulla," the young Caesar confirmed, listening with total attention. "Just as Sulla named Dolabella consul the year prior."

"Correct," Aurelia said, then continued with her line of reasoning. "But Metellus Numidicus, the father, also obtained a triumph for his victories in Africa, in the war that your uncle Marius ended by vanquishing Jugurtha. The Senate only granted Metellus Sr. that triumph to reduce Marius, but that's another matter. The key is: Metellus's father was consul and received a triumph. Metellus Jr. has been named consul but has yet to receive a triumph."

"He surely aims to win one by defeating Sertorius's rebellion in Hispania," Caesar continued, beginning to understand where his mother was going with all this. "Metellus had only planned to be away from the war for a few weeks. He was making a brief visit here to Rome to sort out a family matter. But if he's president of the tribunal, he'll have to remain here, far from the war. And this war will surely be his last opportunity to command an army against a high-ranking popular rebel. His last chance, therefore, to achieve a great victory that could win him the triumph he so desires."

"Exactly, my son," his mother said.

Caesar nodded several times and fell silent.

Cornelia and Caesar's sisters turned the conversation to other matters. Not out of lack of interest or respect, but because they knew that Caesar would be busy mulling over what he had just discussed with his mother.

"I've told you you're the most intelligent woman I know, haven't I, Mother?" Caesar asked after a while, looking back at Aurelia.

"You've told me several times, yes," she replied.

"Well, I stand corrected," her son then said. "You are the most intelligent *person* I know, man or woman. I'd never want to have you as my enemy."

"No, you wouldn't," she agreed, but then smiled warmly to dispel any negative thoughts from young Caesar's mind, wheeling as it was with how to achieve his objective in the reiectio.

"Hispania . . ." he muttered, lost in thought.

"Still, once you've planned your course of action in the reiectio," his mother added with a serious look on her face, "you'll have to work on improving your oratory skills if you want to persuade Metellus to leave the trial."

"I know, Mother, I know."

He wasn't offended by her advice: if his own mother was unaware that he'd feigned clumsiness during the divinatio, then surely the tribunal would not believe him up to the task of recusing any of the judges.

He looked at Cornelia. She was the only one who knew that he'd intentionally underperformed the divinatio. Cornelia heard what Aurelia had said, and, as she sat talking to the two Julias, she threw her husband a complicit glance.

Caesar was desperate to be alone with her after so much time apart.

XLIV

THE PRESIDENT OF
THE TRIBUNAL

Basilica Sempronia, Rome
77 B.C.

THE FIRST THING CAESAR NOTICED WHEN HE ENTERED THE Basilica Sempronia was that the great hall seemed mostly empty. There were only about a dozen people in the audience, including his mother, his wife, and his sisters.

"It doesn't look like the trial has stirred up much interest," Caesar murmured as he sat on the solium that had been placed before the prosecution's table.

Labienus took a seat beside him. "Everyone's given up the case as a lost cause," he explained. "And they don't think . . . they can't imagine that . . ." Labienus didn't know how to finish the thought without injuring his friend's pride.

"And no one can imagine, after my sad performance in the divinatio and the murder of my main witnesses, that I could be capable of offering any resistance worth showing up to see," Caesar said. "Isn't that so?"

"By Jupiter, it's not my fault that people think that," said Labienus, feeling guilty.

"Everyone thinks it," Caesar said, looking toward the tribunal. "But you're not to blame. I was clumsy. That's a fact. Look, Metellus is arriving."

Quintus Caecilius Metellus Pius took his place as president in the center of the tribunal, just as he'd done during the divinatio. The rest of the senators looked at him admiringly.

"He has them eating out of his hand," Labienus said.

"That's why we have to recuse him," Caesar said under his breath. "Our friends, those who sympathize with the popular cause, are they outside, as I asked?"

Labienus nodded. "Not all of them agreed to come, but some did, out of loyalty to your uncle, I believe."

"Yes, I imagine so," Caesar said, never taking his eyes off the tribunal. "No one has much faith in me. I know that any populares who have come today have only done so because I am Gaius Marius's nephew, for better or worse. But it doesn't matter why they've come. Listen: as soon as I mention Metellus's name, go out and tell everyone who it is I am recusing. That will get people's attention." He looked around the immense, empty basilica. "I want this room full before my speech is over."

The praecones, who would assist the tribunal and its president during the course of the trial, were standing now before the tribunal.

"They're about to begin," Labienus said.

The praecones looked to the president.

Metellus had managed to keep from opening his mouth during the entire divinatio, but sooner or later he'd have to give orders on how the sessions should be carried out, and that would require him to expose his speech impediment in public, something that made him enormously uncomfortable. He'd spoken privately with the praecones before the start of the reiectio, instructing them on how to give voice to his instructions, since the president of the tribunal could delegate tasks to the praecones and allow them to direct the trial, calling witnesses and giving the floor to the defense or prosecution. So Metellus did not need to say a word, only nodded slightly to announce the start of the session that morning.

"*Favete linguis!*"* shouted one of the clerks.

Everyone fell silent.

"In the case against the reus† Gnaeus Cornelius Dolabella, the de-

---

*   "Silence!"

†   Defendant.

fense can now take the floor to recuse any member of the tribunal, if they so desire."

Aurelius Cotta stood up and, without moving from his spot, spoke calmly: "The defense is content with the jury that the Senate has selected to preside over this case. My colleague Hortensius and I do not wish to recuse any members of the tribunal, and we defer to their wisdom and intelligence to obtain a just verdict." He sat back down.

The leader of the praecones, who had suddenly become the public voice of Quintus Caecilius Metellus, looked at the president of the tribunal, who once again nodded.

The clerk spoke again, looking into the center of the room: "The prosecution now has the floor in the case against the reus Gnaeus Cornelius Dolabella, to put forth a reiectio against any member of the tribunal, if they so desire."

Gaius Julius Caesar stood up slowly. Today he was going to do everything slowly. At least, until the room filled up. A few curious onlookers had entered, people out for a morning stroll down the Vicus Tuscus, or to do their shopping at the tabernae veteres, who, upon seeing the Basilica Sempronia open, had decided to step in and see what was happening. But, as quickly as they entered, they stepped back outside, disappointed: it was just the trial against Dolabella with that clumsy prosecutor . . . Julius Caesar. Nothing of interest. Everyone already knew how that would end. Curiosity quelled, they continued on their way.

Inside, it was the clumsy prosecutor's turn to speak.

Caesar didn't simply stand up in front of his seat, as his uncle had done, but took a few steps into the center of the room, placing himself before Dolabella, the tribunal, and the defense.

"Many thanks to the president of the tribunal for granting me the floor," he began, looking directly at Quintus Caecilius Metellus. It was a recognition of Metellus's status as maximum authority despite the fact that he was only manifesting his power through the praecones. He took a deep breath before proceeding with his speech. "I take the floor, in effect, to recuse a judge, a senator in this case, since this tribunal, like all tribunals now, are made up entirely of senators . . ."

Here, Caesar saw some glances exchanged among the members of the jury. He was touching on Sulla's reforms, which had decreed that only senators could serve as judges, another example of corruption of justice. "This is always a . . . delicate matter. The reiectio, that is."

Labienus sighed with relief. For a moment he'd been afraid that his friend would go off on a tangent, decrying Sulla's laws instead of focusing on the matter at hand.

"Yes, it is a delicate matter," the young prosecutor continued, "because claiming that there is some conflict of interest between the defendant and one of his judges basically implies that a Roman senator is incapable of impartiality because of a connection with the reus." Here Caesar seemed to take pleasure in using the term reus, looking Dolabella directly in the eye as he said the word. "Yes, a recusal implies that a Roman senator may be less than impartial. The question is, do I have, then, that feeling, that opinion, about one of the fifty-two judges who make up this tribunal?" He paused briefly, as if expecting someone to respond, which he did not. "The answer is no. The prosecution does not, in the slightest, doubt the objectivity, impartiality, or nobility of each and every one of the judges who make up this tribunal. But . . ." Caesar paused. He turned to face the jury: "But the prosecution would like to formally request the recusal of Proconsul Quintus Caecilius Metellus, president of the tribunal."

Murmurs spread through the Basilica Sempronia. Caesar knew that he'd sparked the crowd's interest. He looked at Labienus; his friend stood and left the basilica to inform the populares congregated outside that the prosecutor, Gaius Marius's nephew, had dared to recuse none other than Metellus, the current leader of the optimates in the Senate.

The news quickly spread by word of mouth, first through the forum, then through the entire city of Rome. The conflict between the populares and optimates might have gone dormant, buried by Sulla and his implacable laws, but it had not disappeared entirely. Even the tiniest spark could perhaps set the people's hearts ablaze once again.

Metellus remained silent. It took so little to get the masses riled up. He knew that something as simple as a challenge to the current conservative leader was enough to do it. But Quintus Caecilius Metellus had never let himself be concerned by such matters, and he would not be ruffled by some young upstart with delusions of grandeur who had the nerve to demand his recusal. Even if Marius's blood did flow through his veins.

Caesar knew that he had to lay out a highly convincing argument. "Of course," he said, "I know that the tribunal, including the esteemed senator I am recusing, will listen to my reasoning with the nobility, objectivity, and impartiality that they are recognized for."

He paused.

The praecones looked wildly from the young prosecutor to Quintus Caecilius Metellus. They'd never seen a lawyer, whether it be the defense or the prosecution, dare to recuse the president of the tribunal. They knew that it was possible, from a strictly legal standpoint, and that it had happened before, but they'd never seen it with their own eyes.

Metellus nodded to the clerks.

"The accusator may present his argument," one of them said, giving voice to the president's agreement.

Caesar looked to Labienus, who was returning from outside the Basilica Sempronia. He pressed his lips together and nodded almost imperceptibly to confirm that the great hall of justice was filling with people, just as Caesar had hoped.

The young prosecutor resumed his speech: "I have already stated that I do not doubt the impartiality of the good judges of this tribunal. So then, why would I recuse the president of said tribunal? For one very simple reason: for Rome. Because Rome must be placed above all else. The well-being of the republic, the security of the state, is more important to me than any trial. And what is the biggest threat facing Rome today? What is the greatest danger to our safety?" He paused again, turning around to watch as more and more people entered the basilica. After a moment, he launched into his main argument: "Sertorius."

Merely uttering the name of the popular rebel caused a sudden hush to fall over the room. The audience seemed to hold its breath, shocked into admiration: no one dared to publicly mention the exiled populist whom Metellus had spent the last two years fighting fruitlessly to defeat. But this young lawyer had just said his name in the middle of the Basilica Sempronia, during a trial. He now had the full attention of the judges, all of them wondering where the bumbling young prosecutor was going with this. They hoped he might say something that would permit them to emit a senatus consultum ultimum ordering his arrest and immediate execution. That would be one way to put an end to this cursed trial.

Aurelia, in the audience, squeezed her daughter-in-law's hand. Cornelia understood that if Caesar's mother was worried, it must be because her son was pushing the limits of what could be safely said in front of the optimates.

Caesar could sense the tribunal's tension and knew he had to tread lightly. "I lament, judges of the tribunal, having to mention Sertorius. But I think we can all agree that it would be unwise to ignore Rome's most pressing problem."

Classifying Sertorius as a "problem" was no crime in the eyes of the optimates. Just the opposite. What was this prosecutor playing at? They were confused.

"Sertorius is a threat to the safety of *this* Roman Republic," Caesar continued. For some of the populares now present in the audience, it was as if the young lawyer were trying to suggest that there were other possible Roman Republics beyond this one, ruled by the optimates.

Caesar was playing to one side and the other, moving over shifting sands.

"And if Sertorius is our biggest problem, then Rome must send its best man to neutralize him. And our best candidate for proconsul in Hispania, the only man up to the task, thanks to his vast experience, is none other than Quintus Caecilius Metellus Pius, son of Quintus Caecilius Metellus Numidicus, thus named for his triumphant victory in Numidia, Africa."

Crassus, present in the room, felt snubbed by Caesar's statement. Ever since his success in the battle of Porta Collina, he had considered himself Rome's strongest general. But the Senate looked to Metellus as their natural leader due to his age and experience. Crassus

had also begun to notice, with displeasure, that the Senate was beginning to favor Sulla's other wartime ally, Pompey, with Metellus himself, placing more and more trust in the young man. Crassus took
note of the fact that both the popular prosecutor and the optimate
leaders seemed to completely overlook him. He would not soon forget the slight.

People continued to file into the basilica.

Too many plebes for the tastes of Metellus, Dolabella, and the
other optimates. The president looked to Pompey, and he understood, walking hurriedly out of the great hall just as Labienus had
done before.

In the meantime, young Caesar continued making use of his time
in the reiectio: "Yes, the president of this tribunal's father obtained
his title of 'Numidicus' on the battlefield, fighting for Rome, far beyond the walls of the city. And isn't that where all our legendary battles are waged, our epic victories always obtained? Scipio Africanus,
who first began this custom of recognizing great triumphs by confer-
ring titles on the most victorious Roman generals, obtained his own
name through defeat of the fearsome Hannibal in Africa. Metellus
Sr., for his victories over the Numids. I have two great wishes: first, I
wish for the safety of Rome, and second, I wish that Quintus Caecilius Metellus might have the chance to follow in the footsteps of his
illustrious father, winning a resounding victory and celebrating a
great triumph in Rome. A much *deserved* triumph."

He pronounced the word *deserved* in a somewhat sarcastic tone,
turning to the people who were now crowding into the basilica. The
people laughed. As far as they saw it, Metellus Sr. hadn't in fact ended
the war against Jugurtha in Numidia; that had been done by Marius.
The Senate had granted Metellus Sr. the title of "Numidicus" only to
minimize Marius's merits and diminish his achievements.

Just then Caesar saw that Pompey had returned to the basilica
with dozens of armed men. The optimates had brought in their hired
henchmen to show the young prosecutor and all those present that
they would not be intimidated by a basilica packed with plebes gathered in support of the prosecutor.

The tension grew thick.

Caesar lowered his voice slightly; it was still loud and clear but modulated to seem more serene, more contained. "Here, in the Basilica Sempronia, we stand in the very spot where the great Scipio was born. This building was constructed by Tiberius Sempronius Gracchus, Scipio's son-in-law, who married Cornelia on the very plot where, years before, the home of Scipio Africanus had once stood."

He had said "Cornelia." He was also married to a Cornelia, and his eyes flitted to her for an instant: his young wife looked at him with glowing admiration, swollen with pride, her soul overflowing with love for him. Caesar looked then to his mother, who also seemed proud, and a bit shocked. If Caesar had kept his eyes on Aurelia for a few more seconds, he might've noticed that her eyes showed not only admiration, but also a feeling she wished to hide: fear. His mother was impressed by his persuasive speech, surprised by the enormous improvement in his oratory skills since the divinatio, and terrified that her son could prove too agile, too clever, too dangerous, for the optimates' liking.

But Caesar didn't have time now to evaluate all those feelings. He had to continue arguing the recusal.

Metellus swallowed: he did not like that mention of Tiberius Sempronius Gracchus, who had been Scipio's son-in-law but also father to the Gracchi, the plebeian tribunes who first fought for the rights of the masses and gave rise to the popular political party. He was disquieted by Caesar's speech, yes, most of all because he had not yet figured out where he was going with it.

Caesar spoke again. "Yes, from the bowels of the underworld, Scipio watches us, as do the gods from above. And with their eyes upon us, I feel that I must recuse Quintus Caecilius Metellus from this trial. I do so not to alter a tribunal of justice in my favor, but to provide Rome with the best defense possible, to ensure that our best general is sent to put an end to Sertorius and his rebellion in Hispania. Unless, of course, Metellus would rather hide behind the safety of these walls? Unless Metellus, simply, sadly, is . . . a coward?"

He'd said it.

His uncle Marius had remained resolute as his men thought him a coward, for months, during the campaign against the Teutons. He'd endured it because he knew what he had to do, and that was more important than what everyone thought of him. Was Metellus cut from the same cloth as the great heroes like Marius, capable of withstanding an insult to avoid playing his enemy's game? Or was he too egotistical, too greatly wounded by any insult?

Total silence in the basilica: the young prosecutor had just called the president of the tribunal a coward.

In front of everyone.

And he kept going: "Is he perhaps afraid of losing to Sertorius, afraid that he is incapable of obtaining that long-awaited victory, afraid of never receiving a triumph, never living up to his father's name?"

Caesar paused.

He was sweating.

He'd poured so much energy into his speech, whipped up the tension so thick it could almost be cut with a knife. But he couldn't end on that note—he had to provide the president of the tribunal with a noble exit, a dignified path to accepting the recusal. And not only that: he'd publicly insulted the leader of the optimates. He had to retract his accusations or he might not make it to nightfall alive.

"I don't think so," Caesar continued. "I'm confident that Quintus Caecilius Metellus feels no fear of Sertorius. I believe he can, and will, live up to his father's name. What I think is that Metellus has merely let himself become trapped in the web of this trial. I have the utmost faith that the president of this tribunal is capable of impartiality. But sitting on this tribunal keeps him here, requiring him to neglect his greater duty to defend Rome in the war against Sertorius. This trial keeps him from living up to his father's name. But no, I don't for a moment conceive, by Jupiter Optimus Maximus, by Hercules and all the gods, that Quintus Caecilius Metellus might be a coward."

He'd phrased it in the negative, but he'd repeated, once again, the word *coward*.

The basilica was now packed, the tribunal looked very somber, and there were a hundred armed henchmen spread out around the room. Everyone was silent.

Metellus was staring hard at the young lawyer.

Caesar, undaunted, launched into his final argument. "The president of the tribunal may feel attacked by me, may even consider me his enemy in this moment. But I am not the one keeping him here in Rome, denying him his triumphant victory. It is the reus, Dolabella, who keeps him here, blocking his path to glory."

With that, Gaius Julius Caesar concluded his speech and returned to his seat beside Labienus. And something unexpected happened: the audience began to applaud.

A long applause, a dense ovation, from everyone in the crowd. Only the Senate's henchmen, the judges, and the reus refused to join in.

Metellus glared at Dolabella, his anger lapping at the defendant's face. But Dolabella's mind was elsewhere, stewing in his own rage and mentally calculating how to regain control of the trial.

Metellus then looked at the praecones and raised his left hand with his ring and pinky fingers up, leaving his middle finger, pointer, and thumb curled inward. The clerks understood the message, and the highest ranking among them stood to translate the gesture into words.

"In two days' time, the prosecution will receive a response from the tribunal regarding the recusal. With this the reiectio has come to an end."

The crowd began to file out of the Basilica Sempronia, animatedly discussing everything they had just witnessed.

The fifty-two members of the tribunal immediately convened around Metellus and began to speak among themselves.

Dolabella was left alone in the center of the room, under the watchful gaze of his armed bodyguards.

The Senate's henchmen were firmly planted around the great hall of justice.

Caesar and Labienus remained seated before their table littered with scrolls of notes.

XLV

SHADOWS IN
THE BASILICA

Basílica Sempronia, Rome
77 B.C.
Prosecutor's corner

THE SLAVES WERE SNUFFING OUT THE TORCHES AND CLOSING the windows and doors. The members of the tribunal, the reus, and the lawyers for both the prosecution and defense remained inside the basilica, now thrown into shadow.

"You've managed to divide them. It was genius," said Labienus, looking to the spot where the judges were locked in heated debate.

"He'll give in," Caesar said.

"Who?" his friend asked.

"Metellus. He's eager to return to Hispania and win the great triumph that will make him equal to his father. My mother was exactly right. The trial will be more balanced now: they murdered my witnesses, but I've gotten rid of the president of the tribunal. I've returned the blow. The question is . . ." He scanned the room. "Yes, the question is who they'll appoint in Metellus's place."

Apse of the basilica

"I th-thought he was a p-p-poor orator," Metellus said, his face flushed with rage.

"He was truly clumsy in the divinatio," said Pompey, and the other judges nodded in agreement. "I thought he would perform as poorly or worse today."

"Well you th-th-thought wrong," Metellus declared. "He's exposed me before all of Rome. I d-d-don't have any choice but to return to Hispania and defeat the cursed Sertorius." The angrier he got, the less he stuttered, as if his fury made him forget his speech impediment.

"So you accept his recusal?" Pompey asked.

"Of course. I have to accept it," Metellus said.

"If you've already decided, why did you ask for two days to consider your response?" Pompey asked, voicing the confusion that the other judges felt.

"Because I know Dolabella is going to a-ask me to stay and I'll need time to p-p-persuade him."

"And how do you plan on convincing him?" Pompey asked. "Dolabella has said he would not accept any other president in this trial. You are the only one he fully trusts."

"I already know who w-w-will replace me as president of the tribunal."

"Crassus?" one of the judges asked, but Metellus shook his head. Ever since the battle of Porta Collina, Dolabella had hated Crassus.

"Then who?" one of the other judges asked.

But Metellus remained silent.

Lost in thought.

Center of the basilica

Dolabella did not need to go up to the apse to know what the judges were talking about. Metellus would be informing the judges of his return to Hispania. The young prosecutor had been very clever. Gnaeus Cornelius Dolabella would lose one of his greatest allies on the tribunal. He raised his head and glared at Caesar. The premonition he'd had at the end of the divinatio was coming true. Dolabella saw it perfectly clearly: Caesar was turning out to be quite dangerous, just as Sulla had always said he would. They should've killed him a long time ago. But, as usual, he'd have to do the dirty work himself. When the time was right.

Prosecutor's corner

"He's staring at you," Labienus said.

Caesar looked up and caught Dolabella's eyes boring into him as if he wanted to penetrate his thoughts.

"I think you might have miscalculated," Labienus said. "The president of the tribunal isn't your greatest obstacle—it's Dolabella."

"You might be right. I'll have to keep an eye on whomever they name as the new president, but it's true that Dolabella is our fiercest enemy," Caesar admitted without looking away from the reus, as he liked to refer to Dolabella as often as possible. "Dolabella may be the only one who fully understands what I'm doing."

"And what is it that you're doing?" Labienus asked.

"I'm waging a second war."

"I don't understand . . ."

"The struggle between the populares and the optimates isn't over, my friend," Caesar explained without taking his eyes off of Dolabella. "They may have defeated my uncle Marius and his son, as well as my father-in-law, Cinna, but I'm still here. We all know about the war in Hispania, with Sertorius leading the opposition, but I'm here drawing a new battle line, not with weapons, but with words. Didn't you see how inflamed the people became when I gave my speech? The optimates now fear me. They don't yet realize that there is more opposition brewing here, in Rome. No, for now, the only one who sees it is him: Dolabella." Caesar paused and looked around the gigantic, darkened space. With the torches snuffed out and the windows closed, the basilica was thrown into shadow. And the longest shadow of them all was cast by the furious reus, Dolabella. "Winning this case is more important than ever. Before, it was merely a question of seeing justice served. Now, exiling Dolabella is a matter of survival. That hatred so evident in his eyes can only spell death. My death."

Reus

DOLABELLA

THE
ACCUSED

XLVI

FIRST CRIME:
VIOLATIO

Residence of Aeropus, local aristocratic leader
Acropolis of Thessaloniki
Late 78 B.C.

"AAAH!" SHOUTED GNAEUS CORNELIUS DOLABELLA AS HE wrenched his hand out of Myrtale's mouth. "*Scortum!*"*

The girl took advantage of her attacker's momentary shock to slip away and rush to the door.

Dolabella, governor of Macedonia, turned and waddled after her. He was fat, flabby, and moved with difficulty. Looming over the thin young woman, who was hunched with fear, he looked like a cyclops, as brutal as he was disgusting.

"Scortum," Dolabella repeated through clenched teeth, cradling his bleeding hand. In her terrified frenzy, the girl had drawn blood.

"Open up, open up!" she screamed as she beat on the door with her small fists, white as milk. But it was barricaded by the governor's men.

"I was only planning to force myself on you, but now I'm going to be truly cruel," Dolabella said as he moved closer.

Myrtale looked around, scanning the room for some weapon or object with which to defend herself.

Dolabella saw what she was doing. He stopped.

"Open up!" he ordered the legionaries on the other side of the door.

---

* "Slut," "whore."

This surprised the girl.

The doors opened, but she was not released into the light of freedom. Instead, the icy shadows of several armed guards slipped in.

"Grab her!" Dolabella ordered.

She picked up a fire poker from one of the large braziers used to heat the room during the cold Macedonian winter. The legionaries surrounded her.

The soldiers closed in. She thrashed the fire poker furiously. The guards unsheathed their swords.

"Do not wound her!" Dolabella instructed. "I will be the one to make her bleed!"

Myrtale was clever and beautiful and cunning, but not strong. In one smooth movement, a soldier knocked the iron fire poker from the girl's hand with his gladius. When she bent down to pick it up, the Roman soldiers quickly seized her.

"Hold her arms and legs. Make it easy for me," the governor instructed them.

The legionaries knew how to interpret the order. They laid the girl on the ground: two of them pinned her arms down and two others held her legs apart . . .

"Give me a *pugio*," Dolabella said.

A soldier handed him a short dagger, which the governor used to rip open Myrtale's tunic and underwear, leaving her completely naked from the waist down. She flailed wildly, but the soldiers held her tight, cutting off the circulation to her hands and feet so that she could hardly feel them.

"Perdiccas will kill you," the girl exclaimed, still struggling to escape.

"Oh yes, your dearly beloved . . . I almost forgot about him." Dolabella looked at the other soldiers. "Bring that imbecile in too." He turned back to the girl. "We should let him see what he's going to kill me for, don't you think?"

"Damn you, damn you!" was all she could say before receiving a loud slap to the face that made her head spin.

"Ow!" the governor shouted. The slap had hurt his injured hand. He'd have to see the medicus when all this was over.

The girl's legs were spread wide, her sex laid bare.

Several more legionaries entered the room guarding a chained Perdiccas. The young Macedonian tried to wrench himself from the soldiers' grip—he lurched toward his fiancée lying half naked on the floor, pinned down, with the Roman governor kneeling over her body, laughing as he prepared to rape her. A veteran *optio* who knew how to deal with an unruly prisoner dealt several blows to Perdiccas's gut, leaving him incapacitated.

Gnaeus Cornelius Dolabella stood up and undressed. He liked how things were turning out.

"I'll kill you! I'll kill you!" Perdiccas howled, driven mad with fury and helplessness.

Myrtale closed her eyes and prayed to Aphrodite, begging the goddess to have mercy and strike her dead right then and there, as quickly as possible.

XLVII

SECOND AND THIRD
CRIMES:
REPETUNDIS· AND *PECULATUS*†

Governor's Palace, Thessaloniki, Macedonia
Late 78 B.C.
Three hours prior

DOLABELLA RECEIVED THE LOCAL ARISTOCRATS WITHOUT
standing from his cathedra piled with cushions.

"Well?" he said by way of greeting.

The representatives of the Thessaloniki aristocracy had expected
at least a few words of recognition from the governor. The Macedonians had resisted the Roman yoke for years, but in recent times
they'd shown themselves to be good allies in the battles against the
barbaric tribes that threatened from across the Danube, the Thracians in particular. And they had aided Sulla in his long, arduous
campaign against Mithridates, King of Pontus. Yes, a less hostile
greeting would've been more appropriate.

But Dolabella suspected that the men had come to him with some
problem. He knew that it was best to show unrelenting authority in
cases such as these, so that anyone who wanted to raise demands—or
worse, complaints—would weigh their words carefully.

Young Perdiccas looked to the veteran Aeropus, seeking his permission to speak. Aeropus had more experience dealing with Roman
authorities and was Perdiccas's superior within the Macedonian aris-

---

*   Perversion of justice or corruption; for example, creating arbitrary or unjustified taxes.

†   Unlawful appropriation of public funds, stealing from government coffers.

tocracy. He was also the father of Myrtale, to whom Perdiccas was betrothed.

Aeropus nodded.

Perdiccas stepped forward and faced Dolabella. He would be polite, which was more than could be said for the governor.

"I am Perdiccas of Macedon, accompanied here by Aeropus, leader of Thessaloniki, and all the Macedonians. We offer our cordial greetings to the Governor Gnaeus Cornelius Dolabella of Rome."

The governor merely shifted his weight in his seat.

"Well?" Dolabella said again, gruff and distant.

Perdiccas understood then that cordiality and respect would get him nowhere with this man. So he decided to get directly to the point: "The current situation in which we, the Macedonians, find ourselves, Governor, is untenable. Taxes on grain have made the price of bread so high that many can no longer afford it, and the additional tax to repair the Via Egnatia represents a major expense that has exhausted our resources and left us unable to help those most in need. We Macedonians have proven loyal to Rome, aiding in the battles against Mithridates and the Thracians, for which your Senate named us Allies of the Roman People. Is this how Rome repays their friends?" Perdiccas paused. He noticed two statues displayed on either side of Dolabella's cathedra and he recognized them as having belonged to the temple of Aphrodite. He became even more enraged. "And, what's worse, the Roman authority who has been tasked with assuring the peace and safety of the loyal Macedonian people has pillaged our most sacred temple."

Dolabella took a deep breath.

He exhaled.

He ran his hand over his chin, cleanly shaven by his *tonsor* a mere hour prior.

"Summon Vetus, the engineer," he said by way of response, looking at one of the many legionaries guarding the reception hall.

The soldier rushed off to fulfill the order as the governor turned his attention back to Perdiccas.

"Let's see. One thing at a time. I have been forced to raise the price of grain because of the bad harvests here in your land, requiring me to import wheat from Egypt. At significant added cost. The people want to eat and I can ensure that they have food, but if circumstances beyond my control require it to be brought from farther away, we must all help to cover the cost of transport, shouldn't we? That is the reason for the exceptional tax on grain this year."

Perdiccas was about to respond to the governor's lies. There had been no bad harvests and the grain had not been brought over from Egypt, but grown within the borders of Macedonia. The extremely elevated price was completely unjustifiable. But he felt Aeropus's hand on his shoulder and he understood that interrupting the governor, even if he were lying, was not the best way forward.

"And as for the repairs to the Via Egnatia," Dolabella continued. "The road, so kindly built for you by us Romans to connect the western ports of Dyrrhachium and Apollonia to Byzantium in the East, has been terribly mistreated, it is true. This road is important to Rome, of course, but much more important to your people since it crosses all of Macedonia. It is the backbone of the region; you people use it constantly and benefit from it greatly. I have been obliged to bring in an engineer to repair this road you have destroyed with your overloaded carts in your ceaseless coming and going. You are the ones who use the route more than anyone else, and I for one believe that he who uses it most should pay the most. Do you truly find it unjust that you are asked to finance the repairs of this road used by you, to your great benefit?"

"With all due respect, clarissime vir," Aeropus ventured, "we, the Macedonians, already pay many taxes to Rome, and it would be reasonable to believe that some of those funds could be used to maintain the road—"

"By Hercules! If you use it you have to pay for it!" Dolabella bellowed, angry, irritated, and fed up with the complaints.

Just then a legionary entered followed by the engineer the governor had summoned.

"Ah yes, Vetus," Dolabella said, turning to the man who had just arrived. "Tell us, please, what is the current state of the Via Egnatia?"

The engineer looked at the governor, then at the Macedonian aristocrats. He could sense the tension, especially from the latter.

"The road is in very poor condition, Governor," Vetus finally answered. "Repairs are needed along the entire route, and I have not yet received any of the funds needed to begin work—"

"Silence!" Dolabella ordered, seeing that the engineer was about to ask for the thousands of sesterce and *ases* collected from the special tax he'd levied for the road's maintenance. The governor, in fact, had hoarded the money away in several coffers hidden deep within his palace. He lowered his voice. He fixed his eyes on the engineer: "You may leave. We will speak of the matter later."

Vetus swallowed. He bowed, turned, and left.

Perdiccas and Aeropus did not miss the fact that the engineer had asked for money, saying he had not yet received it. It was all so obvious, so plain to see . . .

"If the price of grain never goes down, harvest after harvest, and the money needed to rebuild the Via Egnatia never makes it to the hands of the engineer hired to repair it—"

"Then . . . what, boy?" Dolabella interrupted. "Are you going to threaten me with a revolt? Like the rebellions other Roman governors have stamped out in the past?"

Dolabella was referring to Alexander's rebellion against Metellus and Euphantus's revolt against the governor Gaius Sextius over an exorbitant increase in the price of grain. But those uprisings were things of the past. It had been many years since the Macedonians had shown violence toward Rome.

Aeropus now decided to intervene in the conversation for the first time, speaking calmly but firmly, taking a few steps forward to place himself in front of the young Perdiccas: "A rebellion, no. That is not the spirit with which we have come here today. We are merely manifesting our concerns over the demands that these new taxes have placed on the Macedonians. We have come to show our dissent for these taxes, Governor, and clarissime vir, which we feel are excessive, whether it be for the transportation of grain or to fund maintenance of the road. And if the governor of Rome can't find a way to reduce them, then we'll have no choice but to submit our demands to higher authorities: we will send representatives from Macedonia all the way to the Roman Senate if necessary."

The room fell silent.

Dolabella looked down from his cushioned seat. He ran his hand over his chin. The Macedonians' denouncement of him before the Senate would be inconvenient, especially since he had recently asked Rome to grant him a triumph for his victory over the Thracians in the North. A serious complaint now could jeopardize that parade through the streets of Rome in his honor. But he was not one to cede to pressure, ever.

Perdiccas and Aeropus studied the statues positioned on either side of the governor's cathedra. They had clearly been stolen from the temple of Aphrodite, and the governor had not said anything to justify that sacrilege. But for the moment they'd decided to focus on the more pressing issue of the unjust taxes. Turning to the topic of religion might stir up heated emotions, and both men still believed they were moving within the sphere of reasonable negotiation.

They were wrong.

Completely.

Dolabella was the kind of man who believed that inciting a certain emotion—terror—could help others to see reason. His reason, that is. He'd proven this time and again, becoming a skilled manipulator of emotions and desires, working with the delicate finesse of a glassblower.

The governor looked up and addressed Aeropus: "If I lower the price of grain and reduce the taxes for repair of the Via Egnatia, do you swear that there will be no violent uprising or any reclamation before the Senate in Rome?"

The veteran Macedonian didn't trust these concessions, so easily granted, but he also knew that the governor had requested a triumph for his campaign against the Thracians and perhaps wanted to keep their complaints from reaching the Senate just as the patres conscripti were deliberating the matter.

"Yes, clarissime vir," Aeropus responded. "I can guarantee that there will be no rebellion or reclamation in Rome if the price of grain is lowered and the taxes on the road are reduced."

Dolabella shook his head. "I don't want you to guarantee it: I want you to swear, by all that is sacred to you."

Aeropus nodded. Looking at the stolen statues as he spoke, and feeling particularly clever in what he thought was his moment of victory, he said, "I swear to you . . . by Aphrodite."

Dolabella caught the subtle recrimination, but for the moment he let it slide. He'd leaned forward in his chair to better hear the man's oath, and once it had been spoken he leaned back again.

He shook his head. "It's not enough. He needs to swear too," he said, pointing to Perdiccas.

Instinctively, the young Macedonian took a step back. It wasn't that he was afraid. Being still young and naïve, he was hardly afraid of anyone or anything. He still had a lot to learn about life. A lot of suffering to endure. He stepped back like a soldier seeking the best vantage point from which to charge into combat.

Aeropus looked at him and nodded.

"Swear it, boy. Do it," the old Macedonian said.

Perdiccas frowned. He had a bad feeling about this, but swearing that there would be no revolt or reclamation before the Roman Senate if the governor lowered his taxes didn't seem like too high a price to pay.

"I swear," he said.

Dolabella smiled and shook his head again. "No, not like that," he said. "Swear like your superior has: swear on what is most sacred to you."

Perdiccas's frown deepened. His future father-in-law had been very clever to swear by Aphrodite, and he wanted to appear clever as well. He couldn't say anything that would anger the governor, but he could say something to flatter the father of the woman he was betrothed to: "I swear by Myrtale, my fiancée, the most sacred person in the world to me."

Dolabella nodded several times, like a priest hearing a solemn prayer. He was enjoying the situation immensely.

"Myrtale, that's a name I've never heard before," the governor commented with genuine curiosity, even as his mind began to swirl with sinister plans.

The young Macedonian puffed out his chest and proudly explained the origin of the name: "Myrtale is the second of the four names that Alexander the Great's mother used throughout her life. She was first called Polyxena; then Myrtale, when she married Phillip II, Alexander's father; then Olympia; and, finally, Stratonice."

"Ah yes, that's right," the governor said, as if he were fascinated by Macedonian history. "Alexander's mother, matriarch of that dynasty you people are so proud of and consider yourselves direct descendants and heirs to."

"Because we are," Perdiccas said.

"Of course, of course . . ." The governor nodded, as if he were in complete agreement. Then, suddenly, changing his tone of voice to a harsh imperative, he addressed his guards: "Seize them!"

The order surprised everyone, soldiers and Macedonians alike. But the Roman guards reacted immediately, unsheathing their gladiī and surrounding the two men, who were still shocked and bewildered by the abrupt turn of events.

XLVIII

THE CURSE OF THESSALONIKI

Aeropus's residence, Acropolis of Thessaloniki
Late 78 B.C.
Three hours later

DOLABELLA ARCHED HIS BACK AND GRUNTED LIKE A HOG choking down its dinner. "Uhhh!"

He pushed against the floor to sit himself up, no easy feat for the obese man.

His now flaccid member dripped semen and blood.

He turned to Perdiccas.

"Well, boy, your fiancée was in fact a virgin. Was." He laughed loudly.

The soldiers, on their leader's slight nod, released the girl.

"Bring in the whore's father!" Dolabella ordered.

Myrtale tried to drag herself away from her attacker, and in a few seconds she was curled up in a corner of the room beside a large window. Dolabella was sweating and exhausted from his efforts, even though the girl had been restrained by four soldiers while he raped her. He wanted to feel the cool air flowing in from the large open window in the cliff that delineated the acropolis of Thessaloniki, high above the rest of the city.

Myrtale watched as the governor leaned out the window. She did not hesitate. She jumped to her feet and launched herself at her rapist, determined to push him to his death even if it meant throwing herself into the abyss along with him.

In the next room

The legionaries addressed Aeropus.

"Get up, old man. The governor wants to see you."

Myrtale's father stood from the bench they'd thrown him onto, fearful of what he was about to encounter. He'd heard his daughter's cries of pain and Perdiccas's shouts of desperation. He didn't need to ask what had happened. All he could do now was assess the magnitude of the defilement.

He slowly followed the guards into the next room, where he knew only disgrace awaited. His life as he'd known it was forever over.

In the main room of the residence

Dolabella felt a furious push from behind. He teetered for a second. But then he placed his hands on either side of the window, stopping his body's fall.

Myrtale shoved with all her might. She was young and healthy and charged with rage, but her small body was not strong enough to push the obese governor out the window.

"Guards, to me!" Dolabella wailed.

The legionaries surrounded the girl, slapping her and dragging her by her feet to the opposite corner of the room, where they kicked her as she curled into the fetal position with her hands over her head to protect herself.

Dolabella caught his breath. It had been a while since death had been so close. Not even in the campaign against the Thracians, where he'd stayed far from the front line of combat. He smiled. It had been an eventful morning; he felt alive. He was pleased with himself.

"Enough, by Jupiter!" he said to his guards, who were still kicking the young woman. "You'd only be doing her a favor by killing her. I want her to live; I want her to suffer."

He laughed again. He was happy. Yes, it had been a long time since he'd seen death so close. He had to go all the way back to the battle of Porta Collina, where, at the start of combat, everything had looked very grim for him and for Sulla. But it had all worked out for them in

the end. He remembered Crassus's insufferable arrogance. That imbecile acted as if he'd singlehandedly defeated the Samnites, when in
fact it was merely his more experienced troops that had led him to
success in battle . . . Dolabella was still bitter about it.

"The curse of Thessaloniki shall fall upon you," Myrtale swore,
loudly enough to infiltrate the governor's thoughts.

"What did you say?" he asked, furrowing his brow.

"The curse of Thessaloniki shall fall upon you . . . and destroy
you!" she shouted, blood dripping from her lower lip, split open by
one of the legionary's sandals.

"The curse of Thessaloniki?" the governor said. Just then, the
girl's father entered the room. "By Jupiter, here we have Aeropus,
man of the house, the great aristocratic leader of Macedonia. Look at
your daughter. She's a little bruised up and no longer a virgin, but if
this imbecile you've selected as your son-in-law will still marry her,
she should be able to bear you grandchildren. The first one may even
be mine, already inside her. But you can all go back to your comfortable, weak little lives. Lives made less comfortable, of course, by all
the money I'm taking from you back to Rome. Lives now stripped of
all honor. But it could be worse, couldn't it?" He moved closer to the
old man, who had no words. "I'm not quite done yet."

Aeropus would not look at him. He only had eyes for his daughter
curled into a ball in a corner of the room, covered in blood.

"Old man!" Dolabella shouted. "Do I have to have you beaten to
make you pay attention to me?"

Aeropus turned reluctantly to the governor.

"That's better," Dolabella said, smiling. "You know what I'm going
to do now?"

He paused. He wanted to make the man speak, force him to ask
what was next, even as his raped daughter sat huddled in fear and his
future son-in-law was subdued through intermittent punches to the
gut by several legionaries.

"No, I don't know," Aeropus replied in spite of himself, because it
was clear that the only way to end that torture was to play along with
the governor's twisted game. "I don't know what the . . . governor
plans to do now."

Dolabella relished seeing the supposed descendants of Alexander the Great groveling, humiliated, utterly submissive. He had been displeased when Sulla had sent him to this far corner of the world but, while here, he had notably increased his wealth and won a great victory that would likely earn him a triumph. Yes, he'd had many good days in this far-flung province, days like this one, when he was able to count another personal victory over the locals who considered themselves so superior yet were nothing but scum. He was on top of the world.

"Now, old man, I will go to your sacred temple of Aphrodite and strip it of all its treasures. I will take each and every statue to adorn my great domus in the center of Rome or to one of my sumptuous villas in the country. I'll also take any silver or gold I find there, of course, leaving your beloved temple empty, with only those ancient Ionic columns left holding it up. That, *old man*," he said, his voice charged with hatred, "is what I'm going to do."

Dolabella had turned to leave the room when Perdiccas dared to speak. "Why . . . why?" the young Macedonian said before receiving another punch that caused him to vomit.

"Release him," Dolabella ordered.

Once freed from the grip of his captors, Perdiccas collapsed. He fell first onto his knees, then to one side, his hands on his stomach. He was choking on his own vomit as he desperately gasped for air.

The governor crouched down to speak to him. "Why am I doing this?" Dolabella asked. Then he nodded several times and continued speaking quietly into Perdiccas's ear. "All this, boy, I do because I can. Do you understand? Simply because I can."

Gnaeus Cornelius Dolabella, governor of Rome, stood up. "Let's go," he said to his soldiers.

The men filed out, leaving utter misery in their wake.

Aeropus saw that Perdiccas was having difficulty breathing and rushed over to help him sit up before attending to his daughter. As he caught his breath, Perdiccas made a solemn vow that he would seek revenge. One of many decisions a man makes that he may or may not live to regret.

"Th . . . thank you . . ." Perdiccas said.

As the men were distracted, Myrtale crawled back to the window, climbed over the windowsill and turned to her beloved. "I am not worthy of you!" she said. "I am not worthy of anyone!"

She looked down at herself, her tunic ripped in a thousand places, her skin scratched and bruised, blood flowing from between her thighs. The pain was the least of her concerns. The abuse she'd suffered had tarnished her reputation beyond repair. Her father's good name, her family's honor ... all lost. It mattered not that she had been violently forced against her will.

"Myrtale! Myrtale, stop!" Perdiccas shouted desperately, trying to stand but still weakened from the blows he'd received. "Stop her!" he then said, looking to his friend Archelaus, who had just entered, and to her father, Aeropus.

The two men merely stood and looked at Myrtale without making any move to stop her from jumping to her death.

Myrtale looked at her father. His face was a blank stare.

She turned back to the window and inhaled the cool air from outside. She peered down at all of Thessaloniki spread out at her feet. She took a step forward. Her body folded toward the abyss below. She began to fall, relieved to put an end to it all ...

No one could say how it happened.

It was inexplicable.

But Perdiccas somehow gathered his strength. He managed to stand and rush to the open window just in time to grab Myrtale, first by her ripped tunic, then by an arm, and finally by her waist, pulling her back into the room.

They fell backward onto the marble floor and he held Myrtale against him.

"Don't go near that window again," he told her. Then, turning to her father, he went on. "She will once again be worthy of me, of everyone ..."

Myrtale nodded. She didn't know what to do, so she would do as Perdiccas wished. Her father would prefer her dead. But Perdiccas wanted her alive. She was confused, but his words were a small ray of hope that cut through her infinite pain and sadness.

Aeropus and Archelaus looked at Perdiccas somberly.

"And how do you plan to make that happen?" asked the girl's father, who thought that his daughter should have been allowed to jump.

"We will seek revenge for this terrible offense," Perdiccas said, one hand on his bruised belly. "We will put an end to that Roman dog."

"Dolabella is a senator and governor." Aeropus almost spat with disdain. "You don't know what you're saying. That's impossible."

But Perdiccas shook his head. "It will be possible," he insisted. "I will find a way. Dolabella is a dead man. And I will marry Myrtale. She has invoked the curse of Thessaloniki, and I will make sure the curse is fulfilled."

XLIX

FOURTH CRIME: *SACRILEGIUM*·

Thessaloniki, lower part of the city
Late 78 B.C.
That same day

DOLABELLA, ESCORTED BY THE BULK OF THE ROMAN LEGIONS stationed in Thessaloniki, went directly from Aeropus's house to the temple of Aphrodite, near the administrative zone of the city and the governor's palace.

"Block all access!" Dolabella ordered, wanting no interruptions while he robbed the temple.

Once the perimeter was secured, he entered the sacred space lined with centuries-old Ionic columns. The large group of legionaries would help ensure there were no unpleasant surprises.

He stood in the center of the temple and turned slowly, admiring the splendor all around him.

"Take everything," he said.

The soldiers looked at one another.

"Everything, clarissime vir?" one of them asked.

"If it can be taken, take it," Dolabella said, still admiring the beautiful statues and carvings, the bronze incense burners, and countless treasures that had been brought to the shrine over the centuries as offerings by the devout people of Thessaloniki. "I want nothing left here except these cursed columns. Everything else comes with us to Rome."

· The crime of stealing from the gods by plundering sacred temples.

This temple could not compare to Delphi or Olympia, both plundered by Sulla, but all the many riches in the shrine of Aphrodite were for him and him alone.

Orestes's home
Acropolis of Thessaloniki

Orestes was a venerated elder, someone people turned to in times of crisis.

Orestes hardly left his home. At over eighty years old, he liked to say that he'd seen everything there was to see: wars, victories, defeats, a Macedonia that was strong and free as well as a Macedonia forced to submit to Rome. He'd lived through revolutions and had accepted that rebellion was no longer an option for them. The world of the dead, now that all his bones ached, began to seem like a desirable destination. He no longer wished to socialize; even female companionship was a thing of the past. His only indulgence, one he turned to more and more often, was the sweet sensation of bewilderment afforded by a jug of fine wine.

But whenever anyone visited to pay their respects and ask for his advice, he listened carefully and offered his honest opinion.

Aeropus, Perdiccas, and Archelaus now told Orestes the long, sad story of the governor's crimes. They bitterly recounted the litany of horrors they had been powerless to stop.

"As we speak, he is pillaging the temple of Aphrodite," Archelaus finished.

Perdiccas hardly spoke. He was still in great pain and felt that he'd used the last of his strength saving Myrtale.

"The temple of Aphrodite," Orestes said to himself.

Not very long ago, he had been the high priest of that temple. To him, that assault was the worst of the governor's offenses. The attack on Myrtale, one more violation among so many, was a shame, especially for the father and the would-be husband, now dishonored . . . But the plundering of their most sacred temple, along with the exorbitant taxes invented purely to fill the governor's personal coffers, both affected the entirety of the Macedonian people.

"They've gone too far this time. I say we revolt. A general uprising across all of Macedonia," Archelaus said. In his youth and naïvety, he still thought that their subjugation to Rome was something temporary.

Orestes shook his head. "It's too late for that, my boy," he said. "Twenty years ago, maybe, but not now. The Romans are stronger than ever and they only continue to consolidate their power. We could incite an uprising, even try to kill the Roman governor before he leaves Macedonia, but Rome's wrath will fall brutally upon us, sweeping through the entire region. They govern all the lands around us from east to west. And they will not permit rebellion in any form as it sets a bad example for their other provinces. No, that is not the way forward. I do not advise revolt."

"So should we just sit back and watch, by Aphrodite? Is that what you're suggesting?" Perdiccas snapped. He was still in pain but seemed to be recovering some of his strength.

Orestes looked at him without a word.

"The young man is beside himself," Aeropus said as justification for his friend's outburst.

"It is understandable," Orestes said. He cleared his throat and, after taking a sip of wine, gave his advice: "Macedonia is part of Rome now. That means we can call upon Roman justice and demand fair compensation. The governor should be forced to return everything he has pilfered from the temple, along with the money he claimed to be spending importing Egyptian grain and repairing our crumbling Via Egnatia. There won't be many consequences, not according to current Roman law, but a good lawyer might be able to impose a hefty fine on him and, more importantly, force him into exile from his beloved city."

Aeropus sighed. It seemed to him, as it did to the rest of them, an insufficient punishment. "Their justice is no good to us. Only Dolabella's death could possibly begin to reverse the indignity dealt to my"—he struggled to continue—"to my . . . daughter. And restore our honor."

Perdiccas then interrupted, "Roman justice may yet serve our needs," he said. "A trial would provide grounds for our presence in

Rome. Dolabella, facing trial, would have to come out into the open in a public place. That's all we need."

Aeropus was impressed by Perdiccas's passion, but these words were pure insanity. "He's constantly surrounded by his guards, armed to the teeth," Aeropus said. "Attacking him in Rome would be impossible, and even if you did manage it, it would be suicide: they'd murder you on the spot."

But Perdiccas could not be persuaded against it. "My life doesn't matter. This trial is all that matters. It will give me the opportunity I need."

"Well," Orestes said, "the girl, you've told me, invoked the curse of Thessaloniki. That may help you, but the trial . . . I don't know . . ."

Orestes fell silent. The old man was thinking.

"What is it that worries you?" Aeropus asked.

Orestes shook himself from his reverie. "It won't be easy. No, it won't be easy to find a Roman patrician willing to bring an accusation against the all-powerful Dolabella. It would have to be someone very brave . . . or insane. Or both."

Port of Dyrrhachium
Three weeks later

Dolabella had fled Thessaloniki immediately after stripping its most sacred temple of all its riches. He was already extremely unpopular because of his invented taxes on grain and the exorbitant fees he'd levied to maintain the Via Egnatia, which had not seen a single repair. Raping a young noblewoman and plundering the temple of Aphrodite had only worsened matters, and all signs pointed to a general uprising. So Dolabella left the city as quickly as he could.

Traveling the Via Egnatia to the port of Dyrrhachium, he was able to see for himself the terrible state of the road. His carts, in fact, on numerous occasions—loaded down with statues, gold, silver, and abundant provisions—became stuck in the enormous ruts along the way. Nevertheless, he was able to advance quickly westward, aided by the several centuries of legionaries who rushed to dislodge the carts as they fell, again and again, into the huge potholes in the road.

But Dolabella was content. Each broken cobble, every hole in the road, every collapsed bridge, was more money he could keep for himself. Why should he care about the state of a road that he never planned to see again as long as he lived? He had accumulated more riches than he'd ever even imagined possible. He had been a wealthy man before accepting this post in the East, having benefitted substantially from Sulla's confiscations of the populares' property. But being appointed governor of Macedonia was the best gift he'd received from the former Roman dictator. Now, at the port of Dyrrhachium, seeing that they needed an entire ship, no less than a large *quadrireme,* to transfer all of his possessions back to Rome, he finally had a clear picture of everything he'd accumulated during his time as governor of the remote province.

He was exultant as he sat drinking wine on a sella his slaves had set out for him on the dock so that he could be comfortable as he supervised the loading process. In a few hours, they would set sail with the high tide, and he and his riches would soon be far away from the hostile land of Macedonia.

"We'll have everything ready in an hour," said Sextus, captain of the ship he'd hired for his return to Rome.

But there was still one concern left in his mind, and he decided to share it with the captain. He gestured for a slave to serve the seaman wine. "Tell me," he said, "what is the curse of Thessaloniki?"

Sextus, who up to that moment had seemed relaxed and happy, pleased to be earning a good sum of money for a relatively easy trip, now tensed, and fear clouded his eyes.

"It's a legend the sailors talk of, but . . . why would the governor concern himself with such nonsense?"

"That's my business," Dolabella said dryly. "Curiosity," he added in a more friendly tone. "I've heard of it and I wanted to know what it referred to. I imagined a seagoing man like yourself would know. But I see I was mistaken."

Wounding the captain's pride had the desired effect. "Thessaloniki was the daughter of the great king Phillip II, father of Alexander the Great," the sailor began. "She was conceived with a concubine, so she was only half-sister to the great conqueror of the East, but she adored her brother. They didn't spend much time together, since Alexander was always with Aristotle, and then at war in Persia and India. The girl was given her name in commemoration of her father's military victory on the plains of Thessali. So the Greek word *níke,* which means "victory," was added to the name of the plain: Thessalia Nike, Thessaloniki.

"They say Alexander visited his sister, bringing her magical waters from the Fountain of Eternal Youth, or that he perhaps simply sent her a jar of the waters of immortality. In some versions, Alexander washes his sister's hair with the enchanted water; in others, it's Thessaloniki herself who does so. Whatever the case, when Alexander died, his sister was so aggrieved that she threw herself into the sea. But Thessaloniki didn't drown. They say that she was transformed into a siren who now lurks in the waters surrounding the Greek coasts, and that sometimes, on the open ocean, she appears to sailors and poses a question. *Ζει ο βασιλιάς Αλέξανδρος,* she says, which means—"

"Is King Alexander alive?" Dolabella translated, annoyed. "I can understand Greek. Just continue with the story."

The captain nodded and obeyed: "The siren wants the sailor to respond: *Ζει και βασιλεύει και τον κόσμο κυριεύει.** As long as she receives that response, everything will be fine and she'll allow the ship to continue its course. But if any seaman is so foolish as to say that Alexander is dead, Thessaloniki transforms into a terrible gorgon, churning up the waters with such fury that the worst of storms will rise up to sink the ship and drown its entire crew." Here the captain paused to take a sip of wine. "I've never come across any mermaids, and I have no desire to. But I've heard more than one drunk sailor tell of an encounter with the siren Thessaloniki, swearing that they only remain among the living because they knew to give the correct answer. All nonsense, I say. The result of too much wine. In fact, I believe Thessaloniki actually died at the hand of one of her sons. Out of jealousy, it seems, because the mother favored one son over the other . . ." The captain was quiet for a moment as he took another sip

*   "He lives and reigns and conquers the world."

of wine. He set his empty cup down before adding, "Although the sea is home to the strangest of creatures. You never know."

Dolabella didn't say a word. He just sat silently staring out at the sea.

The captain stood, taking the governor's silence as his cue to leave.

Dolabella was overcome by a sudden sense of panic. The waters of the bay were calm, but his mind raced wildly. Supposing he encountered that siren invoked by Aeropus's daughter. All he'd have to do was provide the correct response, but still . . .

"Unload the ship," Dolabella said, much to the captain's consternation. "I shall return to Rome by land."

The Trial

V

PRIMA ACTIO

FIRST SESSION
OF THE TRIAL

L

CAESAR'S FIRST WITNESS: MARCUS

Basilica Sempronia, Rome
77 B.C.

LAND.

Caesar stared at the floor of the Basilica Sempronia.

The building had been erected on the very site where Scipio Africanus was born. Caesar now needed to conjure the spirit of that great commander to give his political career a chance at survival. To give himself a chance at survival. The trial had started out badly for him, with the murders of his main witnesses, but he had been successful in the reiectio, in convincing Metellus to recuse himself from the trial. And thanks to his journey to Macedonia, he now had three new witnesses. He began to feel hopeful that he might have a chance at victory.

Caesar looked up to where the judges would enter, anxious to see which of them appeared first. That would be the new president of the tribunal.

He looked around: Labienus, seated beside him, was going over the questions they had prepared for the witnesses who would testify in that prima actio. Prima for so many reasons. The first true session of the trial itself, after all the initial deliberations over lawyers and judges, but also, and most importantly, Caesar's very first judicial session.

He looked into the audience: his mother, his wife, and his sisters were all there. Aurelia, solemn, had fixed her eyes on the door by which the tribunal would enter. Cornelia, for her part, looked di-

rectly at him, her eyes tearful. Just a few days prior she had begged
him to abandon the trial, saying that she feared for his life. His success in the reiectio had put all the optimates on alert, and Dolabella
now saw him as more than a minor nuisance. Cornelia had told him
that his mother was equally fearful and that both women prayed that
he would abandon the trial, even though they had initially supported
his decision to get involved. But quitting now was completely out of
the question, much to his young wife's disappointment, as she sat in
the audience silently imploring him with her red-rimmed eyes.

To Cornelia's right, Caesar could see his sisters talking quietly to
each other. They looked worried as well.

"The judges are entering," said Labienus.

Caesar looked toward the door of the Basilica Sempronia: Pompey headed the committee of fifty-two judges.

"Pompey?" Labienus said, incredulous. "Isn't he too young?"

They both knew that the age laws related to political or judicial
positions could be bent for the right people.

"It makes sense," Caesar commented quietly. "Pompey made a
name for himself in the war against the socii with his brutal efficiency
on the battlefield. Now they want to see if he can be equally efficient
in the courtroom."

"And equally brutal," Labienus added.

Caesar nodded and glanced over to where the adjusters of the
clepsydras* stood preparing to measure the time allotted to each lawyer.

"What do you think of him?" Labienus asked.

"Pompey is capable of anything," Caesar replied, his voice very
sober. "By getting rid of Metellus, we've gotten a less experienced
president, but also maybe a more ruthless one ... It's hard to know
when you're winning or losing a trial. For the moment, I need you to
watch the clepsydras to make sure no one manipulates them. They
may try to speed them up when it's my turn to argue."

"I'll keep an eye on the adjusters."

Caesar then turned to his left. Cotta and Hortensius were sizing

---

*   Water clocks—devices that measure time by the regulated flow of water out of a vessel.

him up as if he were a human sacrifice. His uncle's gaze held a certain sadness and pity, Hortensius's a sarcastic disdain.

Roman Forum
The night before

Rome at night, a sprawling city lacking sufficient torches on its streets, was a kingdom of shadows. A woman walked through the darkness with the swiftness of a girl and stopped outside the tabernae veteres near the forum. She was surrounded by a large group of well-armed slaves who would guard her from the roving gangs of criminals that made the Roman night so dangerous. Still, the risk was great. Here, by the forum, things were slightly safer—perhaps due to the presence of the temple of Vesta, which inspired respect even among the miscreants, or because of the guards outside the public buildings—but leaving the Suburra, the neighborhood she'd slipped away from that evening, cloaked in darkness, meant risking her life. The matrona was moved by precisely that: a life at risk. Not her own life, but the life of a man she loved too much to let him endanger himself. He was embroiled in a trial that would surely destroy him. Even if he somehow managed to win, he would never make it out alive. So, going against everything anyone could ever imagine her capable of doing, she had decided to take that step, to perpetrate that . . . betrayal.

"Domina," said one of the slaves, warning her that a group of men was approaching.

"Don't make a move," she said firmly.

From out of the darkness, their faces covered like common criminals, Hortensius and Aurelius Cotta emerged at the head of the sinister group.

"Don't make a move," she said again.

And her servants remained immobile, clutching the daggers, knives, and other weapons hidden beneath their tunics.

Basílica Sempronia, Rome
Trial against Dolabella, prima actio

The first witness had responded to Caesar's questions clearly and succinctly. Marcus, the engineer, left no room for doubt: the Via Egnatia was in shameful condition from the port of Dyrrhachium all the way to Thessaloniki, the capital of Macedonia, and from Thessaloniki all the way to Byzantium. The road was practically impassable for certain carts, unless the travelers moved in large caravans to help free the vehicles when they became stuck in the countless pits and potholes. The bridges were all on the brink of collapse; the slabs were cracked or missing entirely. Large boulders from rockslides sat in the middle of the road. According to Marcus's expert opinion as engineer, no one had invested a single sesterce in repairing the road for many years, and anyone who said otherwise was lying.

Marcus was categorical.

His testimony was rock solid.

Dolabella was caught in his lie. He had levied a new tax specifically to undertake repairs of the Via Egnatia, but his own engineer had said that he'd never received any of the money to begin them. And it was now abundantly clear that no maintenance had been undertaken for quite some time.

Caesar sat. Calm, tranquil, sure of himself. The trip to Macedonia had paid off.

"The defense may now come forth to cross-examine the witness," said Pompey, who, unlike Metellus, would not let the praecones orchestrate the trial for him.

Gnaeus Pompey spoke for himself, and he spoke well. He did not stutter and, to Caesar's surprise, he seemed unruffled and unconcerned by Marcus's damning testimony.

Aurelius Cotta stood, moved to the center of the room, and looked at the engineer sitting before the tribunal.

The audience packed into the Basilica Sempronia sat in attention.

"Marcus, you are an engineer, correct?" Cotta seemed distracted, studying the floor.

"That's correct," the witness confirmed.

"And some years ago, you worked regularly as an engineer for Rome's public works, did you not?"

"Some years ago, yes, I worked on several of the city's aqueducts and on repairs to some buildings in the forum," he said, proud of his achievements.

Caesar was still relaxed, although he could guess where Cotta was going with this.

"Some years ago, yes. But, with Sulla's rise to power, when Dolabella took over control of certain public work contracts, you were left without gainful employment, isn't that correct?"

"Yes, but—"

"The tribunal asks that the witness respond only to the questions posed. There's no need to provide further explanations," Cotta interrupted quickly. "So, Marcus. You are testifying in your capacity as engineer against Gnaeus Cornelius Dolabella." Cotta was careful not to refer to the defendant as reus, as his nephew Caesar did as often as possible. "And this very man, Gnaeus Cornelius Dolabella, left you without work when he began to oversee Rome's public works projects. Is that correct?"

"It is, but he cancelled my contracts without any justification, only to favor his friends," Marcus said.

"By Jupiter! We are not interested in the witness's interpretation of Gnaeus Cornelius Dolabella's motives for cancelling your public contracts!" Cotta boomed over Marcus to keep him from providing an argument that he didn't want to hear. "Dolabella could've cancelled your contracts for any number of reasons—because he didn't like the results of your previous work, because you didn't stay within budget, who knows why. The only thing that matters here is the fact that the witness clearly feels animosity toward the man I am tasked with defending. So the witness's testimony could easily be motivated by revenge and a simple desire to damage the defendant."

Marcus shook his head and tried to argue, but Cotta peppered the man with quick questions, leaving his head swimming: "What was your motivation for traveling to Macedonia to study the road so painstakingly? A long journey and a costly one. You must've spent many a sesterce, if not silver denarii. The real question, the question that will allow the tribunal to judge the credibility of this testimony is: Who paid for your trip to Macedonia?"

Marcus swallowed. He ran a hand over his dry lips. Lying to a Roman tribunal was a bad idea. It wasn't that there was any serious punishment for giving false testimony, but anyone perceived of having lied in court was looked down on. And public disdain was bad for business.

"Gaius Julius Caesar paid my way," he at last admitted.

"The accusator?" Cotta said, feigning disbelief as he pointed his index at his nephew.

"Yes," the engineer said.

Caesar jumped up from his seat. "The engineer who Dolabella hired to rebuild the Via Egnatia," he said loudly and quickly, without asking permission from the president of the tribunal, "would have testified that he was never able to start any repairs because he was never given any money to do so. He was found dead, murdered with a dagger to the back. That's why I had to ask another engineer to certify the abominable state of the road—"

"The defense has the floor!" Pompey thundered.

Caesar went silent, but remained standing.

"I could remind the young prosecutor that it is rude to interrupt, but it doesn't matter," Cotta continued smugly, as if he'd expected that outburst and was unfazed by it. "We all lament the death of the engineer. The fact is that our prosecutor could've sought out one of that engineer's assistants, but no, it was much easier and more convenient to pay, yes pay, another witness, someone easily influenced and manipulated. Not just any engineer, but one who felt animosity toward the defendant, who could be paid to testify to anything the prosecution told him to." Cotta turned back to the engineer. "What a shame that perjury is not punished as it should be by our laws. But the gods will surely see to anyone pedaling such obvious lies before a tribunal of justice! By Jupiter, this is no testimony, it's a pack of lies, bought and paid for!"

Cotta fell silent.

Caesar was about to object, but Pompey spoke before he got the chance: "Does the prosecution have another witness?"

Caesar understood that the president of the tribunal considered the engineer's testimony to be over. There was nothing he could say to change it.

He looked down.

He sighed.

He had to get his thoughts in order.

LI

CAESAR'S SECOND WITNESS: ORESTES

Basilica Sempronia, Rome
77 B.C.

CAESAR WAS CONFUSED. COTTA HAD DISMANTLED HIS WIT-ness's testimony, destroying his credibility and making it seem as if he'd been bribed. Caesar would have liked to object, but he didn't have a clear argument and Pompey wouldn't have granted him the floor anyway.

"Does the prosecution have another witness?" Pompey asked again. He enjoyed watching Gaius Marius's nephew squirm.

"Orestes," Labienus whispered.

Caesar nodded, still staring at the floor, then he took a deep breath and collected himself. "The prosecution . . ." He swallowed, shook his head, and looked Pompey directly in the eye. "The prosecution now requests the presence of the venerable Macedonian elder Orestes, former high priest of the temple of Aphrodite in Thessaloniki," he said loudly and clearly. Then he sat for a few seconds as the old man painstakingly made his way to the witness stand.

"It's like they'd prepared their arguments perfectly," Labienus said, "as if Cotta had them all memorized ahead of time."

"No," Caesar said. "It's as if someone fed them information. How could they have known that we'd paid for the engineer's trip? Or that Marcus was left without work when Dolabella rose to power with Sulla? They could've figured it out, of course, but we returned from Macedonia only days ago—they wouldn't have had time. It's . . .

strange. They have information. *Someone* has given them information."

Labienus didn't know what to say.

Old Orestes was now sitting before the tribunal.

Roman Forum
The night before

"Don't make a move," the woman said again.

Her slaves relaxed their grip on their daggers. They had no desire to instigate violence: the approaching group was equal to their own in size. If the knives came out, many from both sides would fall. But the domina seemed to have everything under control, and they hoped their masters would be able to work things out peacefully.

"What is it that you wanted to tell us?" one of the masked men asked.

"I will tell you whatever you want to know to make sure Caesar loses this trial," she said. "What do you need?"

The masked men exchanged a glance. One of them turned to the woman, about to ask why she would betray Caesar. Then he thought better of it and said instead, "We need to know who the new witnesses are and everything about them. Their weak spots."

The woman hesitated, glanced around at the shadows, then fixed her eyes on those hooded faces.

"So be it," she said.

Basilica Sempronia, Rome
Trial against Dolabella, prima actio

Caesar slowly stood. He'd been so confident about Marcus's testimony, but after Cotta's cross-examination, it was as if the power had been drained from the engineer's words.

When Caesar had first met Orestes, in Macedonia, he'd been convinced that the old man was going to be his strongest witness in the trial. But in the past days, that had begun to change. The elderly priest clearly wanted to help justice prevail, but the journey from Macedonia to Rome—first by the cursed Via Egnatia (in terrible condition, no matter what the defense said), then by ship, and then up through southern Italy to Rome—seemed to have depleted the man's energies. Caesar had wondered if old Orestes would even have the strength to appear in the Basilica Sempronia on the day of the prima actio. He'd made it, but the young prosecutor was now nervous about his testimony. Orestes, who at the start of the journey from Macedonia had recited passages from Sophocles and Euripides with a stirring passion, had begun to shut down. He was hard of hearing, so questions had to be repeated loudly. And while he retained memories of the distant past, he forgot recent events or conversations from only a day prior.

Nevertheless, with Caesar's original witnesses murdered and the engineer's testimony now discredited, he knew he had no choice but to call the aging priest before the tribunal. He would have to use all the tricks he had up his sleeve.

Caesar walked to the center of the room. He turned to Orestes and spoke loudly and clearly, looking the old man in the face so that he could see the movement of his lips. Anything to help him understand what was being said.

"Your name is Orestes, and you were once the high priest of the temple of Aphrodite in Thessaloniki, on the eastern coast of Macedonia. Is that correct?"

"It is," the old man confirmed, his voice somewhat shaky but audible to everyone present.

"And, for this reason, along with the fact that you've lived an honorable and dignified life, is it true that you are a venerated elder in your community?" Caesar asked, still looking directly at Orestes and speaking clearly.

"People know and respect me, I think, yes."

"And they consult you on important matters, ask for your advice?"

"They often do, yes."

Caesar nodded. He turned slowly, looked at Dolabella, pressed his lips together, and then again faced his witness. "And is it true that when Perdiccas, Archelaus, and Aeropus, respected members of their community, came to you for advice on how to respond to the actions of the governor, Gnaeus Cornelius Dolabella, reus in this trial, you advised them to turn to Roman justice, urging against a violent uprising?"

"That is correct; that is the advice I gave."

Caesar nodded again and looked for a moment at the members of the tribunal: the Roman senators, despite being predisposed to exonerate Dolabella of all crimes, showed genuine interest in what the old priest had to say. And just as Caesar had thought from the start, a respected elder—a priest, no less, someone wise, knowledgeable, and well educated—would always make the senators take note. It was difficult, if not practically impossible, to sway them from their intent to declare Dolabella innocent. But sowing any doubt, any call to conscience, could constitute a crack in their impenetrable wall.

"And is it true that, during his time in Macedonia, the governor, the reus in this trial, Gnaeus Cornelius Dolabella, imposed fictitious taxes for repairs to the Via Egnatia that were never carried out? Is it true that he increased the price of grain, claiming that it had been imported from Egypt when in reality it came from within Macedonia? And is it true that the reus stole statues and other treasures from the temple of Aphrodite in Thessaloniki and that, still unsatisfied even after all these crimes, he forced himself upon and raped Myrtale, a young aristocratic woman who had been widely respected as a chaste virgin up to that point?"

"Yes, the governor did these things," Orestes confirmed with all the strength his feeble voice could muster.

The old man's voice may have been weak, but his affirmation carried as powerful, credible, and damning. The senators of the tribunal shifted uncomfortably in their seats, adjusting their cushions and togas.

"The man speaking these words is not someone I have paid," Caesar continued. "The Macedonians financed his journey to Rome, with the little money, I must point out, that the reus has left them. This is not a man who had any hostility toward the reus before he began to govern Macedonia and make life miserable for the local community. Orestes is a wise elder, a priest, an upright citizen of Macedonia, venerated by all who know him. He is a man who respects our laws, our justice. And, when confronted with his compatriots' understandable outrage and desire for revenge against an unjust and ignoble envoy of Rome, a corrupt governor who dishonors our great republic wherever he goes, this man, Orestes, advises against rebellion. He urges the aggrieved parties not to incite violence against Roman authority, but to turn to our laws, our justice, and expose the reus's crimes to this esteemed tribunal so that they might render their just verdict.

"This revered elder, who not only accepts but also respects our laws, sits here before us confirming that the reus Gnaeus Cornelius Dolabella perpetrated abominable crimes. Crimes made all the more atrocious for having been committed by a delegate of Rome sent to govern, to advocate for, this province. But, instead, the reus has only violated, plundered, and humiliated the people he was meant to protect. The defense may be tempted to justify such crimes, to say that violations sometimes occur unwittingly, that a territory may be exploited or a temple pillaged out of greater necessity, for example in times of war. They may try to remind us that Sulla, whose laws dictate the proceedings of this judicial session, plundered the temples of Olympia and Delphi to collect funds when our troops were up against the fearsome Mithridates of Pontus. In this case, in Macedonia, there is no such excuse to justify or absolve the crimes committed by the reus, Gnaeus Cornelius Dolabella, against the inhabitants of this Roman province. Everything done by the accused was for his own personal gain, never for the greater good of the Roman Republic."

Caesar then asked Orestes to provide details on the statues missing from the temple of Aphrodite. He asked him to describe how he'd seen them being loaded into the governor's carts, and to tell the court about the other treasures pillaged from the temple. And the old man was able to provide many convincing details. He spoke slowly, not very loudly, but clearly enough to be perfectly audible, with a contained outrage over what had happened in that place so sacred to him and to all Macedonians.

"By Jupiter! There are no further questions!" Caesar exclaimed, satisfied with the elderly priest's responses.

"He did well," Labienus said when Caesar sat down beside him.

"Yes," Caesar agreed as he poured himself a cup of water, "but it's Cotta's questions that worry me. And how Orestes will react. He's sweating. Can you tell? He's exhausted. Maybe I should've been briefer."

Labienus looked at Orestes: the old man, it was true, was sweating and looked even older and more tired. "Maybe," he said, "but the testimony was excellent. And we needed it."

Caesar nodded and took a sip of water.

Meanwhile, Aurelius Cotta was pacing back and forth in front of the witness, looking down at the floor. This time, the veteran defense lawyer seemed at a loss. But it was an act. He began to speak, looking at the audience, his back to the witness, so that the old man could not see his face or his lips: "So now we're supposed to believe that this elderly foreigner," Cotta said, emphasizing these last two words with slight disdain, "witnessed, with his own eyes, Governor Dolabella's supposed pillaging of a sacred temple. Is that right, old man?"

Orestes did not react to the question. Cotta had classified him as an elderly foreigner, but he was aware that the man's noble, venerable appearance had made a good impression on many members of the tribunal, so he was now out to belittle him in their eyes. If the information he and his colleague had received the night before was correct, it would be easy. But he still feared that Caesar's supposed betrayer could be setting a trap for him. So Cotta was extremely cautious.

"I have asked, old Orestes, if we should believe what you've said," Cotta repeated, still with his back to the witness, in a voice audible to everyone in the room, but not loud, without making any effort to project it.

The witness again did not respond.

"I now wonder whether this elderly foreign man refuses to respond out of disdain for my questions, disdain for the defense, or disdain for this tribunal. Or is it that you only understand Latin when spoken to by the prosecution?" And here Aurelius Cotta turned toward the witness and the judges.

Orestes remained silent. He was an educated man. He didn't have any problem understanding Latin, even if Greek was his native tongue. But since Cotta had stood with his back to him and had not spoken loudly and clearly, the old man was confused—he wasn't sure whether he was being questioned or not.

Then Cotta decided to share another theory with all those present in the Basilica Sempronia. "Or is it that this old man is simply hard of hearing?"

A murmur ran through the room.

Pompey looked to one of the praecones, who stood and demanded silence: "Favete linguis!"

The audience quieted.

"But, by all the gods, a person can be hard of hearing and still witness the pillaging of a temple," Cotta continued, increasingly more confident. "Good eyesight is all that's required there. We should ask nothing more of this *noble* elder," Cotta said with a sarcastic smile.

Hortensius, his defense partner, laughed from a corner of the room and was joined by several members of the public. Cotta knew that as he reduced Orestes to a sad sack of bones, it was all the more ironic to aggrandize him with adjectives that implied social prestige.

"Orestes!" he continued, shouting as if speaking to someone who was stone deaf and also lacking in intelligence. "When you supposedly observed the governor pillaging the temple of Aphrodite, did you do so from a distance?"

Now that the lawyer was facing him, Orestes responded immediately. "The governor had his troops stationed all around the square," he explained, "but I personally saw him exit the temple of Aphrodite, and his legionaries were carrying statues out of the temple along with the rest of its treasures."

"From what distance?" Cotta replied, practically shouting.

"I don't know . . . some fifty paces. Maybe a little less . . ."

"I see." The lawyer turned back to face the public but continued to speak in a booming voice, glancing back at the witness. "Well, in this room, for example, the prosecutor's sisters are present here among us. Does the witness know these women?"

"I do," he said.

Caesar and Labienus both tensed.

"I have dined in the prosecutor's home during my stay here in Rome," Orestes clarified.

"Perfect," Cotta said. "Nothing wrong with that. What interests me," the lawyer continued, "is that the witness is familiar with these two women's faces and that they are present here today, in the audience, fewer than thirty paces from where I stand. I can see them perfectly. Could the witness please point these two women out to me?"

Orestes understood the question and looked out into the audience, but his tired old eyes could only see blurry faces.

Cotta went further: "Could the witness, from where he's seated, point out *any* woman in the audience?"

Orestes squinted into the room, but everything looked cloudy. "Not at the moment," he admitted. "My vision has deteriorated in recent weeks. I could see better before."

"Of course." Cotta now spoke to the audience without looking at the witness or raising his voice and said, "I'm sure he could hear perfectly before he left home, too."

"What?" Orestes asked. "I didn't catch that last bit . . . Was it a question?"

Hortensius once again laughed as did a large part of the audience. More serious in Caesar's eyes was the fact that a good number of the senators sitting on the tribunal joined in the mockery as well.

But Cotta had not yet finished.

He turned once again to the witness and spoke to him in a loud, clear voice, making sure he understood: "Tell me, did you dine in the home of the prosecutor last night?" he asked.

Orestes was about to respond, but then seemed to think better of it and remained silent, blinking with his mouth hanging open before the questioning eyes of the jury.

"The witness need not be fearful," Cotta continued calmly. "It is perfectly acceptable for a witness to dine and converse with a lawyer who has called them to testify in a trial. There's nothing wrong with that."

Orestes remained silent.

Cotta decided to put words to that silence. "Of course, what could be occurring is that the witness does not remember whether he dined in the home of the prosecutor last night."

Orestes nodded slightly but stopped short of answering, well aware that admitting to his poor memory would make him look bad.

"Did the witness dine in the home of the accusator last night?" The question echoed mercilessly through the great hall of the Basilica Sempronia.

Roman Forum
The night before

"Who was at the domus tonight?" one of the masked men asked the woman, to her surprise.

"What does that have to do with the case?" she asked, not wanting to give the men any extra information beyond what was strictly necessary to ensure that Caesar lost the trial.

"It will help me in the interrogation tomorrow," one of the masked men explained.

The night was black indeed, here near the tabernae veteres in the forum, yet the thoughts of the conspirators were just as dark.

Basilica Sempronia, Rome
Trial against Dolabella, prima actio

Orestes could not remember. So he chose to lie. "Yes, I dined last night at the home of the lawyer for the Macedonian cause."

"I happen to know that's not true," said Aurelius Cotta.

The defense lawyer did not reveal his source, but the response was enough to make Orestes question his faulty memory and throw him into a state of total confusion. Cotta was aware that he was being cruel to that elderly man, but there was no room for compassion in an interrogation. "The witness did not dine with the prosecutor last night," Cotta continued, "but it would seem that the witness does not remember that. Does the witness remember whether he had breakfast this morning?"

"I always do," said Orestes, but he wasn't completely sure. His long-term memories were more clearly defined, but the recent past was diffuse, blurry. He didn't understand what was happening.

"Can the witness then tell us what he had for breakfast? Goat's milk? Porridge? Nuts? Or wine, perhaps?" Cotta said.

Orestes did not remember what he'd had for breakfast, was not even sure that he'd eaten breakfast at all, and lying again did not seem like a good idea since the lawyer seemed to know everything already.

"I cannot seem to recall," he admitted.

Caesar shook his head. Orestes's failing memory wasn't obvious enough that a slave could have leaked the information. Who was betraying him, then?

Just then, Cotta had a brilliant idea.

"Does the witness recall that, earlier in this interrogation, I asked him to point out someone in the audience?"

Orestes had a foggy recollection. "Yes."

Cotta licked his lips before proceeding: "Who did I ask the witness to point out?"

Orestes opened his mouth, then froze.

"Who?" Cotta repeated.

Total silence in the room.

"I cannot recall," Orestes admitted after a few seconds.

Cotta knew that he didn't need to ask the man anything else.

He turned back to the audience, then to the judges, and spoke with the assuredness of someone stating an incontestable fact. "He can't hear. He can't see. And he can't even remember something asked of him mere minutes ago. The prosecutor may try to convince us that the witness's mental deterioration is something recent, but I don't believe that to be the case. Judges of Rome, this is not the testimony of a venerable elder, a former priest of the sacred temple of Aphrodite in Thessaloniki. No, this is the testimony of a decrepit old man who is deaf, blind, and senile. And we're supposed to believe what this witness says he supposedly saw or heard? What he thinks he remembers happening in Macedonia several months ago?

"The prosecutor first provided a testimony paid for out of his own pocket. He now presents us with a witness so old he can't see, hear, or remember. And it makes me wonder if this poor man hasn't been coached by the prosecutor to repeat what he wanted him to say. The first witness, bribed and paid for. The second, a senile old man manipulated by the prosecutor. Yes, we knew that the lawyer for the prosecution was young and inexperienced, but sincerely, I expected more from him."

And with this, Aurelius Cotta paraded across the basilica like a triumphant consul through the streets of Rome and took his seat beside Hortensius, who congratulated him heartily.

At the table for the prosecution, the mood was one of utter defeat. "They didn't just know a lot about our witnesses," Labienus whispered to Caesar. "They knew everything."

Caesar did not respond. He looked into the audience, searching for the face of the person who had betrayed him. His sisters looked back at him, very grave. His mother met his gaze, dignified and still as an Egyptian effigy. But his young wife Cornelia averted her eyes, tears visible on her face. Why was Cornelia avoiding him?

"All that's left is the girl's testimony," Labienus continued. "What should we do?"

The room was abuzz with dozens of overlapping conversations about the last interrogation. It was becoming clear to everyone that the prosecutor was not able to support his accusations.

Old Orestes seemed confused, withdrawn, as he walked with his head down back to the place where Perdiccas, Aeropus, and Archelaus waited for him. He didn't understand what was happening, but he could tell it wasn't good.

Just then, Pompey's powerful voice rose over the tumult: "Does the accusator have any more witnesses?"

Caesar remained silent.

The question was like a sword to his throat, pressing against his jugular.

"Should we call her?" Labienus asked again quietly.

"We have to. We don't have anyone else," Caesar muttered, standing up.

LII

CAESAR'S THIRD WITNESS: MYRTALE

Basílica Sempronia, Rome
77 B.C.

MYRTALE FINISHED GIVING HER TESTIMONY. CAESAR HAD asked only a few questions. The girl had been clear, direct, and brutal. She spoke unequivocally and did not cry, but showed a restrained emotion that was even more effective. She gave a concise but scathing account of how the reus, Dolabella, had entered her home and, taking advantage of the fact that both her father and Perdiccas were absent, had beaten her, thrown her to the ground, and ordered several legionaries to pin her down. Then he raped her. She then explained that she tried to commit suicide and how Perdiccas had stopped her at the last moment, and that her only hope of finding some redemption and peace was for a Roman tribunal to condemn her rapist. Her very honor depended on this trial.

"Thank you," Caesar said, not feeling the need to question her any further. She was not senile and had not been bribed. She was a compelling witness, a young, intelligent woman who'd been brutally raped by a governor in a grotesque abuse of his power.

Caesar sat down and, very seriously, looked to the defense. He was expecting his uncle Cotta to cross-examine the witness, but it was Hortensius who, pressing his lips together and exaggeratedly nodding his head, as if he approved of the testimony he'd just heard, stood and, with the practiced calm of someone who has rehearsed every move, approached Myrtale.

"A woman," Hortensius began. "First a purchased testimony, then

a senile old man's. Now the prosecution presents us with the testimony of a *woman*."

Caesar frowned. Roman law permitted women to give testimony
in trial. It wasn't even all that uncommon. He had not expected the
defense to focus on that. Where were they going with this?

Roman Forum
The night before

"With everything you've told us, we have enough to discredit those
two witnesses," said the masked man. "But we need to know if the
girl who said she was raped is going to testify or not."

Here the woman hesitated. Somehow revealing anything about
the girl seemed an even greater betrayal. But nothing was more important to her than saving Caesar.

"Yes, the girl will testify," she said.

"Then we need you to give us something to discredit her."

Basilica Sempronia, Rome
Trial against Dolabella, prima actio

Hortensius projected his well-modulated voice in a way that made
his words echo loudly through the cavernous space. "We are now
asked to believe a woman." He raised his voice even further as he
threw up his arms: "A woman!" And to keep Caesar from saying that
a woman was as capable of testifying as any man, he went on, swag-
gering around the room. "Of course, a woman is permitted to testify
in trial, something I always found absurd, but"—he turned his palms
up as he looked at the audience—"it is legal by Roman law. We will
allow it. However, I can't help but question the validity of any testimony given by a woman. Do I have to remind those of you present
here that the first woman, Pandora, was nothing more than one of
Zeus's poisoned gifts, as we see in the most ancient texts? Women
are the source of all conflict among men, poor mortals that we are.
The immortal gods who look down on us and help guide us also, on
occasion, punish us. Prometheus stole the flame that was sacred to

man, and he warned our ancestors not to accept any gifts from Zeus. But did our elders heed him? No. Zeus's gift came in the form of a woman: Pandora. And Epimetheus accepted her, took her as his wife, and begot offspring from her. And what did Pandora do? She opened her famous box and released all evils into the world, evils that still torment us today.

"All lies are female, incarnated in the goddess Apate, whom we call Fraus, since she is the mother of trickery and fraud. And in this way, from Pandora to Fraus to the present day, woman brings not only misfortune, but, in the case at hand, falsehoods and lies. Minerva lied to Ulysses when he finally reached Ithaca, telling him that Penelope had taken another husband. And only when wise Ulysses discovered that the person speaking to him was Minerva in disguise did she stop lying and tell the truth. It is woman's inclination to lie. Even goddesses do so. By all the gods: even the Trojan War was the fault of a woman! Is that all the prosecution has to present us with, another fraudulent testimony?"

Caesar remained silent. The argument was unexpected and he could think of no rebuttal. He knew he had been betrayed, and he increasingly suspected that the traitor was a woman . . . perhaps even his own wife, who knew all the details that the lawyers for the defense had made use of. Talking to Cornelia always put his mind at ease; he'd shared everything with her. No, it couldn't be. His thoughts swirled and he had no words for Hortensius.

Hortensius was pleased to have left his opponent speechless. He then turned to Myrtale, whom he had yet to ask a single question. "When the governor arrived at your home, woman, what were you wearing?" the lawyer asked.

"What was I wearing?" Myrtale repeated, incredulous.

"Do we have another witness who is hard of hearing?" Hortensius turned to the audience. "It would seem that deafness plagues the Macedonians." He laughed, as did many of those present in the room, including almost all of the judges.

"I was wearing a tunic!" Myrtale shouted to make herself heard over the laughter.

Hortensius turned back to her. "She can see, hear, and even speak,"

he commented mockingly, to more laughter. But then his expression
turned grave. "Just a tunic? Is that the type of clothing with which a
young Macedonian woman typically receives men?"

"No, we would normally wear a mantle as well, like the *palla* I see
the Roman women wear when they leave home."

"But you were wearing only a simple tunic, and you opened the
door in that state," Hortensius insisted.

"It was the governor of Macedonia," Myrtale explained. "Should I
have refused entry to the governor sent by Rome to rule Thessaloniki? Is that what I should have done?" she added in a defiant tone.

Hortensius stood immobile before the witness.

There was silence in the room.

Caesar admired the young woman's integrity.

"Leave the questions to me, girl," said Hortensius. "The witness is
only required to respond. But since you asked, I shall give you an
answer: any woman who considers herself decent wouldn't have
opened the door in that state of undress—she'd have ordered her
slaves to admit the esteemed guest while she retired to her private
bedchamber to dress herself appropriately. That's what you should
have done, girl. Any decent woman would never have presented herself provocatively before the governor. But you chose to welcome
him in as a prostitute would, and like a harlot you gave yourself to
him, in an attempt to later falsely accuse him."

"If I gave myself to the governor like a harlot, he forgot to pay
me," Myrtale replied, once more with a boldness that surprised the
defense and everyone present in the room.

Caesar looked down. The girl's courage impressed him, but his
mind was on other matters. "They know everything," he said to Labienus quietly.

"Everything?"

"About how she was wearing little clothing when she let Dolabella
in," Caesar explained in a whisper. "I only told that to one person."

Labienus swallowed but did not answer.

Hortensius continued with the interrogation, now angry. He
wanted to wipe any vestige of defiance from the face of the young
woman who dared to challenge him in this hall of justice, his terri-

tory. "Was there any other man present when you received the governor?"

"No, but I couldn't leave the governor—"

Hortensius didn't let her finish. He barraged her with a torrent of accusations: "You received him half naked, alone, without a male chaperone, without your father, your brother, or any other male relative present. You wanted this to happen. You made it happen." He then turned to the public. "She bamboozled him, bewitched him, in an attempt to ruin the governor's reputation, as I've previously suggested, because this entire trial is a farce created by foreigners to discredit a Roman envoy. It is nothing more than a cry of rebellion. They pretend to follow our laws, but they are cunning, attempting to undermine our authority from within our system. They are much more dangerous this way than they would be on a battlefield, where our legions have already demolished them. So they try to destroy us here, in Rome, to bring our government down from the inside. And they do so aided by enemies of the Senate"—here he looked at Caesar—"who, whether out of perversion or naïvety, I don't know which is worse, assist them in their treachery, speaking for these liars here in the Roman Forum, in the Basilica Sempronia, in the very heart of our great city."

Myrtale opened her mouth to say that she hadn't had the chance to refuse the governor's entry into her home since he burst in, but Hortensius threw up both hands to silence her. She was overwhelmed at having to defend her honor all alone before so many people.

"A woman. A girl, no less," Hortensius continued. "A woman must not only be chaste, but also appear to be."

"That man raped me!" Myrtale shouted desperately, pointing at Dolabella. "He raped me and ruined my life," she said, tears in her eyes.

Hortensius, merciless, leaned over her, sprinkling her face with spittle as he now shouted, "All lies! Falsehoods, crocodile tears intended to manipulate us!" He bent closer to speak into her ear as if he were telling her a secret, but spoke loudly, so that everyone could hear: "Tears will do you no good here." He straightened and addressed the tribunal. "One purchased witness, another one senile, and now a harlot. These have been the testimonies presented by the prosecution."

Myrtale was sobbing.

The judges frowned down at her.

Pompey then looked up. It was getting late. He would end the trial for the day.

Caesar glared at Cornelia.

LIII

BETRAYED BY
YOUR BELOVED

Rome, 77 B.C.

CAESAR STORMED FROM THE BASILICA SEMPRONIA ALL THE way home to the Suburra almost without seeing, his eyes bulging and his jaw clenched with the fury he held in his guts.

Labienus rushed to keep up, and they did not speak a single word the whole way there. He had never seen Caesar so furious.

They reached the Julia family domus and the young pater familias burst into the atrium like a lion in a *venatio.* But this fierce beast was not going to be hunted down and killed for the public's entertainment, at least not at the moment. He was the one on the hunt.

"Where is she?" he demanded of one of the slaves, who looked confused. Not even Labienus knew whom his friend wanted to see, as he repeated once again, "Where is she?"

Labienus began to understand, finally, why Caesar had been staring into the audience during the trial: his friend thought that someone in his own domus had betrayed him by leaking information to Dolabella's defense. And, Labienus was now almost certain, the person his friend suspected was his own wife.

"By all the gods!" Caesar boomed. "Where is Cornelia?"

The slaves didn't know how to respond.

"What are you going to do?" Labienus asked. He didn't believe Cornelia capable of betraying Caesar, and he couldn't see how her husband could even think such a thing.

Caesar was blind with rage. He stormed through every room, finding them all empty. "Cornelia!" he shouted. "She knew everything. I told her everything. I talked to her about each and every one of my witnesses in the trial and she . . . she . . ." he said by way of explanation, not finishing the thought.

Labienus remained silent. He was processing this information.

Caesar turned back to the slaves.

"The master's mother, sisters, and wife have not yet returned from the forum," the atriense said. "They said that they would stop to look in on mistress Cornelia's mother on the way back from the trial, since she seems to have fallen ill . . ."

"Well send someone, have her brought to me!" Caesar yelled, stopping short of hitting the poor slave who had knelt before her furious master.

"What's going on?" Cornelia's voice echoed across the atrium. "Why are you shouting for me?" she asked innocently.

Her soothing tone calmed him slightly.

She was still walking toward him, trustingly. "Aurelia decided to sit awhile longer with my mother, who is unwell. But I wanted to get back quickly because I saw how bad a time you had in the basilica today, and I wanted to be with you as soon as possible. Your sisters are with me."

At that moment, as if to verify what she'd just said, Caesar's sisters appeared in the atrium, alarmed by the anger on their brother's face. In her infinite love for Caesar, her youth and innocence, in her devotion and loyalty to him, Cornelia was unable to see the rage that he felt toward her at that moment. She was incapable of imagining that he could ever suspect her of betrayal, much less that he'd want to do her any harm. She saw that he was angry, furious—that was obvious—but she believed it to be over the disastrous day in trial.

"What's wrong, Gaius?" she asked innocently, finally intuiting that she was missing something.

"What's wrong? Do you really have to ask what's wrong?" he repeated, pacing around the atrium and gesticulating until stopping in front of her. "You didn't see it?"

"What should I have seen?" she asked, very serious, nervous.

"My witnesses, one after the other, discredited by the defense, who knew everything about them," Caesar explained. "Everything."

Cornelia sat on the edge of a triclinium.

"They knew everything, Cornelia. They knew things that I only told you."

Silence.

Thick. Dense. Labienus was afraid of what his friend might do.

Cornelia only feared what Caesar might think of her.

"And you think that I've betrayed you, that I've told those things to Dolabella's lawyers?" the young woman asked, with tears in her eyes.

Caesar, scowling, moved closer to her.

Labienus stepped in front of him. "You're upset. You don't know what you're saying."

"Get out of the way," Caesar snapped. "This is between me and my wife."

Labienus held his friend's gaze for a long moment and then, against his better judgment, stepped aside, still ready to intervene if necessary.

Caesar crouched down in front of Cornelia and looked her in the eye. "No," he said, his voice surprisingly composed but icy, charged with controlled rage. "I don't think that you went and deliberately spoke with Dolabella's lawyers. I don't think you've knowingly betrayed me. How could I think that?"

She nodded, crying silently from the stress of the situation but now somewhat relieved. "You don't think I intentionally betrayed you, but you think that somehow, somewhere, I said something about your witnesses and it reached the ears of Dolabella's lawyers and that's why all your testimonies were destroyed today in trial. That's what you think."

Caesar sighed and nodded. "Yes, that's what I think."

She nodded again as the tears ran down her cheeks. "I haven't talked to anyone about what you told me," she assured him, as she mentally recounted all the conversations she'd had in recent days, thinking about what she'd said and to whom.

"Think about it, Cornelia," Caesar said sternly, his rage now beginning to fade. Seeing her so frightened and upset, feeling responsible for his failure, melted his anger. He felt ire mixed with compassion. Rage with love. Disappointment with understanding.

Cornelia thought... "No, I haven't talked to anyone about the witnesses," the girl said, but then she seemed to remember something. "Unless..."

"Unless what... what?" Caesar grabbed her by the arms, not aggressively, but merely to coax the answer from her.

Cornelia's mind was racing. Everything suddenly fit into place, but the full picture was too terrible. She couldn't say what she was thinking so she tried to come up with an alternative. "Unless one of the slaves heard us talking..." she suggested, to buy time as she thought about whether her suspicions could really be true. "Yes, maybe one of the slaves overheard us, like when we used to listen to our fathers as kids, remember?"

"Like when we found out we were going to be married," Caesar said.

"Something like that."

Still crouched beside his wife, Caesar looked around: the atriense and other slaves were present in the atrium.

"Do you think one of the slaves is spying on us? Do you think, Cornelia, that I should question them one by one until the traitor confesses?"

Caesar rose.

Caesar was taken aback by the notion of betrayal among the slaves in his home, who were much better off than they would be with most families. The family never punished anyone unjustly, and when his father died, they had freed several of the older slaves by Caesar Sr.'s express wishes. They even paid their slaves generously, allowing them to save up to buy their freedom, an arrangement that had always worked well. But maybe, if his wife agreed, he should interrogate them... Cornelia was shaking her head. He crouched back down beside her.

The girl would not allow any injustice to take place. "No, I don't think it was the slaves," she muttered. "I don't think it was any of them. They are very loyal to you, I'm certain."

The atriense and the rest of the servants breathed sighs of relief, impressed that their young mistress had defended them when it would have been easier to let suspicions fall squarely upon them.

Caesar spoke to his wife: "You know more than you're saying. You know who betrayed me. You talked to someone. To who? Someone in the forum? At the market? Did you tell your mother about the trial during one of your visits? Or one of the senators? One of my uncle Marius's former guards? Who did you talk to, Cornelia? If it wasn't one of the slaves, you must've talked to someone about all this. Why are you keeping quiet? Who are you protecting?" He took her again by the arms, gripping her tightly, not to harm her but simply to transmit his rage over her silence.

And she understood that he would not stop questioning her until he received an answer. But the truth was too horrifying to say aloud, so she remained silent, tears still in her eyes.

"Who did you talk to, Cornelia? By all the gods! I'm not blaming you, but you have to tell me! Who did you tell about the witnesses? Who?"

"She told me," came a voice from behind him.

Caesar turned and saw the straight-backed, poised figure of his mother standing between the columns of the atrium. He dropped his young wife's arms, stood, and stared at Aurelia, confused and bewildered.

Aurelia handed her palla to the atriense, who was glad that the mistress had arrived to set things straight. "Cornelia told me the details of Myrtale's abuse," Aurelia explained coldly, calmly. "I saw that you were worried, so I asked your wife and she told me of your concerns over having Myrtale testify. You feared they might find out that she received Dolabella alone and wearing what a Roman tribunal would consider inappropriate attire. I've witnessed Orestes's deterioration, his forgetfulness, here in this atrium, during the meals we've shared with him. And I know how your trip to Macedonia with Labienus and Marcus the engineer was financed. I had all that information and I shared it with Dolabella's lawyers. With my brother, your uncle, it's true."

Aurelia asked a slave for water. "I can't believe you'd ever think

Cornelia might speak of your witnesses to anyone she didn't trust completely," Aurelia continued. "The girl worships the ground you walk on, Gaius. By all the gods, Cornelia is smart and loyal to you beyond anything imaginable! She's not capable of letting something like that slip. How could that girl talk to anyone but me about something as delicate as your witnesses' weak spots?"

Caesar sat on a triclinium.

Just then, the voice of a young child rang out across the courtyard: "Mama, Mama!"

Little Julia, trailed closely by her nursemaid, rushed to her mother and hugged her.

"All the shouting frightened her, domina, and she got away from me," the slave explained.

Cornelia hugged her daughter without saying a word.

"Get up, little one, go to your room and wait for your husband; take your daughter with you," Aurelia ordered Cornelia.

Cornelia nodded, still stunned, and ushered her daughter out of the atrium. Aurelia then addressed the slaves and Labienus: "Everyone out, back to your *cubicula* or to your work. You too, Labienus. Go home. Tomorrow is a new day, and my son will need you to aid him in trial, as you always do." She sighed before adding, "That cursed, unending trial."

Everyone dispersed.

Aurelia didn't usually give instructions in her son's presence, but when she did, as long as Caesar himself did not contradict her, everyone obeyed. She spoke with an air of authority that made her orders indisputable.

Caesar was silent.

Aurelia and her son were alone in the atrium. For a long moment, she stood over him as he sat, the only sound the crackle of the torches that the slaves had lit.

"Punish me if you wish," said Aurelia.

"And how would I do such a thing, Mother?"

She sighed and took a seat beside him.

They both seemed drained and defeated.

"Why did you do it?"

Aurelia stood, turned around, and looked away from him as she spoke, something unusual for her. She began to walk around the atrium as she explained herself.

"I was trying to save you. If you win this trial, they'll see you as the new leader of the popular faction, the new Marius. At first I was only worried about your losing the trial. I knew you'd damage your political career if you lost, and that saddened me, but it was your decision to take on the role as prosecutor. You were terrible in the divinatio, but I later realized that you were only pretending to be incompetent so they'd select you as prosecutor. Then, in the *reiectio,* with your powerful speech that convinced Metellus to recuse himself, I saw that you could disrupt the tribunal, even though they've all been bought off by Dolabella. It was very unlikely, highly improbable, but I no longer thought it impossible that you might win the trial. You had good witnesses, and you were going to uncover many weak spots in Dolabella's defense. So to keep you from getting too close to victory, I had a secret meeting with the defense, and I gave my brother enough information to discredit your witnesses. Which he did. Now I know you won't win, but it's too late. I saw how Dolabella looked at you today. It's the same look he had in his eyes during the reiectio. He's already condemned you to death, and he's just waiting for the end of this horrible, cursed trial that's driving us all mad, making me betray you, causing you to doubt Cornelia, who's more loyal to you than anyone in the world. It will probably be the death of you, all for what? For nothing. I betrayed you because I thought it would save you, but I was too late. Dolabella is going to come for you as soon as he can. I've only hurt you, Cornelia, everyone. It was wrong of me."

Aurelia sat on a solium. Her throat was dry and she needed water, which she'd asked for when she first arrived, but she'd instructed everyone to leave, and her final order had prevailed. She didn't want to call the slave back in now.

"You were wrong to betray me, Mother. And I was wrong to suspect Cornelia. Neither one of us has behaved with honor."

"No, neither one," she agreed.

Caesar stood, moved to another seat closer to his mother, and rubbed his face.

"What are you going to do, son?"

"I'm going to rest and think about all this. You're right, this trial is driving us all mad and causing strife among us—between my uncle Cotta and me, you and me, Cornelia and me. I need to relax and try to clear my mind." He looked into his mother's eyes. "I take it that I should expect no more betrayals, Mother?"

"If you can find some way to win this trial, I won't try to stand in your way. I won't be the one to reveal anything else to anyone."

"Good. I'm going to lie down . . . and apologize to Cornelia." He stood up, walked over to his mother, and bent to give her a kiss on the forehead. "Goodnight. Thank you for trying to save me." Then he added quietly, almost whispering, "I'll survive this, you'll see. You raised me to be victorious." He walked away, but as he was about to leave the atrium, he turned back to her. "I've been condemned to death before, Mother, remember?"

"I remember," she answered. "By Sulla."

And he repeated: "By Sulla."

Caesar entered his bedroom to find Cornelia curled up on the bed still upset over everything that had happened. Their daughter had been taken away by the nursemaid, leaving Caesar and Cornelia alone.

He sat on the bed, not daring to touch her.

"I'm sorry," Caesar said. "There's nothing I can say or do to reverse the way I've treated you today."

Cornelia, sitting on the bed, hugged her knees to her chest.

"You once risked your life for me," she said.

"Yes. By defying Sulla."

Everything always came back to Sulla.

"Do you still love me that much?" she asked.

It was not a proper question for a Roman matrona to ask her husband, but their marriage—both of them so young, especially her—was unconventional, at least where emotions were concerned. They felt deep love and endless passion for each other. It was normal in Rome for a woman to marry as a teenager, practically still a girl, to a man of thirty or forty, but she had married a young man, barely out of his teens himself. And they had truly fallen in love.

"Yes, I still love you just as much," he said. "I don't know what got into me earlier. My mother is right: I should never doubt you. You're too smart to discuss what I tell you with anyone outside the family. You could've never imagined that my mother would do what she did. It wasn't your fault."

"No, no one could've ever expected your mother to do that, even though I understand that she did it to protect you," Cornelia said.

"Yes, but even so, I should've never doubted you," Caesar said again. He brought his hands to his head.

She leaned over and moved his large, cold hands, placing instead her small, warm fingertips on her husband's temples.

"Is your head hurting again?" she asked in a soft voice.

"Yes. But your hands always help."

They sat that way for a while, Caesar on the edge of the bed, Cornelia kneeling on the sheets, half naked behind him, massaging his temples, relaxing him.

Caesar's headache melted away. They were becoming more and more frequent, but he hadn't seen a doctor about it.

"This trial is driving me crazy," Caesar said.

"No," she replied, still rubbing his temples. "No, my love, you were already crazy. Only a madman would have defied Sulla. You're a lunatic who thinks he has to stand up to every miserable criminal out there. That's why I love you."

Caesar sighed.

She continued massaging his head and speaking quietly into his ear. "You're twenty-three years old, but you're as wise as a man who's lived a hundred years, my love. With everything you've suffered, fought for, it's as if you've lived that long."

"I don't know . . . but it feels like it sometimes . . ." he said.

Caesar closed his eyes.

The trial was a lost cause. He'd been insane to have agreed to serve as prosecutor in the first place. Maybe, like Cornelia said, he was a lunatic. And he'd been through so much already . . .

Caesar relaxed as Cornelia's soothing fingertips eased his tension. His wife's faith in him remained unshaken. Cornelia was his refuge.

He kept his eyes closed. Yes . . . It all went back to Sulla, Dolabella's mentor . . . Sulla . . . Lucius Cornelius Sulla . . .

SULLA

*Mortal enemy of Gaius Marius
and Julius Caesar*

*Two-time consul
Dictator of Rome*

LIV

IN THE HANDS
OF THE GODS

Rome

Late 82 B.C.

Five years before Dolabella's trial

IT TOOK CORNELIA SEVERAL DAYS TO RECOVER FROM THE difficult childbirth. She was only fifteen years old, and it had been a traumatic experience. She had survived, but she was left drained. Exhausted. The events taking place in Rome were nothing to be cheerful about either.

Caesar, constantly at her side, gave her the bad news in small doses: Sulla's victory at Porta Collina was not the only thing that had happened during those terrible days. The popular faction had been destroyed, and its allies, the socii, defeated and forced to retreat. The crowning glory of the optimates' complete victory was that Praeneste, where Gaius Marius's son had taken refuge, had fallen to the conservative forces. The news was confusing, and it wasn't clear whether Marius Jr. had committed suicide or had been executed.

"Either way, he's dead," Caesar somberly declared.

But he decided to spare his recovering wife the latest rumor circulating through Rome: Sulla had asked for Marius Jr.'s head to be sent from Praeneste so that he could mount it on a spike in the forum, as he'd previously done with the head of Plebeian Tribune Sulpicius in his first military advance on Rome. Sulla had also decided to adopt the title of *Felix,* for his felicitous victory over all his enemies, the total defeat of the populares, and the fact that Rome was now under his complete control. The gesture made it clear there was no chance of reconciliation between the two parties.

Cornelia stood slowly, and, aided by Caesar, tried to walk from one side of the room to the other. "Gaius Marius is dead," she began. "His son is dead; your father and mine both dead. Sertorius, our last hope, has fled to Hispania, where he fights for survival. Sulla now rules the city with an iron fist. He has absolute power. We are trapped in Rome, Gaius, in *Sulla's* Rome. He'll come for us. He'll kill us. Because you are Gaius Marius's nephew and I am Cinna's daughter. And to top it off, we're married. He'll kill us all. Including our little Julia."

Caesar didn't know what to say. The thought of his newborn daughter's death caused the blood to freeze in his veins.

Aurelia had entered the room and heard her daughter-in-law's laments. She walked over and hugged the girl as she spoke. "Things are going to get difficult. Very. But we have to stay calm and remain unified. We are all alive and well. We'll find a way to survive this madness together."

The words seemed to soothe Cornelia as she moved from Aurelia's arms back into her husband's embrace. "You will protect us, Gaius," she said. "I don't know how, but I know you will. You descend from Aeneas. The gods will save you."

Caesar hugged her and closed his eyes.

He was overwhelmed by the task of protecting his wife, his mother, his daughter, and his sisters, but it was his unquestionable duty as pater familias. It mattered little that he was only eighteen and that Sulla was a tyrannical senator with all of Rome under his control. Standing up to him alone would be suicide. But with the gods on his side . . . Rome was now ruled by a man who hated the Julia family and everything they represented. Caesar was still but a young man, no match for the all-powerful Sulla. And yet Cornelia believed that the gods might aid him. He was a pious man, like all good Romans, but he wasn't sure if a few sacrifices would be enough to ward off Sulla's insatiable lust for violence.

Caesar's mind whirled.

Sulla had won control of the largest Roman army ever through bribery. He had then purchased the loyalty of the second army sent to defeat Mithridates, as he did again with the army Cinna had recruited. The Samnites had been massacred at Porta Collina and Marius Jr.'s troops annihilated at Praeneste. There were no armed forces left to stand up to Sulla. But there was still the army of the gods. Or rather, the representatives of their divine power here on earth.

One last army.

Cornelia had gotten to the crux of it.

And his uncle Marius, from wherever he was, still protected him.

"How clever of him," Caesar said.

"Who?" his mother and wife asked in unison.

Caesar looked at them with a gleam in his eyes. "Marius," he replied.

"Marius?" Cornelia asked, confused.

"We're not so alone," he said. "You're right, Cornelia: the gods will help us. Jupiter will help us."

LV

SULLA'S DICTATORSHIP

Roman Senate
82 B.C.

"**H**OW LONG WILL THIS DICTATORSHIP LAST?" ASKED
Dolabella. He was the only senator bold enough to question Sulla so
directly.

Sulla, from the center of the huge Curia Hostilia, did not take offense. In fact, it had been decided beforehand that his second-in-
command would raise the issue of his term limit as soon as Sulla
concluded his speech to the patres conscripti. This would give Sulla
the opportunity to make it abundantly clear that he did not plan to
relinquish his absolute power over Rome, ever.

"What do you mean, 'how long will this dictatorship last?'" Sulla
boomed from the center of the room. Then he smiled before answering. "I will remain dictator for as long as necessary."

And with that, the meeting of the Senate was concluded.

That is to say, Sulla decided he had said enough for that morning.
They could continue the next day. He planned to submit the Senate
to as many sessions as it took to pass new laws and take control over
each and every state institution in Rome. Tirelessly. Systematically.
But that morning a lovely gift had arrived from Praeneste and was
now on display in the forum. He was eager to see it. He couldn't wait.

As the senators filed out to see his "gift," Sulla relived his meteoric
rise to power. Emerging from among the ranks of the optimates, he
had become their unequivocal leader, making ingenious political and

military maneuvers to ensure that the popular faction had been reduced to nothing. And now he controlled everything.

Sulla smiled: he'd started off as one of Marius's lieutenants in Africa, his quaestor, then rose to military tribune in the war against the Cimbri and the Teutons, before becoming praetor of Rome, governor of Cilicia, and a celebrated commander in the war against the socii. Finally he was named consul. That was more than most men even aspired to. But his military and political career had been unstoppable as he'd won control of the Roman troops over Marius, then marched the legions against Rome to knock the populares from power and take total command of the troops that would stop Mithridates, the fearsome King of Pontus, from taking control of Greece and beyond. While it was true that Marius and his ally Cinna had taken advantage of his absence to install a popular government in Rome, first Marius's death and then Sulla's return from the East after having come to an agreement with the King of Pontus had led to the populares' eventual loss of power when they were defeated in the brutal civil war. Yes, things had worked out very well for him.

Sulla had now declared himself absolute dictator of Rome.

And he was determined to root out any remaining semblance of popular resistance so that no one would ever again talk of extending the rights of citizenship and the vote to the allied cities or to the people of the lower social orders who were not aligned with the more conservative senators.

Dictatorships were not the norm. Gaius Servilius had been named dictator for a brief period during the Second Punic War, but for over a century, there had been no other dictator in the Roman Republic. Hence the patres conscripti's surprise.

But Sulla wore a wide smile as he left the Senate building chatting with the other senators: "We will now be the ones to decide what happens in Rome," he said. Everyone, even his most staunch supporters, knew what he really meant: he and he alone would determine the fate of Rome. "It's a new order . . . a new reality."

Silence.

No opposition. Not a hint of dissent. Fear makes men go mute.

They all dutifully followed him outside.

There, proudly displayed in the center of the forum for all Romans to see, was Marius Jr.'s head mounted on a spike.

Sulla approached slowly, savoring the moment. He'd defiled Marius's ashes and now he'd had his son's head cut off and exhibited before him. Sulla knew what he had to do: he had to celebrate.

"First learn to row, before you try to steer,"* he said, laughing, as he turned around and began walking home, practically weeping with joy. His worst enemy, Gaius Marius, was gone. He had now done away with his son as well. It was a moment to be celebrated.

Sulla's domus, Rome

"What steps are you planning to take now?" Dolabella asked as they walked to Sulla's domus. He wanted to find out how far Sulla would go to instate a new regime, one fully in line with the ideas of the most conservative optimates.

"We will start by overturning the populares' laws, one by one, in the Senate," Sulla explained. "But we mustn't forget about the judiciary."

"The judiciary?"

"Citizens of the equestrian class† or even lower orders are currently allowed to sit on tribunals, meaning we optimates, if we happen to be brought to trial for something, are often judged by ignorant jurors unfavorable to the senatorial class. We will reform the judiciary system so that our government, our administration, our legislation, our senators, can never be brought to trial, and, if it happens, exoneration is all but guaranteed." Sulla smiled.

"And how do you plan to make things so easy for us?" Dolabella asked, doubtful.

"I will pass a law stating that only senators may sit on a tribunal of justice," he said, taking confident strides.

---

* As quoted by Appian of Alexandria, *Roman History, The Civil Wars,* Book I, Chapter X, paragraph 94.

† Members of the equestrian class, also known as *equites,* ranked just below the senatorial class in wealth.

Dolabella could only admire Sulla's audacity. The new dictator of Rome aimed to reduce all their problems to nothing. He began to understand that his mentor was planning to annihilate any remaining Roman institution that could possibly oppose the new regime, this new reality that he'd mentioned that very morning.

"There's still Sertorius," Dolabella pointed out, keeping pace alongside Sulla.

"It's true, Sertorius is a nuisance, but we will deal with him in due time. For now, he's far away, hiding out in Hispania. I'll send someone to take care of him. Maybe Metellus, who's so eager to receive a triumph. If he could defeat Sertorius in Hispania, he might finally be able to live up to his father's name." Sulla seemed to be speaking more to himself than to Dolabella. "Yes, I'll send Metellus to deal with him. I'm more concerned with the loose ends I have to tie up here in Rome."

They reached Sulla's domus and Dolabella arranged himself comfortably on a triclinium beside the dictator of Rome before asking about those loose ends, which had piqued his curiosity: "What is there still left to tie up?"

The slaves were passing around trays of meats in fragrant sauces. The wine flowed abundantly.

Sulla did not respond.

Or rather, he did not respond with words. Instead, he looked to his right, toward the triclinium where his daughter Emilia and his son-in-law Acilius Glabrio lay enjoying his hospitality. Emilia was his stepdaughter, daughter of Cecilia Metella, the dictator's recently deceased wife. But Sulla had raised the girl as if she were his own blood. Not out of any special fondness for her, but because that was expected of a stepfather according to traditional Roman customs. Her husband, Acilius Glabrio, was a young senator with a promising political career ahead of him, especially now that his father-in-law had become the self-appointed dictator of Rome. But Sulla's eyes now fell on him.

Dolabella, who understood what his mentor was thinking, nodded and remained silent. Acilius had dared to criticize his father-in-law for proclaiming himself dictator without providing the customary limit to his term.

Most conservatives agreed that ending the popular rule in Rome
called for a firm hand, but many felt that the dictatorship should only
last for a specified period of time. No one dared, however, to make
such criticisms public after seeing how ruthless Sulla had been with
his enemies, executing the populares by the hundreds and counting.
Anyone who defied Sulla saw their property seized immediately,
confiscations becoming the order of the day. Dolabella had dared to
ask Sulla about the duration of the dictatorship, but that had been
agreed upon ahead of time with Sulla himself. Acilius, for his part,
although a conservative—if not, Sulla would've never allowed him to
wed his stepdaughter—was suspicious of a dictatorship. The title
that Sulla had arrogantly bestowed upon himself summed up his
powers: *dictator legibus scribundis et rei publicae constituendae,* meaning a
dictator who could pass laws and reorganize the government as he
saw fit. Absolute power. Without any mention of a term limit to said
power.

"Acilius," Sulla said.

Dolabella knew that tone well. He arched his eyebrows and sighed
as he looked into the bottom of his cup. Acilius's future no longer
looked so bright: the young man had mistakenly believed he could
criticize Sulla simply because he was married to his stepdaughter.

"Acilius," Sulla said again, irritated at having to repeat himself.

"Yes . . . Father," Acilius answered.

Sulla smiled.

"Do you think, because you now call me Father, that you are safe?"

A hush fell over the room.

The guests stopped eating and drinking.

The slaves froze like statues; the only sound was a fountain inside
the residence. Sulla's harsh tone had immobilized everyone.

"I don't understand . . ." Acilius began, but Emilia's hand on his
arm stopped him.

She knew that it was unwise to challenge her stepfather, and especially so in the presence of guests. Anything her husband said would
only make things worse.

"Do you believe, Acilius, that a son should publicly criticize a father over political matters?" Sulla asked.

Acilius pulled away from Emilia, severing his tie to his only supporter. She curled up on the triclinium as if trying to distance herself
from her husband and avoid her stepfather's ire.

The young man now understood where all this was going, but he
thought his father-in-law was overreacting.

"Perhaps I did not express my doubts over this . . . dictatorship in
the proper place, but I think that specifying a term limit—"

"Do you think your opinion matters, boy?" Sulla interrupted.
Acilius, despite his youth, was still a Roman senator, and Sulla was
being intentionally insulting. "By Jupiter, no, it does not matter at all.
If you had dared to be so impertinent in private, I could have at least
reprimanded you in private. But you criticized me publicly. Do you
need reminding that mere weeks ago the populares ruled Rome at
their will? It took a long civil war to restore control to those of us
ordained by god to rule this city, this republic, and its provinces. I
won't allow any criticism, much less from members of my own family.
If there's one thing we optimates need now, it is unity. And you have
broken it." Sulla paused, took his time to finish his cup of wine in
dense silence, and finally rendered his sentence: "Stand up and leave,
Acilius, and never return to this domus."

The young man's mouth fell open. He was still lying on the triclinium beside his wife, and he looked at her and then to his father-
in-law.

"Consider yourself officially divorced," Sulla said.

Acilius, looking shocked, slowly stood.

"She's pregnant," he announced. "We were going to tell you tonight."

Sulla held his empty cup out and a slave rushed over to refill it. He
took another long drink, set his cup on the table, and fixed his eyes on
Acilius.

"Well, boy, you've told me," he said. "Now leave. And consider
yourself fortunate that you are the father of my stepdaughter Emilia's
future child; it is the only thing saving your life. Now go, by Jupiter,
out of my home, for good!"

Acilius Glabrio, without so much as saying goodbye to his wife,
exited the atrium, dumbstruck by his unexpected fall from grace.

The tension subsided after Acilius left; the guests returned to their food and wine and the musicians broke into lively song in an attempt to lighten the mood of the long *comissatio* around the banquet table. Everyone relaxed. Only Emilia stared sullenly at the floor. She loved Acilius. Her now ex-husband's criticism of Sulla had been reasonable but poorly timed. She was now pregnant, divorced, without a father for her child. And terrified. She sat in silence.

"Do you think you were a bit, let's say . . . harsh with Acilius?" Dolabella dared to ask. "After all, he is . . . well, *was,* family."

"No, my friend. I was not too harsh at all. It's only practical, from a political point of view," Sulla argued. "If I am this tough on dissent within my own family, everyone outside my family will think twice before disagreeing with me, especially in public."

"Without a doubt," Dolabella admitted as he nodded for a slave to serve him more wine. "So, does that tie up all the loose ends?"

Once more, Sulla did not respond out loud—he now had a stepdaughter to marry off. He still had to formalize the divorce, of course, but that could be taken care of the very next day. What mattered was that Emilia was . . . available. A perfect opportunity to seal a new, more useful political alliance. Sulla had very loyal followers, such as Dolabella, but there were other Roman eagles flying too high. It would be better to tie a few of them down. A marriage could do the trick.

Dolabella watched as the dictator slowly turned his head and stopped when he came to one of his guests of honor, Pompey, lying on a nearby triclinium.

He mentally reviewed the events and actions he'd already given so much thought to. Pompey was a young senator in stunning ascent. Punishing on the battlefield, he had earned the nickname *adulescentulus carcifex,* the "adolescent butcher," for his brutal and ruthless performance in the war against the socii. The young patrician had limitless ambition, and Sulla wanted to keep him on his side to ensure that he could enjoy his final years in peace. Organizing Rome around a dominant order of optimate senators required strong, implacable leaders whose pulse did not quicken when called upon to punish, execute, or even charge into battle if necessary. In the recent civil disputes, Pompey had been wise enough to position himself squarely on Sulla's side, skillfully and efficiently commanding three legions against the populares' troops. But unlike the majority of those in attendance and the optimates in general, Pompey did not come from a noble lineage: his father had been a *homo novus,* the first of his bloodline to become a senator. Joining Sulla's family would constitute a huge boost for Pompey's career and ensure a very promising cursus honorum as he rose among the ranks of the conservative senators.

Pompey, feeling Sulla's eyes on him, held his gaze, not arrogant, only attentive. It was as if he could read his mind. And, he had to admit, Sulla's thoughts aligned with many of his own objectives. But, always cautious in the presence of the commanding dictator, he waited to hear Sulla's proposal.

"You, Gnaeus Pompey, will wed my daughter Emilia."

Sulla did not wait for acceptance. He looked away from the man he had chosen as his future son-in-law and turned to the slaves to loudly order more wine and food to celebrate the wedding that was soon to take place. He said nothing about the fact that Pompey was already married.

Emilia sighed. She felt nothing for the man her stepfather had chosen, but being wed to one of his closest allies would at least provide her some security. The child she carried inside her would be protected and that put her mind at ease.

Pompey took a sip of wine. He had not accepted Sulla's proposal, but it was clear that the dictator would not allow him to reject it. He was already married, to Antistia. It had not been a love match, at least not at first. Pompey had been accused of corruption and misappropriation of funds in the distribution of the spoils from the sacking of Asculum. He could've found himself in dire straits since, in fact, the allocation had not followed all the formalities of Roman law and custom. He therefore chose the easier route and, before the trial began, courted and married Antistia, daughter of the president of the tribunal set to try him.

Pompey took a drink of wine as he thought of that well-planned marriage and how it had ensured he was absolved of all charges. Later, it was true: to his surprise, he had begun to care for the girl, who had always been a good wife. He didn't want to set her aside. And, of course, it was not fair to do so. On the other hand, opposing Sulla could be the beginning of the end for him.

Gnaeus Pompey raised his cup and his voice: "To the happy union between me and Emilia, daughter of Lucius Cornelius Sulla, dictator and savior of Rome!"

"I'll drink to that!" Sulla answered, raising his cup.

The guests imitated his gesture, lifting their cups high.

Everyone seemed joyful.

Antistia was not present.

Pompey looked down. He would not return home that night. He would stay at a friend's domus and communicate his written request for divorce to Antistia in the morning. Women were so emotional in certain matters, and Pompey did not feel like having to endlessly explain himself. Antistia would have to leave the house, and he would return to the domus in a few weeks, perhaps with his new wife Emilia already in tow.

"That's it then?" Dolabella asked Sulla quietly. "Have you now tied up all the loose ends?"

Sulla shook his head.

"No," he said, "there's one more, but he's not here."

"Who?" Dolabella inquired.

"Caesar."

Dolabella furrowed his brow, truly surprised. "Caesar? Gaius Julius Caesar? That boy? He's nobody. He has yet to make a name for himself in any military campaign, he's never participated in a single trial . . . We don't even know if he can speak. Are you truly worried about him? How old is he, nineteen?"

"Eighteen," said Sulla, who had carefully studied the young man in question. "And he's flamen Dialis," he added.

"Who cares about a flamen Dialis?" Dolabella asked, worried that Sulla was becoming paranoid in his old age. "He's just a priest; he has no political power at all."

"It's a prestigious position as far as the people are concerned, as far as everyone is concerned," Sulla argued.

"Well, he was appointed by Marius and Cinna. If that's your concern, you could remove him from the post. You have all the power now. Limitless. You'd simply have to give the order and he'd no longer be high priest of Jupiter."

"That's not good enough," Sulla said, very serious.

The other guests were talking among themselves, not paying attention to the conversation between Sulla and Dolabella. Dolabella listened carefully to his mentor. He was trying to determine whether he was still the brilliant man he had learned so much from or if he was in fact losing his good sense. If that was the case, it might now be his moment . . . but Sulla continued.

"No, stripping him of his post is not enough. In fact, I'd prefer to bring him into the fold, to our side. Like we've just done with Pompey. I will order Caesar to divorce Cinna's daughter and marry some young patrician girl from an optimate family closer to our . . . way of seeing things."

Dolabella tilted his head and sighed before making a final judgment on Sulla's words: "I think you're overreacting."

"No I'm not," the dictator insisted. "Caesar is Gaius Marius's nephew. No one yet knows what he's capable of. I want him with us. Not against us."

Dolabella nodded a few times. Marius was still a legend in Rome. And it was true, after the death of Marius's son, Gaius Julius Caesar was his only relevant family member left alive. Sulla didn't seem to be losing his good sense. He simply wanted to remain cautious and anticipate future dangers. His cleverness and intuition had helped him seize control of Rome, after all.

"Maybe you're right," Dolabella admitted. He took a drink of wine as a doubt crept into his mind: "But what if Marius's young nephew, this Gaius Julius Caesar, refuses to divorce his wife?"

Sulla said only one word as he turned his palms up: "Then . . ." He didn't need to finish the sentence.

Dolabella did not require further clarification.

LVI

CAESAR'S DIVORCE

Julia family domus
82 B.C.
A few days after Sulla's feast

"AGREE TO IT," CORNELIA SAID. SHE WAS SITTING IN A CORNER curled up like a frightened animal but spoke in a surprisingly calm tone for a distressed fifteen-year-old girl. "Agree to it," she repeated, then buried her face in her hands to muffle a sob.

Her words said she was releasing Caesar, but her gestures, her body, her tears, begged him not to leave her.

With his father, his uncle Marius, and his father-in-law Cinna all dead, the eighteen-year-old Caesar had no trusted older man to advise him. Gathered in the Julia domus were Cornelia, his best friend Labienus, his uncle Aurelius Cotta, and his mother. There was much debate over what Caesar should do.

Sulla had sent a soldier to convey an order: Caesar was to present himself at the domus of Rome's dictator. The messenger had been asked to wait for the boy, who was expected to comply immediately. There was no mystery as to the meeting's subject, since the message had been quite clear. "Lucius Cornelius Sulla requires the presence of the young Gaius Julius Caesar to discuss his divorce from Cornelia, daughter of the criminal Cinna, and his new marital bond to a patrician girl more appropriate to his personal relevance," the messenger had said. He stood waiting, still as a statue in the center of the atrium, as Caesar wished more than ever for a proper pater familias strong enough to reject the pressures of this unjust dictator. Or experienced enough, at least, to know how to act as prudently as possible.

Young Caesar stood beside Cornelia and rested his hand on her shoulder.

"Answer his summons and agree to the divorce," she said. "I don't want them to hurt you," she added, now with more conviction.

Aurelia looked at her son: even the great Scipio Africanus, who had to take charge of his family at a young age, had been twenty-five when he'd been burdened with the responsibility of pater familias. Caesar was only eighteen and up against the all-powerful Lucius Cornelius Sulla. Without his father, his father-in-law, or his uncle Marius, what could he do but blindly obey the dictator? Which was what her brother Aurelius Cotta had advised him.

"The boy must do as Sulla demands. He has no choice."

Aurelia knew it was the logical course of action. And yet she could see the blazing fury behind her son's icy gaze, and she knew that his indomitable, rebellious spirit would likely drive him into a confrontation with Sulla. One he could not win. She had raised her son to always stand firm in his convictions ... But she'd never expected him to be tested so severely at such a young age. Or against such a formidable foe.

"What do you think I should do, Mother?" Caesar asked.

Aurelia nodded, but did not answer. She circled the atrium lost in thought: if she had poisoned Cornelia when she'd had the chance, everything would be so much simpler now. But the girl had been pregnant and she was now the mother of Caesar's daughter. Also, Cornelia had always been steadfast in her loyalty. Eliminating her was no longer an option. For better or worse—much worse, as was now the case—Cornelia was a part of the Julia family. Everything had to be handled differently.

She turned to the centurion messenger still waiting in the atrium: "My son will answer Sulla's summons, but he needs to prepare himself for such an audience," she said in a submissive tone, but with the authority of a seasoned domina. "We would like some privacy. I suppose it wouldn't be too much trouble for you to wait in the street for a few minutes, would it?"

The soldier considered the request. He had received clear instructions and would not let himself be manipulated. He hesitated.

"You have a weapon, centurion, and it is in plain sight," continued Caesar's mother. "In plain sight of the flamen Dialis. That is sacrilege. Do you not fear the gods?"

The officer remained silent, but he covered his gladius with his cape so that it was no longer visible.

"I can stand outside for a moment," he said. "But an entire century of soldiers waits in the street and there is no door that will block us if Sulla's summons is not answered immediately."

"He'll answer," Cornelia said. "Now please..." she gestured toward the door.

The officer saluted them with a fist to his chest, turned around, and left. The slaves closed the door behind him and secured it with a thick crossbar that, nonetheless, as the centurion had warned, would be utterly insufficient against eighty armed men should they wish to enter.

"We only have a few minutes," Aurelia said, looking in turn at everyone present. "We have to make the most of them."

She had their full attention. Cornelia seemed to snap out of her state of despair as a gleam of hope crept into her wide eyes.

"Gaius," Aurelia began, moving closer to her son, "you must appear before Sulla. I will look after Cornelia, don't worry. But you can't go to Sulla's house alone." She turned then to Labienus. "This is the moment that will test your friendship. Will you accompany my son to his audience with Sulla? It will be dangerous. Perhaps even deadly."

"I will do it," he said without hesitation. If his dearest friend Caesar was brave enough to stand up to Sulla, he would stand alongside him, even if it cost him his life. Better to die standing than kneeling before this vile and greedy dictator.

"Good." Aurelia turned to her brother. "You have given your opinion and it is logical: Gaius should agree to divorce Cornelia and marry whomever Sulla chooses for him. But Caesar"—she turned to her son—"will do whatever he thinks best, what his head and his heart tell him to do. I would venture to guess that he's going to say no, for two reasons: because I raised him to never bow down to anyone, and because . . . because the boy is in love with Cornelia. She has proven herself forever loyal and it is only proper and fair that he repay her loyalty with his own."

She moved over to her daughter-in-law. "Don't worry, little one: Sulla has not yet started killing women and children. Not because he doesn't want to, but because it would make him too unpopular. He may confiscate our lands, money, and possessions. He may make our lives miserable. But we have many friends in Rome. We will survive, don't worry." She turned back to Caesar. "You will have to leave the city. You'll take the money, everything we have in the house."

"Mother, no. You'll need the gold and sesterce," Caesar began, but Aurelia interjected.

"No, my son, you're going to need it much more than we will. I'm sure of that. As soon as you disobey Sulla's orders, if that's what you decide to do, those soldiers waiting outside will return to strip the house of everything valuable. It would be better for you to take it. I know you'll put it to good use." She paused and sighed. "May the gods protect you, my son. Never forget that you descend from Aeneas. Be brave but not rash. Be just, but not foolish. Remember your uncle Marius's advice. It doesn't matter if they call you a coward. All that matters is that you win in the end. Now there is nothing more to say. They're waiting for you. And they're getting impatient. Go lightly."

Gaius Julius Caesar nodded his head.

"Not everything has been said, Mother. There's one more thing." He knelt beside Cornelia as she sat crumpled on the floor crying. "I have to say goodbye to you, Cornelia. Listen to me. What my mother says is true: I love you, with all my heart, and I will always love you. Whatever happens, whatever you hear, remember that." He stood up and walked quickly to his mother's *cubiculum,* where he collected several sacks of gold and silver coins that they kept in the house, regretting that the rest of it was at their villa outside the city which would soon be confiscated by Sulla.

"I'm going with you," Labienus said when Caesar returned to the atrium.

Caesar smiled. A loyal friend was worth more than gold. But money was useful. Always. "Are you sure?" he asked.

"Like when we were boys and we got into that fight," he laughed, trying to lighten the mood.

"Let's go, then," Caesar said.

They walked to the door. Then Caesar stopped.

"My *apex*," he said.

Cornelia stood and rushed into their bedroom to grab the hat worn only by the high priest of Jupiter. She returned to the vestibule and placed the apex on his head. It would remind everyone that Caesar was no ordinary citizen. He was flamen Dialis, the most sacred priest in Rome.

Waiting in the vestibule was the lictor assigned to guard the high priest of Jupiter. The man was dressed in a white toga and carried a *fasces,* a long sheath of sticks tied together. This was meant to symbolize power, since one wand was easily broken, but many together were much stronger. When a lictor escorted someone beyond the *pomerium*—the central, sacred part of the city—he would also carry a hatchet affixed to the fasces. Few people had the right to walk the streets of Rome proceeded by a lictor: councilmen had two, magistrates six, and a consul or dictator was surrounded by twelve. That is, until Sulla had proclaimed that he would be escorted by twenty-four lictores, one more example of how his dictatorship broke with typical Roman traditions and customs. The flamen Dialis was escorted by a single lictor, the only nonpolitician bestowed with this privilege.

Caesar looked at the man. "My one lictor against Sulla's twenty-four," he said with a sad smile. "A clear sign of how greatly outmatched I am."

Caesar was not intimidated as the slaves lifted the heavy crossbar and the door opened, revealing the eighty legionaries guarding his home. He stepped outside and the *centuria* surrounded him, ready to take him by force if necessary, to the home of Lucius Cornelius Sulla, dictator, ruler, and absolute master of Rome.

Caesar noticed that all of the legionaries covered their gladii with

their capes as they saw him emerge wearing his apex and accompanied by the lictor. He knew he was walking into a potentially deadly
situation, but he felt protected by his uncle Marius, who watched
from Hades below. He was flamen Dialis, after all. How far would
Sulla go to pressure the high priest of Jupiter?

LVII

SULLA'S PROPOSAL

Sulla's domus, Rome
82 B.C.

CAESAR AND LABIENUS ARRIVED AT SULLA'S HOME, ESCORTED
by a century of armed soldiers. Sulla's mansion was gigantic and had
not one, not two, but five atriums, the first of which served as vestibule. There, they crossed paths with Pompey, who was leaving an audience with his new father-in-law after formalizing his divorce from
Antistia and marrying Sulla's stepdaughter Emilia.

Caesar and Pompey stared each other down.

Caesar's gaze was defiant, Pompey's penetrating as Medusa's, as if
he were trying to turn the younger man to stone. The visual standoff
lasted only a few seconds before Pompey left without saying a word.

"He hates us," said Labienus.

Caesar simply nodded. He knew about Pompey's divorce and re-
marriage. If someone so cruel and violent had ceded so readily to
Sulla's pressures, perhaps it would be wise for him to do the same, as
his uncle Cotta had suggested.

"Enter!" the messenger shouted.

Caesar and Labienus, along with the lictor, passed into the second
atrium, which the dictator reserved for audiences. To their surprise,
they found it practically empty except for Sulla and his right-hand
man, Dolabella, who was expected to be named consul for the up-
coming year. Each man reclined on a triclinium surrounded by the
legionaries posted along the sides of the gigantic patio.

Caesar, Labienus, and the lictor had all been frisked several times to make sure there would be no surprises. The excessive number of armed guards were merely there to intimidate them, a symbol of Sulla's ironclad control.

Caesar noticed that none of the legionaries made any attempt to hide their weapons in his presence.

Dolabella rose from the triclinium. "Well, by Jupiter, who do we have here? Gaius Marius's fearsome nephew." He stopped a few paces from Caesar and circled him slowly. "I don't see what's so fearsome about him. Seriously, Lucius," he added, turning to Sulla, "I think you're overreacting."

He threw a brief glance at Labienus, then returned to his seat.

Sulla had not said a word as he reclined eating nuts and cheese that had been set out on a low table before him.

The lictor took a few steps to one side, leaving Caesar and Labienus alone in the center of the atrium. He was a lictor, not a hero.

"Are you hungry?" the dictator asked casually, without looking up but at least acknowledging their presence. He was not a man to overlook anyone. And the fact that Caesar had brought a lictor and wore the priest of Jupiter's apex as a reminder that he was flamen Dialis did not escape him.

At Sulla's question, Labienus merely shook his head. Caesar, however, responded boldly: "Yes, we are hungry. Hungry for freedom . . . clarissime vir."

Sulla stopped chewing.

There was a dense silence. Caesar's challenge to the dictator's authority had not been softened by his use of the appropriate form of address.

Sulla ran his tongue over his teeth. There was a bothersome piece of almond stuck between his back molars. He managed to dislodge it with the tip of his tongue and swallowed it with a sip of wine.

"I was offering you something to eat," he eventually said, as he set his cup on the table, still not looking at the young men.

"We do not want any food," Caesar replied.

"Good," Sulla said, "then we can get straight to the matter at hand, young Gaius Julius Caesar. Do you know why I have summoned you?"

"I do . . . clarissime vir."

Sulla smiled. "I expect a more precise answer from you, boy."

Caesar took a deep breath, then exhaled. It didn't make sense to be defiant every step of the way. "Lucius Cornelius Sulla is displeased with my marriage to Cornelia, daughter of Cinna, who was an ally of Gaius Marius, my uncle, both clear enemies of the senator and now dictator of Rome. And as the centurion informed me, the dictator would like me to divorce my wife and immediately remarry a young patrician girl of his choosing. He would like me to marry into the family of a conservative senator, into the group clearly opposed to what my uncle defended for years: the redistribution of wealth and lands among the people and the concession of Roman citizenship to many more than currently enjoy it. I'm summarizing, but I think I've been fairly precise."

Sulla thought for a moment before he spoke, chewing a slice of cheese as he carefully studied the young man's stubborn countenance.

Dolabella lay watching with amusement. The situation was made almost comical by Caesar's obliviousness to his enormous inferiority, his total insignificance in the face of the all-powerful and implacable Sulla. The dictator's silence did not bode well for the pater familias of the Julia clan. The boy might not even make it out of the atrium alive.

"Yes, that was sufficiently precise," Sulla agreed, always cold, distant, pensive.

Another silence.

"I don't plan to do it," Caesar added.

"Do what?" Sulla asked, almost bored.

"Divorce my wife."

Lucius Cornelius Sulla let out a long, unhurried sigh, then lifted his thick body from the triclinium. He approached Caesar, and, when he was about a foot away, without saying a word, slapped him. Perhaps because the young man had not been expecting it, or perhaps because the tyrant still had the strength of a soldier, he split Caesar's bottom lip open.

Labienus lurched forward to intervene, but as he did so, dozens of legionaries stepped from the shadows, unsheathing their gladii. Labienus froze. Caesar repressed a violent reaction.

Very slowly, Sulla lay back down on his triclinium. Dolabella smiled broadly and sipped his wine.

"That was for your impertinent tone," the dictator explained. "I can understand that you might refuse to divorce your wife and marry the girl I select, but I will never let an *adulescens* upstart talk down to me in my own home. Is that clear, boy? Or do I have to ask one of these soldiers to clarify my meaning? They can be very convincing."

Caesar quickly swallowed his pride. His uncle had taught him not to enter a battle he couldn't win, and it didn't make sense to receive a beating for no reason.

"I understand, clarissime vir," he said. "But I'm surprised that he who calls himself protector of the most ancestral habits and customs of Rome would dare to slap the high priest of Jupiter."

Sulla sneered and fluttered his hand at Caesar. "Yes, I see that you wore your apex and brought your lictor; but your appointment as flamen Dialis by the miserable Cinna is, in my opinion, open to question, like everything the man did. But that aside, let's get back to the matter that brings you here, by Jupiter, since you love to mention him. Will you or will you not divorce Cinna's daughter?"

Caesar considered his response carefully: "With all due respect . . . no, clarissime vir."

"With all due respect," Sulla repeated sarcastically, and looked at Dolabella. "Did you hear that? With all due respect . . ." He let out a loud laugh and several of the legionaries joined him. They were veterans of the war against Mithridates who had followed the dictator halfway around the world. They loyally shared in his laughter and used their force to enact his rage. They dutifully did his bidding, whatever that might be.

Their laughter was humiliating, but Caesar did not say a word. Inside, he was seething, shocked that Sulla would show such open disdain to the flamen Dialis.

Sulla stood again.

Dolabella was intrigued—it was unusual for his mentor to stand up from his triclinium at all. Standing twice during a single audience was something he'd never seen him do.

Sulla approached Caesar, whose lip was red with blood. The dictator of Rome stopped in the same place he'd stood moments before and once again raised his hand. Caesar closed his eyes and turned his face, but he did not step back, prepared to endure another blow. But the second slap never came. He opened his eyes and saw Sulla standing before him, scratching his ear.

"You disrespect me," the dictator said. "You disrespect me because you think you are better than me, than him." He gestured toward Dolabella before once again facing Caesar. "You think yourself better than all the optimates. You think yourself superior because you are concerned with the scum of Rome, with all the miserable beggars in rags who were born to serve us. And because you care about the poor people of Italy who demand Roman citizenship, which they do not deserve. You think you're better than me; you consider yourself more just, more intelligent, a more upright Roman citizen. But you are not more just or more intelligent or more upright. Your uncle's blood runs through your veins, the blood of the greatest traitor Rome has ever known. He destroyed the natural order of things, but I am here to restore things to the way they should be. The oldest patrician families will rule, lead, and guide the Roman state. I'm here to establish a new order where all dissent ceases to exist. And I am prepared to apply as much force and violence as necessary to ensure it. You disrespect me for my use of violence. You disrespect me because you consider yourself more virtuous, but I see something in you, boy, that you are not even aware of."

Sulla leaned in so close that his breath, heavily perfumed, washed over Caesar's face. "What you don't know, what you aren't capable of even imagining, is that you are just like me. Maybe not yet, but you have all the makings of a man just like me, and you will end up just like me. That is, if I decide to let you." Here he took a few steps away and turned his back for an instant before resuming his speech. "I do not disrespect you. I judge you for who you truly are. Which is why I want you on my side. We, the great families of the Senate, need the best of Rome with us in this new order. But I need you to swear your absolute loyalty and submission, starting by divorcing Cinna's daughter and marrying whomever I deem appropriate. I'm giving you an opportunity, boy, a much greater one than you surely deserve. Think carefully before you speak."

With this, Sulla concluded his speech and returned to his triclinium. He sipped his wine as he waited for young Caesar's response.

"I am nothing like you, clarissime vir, and I predict that, under your regime, I will never become a senator. I am sorry for that. I understand that in saying this, my political career is over before it has even begun, but even so, I do not plan to divorce Cornelia."

"Why not?" Sulla asked, genuinely curious. "Just to defy me?"

"I do not like to take orders from anyone, clarissime vir, but there's another reason as well."

"What is it?"

"I love my wife."

"It was an arranged marriage, merely a way to seal the alliance between Cinna and your uncle." Sulla turned up his palms and raised his eyebrows to show his confusion.

"Be that as it may, clarissime vir, I love my wife. I pledged loyalty to her. And I am a man of my word."

"I am also a man of my word," Sulla replied with icy calm. "And I have vowed that this new order will not be threatened by any of Marius's relatives or supporters. I still have Sertorius to deal with, but I'll root him out in Hispania, have no doubt about that. So that leaves only you, here in Rome."

Caesar braced himself for the punishment he knew would come.

"You may leave," Sulla said.

The young man blinked and furrowed his brow. The legionaries sheathed their gladii and moved back into the shadows of the atrium. Caesar looked at Labienus, who was equally shocked. Both turned on their heels and quickly left, trailed closely by the lictor, before the dictator had time to change his mind and execute the two of them, or the three of them even, right then and there.

Sulla and Dolabella were left alone in the atrium guarded by the many soldiers.

"Why did you let him go?" Dolabella asked. "If you're so worried about him, why not just kill him?"

"Not here. Not in my home. There are still many populares left in Rome. And even if I question his position as flamen Dialis, the plebes see him as the high priest of Jupiter. I have to fix that first, to strip him of his priesthood. In the meantime, we'll see what he does. I need a reason to accuse him of wrongdoing, any little thing. Then I'll put him in front of a tribunal, controlled by us, and execute him. Doing it legally will make it much easier."

LVIII

A DEADLY
CONFRONTATION

Julia family domus, Rome
82 B.C.

"**W**HY HAVE YOU RETURNED?" AURELIA ASKED.

"I want to show him that I'm not afraid," Caesar replied.

"Well you should be afraid, boy. You should be very afraid," Aurelius Cotta said.

Caesar did not respond. He simply hugged his wife, who was crying and terrified.

"I don't want anyone to hurt you because of me," the girl said between sobs.

"This is about more than our marriage. He'd hate me no matter who I was married to." Caesar looked at his mother. "Marius warned me, but I didn't believe him—he told me that they would never forgive me for being his nephew."

Aurelia sighed. Her son should've left Rome, but he was stubborn and determined. He was either brave or insane. Time would tell.

Two days later a messenger from the Senate appeared at the Julia family domus.

Caesar read the message aloud to his mother, his uncle Cotta, his young wife Cornelia, and his friend Labienus who were all present.

"They've stripped me of the priesthood. I'm no longer flamen Dialis," he announced. "He'll stop at nothing. He respects nothing. Nothing except violence."

"I was afraid of a much more extreme reaction," Aurelia said.

"Stripping you of the priesthood is only the beginning," Cotta warned.

No one said a word.

Cotta was right. It would be a slow process. Carried out meticulously, like a surgeon performing an extremely delicate surgery. Sulla wanted to excise Julius Caesar from public life in Rome. And he would go as far as necessary to do so.

"He never even accepted my appointment as flamen Dialis because he doesn't recognize any of Marius's or Cinna's laws. This is just a formality to justify his action to the senators and plebes when he . . ." Caesar paused for a few seconds as he paced the atrium. He abruptly stopped and glanced back with a gleam in his eyes. "Yes, I'll play his game, with his pawns, his rules, his new regime. I'll present myself as candidate for the *quindecimviri sacris faciundis,*" Caesar growled, fierce as a consul charging into combat. "It's a lower priesthood than flamen Dialis, less prestigious, but it's elected by the legislative assembly, not by the Senate. Sulla does not control them. It depends only on the will of the people."

Everyone was surprised. To Cotta's eyes, the confrontation was as unequal as it was absurd. Aurelia admired her son's determination, but at the same time, she was wary of his presenting himself for the election. Sulla would surely see it for what it was: a public challenge to his authority.

Sulla's domus
A few days later

"He did what?" Sulla asked.

"He nominated himself for quindecimviri," Dolabella said again. "He knows they're elected by the legislative committee, far outside our control. It's a clear provocation."

"It is, without a doubt," Sulla agreed. "But the voters of that committee are just as corruptible as our comrades in the Senate. And they come at a much lower price. Buy as many votes as necessary; he will not be elected. Oh, and order his properties confiscated. I don't want him to be able to enter into a battle of bribes." Sulla paused.

"Cinna had a lot of money; confiscate his daughter's dowry as well. That should make it impossible for him to buy any votes. That will weaken him." He gritted his teeth and smiled. "This is fun."

"What is?"

"Closing in on him, one step at a time, tightening our grip around him. Suffocating him little by little. It's more entertaining that way."

Dolabella nodded and left the atrium to communicate Sulla's instructions to several men waiting in the vestibule. There were orders to give, elections to be rigged, and many votes to purchase.

Julia family domus
Fifteen days later

Caesar lay slumped on a triclinium. His mother, his wife, his uncle Cotta, and Labienus listened as he spoke.

"I've only made things worse by defying Sulla. Not only has he confiscated our family's property, he's stripped Cornelia of her dowry. And I didn't even get elected as quindecimviri. Sulla bought all the votes he needed to make sure of that. The people are as easily corruptible as the senators," Caesar said. At the tender age of eighteen he'd had his first dose of cold, cruel reality. If the very people whose rights he was fighting for would abandon him over a handful of sesterce, did that fight even make sense?

Aurelia knew what he was thinking. "The people's representatives can be corrupted, yes, but that doesn't change the fact that the great majority live in terrible conditions, dying of hunger in the streets, oppressed by the abuses of a few select senators. The people still deserve to be defended. But this is a fight, son, that you can't win. At least, not now. Not against Sulla at the height of his power. We have to concentrate on your survival. We have to get you out of Rome as soon as possible. With whatever money we have left. Sulla will soon issue an order for your arrest. He wanted to make you look ridiculous in the public elections first, but now he'll come for you personally. Take everything we have and leave Rome. All the gold in the sacks is for you. Our friends will help Cornelia, little Julia, and me."

Caesar, slouched on the triclinium in defeat, nodded.

His mother added a few words of encouragement: "He hasn't beaten you, son: you did not divorce Cornelia, which is what he wanted. And he did not force you to join him. But he is out to win this confrontation. And it is a deadly one. You have to leave Rome. I will rally all the support I can for your return. And if that doesn't work, there's another solution. It simply requires patience."

"What solution is that, Mother?"

"Sulla is old. He won't be alive for too much longer. That will be your chance, but until then, I will work here in the city to make it safe for you to return. Now leave Rome before it's too late."

LIX

FUGITIVE FROM ROME

Vía Apía, Rome
81 B.C.

THEY LEFT AT NIGHT UNDER THE CLOAK OF DARKNESS, HEADED south. Caesar and Labienus walked quickly down the Via Apia, a centuries-old thoroughfare, constantly looking over their shoulders. They feared the night patrols, but they'd managed to leave a few hours before Julius Caesar's arrest warrant was issued by the Senate. That gave them an advantage.

"This old road needs to be repaired," said Caesar.

He was right. Repair of the road had been a source of debate in the Senate, but with so many disputes between the populares and the optimates, funding had never been approved.

"Well," said Labienus, "let's focus on your survival first, as your mother would say. Then you can take care of the Via Apia."

He meant it as a joke, but Caesar responded in total seriousness. "Yes, I'll take care of it someday," he said, staring down at the old loose stones.

Labienus shook his head and smiled. Caesar's ambitions never waned, even when on the run as a fugitive from Rome.

They continued their journey.

The night enveloped them.

There was no moon, and the darkness was impenetrable as they felt their way through the night, following the course of the old road.

They walked for hours, until they were as far away from the city as their feet could take them.

"Dawn is breaking," said Labienus.

They were exhausted.

"You're right," said Caesar. "Let's get off the road to rest for a while."

Sulla's domus, Rome

"He's escaped," Dolabella announced, standing before Sulla.

No one had been able to find Caesar in the city by the Tiber.

"We were too slow," Sulla commented. "We should've known that he'd flee as soon as he lost the election."

"Maybe we should've acted sooner, had the Senate issue the arrest order before the legislative council met to vote," Dolabella ventured.

But Sulla shook his head: "No, absolutely not. It's one thing to arrest someone who has lost an election and another thing to arrest the winner."

"But the elections were . . . rigged," Dolabella reminded him.

Sulla's face twisted into a scornful expression. "So many things in life are rigged . . . People will talk, of course, but as far as the public is concerned, he's a loser and that's what matters. His supporters must be disappointed to see this promising young leader lose his battle with us. They'd hoped he might replace Marius or Cinna. If he'd been smarter, he would've fled immediately after meeting with me a few weeks ago. If he'd never presented himself at that election, he could've at least escaped with what he had left of a reputation intact. But whether the elections were rigged or not, his supporters now see that he is no match for me. He's arrogant and overreaching but not very intelligent."

Dolabella nodded several times. Everything Sulla was saying, as always, made perfect sense.

"How many legionaries do we have in Rome?" the dictator asked.

"A hundred and twenty thousand," Dolabella answered. The entire army that had been deployed against Mithridates in the East and then against the populares during the civil war, in addition to the legions from Ancona, were still posted in Italy to ensure Sulla's consolidation of power.

"Good. Let them all search for him. I want Caesar, dead or alive. Either kneeling before me or lying cold at my feet. Let them hunt him down like a pack of wolves hunts its prey. Like the most heinous of criminals."

Italy
Several weeks later

Life on the run was desperate, sad, and humiliating. Caesar was overcome with a sense of melancholy and defeat, as the only imaginable end to his predicament was the death of his pursuer, at fifty-seven years old.

"Sulla eats a lot," Labienus pointed out one afternoon beside a small fire they'd built deep in the mountains. "He's fat and he drinks wine constantly. I wouldn't be surprised if he dropped dead out of nowhere in the middle of one of his unending orgies."

Labienus visited Caesar intermittently. He was the only one who knew where he was, bringing food to the most remote locations. Caesar worried that his friend might be putting himself at risk by helping him, but he had no choice but to accept his aid. He had to avoid the villas of all friends and acquaintances of the Julia family and his uncle Marius. They were all being watched. Labienus did not return to his home but slept in the domuses of different friends in the Suburra, so densely populated that it was easy to get lost in the crowd. It would have been impossible, however, for Caesar himself to hide anywhere in the city: thousands of legionaries patrolled the streets, and there were checkpoints at every entrance to the urbe.

Caesar knew that his friend was risking his life to help him, but he also knew that without him he'd be dead by now. He had enough money—his mother had given him everything. But going into any village to buy food in a public market was too great a risk. Sulla's legionaries were indeed everywhere.

Time passed.

The situation became increasingly unbearable.

"It's getting harder and harder to avoid the legionary patrols," Labienus said. "By all the gods, I was surrounded and questioned just for leaving Rome yesterday. The checkpoints on the roads are tighter, and now they're sending entire centuries into the mountains to hunt for you. Sulla has ordered them to leave no stone unturned in all of Italy. You might need to go farther away. To the East, or"—he hesitated—"to Hispania, with Sertorius."

"I've considered both options," Caesar admitted, looking off to the horizon as the sun set over the mountains. "In the East, there will be fewer soldiers hunting me, but all the ports of Italy are being watched. I would likely be betrayed to Sulla's legionaries before I even set sail for Greece or Asia. I'd have just as much trouble getting on a ship to Hispania, but beyond that, Sulla would see it as a clear provocation if I went and joined Sertorius. He might retaliate against my wife, my daughter, my mother, my sisters . . . I can't do that to them."

Labienus sighed. Caesar's words were sadly true. "But they're getting closer and closer."

"I know," Caesar said. "I have to go into the swamps."

There was a silence.

"That's dangerous," Labienus finally said. "The air there is rotten. You could get sick or even die."

"I'm already dead if I stay here. Look." He pointed through the trees down to the base of the mountain, where a group of legionaries milled about, examining each rock and clump of dirt as if they had taken Sulla's orders literally.

Labienus and Caesar looked at each other. They hugged.

"I'll come back to this very spot in fifteen days," said Caesar. "Meanwhile I'll go where the soldiers will never think to look for me, down into the swamps. They won't follow me there for fear of the swamp fever. But I will survive. Go down to meet them. They won't do anything to you, as long as they don't see you with me."

"Be careful, by Jupiter."

"I will survive," Caesar said again with a smile. Then he picked up the food and the wineskin full of water that his friend had brought and began his march down into the humid, swampy marshland on the north side of the mountains, where no one in their right mind would ever enter, where only illness and death awaited.

Foothills near Caesar's hideout in the swamp
Two weeks later

The first time Labienus met with Caesar after he'd gone into the swamps, he found his friend somewhat worse for wear, weaker and thinner. Initially he attributed it to the harsh living conditions and scarcity of food, but as he descended the mountainside, leaving Caesar to head back into the dark, damp, desolate marsh, Labienus realized that he had brought his friend enough food to survive comfortably: bread, cheese, nuts, dried meat, wineskins of clean water, as well as plenty of *buccellati,* the crackers typically eaten by the legionaries that were extremely lightweight and easy to keep, even in the inhospitable swamplands.

Two more weeks passed and Caesar was more than just weakened, with dark circles under his eyes and a sad expression resulting from so many days alone in the swamps. This time the young pater familias of the gens Julia was sweating profusely and trembling uncontrollably.

"You're sick," Labienus said. "You have to come with me, to our villa."

"No!" Caesar objected. "By Jupiter! That would put . . . your entire family . . . at risk . . ." He spoke haltingly. Each word represented a major effort.

Labienus thought quickly. Caesar was in no condition to make decisions. It was true that taking him to his family's villa was very risky, but . . . was there any alternative? "Don't go back into the swamp," Labienus ordered Caesar. "Stay here. I'll return as soon as I can with a doctor and we'll see what he says. Agreed?"

Caesar slumped to the ground and nodded as he covered himself with the clean blankets his friend had brought him.

Titus Labienus did not feel comfortable leaving Caesar alone, but there was nothing more he could do for him. He began the long hike back down the mountain and into the nearest town, where he went directly to the home of the Greek doctor who had treated several members of his family. Leaving the village, however, they passed a tavern crowded with legionaries. Many of them recognized the young man as well as the old man accompanying him. Among the soldiers was Cornelius Fagites, a veteran centurion with a huntsman's instinct. Before joining the army, he had been a bounty hunter, tracking down fugitive slaves. And he'd been good at it. But except in the case of a renowned fugitive, the rewards were very small, and so he'd decided to enlist in the army as a more stable way to earn a living.

Everyone knew that young Labienus was a good friend of Caesar's, the most wanted man in all of Italy, so when Cornelius had been ordered to set up a watch outside Rome, he'd chosen the town near Labienus's country villa. But his men hadn't seen anything, or so they said. Cornelius was getting old, a bit too old for the tireless task of chasing fugitives from justice, and he had not questioned his men's explanations. But that day, his instincts forced him into action.

"Let's see where he goes," the centurion ordered.

His men followed him grudgingly. They were happier in the tavern, but it was true that they hadn't patrolled the area in days.

"We've followed him before," one of the legionaries said. "And he either returns home or goes into the mountains to hunt."

"Into the mountains?" Cornelius asked, as they followed Labienus and the doctor at a safe distance along a busy road where the cart traffic allowed them to go unnoticed.

"Yes, into the mountains, near the swamps."

"And have you followed him farther?" Cornelius inquired without stopping.

"Well, to his house, yes," the optio explained, beginning to understand that they had made a mistake. "When he goes into the mountains, we follow him for a half day. Then we come back down and wait for him near his villa. He always returns with something he's hunted. That's why—"

"That's why you assumed, without actually knowing, that he was going out to hunt and only to hunt. Does he take provisions with him, water and food, when he goes up the mountain?" the centurion asked, increasingly irritated.

The optio blinked several times before responding. "Yes, lots . . . But we thought they were provisions for his hunting expedition."

"When does he return from the hunt?"

The optio swallowed. "The next day," he admitted quietly.

"And you never thought it strange that he carried so many provisions for a single night?" Cornelius Fagites asked, furious at his men's stupidity. And furious with himself for his oversight.

Just then, much to the optio's relief, Cornelius was distracted—Labienus and the doctor had left the road and were heading up the mountainside.

"Is it common for him to take the doctor along when he goes hunting?" Cornelius asked sarcastically. "By Jupiter, what a pack of morons!"

Julius Caesar's campsite, south of Rome

Labienus and the doctor found Caesar lying on the ground, curled up and shivering even as he hugged the blankets tightly. Night was already upon them.

"How long have you been feeling poorly?" the doctor asked, crouching down beside the trembling man.

"A few days . . . This morning it started to get . . . worse . . ." Caesar explained, struggling to speak.

The doctor examined his face, placed his hand on the young man's forehead, and asked, "Is this the first time you've felt feverish?"

Caesar shook his head.

"Do you think it's been about four days now? And before that, maybe, always four days at a time, then you feel better?"

Caesar's mouth fell open in surprise.

"Yes . . . It's happened a few times . . . But it always goes away . . ."

"It'll never go away as long as you stay in the lowlands, boy." The doctor looked at Labienus. "By Asclepius, he has the swamp fever.* It's caused by the rotten gases that come off the stagnant water. We

---

* Malaria, common in the damp, swampy zones of Italy at the time.

have to get him out of here or he'll only get worse. He's young and if we can get him somewhere safe and dry soon, he'll likely recover. If he stays here, he'll die. No amount of food or water will cure him. He has to leave this place."

"I'll think of something," said Labienus.

"I can't go to your villa . . . or to anyone else's . . ." Caesar said, anticipating his friend's thoughts. "Anyone who helps me will be executed."

The doctor's eyes went wide as he realized that the feverish young man was the fugitive being hunted by every single soldier in Italy. "I shall leave now," he said. Returning at night with no light was certainly dangerous—he could get lost or fall off a cliff—but the Greek doctor was more fearful of retaliation from Sulla's men. "Pay me the sum we agreed upon and don't ask me to help this fugitive again."

Labienus was furious. Moonlight fell on the doctor's face as he stretched out his open palm to receive his coins.

"Pay the man . . ." said Caesar. "Use my money." He pointed to one of the bags of denari and sesterce that his mother had made him take before leaving Rome.

Labienus, controlling his rage, took a few coins from Caesar's bag and placed them in the doctor's hand.

"It's nothing personal," the doctor said, seemingly ashamed for refusing to stay and help, "but Sulla wants your friend, dead or alive, and I don't want to be associated with him in any way. This is not my war. Place damp cloths on his forehead during the night. That will lower his fever. And take him somewhere else as soon as day breaks. That is the hour when the fever will begin to dissipate."

Labienus didn't say a word.

The doctor closed his fingers around the coins and disappeared into the shadows of the night.

"May the gods lead him off the edge of a cliff," Labienus said angrily.

"You cannot blame . . . the man . . . for being afraid," said Caesar, still lying huddled on the ground. "It's Sulla's fault . . . Don't be angry with the man who has helped us."

Labienus sat down beside his friend and began to wet a cloth with some fresh water. "You're too forgiving of people, Caesar," he said as he placed the damp cloth on his forehead. "That generosity will be your undoing."

They did not speak any more that night. Caesar did not have the energy to argue, and Labienus did not feel like talking.

Labienus slept.

But Caesar did not.

Perhaps because of his feverish state, perhaps because he had been pushed to the limits of his strength, he began to question everything: What sense did his defiance of Sulla even make? Wouldn't it have been easier to do as Pompey had done and give in to the dictator's pressure, divorcing Cornelia and marrying whomever the tyrant chose for him? What was he going to achieve with his resistance, his stubbornness, his endless conflict with Sulla? Wouldn't his wife, his mother, and his entire family be better off if he'd submitted docilely to the dictator's orders? Cornelia would have been devastated, without a doubt, and he as well, but wouldn't she be happier divorced from him than married to an outcast, a rebel, a fugitive whom Sulla himself had declared an enemy of the state?

He was drenched in sweat.

And he doubted every decision he'd made.

He no longer knew what was right and what was wrong.

But Cornelia had not wanted him to divorce her. His mother, too, had supported his decision. And Labienus was always there for him, unfailingly. Why did they all support him, a foolish young man not even twenty years old? What did they all see in him?

He balled up into the fetal position.

He knew exactly what they saw in him, especially Sulla. He was the nephew of Gaius Marius, the greatest of all the popular leaders, the only man Sulla had truly feared in his entire life. And that led to another thought: Why would the all-powerful dictator bother to unleash the full force of his fury on him? Remembering the fact that all the legions of Rome had been sent to look for him helped him see that perhaps, as his mother had said, he was much greater than he himself even imagined. If Sulla had to send tens of thousands of legionaries to hunt for him across all of Italy, maybe it was because he, Julius Caesar, was, in fact, someone to be feared.

The thought emboldened him.

He was Marius's nephew, and he would become the great man that his mother, his wife, his sisters, his friends, and his family expected him to be. He couldn't let them all down by surrendering, giving in. Just as he hadn't given in when Sertorius attacked him on the Campus Martius. Caesar finally understood, in that moment, what Marius had been trying to discern that day in Rome, when he submitted his young nephew to that endless round of blows at Sertorius's powerful hands. His uncle wanted to see if he was the kind of man who would surrender and beg for mercy, or the type who would never give up and never, ever, surrender.

He was descended from Aeneas, from Mars and Venus.

He then recalled how Sulla had profaned his uncle's tomb, and how he had sworn to himself that he would never submit to that tyrant. It was his destiny to challenge Sulla and any other despot that might replace him. It was his destiny to change Rome.

As Caesar was lost in these thoughts, Morpheus's embrace finally found him and he fell into a fitful sleep.

The mountainside
Dawn

———————

Labienus woke with the first light of day and quickly scanned the area.

"By Hercules, they're nearly upon us!" he exclaimed, shaking Caesar out of his exhausted, feverish slumber.

"Who?"

"The legionaries," Labienus said, looking down the slope of the mountain. "They've either followed me or the doctor has betrayed us, or both. I don't know, but they're very close now." He turned to Caesar. "You have to flee. Back into the swamp if necessary."

Caesar shook his head.

"No . . . I can't . . . I'm too weak. And that doctor, traitor or not, seemed to know what he was talking about. The swamp is not an option anymore . . . Not in the state I'm in."

"But they'll arrest you and turn you in and—"

Caesar cut him off. His fever had decreased considerably, just as the doctor had said it would at that hour, and he was able to think more clearly. "Take my money and go. You can avoid them if you leave now. There's no hope for me, I'm too slow."

"I won't abandon you. Much less when you're so weak. And how could I take your money? What sense does that make? You're delirious. It must be the fever."

"No, I assure you I am now fully lucid." Caesar stood and looked down at the approaching legionaries. "That money won't do me any good. The soldiers will rob me as soon as they get here. But in your hands, it can be used to negotiate. Go to your villa, where most of what I took from my mother is safely hidden away, but take these sacks as well. You'll soon have news from me. They won't turn me in to Sulla. You'll see. If those elections taught me anything it's how easily corruptible a man can be. All it takes is the right sum of money." He smiled. "I'm learning from my enemy. Sulla is vile and despicable, but he could teach us a thing or two."

Labienus began to understand his friend's plan. It was risky, but it made sense, so he did not argue. He picked up the sack of coins, rested his hand on Caesar's shoulder for an instant, and without a word, he turned around and absconded into the trees to remain out of view as the legionaries ascended the slope.

Caesar sat, waiting to be arrested.

In a short while he found himself surrounded by several armed soldiers.

"Who is the officer in charge?" Caesar asked in an authoritative voice that they did not expect to hear from the wanted man.

"I am," Cornelius Fagites said, gasping for breath as he reached the top of the slope. He was definitely too old for this.

"I want to speak with you. Alone," Caesar said.

"I don't think you're in any position to negotiate," Cornelius replied, annoyed at having to climb half a mountain to capture this fugitive.

"I think you'll find I'm actually in a great position to negotiate. Alone," Caesar said.

The veteran centurion sighed. He looked at his men, who had spent months in his service, and they all stepped back so that their commanding officer could speak with the fugitive in private.

"The climb up the hill was hard on you," Caesar commented.

"It's a mountain," the centurion argued.

Caesar smiled. "No, centurion, this is just a foothill at best, but the years take their toll. I'd say it must be about time for you to enter retirement, which I'm sure is well deserved . . . and could be well compensated."

Cornelius could read between the lines. "How much are we talking about?"

Caesar knew he needed to get straight to the point. He was talking to a practical military man like his uncle Marius, who was never one for subtlety. "Enough money to last you the rest of your life without having to reenlist."

Cornelius considered the offer. He wanted to leave military service but did not know what he would do for money if he retired. Although he'd been paid well in recent years, saving was not his strong suit; wine and prostitutes were expensive pastimes for a Roman officer.

"You'll have to buy my men's silence as well," he pointed out.

"How many?"

"An entire century. Eighty."

Caesar looked around: there were barely thirty soldiers with him. "There's not even half that here," he commented.

"But the others will ask questions. We have to keep them all quiet or else it won't work."

Caesar nodded. "All right. Thirty silver denari for each of your men. And three thousand for you."

"Three thousand denari would provide me with a very poor retirement. I want fifty silver denari for each of my men and fifteen thousand for me."

"Fifty for your men. Six thousand for you."

"Twelve thousand."

"Let's meet in the middle," Caesar proposed, calm and cool as he negotiated the price of his own life: "Forty denari for each of your men and eight thousand for you."

Cornelius knew that forty was enough for his legionaries; they would accept it. But he wanted to increase his own payout: "Nine thousand for me."

"Eight thousand five hundred," Caesar countered.

"Eight thousand eight hundred," Cornelius pressed.

"So be it," Caesar agreed. "Forty silver denari for each of your men and eight thousand eight hundred for you."

"Give me the money."

Caesar laughed loudly. "So that you can slit my throat and make off with it?" He stopped laughing. "Take me somewhere dry, far away from these cursed swamplands, and I'll tell you where to send a message written in my own hand. You'll have the money in three days' time." He knew that on the fourth day his fever would return. He had to make sure he was free by then.

Cornelius pressed his lips together and furrowed his brow.

"So be it, by Jupiter. But if there's no money by the third day, I'll wrap you in chains and march you to Sulla myself."

"You'll have your money," Caesar decreed.

Cornelius Fagites's tent
Three days later

Labienus entered the centurion's tent with a sack in his right hand. His friend's letter had contained very precise instructions on how the ransom should be delivered. Labienus deposited the sack of silver denari on the table beside the centurion's cup of wine.

"Is it all there?" he asked.

"There? In that small sack, twelve thousand denari?" Caesar said. "Impossible." He looked at his friend. "Did you bring all of it, like I asked you to?"

Labienus nodded and looked toward the door of the tent. "The rest is outside with my slaves, who are guarded by the officer's men."

"Let's go then," said the centurion, greedily finishing off his wine.

"I wouldn't open the coffers in the presence of your men," Caesar advised him. "They might find the distribution less than satisfactory."

Cornelius Fagites looked at Caesar and chuckled. "By Hercules, you're right!"

He stepped out to order the coffers brought into the tent. Labienus took the opportunity to speak to Caesar in private: "How do you know they'll let us go?"

"He's tired. Of the army, of war, of everything. He has nothing to gain by turning us in. Sulla is not known for his generosity. Cornelius will let us go. He'll give the forty denari to each of his soldiers, put the rest away for his retirement, and I'll go back on the run. Broke, but free. That calls for a drink."

Caesar picked up the pitcher of wine and filled two cups to the brim, as if he were not a fugitive and prisoner but the official in command.

"The centurion will go on like nothing's happened for a few months, until it's time for him to leave the army. A few weeks pretending to work, drinking wine, his men contented by the money they've received, and then he'll retire in comfort."

Caesar handed his friend a cup. "Will you drink with me? To my ruinous freedom?"

Titus Labienus shook his head as he accepted the wine Caesar offered, smiling. "Either the fever has made you delirious or you're completely insane."

Caesar rejected both notions. "No, my friend. I have simply reached a greater understanding of human nature." He emptied his cup, set it on the table, and looked at Labienus. "I am once again a fugitive."

THE FIRST
VICTORY

Caesar's first victory was not on the battlefield. It was a silent win, feverish and miserable, as he spent weeks and months dragging himself through the most inhospitable corners of Italy, always on the run, always fleeing . . . awaiting either death or permission to return to Rome.

Sulla's domus, Rome
81 B.C.

Parading through Lucius Cornelius Sulla's domus that morning were the high priestess of Vesta, respected magistrate Marcus Aemilius Lepidus, Aurelius Cotta, and even Caesar's mother, all of them begging him to pardon the young fugitive. Even Crassus, Metellus, and other prominent optimates had asked Sulla to stop pursuing the boy, not out of pity, but because the legionaries' continued failure to capture Caesar had made a legend of this young man who dared to defy the authority of the new regime. Sulla agreed with this last point, but still . . .

Aurelia left the dictator's atrium, and Sulla let out a long sigh. He was alone with Dolabella and Pompey, who had been present through the endless series of petitions that day. Pompey was fierce on the battlefield, and Sulla liked to keep him close, even if he was too young to weigh in on political matters.

"What do you think?" Sulla asked Dolabella.

"I don't know what to say," he replied. "Of course the mother would beg for her son's pardon, and the same goes for his uncle Aurelius Cotta, without doubt the most moderate member of the Julia clan. He was smart enough to pitch the pardon as a way of appeasing the many populares who have been forced to submit to us and purged from our government. But the fact that they've managed to get the high priestess of Vesta to support their petition for clemency means that the matter of this young fugitive has become something bigger. That seems to be what Crassus and Metellus think as well. I don't understand why Lepidus would support Caesar, however."

"Lepidus is disloyal," said Sulla. "He knows I don't like him and that I will limit his political ascent. He has great ambition and prefers to give orders, not take them. I believe he plans to emerge as leader of the populares, now beheaded and dismembered. And what better way to gain their favor than to demand I pardon the nephew of their greatest leader?"

"It's quite possible," Dolabella agreed, "but beyond Lepidus's political leanings, the populares are as good as dead here in Rome. Though we have yet to end Sertorius's rebellion in Hispania and, as others have pointed out, young Caesar's ability to escape us time and again is starting to make us look foolish. It's almost as if his arrest order has created a rallying point for the populares across Italy. They have no military might, only scant influence at best, but it might be worth considering . . ." He measured his next words carefully. "Yes, it might be, perhaps, more convenient to consider pardoning him."

Sulla sighed. He turned to Pompey. He would see what the boy had to say on a political matter, for once. "I agree with Dolabella," Pompey said. "Caesar is nobody. This endless, fruitless persecution only makes him seem more important than he is, as Crassus and Metellus have pointed out."

Sulla shook his head several times as a cynical smile spread across his face. "By Jupiter Optimus Maximus, how simpleminded the two of you are . . . and everyone else." The dictator was disappointed that no one seemed able to grasp the full scope of the situation. "This boy's uncle was Gaius Marius, the most terrible enemy we optimates have ever seen, a threat to our very existence. Marius nearly decimated all the power we'd built up over so many years. Have you all forgotten that not even a year ago we were fighting his men in Italy?

And, as you point out, his supporters are still resisting us in Hispania, under Sertorius's command."

Sulla paused. He needed time to think. He believed that pardoning Caesar was a mistake, but it would also be unwise to go against all his main allies in the new regime. They didn't see the young man's hidden threat. Sulla recalled his defiant gaze. A boy of barely eighteen who dares to confront the dictator of Rome is a boy with boundless potential. Why was that so hard for everyone else to see?

Sulla sighed before speaking again: "So be it. I will pardon the cursed Julius Caesar. But I am only doing so to keep from looking ridiculous. Gnaeus Dolabella is right. Every day that goes by with a hundred and twenty thousand legionaries hunting him and no arrest makes us look more foolish. I don't want to create a living legend out of someone who, for now, is no one. He has never participated in a public trial or fought a single battle, that is true, but you are both wrong. Everyone is wrong to think him insignificant. I am certain that, if he doesn't die young, he will grow strong. And then he will be a true danger.

"But I'm an old dog. It will be you, Dolabella, or you, Pompey, who will have to take down this boy you so greatly underestimate. The ire in my gut tells me to continue the hunt. But pardoning him will ensure me greater peace in my final years, without the legend of the supposedly indomitable Julius Caesar constantly looming. A legend gives the enemy something to hold onto, it gives them hope. And it is important to stamp out all trace of hope; only then can the enemy be truly defeated. I shall pardon him. But mark my words: do not ignore young Julius Caesar."

Sulla took a long sip of wine. Then he set his cup on the table and looked first to Dolabella, then to Pompey, and said, "*Nam Caesari multos Marios inesse.*"*

---

* "... for in this Caesar there is more than one Marius"; said by Sulla about the young Caesar, according to Gaius Suetonius in *De Vita Caesarum,* VII, Julius Caesar, 1.

The Trial

VI

SECUNDA ACTIO

SECOND SESSION
OF THE TRIAL

DOLABELLA'S
TESTIMONY

Basílica Sempronia, Rome
77 B.C.

CAESAR WAS ARRANGING THE MANY SCROLLS SPREAD ACROSS the prosecutor's table. To his right, his friend examined the audience gathering in the basilica.

"There's a large crowd," said Labienus. "And we haven't summoned them."

"Would you rather there were fewer people?" Caesar asked, distractedly going over his notes.

Labienus did not respond.

"I take your silence to mean that you would've preferred a smaller audience," Caesar said in a surprisingly relaxed tone. "After the disaster of the prima actio, the fewer people to witness my failure in this second session the better, right? Am I wrong, my friend?"

Labienus sighed before responding: "No, you are not wrong."

Caesar nodded and looked around. Dolabella was already seated in the center of the room, prepared to give his testimony. The judges were taking their places. In the audience, his wife, mother, and sisters looked at him with a mixture of pride and worry on their faces. Caesar acknowledged them with a brief nod and a somewhat forced smile: he had reconciled with his mother, but he still felt the sting of her betrayal. He understood that she was only trying to protect him, to keep him from receiving the full force of Dolabella's ire. With the trial rigged against him anyway, his mother had thought it best to make him seem like a lesser threat. After all, no one in Rome believed that Dolabella would truly be punished. Only Caesar, it seemed, held on to that delusion as he sat in the basilica, his guts roiling as if he were preparing to charge into combat.

"Hortensius is standing," Labienus said.

Caesar tracked the defense lawyer's movements, still lost in thought, recalling his reconciliation with Cornelia. She had forgiven him for doubting her. His wife was his greatest supporter, a soothing balm that helped replenish his strength.

"You're going to go after him with all you've got, aren't you?" she had asked him that morning as she helped him dress.

"Yes," he'd responded, and then turned to her as she finished adjusting his toga. "You know what? I think my mother, by betraying me, has unwittingly given me a second chance in the trial."

Cornelia gave him a perplexed look. "I don't see how."

"Dolabella and his lawyers, the tribunal and the public, they all think there are two Julius Caesars. They've seen two very different men in the basilica: first a clumsy orator during the divinatio, when I secretly let Cicero destroy me to assure I'd be named accusator. Then the brilliant Julius Caesar in the reiectio, when I convinced Metellus to recuse himself. Everyone was left wondering which of those two Julius Caesars would prevail during the trial. Now, after that disaster in the prima actio, with Hortensius and Cotta completely undermining my witnesses, everyone is convinced that I'm simply a bumbling amateur."

"And today my true Julius Caesar will return for the reiectio. The bold, brave man I love so dearly, who confronted Sulla for me even though it almost killed him," his wife said.

"Yes, today your true Julius Caesar will return. The brave, bold man you love who defied Sulla for you. But today I'll have to confront his hound Dolabella."

Cornelia had wrapped her thin arms around Caesar and hugged him tightly as she whispered in his ear: "May the gods protect you."

Caesar blinked.

"They're starting," Labienus whispered.

During the time it took for an entire water clock to empty, Dolabella answered an exultant Hortensius's questions, one by one.

Caesar listened to each answer, every word the reus spoke, paying close attention to his categorical denial, his relaxed demeanor, the defiant way he looked at the audience. Dolabella was calm and collected as Hortensius asked his questions and seemed satisfied with his answers. The defense was so confident in this testimony, in fact, that Dolabella was their only witness.

"The prosecution alleges that the Via Egnatia is in poor condition throughout the entire province of Macedonia. Is that in fact the case?" Hortensius asked.

"It is," Dolabella admitted, to Caesar and Labienus's surprise. "It's true that the road is in poor condition, but it's not as bad as they have suggested. It had been severely abused and neglected by the Macedonians and was in truly pathetic shape when I arrived in the province. The repairs funded by my government have made the road passable, but without doubt, there is more work left to be done."

"Perfect," said Hortensius. "That clears that up. The taxes levied for the repair of the road were used, then, to that end."

"That is correct," Dolabella assured him.

"In the same way that the tariffs on grain were used to transport said grain from Egypt, correct?"

"Exactly."

"Good. We still need to clear up two claims made by the prosecution against the former governor of Macedonia, former consul, and brave commander granted a triumph in the streets of Rome," Hortensius said, seeming to enjoy reciting his defendant's hefty cursus honorum. "The first claim, the matter of the temple of Aphrodite in Thessaloniki and its plunder; and the second, the lies spouted here by a young Macedonian woman, unmarried, unchaste, a truly shameless girl, to put it mildly. But let's go first to the matter of the temple. Was the temple of Aphrodite in Thessaloniki, so sacred to the Macedonians, in fact pillaged?"

"It was," Dolabella admitted. "But it had already been plundered before I arrived in the city. The Macedonians are not a particularly religious people who bother to take care of their temples. When I arrived in the capital I found that the temple had already been stripped of its statues and all items of value."

"I see," Hortensius continued without batting an eye, taking his client's audacious lies as unquestionable truths. "We're left, then, with the accusations of that dishonored Macedonian woman, which this tribunal has already been forced to hear. Can the former governor enlighten us as to what truly occurred between himself and that woman?"

"Easy to clear up. She summoned me to a meeting," Dolabella began. "It seemed unusual that a young woman, no matter how aristocratic the family, would take the liberty of inviting me to her home, but I agreed to go, out of courtesy. When I arrived, she was alone and wearing clothing more appropriate for an intimate encounter, and she insinuated herself to me repeatedly. I am a widower and I decided to accept her sexual invitation, thinking that if she wanted to be dishonored, that was her prerogative. I supposed she held out some hope that I would wish to bring her to Rome and offer her a life of luxury at my side. But, the fact is, I would choose a Roman woman over a Macedonian any day." He chuckled and was met with laughter from Hortensius, some members of the audience, and a portion of the tribunal.

Myrtale herself, along with Perdiccas, Aeropus, Archelaus, Orestes, and the other Macedonians, gritted her teeth and clenched her fists as the laughter fanned the flames of their bitter fury over Dolabella's blatant lies.

"I think everything is now perfectly clear," said Hortensius as the laughter died down. "The defense has no further questions and no further witnesses. We do not wish to drag out this drama or bore the judges of this tribunal."

Pompey then gave the floor over to the prosecution.

Caesar did not stand. He simply sat staring at Dolabella.

The two men had never exchanged a single word, not even when Caesar had been summoned to an audience at Sulla's home five years prior. They had sized each other up, but they had not spoken directly. Only Sulla had addressed him.

At last, Caesar stood and slowly took his place in the center of the room.

He looked at the audience.

He took a deep breath.

He projected his voice.

"*Testis unus, testis nullus,*"* the young prosecutor began. "A single witness is as good as no witness. The defense wishes to conceal their inability to find a single outside witness to support the reus's version of events. They claim it is to keep from dragging out a case that they consider to be a spectacle. This is interesting: the defense would have it that this is all a stage act, a comedy perhaps, a farce. What part do the judges play in this so-called farce, according to the defense, I wonder? But I won't continue that line of thinking, since I see that the reus's lawyer is about to stand up and tell me not to put words in his mouth. Let's return, then, to the witness who has testified in defense of the reus. The only witness, the reus himself." He turned now to Dolabella. "I was able to find witnesses, several in fact, willing to testify against the reus, as I explained during the divinatio. My two main witnesses were the high priest of the temple of Aphrodite during the reus's term as governor of Macedonia, and the engineer hired by the reus to, supposedly, repair the Via Egnatia. Those witnesses would have testified that the reus looted the temple and that the reus never invested a single sesterce in the repair of the Roman road that traverses Macedonia. But those two men were murdered. Both of them. Both murdered by unknown persons, both stabbed to death," Caesar said, as he walked to the table where Labienus sat and lifted a scroll to reveal a knife, clean and gleaming, and held it up for everyone to see. "Both stabbed to death, yes, a dagger stuck into the back of both witnesses, one after another. And the hired hitmen left the daggers behind in the wake of their abominable crimes. A dagger much like this one."

Dolabella remained silent. For the moment, the accusator was only insinuating that he had given the order for the murders. He was curious to see if the young lawyer would dare to directly state the accusation.

Caesar swallowed. He was going to go for it. Dolabella was already planning to kill him, so what did he have to lose?

---

* "A single witness is a null witness." This phrase appears in the Latin version of the Bible, in the book of Deuteronomy, and is also included in the Justinian Code, after Caesar's time, but that does not mean it hadn't been used informally well before then.

"And I am certain that these daggers," he said as he held the sharp, shining blade with its ivory handle up high for everyone to see, "were wielded by Gnaeus Cornelius Dolabella's hired hitmen."

Hortensius shot to his feet.

"That is a gratuitous and unfounded accusation," he objected. "Is our defendant going to be blamed for all the murders that occur every day across Rome and its many provinces?"

Caesar turned to Hortensius. "No, not all of them, I suppose," he said, making part of the audience laugh.

Pompey gestured toward the praecones, furious that he was losing control of the session. The eldest clerk stood up and demanded silence in the room: "Favete linguis!"

The laughter died down, and Caesar resumed his speech before the president of the tribunal could call him to order. "Not all of them, no, but I am wholly convinced that the hitmen who murdered my witnesses, leaving identical daggers in the backs of both innocent men, were hired by the reus." He looked directly at Dolabella now. "Isn't that right?"

Gnaeus Cornelius Dolabella's face lit up with a smile. The young prosecutor's enormous clumsiness seemed almost unbelievable. All he had to do was deny the accusation, it was that simple. It was the word of a respected Roman senator against the accusations of a young and inexperienced lawyer.

"No, I did not order their deaths. Everyone in Rome knows that my men don't carry daggers with ivory handles. They carry much sharper blades, with red-and-black hilts. Nothing like the knife the accusator holds in his hand. So the daggers found in the backs of your witnesses could not have belonged to my men."

Caesar froze in the center of the room. He seemed surprised for a moment, defeated once again. But just before the murmurs began, he spoke up: "The dagger I hold in my hand is my own," he said. "A gift from my wife. Perhaps I led the reus to falsely believe that the dagger I hold was the one used by the murderers, but that is not the case." He walked back to the table where Labienus sat. He stood to one side and lifted the scrolls to reveal two daggers with dried blood on their blades.

Caesar set down the dagger that Cornelia had gifted him and held up the other two, lifting the handles, red and black, for everyone to see.

"*These* are the daggers that killed the prosecution's witnesses, which the reus has been kind enough to identify as the ones used by the men in his hire. And I have witnesses, live ones, who can testify that these, in fact, were the very knifes found in the backs of the Macedonian priest and the murdered engineer."

Dolabella gritted his teeth and muttered under his breath, breathing heavily. He looked to Cotta and Hortensius, who stood. "That proves nothing. Purely circumstantial," he argued. "Our defendant's men are not the only ones who use that kind of dagger. And we can't even be sure if those knives were, in fact, the ones used in the murders."

Caesar smiled before responding. He'd managed to get Dolabella, almost without realizing it, to testify against himself.

"It is perhaps circumstantial, but whether it proves anything is a matter to be determined by the fifty-two judges of the tribunal. Because we are not in the theatre watching a farcical comedy, or in the Circus Maximus enjoying a spectacle. We stand before a tribunal of justice in the Basilica Sempronia of Rome." He turned now to the judges. "To the testimonies supplied in the prima actio, I'd like to add the reus's testimony . . . against himself." He turned back to Hortensius. "Or is the defense now going to argue that the reus is a liar? Or that the reus is a senile old man who doesn't even remember the color of the daggers used by his personal guard? That would be interesting to hear."

Laughter once more spread through the room.

Under Pompey's attentive gaze, the praecones called the court to order and silence once again fell over the Basilica Sempronia.

Everyone thought that Caesar had finished interrogating the defendant; in fact, the prosecutor had walked back to his corner, but he stopped short, turned, and faced Dolabella: "One last question: Does the reus believe that the Macedonians deserve justice, Roman justice?"

The defendant leaned back in his seat and tilted his head, looking at Caesar out of the corner of his eye. It was a totally unexpected question and seemed to have nothing to do with the case. According to Roman law, the Macedonians had the right to bring the former governor of their province to trial as long as another Roman citizen, like Caesar, agreed to prosecute him. That was a fact. But the young lawyer was asking whether he thought they deserved this right.

Dolabella walked right into the trap. He was so confident in the notion that the tribunal would exonerate him on all counts that he didn't see any harm in speaking his mind. He failed to see how giving his honest opinion could damage him in any way. So he straightened his back and responded loudly and clearly. "Personally, I don't think that the Macedonians or any other non-Roman people should be allowed to abuse our judicial system. Rome is for the Romans, and Roman law should be applicable only among Romans. Especially in the case of a defeated people such as the Macedonians, who forget they are now merely subjects of Rome and that they exist at the mercy of our generosity. They live in the past, in the times of their great Alexander. But Alexander has been dead and buried in the ground for centuries . . ."

He was about to say, "in Alexandria," where the tomb of the great Macedonian conqueror lay, but just then a thunderous boom echoed through the Basilica Sempronia, silencing him. It was an unexpected sound since the day had started out bright and clear. But a sudden storm must now be rolling in. Dolabella refused to consider other alternatives. But he stopped speaking.

The former Macedonian governor, breathing shallowly through his mouth, sat motionless as he looked out at the audience, his eyes scanning the crowd until, suddenly, he found Myrtale, her icy glare fixed on him.

He saw her turn to one of the other Macedonians, but he couldn't hear what the girl was saying. It didn't matter, he could guess.

"He's said it," Myrtale hissed, her heart pounding with a sense of triumph. "He's said it."

Caesar, like everyone else, was jarred by the thunderclap, but he knew nothing of the curse of Thessaloniki, so he resumed his line of questioning without another thought to the brewing storm. "It's interesting to note that the reus thinks this trial should've never taken place," he said with a smile.

There was no more thunder.

Dolabella looked away from Myrtale and shook off the strange, dark thoughts about the sudden thunderclap that foretold torrential rain. He turned his attention back to the prosecutor. "I follow the laws and therefore accept this trial," he said, not wanting the judges to think he was questioning their authority. Truth be told, he despised the tribunal; he'd paid them a fortune to sit and pass judgment on him. But he knew it would be unwise to openly express his disdain or make them look ridiculous in public. Bribed or not, he couldn't belittle the judges before the entire basilica. "I was referring to the fact that foreigners have been allowed to abuse our laws and unjustly accuse a senator of Rome. I would change that law if I could, but the law exists, and I am here, following it. I follow the law."

"That is what it all boils down to, isn't it?" Caesar replied. "Whether we truly believe that the reus followed Roman law during his term as governor of Macedonia." He walked back to the prosecution's table and addressed the tribunal. "I have no further questions," he said before the defendant had time to object.

LXII

THE DEFENSE'S
FINAL STATEMENT

Basílica Sempronia, Rome
77 B.C.

C AESAR HAD BEEN VERY SKILLFUL IN HIS INTERROGATION of Dolabella, almost seeming to have coaxed a confession of murder out of the defendant. Hortensius knew that even though the tribunal was predisposed to exonerate his client, it was still a public trial and the basilica was packed. The political situation in Rome was tense— it was crucial that Dolabella be made to look as good as possible in front of the masses, just as it was important for Caesar to be fully discredited.

The eternal struggle between the optimates and the populares still remained latent, like a dormant volcano that might erupt at any moment. The defense lawyers understood that Dolabella was paying them not only to achieve a favorable verdict, but also to repair his public image. The former governor of Macedonia had bribed the entire tribunal and would surely obtain a not-guilty verdict. He had hired the services of the best lawyers in Rome to ensure that the people would overlook his excesses in Macedonia and view him as a just and upright politician.

Hortensius stood to give the defense's final statement.

Aurelius Cotta had decided to remain in the background after the conclusion of the prima actio since he did not relish destroying his young nephew's reputation. He felt sorry for the boy, but he had warned him against prosecuting Dolabella. It was now impossible to extract him from the punishing maws of Roman justice. Hortensius was about to do away with any shred of credibility Caesar had left. The trick with the dagger and the way he'd managed to make Dolabella look ridiculous had been a stroke of brilliance, but it would now be entirely overshadowed by the firestorm that Hortensius would unleash on the prosecutor. It would be brief but intense.

"Good justices of the tribunal," Hortensius began, pacing the floor and making sweeping gestures with his arms. "I will be very concise and succinct. Not because I consider this to be a farce, as the young prosecutor would have you believe that I or the reus ... I mean"—he quickly corrected himself—"senator and former governor Dolabella consider it to be." He was nervous, absurdly nervous, after Caesar's successful interrogation. "I will be succinct," he said again, trying to focus on his speech, "because my defendant's innocence is so obvious and the prosecution is so greatly lacking in evidence that I do not need to trot out complex arguments that would only distract us from the matter at hand. The prosecution's first witness was an engineer who was bribed by the prosecutor himself, subtly perhaps, but bribed nonetheless, when he paid said engineer's way to Macedonia. Then we were submitted to the ramblings of a senile old man who can neither see nor hear, and finally forced to listen to accusations made by ... a woman. And women, we all know, are inclined to the most grotesque exaggerations, if not outright lies. Not to mention the fact that she is unmarried, and unchaste. This is all the prosecution has been able to muster for the occasion. As good as nothing. Not a single testimony worthy of consideration by a Roman tribunal. Lies levied against a respected senator, former consul, defeater of the Thracians, a generous governor who took it upon himself to improve the conditions of his province, procuring grain from as far away as Egypt so as to avoid widespread famine, reconstructing the Via Egnatia, which was badly damaged by overuse. They would blame him for the inexorable decline of Macedonia. Yes, their land was once glorious, perhaps, in the past, but it was already well on its way to social and economic collapse. The shameless, dishonorable people of Macedonia would loot their own temples and spend their days blaming innocent Romans for their own indignities, weaknesses, and crimes.

"For these reasons, I am confident that the tribunal will find Gnaeus Cornelius Dolabella completely innocent of everything he's been unjustly accused of during the various sessions of this trial. A trial that, nevertheless, has shed light on one fact." Here he turned to Caesar: "It has become abundantly clear to all of us that Gaius Marius's hatred of the optimates is hereditary, passed on from uncle to blundering nephew. Because, make no mistake, this is not a trial for corruption. No. It is nothing more than a crude, bumbling, spiteful attempt at political persecution."

Here Hortensius concluded his speech and sat down next to Cotta, who simply nodded in recognition of the persuasive closing remarks. He'd seen Hortensius speak much more brilliantly and incisively on other occasions. But, unfortunately for his nephew, it was still a flawless argument. Even if Dolabella was guilty, his nephew had been unable to provide sufficient evidence or argue with the necessary skill. Caesar was now standing in the center of the room. Cotta was genuinely curious to see how he would try to save the unsalvageable.

LXIII

CAESAR'S FINAL
STATEMENT

FIRST CITIZEN: Methinks there is much reason in his sayings.
SECOND CITIZEN: If thou consider rightly of the matter,
Caesar has had great wrong.

—SHAKESPEARE, *Julius Caesar*, ACT III, SCENE II

Basílica Sempronia, Rome
77 B.C.

CAESAR BEGAN SPEAKING TO THE TRIBUNAL, HIS EYES FIXED
on Pompey. "I will not be brief. I will be honest. I will not be succinct.
I will be exhaustive. Because exhaustive is the list of crimes committed by the man accused here today, Gnaeus . . . Cornelius . . . Dolabella," he said, fixing his eyes on the reus as he pronounced his
praenomen, nomen, and *cognomen* like some obscene insult. He looked
back at the president of the tribunal before he had the chance to warn
him that he was wasting precious time. "Yes, I will be exhaustive. I
will be honest, but I will remain within the time allotted to me by the
water clocks."

Pompey held his gaze.

Caesar began his speech.

He was up against lies, murders, and blatant corruption, and all he
had were his words. "To truly understand what this trial represents,
here, in the Basilica Sempronia, in the heart of our Roman Forum,
we must first answer one question: What is truly at stake? What is it

that is being decided?" He spoke with his hands on his hips, looking from the audience to the tribunal to the defense to the reus, turning as he paced slowly across the floor. "What is this trial really about? By all appearances, we could say that this case is about the illegal actions of the reus during his term as governor of Macedonia. Those crimes, certainly, are what have brought us here. But this trial has implications far beyond that. The defendant's crimes are like a nut surrounded by a hard, protective shell. The shell is as important as the nut itself. In this case, the shell is Roman justice. Without it, this trial would not exist, nor the concept of crime, or crimes, in this case, that the reus, Gnaeus Cornelius Dolabella, is being tried for. And the future of Roman justice, of Rome itself, perhaps, is also on trial. I stand here today arguing the case of the Macedonian before all of you present, the judges of the tribunal, the reus, the lawyers for the defense, and the public. But also attentive to this case, waiting for news, are the good people of Macedonia and, I'd dare say, the inhabitants of all the provinces governed by Rome. And they are paying close attention to what is done and said in this trial because they want to understand our laws and comprehend the reach of our justice.

"The people of Hispania, Cisalpine Gaul, Africa, and Italy; of Sardinia, Sicily, and the better part of Greece and Macedonia; no doubt understand the reach of our weapons, our legions. But now they are trying to determine whether we are merely brutal conquerors or if we can be, also, just rulers. Are our laws worth following? Are we, as rulers, worthy of their loyalty? It may seem, on the surface, that we are simply here to judge the crimes of a bad governor. But we, as Romans, who consider ourselves destined to rule other nations, have to know that what we are truly deciding here, today, is whether we deserve, by Jupiter, by Mars, by Venus, by all the gods, to govern, justly and effectively, these other nations!"

There was total silence.

"A smoke screen . . ." Hortensius whispered. "Just words."

"Just words," Cotta agreed, "but well put. And the people are listening." He turned his eyes to the public and Hortensius also looked to the citizens crowded into the Basilica Sempronia that morning.

It was clear that Caesar had captivated all those present, and his words seemed to resonate especially with the sympathizers of the popular cause, who were among the majority in the crowd. They wanted to see if he would question the regime built by Sulla and maintained by the optimates.

Caesar had the Macedonians' full attention, obviously, since the trial involved them directly; but the judges and the rest of the conservative senators followed his words closely as well. The young lawyer's speech was starting to sound like a challenge to the current system. And they were highly interested in keeping things as they were, with all the power in their hands. They were curious to see how far he would take his criticisms.

All those gathered in the basilica were hanging on Caesar's every word.

The optimates had their guard up. As president of the tribunal and leader of the conservative senators now that Metellus had returned to Hispania, Pompey was willing to let Caesar speak, if only to maintain appearances, but there were limits to what he would allow the young man to say publicly.

Caesar knew that he was the focus of all eyes and thoughts. For better or worse, this was his moment.

"The defendant's lawyer, Hortensius, was very brief in his attempts to exonerate the reus of his crimes. He aims to reduce the long list of egregious offenses to merely a few slight indiscretions that should not even be attributed to his client. He'd have us believe that the temple of Aphrodite was looted before the reus arrived in Thessaloniki; that a testimony from the defendant, Dolabella himself, is enough to prove that grain was imported from Egypt; that a road was repaired. That the murder of both of my initial witnesses is pure coincidence. And when I bring new witnesses, they accuse them of having been paid, of being senile, or female, all discredited. The reus is therefore innocent, they argue. As if the Macedonians had nothing better to do than travel all the way from Thessaloniki, spending the little money they have left after Dolabella's greedy tenure in their province, to demand a long trial for made-up crimes. As if a violated woman somehow derived pleasure from humiliating herself in public before hundreds of strangers. What sense does it make for these

Macedonian men, for this woman, to waste their money and demean themselves over fabrications?"

Caesar stopped. He ran a hand over his dry mouth. He needed water, but he didn't want to stop for a drink. Not yet. His speech was going well. He had managed to rouse the ire of many of those present, more inclined to believe him than Dolabella's lawyers. He could see it in the eyes of the citizens, watching him intently. He had to continue.

"No, I will not be brief!" he said, inflamed. He glanced at the water clock and then addressed Pompey. "I beg the president of this tribunal to urge the adjuster to keep away from the clepsydras. The fact that the defense has chosen not to use all their time does not mean that I should have to do the same. The water clocks are full, all six of them. I will speak until they are empty, as is only fair. Now that they have been filled, I don't see any need for the adjuster to remain beside them."

Pompey looked at Caesar with a bored, impassive expression.

As Caesar had guessed, Pompey had given the water clock adjuster instructions to manipulate the clepsydras during the prosecution's final statement, if necessary, to keep him from going on for too long. He never imagined that the young prosecutor would notice, but thanks to Caesar's direct, public challenge, with all eyes on him, Pompey had no choice but to nod for the adjuster to move several paces away. Pompey filed Caesar's affront away in his memory. And Pompey was not one to forget an insult, ever.

Caesar nodded, still in the center of the room. He ran his right hand through his hair. It was getting long and he liked the feel of it, but he'd noticed that it was beginning to thin. That worried and irritated him, but he was now focused on other matters. He went on: "No, I will not be brief, but neither will I be excessive. I will be deliberate, going over everything that has happened here. The defense claims that the reus did not keep the money he collected to repair the Via Egnatia, but even the reus himself admits that the road in question is in terrible condition. His justification is that when he arrived in Thessaloniki it was much worse. By all the gods: in two years as governor he should've been able to not only repair a road, but to build a new one entirely! Thank the gods that the rest of our governors, praetors, consuls, and proconsuls have not been as unskilled in infrastructure as Dolabella. If they were, Rome would be totally isolated from the rest of the world, without a single road, even in poor condition, to lead us anywhere. One term as governor is enough to build two roads from Dyrrhachium to Byzantium, one to get there and another to get back."

Laughter rang out through the Basilica Sempronia.

Hearty laughter that did not immediately die down.

The praecones worked to silence the crowd.

Caesar used the opportunity to quench his thirst, his throat parched from so much talking and from the stress of the moment. He drank slowly.

He returned to the center of the room.

Everyone looked at him.

"In addition to denying the reus's illegal misappropriation of public funds, the defense has also tried to discredit my witnesses and my arguments. 'They expected more of me,' they say. In their attempt to discredit me, they have disregarded the heartfelt testimony of a young woman who saw her honor disgraced. They have mocked her and accused her of lying, the only argument being . . . that she is a woman. And to support this ridiculous claim, the defense's lawyer turns to mythological stories showing the ways women have negatively impacted the course of history. But his compilation of myths is clearly partial. Because we could just as easily list others in which women are free of all guilt and just as trustworthy as any man, even more so, perhaps."

"I'm not so sure about that," Hortensius interrupted, standing and spreading his arms as he let out a fake laugh that a few optimates and their supporters joined him in.

Caesar turned to Hortensius, accepting his challenge: "I would remind the defense that we are on my time, but nonetheless, let's examine the question of a woman's honor, or lack thereof. First we have the god of trickery, Dolos, who is not female but male. Women are often accused of being inconstant and changeable, but in *The Odyssey*, Penelope remained faithful to her husband Odysseus for his entire time away from Ithaca, in a difficult challenge to her loyalty that I'm not sure many men here could successfully endure."

Caesar paused his speech to look Pompey in the eye. All of Rome knew that the president of the tribunal had married Antistia, his first wife, to manipulate a tribunal where his father-in-law served as judge, only to later abandon her at Sulla's request. Pompey was no example of fidelity. He was faithful only to his ambition.

Pompey did not say a word. He merely noted this indirect criticism. Caesar was mocking not only the defense but the president of the tribunal as well. Perhaps the verdict was not what mattered most to him.

"Penelope was loyal," Caesar continued. "To the end. But we should also recall that Rome was created by the descendants of Aeneas, and Aeneas himself descends from none other than Venus. Rome, in its divine origin, has the blood of a goddess. And our city's most scared deity, whose circular temple stands only a few steps from this basilica, is another goddess, Vesta. It is her flame that burns eternal, protecting the city, assuring that, as long as it burns, Rome will prosper. And who have we charged with the protection of this sacred flame? It is not guarded by armed legionaries or veteran warriors. The temple is not surrounded by gladiators prepared to fight to the death to protect it. No, since ancestral times, Vesta's sacred flame has always been watched over and tended by six virgin priestesses. This is whom we charge with the protection of what is most cherished. Six women: the vestal virgins."

Caesar paused, rhetorically. He wanted to see if Hortensius had any new comments to add, but he'd managed to quiet the defense. It was as if the entire trial were changing course.

The first water clock emptied. The liquid from the second one began to spill out, drop by drop.

Gaius Julius Caesar confidently resumed his speech. "It has been argued that a woman, Helena, and her infidelity, caused the terrible Trojan War. That would seem to be the case, if we take Homer's *Iliad* as fact. But the same events narrated by Euripides, who follows the version told by Stesichorus, authors that the reus's lawyer should read, tell us that Helena had nothing to do with that blaze. We could spend hours trotting out examples from Greek and Roman authors, both contemporary and classic, where women are not unfaithful, not inconstant, not liars." He looked at the water clocks. There were four left out of six; hadn't the second one emptied exceedingly fast? "But I don't want to bore the tribunal or to deviate from the central point of this trial. I only wish to highlight the fact that Myrtale, the young Macedonian woman violently dishonored by the reus, should not be discounted simply because she is a woman." He walked toward Hortensius as he continued speaking. "I also expected more of the defense. I may have made errors or missteps in this process, but this is my first trial. The reus's lawyers have no such excuse, since they are expert litigators. Their problem is not lack of experience, no. Their problem is that their reus is indefensible and they have no *living* witnesses willing to testify in his favor, not even with all the gold the reus has managed to accumulate through illegal means, robbing, and plundering. Because, make no mistake, the man who sits before us accused of these crimes is a thief, an extortionist, a murderer, and a rapist. A criminal."

Applause in the room.

And shouts. The first cries of "Criminal!"

It was clear that the people did not sympathize with Dolabella and only a small spark was needed to light the flame of indignation. Dolabella was a symbol of Sulla's tyranny, the populares' defeat, and the optimates' oppression of the people going all the way back to the murder of the Gracchi, the Drusi, Saturninus, and so many others who'd fought for their rights. Dolabella symbolized Marius's defeat. But Marius's nephew was now speaking to them. And he spoke well.

Pompey eyed the door, where a veteran of Sulla's former legions stood. The retired officer nodded and turned to give word to someone outside. Pompey had suspected that the prosecutor might attempt to instigate the plebes and had forces standing by to control the situation if necessary.

Caesar watched as several dozen men dressed as everyday citizens, but surely armed with more than just daggers, entered the basilica and fanned out through the room. He had to measure his words carefully. It was time to get serious, solemn, grave.

He raised his arms.

The insults ceased. The voices quieted.

Hortensius jumped out of his seat. He didn't like seeing the boy so focused, so in control of the situation, and he felt the need to discredit his arguments, to destroy his rhetoric. "Women cannot be trusted," Hortensius insisted. "They all carry within them a Clytemnestra who, shan't we forget, murdered her husband Agamemnon when he returned from the Trojan War."

Caesar lowered his arms.

He did not express surprise or anger at Hortensius's interruption. He knew that the man was acting out of desperation. Caesar had the upper hand now. Clytemnestra was another unfaithful, murderous woman whose story had been told over and over, almost always incompletely.

Caesar was about to get to the crux of his argument, but he couldn't let the example go uncontested. "Clytemnestra, Agamemnon's wife," said Caesar, walking to where Hortensius sat, "did kill her husband. But it's not so clear that it was murder. The debate is still open as to whether she murdered him . . . or justifiably executed him for his crimes. The story of Clytemnestra, as opposed to that of the faithful Penelope, is rarely told in its entirety: Clytemnestra killed her husband Agamemnon, but he had returned from Troy with a new lover, Cassandra, and if that weren't motive enough to anger a wife, everyone seems to have forgotten that Agamemnon also killed his own daughter, Iphigenia, sacrificing her so that the gods would favor him in the Trojan War. Agamemnon murdered his own daughter, Clytemnestra's daughter. We could debate for hours over whether Clytemnestra did the correct thing or not upon avenging the death of Iphigenia, but there is no doubt that Clytemnestra had justification for killing Agamemnon. In the same way that Myrtale, the young Macedonian woman, has justification for accusing Gnaeus . . . Cornelius . . . Dolabella . . . of rape."

Silence.

Silence from Hortensius.

Silence in the room.

Caesar gravitated again to the center of the basilica.

He raised his arms, and silence fell: "But at the start of my speech," he continued, "I said that this trial goes much further than the crimes perpetrated by Gnaeus Cornelius Dolabella. I believe that this trial is about Rome itself, about us, and what kind of justice we want to see for ourselves and for all those we govern. And this is something we should consider very carefully. Because we can impose ourselves by the force of our weapons in conquest. But we will only keep what we've conquered over time by the force of our justice. Justice for all, not for the few. I recall the words that Thucydides attributes to Pericles, when the illustrious ruler gives his famous discourse in commemoration of his fallen compatriots in the long Peloponnesian War."

Here Caesar quoted Pericles in Greek, but he did not wish to speak only to the few judges of the tribunal who could sufficiently understand the language. He wanted to reach the Roman people in the crowd congregated there in the Basilica Sempronia. And so, after citing Pericles's original words, he translated them so that everyone present could understand: "Our constitution does not copy the laws of neighboring states; we are rather a pattern to others than imitators ourselves. Its administration favors the many instead of the few; this is why it is called a democracy. If we look to the laws, they afford equal justice to all in their private differences ... But all this ease in our private relations does not make us lawless as citizens. Against this fear is our chief safeguard, teaching us to obey the magistrates and the laws, particularly such as regard the protection of the injured."*

Caesar paused again, letting the people gradually process the meaning of those words. He knew that he had to guide their thoughts, so he continued, speaking unhurriedly, even though the water seemed to be rapidly disappearing from the clepsydras.

"Let's examine this, let's consider the significance of these words.

---

* Thucydides, *The Peloponnesian War* Book 2, Chapter 37, paragraphs 1–3. In Greek, the quotation reads: Χρώμεθα γὰρ πολιτείαι οὐ ζηλούσῃ τοὺς τῶν πέλας νόμους, παράδειγμα δὲ μᾶλλον αὐτοὶ ὄντες τισὶν ἢ μιμούμενοιετέρους. καὶ ὄνομα μὲν διὰ τὸ μὴ ἐς ὀλίγους ἀλλ᾽ ἐς πλείονας οἰκεῖν δημοκρατία κέκληται· μέτεστι δὲ κατὰ μὲν τοὺς νόμους πρὸς τὰ ἴδια διάφορα πᾶσι τὸ ἴσον (...) Ἀνεπαχθῶς δὲ τὰ ἴδια προσομιλοῦντες τὰ δημόσια διὰ δέος μάλιστα οὐ παρανομοῦμεν, τῶν τε αἰεὶ ἐν ἀρχῇ ὄντων ἀκροάσει καὶ τῶν νόμων, καὶ μάλιστα αὐτῶν ὅσοι τε ἐπ᾽ ὠφελίᾳ τῶν ἀδικουμένων κεῖνται.

We may call our form of government a 'democracy,' but to truly be democratic, our laws, as Pericles points out, must defend the interests not of the very few, but of the majority. Or at least that's how I interpret it. And equally important, and I am certain there will be consensus among all those listening to me today: we don't want to simply imitate others, but to instead serve as a model for others to follow. And this point is key.

"We have proven time and again, through great pain and suffering, that ignoring the people we govern is a grave error. It was only a few years ago that the Marsi rebelled and were joined by our Italic allies. This was because they did not consider themselves to be justly governed. Only after much bloodshed did we reach agreements with them. Our laws affect not only the Italic people, but all those who reside in any province governed by Rome. And each representative of Rome sent to these provinces as governor must be absolutely exemplary in his behavior. He is there not simply to maximize his own personal gains, as the reus seems to have believed. He is there, in this case in Macedonia, to represent each and every one of us, the citizens of Rome. The Macedonians are here today because they accept our laws and understand that these laws rightfully extend to them as well. They chose to avoid violence against the reus, Dolabella, the blatantly corrupt governor who, unfortunately for all of them and for us, was sent to Thessaloniki. And because of this, it is important that we seek justice for the injured, as Pericles refers to those who suffer injustice. But, what's more . . ."

He had reached the prosecutor's table, where Labienus had refilled his cup of water. Caesar took a few sips. He set it back on the table. *Water,* he thought. He scrutinized the water clocks: there were three left. The adjuster was still several steps from them, but it was obvious to Caesar that the clepsydras had been somehow manipulated. The water was disappearing too quickly. The second clock had been emptied in seconds, or at least it had seemed so. He turned around, then, to face the defendant: Dolabella shifted in his seat, as if he couldn't find a comfortable position. Caesar liked watching him squirm.

Pompey, for his part, was scanning the audience for the men he'd called in to control the room if things should get out of hand. He then looked at the defense lawyers, the water clock adjuster, the audience, Dolabella . . . and finally, Caesar himself.

The young prosecutor met his gaze and held it.

Caesar walked back to the center of the room. And he continued. "Pericles also talks to us about fear. What fear is he referring to? He's talking about a very concrete fear: fear of the law. Fear of breaking it. And that fear is essential in any government that must depend on the will of its people. The fear inspired by our legions on the battlefield makes our enemies either retreat or submit, but it is the fear of punishment for breaking the law that dissuades vile persons such as Gnaeus Cornelius Dolabella from wallowing in corruption like a pig in his sty."

"Corrupt!"

"Dolabella is crooked!"

"A corrupt pig!"

The audience once again interrupted Caesar's speech with insults hurled loudly at the reus. Never before had the prosecutor been so scathing and direct in his attacks on the defendant, and the crowd was ready with their jeering responses.

Pompey looked to the door. More men were entering, equally well armed, he knew, although they had not yet exhibited a single dagger or gladius. Even so, Caesar could feel the weight of sharpened metal accumulating in the Basilica Sempronia. And he didn't know for sure, but he suspected that Perdiccas, Archelaus, Aeropus, and the other Macedonians wore multiple weapons as well.

Distracted by the tumult of shouts and insults that continued to rain down on the reus, Caesar missed the note passed from Dolabella to one of his slaves. The servant immediately rushed to one of the praecones as the other functionaries continued calling for order in the court. As the crowd reacted to Caesar's words, the clerk took the small rolled-up scroll that Dolabella's slave handed him and carried it to the president of the tribunal without anyone else noticing.

Pompey unrolled it and read to himself:

*"I have the very unpleasant feeling that I have before me, in the center of the basilica, the reincarnation of Gaius Marius. You know what has to be done with the young Caesar. Sulla was right."**

Even though Pompey hadn't seen where the unsigned note had come from, he looked immediately at Dolabella, who sat distractedly studying his nails, as if the proceedings had nothing to do with him. Dolabella had made up his mind to have Caesar killed as soon as this farce of a trial was over, and he was analyzing the different ways he could do it. For him, planning the death of someone who dared to challenge him was comforting, and he delighted in thinking about how and when the death of his enemy would take place. The note he'd sent to Pompey was not a request for permission to execute Caesar. For some time now, ever since Sulla's death, Dolabella had not asked anyone for permission to do anything. It was just a courtesy to Pompey, the young emerging leader of the optimates.

Caesar walked back to the table where Labienus sat and took a few more sips of water.

His friend spoke to him in a low voice: "The adjuster . . ." he said.

Caesar turned to the water clocks: the clepsydra adjuster was stepping away from them, but it was clear that he had further manipulated Caesar's time. In fact, Caesar had the feeling that his entire life was counting down to a predetermined end. A violent end. The question was how many more arguments he could lay out before the remaining clocks emptied. And how many of his objectives he would be able to achieve before his life ran out.

Caesar walked back to the center of the room.

He faced the tribunal.

Silence, after much insistence from the praecones, had been restored.

"Yes, judges, this trial is not only about Dolabella's crimes, but about the very essence of who we are, of who we want to be: Conquerors or liberators? Do we want to be tyrants? Or do we want to be

---

* "Habeo ingratissimum sensum tenendi Caii Marii novam incarnationem ante me in medio basilicae. Iam scis quod cum iuueni Caesare faciendum erit. Sulla recte dicebat."

legends, like Darius or Alexander, who not only conquered, but who were so generous to the territories that they annexed that they were loved and adored by all the inhabitants of their empires? That is what is being decided here in this trial. For Aristotle, a true politician, a true ruler, is a virtuous one, willing to act for the common good. Similarly, the verdict of guilty or innocent in this trial should set aside personal affinities to consider the entirety of everyone affected by this case: the defendant, on one hand, and on the other, everyone harmed by him. We should not, in this case, distinguish between Roman citizens and non-Romans, much less when this latter group has accepted our laws as their own.

"There are those who say, as I have heard in the forum on more than one occasion, that there should be more laws, to cover cases like this one. I say we do not need more laws. More laws only means more corruption. The problem will not be solved by endless legislation, but by making sure that the laws we already have are enforced. I know," he opened his arms wide before the audience, as if he were including everyone in his speech, "we all know, that the reus is secretly pressuring the judges, that he has practically bought them off, that he uses the many means at his disposal to ensure they exonerate him of his crimes. It reminds me of Plautus's famous words: 'It would be unfitting, of course, for unjust favors to be obtained from the just.'* I think, I *need,* to believe that the tribunals of Rome are just. In the same way that what Dolabella seeks is, to put it mildly, paraphrasing the noble Plautus, unjust."

He paused to take a breath. He looked at the water clocks. Time was short. He could've complained about it, but things were already very tense. The more prudent thing to do was simply wrap up his final argument. Even if the manipulation of his time was unfair.

"I have provided testimonies and proof of Gnaeus Cornelius Dolabella's crimes, but, in case any doubts remain, let us look to his past behavior, as well as his present lifestyle: parties, banquets, decadence, unlimited luxury, prostitutes, and every excess imaginable are in-

* *"Iniusta ab iustis impetrari non decet."* T. Maccius Plautus, *Amphitryon, or Jupiter in Disguise.* Prologue, line 35.

dulged in by the reus on a daily basis. Because, returning to Plautus, 'Ill-gotten, ill-spent.'* And that is the case. If Dolabella had amassed his fortune through hard work and effort, he would surely spend it with more restraint. His extreme ostentatiousness belies his wealth's dark, sinister, criminal origin: his money was stolen from the Macedonians through illegal taxes and plundering of their temples. And if we allow the accused to be exonerated of these crimes against the Macedonians, simply because he is a Roman citizen, all of us here in Rome will have to continue living under the threat of this same criminal. And so, I ask the tribunal to remember the wise maxim *multis minatur qui uni facit iniuria.* Yes, honorable iudices of the tribunal, he threatens many who does injustice to one.† And if the tribunal exonerates Dolabella of his crimes, they will be committing an injustice against us all, against the entirety of the citizens of Rome who dutifully follow the laws, as well as the Macedonians who agree to accept our laws and customs. I've read the Greek phrase: Δεῖ ἐν μέν τοῖς ὅπλοις φοβερούς, ἐν δὲ τοῖς δικαστηρίοις. And I agree. Yes, 'one must be implacable on the battlefield but compassionate in the courtroom.' But, I'd ask, compassionate with whom? And I would respond that the iudices should be compassionate with the injured parties, compassionate with the Macedonians," Caesar said, making use of Cicero's advice.

"The lawyers for the defense have not missed a single chance to remind the court that I am here to serve as prosecutor. It is true, I am in fact the one who brings these charges against Dolabella. But I am also, here and now, doing something much more important: I am defending the Macedonians, who have suffered terrible injustices at the hands of the corrupt Dolabella. I defend the Macedonians for the common good of us all, Romans and non-Romans alike, all subject to the laws of the fair and just Roman Republic that we so love. I am here not merely to defend the Macedonians but to defend justice, to defend the citizens of Rome, who are tired of corrupt senators going unpunished for their endless crimes. Dolabella has

---

* "*Male partum, male disperit,*" from Plautus's *Poenulus,* translated by Paul Nixon.

† Attributed to Publius Syrus, but was likely used popularly before him.

sullied the name of Rome. He was tasked with administering peace but has instead created a perfect storm for rebellion and war."

Silence.

All eyes were on Caesar.

"And precisely because we were implacable with the Macedonians on the battlefield," he continued, "we must now, in our hall of justice, be compassionate, sensitive to the claims of these Macedonians, whatever those claims may be. We must be just. We must listen to their grievances and compensate them in accordance with their suffering. The fifty-two judges of this tribunal, senators, optimates, specifically, consider themselves to be the best of the best. Well then, by the gods, let them prove it, I say! 'The corruption of the best is the worst of all.'"* He lowered his voice but charged each of his words with authority. "Prove to us, iudices, that you stand against this injustice, since, as Democritus said: Μούνοι θεοφιλέες, ὅσοις ἐχθρόν τὸ ἀδικέειν. Yes, the gods love the enemies of injustice. And may the gods have reason to love us all, Roman citizens and Macedonians alike. May all those whom we govern have reason to respect us. A bad apple will spoil the bunch, as they say, but if it is removed, the rest will remain resplendent."

He looked, once more, to the water clocks. There was only one left and it was running out.

"I, for one, believe in justice. I believe in Rome. I know that the defense has played at denying the truth, denying the reus's crimes, trying to confuse us, but may the judges remember: 'Η Δίκη γάρ καὶ κατά σκότον βλέπει.' Yes, may the members of the tribunal remember that 'justice can be seen even through darkness.' As judges, as enforcers of our laws, you must see through the shadows of the defense's fictitious, invented tales. You must see the defendant's total disrespect for all that is just and decorous and honorable. That is why I beg the gods to shine down on this tribunal so that Gnaeus Cornelius Dolabella may be condemned for all his atrocious crimes, so that we may remove from our resplendent city the most rotten, poison-

---

*   "*Corruptio optimi, pessimal.*" Later attributed to Saint Geronimus, probably commonly used before that.

ous, and despicable of apples imaginable. A rotten apple that will bring Rome not wealth and prosperity but more war and rebellion from all those forced to suffer under his corrupt power!"

He paused for an instant. He needed to catch his breath before getting to the most important part of his argument.

The audience was shouting insults at Dolabella and there was some applause for Caesar, but he raised an arm and they fell silent.

He ran a hand through his hair.

He turned to the audience, scanned it until his eyes found Cornelia's. He felt love emanating from her gaze. He then located his mother and registered her approval. Finally, he turned to Dolabella, whose face was a mask of hatred.

Julius Caesar took a deep breath. Time was running out. His voice boomed through the basilica: "Dolabella sits trial here, today, for his terrible crimes. But there is something much more important on trial in this basilica as well. I stand here representing not only the Macedonians. I stand here representing all of Rome. The defense would have us believe that Dolabella is Rome, but that is not the case. In this trial, Dolabella is not Rome. The judges are not Rome. Rome and the interests of the Roman people are represented here, today, in this hall of justice, by me and me alone. Today, here and now, I. Am. Rome."

He raised his arms.

The final water clock emptied its last drops.

The audience let out a resounding ovation.

Pompey looked on wearing a grave expression.

Dolabella, seemingly composed, was seething inside.

Cornelia had been moved to tears.

Aurelia was proud but fearful.

"Pretty impressive," Labienus said, congratulating Caesar as soon as he sat down beside him. "Like in Lesbos."

The applause continued. Caesar looked at Labienus. His eyes were blazing and his heart pounded as he responded, "Yes. Like in Lesbos."

LABIENUS

Caesar's lifelong friend
Second-in-command during the
conquest of Gaul

LXIV

THE LAND
OF SAPPHO

Mytilene, Island of Lesbos, eastern Mediterranean
78 B.C., a year and several months before Dolabella's trial

> *That man to me seems equal to the gods,*
> *the man who sits opposite you*
> *and close by listens*
> *to your sweet voice*
> *and your enticing laughter—*
> *How dear and fair was*
> *The life that we girls lived together*
> *Then, with violet crowns and sweet roses*
> *You covered your wavy curls.* *

CAESAR ROLLED UP THE SCROLL AND LOOKED OUT AT THE
sea.

Reading Sappho there on that island, where the poetess had been
born, felt right to him. He knew that he would soon have to go into
combat with the Mytilene troops defending the city against the Romans, but Sappho's poems to her beloved soothed his nerves, reminding him of his wife's warm body, her complicit caresses in the
night, her sly smile at dawn. And those memories gave him renewed
energies for a day he knew would be intense: Lucius Licinius Lucullus, the *proquaestor* sent to command the Roman troops, had sum-

---

* *Poems of Sappho.* Translated by Julia Dubnoff.

moned him and Labienus to his campaign tent. And Caesar predicted they were in for a dangerous mission.

Was he afraid?

He furrowed his brow as he set aside the scroll of Sappho's poems.

He nodded to himself in the deep silence of that dawn on the eastern Mediterranean.

Yes, he was afraid.

In truth, he had many fears: he was afraid of failing, of not living up to what was expected of him, of not being the worthy nephew of Gaius Marius. At just twenty-one years old, he had been named *tribunus laticlavius** alongside his friend Titus Labienus, and he feared that the legionaries would refuse to obey him because of his youth. And yes, he was afraid of combat itself, of how he'd react to the blood and frenzied violence of battle on the front lines. Up to now he'd only participated in training exercises, at the Campus Martius and at the Roman encampment at Lesbos. He had been on the periphery of a few skirmishes. But he would soon test his mettle in direct combat against fierce adversaries of Rome. And that was something entirely different. This would be no mock battle against instructors or an ambush of enemy scouts. This time, he was certain, it would be perilous.

Several small kingdoms in Asia and on the islands of the Aegean had joined forces with the fearsome Mithridates as he swept through the region. The civil war between the optimates and the populares had caused Rome to pull out of Asia, but they were now determined to recover all the territory they had lost. The Senate had given the order to punish every city-state that had betrayed Rome in its moment of weakness.

The island of Lesbos was one of those territories that had turned away from Rome. But its inhabitants, while untrustworthy, were not stupid. They knew of Rome's retaliation against nearby cities and also of Lucullus's military expertise. The brilliant naval commander had been appointed by Sulla himself to keep Rome's control of the East. So the people of Lesbos had barricaded themselves inside the

---

*   Second-in-command of the legion.

fortress at Mytilene, on the island's largest bay. They had reinforced the walls and had abundant supplies of food and deep freshwater wells inside the fortress; they were well prepared to resist a Roman siege, which they predicted would be long and arduous. There was a chance they would lose, but there was also a chance that they could hold out for so long that the Romans would decide to move on. Mytilene was but a small enclave, and Rome, despite its superior military might, could not afford to waste too much time on them when their troops were needed so many other places along the eastern Mediterranean. The Mytilenes were convinced that if they could resist for a few months, Lucullus's cohorts would be called to another part of the region more vital to Roman interests. Or, if they could cause enough losses on the Roman side, they might be able to negotiate a pardon from the Senate in exchange for the establishment of a permanent military base at Lesbos. It would be a defeat of sorts, but it would mean survival. Avoiding the burning and total destruction of their homes, families, and everything they owned would feel like a victory. They knew that the Romans were out for brutal revenge against those who had betrayed them, but they also knew that they were pragmatic and, if the siege became too long and difficult for them, anything was possible.

They had successfully resisted for several weeks.

Julius Caesar heard footsteps behind him.

He knew who it was. He stood up from where he had been reading Sappho.

Caesar adjusted the gladius at his waist and turned around.

"I've been looking everywhere for you," his friend said.

"I wasn't hiding. Just reading in this beautiful spot," Caesar replied. "I was about to go back and have a cup of wine, but I was waiting for you."

"Let's go," Labienus said, turning on his heels.

Sulla had grudgingly pardoned Caesar, after being repeatedly petitioned by dozens of Caesar's friends and family members, as well as several public figures, including the high priestess of Vesta. He had removed the order for the boy's execution, but it had been strongly suggested that Caesar should stay well away from Rome, at least for a while. Sulla wanted to guarantee his control over the city by the Tiber without any interference from Gaius Marius's nephew.

Caesar was allowed to spend a few weeks at home recovering from his months on the run, where the fevers he suffered in the swamps finally subsided. He enjoyed his wife's warm embrace, his young daughter Julia's laughter, his sisters' company, and his mother's advice. A brief respite that the pater familias of the gens Julia cherished. But eventually the time came for Caesar to kiss his wife goodbye, hug his daughter, receive his mother's blessing, and bid his sisters farewell as he marched east to join the legions stationed there. Labienus, ever loyal, had accompanied Caesar on his voyage.

"Where have you gone off to now?" Labienus said, shaking Caesar from his daydream.

They had just returned to their tent in the military encampment. Caesar had not said a word during the short walk from the beach.

"I was ... in Rome," he responded honestly, "thinking about my family."

Labienus nodded and tried to bring his friend back to the present: "Do you think he'll send us on another diplomatic mission?"

Caesar had poured two cups of wine and handed one to his friend. As soon as he'd arrived, Lucullus, aiming to reinforce the Roman fleet on the eastern Mediterranean, had sent Caesar and Labienus to Bithynia to demand a squadron of ships from King Nicomedes IV. Caesar had fulfilled his mission, but a rumor had been started saying that he had slept with the king in order to obtain the ships. Passive homosexuality, giving yourself to another man, was frowned upon in Rome, and Caesar was certain that these rumors were spread by his enemies in an attempt to damage his public image. He was concerned that they might reach the ears of his wife Cornelia.

"She will never doubt you," Labienus said, reading his friend's thoughts.

"Cornelia, you mean?" Caesar asked.

"Cornelia," Labienus said.

Caesar nodded. It was true: she would never doubt him. Others might, but not her. His mother would not doubt him either.

Nevertheless, it was true that the king of Bithynia, known for his excesses, had pressured Caesar and even threatened not to concede the ships unless Caesar slept with him. But Caesar simply responded that the king should do as he pleased, that he would simply communicate the refusal to the proquaestor Lucullus. He, Caesar, might be demoted for his failure, but Lucullus would send several legions to Bithynia to remind the king of his pact with Rome and his obligation to provide ships when required. The proquaestor was not one to accept refusal.

Caesar recalled how Nicomedes's face had soured as he banished Caesar from his reception hall in Nicomedia. But the next day he had received a note from the king with information on where the Bithynian ships would be waiting, ready to serve Rome. The rumor about Caesar sleeping with the king, however, spread across all of Asia. Lucullus never asked him how he had managed to obtain the ships. In fact, the proquaestor, nothing if not pragmatic, was unconcerned with the process, only with the result.

"First your family, and now you're thinking about our mission to Bithynia," Labienus said. "Is there any way to keep you in the here and now?"

Caesar smiled.

"Do you think he'll send us on another diplomatic mission?" Labienus asked again.

"No," Caesar said, shaking his head. "Lucullus has come to end this siege, and I have the feeling that he's going to assign us a very active role."

"A military role?"

Caesar simply nodded.

Labienus now understood why Caesar seemed so nervous. Rumors did not kill, but swords, spears, and arrows did. Neither man had ever seen real combat. They both drank deeply from their cups, staring down at the ground, lost in thought.

LXV

LUCULLUS'S
ORDERS

Roman camp at Mytilene, Island of Lesbos
Asian proquaestor's tent
78 B.C.

THE MEETING TO DISCUSS THE SIEGE WOULD NORMALLY HAVE
occurred in the praetorium, the military command center for the
troops at Lesbos. And Minucius Thermus, *propraetor* charged with
the task of stamping out the final cells of resistance against Rome
in the region, should have been the one to summon the tribunes and
other military officers there.

Yes, that would've been the logical, habitual order of things.

But Lucullus had sailed to Mytilene. And Lucullus had been one
of Sulla's top men in the social struggles, in the battles against Mithridates of Pontus, and most recently in the civil war. Nothing else
needed to be said about him. Sulla had blind faith in that dark silent
man, taciturn, intimidating, and severe.

Despite the fact that he was the *de iure* commander of those troops,
Minucius Thermus sweated as he stood before Lucullus in the center
of the tent from which the army's funds were managed. Lucullus held
the rank of proquaestor, rather than commander. But to Sulla, money
was the key to everything, and so he chose to name his closest men as
quaestores or proquaestores, rather than praetors, legati, or tribunes.
Minucius Thermus understood this perfectly, just as he understood
that his failure to take the city of Mytilene would not please Sulla,
who still controlled everything, despite the fact that he claimed to
have retired from public life. No, Lucullus's arrival did not bode well

for Minucius Thermus. He feared that, at best, his political and military career would be forever marred by his slow progress in that cursed siege, his chances for promotion perhaps even halted *in aeternum*. At worst, Sulla could decide to punish him for his inability to take control of the island in a timely manner.

"As you must imagine, Minucius," Lucullus began without any preambles or greetings, "the Roman Republic is not satisfied with the progress of events here in this little corner of the Aegean."

Minucius Thermus knew that when Lucullus said, "the Roman Republic," he in fact meant Sulla.

"The city of Mytilene is much better fortified than it appears to be at first sight, proquaestor. Its walls are impenetrable. I wouldn't go as far as to say they are unassailable, but with the forces I have on the island, I don't see any way to proceed beyond a long, slow siege."

Lucullus sat on a comfortable cathedra at the back of the tent beside a table set with cups of wine. Two. But the proquaestor did not invite the other officer to join him in tasting the drink of Bacchus.

Lucullus took a long sip.

He set the cup down.

He looked at Thermus.

"A long siege only fans the flames of Mytilene's resistance and allows the island of Lesbos to be an example of rebellion in the East, where Mithridates is still greatly admired. This displeases the Senate. Your inability to succeed here, Minucius, is not making you look good in Rome's eyes."

The propraetor swallowed. Now he was quite certain that when he said, "Rome's eyes," he really meant "Sulla's eyes." Minucius did not fear Rome. But Sulla, with his vengeful reactions, was truly terrifying. He wiped the sweat from his brow.

Lucullus smiled. He had the propraetor exactly where he wanted him.

"But I know you've tried hard, Thermus, and . . . Rome knows it too. That's why we're going to give you a second chance to take the city."

"Thank you. I will follow whatever orders the proquaestor deems best."

Lucullus settled comfortably into his seat and looked Thermus in the eye: "I've come up with a plan, but it requires a couple of young officers—brave, impulsive men. I had thought of Julius Caesar and his friend, the one who's always with him."

"Titus Labienus, proquaestor."

"Yes, that's the one. I want to talk to them."

Minucius Thermus was about to get up to send word to the young tribunes, but Lucullus raised a hand. "I've taken the liberty of summoning them myself. I expect them at any moment."

Thermus nodded.

Lucullus sat observing a glass platter piled with exotic red fruits he'd had brought by boat from Cerasus. "Wine?" he asked, finally offering the other officer.

"Yes, thank you," Thermus said, reaching for a shimmering golden-colored cup. When he picked it up, he realized that it was actually made of gold. The proquaestor, like all the optimates, enjoyed luxury.

They drank and made small talk, even though the weather would not change their plans of attack on the besieged city.

"They have arrived," said a centurion, emerging through the curtain that covered the entrance to the tent.

"Let them in," Lucullus ordered.

Minucius Thermus, for his part, was very curious as to what Lucullus's new plan would be. He thought Caesar an odd choice, given that he had been singled out by Sulla as an enemy of Rome. Sulla had pardoned him, it was true, but Thermus was confused as to why Sulla's envoy would seek out a young man fallen from grace, only grudgingly forgiven, as the person tasked with taking the city.

Caesar and Labienus appeared in the entrance to the tent.

Lucullus was still seated. He did not offer them wine. They did not expect him to.

Julius Caesar, in fact, did not expect anything positive from Sulla's trusted commander, but his superiors had summoned him and he had no choice but to comply. Lucullus had already sent him on one complicated mission to Bithynia. He did not expect this second task to be any less difficult. It was more likely to be quite dangerous.

"We meet again, tribune," Lucullus began.

"Yes, proquaestor."

Lucullus began to lay out his plan, looking first at the ground, then at Minucius and, lastly, at Caesar and Labienus. When the details of his strategy for taking Mytilene had been explained in broad strokes, he went into more detail about the part that most directly required Caesar's and Labienus's efforts.

Minucius Thermus listened very attentively and in silence, his brow furrowed, drinking from his cup from time to time.

Caesar and Labienus stood firm, exchanging brief surprised glances between them, but without a word.

"Any questions?" Lucullus asked when he had finished speaking.

Minucius simply fixed his gaze on the bottom of his empty cup. Labienus shook his head. But Caesar had a few . . . doubts.

"It would appear that the proquaestor has assigned the tribune Labienus and myself to carry out the most dangerous part of the plan."

"Also the most important," Lucullus said with a smile.

"That's true, proquaestor," Caesar admitted, "but I would prefer to do this . . . alone."

Lucullus was puzzled by the young tribune's response. But the boy had defied Sulla, after all, so it made sense that he would speak up for himself.

"What I'm offering is the chance to become heroes," Lucullus argued. "Does the tribune Julius Caesar perhaps want all the glory for himself? Is he unwilling to share it even with those considered to be his friends?"

Labienus stood in silence, unsure what to think.

"Let's say, proquaestor," Caesar continued, "that I prefer to assume all the risk myself."

"Is the tribune Julius Caesar perhaps frightened?" Lucullus then asked with a cynical smile.

"The proquaestor can think what he likes of me. I always follow orders." Then, remembering that he'd refused to divorce Cornelia when Sulla had demanded it, he qualified this statement: "Military orders, that is."

There was a thick silence.

"I agree to carry out the plan as indicated by the proquaestor," Labienus said, speaking for the first time in that meeting, "alongside the tribune Julius Caesar."

"By Jupiter!" Lucullus stood up and walked to the table to serve himself more wine. "Your loyal friend seems to have more resolve than you do, Caesar."

"I understand the risk," Labienus said to Caesar, who had not expected him to be so determined to participate in this insane plan. "And I won't leave you alone. I think that, together, we can pull it off."

"More resolution and more courage than the tribune Caesar, don't you agree, Minucius?" Lucullus said, sitting back down on the cathedra with his cup of wine mixed with a splash of water to soften it. "It is clear that the plan has its risks. But Sulla is offering Gaius Julius Caesar a chance to redeem himself, fully, in his eyes. Carry out the plan, help us take the city of Mytilene, and I will send a positive report to Rome and to Pozzuoli, where Sulla resides now that he has retired from more active public life."

Another silence.

"Unless Gaius Julius Caesar is too . . . afraid," Lucullus said.

Caesar thought for a moment before responding, but when he did, he was categorical: "I am afraid," he said. "But I will follow my orders."

Caesar and Labienus left the tent.

"He admits to being a coward," said Minucius Thermus.

Lucius Licinius Lucullus ran his fingertips over his lips. "I don't think he's a coward. It takes great courage to admit before your superiors that you are frightened to take on a mission that is, by all appearances, very dangerous. That Julius Caesar is . . . unusual."

The proquaestor sat with his brow furrowed, suddenly having second thoughts. But he answered to Sulla. And Sulla was a man who liked to see his orders carried out exactly.

Roman camp outside Mytilene

"By Hercules! Why did you have to get involved? I'm the one who needs to redeem myself to Sulla, not you." Caesar was angry. "If you'd gone along with me you'd already be free of this insane plan and could be safe with the bulk of the troops when it plays out."

"I need to redeem myself to Sulla as well," Labienus replied calmly. "Sulla hates not only you, but everyone who has helped you in any way. I am your friend, loyal to the death, and that has tainted me in his eyes. It's too late for me. The only thing I can do is help you get on the right side of Sulla, of Rome, of the Senate. I know that the only way my name will ever live on in history is by making sure that yours does. You will do great things, and I will be there with you. And I'm certain that, when someone writes about your military achievements, they will note my name in the annals as one of the men who aided you. And in this way I will be remembered. But now we're going to focus on Mytilene, on surviving, on returning to Rome, to do the great things that await us. Think of Cornelia, let her guide you."

Caesar stopped short as his friend walked on. Labienus, perhaps, had not properly weighed the risks of the mission, but it was certain that he was a loyal friend.

Labienus turned around. "Shall we?" he asked. "I feel like a cup of wine or two, and the proquaestor was not kind enough to offer."

Caesar laughed, releasing some of the tension from the meeting with their superiors. "Let's go, my friend," he said. "By Jupiter, let's have a drink."

LXVI

CAESAR'S
EXTERMINATION

Roman camp at Mytilene, Island of Lesbos
Proquaestor's tent
78 B.C.

LUCIUS LICINIUS LUCULLUS AND MINUCIUS THERMUS RE-
mained in the proquaestor's tent.

"It's an interesting strategy," Thermus said. "And it could let us
successfully take Mytilene, but . . ."

"But what?" said Lucullus. "By Jupiter, if there's one thing I hate
it's an unfinished sentence."

"The plan has one weak spot," Thermus mustered the nerve to
say.

"What weak spot?"

Thermus realized that Lucullus would not be satisfied until he
spoke his mind. "The currents around the island are . . . impetuous,"
he ventured. "It might prove difficult for the ships to sail back with
the troops, as you've planned."

"You don't say?" Lucullus relaxed into his comfortable high-
backed chair.

The sarcastic tone reminded Thermus that his superior was an
expert navigator who, without a doubt, would've noticed the currents
as he approached Lesbos in his own ship. The proquaestor knew very
well that the ocean streams and the changeable winds could delay the
Roman fleet's return, thus jeopardizing the plan presented to the
young tribunes. Minucius Thermus's eyes opened wide and his

mouth fell open. He had just comprehended the true objective of that mission.

"And if our fleet is delayed, the young tribune Julius Caesar will be surrounded by the enemy, without enough troops to defend himself and he will be . . ."

"Exterminated," Lucullus said. "This is what Sulla has asked me to do. He does not care about Lesbos; Mytilene is of no consequence. It doesn't matter if we have to abandon this siege. The most important thing, to Sulla, is assuring the death of that young upstart who dared to defy him."

Minucius Thermus thought for a moment before responding. "But Sulla has pardoned Caesar."

"Have you never in your life changed your mind, Minucius?"

Thermus sighed, set his cup on the table, and nodded. "Yes, of course I have. But won't Caesar suspect something? He's young and inexperienced in combat, but he's good at identifying loyalties, and . . ." He was searching for the right word but didn't dare to say it.

"And conspiracies," Lucullus concluded. "Let's call things by their names, although Sulla would prefer to call it an 'execution.' And yes, I thought that mentioning our great leader when I laid out the plan might put the boy on alert, but that was an express order from Sulla. When Caesar finds himself surrounded by the enemy and realizes he's fallen into a trap like a child, an idiot, worse yet, a fool, as the enemy's swords run through him over and over, it will be clear in his mind that Lucius Cornelius Sulla has finally gotten the better of him."

"But, by all the gods, won't Caesar see through the plan?"

"An interesting thought," Lucullus admitted. "But Julius Caesar cannot refuse a direct order from his superiors. He might suspect something, but he can't possibly think us capable of risking five hundred legionaries just to end his life. Caesar is noble at heart, and that makes him blind to certain things. But to Sulla, to me, and to you too, if you know what's good for you, the ends always justify the means. Personally, I don't see how Marius's young nephew could ever be the formidable enemy Sulla thinks he will become. But our leader is obsessed with him, and I won't be the one to stand in the way of one of his deepest desires. He wants Caesar dead and so Caesar will be dead, tomorrow. Now let's drink some more wine and give the orders for the legionaries to break camp as quickly as possible and board the ships of my fleet. It is time to send a message to the defenders of Mytilene that we, the Romans, will abandon the siege tomorrow at dawn. Or so it will seem."

Minucius Thermus raised his cup and drank in silence, not wanting to leave any doubts about his loyalty to Sulla. Lucullus emptied his own cup, hoping the wine would make it easier to risk five hundred soldiers for the life, or death, rather, of a single man. Lucullus would have to drink a lot that night, drowning his conscience in alcohol to be able to carry out Sulla's cursed orders.

LXVII

AN IMPOSSIBLE
MISSION

Mytilene, Island of Lesbos
78 B.C.
The walls of the city

THE SENTINELS PEERED AT THE HORIZON AS THE SUN BEGAN
to show its first rays. Everything seemed normal until one of the
younger scouts, with keener vision, furrowed his brow in a marked
gesture of confusion.

"They're leaving," he said in a low voice.

"What are you saying?" asked one of his more veteran comrades.

"The Romans . . ." the young soldier said. "They've boarded their
ships and they're leaving."

Everyone looked where the sentinel was pointing.

"By Demeter! The boy is right!" the commanding officer confirmed, invoking the mother goddess so beloved in that land.

As the sun rose, they could see the sails of the Roman fleet
stamped along the line of the horizon moving away from the island.
The glowing rays then stretched to the Roman camp some two thousand paces beyond the city, abandoned.

Palace of the satrap of Mytilene

Anaxagoras had been named satrap and *strategos*, singular and maximum ruler of the Island of Lesbos by Mithridates VI, King of Pontus, the scourge of the Romans in the East. Mithridates ruled the
destiny of the entire region, from the Euxine or Black Sea to Syria,

from the borders with Parthis to the coasts of the Greek cities. And
he had decided to gift Anaxagoras with rule of that island in appreciation for his important contribution to the battle of Mount Scoro-
bas, where the King of Pontus had massacred the Roman armies. A
truce was then extended to Mithridates by the Roman commander
Sulla, who had his own problems to solve back in Italy. But, with the
civil war now quelled, Sulla wanted Mithridates to understand that
the peace treaty did not mean the King of Pontus would be allowed
to maintain control of the East. It had merely bought Sulla the time
he needed to defeat his enemies in the popular faction. Once he had
obtained absolute control of the Roman Senate and the rest of the
state institutions, Sulla had sent his legions back eastward.

Anaxagoras had enjoyed a period of peace and opulence on that
island, indulging in its famed wine, living from banquet to banquet,
and lying with slaves and non-slaves alike. But that all ended when
Rome sent first Minucius Thermus and later Lucullus to darken his
doorstep. Anaxagoras began to see that the party would soon come to
an end, but he wasn't certain that this end would be determined by
the Roman troops. A prolonged resistance would buy him some time.
He would wait to see if Mithridates made a move and in the meantime test the number of losses the Romans were prepared to suffer in
a long siege. He believed they might decide to simply leave Lesbos.
So the news from the sentinels at the wall that morning was quite
interesting.

"They're leaving? Are you sure of what you're saying?" Anaxagoras
asked, seated on a comfortable throne piled with pillows in the center of the great reception hall.

"Yes, Lord Protector of our Land!" the sentinels said, kneeling before their leader.

"I myself have confirmed it, Lord Protector," said Pittacus, the
second-in-command on the island. "I climbed to the top of the wall
and saw the sails of the Roman fleet moving away along the coast."

Anaxagoras leaned back on his throne. He couldn't think straight.
He had a hangover from the night before and had been fornicating
with a young slave woman all morning. He ran his hand over his forehead.

"Bring me water," he said, as he tried to get his thoughts in order.

Anaxagoras did not like Pittacus, a man with a dark past as a mercenary. The man had come from Anatolia and had adopted the surname of an ancient wise man of Mytilene in order to make himself more popular among the subjects of Lesbos. Before, Pittacus had been named . . . Anaxagoras shook his head. He couldn't remember. It didn't matter anyway.

"What do you make of this, Theophanes?" Anaxagoras asked, looking across the room.

Theophanes was a local aristocratic leader of the city. Anaxagoras suspected that he would prefer to be governed by the Romans than by Mithridates, but he was an intelligent man and Anaxagoras valued his advice, in addition to the fact that he served as a bridge to the citizens of Mytilene. The man, for the moment, was useful in keeping the locals loyal to Mithridates.

"I also ascended the wall and, in fact, it is clear that the Romans have moved their fleet away."

Theophanes's careful explanation did not escape Anaxagoras. "Are you saying that they might have done it to make us think they are leaving when, in fact, they have all their troops hiding in some place we can't see from the wall?"

"That's a possibility, of course, my lord," Theophanes admitted without using the satrap's full title, "but it is true that the Roman camp appears to be abandoned—"

"And there's nowhere to hide their men," Pittacus interrupted.

"There's the small forest beside the sea," Theophanes objected.

"Small, as you say," Pittacus insisted. "No more than three or four hundred soldiers could hide there, definitely not the huge legions camped until just yesterday before our walls."

Anaxagoras sighed: as usual, his top advisors disagreed. A slave arrived with fresh water and the satrap drank deeply from a bronze bowl plated with lead. He quenched his thirst then pushed the slave away and turned to his council.

"It is quite possible that the Romans have gotten tired and decided to leave. Or perhaps they were needed elsewhere. King Mithridates controls these lands and, just as the Romans aim to punish his supporters, Mithridates himself is launching attacks on cities allied with Rome. But of course, it could also be a trick. Perhaps the Romans have simply moved their troops to the other end of the island so that we'll relax and they can take us by surprise. Whatever the case, by Apollo, we have to find out what is truly going on." He paused briefly before announcing his decision: "We will take the army outside the city to see what is happening."

"We could send scouts," Pittacus suggested.

"We could, but any soldiers hidden nearby would annihilate the scouts. We can't afford to lose a single warrior, let alone an entire patrol. It's safer to take the bulk of the troops to explore the island. We will leave archers on the walls. And, most important, the gates will remain open in case the entirety of the Roman army is hidden somewhere on Lesbos and we have to quickly turn back."

Pittacus tried to argue, but Anaxagoras spoke over him: "By Apollo! This is my decision!"

Everyone in the room bowed to the satrap.

"Pittacus, arrange the departure of the troops and position the archers on the wall. You will remain in command of the city in my absence. Theophanes, you will come with me."

There was nothing more to be said.

*Forest beside the sea, two thousand paces
from the wall of Mytilene*

"What should we do?" said Titus Labienus, looking nervously toward the gates of Mytilene. "They're marching out with everything they've got."

"That was the idea, remember?" Caesar replied, his gaze shifting constantly between the enemy troops and the horizon. "But they've gone too far."

"Who?" Labienus asked without taking his eyes off the Mytilene army.

"Our ships: Lucullus and Thermus have sailed too far into open water."

"Well, they had to make it look like we were really leaving."

"Still. There's something suspicious about this entire plan," Caesar continued. "Let's stay here for now, concealed by the trees. The enemy will surely march straight to the abandoned camp to see if there's anything they can scavenge."

Titus Labienus could see the tension on his friend's face. He looked then to the sea and it was true, not a single sail remained visible. The fleet had left behind a cohort of 480 men here on the island, with the plan to ambush the enemy and keep them from returning to the safety of the walls as the Roman ships returned with the bulk of the legionaries. But . . . if Lucullus and Thermus took too long getting back, Caesar and the rest of the cohort would be annihilated.

Labienus and Caesar exchanged a glance.

"If the ships don't appear, this mission is . . . doomed. But for now, we have to continue with Lucullus's plan," said Caesar.

Labienus did not miss the fact that his friend had said *for now.*

LXVIII

A MESSENGER

Mytilene, Island of Lesbos
78 B.C.
Command ship of the Roman fleet, far from the coast

ON THE AEGEAN SEA, SEVERAL MILES FROM LESBOS, LUCIUS Licinius Lucullus watched as the island disappeared on the horizon. Still he did not give the order to turn around.

"If we can't see the coast, they can't see us," Minucius commented.

The proquaestor looked up at the tall central mast of the ship, the sails filled with wind pushing them farther and farther from Lesbos. "That's our plan. Don't forget the main objective of all this."

"I know, proquaestor, but, if I may, I think we've gone far enough, and the rest of the legionaries will begin to think so too. We've left an entire cohort behind and everyone is expecting us to return to help them. That is, everyone expects us to return . . . on time."

Lucullus nodded, but he wouldn't let anyone twist his arm. "I will decide when the moment is right, and—"

"A boat!" one of the lookouts shouted.

Lucullus and Thermus saw a small boat approaching with a few legionaries on board.

"Messengers from Rome," said Minucius Thermus.

"No doubt," Lucullus agreed. "Let them come aboard and send them straight to my cabin. In the meantime, stay the course away from Lesbos."

Abandoned Roman camp

Anaxagoras walked through the Roman camp with an air of authority. He was an experienced warrior and knew that he had to always maintain the appearance of an alert, decisive leader. He was not concerned by the Romans' sudden departure. It could simply mean that their supreme leader, King Mithridates, had launched an attack and that the Romans had been forced to call in some of their troops spread across the East. Or, better yet, perhaps the all-powerful King of Pontus had forced a full retreat of the Roman armies in Asia, as he'd done some years prior through a pact with Sulla.

The satrap looked around. Whatever the Romans' reason for leaving, there was plenty to pillage. In their hasty departure, the legionaries had left half of their camp behind. Strewn all over the ground were blacksmithing tools, cooking utensils, swords and daggers. There was no silver or gold, which disappointed him, but soon some soldiers found several sacks of grain, which would certainly help replenish the supplies that had been depleted during the siege.

"They've found something else," Theophanes said, pointing to a group of soldiers gathered at one end of the camp.

Anaxagoras had insisted on bringing Theophanes along because he knew of the Romans' tendency to make agreements with the local aristocrats, and he did not trust Theophanes enough to leave the city under his command. The man was capable of shutting the gates, leaving the troops faithful to Mithridates locked outside. Whereas Pittacus, despite his great ambition, was loyal to the King of Pontus and would never wish to face his ire.

"Let's go check it out," Anaxagoras said, as flanked by his guards, he moved toward the spot where the group of men had gathered.

Command ship of the Roman fleet, proquaestor's cabin

"The messenger has arrived," Minucius Thermus said. "He is being brought aboard."

"Good. Wait, did you leave the spears in plain sight at the camp, like I ordered?" Lucullus asked, as if suddenly remembering a detail that might alter his plans.

"Yes, more than five hundred pila, ready to be launched," Thermus confirmed.

"Good, that's good," Lucullus said, settling into the wide cushioned seat as he waited for the messenger to arrive.

Just then an optio entered. "Message from Rome, proquaestor," he announced.

"Let him in," Lucullus ordered. "Leave me alone with him," he said to Minucius Thermus.

The order wounded Thermus's pride, but since he was dealing with one of Sulla's most loyal friends, he chose to simply give a military salute, raising his fist to his chest, and turned to leave just as the proquaestor gave another order.

"Turn the fleet around. It's time to make our return to Lesbos, or, as you said, the army might believe that we have abandoned their comrades. And we don't want them to think that."

Thermus looked at the proquaestor, nodded, and left the cabin. On the way out he passed the messenger, who was carrying a rolled-up scroll sealed with wax. Thermus was quite curious as to what the message might say, but he had instructions to give, and so he climbed the steps up to the deck.

Forest of Lesbos, beside the sea

"Should we make a move?" Labienus asked.

"Not yet," Caesar responded. "Not until we see the sails of the fleet returning."

That seemed sensible to Labienus.

The sea, however, only showed the flat line of an empty horizon.

Abandoned Roman camp

"Spears?" Theophanes said, baffled, as he stood over the inexplicable pile of weapons Anaxagoras's men had uncovered.

"Many of them, my lord," one of the soldiers said. "Hundreds, maybe more."

"That's strange," Theophanes said. "Why would they leave behind an entire horde of spears? The odd sword or dagger forgotten in haste is one thing, but abandoning such a large number of weapons is quite peculiar."

"And they're good," Anaxagoras added, holding one up, contemplating its weight and the exact point by which to launch it at some imaginary enemy. "Perfect Roman pila."

Theophanes looked at him in confusion. He was well versed in history and literature, but not in warfare.

"The pila is a Roman spear perfectly designed to penetrate an enemy shield," Anaxagoras explained. "It will always wound, kill, or render the defensive armor useless. It's very difficult to remove."

Anaxagoras was not at all suspicious of having found those weapons left behind. He'd seen many strange things in war, and this was by no means the most peculiar.

"Take them," he ordered his men.

Command ship of the Roman fleet,
proquaestor's cabin

Lucius Licinius Lucullus read the letter that had arrived from Rome.

Then he read it again.

"By Jupiter!" he exclaimed, and immediately turned to the messenger: "When?"

"A month ago, proquaestor."

"Do not leave this cabin and do not speak to anyone. There is water and food for you here. Do you understand your orders?"

"Yes, proquaestor."

The messenger did not seem surprised by his superior's reaction. Considering what had happened in Rome—or south of Rome, to be precise—it seemed well warranted.

"This changes everything," Lucullus muttered to himself as he slowly stood and walked to the door. "Everything," he repeated as he climbed up to the deck.

LXIX

CAESAR'S FEAR

Mytilene, Island of Lesbos
Forest beside the sea
78 B.C.

"I CAN SEE THE FIRST SAILS," SAID LABIENUS QUIETLY.

Caesar seemed to be lost in thought. "Yes," he finally responded. "They should soon reach the coast. But I'd prefer to wait a little longer."

Labienus looked toward the abandoned camp. "The soldiers are beginning their return to the city," he pointed out.

They both observed the enemy army, somewhere between two and three thousand men. The Roman cohort would be even more outnumbered than expected.

"They've brought out pretty much everyone they have," Caesar said, putting words to both of their thoughts.

"They are being cautious," Labienus said.

"That Anaxagoras knows what he's doing," Caesar continued, "and I don't like it. He suspects it might be a trap. And our ships are still too far away. But you're right, if we don't leave now, the proquaestor's entire plan will fall apart. And if it does, they'll punish us for disobeying orders. They may even accuse us of outright rebellion."

Caesar and Labienus knew little of Anaxagoras, leader of the army posted at Mytilene, except that he had entered into negotiations for a possible surrender of the city, but it had never occurred. But now Caesar recalled that the satrap had been spoken of as a skilled warrior who was above all prudent, like his uncle Marius.

"Should we make our move, then?" Labienus asked.

Gaius Julius Caesar ran the back of his hand over his forehead.

He was sweating.

Was he frightened?

Yes.

There was no use denying his feelings.

This was not a mock battle at the Campus Martius, not a training session.

This was war. Real. Ruthless.

He was about to go into combat for the first time in his life.

He was twenty-one years old.

Labienus began giving orders to the six centurions under their command, as Caesar remained rooted to the spot, petrified. He swallowed: Scipio had entered combat for the first time at age seventeen. To save his own father. But Caesar, nevertheless, felt the icy grip of fear.

No, he decided, he would never be a man of great military accomplishments.

He would have to stick to the forum, to words, public speaking, and the halls of justice.

That is, if he managed to survive that morning.

"The men are ready," Labienus said, once again beside him.

But Caesar remained silent, immobile.

Labienus understood what was happening. "I'm scared too," he admitted quietly. "It's the first time for me as well. You know that. But we have to move, my friend. We have to fight. This is what we've trained for. This is what we are. We are more than just soldiers. We are warriors."

Gaius Julius Caesar was held captive by fear.

Titus Labienus didn't know what to say. He considered ordering the attack; that would surely force his friend into action. The proper thing was for Caesar, as commanding tribune, to give the order. But he was frozen in place.

Just then, Labienus had an idea. He leaned over and whispered five words into Caesar's ear: "Remember you are Marius's nephew."

But it didn't seem to work. Marius's nephew remained still as a statue. And with him, the history of the world stood still as well.

LXX

THE EYES OF
ROME

Puzzuoli, Campania, south of Rome
78 B.C., a month before the battle of Mytilene

G NAEUS CORNELIUS DOLABELLA ARRIVED AT SULLA'S VILLA
at dusk. Although Dolabella had traveled by ship from Ostia and not
over land, the journey had been tedious and exhausting. Dolabella,
like his mentor, was used to luxury and convenience, but the uncomfortable trip was a necessary one: Sulla had summoned him to his
residence in Puzzuoli, and that could only be a good thing. That
could only mean power. As everyone knew, the fate of Rome was decided from this villa, where Sulla had retired from political life,
claiming health problems. In reality, it was a clever strategy to protect
himself from the many conspiracies so common in Rome. Formally,
Sulla had handed power over to a conservative Senate bolstered by
the abolition of popular laws. Under Sulla's reforms, the Tribal Assembly of the People and the Plebeian Tribunal were weakened to
such an extent that all power was now concentrated in the Senate.
Sulla had abdicated his dictatorship, nominally, but he still controlled
every move the Senate made.

Puzzuoli was a combination of luxury villa and fortress, much
easier to safeguard against murder plots than anywhere in overpopu-
lated Rome. It was a bastion of safety guarded by veteran warriors
from the campaign against Mithridates and the civil war. The small
city was a military checkpoint, and to get from the port to the villa,
Dolabella had to show, on five separate occasions, the letter sent by
Sulla as proof that he'd been summoned.

Finally, Dolabella reached the great villa.

He passed through the immense wooden gates in the wall surrounding the residence and moved between the cypress trees lining either side of the road snaking up to a plateau with sweeping views of the Bay of Puzzuoli. At his feet sat homes, temples, and the large military camp where the bulk of the troops loyal to Sulla were posted. Attacking him here would be very difficult, if not impossible. The former dictator had also been astute in choosing a town beside the sea, where a small fleet of ships were kept at the ready in case he had to flee to some other location on the Mare Internum to hunker down and wait to return to power. Very recently, in fact, there had been an attempt at rebellion against him. Aemilus Lepidus, a Roman consul, had moved over to the side of the populares, distributing grain to the plebes and allowing men exiled by Sulla to return to Rome. He had also restored many lands and holdings to prominent populares who had seen their wealth confiscated by Sulla.

"Just a moment," the slave who was guiding him said.

As Dolabella waited, he thought over those recent events, once again admiring his mentor's intelligence: Sulla, from his home here in Puzzuoli, had ordered Lutatius Catulus and Gnaeus Pompey to defeat the troops that the rebel consul Lepidus had managed to gather in Italy. Lepidus had fled to Sicily, where he later died, as his second-in-command took refuge in Hispania, like so many other populares before him. Sertorius, Marius's former lieutenant, still held a large part of that territory in rebellion against Rome, despite Metellus's attempts to defeat him.

Dolabella nodded to himself. Sulla had successfully put an end to that political and military conflict, all from the calm and safety of his retirement in Puzzuoli.

"This way, clarissime vir," said the atriense as Dolabella entered the gigantic villa from which the entire Roman world was governed.

Dolabella passed through several rooms decorated with frescos of landscapes, hunting scenes, and finally, erotic encounters. He crossed two atriums with large *impluvia* in their centers until reaching an antechamber that opened onto the villa's largest atrium. The doors were closed.

"The *clarissimus vir* may wait here; the master will be out shortly. There is water and wine for my lord."

Dolabella was left alone. He walked over to the table and served himself some wine with water. The doors to the villa's main atrium remained closed, but once the slave's footsteps retreated, Dolabella could clearly hear dry cracking sounds, each followed by a wail of pain. Someone was being whipped. He recognized the sound immediately, since he himself frequently ordered his slaves be submitted to long whippings when they did not fulfill their duties to his liking.

More whip cracks.

The dry, perfect blow of leather against human flesh. And more wails of pain, in a different voice. They were whipping more than one slave. Female. Several female slaves. There was a cadence to it, a certain rhythm, as if someone were carefully orchestrating the concert of whip cracks and moans.

Suddenly the atrium doors opened and Lucius Cornelius Sulla emerged, dressed in a beautiful purple tunic. As the doors began to shut behind him, the former dictator turned and said a few words to someone on the other side. "Wait until I return to resume the whippings, Valeria. I don't want to miss a single whimper."

"As you wish, my love," came a sensual yet somewhat slurred female voice, as if she'd had too much wine. Or could it have been opium? With Sulla, anything was possible.

"Dolabella!" Sulla shouted, turning to his friend. "Thank you, thank you, thank you for coming. I know it is enormously uncomfortable, but it's a thousand times safer than Rome. I refuse to let myself be stabbed to death in the forum like so many others. I won't be the one to make the mistake of trusting senators. No, there are too many power-hungry men who would conspire against me." Sulla laughed heartily, his jowls jiggling. Despite his sixty years and his large belly, he still seemed full of energy and not at all prepared to loosen his iron grip on Rome.

"It's always a pleasure to see Sulla, even if I have to sail the sea and be stopped infinite times by your soldiers. I bring letters from Rome."

Dolabella held up a handful of sealed scrolls.

"Anything from Lucullus, in the East?" Sulla asked, genuinely interested.

"No, no news from that front," Dolabella answered, unhappy to disappoint his mentor in any way. "But I have letters from Catulus and Pompey. They have put an end to Lepidus's uprising."

"I know, I know. They are efficient, especially Pompey," Sulla commented. "It's clear that he is the eagle in ascent among us. He'll make sure that my laws remain in effect for a long time and that, by consequence, our privileges will endure. The only thing that interests me now is hearing from Lucullus," the dictator replied, somewhat annoyed. "But come, leave the letters and sit with me."

Dolabella placed the scrolls on the table and Sulla led him by the arm to a corner of the room, seemingly wanting as much privacy as possible for their conversation.

"I asked Lucullus to do something very important, and I'm eager to hear how it's going. Lucullus has never let me down. Neither have you. There is a lot at stake in the East. The problem of Mithridates is not yet solved. Cinna's rebellion forced me to negotiate peace with that cursed King of Pontus when what I should've done was annihilate him. He's a problem, and Lucullus, or you, or someone else, will soon have to solve it. I need men I can trust in that part of the world. Which is why I want you to take charge of Macedonia. I know it's far away, but it's where I need you. I want to settle things in the East and then find someone to stamp out Sertorius's rebellion of the populares in Hispania, if Metellus doesn't prove up to the task. For now I have my sights set on Asia, with Lucullus at the helm, and I want you in Macedonia, in the rearguard. What do you think, my friend?"

Dolabella knew that, although Sulla was trying to frame it as an offer, he was in fact giving an order. There was only one path to take with the former dictator. But along the way, Dolabella knew he would get rich. The other option, opposing Sulla's plans, would only mean death, sooner or later.

"I will go wherever Sulla needs me most."

"Very good, very good, by Jupiter, my friend. I like that," said Sulla, clapping him on the back. "Good. With that out of the way we can relax. I'd like to invite you into the atrium, where I think you will enjoy yourself. I've discovered some new pleasures."

Sulla rapped on the door three times, paused, and knocked three more times. The wide wooden doors opened and the former dictator, followed closely by his guest, entered the villa's central atrium.

"I've discovered new pleasures," Sulla said again, taking Dolabella by the arm. "Have you ever made love surrounded by screams of pain? It's extasiatic. Is that a word? If not, it should be."

Along two sides of the atrium, some thirty young women were tied to the wall, their arms outstretched. Beside each one stood a hardy, muscular slave with a whip. The women were all completely naked, and most of them had lash marks on their backs, arms, legs, and buttocks... Some were bleeding. Others had clear wounds that had not yet begun to bleed; only a few of them seemed unharmed.

Dolabella looked around, his eyes wide, as a dark, admiring smile spread across his face.

"I swap them out so they last longer," said Sulla. "After every hundred whiplashes I let them rest for a few days. Some die. They bring me more. I spend a fortune on slaves, but it is extremely pleasurable." He moved away from Dolabella toward a woman reclining comfortably in the midst of all the horror, as if it had nothing to do with her. "Valeria, my beloved. Dolabella has come, from Rome."

The young wife of the former dictator reclined on a triclinium in the center of the atrium, wearing only her intimate tunic, one breast uncovered, the other held by an actor who was dressed as a woman. It was Metrobius, Sulla's close friend of many years.

A few steps away, just to the right of Valeria and Sulla's triclinia of honor, was an empty divan. Sulla gestured for Dolabella to make himself comfortable. On the other side of the atrium, the actors Roscius and Sorex were each manhandling a naked, bloodied slave. The women, semi-unconscious from the beatings, sobbed.

More sobbing.

From every corner.

The order given by the former dictator to pause the punishment had provided the women with a brief respite, but they were all crying—most of them in pain, and a few who had only recently been tied to the wall out of pure terror, because they saw the state of the others and knew the terrible fate that awaited them.

More slaves came in bringing food and drink for Sulla, his wife, and the other participants in that orgy of sex and blood, ecstasy and horror. Dolabella accepted the offerings from several delicious-smelling trays of food as he was handed a luxurious golden cup, over-flowing with wine.

"Drink, my friend, drink," the former dictator insisted. "And eat . . ."

Dolabella was hungry, and the spectacle only increased his appetite. He was witnessing a new way of enjoying life and wealth. He would have to do something like this one day, but so many slaves . . . were expensive, as Sulla had said. Very expensive. Of course, he had just been appointed governor of Macedonia, an excellent opportunity to increase his wealth and enjoy exotic luxuries. He could perhaps do something like this in . . . what was the capital of Macedonia again? Thessaloniki? Dyrrhachium? But he was more excited by the notion of forcing himself on freeborn women, snooty local aristocratic girls, than he was by the thought of torturing slaves. He would have to return to that idea.

Dolabella picked up an unidentifiable vegetable seasoned with a tasty sauce and began to eat as Sulla gave the order to start whipping the slaves tied to the wall. The food was good, but it had an unusual flavor.

"What is this?" Dolabella asked.

"Asparagus in oyster and lobster sauce," Sulla said. "It's an excellent aphrodisiac. And wait until you try the meat. Exquisite."

They spoke calmly amid the howls of pain. Metrobius stood up from the dictator's wife and pranced across the atrium in an imitation of a woman's gait, with exaggerated feminine gestures. Sorex stood behind Metrobius and, with very precise movements, mimed tying Metrobius up as the actor played the part of a laughing, crying, shouting, moaning slave.

The brief skit delighted the former dictator and his wife, who laughed loudly.

Dolabella felt right at home. This was exactly what he wanted for himself. He planned to make Thessaloniki—he was now more certain that was the capital of Macedonia—his own Puzzuoli. He swore to himself, before the gods, that he would tie up and possess the most beautiful women of Macedonia after taking the province in his iron grip. But first he had to focus on increasing his wealth so that he could later enjoy his money in peace and quiet in a villa somewhere outside Rome.

Still mesmerized by the luxurious life led by the ruler of the Roman world, Dolabella returned to Sulla's concerns in the East. There was something he was still curious about. "What is it that you asked Lucullus to do for you?" he asked.

"Mmmm," the former dictator replied, chewing. He seemed to hesitate. But he had all of Rome under his complete control. Pompey, his armed muscle in the capital, had put an end to Lepidus's latest attempt to overturn his regime. He no longer needed to hide anything. And anyway, in Puzzuoli, surrounded by his loyal legionaries, he was fully protected. He could reveal his secret plan to Dolabella: "I ordered Lucullus to put an end to Julius Caesar."

"I thought you'd pardoned him," said Valeria, who was following the conversation.

"That's what I said in Rome, publicly," Sulla admitted. "It was a minor concession to secure power, since so many people interceded on behalf of Marius's cursed nephew. I remember at the time, I thought: *dum modo scirent eum, quem incolumem tanto opere cuperent, quandoque optimatium partibus, quas secum simul defendissent, exitio futurum; nam Caesari multos Marios inesse.*[*] That's what I said. And I considered forgetting all about the matter. But I refuse to leave this world only to watch from Hades as that young fool undoes everything I've worked for. He's still Marius's nephew, and I won't go out of this world with him still in it. I've instructed Lucullus to do whatever it takes to make sure Caesar falls in combat. The siege of Mytilene will be the begin-

---

[*]   "Have your way and take him; only bear in mind that the man you are so eager to save will one day deal the death blow to the cause of the aristocracy, which you have joined with me in upholding; for in this Caesar there is more than one Marius." Gaius Suetonius in *The Lives of Julius Caesar,* VII, Julius Caesar, I.

ning and end of Julius Caesar's military career. Lesbos will be his tomb."

Sulla laughed.

The others joined him, but their laughter was soon drowned out by the slaves' cries. Sorex returned to the slave he had been lying with. The girl, exhausted from the brutal torture she'd received, let herself be taken, through muffled sobs, like a bloodied ragdoll. Metrobius, despite being dressed as a woman, sucked at Valeria's breasts like a ram in mating season. The dictator's wife gave herself over to the actor and Sulla watched on with a smile, entertained by the spectacle of blood, screams, sex, and debauchery.

Dolabella stood up. "By Hercules! A toast, then, to the death of Gaius Julius Caesar! Someone we will never have to worry about again!"

"I drink to that, my friend," said Sulla, exultant. "Lucullus will eliminate that impertinent boy who dared to defy me. And he will settle our troubles in the East. Then, I will send Pompey to Hispania to exterminate Sertorius and the rest of the populares hiding out there, since the old stutterer is incapable of doing it," Sulla said, the wine allowing him to express what he truly thought of Metellus. "That is the plan, my friend. The two of us can sit back and relax, you in Macedonia, and me here in Puzzuoli. Nothing can go wrong. I have everything perfectly under my control."

Dolabella left the atrium several hours later, seeking a bedroom in which to rest. He was euphoric. The world belonged to those like Sulla, like him, who held great wealth and great power. They could never be challenged. No one would dare. The young Caesar had ignored Sulla's orders to divorce his wife Cornelia, and now he would be wiped from the face of the earth. That was the way the world worked, the way things would always be. Freedom was only for those who governed, for those who ruled. All others were their slaves, destined to do their bidding.

He was drunk.

They brought in one of the slave girls to keep him company. She was naked, her back in shreds, and she was trembling with pain, with pure terror.

Dolabella fell asleep.

The slave curled up in a corner and continued crying for hours, until her exhaustion won out and she fell asleep as well.

Central atrium of Sulla's Villa

The orgy continued.

Endlessly.

Sorex was now penetrating Valeria, who moaned with pleasure.

Metrobius, still dressed as a woman, danced in the center of the atrium.

The whiplashes were doled out mercilessly.

The slaves wailed in pain.

Sulla walked among the tables crowded with food and drink, wobbling from so much wine, laughing uncontrollably. His face was red, and he was clumsy in his movements but content at the center of his world, happy in his great victory over everything and everyone.

Then he began to wretch.

He doubled over with the first spasm, then lay down on a triclinium and began to vomit.

He laughed between heaves.

Once he'd expelled everything he'd ingested that day, he stood up and went for more food. And drink. He remembered Caesar, in the East, far from all his friends in Rome, under Lucullus's command, and he started laughing once again: Marius's cursed nephew was, at long last, a dead man.

LXXI

A FRIEND'S LIFE

Mytilene, Island of Lesbos
78 B.C.
Forest beside the sea

Gaius Julius Caesar remained paralyzed with terror. "You are Marius's nephew."

Labienus's words echoed through his mind. "Call the centurions," he finally said.

Labienus sighed with relief. His friend was beginning to respond. He didn't doubt Caesar's courage, but it was his first battle, and no one ever knew how they would react in the face of a real war when the time came. Labienus had seen his friend train at the Campus Martius in Rome and in the camps where they'd been stationed. Throughout his entire military training, Caesar had excelled in all areas: hand-to-hand combat, speed, skill, and resistance. If he could get over his nerves, Labienus was sure that Caesar would do well in combat. And they needed him, because the situation was a difficult one. The proquaestor's plan was insane, especially for the centuries who had been left behind on the island to wait for the return of the Roman fleet.

In an instant, Labienus and the six centurions who led the cohort were gathered around Caesar.

"I'll take command of the first century and position us directly in front of the gates to Mytilene, safely beyond the reach of any archers on the walls. Labienus will be to my right with the second century, and there will be another to his right. The rest of you on my left. We will block Anaxagoras's army as they return from our abandoned camp. The enemies outnumber us five to one, but our mission is only to delay their access to the gates of the city until our fleet returns with the rest of the army. Then we'll outnumber them, and they'll be trapped outside their walls, allowing our legions to annihilate them. Any questions?"

No one said a word. They had imagined some such plan when the bulk of the legions left and they stayed behind. Now everything had been spelled out clearly for them.

"The sails are getting closer," Labienus said, pointing out to sea.

Between the trees, they could make out some of the ships of the Roman fleet returning toward the coast. The sight of those sails on the horizon was a relief and boosted morale among the centurions and legionaries, who were terrified by the enemy's great numerical superiority. Seeing the fleet returning, things seemed less dire. It was only a matter of resisting for a little while, as the young tribune in command had said. They could do that. And then they would take the city once and for all. And there would be spoils, money, wine, and women. The future looked bright.

Abandoned Roman camp

"By Demeter, Apollo, and all the gods!" Theophanes exclaimed.

Anaxagoras turned and fixed his gaze on the sea, where the leader of the local aristocracy was staring with a look of shock: the Roman fleet was returning.

The satrap merely gritted his teeth and grunted. He was a man of war, and battles often took unexpected turns. Somehow, as strange as it seemed, this did not surprise him.

He furrowed his brow, thinking quickly.

The Roman ships were still far away, and the winds and currents were against them. Anaxagoras could simply march his troops back to the city and everything would be the way it had been before they'd left. They had enough food and water to last months. Mithridates's help would arrive soon, and the Romans would have to leave for good. And their little outing had not been in vain: they'd gotten to stretch their legs and enjoy the feeling of freedom for a bit, they'd gathered food left behind by the Romans in their retreat, and they'd also confiscated more weapons from the enemy.

"Over there, Lord Protector!" one of the officers shouted.

Anaxagoras turned toward the city and saw the Roman troops trailing out of the forest, blocking their route back to Mytilene.

"It was all a trap," said Theophanes, his voice filled with misery.

Anaxagoras did a quick calculation: "There are barely five hundred of them. We have five times that many men. We can easily breach their lines and be safely back behind the walls in no time . . . Pittacus will keep the gates open . . ." He looked to the sea. "Poseidon and Aeolus will not make things easy for those Roman sailors. We have time. And we have pila. Plenty," Anaxagoras said, watching as his soldiers picked up the spears that the Roman army had left behind. "Yes, Theophanes, this is a trap, but I'm not certain it was laid for us." He looked at the Roman centuries blocking their route back to Mytilene. "I wonder who they've put in command of this suicide mission."

"Is this what we've been reduced to?" Theophanes said quietly, almost to himself, but in a clear message to Anaxagoras. "Pawns used to resolve their internal disputes? Now we're tasked with doing the Romans' dirty work?"

But the satrap of Mytilene was unconcerned by those words. "I don't do anyone's dirty work," he argued as he held up one of the Roman spears. "This will be a quick, clean execution: we'll wipe out those five hundred legionaries, or most of them anyway, and return to the city. Mithridates will soon reward us for our efforts. I don't give a damn about the quarrels among the Romans. I fight to defend the interests of the King of Pontus, and you, Theophanes, should do the same."

There was no more debate.

"Distribute the pila among the men!" Anaxagoras ordered his officers. "Form a phalanx and await my order to advance!"

Atop the walls of Mytilene

Pittacus observed the movements of the Roman centurions as well as those of the phalanxes Anaxagoras had formed. He could see the Roman fleet approaching the island of Lesbos.

"Ready the archers," was his order to the officers. "If the Romans try to retreat to the walls when they see Anaxagoras's advance, massacre them."

On the ocean, near the coast of Lesbos

"Row! Row!" ordered the captain.

The ship's slow advance was exasperating. The coast was very close, but the distance seemed to remain static. The wind was against them. They had lowered the sails. It was now a matter of reaching land by the sheer force of their oars, but even with all the sailors rowing as hard as they could, they were barely able to make any headway.

It was taking too long.

Minucius Thermus could feel the tension among the legionaries aboard his ship.

"They're all worried we'll be too late," he commented quietly to Lucullus.

The proquaestor nodded. Before having received that letter from Rome, he would've smiled at the notion. The calculated delay to reach the coast would ensure young Caesar was annihilated, the mission's main objective. Now, after reading that message, he saw things differently. But Fortuna was a capricious goddess and the plan was already under way. The young tribune would be massacred on Lesbos, at the gates to the city of Mytilene, along with six centuries of Roman soldiers. Lucullus lamented the loss of those 480 legionaries. That sacrifice, which only an hour earlier had seemed necessary to satisfy the wishes of the all-powerful Sulla, was now revealed for what it truly was, a senseless waste of troops who were greatly needed elsewhere if they hoped to ever end the eternal conflict between Rome and the King of Pontus.

"It's a shame," Lucullus said. "It would be good to save at least part of that cohort."

The comment confused Minucius Thermus. He began to understand that Lucullus had changed his mind. He had an inkling as to why. "May I ask, proquaestor, what the letter from Rome said?" he asked cautiously.

Lucullus did not respond. He simply kept his gaze fixed on the coast of Lesbos.

Roman cohort at Mytilene

"Maintain the formation! *Testudo,* on my order!"* Caesar bellowed, looking around at his men.

He arranged the six centuries of his cohort in such a way that their front line was as wide as the one presented by the enemy. As the phalanx advanced threateningly toward them, Caesar noted the wide spaces between his centuries, and he knew that the enemy troops would be able to breach their ranks. But if he brought the centuries closer together, they could easily be surrounded. This way, any enemy that breached their lines might be able to attack a century's flank, but they would also be trapped between one Roman military unit and another and could be attacked from two sides if Caesar ordered it.

Still, the odds were not good.

Caesar peered at the horizon: the ships had lowered their sails. The wind was not in their favor. They were now rowing their way to shore, making their approach even slower. That was not a good sign.

He thought of Cornelia, of his daughter Julia, his mother, his sisters . . . It was very likely that he would never see any of them again.

But Caesar had no time for wistfulness.

He gulped as he watched the enemy army advance.

The phalanx commanded by Anaxagoras was some five hundred paces out and moving quickly. They were not carrying the long *sarisa*

---

* *Testudo* is Latin for "tortoise" and describes the Roman army's famous formation in which a group of legionaries used their overlapping shields to cover themselves and their comrades from arrow fire from above and all sides—like a turtle taking refuge within its shell.

pikes typical of a phalanx, but were instead brandishing short spears ready to be thrown. The sight put Caesar on alert.

"Testudo, testudo!" he shouted at the top of his lungs.

The Roman shields went up.

The centuries were protected by their armor.

It was about to rain iron.

Mytilene phalanx

Just behind the line of combat, Anaxagoras waited for the precise moment to launch the pila. If the cursed Romans hadn't formed those completely closed ranks and taken cover under their shields, he was certain that his men would've been able to devastate the enemy in a matter of minutes without any need for hand-to-hand combat. The Roman defensive formation would allow them to resist for a while. But his troops, with their clear numerical superiority, would soon win out.

He looked back toward the sea. The Roman ships were still rowing with difficulty and had not yet reached the shore. He had plenty of time to carry out his massacre. War was best done slowly and methodically—not something to be rushed. A lack of haste made the enemy all the more uneasy; it gave them time to see the inevitability of their defeat, of their death. And more often than not, panic ensued. And when the enemy began to panic and flee, everything was easier. So Anaxagoras did not hasten his men along.

He took his time.

He waited determined.

He could feel the impatience radiating from Theophanes, a useless man who knew nothing of war, only of truculent words and surrender. Yes, Theophanes's impatience gave Anaxagoras even more confidence. He knew what he was doing.

He counted down from ten between gritted teeth, to make sure they attacked in the precise moment: Δέκα, ἐννέα, ὀκτώ, ἑπτά, ἕξ, πέντε, τέτταρες, τρεῖς, δύο, εἷς . . . * When he got to zero he shouted, "Now! Launch the pila, now!"

---

*   Countdown from ten in Greek.

Roman centuries outside Mytilene

Caesar watched as the sky darkened and a dense cloud of spears descended upon them. It would surely cause casualties among his men.

The javelins whistled through the air as they arced to the ground in their merciless descent. The spearheads punctured the Roman shields, and the sounds of the shafts snapping off was like a roll of thunder through the young tribune's head. He heard the screams of his legionaries as they saw their arms, held high in defense, penetrated by that iron rain.

"Aaah!"

Everywhere, wails of pain.

Caesar's shield remained intact. He was in the first line of combat, as his uncle had been at the battle of Aquae Sextiae, to give an example of fearlessness. But the enemy had aimed at the center of the Roman formation in order to do the most damage possible. And they had succeeded, causing many deaths and even more injuries. Still, each quadrant of each Roman century had been able to hold its exterior lines as the dead and badly wounded were moved to the center of each testudo. Many. Too many. A legionary beside him lowered his shield. A spear had punctured his arm and he could no longer hold it up.

"I'm sorry, tribune," the soldier apologized with tears of pain in his eyes.

"It's all right," Caesar responded. "Now we'll enter hand-to-hand battle. Keep your shield . . ." He was going to tell him to keep it close to his chest, to defend his torso in the clash with the enemy, but he realized that the spearhead had split the shield and remained lodged in the wood, rendering it practically useless.

Caesar's heart stopped for a brief instant.

It was a moment of revelation.

His eyes remained fixed on the spear launched by the enemy. Only the Roman pila split that way, the wooden part bending and breaking as the iron was embedded in the shield, impossible to remove . . .

He looked around and saw that the spears in all of his men's shields were Roman pila, dozens, hundreds of them. Their own weapons had been used against them, wounding and killing many legionaries. How had Anaxagoras's men gotten ahold of those spears? Were they left at the Roman encampment? But . . . why would Lucullus and Thermus have left so many pila behind? They should've been loaded onto the ships. His mind raced under the pressure of battle as he quickly assessed the situation. Finally everything made sense. Lucullus was Sulla's man in the East, and Sulla had wanted to see Gaius Julius Caesar dead ever since he'd refused to divorce Cornelia. Sulla was not known for forgiveness; the public pardon had been, in truth, a farce. Sulla still despised him, and feared him, simply because he was Marius's nephew. Caesar remembered his uncle's words. "Your enemies, my enemies, will forgive you anything except one thing: Sulla, and Dolabella, his hound, will never forgive you for being my nephew. I'm sorry, my boy, you'll have to live with it. You'll have to try to survive under these unfavorable conditions."

It was now abundantly clear that this whole battle was nothing more than an elaborate murder plot, six Roman centuries being sacrificed to ensure the death of one man.

The Mytilene troops continued advancing.

His men maintained their testudo formation, the howls of the wounded rising up all around. He glanced out to sea: the ships had not yet reached the coast. Lucullus would blame the wind and currents, but the proquaestor was an expert sailor. He would never make such a basic mistake. Never, that is, unless it wasn't a mistake at all. It had all been carefully calculated. Abandoning the pila to facilitate Anaxagoras's massacre had been Sulla's final touch.

The enemy phalanx continued its advance.

Caesar thought quickly. He had three options: the first was to retreat as quickly as possible back into the woods. But this would be taken as an act of cowardice and a defiance of the orders they had received. It would mean, at the very least, a *gradus deiectio,* a demotion, or even an *ignominia missio,* a dishonorable discharge from the army. But more likely, Lucullus would deem him a military rebel and decapitate him in front of all the legionaries. If he wasn't first run through with an enemy spear as he fled, that is.

The second option was to follow the proquaestor's orders to the letter and try to hold the position for as long as possible, delaying Anaxagoras's return to the city and giving Lucullus and Thermus time to arrive with the bulk of the Roman army. But the fleet had not yet even reached the coast. That would be suicide. Some two-thirds of the 480 Roman soldiers they'd started with remained alive. Almost all of them would certainly die as the enemy phalanx plowed through them and returned to the safety of the walls, making it impossible for Lucullus to take the city when he finally arrived. Anaxagoras would simply kill them all, then march his men back into Mytilene and close the gates, having saved his army.

The phalanx was nearing.

He had to do something.

Making a decision, any decision, that was the most important thing.

"Pila! On high!" Caesar howled.

His men prepared to launch their spears.

The enemy was close. Almost directly upon them.

"Now! Launch! By Jupiter!" Caesar ordered.

He watched as even some of the injured men made a concentrated effort to launch their spears against the enemy.

The enemy phalanx suffered losses.

Many.

But there were so many of them.

Caesar saw Anaxagoras quickly close the holes in his ranks created by the casualties from the Romans' defensive broadside. Then they resumed their advance.

Lucullus's ships, meanwhile, seemed to be stopped dead at sea.

Caesar swallowed and again thought quickly.

He had three options. Yes, three. There was a third option that did not involve fleeing into the woods or standing to meet their death. If he didn't follow Lucullus's plan, everyone would think he was a cursed coward . . .

He suddenly remembered the advice his uncle had given him that day in the tavern beside the Tiber, when he'd told him and Labienus about the battle of Aquae Sextiae. The words were etched in his mind as if they'd been carved in stone: "It doesn't matter if they insult you. You can pretend to be a coward and not be one, you can pretend to be clumsy even though you are agile. The only thing that matters is the final victory. It doesn't matter if they call you a coward. Don't go into combat unless you believe you can win. Later, in time, all that will be remembered is that: the winner. Everything that happened before is erased. Remember this, boy, and never enter a battle you can't win."

The phalanx was almost upon them. They were outnumbered five to one.

"This doesn't make any sense," Caesar muttered to himself.

Anaxagoras's men would annihilate them.

But there was a third option.

"To the city, everyone, follow me!" Caesar commanded, pointing, much to his men's surprise, to the walls of Mytilene.

Phalanx of the Mytilene troops

Anaxagoras looked on as the six Roman centuries broke formation and began a quick retreat . . . not toward the forest, but to the city. He smiled: it was the panicked retreat he had hoped for. Now they would be even easier to defeat. Why would they flee to the city, where the archers defended the walls, when the logical thing would be to escape back into the forest and try to hide there until the rest of the Roman troops arrived? Not that it would've saved them—Anaxagoras calculated that the Roman fleet was so delayed, his troops would've had ample time to massacre the centuries in the woods and then return to the safety of the city. In any case, retreating to the walls would, for those legionaries, only accelerate their death.

He observed the Roman retreat with his brow furrowed. And then he understood it. It was no retreat. It was a full-scale attack. An attack with only a slim chance of success, but with a chance nonetheless, whereas facing his phalanx head-on was suicide. From one warrior to another, he couldn't help but admire the intelligence of whoever was in command of the cohort.

"They've lost their minds," said Theophanes. "The archers will pick them off one by one. It's going to be even easier than we thought."

But Anaxagoras shook his head. "The commander is not crazy," he argued. "We have archers there, but no soldiers. If they reach the gates, we'll have a problem. And if Pittacus is forced to close the gates, we'll have an even bigger one. No, the Roman in command of those centuries is not crazy, whoever he is." And he turned to his warriors: "Pick up the pace!"

Anaxagoras realized that, all of a sudden, time was of the essence.

Walls of Mytilene

Pittacus watched as the movements of Anaxagoras's phalanx and the six Roman centuries unfolded at his feet. He was calm but attentive to everything that was happening. He looked on as the enemy fleet neared land. He understood that it had all been a ruse to draw the Mytilene troops from behind their wall, but everything was under control: the Romans had not left behind enough legionaries to truly block Anaxagoras's return to Mytilene. The satrap had been smart to march out with the entire army. Any less and they wouldn't have been able to withstand the ambush, but this way they would annihilate the Romans as they returned to the city and close the gates behind them. The Romans would have achieved nothing except the loss of a few hundred men. Senselessly. But . . . what were the Romans doing now? Fleeing. After Anaxagoras's brutal rain of spears . . . but they were running in formation, in an orderly fashion toward . . . toward the open gates of Mytilene.

"Archers! At the ready! At the ready, by Apollo!" Pittacus wailed at the men posted along the wall. "Take aim at the Romans! Take aim!"

Roman centuries outside the walls of Mytilene

"To the city, to the gates!" Caesar commanded. "By Jupiter, everyone follow me! To Mytilene!" Marius's words echoed in his mind: "Remember this, my boy, and never enter a battle you can't win."

Titus Labienus was confused by the order.

"To the city! To the city, by Hercules!" Caesar shouted over and over. "Maintain the testudo, but move quickly, to the city! To the gates!"

Labienus always thought a little more slowly than his friend, but he was beginning to see that this plan might be the best option: fleeing to the forest would mean defying direct orders; battling Anaxagoras's phalanx was suicide. This way, they could perhaps take control of the gates. It was insane, but it was possible. Difficult, but at least it gave them a chance.

"To the city! In testudo!" Labienus said, and the centurions repeated the order.

They knew, as they approached the walls, that there would be a firestorm of arrows launched by the archers defending the city, which was why they had to maintain the testudo formation. But their objective was to get through the city gates, and they wouldn't be able to fit all at once, so the maneuver had to be carried out in an orderly fashion.

And the order soon arrived: "Through the gates in battle formation!" Caesar shouted. "In battle formation, by Hercules!"

With Marius's military reforms, all the centuries of a cohort now carried the same armaments, and the only thing differentiating one cohort from another was their amount of experience in battle. All centuries were well trained in the specific combat formations, which officers and soldiers alike understood perfectly. So, hearing Caesar's order, the third century immediately situated itself ahead of the rest and was the first to be peppered by the city's archers. But after the brutal rain of pila, those arrows were not quite as terrifying. The men were protected by their shields, and despite some injuries, were able to continue their advance. The sixth century immediately fell in line behind the third, followed by the second, with Labienus at the head. After them came the fifth century, followed closely by the first, led by Caesar. Forming the tail of that Roman serpent, shields held high, came the fourth century of the cohort. It was an old formation that harkened back to the times when the different centuries had different armaments, but it was the order that everyone knew and it allowed them to move automatically, in perfect synchronicity. There was no time to stop and think. Luckily, the legionaries could tell that Julius Caesar was thinking for everyone.

Walls of Mytilene

"By Apollo! Kill them all!" Pittacus howled. He looked on as the Roman shields deflected their arrows and, leaving behind the few felled by the archers, the surviving Roman centuries neared the gates of the city, still open to facilitate Anaxagoras's return. He struggled to process the surprising turn the battle had taken.

Pittacus considered closing the gate to leave the enemy locked outside, but it took a long time to move the heavy doors and then barricade them. Opening them later, after Anaxagoras had annihilated the centuries, would take a long time, and the Roman fleet carrying the bulk of their army had now reached land. Everything had suddenly become more complicated. All because whoever commanded those six centuries had gotten the crazy idea to rush the gates of Mytilene. No. It was better to leave the gates open. A few of the legionaries might make it into the city, but Anaxagoras's men would be close behind them, and once the Mytilene army was safely inside, they could close the gates, leaving Lucullus and Thermus's troops out in the cold. That was essential. After that it would be easy to hunt down any remaining Romans trapped in the city. With the return of Anaxagoras's troops, it would be easy enough to root out any stray enemy left within the walls.

"Should we close the gates, my lord?" asked an officer.

"No," Pittacus replied. "We will wait for Anaxagoras to return. Gather all available men and try to keep the cursed Romans out."

Troops of Mytilene outside the city

Anaxagoras reorganized his troops in a long formation, like a second snake trailing the one formed by the Romans. Getting back into the city was now the priority. Once inside, they could annihilate the enemy. He could tell that Pittacus was thinking along the same lines, since he had left the gates open.

"Good. Everything can still work out," he muttered under his breath.

Outside the gates to the city

The Romans suffered more losses through the incessant rain of arrows, but the third and sixth centuries were already passing through the gates. There, they encountered dozens of enemy warriors. Although the tenth cohort, under Caesar's command, had little combat experience, they were well trained, had just survived a merciless onslaught, and had seen many of their friends fall in combat. They were brimming with raw hatred of the enemy. And now, finally, they were able to enter hand-to-hand combat, which is what they'd been trained to do.

The first line of soldiers held up their shields and ruthlessly slashed at their opponents through the cracks in their defensive armor. Behind them, the other soldiers held their shields over their heads to protect themselves from the archers, who were still shooting from atop the wall.

The legionaries in the first line of combat made way for themselves by sheer brutal force. They pushed the enemy back using the *umbones* of their shields as they wielded their blades with an almost hysterical fury, pulsing with adrenaline, fighting for their lives.

For survival.

They sliced at the enemy as if there were no tomorrow.

The first two centuries made quick work of the few men Pittacus had been able to muster up against them. From atop the wall, where he commanded the archers, Pittacus now saw that the soldiers at the gates had fallen and ordered his men to fire at will.

The Roman soldiers held their shields high as they flooded through the gates. But they were unsure what they were supposed to do once inside the city. Where were the two tribunes? They needed new orders . . .

Things were not going exactly as planned.

Because Labienus had fallen in combat.

An arrow had pierced his leg. He wasn't dead, but he was lying on the ground some two hundred paces from where the Roman soldiers swarmed the gates of the city.

Caesar arrived at the gates and saw the troops milling around chaotically. He scanned the group for Labienus but didn't see him anywhere. First he had to organize his men.

"Third, sixth, and second centuries, inside the city, all of you!" he ordered. "Seize control of the chains that open and close the gates and guard them with your lives! Kill anyone who gets in your way! Let me know when you have the chains in your hands, by Jupiter!"

These men now had clear instructions and, led by their centurions, sprang into action. The centurion of the sixth century had died in combat.

"The fifth, first, and fourth, with me, outside the wall, we'll fend off Anaxagoras's men!" he shouted. Only after he had given his orders did he ask, "Where is the other tribune?"

"He has fallen wounded, there, among the dead beside the wall," the centurion said, pointing to the spot where Titus Labienus lay on the ground, using his shield to protect himself from the arrows still being launched by the archers from above.

Anaxagoras's men were quite close to where Labienus lay and were advancing quickly. Caesar watched as they moved among the fallen Romans, methodically running their swords through each of the wounded or dead as they made their way to the gates to the city. Anaxagoras wanted to make sure no Roman was left alive. Labienus was a dead man. It was only a matter of time, very little time, until one of Anaxagoras's soldiers pierced the wounded tribune with his blade.

LXXII

CAESAR'S
ORDERS

Mytilene, Island of Lesbos
78 B.C.
Outside the city's main gate

CAESAR TURNED TO THE LEADER OF THE FIRST UNIT. FOR the second time, Gaius Julius Caesar dictated his own combat orders. His first order had been to take control of the city gates. Or attempt to. Whether they would succeed was yet to be seen. Making decisions and giving orders was starting to feel easy, but he didn't have time to reflect. Labienus was in danger.

"Maintain this position! I'm going after the wounded tribune. If Anaxagoras catches up to us, your mission is to close the gates to the city. Is that clear? No matter what happens, whether tribune Labienus and I are inside the city or not, your mission and the mission of the rest of the men is to close this gate before Anaxagoras's soldiers get here. Understood?"

The centurion nodded, but he seemed confused.

"Tell me that you've understood, damn it!" Caesar shouted.

"I understand, tribune!"

Caesar rested his hand on the man's shoulder for an instant and gripped it firmly in a sign of appreciation. The centurion was twice his age, but he looked at the young tribune with awe and admiration. Caesar then turned around. He took a deep breath. He'd have to run as fast as he could. He threw his shield to the ground; it was too heavy and would only slow him down. They could use Labienus's shield to protect themselves for their return to the gates.

Caesar took off at a sprint, zigzagging unpredictably. Arrows fell around him, but his speed and constant changes in direction made it difficult for the enemy archers to calculate his position when they shot from on high. Soon, Pittacus ordered them to concentrate their energies on the base of the wall around the main gate, where the Romans were clustered. He didn't want them to waste arrows on a moving target that was difficult to hit.

Caesar reached Labienus.

"Can you stand?" he asked.

"I don't know..." Labienus answered. "I don't know...but... you're insane, go back...leave me," he said, his words punctuated by the pain of the arrow stuck in his left calf.

"Stop talking and stand up, by all the gods!" Caesar ordered, tugging at his friend's arm. "Up!" Caesar pulled Labienus to his feet with surprising strength.

"I can't...walk!"

"Shut up and walk or I'll kill you myself!" Caesar spoke with such authority that Labienus stopped arguing and began to stumble along, aided by his friend.

Caesar supported Labienus's weight with one arm, and with the other he held his friend's shield to protect them from the arrows that still fell intermittently around them. Not many, because Anaxagoras and his men were drawing near, and the archers on the wall, by Pittacus's orders, were focusing their arrows on the Romans trying to seize control of the huge iron chains that opened and closed the gates to the city.

The leader of the first unit looked toward the tribunes. Anaxagoras's men seemed to be right on their heels.

"They'll never make it," an optio said.

The centurion nodded. "No, they'll never make it," he agreed, cursing the gods, fate, Fortuna, and all the cursed soldiers of Mytilene.

The centurion was a veteran of the first war against Mithridates. He'd been in combat on several occasions and had fought under superiors who were sometimes intelligent and sometimes bumbling, some cowardly, some brave, some quick to make decisions and other heart-achingly slow. He'd seen many patrician men, named tribune simply because of their noble birth, who were incapable of leading armed men, who refused to enter hand-to-hand combat on the front line. And he'd seen many of his comrades fall because of poor leadership. But he'd never seen a patrician tribune display such bravery and courage as Julius Caesar, risking his life to save another officer.

"Damn it all!" the centurion said. He turned to the optio and the other centurions and said, "As soon as you have control of the chains, begin to close the gates! I will take the first unit to aid the tribunes!"

The other officers understood the importance of closing the gates so that Anaxagoras's men would be forced to face the bulk of the Roman army, now ascending from the beach under Lucullus's command. And the officers and legionaries alike all admired the courage of their tribune and thought it right that the centurion should take a unit to help him save his comrade. It was risky, but at the very least it would give them a chance.

"Let's go! By my cursed fate, let's go!" the centurion howled.

Outside the walls of Mytilene
Rearguard of the phalanx, Anaxagoras's position

The satrap saw the tribunes dragging themselves toward the gates. Their heads would make a nice trophy. Yes, he would decapitate them before all the citizens of Mytilene and then mount their bloodied skulls atop the wall as a warning to the rest of the Romans.

He smiled, thinking of his imminent victory. He admired the tribunes' bravery, but war was war . . .

They were closing in on the tribunes when he saw a Roman unit leave the gates in an attempt to aid them. But he immediately forgot about the tribunes as he noticed that the gates now seemed to be controlled not by Pittacus but by the Romans. If the legionaries managed to close the gates, they'd be locked outside the city. He looked back: Lucullus and Thermus's huge army was ascending from the beach in combat formation. They would see their many fallen comrades along the way, and if there was one thing Anaxagoras had learned in his past encounters with the Roman legions, it was that the legionaries fought especially fiercely when avenging the lives of their friends.

His smile faded.

War, sometimes, was fucking war.

Outside the walls of Mytilene
Caesar and Labienus's position

"Walk, damn it!" Caesar shouted.

"I can't, by all the gods, leave me!" Labienus replied weakly.

His complaints fell on deaf ears, as Caesar continued urging him along, never flagging for an instant.

They advanced at a painstaking pace, and both men were certain that Anaxagoras's troops would overtake them, when suddenly, the first century rushed toward them and placed themselves between the tribunes and the satrap's front line.

"Attack! Attack!" the centurion howled.

Caesar couldn't believe it. It was as if the legionaries were injected with such rage and energy that now anything seemed possible. Two soldiers rushed to Caesar.

"We will take the tribune," they said.

Grateful to be relieved of laboriously dragging Labienus to the gates, Caesar placed his wounded friend in the care of those legionaries and, gladius held high, using Labienus's shield for protection, he positioned himself beside the leader of the first century as the enemy phalanx descended upon them. He shouted for the men to form a testudo, small now, since half of the unit had already fallen, and he began to slash at the enemy like any other legionary. Furiously, with punishing brutality. It wasn't hard. All he had to do was imagine Anaxagoras's warriors as nothing more than mercenaries sent by Sulla, trying to execute him. Which was, in fact, what they were, unwittingly.

In the midst of that chaotic bloodbath, Caesar found himself able to keep a level head and ordered a retreat to the main gate, which was still open.

"Quickly, centurion, or we'll be locked out," Caesar shouted.

The officer nodded.

"Retreat, quickly!" the leader of the first century said to his men.

Arrows fell all around them, but they were very close to the gates as they slowly, creakingly began to close. The Roman centurions had at last taken control of the chains and, following orders, they began to turn the huge wooden wheels that shut the heavy iron doors, blocking access to Mytilene.

Atop the walls

Pittacus watched helplessly as the gates began to close. With all the soldiers outside with Anaxagoras, he hadn't had enough men on the ground here to fend off the Romans. And now his archers were running out of arrows.

There was nothing he could do except look on as the disaster unfolded at his feet.

All was lost.

Or was it?

He scanned the wall. He had with him approximately three hundred archers.

He took stock of the battle below: the enemy had brought little more than two hundred men into the city, since, between Anaxagoras's spears and the archers' arrows, the Romans had lost half of their troops. The battle would be evenly matched.

Pittacus craned his neck and peered down at the gates. He would take his archers and defeat the Romans to retake control of them.

Outside the gates of Mytilene
First century

"Throw down your shields and run to the gates, by Jupiter!" Caesar shouted as he saw the enemy archers abandoning the walls.

The first century's push had halted the initial onslaught of Anaxagoras's warriors, who were now waiting for more men to join them before charging again. The Romans took advantage of the pause in combat to retreat as quickly as possible to the gates, which slowly but inexorably, were closing, as per Caesar's orders.

Labienus, aided by two legionaries, made it safely into the city. Behind him were the surviving members of the first century who had come to his rescue, the centurion among them. Finally, when there was barely enough space to pass between the gigantic iron doors, creaking with the immensity of their weight as they swung closed, Gaius Julius Caesar slid through. Along with him, three of Anaxagoras's soldiers who had taken off in pursuit of the Romans slipped in as well. A fourth Mytilene soldier became trapped between the doors as they closed. They heard the crunch of his bones as the gates, more slowly now but just as unstoppably, continued to close—until the poor soul's body was crushed by the pressure, exploding in a rain of blood that showered down on all nearby. And in the midst of that red rain, Caesar lunged at the enemy warriors who had followed him in. The surviving soldiers of the first century quickly followed suit and, in no time, Anaxagoras's men were attacked from all sides, stabbed in the neck and chest at once, falling dead in an instant.

"Push! Push!" Caesar ordered, seeing that the gates could not close all the way, obstructed as they were by the skull of the soldier trapped between the two iron doors.

The soldiers obeyed and soon the skull exploded and a new rain of blood drenched Caesar. And then they heard the final, loud clang, a beastly metal snap announcing that the gates of Mytilene had been completely closed.

Anaxagoras's phalanx

Anaxagoras and his men outside the wall numbered 2,500 well-armed warriors, but directly behind them, one entire Roman legion and several additional *vexillationes* from the proquaestor's fleet were coming up from the sea. Over eight thousand legionaries in combat formation.

Roman army under Lucullus's command

Lucullus and Thermus disembarked.

Beyond their dark political maneuverings, both were competent military officers. Caesar and Labienus had altered the established plan, but the result was even better than anticipated: they had not only managed to block Anaxagoras's return to the city, but to completely prevent them from taking refuge behind the walls, closing the gates of Mytilene with the enemy warriors trapped outside on the battlefield.

"If our men inside can maintain control of the gates, we have them," said Minucius Thermus.

"Effectively, yes," Lucullus agreed.

His voice belied a certain surprise and a hint of admiration. Julius Caesar should be dead but nevertheless seemed to be quickly transforming into a military hero that morning on the Isle of Lesbos. A place so remote it took weeks for news to arrive from Rome. Weeks. Lucullus frowned.

And in a matter of weeks, everything could change in Rome before they even had an inkling of it in the East.

"Caesar may still fall in combat," said Thermus, trying to anticipate Lucullus's thoughts. He'd expected the proquaestor to be angry over the fact that Caesar had strayed from the original plan, to astonishing success. "It's going to take us hours to put an end to Anaxagoras's men. Hours in which Caesar will have to survive inside the city with only a handful of men."

"Hours," the proquaestor repeated mysteriously, showing no hint as to whether that delay was good or bad.

Inside the city of Mytilene

Labienus was leaning against the wall. The gates were closed. They could hear Anaxagoras's men pounding on them from the outside, cursing in a Greek that both Caesar and Labienus could understand perfectly:

"Open up, cursed bastards, open up!"

Caesar and Labienus exchanged a glance.

"Now we wait," said Caesar. "We must make sure that this gate remains closed no matter what."

Labienus simply nodded. His leg was still bleeding and his face was pinched with pain.

"Tie something, your gladius belt, anything, around your thigh," Caesar said. "That will stop the bleeding and make it easier for the doctors of the legion's valetudinarium to treat the wound later."

Labienus nodded and took off his belt. When he looked back up, after applying the tourniquet to his leg, his friend was already talking to the centurions, organizing the defense.

"Testudo!" Caesar shouted. "Attack anyone who comes near!"

It was a straightforward plan, easy to follow.

Pittacus and his archers descended from atop the walls. It was clear that their arrows would not be enough to defeat those miserable Romans who had infiltrated their city.

"Let's go, everyone, with me!" Pittacus ordered.

It didn't make sense to leave any archers on the wall when it was their own men outside on the ground below. Pittacus knew that they would have to break through the Roman defense formation guarding the large pulleys that activated the gates' opening and closing mechanism.

He positioned himself at the head to lead by example.

The soldiers under his command brandished their spears and swords, anything they could find, against the Roman testudo formation.

Outside the walls of Mytilene

Lucullus saw the long front line of battle presented by Anaxagoras and decided to build a formation similar to the triplex acies* but with certain variations: they didn't have the tenth cohort, since Caesar had taken them into Mytilene and closed the gates to the city, meaning there were only two cohorts on the front line of com-

---

* Triple battle order, with the legionaries arranged in three ranks.

bat, which was not enough to take on the phalanx. So he ordered all
the auxiliary troops and the vexillationes to the vanguard. Behind
them the seventh, ninth, fifth, sixth, and eighth cohorts would follow in a second line. Bringing up the rear, the first, second, third,
and fourth cohorts would form the third line typical of the triplex
acies.

The auxiliaries and the additional units charged furiously against
Anaxagoras's phalanx. Any man who served as a member of Rome's
auxiliary troops with bravery and efficiency for a period of twenty-
five years would receive citizenship and a small plot of land to culti-
vate. It was a good incentive for the long term. In the short term,
pillage and plunder, the promise of spoils from the city they would
sack that day, were powerful motivators.

Anaxagoras and Theophanes ordered the phalanx to charge, in
turn, at the Roman auxiliary soldiers.

The clash was brutal. The phalanx's long pikes caused injuries
among the Roman auxiliaries, but not enough to break their attack
formation. There were losses, but the Roman lines remained tight.

By Lucullus's orders, the auxiliaries, many wounded in body and
in pride, withdrew down the passageways that the seventh, ninth,
fifth, sixth, and eighth cohorts opened up to make way for them as
fresh legionaries surged forward to the front line, eager for battle.
Putting an end to that long siege and adding to their salaries through
plundering was a motivating factor for the regular soldiers as well.
But above all, taking the city meant the chance to finally leave this
remote island they were all so sick of.

The clash was violent as the Mytilene sarisas fell upon the Romans. But unlike the pila, the long Greek spears often passed directly
through the Roman shields without damaging them or could be broken off with a swipe of a gladius, so that the legionaries remained
protected as they began to slash furiously at the enemy.

Anaxagoras's phalanx began to break apart in several spots.

Lucullus watched the battle and predicted they would succeed,
but he foresaw many losses among his men. Anaxagoras would go
down fighting, and fighting hard. The proquaestor knew he needed

to send replacements to the front lines, but he couldn't decide whether to send the auxiliaries or his more experienced cohorts, who remained in the rearguard.

Lucullus ran his hand over his mouth, weighing the options. "Take a couple of the more experienced centuries to the front line along with the auxiliaries," the proquaestor said to a nearby tribune. "Have the more experienced warriors surround Anaxagoras himself. I want him dead. I want him dead . . . now."

Inside the city of Mytilene

Caesar was fighting on the front line to maintain control of the gates.

Pittacus was on the front line as well, leading the Mytilene archers.

Caesar identified the enemy leader, and as he made his way through spears and swords with the legionaries in testudo formation, he reached the spot where Pittacus stood fighting.

Caesar attacked viciously.

Pittacus screamed in pain.

Their leader fallen, the archers retreated almost instinctively. Once a few men began to flee, the others quickly followed suit, scattering through the streets in search of places to hide. They didn't realize it would do them no good.

Caesar, escorted by several legionaries, quickly rushed to the top of the wall.

Outside the walls of Mytilene

Anaxagoras didn't see it coming. He was fighting on the front line to set an example, and he didn't have enough perspective to realize that the Roman troops were concentrating around him.

He was pierced by a dozen Roman gladiī all at once.

His phalanx could've dispersed immediately, as had happened inside the city after Pittacus fell, but Theophanes took over command and ordered a tactical retreat of several dozen feet, distancing the phalanx from the first line of Romans. Then he set off on his own to negotiate surrender terms with the Roman leaders, accompanied only by a few Mytilene aristocrats who Anaxagoras had brought along as hostages in their flight from the city. By the time Anaxagoras's men realized what was happening, Theophanes and his friends were safely talking terms inside the Roman proquaestor's tent and the legionaries had resumed their charge against the enemy ranks, attacking relentlessly.

Soon the Mytilene were annihilated. They had bravely defended themselves, refusing to surrender until the end of the day, with only a few hundred men standing.

"They are strong," Lucullus said to Thermus from atop a hill where he could take in the scene. "They will make good slaves."

Thermus nodded. The battle had gone in their favor, but there was still one matter to settle: Julius Caesar was still alive, comfortably watching the annihilation of the enemy phalanx from atop the wall like a spectator in the coliseum.

Lucullus looked at Thermus and understood his concern but refrained from saying anything. The proquaestor, escorted by a dozen legionaries, simply walked down the hill, crossed the field of corpses, and approached the walls of the city. A few paces from the main gate, Lucullus gazed up to the top of the wall.

Caesar looked down.

Their eyes met.

"Open the doors, tribune!" Lucius Licinius Lucullus boomed.

Caesar heard the order, but he did not move: this was the man Sulla had sent to force him into a deadly trap. His blood boiled, but he was a mere tribune, and his superior, the most powerful man in all the East, had just given him very clear orders in front of everyone.

Labienus, leaning on the wall near the gates, his left leg badly wounded, glanced up at Caesar where he stood atop the walls. His friend looked as terrified as he had before going into combat that morning, which felt like a lifetime ago. Labienus recognized the proquaestor's commanding voice, and the other legionaries who controlled the gates all knew it was Sulla's envoy in the East who had given the order.

Caesar slowly inhaled, filling his lungs with calm. He then turned to the legionaries of the first century of the tenth cohort, his cohort, and, loud and clear, gave his last order of the day, the last order Caesar would give at Mytilene: "Open the gates!"

LXXIII

THE CIVIC
CROWN

Island of Lesbos, outside the walls of Mytilene
78 B.C.
Proquaestor's tent

CAESAR OPENED THE GATES TO THE CITY, AND THE ROMANS
took Mytilene.

Theophanes, the leader of the local aristocracy, had surrendered
to Lucullus. He portrayed Mytilene as a victim of the King of Pontus's desires for annexation and expansion. He argued that they had
never wanted to leave Roman protection but were invaded by Anaxagoras's army.

Lucullus appreciated Theophanes's cooperation, but he didn't believe his excuses. He knew that the citizens of Mytilene had been
playing both sides, so he ordered the sacking of the city. The legionaries needed to be compensated for all those months of siege, especially with the many losses they'd suffered. The cohort Caesar led,
which had taken control of the gate, had seen great losses. Many men
had fallen in combat with Anaxagoras's phalanx as well.

Theophanes accepted the sacking of the city, but in exchange for
his cooperation with Lucullus's troops, the lives of the citizens of
Mytilene would be spared and the Romans would not burn the city.
It was still a harsh punishment, but Theophanes persuaded the rest
of the citizens of Mytilene to accept the pact.

"If we were negotiating with Sulla instead of Lucullus, nothing
would be left of Mytilene except a grazing field," he said, "as with
Athens a few years back."

Theophanes, now in the proquaestor's tent, was trying to hammer out the details of the sacking and set some limits. "How long will the sacking last?" he asked.

But before Lucullus could respond, Caesar entered.

"Sorry," said the young tribune. "I was summoned by the proquaestor. No one notified me that he was in a meeting." He turned, prepared to wait outside until the negotiations were concluded.

Theophanes glared at him. This was the officer who had been so bold as to take the gates of Mytilene and, in consequence, delivered the entire city into Roman hands.

"Wait, tribune, you don't need to go," Lucullus said, turning to Theophanes and repeating his last question: "You wanted to know, how long will the sacking last?"

"Yes," Theophanes replied, eager to hear to what extent Rome would punish them for having let themselves be controlled by Mithridates's troops.

Lucullus took a sip of wine, exchanged a sidelong glance with Minucius Thermus, and said, "The sacking will last until the fire begins."

Theophanes looked perplexed. "Fire? What fire?" he asked in disbelief.

"The fire we will set to burn Mytilene to the ground, of course," Lucullus said, amused that the man he was speaking to failed to understand something so obvious.

"But ... but ... that's not what we agreed," Theophanes sputtered, beginning to sweat.

Caesar witnessed the conversation with consternation. He bit his tongue to keep from interjecting.

Theophanes was still arguing in a desperate attempt to avoid the destruction of his home. "If I had stoked the flames of resistance in the city, you'd still be fighting in the streets of Mytilene and would have suffered many more losses among your men." He realized that things could be even worse. "Are you going to kill us all too?"

There was a dense silence.

Lucullus set his cup down. "If it's not necessary, no," he stated.

Theophanes panted with fear as he wracked his brain for some convincing argument to save Mytilene. He looked back up and with his eyes fixed on the proquaestor, made a desperate threat: "If you burn the city, I will travel the entire East letting everyone know that Lucius Licinius Lucullus is not a man of his word. You won't be able to reach another agreement in the entire region. With anyone."

Lucullus did not seem concerned at the prospect, responding with utmost calm. "If I kill you, you won't be able to tell anyone, will you?"

"Then you've already decided to go back on your word. You're going to burn the city and kill us all."

"I have no plans to kill the citizens of Mytilene, but if you insist on making threats, your death may become necessary. Executing you would certainly serve as a good. The fire is necessary. We have to send a clear message that Rome will be merciless with any city that joins Mithridates. Our war with the King of Pontus will be long yet, and Rome's strength must remain utterly clear. For everyone and—"

"Perhaps the fire isn't the best idea, proquaestor," Julius Caesar interrupted, much to the shock of everyone present.

The men looked at the tribune. Theophanes had a spark of hope in his eyes; Minucius Thermus's face showed surprise; Lucullus seemed irritated yet slightly intrigued.

"Not the best idea?" said the proquaestor, catching Thermus's eye. "It turns out that the tribune is not only bold in combat but is also quite the diplomat."

Caesar understood that it was unwise to interrupt his superior, but now that the mistake had been made, he would speak his mind. "The burning of Athens in Greece didn't solve anything," he said. Then, before Lucullus could argue, he continued. "Yes, Greece fell to Sulla, but the rest of the East perceived Rome as cruel and ruthless. That allowed Mithridates to present himself to the people of the region as a liberator, as the only person capable of freeing them from the terrifying giant that is Rome. And that's what many believe, no matter that in truth he's a tyrant motivated only by personal ambition. The proquaestor could burn Mytilene and all of Lesbos, and that will definitely inspire fear, but only fear. It will not help forge any alliance that will allow us to control this enormous territory and guarantee a more lasting peace."

"By all the gods, are you suggesting we should let this long rebellion at Mytilene go unpunished?" asked Lucullus. "Is that what you're proposing, tribune? You have just opened the gates to the city and now you talk of controlling the entire East. I think you might be getting ahead of yourself, boy."

Caesar was undaunted. Theophanes listened, impressed: the officer was debating with the all-powerful proquaestor of Rome like a peer. He had heard gossip about this tribune circulating through the camp—something about how he had confronted none other than Sulla himself in the recent past. Seeing him speak so freely before the proquaestor, he began to think that the rumor might be true.

"No, we should not let a rebellion like the one here at Mytilene go unpunished," Caesar said, "but we have to find a middle ground, a balance between strength and cruelty, between authority and tyranny. In Hispania, Hannibal took control relatively quickly by combining military might with pacts and agreements. He even married an Iberian woman, Himilce, to strengthen the ties between himself and the Iberians that he was forcing to submit to him."

Lucullus laughed. "Now you're suggesting I should take an Eastern wife? I'm not sure I'd tempt my fate with a third marriage," he said, making light of the young man's serious arguments. He cut his laughter short, stared at Caesar, and then added, "But finish, since you've started, and tell us what you think we should do."

Caesar nodded. "No, I'm not suggesting that the proquaestor should remarry, it was only an example of a pact that Hannibal used to take a territory without having to resort to systematic violence and cruelty. Cruelty, in the end, only generates bitterness, and bitterness leads to rebellions in the conquered lands. Scipio adopted a line of action very similar to Hannibal when he arrived in Hispania: he besieged New Carthage, the Carthaginian capital of the region, and took control, but when he did so he freed the Iberian prisoners. Scipio fought several fierce battles with the Iberians but was generous in his victory and, in a short time, he took control of Hispania."

"Which proves that Hannibal, even with his marriage to the Iberian woman, had not managed to make lasting alliances with his combination of force and generosity," Lucullus argued, given over completely to the debate.

"That's because Scipio used the same technique. Mithridates uses only force—and offering only force, the battle for control of the East will be eternal. That's what happened when Cato took over for Scipio in Hispania, leaving a trail of blood and fire in his wake. It took decades after that to regain control of Hispania. Here, it's the same. If Mytilene is burned to the ground, Mithridates's image as the regions' savior from Rome will only be reinforced. If, however, we are generous with Mytilene in their defeat, other cities in the East might come over to our side, thus weakening the King of Pontus's position . . . reducing the number of battles and the number of dead legionaries."

Lucullus tilted his head. "You may be right . . ." he admitted. "But Hispania is rebelling now," he added, referring to the uprising led by Sertorius and other populares who had taken refuge there.

"It's not the Iberians who are rebelling," Caesar argued. "What's happening in Hispania is"—he weighed his words carefully—"the prolongation of the unresolved conflict between the populares' demand for reforms and the optimates' full opposition to those reforms. It is not an Iberian rebellion."

Lucullus nodded again. "You may be right," the proquaestor repeated, "but there are other matters to consider: my men need gold and women. How do you plan to give it to them if we don't sack and burn the city? If we don't take their daughters and wives and slave women, boy? Or are you suggesting that I make the legionaries go without their spoils after so many months of siege? I'd have the cities of the East on my side and my own army against me."

Here Caesar turned to Theophanes, who understood and began to propose solutions. "I can get Mytilene to gather a huge quantity of gold and silver to be distributed among the soldiers. And I can get women from the Cilician pirates. Without a sacking. The gold and silver immediately. The women in a few days. The legionaries will be fully satisfied."

"Without sacking and burning the city," said Lucullus as if skeptical. "And we'll send this message of Roman generosity to the East, which could weaken Mithridates." The proquaestor was talking to himself more than anyone else.

No one spoke.

Lucullus nodded. "So be it," he agreed. To Theophanes, he said, "I want all your gold and silver here by tomorrow. We will distribute it among the men. The money will appease them for a few days, but those women will have to come soon."

"Everything will be done just as we've agreed upon here, pro-quaestor," Theophanes said, still incredulous at the turn the negotiation had taken. Moments ago it seemed that his city would be razed to the ground, its women abused and raped, and he executed. Now, suddenly, everything had changed. They would go broke turning over all their gold and silver to the Romans and spending what little they had left buying slave women from the Cilician pirates, but they could at least rebuild and be reborn after it was all over. Plundering, burning, massacre, and rape, on the other hand, would take his people generations to recover from.

Theophanes bowed to the two commanding officers, stared for a moment at the young tribune who had unexpectedly defended his cause, then left the tent.

Caesar knew that Theophanes would remember his face forever. For better or for worse, he couldn't say. Only time would tell if their paths would cross again.

Lucullus looked to a slave, who refilled his wine.

"I was summoned, proquaestor," said Caesar, "but I understood that it was for another matter."

"That is so," Lucullus confirmed, "but now the battle has been won and the matter of whether to burn the city has been settled as well," he continued in an affable tone, seated on his comfortable ca-thedra, drinking wine.

The more he thought about it, the more he liked the way the capture of Mytilene had turned out. But it was true that he had summoned the bold young tribune, who was also apparently a shrewd negotiator, for another reason entirely. Lucullus now grasped that this boy, based on his oratory skills, was perfectly capable of persuading the king of Bithynia to provide ships for the Roman fleet without giving in to his sexual demands.

There were several cups of wine on the table and a bowl of small red fruits.

"Drink with us," Lucullus said, offering him a cup.

Caesar hesitated. He valued his life over any possible punishment. "I'm exhausted, proquaestor," he answered. "I'd prefer not to drink."

Lucullus was shocked. A superior never truly offered anything—he ordered it.

Thermus couldn't believe the young tribune's audacity. He was beginning to believe the stories they'd told about Caesar's having refused to divorce his wife and living as a fugitive from Rome for months as a result, even falling ill in the swamps in central Italy.

Lucullus pressed his hands together over his mouth for a few seconds, then separated them and continued speaking, ignoring the young tribune's insult. "You have fought courageously. You modified my plan without consulting me, but the result was successful since the main objective of capturing the city was achieved. You also saved that tribune friend of yours . . . What's his name?"

"Labienus, Titus Labienus, proquaestor," Caesar replied.

"That's it, Labienus," Lucullus said. "Your actions, without doubt, make you worthy of a military honor. I think a civic crown would be appropriate, considering that you heroically saved the life of another officer in combat. And so that is the honor I shall confer on you."

Caesar was silent, pensive, confused. Why would an honor like that come from the man whom Sulla—he was sure of it—had sent to kill him? He'd offered his opinions on the fate of Mytilene, but he'd done so for the general good of Rome in the region, not because he trusted Lucullus.

Thermus was equally bewildered. He didn't see the sense in honoring a man Sulla wanted dead.

"You're a strange one, Gaius Julius Caesar," the proquaestor continued. "You don't seem happy about being granted this honor, you reject your superior's offer to partake in a cup of wine in his company, you interrupt me as I'm negotiating the terms of a surrender, and you even have the nerve to argue over these terms. You argued intelligently and convincingly, I'll give you that, and without fearing punishment for interrupting me. You are certainly ... peculiar. Would you at least try a few of the delicious fruits I've had brought over from Cerasus? I think they might sell well in the markets of Rome, and I plan to bring several trees by ship when we return. Why don't you try one and tell me what you think? I'm curious to hear your opinion. You seem like a man with a strong intuition, which is why you rushed the gate at Mytilene instead of trying to resist Anaxagoras's phalanx. An intuitive man with good fortune."

Caesar eyed the bowl filled with the unfamiliar red fruits but did not move to try one. He stood, deliberating. Refusing again would be unwise, but the proquaestor's insistence that he drink and eat ... made him uncomfortable. To him, Lucullus was still the man Sulla had sent to end his life. He was certain that the plan to attack Mytilene had been designed to ensure that he died in combat. He recalled the pila that Lucullus's men had mysteriously abandoned at the camp. If the proquaestor wanted him dead, he'd have to execute him. He wasn't going to make things easy by eating some poisoned fruit.

Suddenly Lucullus understood that Caesar must have realized that the insane plan had in fact been a complicated plot to do away with him. His refusal to drink or eat now made sense. It wasn't out of disrespect for his superior; the young man merely wanted to stay alive.

Lucullus stood, walked to the table, and picked up a handful of the red fruits. "I like them," he said. "They're sweet, juicy. It's a fleshy little fruit with a pit in the center." He took another, this time without looking at the bowl, at random, and brought it to his mouth, ate it, and spit the pit on the ground.

Caesar understood the gesture. The proquaestor could have poisoned some fruits and not others, but he had picked the last one up without looking. He walked to the table, chose a fruit, and ate it, savoring the flavor. He spit the pit into his hand and placed it on a plate beside the bowl.

"They're good," he said. "They will sell well. Those trees are a good investment."

Lucullus nodded. "You may leave. Tomorrow you shall receive your civic crown."

Caesar gave his superiors a military salute and departed.

Thermus and Lucullus were left alone.

"I don't understand you," Minucius Thermus commented, not trying to conceal his confusion. "You've come to Lesbos to annihilate Caesar, under Sulla's instructions, and now you're going to grant him a military honor. Sulla will kill you. He'll kill us both, if I can't manage to convince you not to."

Lucullus didn't blink at Thermus's comments. He simply looked into his now empty cup. "Sulla is dead," said Lucullus.

Silence. Minucius Thermus was stupefied.

"Do you remember the messenger who boarded the ship?"

Thermus did not respond.

"That was the news he brought from Rome."

Thermus shifted his gaze, then, after a moment, spoke to his superior: "So . . . you're going to honor him?"

"He saved a man, another officer, risking his own life to do so. He probably saved many more lives in rushing the gates to the city and, without a doubt, his action is what assured Mytilene's surrender. He has earned a civic crown. I have to take control of the East. It's my mission from the Senate. Do you think the troops will respect me if I don't grant honors to men who clearly deserve them? Do you think I'll be able to maintain discipline if I don't conform to military tradition? I'm demanding of my men, but I always reward them when they act heroically. And that young Caesar has been heroic."

Lucullus was exhausted and irritated over having to explain something so obvious.

Minucius Thermus nodded in approval, in light of the former dictator's death. "With Sulla dead, nothing will be the same in Rome when we return," said Thermus. "Who will rule now?" he asked, concern creeping into his voice.

Lucullus pressed his fingertips together. "Let's see. Old Metellus is in Hispania fighting Sertorius. But there are several eagles on the ascent in Rome. Crassus is one of them, but to my mind Pompey is stronger. He is sure to take over leadership of the optimates sooner or later. But the populares aren't done for yet: Sertorius has grown strong in Hispania; and in Rome, this very year, Lepidus's rebellion showed that the populares still have a foothold there. I want a peaceful retirement. Killing Marius's nephew would single me out as an enemy of the populares, and it's not altogether impossible that they could return to power and seek revenge. I have no interest in being dragged into that eternal war between one side and the other. I am truly . . . exhausted. And, in the end, Sulla publicly pardoned Caesar, did he not?"

"He did," Thermus admitted.

"Well then, he's pardoned. He's earned a civic crown for his bravery. Whatever happens to that young tribune from here on out is no concern of mine. I'll complete my mission in the East, and then I'll plant those trees in Rome and send their red fruits to be sold in the markets. Mithridates, the social war, the civil war . . . I'm sick and tired of so much war."

He then stood and brought another of the red fruits to his mouth: "I got the trees in Cerasus. I'll call the fruits . . . *cerasi.*"*

Field hospital

As he stepped into the valetudinarium, Caesar saw the leader of the first century lying on one of the beds. It was the man who had decided to help him when he went to Labienus's aid.

"Are you well, centurion?"

The officer had bandages on one arm and one leg and could not sit up to salute. "The doctor says the wounds are superficial. I will recover, tribune," he answered, surprised that the young aristocratic boy would concern himself with his well-being.

"I hope so. Rome needs officers like you. What's your name?"

"Gaius Volcacius Tullus, centurion of the first century of the tenth cohort of the legion—"

"I know which legion you're in, centurion," Caesar interrupted him with a smile. "Perhaps we shall fight together again someday."

---

* Cherries, brought to Rome by Lucullus in the first century B.C.

"It would be an honor, tribune."

Caesar nodded and continued walking between the beds of wounded until he came to Labienus. "How are you?" he asked his friend.

He laughed. "I'll survive. You'd better hope I do anyway, or they might take back your civic crown."

Caesar laughed along with his friend, then turned serious. "I don't understand Lucullus. First he lays out a strategy designed to ensure we perish in combat. I'm convinced that Sulla sent him here to Lesbos with the mission to eliminate me. And you too, since you insist on following me everywhere," Caesar joked. "I can't make sense of this civic crown."

"There's a rumor going around the camp," Labienus said.

"What rumor?"

"They're saying that Sulla is dead."

Caesar sat down, slowly, on a stool beside his friend's bed. "How did it happen?" he asked. "A conspiracy?"

"No. An orgy at his villa in Puzzuoli. Too much food, too much drink, too many women. He died like the miserable swine that he was."

Caesar nodded, pensive. "That would explain things," he admitted. "Yes, his death would explain Lucullus's actions."

They sat quietly for a few moments. An instance of calm after so much chaos, bloodshed, and death.

"What are you going to do?" Labienus asked.

"Return to Rome," Caesar replied decidedly. "I miss Cornelia, my daughter, my mother, my sisters, everyone. And I miss Rome."

"Do you think Lucullus will allow it?"

"With Sulla dead, yes. We were successful in the diplomatic mission to Bithynia and have fulfilled our duties in Lesbos. If we ask him, he will let us return."

Labienus nodded. "What does a civic crown look like?" he asked after a few moments.

"It's made of oak twigs, with leaves and acorns," explained Caesar. He'd long been interested in everything military, something he got from his uncle Marius, so he knew all the possible honors granted by the Roman army. "It's not made of gold," he said, laughing again.

"It's not its value that matters. It's what it represents," Labienus said, placing his hand on his wounded leg and looking at his friend with eternal gratitude.

"It's what it represents," Caesar agreed.

The Trial

VII

SENTENTIA

FINAL VERDICT

LXXIV

UNANIMOUSLY

Basilica Sempronia, Rome
77 B.C.
Prosecutor's corner

CAESAR TOOK HIS SEAT BESIDE LABIENUS.

"You did well," his friend said, placing his hand on his shoulder.

The large crowd packed into the basilica was still applauding Gaius Julius Caesar's final speech. But his grave expression remained unchanged. He was arranging his notes, rolling up the scrolls, when a crown of oak leaves slipped out from between the pages, dry and brown.

"You brought it," Labienus said. "The civic crown."

Caesar smiled slightly then turned serious again.

"I hoped it might bring good luck," he said. "But I don't think even the crown can save us here in the Basilica Sempronia before these fifty-two bribed judges."

The senators of the tribunal crowded around Pompey.

Dolabella was staring fixedly at them. Caesar was as well.

Just then the accused turned his head and met Caesar's eyes.

They locked eyes and stared each other down.

It was Dolabella who broke away first, but Caesar knew that this was no sign of weakness on the part of the accused. Dolabella simply wanted to look back at the senators gathered around the president of the tribunal.

It would be a brief deliberation.

Caesar and Labienus could tell that the judges would not request time to discuss the verdict. They simply gathered around Pompey, murmured a few words, and received his nod of approval in response. In no time, they had all returned to their seats.

The president of the tribunal remained standing. Gnaeus Pompey knew that Dolabella was watching him; he knew that the sentence was unjust; and he knew that there were many more things at stake in that trial beyond Dolabella's corruption. Pompey had picked up on the warnings of rebellion in Caesar's speech. And he knew that his response had to send an unequivocal, indisputable message. He took a few steps forward and faced the crowd that had just cheered wholeheartedly for Caesar. His verdict rang out loud and clear through the basilica: "Innocent," he said. "Unanimously."

Dolabella was declared innocent by the tribunal. Innocent of all the crimes he'd been accused of: the creation of false taxes for personal enrichment, raping Myrtale, plundering the temple of Aphrodite. He was innocent, they believed, of generalized *corruption* since there had not been sufficient evidence to prove his guilt. Innocent on all counts.

Dolabella relaxed in his seat and smiled.

Pompey stepped back and sat on his cathedra, a grave look on his face.

The hundreds of citizens who had applauded Caesar's final speech were now mute. It was as if, all of a sudden, their hopes had crashed up against an immutable wall. Nothing would ever change in Rome.

Caesar remained seated, staring down at the floor. He was the living image of defeat.

Center of the basilica

Dolabella rose, exultant, and was soon surrounded by the optimate senators who had been in the audience and even some members of the tribunal, who were shamelessly congratulating the defendant.

Prosecutor's corner

Caesar remained seated.

The verdict was not unexpected, but the fact that it was unanimous came as a shock. Caesar had not managed to convince a single judge to dissent.

"Not a single one," he muttered to himself.

Labienus stood. "This place is full of armed men hired by the optimates. It would be wise for us to leave quickly. I've called some of your uncle Marius's men to escort us to the Suburra. We'll be safer there since the optimates and their thugs don't like to go into that neighborhood. They prefer to ambush their enemies in the forum. We should go, now."

Caesar was in a daze, as if struck dumb by the magnitude of his failure.

"Not a single one," he said again. "I'm finished, just like my uncle Cotta predicted."

Among the crowd

"Let's go, child," Aurelia said to her daughter-in-law.

Cornelia was looking at Caesar. "He's devastated," she said. "I have to go to him."

"No! We are not safe here!" Caesar's mother whispered harshly. "You can console him at home," she then added in a softer tone.

The girl had shared her husband's blind faith in a guilty verdict and was deeply disappointed by the result. But she did not have the energy to oppose her mother-in-law, so she simply obeyed. Both women left the basilica, escorted by the Julia family slaves.

On the street outside the basilica

Perdiccas, Aeropus, Archelaus, Myrtale, and the rest of the Macedonians who had traveled to Rome to attend the trial were gathered in the street. Old Orestes had stayed behind at Caesar's house; his health had continued to deteriorate to the point that he was too weak and ill to leave the Julia domus.

"We tried Roman justice," said Perdiccas. "Now we'll do it my way."

Archelaus and Aeropus exchanged a glance and then turned to the other Macedonians.

They all nodded.

Perdiccas pulled a dagger from under his tunic.

The others exposed similar knives.

"I want one too," said Myrtale, to their surprise.

Perdiccas looked to the girl's father.

"Give it to her," Aeropus said.

"Take this one, Myrtale," he said, handing her his dagger. "I have another."

Inside the basilica

Dolabella did not rise to greet Pompey as he approached. "Away with you all, by Hercules! I will speak to him alone," Dolabella said to the men around him.

"Do not make a move yet. The time is not right," Pompey said as soon as he reached Dolabella, not even bothering to congratulate him first.

Dolabella smiled cynically. "I knew you had no guts. Sulla was right about the boy. I put it down in writing for you the other day, but I see you don't have the courage to do what needs to be done. Caesar, Marius's cursed nephew, must die. Today. We cannot let him grow and transform into a new Marius. None of us were able to see it before, including me. Sulla could see it. But the fact that you still don't see it is deeply disappointing. Look at what he's done, at only twenty-three years old. He's taken on you, me, everyone. He defied Sulla himself at only eighteen. He received a civic crown at twenty-two. Do you truly want to wait and see what he'll grow into?"

"I exonerated you of all crimes. And it was unanimous," Pompey said, reminding Dolabella of his loyalty to him and to the optimates.

"It's going to take more than a verdict to stop Caesar."

"But he's broken, defeated. Look at him." Pompey gestured toward the door, where Caesar, shoulders hunched, head down, was shuffling clumsily out of the building. "His political career is over and he knows it. He was no one and now he will never be anyone. Killing him is unnecessary. And it's not the right time. Lepidus's popular uprising is still fresh in everyone's memory. We should not needlessly stoke the ire of the defeated populares."

Dolabella looked at Caesar and shook his head. "He'll pull himself back up. I won't allow it," he said, as if he hadn't even heard Pompey's warning.

Dolabella turned then to his slaves and the optimates' hired thugs who had been summoned to the basilica by Pompey, now gathered nearby awaiting their orders.

"Follow me," he said without raising his voice, in the authoritative tone that some people are born with and some can never muster.

The daggermen followed him unquestioningly.

Dolabella paid higher than any other senator, and that argument was as unshakeable as the verdict they'd just heard.

LXXV

ANOTHER KIND
OF JUSTICE

Roman Forum, outside the Senate building
77 B.C.

THE MACEDONIANS WERE STILL GATHERED ON A STREET corner near the tabernae veteres. They were waiting for Dolabella to leave the basilica. The plan was simple: they would follow him until he turned onto some less crowded street and then surround and kill him. They knew he would be protected by several guards. None of the Macedonians expected to get out of the skirmish alive. They weren't even certain they would be able to achieve their objective. But it didn't matter; they had to at least try.

They'd followed the advice of old Orestes and appealed to Roman justice.

Roman justice had now spoken. And it had not restored their honor or provided any restitution for their losses.

It was now time for *their* justice.

Lightning flashed overhead in the dark sky and immediately thereafter thunder boomed over the city of Rome.

It began to rain.

It had been raining for days, ever since the prima actio, already a distant memory.

"It's Thessaloniki. Alexander's sister is coming for him," said Myrtale in a low voice that was nonetheless audible to the rest of the group.

"There is no sea here for any mermaid to rise up from, my child," said Aeropus.

"Yes, but the river is swollen from the recent rains," she argued, placing her entire faith in the vengeful siren of Thessaloniki, which gave her something to hold on to. She had been dishonored and was despised by even many Macedonians. Perdiccas, who had saved her when she tried to take her own life after being raped by Dolabella, had hardly spoken to her since he began to understand that the trial would not restore her honor. The curse of Thessaloniki was the only thing keeping her standing through that ordeal, giving her the strength she needed to get up every day and attend the trial. But the trial had proven useless, futile. So Thessaloniki was all she had left.

"She will help us," the girl said as the rain fell harder. "He said it. Dolabella said the words loud and clear in the basilica. He said that Alexander was dead and buried." The girl looked up at the sky, eyes blazing. "And she heard it. Thessaloniki heard him. She will come for him."

They all covered their heads with their hoods and watched the door to the basilica. They stepped aside as Caesar's wife and mother walked by.

Inside the Basilica Sempronia, near the exit

"There's my mother, with Cornelia," said Caesar.

"No." Labienus stopped him. "We can't go with them, it's not safe. We have to take a different route."

"A different route?" Caesar was still stunned by his failure as he rolled up his notes and put away the civic crown that had not brought him any luck. At least not enough. He seemed unable to focus on the urgent matter at hand: escaping Dolabella's hired daggermen.

"Look," said Labienus, pointing to Dolabella, who was surrounded by some twenty thugs, all making their way through the crowd directly toward them. "They're coming for us. For you. Follow me. We'll get to the Suburra, but we'll take a different route. We have to keep those brutes away from your family."

Caesar at last began to react, eager to protect his wife and mother from Dolabella's assassins even if his own life no longer mattered to him. He would never be able to make a name for himself after his colossal failure in this hall of justice. The fact that the whole thing had been rigged mattered little.

"Let's go," Caesar said, following his friend.

Leaving the basilica, they were joined by a dozen of his uncle Marius's former soldiers.

"I'm sorry there aren't more of us," one of the men muttered. "Everyone is too afraid of the optimates these days."

"It's fine," said Labienus. "We'll go to the river and walk along it to the Suburra. We have to avoid the forum."

"That would be wise," the man replied. "There are several groups of armed men on the corners leading from the forum. And they're not our men."

Here, they came upon the Macedonians, and Perdiccas approached them.

Marius's men placed themselves between Caesar and the young Macedonian.

"Let him through," said Caesar.

The men made way and Perdiccas stepped in front of Caesar. "Innocent. Of all crimes. That's your famous justice?"

Caesar didn't know what to say. But the Macedonian man did not stick around to wait for an explanation. He simply walked away and rejoined his friends. He had other, more pressing matters to attend to.

The rain began to fall harder.

"Let's go, by Jupiter!" Labienus exclaimed. "Or Dolabella's thugs will be upon us!"

They walked quickly downhill toward the Tiber.

Outside the basilica a moment later

Dolabella and his men emerged from the basilica and looked around.

"By Hercules! Where is he?" Dolabella growled, fat raindrops hitting his face.

"They are headed to the river!" said one of his men.

"After them," Dolabella ordered.

Not even the worst of storms could stop him. Not now. He had suffered this young upstart's insults for weeks through the farce of a trial, but it was finally over. He'd played his part for the audience and now he'd settle his personal matters his own way. Everyone was rushing inside to take refuge from the storm, and that left the streets empty for him to execute his particular brand of justice. He was charged with adrenaline like the night when he'd hunted down Saturninus and stoned him to death in the Senate building. With Caesar, he would not use stones, but knives.

Beside the tabernae veteres

"There they are," said Archelaus without raising his voice, as he saw Dolabella and his men leave the basilica.

"Let's follow them," said Perdiccas, and the group of armed Macedonians took off in pursuit of Dolabella and his hired daggermen.

Forum Boarium, beside the Tiber

Caesar and Labienus were no longer walking quickly. They were running. Ten of Marius's closest men trotted behind them, fierce warriors who had battled bravely in Aquae Sextiae and other epic battles, but who were now old and flagging.

"We have to go . . . slower . . . or we'll be left alone . . ." said Labienus.

Caesar came to a standstill.

Labienus was about to say that they just needed to slow down a little, not stop altogether, when he saw why his friend had halted abruptly: a group of armed men, doubtlessly hired by Dolabella, was blocking the road ahead.

"To the docks," Labienus said.

They had nowhere to turn except into the port of Rome's central market. But once they went in, there was no way out.

The storm was gathering strength. They were soaked to the bone, but that was of no consequence. The Tiber raged past on one side, swollen from the several days of torrential rain Rome had seen.

"It's about to overflow," said Caesar.

Dolabella reached the port along with the assassins who had escorted him from the forum, now joined by the men who had cut off Caesar and Labienus's path. The senator now had over forty armed men to Caesar's ten veteran soldiers. When Dolabella went on the hunt, he made sure he would capture his prey.

Caesar and Labienus raced over the boards of the dock until they reached the enraged waters. Attempting to swim away down the turbulent Tiber was not an option. The river had already washed out entire trees and many boats whose ties had been ripped free by the rushing current.

Caesar walked back to the veterans. "Do you have gladiī for us?" he asked, looking at Dolabella's men, now advancing down the dock.

"We do," one of them said, handing him a dagger. Someone else provided one for Labienus, who took his place beside Caesar.

"They're going to slaughter us," Labienus muttered through gritted teeth.

"They're going to slaughter us," Caesar agreed.

It was clear that things would not end well for them.

They had managed, just barely, to save their necks in Lesbos, but there was nothing to stop the execution from being carried out this time.

The boards trembled as the angry waters shook the posts anchored in the riverbed. It seemed as if the dock might give way at any moment.

The optimates' hitmen stepped aside as Gnaeus Cornelius Dolabella, heavy and slow-moving, made his way down the dock that extended over the raging river.

"I'm here to finish what Sulla started!" he shouted at the top of his lungs to make himself heard over the sound of rushing water, howling wind, and lashing rain. "Did you really think you could sit there for weeks, accusing me before all of Rome, and not suffer any consequences? I stayed quiet during the trial because Metellus and Pompey and the others think we need to keep up appearances, but this farce ends today. For you, boy, the show is over. And it is not one of Plautus's comedies. You escaped that trap in Lesbos because Lucullus is a bumbling idiot, weak, like the rest. But I never fail: this time, you will not make it out alive. You die here, today, in the heart of Rome," Dolabella said, then laughed as he turned to walk away. "Kill them! Kill them all!"

Dolabella left his men, eager to get off the unstable dock that was shaking ever harder from the force of the current. He would wait calmly in the Forum Boarium, on dry, solid ground, for Gaius Julius Caesar's execution to be carried out. He was accompanied only by the two bodyguards who went everywhere with him.

The rain was now falling so hard that they did not notice the Macedonians approaching until it was too late. Archelaus plunged his dagger into one of Dolabella's bodyguards and Perdiccas stabbed the other one.

Dolabella suddenly found himself completely alone, surrounded by Macedonians.

"To me! To me!" he bellowed, ordering his men on the dock to come to his aid.

Myrtale was the first one to thrust her blade into Dolabella's soft, flabby flesh. She stabbed him in the lower belly. A painful wound but not very deep. Not mortal. The girl, despite her rage and hatred of the former governor, was not strong enough to penetrate the thick layer of fat around his belly. She was about to try again when Dolabella's hired daggermen arrived at a sprint, answering his call. They were highly motivated to save their boss; if he perished, there would be no one to pay them for the day's work.

Archelaus took a knife to the shoulder and old Aeropus, Myrtale's father, was stabbed in the back. In a matter of minutes, there were multiple injuries and two dead among the Macedonians as Perdiccas shouted for them to retreat and regroup around Myrtale several meters from where they had ambushed Dolabella.

The senator pressed his hand to his stomach, trying to staunch the flow of blood as the rain continued to pour down from the heavens.

Behind them, Caesar and Labienus, along with their men, rushed from the dock, which was growing more unsteady by the second.

More lightning. As if the gods were unleashing all their fury on Rome that day.

Rolls of thunder.

Water and wind.

Water everywhere.

And the river continued to rise.

Caesar led his men around Dolabella's assassins to join the Macedonians, who, without any words of welcome or display of acceptance, tacitly absorbed the additional manpower like another weapon as they once again charged at Dolabella. The assassins now only outnumbered their enemies two to one, not four to one as before. This made them uneasy, since they were not experienced warriors or even former gladiators, merely hired daggermen accustomed to ambushing unsuspecting victims under the cloak of darkness. Hand-to-hand combat against veteran soldiers and the Macedonians out for long-awaited revenge was not something they were comfortable with.

In a matter of minutes, there were many wounded and several dead among Dolabella's men without any losses from the combined force of Caesar, Labienus, Marius's veterans, and the Macedonians.

The senator saw that his men were retreating to the dock. He had no choice but to rush back onto the unstable boards extending over the furious Tiber.

Caesar and Perdiccas both hesitated, unsure of what orders to give. Their only option, with Dolabella and his thirty hired assassins packed tightly onto the narrow dock, was a frontal attack. And the hitmen would be more difficult to defeat without the element of surprise. They were fighting not only for money now but for their own survival, a lethal combination of desperation and deadly weapons.

Caesar, Labienus, and Perdiccas were still debating what to do when Myrtale raised her arms to the sky, gripping the blade stained with Dolabella's blood. Looking up at the clouds, she shouted a prayer: "Thessaloniki, beloved sister of Alexander the Great, who lives and reigns over us all! That man who walks the boards of the dock has declared your brother dead and buried! He said it loud and clear! Unleash upon him and his men the full force of your rage! Rain down upon him the fury of the Macedonians! May the gods punish him justly for his heinous crimes and drag him down to Hades!"

The Tiber roared as if a thousand gorgons had emerged from its waters, as if Neptune and the sirens of all the seas had concentrated their power into that river, at that exact point, in that exact moment, as the water rose up and crashed violently against the boards. In a matter of seconds, it had swallowed the dock, taking Dolabella and his men along with it. The senator's final words were a howl that no one heard over the tempestuous waters: "No! Damn you all! Noooooo!"

Perdiccas felt Myrtale embrace him as she began to cry.

He hugged her to him as he had done before the despicable Dolabella had arrived in their lands.

Caesar and Labienus, stunned by the Tiber's power, merely looked out at the river, where a wounded Dolabella struggled in vain against the current. They watched as the man thrashed about in an attempt to keep his head above the surface, shouting and cursing everyone and everything. Then, after a few seconds, they could see only his hands, then one hand, then nothing.

Only water, water, and more furious water.

Gnaeus Cornelius Dolabella was swallowed up by the Tiber and was never seen again.

The taverns along the port had to be rebuilt after that storm, and in them, they told the tale of the siren Thessaloniki who had dragged the senator's body to the depths of the sea. There, they say, at the bottom of some remote bay, she dances and laughs over his rotting corpse, lying at her feet in eternal torture, deprived of everlasting peace in the kingdom of the dead.

LXXVI

CAESAR, CAESAR, CAESAR

Julia family domus, Rome
77 B.C.
Half an hour after the fight on the dock

CAESAR AND LABIENUS BURST INTO THE JULIA DOMUS, THEIR togas soaked with rain and stained with blood.

Cornelia, terrified, threw herself at Caesar and began to pat him down, trying to find the source of the blood. "They've killed him! They've killed him!" she wailed.

Aurelia looked on, her face pale.

Cotta, invited over in Aurelia's attempt to heal the rift within the family, also witnessed Caesar's dramatic entrance. And it was true that his nephew appeared to be gravely wounded.

"I'm all right, Cornelia," Caesar said to his wife. "I'm all right. It's not my blood. It's the blood of Dolabella's thugs."

"They attacked you?" she asked, still patting her husband's toga with her small hands, as if she didn't trust his words, afraid he was trying to hide his injuries to keep from frightening her.

Aurelia told the servants to attend to the young men.

"They followed us from the forum," Labienus explained before taking a sip from a cup of water offered to him by a slave.

"From the forum?" Cornelia repeated, somewhat calmed after not finding any wounds on her husband's body.

"Yes," said Labienus. "We ended up at the port. They had us cornered, but then the Macedonians showed up and everything changed. They murdered Dolabella."

Caesar shook his head. "They didn't murder him," he said. "The Macedonians did not murder Dolabella. They executed him."

Labienus and Cotta both tried to speak, but Aurelia interrupted them in an authoritative tone: "The explanations and debates can wait. You two go to Gaius's bedroom and change out of those wet, bloody togas. Put on some clean, dry clothes, and in the meantime we'll set out some food inside the house, where we'll be protected from this endless rain."

Caesar nodded.

"So we really don't need to call a doctor?" his mother leaned in and quietly asked.

"I'm fine, Mother, it's not necessary. They haven't taken me down. Yet."

Aurelia watched him walk away accompanied by Labienus and Cornelia. Caesar's mother was left with that final word echoing in her mind: "Yet."

Roman Forum, outside the Senate building

Taking refuge from the rain between the columns of a temple, Pompey watched Dolabella's men speaking among themselves in hushed tones with clear signs of concern on their faces.

He could tell that something was wrong, but for the moment, he simply observed. Several senators rushed across the forum toward the Curia, their hoods up to shield themselves from the heavy rain. Nearby stood a group of Sulla's former soldiers who now answered to Pompey, after fighting under him to put an end to Lepidus's uprising.

Pompey looked toward the group of armed men awaiting his orders. He liked knowing that they were there, ready and willing to do whatever needed to be done that afternoon. Or that night.

Julia family domus
Nightfall

By the time they sat down to eat, there was barely any light left in the leaden sky. The rain had let up and only fell intermittently, as if the gods had taken pity on the soaked, muddied city with the Tiber River straining at its banks.

The family was gathered inside, safe from the inclement weather, as Caesar and Labienus recovered from the attack on the dock, discussing what had happened and, more important, what might occur next.

"It's justice," Caesar said. "Our basilica of justice, our Roman law, did nothing for them. So the Macedonians sought it out for themselves in the streets. Or rather on the docks, under a furious sky beside the enraged Tiber."

"That's not justice, boy. It's revenge," Cotta argued, livid. "By Jupiter! This will bring consequences. There will be more bloodshed, you can be certain!"

"Repeated injustice, Uncle, often leads to violent reactions. Dolabella and all the optimate senators who you seem to have become so cozy with lately have been committing constant injustices when it comes to lands, wealth, and rights. Just a few years ago, the Italic people rebelled against Rome, demanding citizenship and other fair concessions. Now the Macedonians have had to execute one of our shamelessly corrupt senators after our courts denied them justice for his criminal treatment of them. I agree that it is wrong—it diminishes Roman authority and, if it continues, the republic will become ungovernable. We have to make changes, profound transformations, starting with rooting out all the corruption. That's what this trial was about, Uncle. Only you and your friends didn't see it, or didn't care. Rome is headed for another large-scale civil dispute if we don't undertake a total restructuring of the distribution of rights and obligations—"

"Save your speech, boy," his uncle interrupted. "Whether or not you are correct, your political career was over the moment you agreed to take part in the trial against Dolabella. Your first appearance in the forum was a resounding failure. Hortensius destroyed you. I'd be shocked if you could even become elected councilman. I told you to stay out of it."

"You played dirty," Caesar snapped, looking at his mother.

Aurelia sighed and lowered her head.

"We did what we always do. I have to use any resources at my disposal to discredit an opponent's witnesses," Cotta said.

"So there are no limits to how far you'll go?" Labienus asked.

"There are no limits in a trial, boy, no, there are not. I told you a thousand times not to get in over your head, by all the gods."

"You are a traitor to this family," Caesar said, furious.

"I'm sorry, Aurelia," Cotta said, seeing the pained look on his sister's face. "I warned him not to get involved, but he wouldn't listen. Your son never listens to reason, only to unwise advice," he said, throwing a glance at Cornelia.

The girl was about to respond, but Caesar placed a firm hand on his wife's shoulder and she bit her tongue.

"This trial has been a strain on everyone," Aurelia said. "We all acted as we thought best and we all had our own reasons, but now it's time to put the whole thing behind us and try to heal our familial bonds. I sense that tumultuous times are again upon us and we'll need each other now more than ever. We have to stick together."

"I hear something . . . outside," said Caesar.

Everyone stopped to listen. Silence, not even the patter of rain, since the storm had finally relented.

Aurelius Cotta thought his nephew was simply trying to change the subject, to avoid the unpleasant conversation. But the boy needed to face the truth. His cursus honorum was already unsalvageable, but if he continued talking about reforming Rome, he'd surely meet a violent death in a matter of months, weeks even. Especially now that Dolabella had been murdered. The more radical senators would demand revenge and Caesar could easily be one of their first targets.

"I don't hear anything," said Cotta.

Julius Caesar ignored him and walked to the far corner of the room. The densely packed Suburra that spread out all around the residence in a maze of narrow streets was home to thousands of poor families, the maligned plebes of Rome.

"Yes, I hear something," said Cornelia, who had stood up to join her husband.

She stopped beside him as he nodded and held up a hand so that no one would speak.

Cotta sighed and shook his head, looking down at the floor.

Labienus took a sip of wine. It tasted of bitter defeat.

Aurelia walked into the atrium and looked up at the star-studded sky, not a cloud in sight. She heard something as well. It was as if a crowd of people were all shouting in unison. By the gods! She hoped it wasn't the senators' daggermen already coming for her son in retaliation for what the Macedonians had done to Dolabella.

"Do you hear it now?" Caesar asked.

Labienus tilted his head. He heard it too. He set his cup down and walked over to where Caesar and Cornelia stood.

Cotta frowned. He heard something now as well. The sound of shouting, a mob moving closer, howling something incomprehensible.

Aurelia turned to the slaves: "Open the windows to the street!" And then added, terrified, "But keep the door locked!"

The domina's orders were carried out and the shouts from the crowd surging the alleyways of the Suburra suddenly became clear: "Caesar! Caesar! Caesar!"

Julius Caesar turned slowly to his mother. She blinked. She couldn't believe what was happening. Cotta, beside her, was equally incredulous, his face showing absolute bewilderment.

"Caesar! Caesar! Caesar!"

The shouts ... cheers ... came ever closer. The people of Rome had been abandoned, left utterly leaderless as their representatives had been murdered, one by one, for the past decade, leaving the all-powerful Senate in total control. Gaius Marius was dead, Saturninus dead, the Gracchi dead, Drusus, Glaucia, Cinna, and Lepidus, all dead, along with so many others. But they had just found someone to replace those men. Someone young and energetic who had not been afraid to take on the formidable Dolabella before a corrupt tribunal. He'd known that the unscrupulous senator would buy the best lawyers; he'd known that the water clock adjusters would rob him of his time; he'd known that the odds were stacked against him. But he had tried anyway, because it was the right thing to do. And yes, he had lost. But the Roman people didn't seem to care about that loss; it had been rigged, like everything else ...

"Caesar! Caesar! Caesar!"

The unprecedented courage, boldness, and self-confidence that the young Caesar had shown before the corrupt senators had sparked a flame of hope. Maybe, just maybe, things could change.

"Caesar! Caesar! Caesar!"

"Are you sure, Uncle, that I've truly lost this trial?" said Caesar. "The verdict might not have gone in my favor, but it seems that the people view things differently, don't you think?"

Aurelius Cotta served himself a cup of wine, filling it to the brim. He drank steadily until he'd emptied its contents. His nephew was exultant as the cheers grew louder in the street.

"Caesar! Caesar! Caesar!"

It was the first time that the Roman people would gather to chant that name. The first in a long history of that name chanted in unison across the centuries. With Caesar, many things would happen for the first time in history.

The young lawyer stopped before his uncle. He was waiting for an answer to his question.

"The people, as you say, boy, might see things differently, but the senators do not. And they are the ones in charge."

"You predicted a few moments ago that I had reached the end of my political career, that my cursus honorum was hopeless," Caesar continued defiantly, "but I think perhaps this trial is not the end of anything. No, it's the start of everything. The start of something big."

"Caesar! Caesar! Caesar!"

His eyes still fixed on his uncle, Julius Caesar gave his orders: "Open the doors! I will greet the people of Rome!"

The slaves hesitated and looked to Aurelia, but the matrona gave no response. It was not her place to contradict the wishes of the pater familias, and so the doors to the Julia family domus were thrown wide.

"As your uncle, because you are family, out of love for your mother, I have to warn you, boy: the senators will come for you. All the cheering in the world won't change the fact that a death sentence hangs over your head. You should leave Rome, at least for a time. Until things calm down."

Caesar turned to his uncle, prepared to respond . . .

Inside the Senate building
That same night

News of Dolabella's death reached the senators along with the news that crowds were cheering for Caesar in the streets of the Suburra.

They all agreed that something should be done, but no one dared to make a rash decision.

Their top leader, Metellus, was in Hispania fighting Sertorius's popular rebellion. There seemed to be no way to put an end to the scourge of populares abroad. And now, suddenly, right here in Rome, was another figure for them to rally around: Caesar.

"The entire Suburra is cheering for him!" a senator exclaimed as he joined the other optimates gathered after the trial to discuss the developing situation.

"It would be unwise to kill him . . . Not tonight . . ." said another.

At that moment, Marcus Tullius Cicero stepped forward and stood at the center of the group, beside Pompey. Cicero had kept silent throughout the entire trial. Although he moved freely through the Senate, he was not clearly affiliated with the optimates and was not allied with the populares by any means. He always expressed perplexing opinions.

All the senators, including Pompey, gave him their attention.

"It would be unwise to kill him, but we should encourage him to leave Rome," Cicero said. "We cannot allow the young Julius Caesar to think he can win in the streets of Rome what he is unable to win in our halls of justice."

No one responded.

Someone had to set Caesar straight. At only twenty-three years old, he was already beginning to intimidate those in power.

"I will go," said Pompey, rising, his voice calm.

Everyone agreed. With Metellus gone from Rome, Pompey was beginning to emerge as their leader in the city.

Julia family domus

Caesar turned to his uncle. "I appreciate your advice, because I know that you give it as a concerned uncle. So I will follow it; I will leave Rome."

Gaius Julius Caesar, accompanied by Cornelia, crossed the threshold of the Julia family domus. The Roman people welcomed him warmly, shouting his name. The young man had dared to stand up to the greedy senators who hoarded the wealth and power for themselves, leaving the people they governed exhausted, submissive, stripped of all resources. He was so young, so inexperienced, so alone. But he was also something else: he was Marius's nephew.

"Caesar! Caesar! Caesar!"

Julius Caesar paused for an instant and turned to his uncle Cotta and his mother.

"You were right, Mother."

"Right about what?" she asked.

"I'm not strong enough to take on the senators," he said. "But I will get stronger, Mother. I will get stronger."

Cotta sighed.

Aurelia looked at her son, her eyes brimming. She was afraid for him, but she was filled with pride. Her son's unflagging bravery helped assuage her fears.

The cheers continued all around.

"Caesar! Caesar! Caesar!"

"Come, Cornelia, come with me. And you, Labienus, are you coming too?"

Cornelia and Labienus both stepped forward. Julius Caesar, flanked by his wife and his best friend, walked out to greet the people of Rome.

Epilogus

————

POMPEY WAS ESCORTED BY TWO HUNDRED VETERANS LOYAL to the optimates as well as another hundred daggermen and retired gladiators on the Senate's payroll. He knew that the streets would be chaotic and that the Suburra was a dangerous place for senators. But, as he had hoped, the more prudent Romans took to the safety of their homes as soon as they saw Gnaeus Pompey appear between the *insulae* with his display of military might.

Julia family domus

"You know the senators are going to kill him eventually, don't you?" Cotta said to his sister.

"It's possible," Aurelia admitted. "But maybe, by the time they manage it, he'll have changed everything. This is just the beginning. My boy is going to make his mark on the world. And neither you nor the senators will be able to stop him. My son descends directly from Julus, son of Aeneas. The blood of Venus and Mars runs through his veins. And I pray to Venus and Mars that they might protect him and guide him in peace, and in war. Because there will be wars, this I know. It is his destiny."

Outside, the cheering continued: "Caesar! Caesar! Caesar!"

Streets of the Suburra, Rome

Caesar, accompanied by Cornelia and Labienus, greeted the cheering crowd with a wide smile. Suddenly, from the southern end of the street, the cheers began to die down as the people were pushed aside to make way for the sturdy, corpulent figure of Gnaeus Pompey, escorted by dozens and dozens of armed men.

"Are they coming to arrest you?" Cornelia asked, gripping her husband's arm.

"I don't think so," Caesar answered quietly. "Not here, not now, before all of Rome. That would only make me legendary in the people's eyes."

"Are they coming to kill you, then?" she asked, even more terrified.

Caesar looked around. He saw that many of the people who had been recently cheering for him had not fled but had instead picked up stones or were flashing knives, their sharp blades gleaming in the light of the torches they carried.

"The senators only kill when it's easy for them," Caesar said. "They're here for another reason."

Pompey stopped a few steps from Caesar. He had also noticed the stones and knives held by the mob gathered there in the street. He knew that if he tried to arrest Caesar or attack him, rioting would break out across the city. And with the bulk of the Roman legions off in Hispania fighting Sertorius's rebellion, it was no time to incite a popular uprising in Rome. Pompey chose to be firm but cautious.

"I've come to give you some advice," he said.

"What is your advice?" Caesar asked, standing tall.

Cornelia was pressed against him, looking at the ground, trembling, but trusting in her husband's boldness and bravery. Labienus stood on the other side of him, as defiant as Caesar himself, ready to charge into combat for his friend and fight to the death if necessary.

"My advice is that you leave Rome," Pompey said.

A few beats of silence followed as Caesar and Pompey locked eyes in an intense, powerful stare. It was a clash of two emerging titans, a foreshadowing of what would become a confrontation of dimensions as yet unfathomable to those gathered on the streets of the Suburra in the center of Rome. It had started with the trial of a corrupt senator, but, thanks to Caesar, it had become something much larger. It could so easily lead to total chaos . . .

Caesar knew it was not the time or the place for violence. He'd learned that from Marius: fight only in the right place, at the right time.

"Very well," Caesar responded. "I'll leave Rome."

Pompey gave an almost imperceptible sigh of relief.

The soldiers and daggermen seemed to relax as well, and the citizens crowding the streets lowered their stones and knives. They were disappointed. Yet another leader abandoning them.

"I will leave," Caesar said again, "but I will return."

And as soon as he had uttered those words, he turned around, accompanied by Cornelia and Labienus, and began walking back to his house.

But I will return! the Roman people had heard him say.

The cheers resumed, with even more enthusiasm than before: "Caesar! Caesar! Caesar!"

Pompey, sure that he and Caesar would encounter each other again, turned on his heels. His men opened a path for him through the crowd of people cheering incessantly for the loser of the trial against Dolabella.

"Caesar! Caesar! Caesar!"

Victory or defeat, sometimes, is a matter of perspective.

A ship on the open ocean, Mare Internum
Two days after the battle
at the port of Rome

———————

Perdiccas's arms were bandaged, but his wounds were not deep. Aeropus, Myrtale's father, had perished in the conflict with Dolabella's men. Archelaus was weak, but resting in the ship's hold, recovering. Old Orestes hadn't had the strength for another journey and so had remained in Rome.

Myrtale embraced Perdiccas from behind.

"What do you think will become of that noble old man?" she asked.

They had been talking about Orestes as they climbed up to the deck.

"The Roman lawyer said he'd look after him," Perdiccas responded.

"Julius Caesar?"

"Yes."

"Do you think he will keep his promise?"

"He's never gone back on his word. His justice failed us, but it failed him as well. He fulfilled his commitment, and he helped us board this ship to flee Rome. He'll look after old Orestes. I'm sure of it."

They were standing on the ship's bow.

Myrtale hugged Perdiccas tightly.

"As soon as we arrive in Thessaloniki we shall marry," he announced. "And put all of this behind us."

She didn't say a word. She simply buried her face in Perdiccas's shoulder as the cool sea breeze enveloped them.

"We'll have smooth sailing," he said. "I can sense it."

"Thessaloniki and the other sirens will protect us," she said.

They stood in silence, listening to the sound of the wind in the sails and the ship's keel breaking against the waves.

"Do you think we'll ever hear of him again?" Myrtale then asked. "Caesar, I mean."

Perdiccas slowly nodded and, without taking his eyes off the horizon, responded confidently: "I'm certain we will hear plenty more of Julius Caesar before all is said and done."

ACKNOWLEDGMENTS

I *Am Rome* WAS MADE POSSIBLE THANKS TO THE HELP AND support of many people who were essential to the development of this novel.

First of all, I'd like to thank Alejandro Valiño, professor of Roman law at the University of Valencia for his crucial input. Professor Valiño's deep knowledge of every one of the multiple facets of a trial in Rome in the first century B.C., specifically 77 B.C., under Sulla's laws, was invaluable when it came time to re-create a trial in this historical context in that precise moment in the Ancient Roman Republic.

I am very grateful as well to Carlos García Gual, emeritus professor of Greek philosophy at the Complutense University of Madrid and member of the Royal Spanish Academy of Language, for checking some chapters of this novel.

Thank you also to Julita Juan Grau, professor of Greek at the IES Luis Vives of Valencia, and Professor Rubén Montañés from the Greek department of the Universidad de Juame I de Castellón, for advice on everything related to the different quotes from Latin and Greek that appeared in the narration.

Thanks to my brother Javier and my sister-in-law Pilar for being early readers of *I Am Rome* and communicating their suggestions on how to improve the text.

Thank you to my editors Carmen Romero and Lucía Luengo for being with me from the start of my professional career as a writer and thanks to Nuria Cabutí, Juan Díaz, and the administrative, commercial, communications, design, and editing departments at Penguin Random House for their faith in me during what has been, without doubt, my greatest literary challenge: narrating the entire life of a figure who changed the course of history.

Thank you to my agent, Ramon Conesa, and the Carmen Balcells literary agency for guiding me through the complex world of publishing in the twenty-first century and offering their constant advice and support.

Thank you to my daughter Elsa, for growing up alongside me surrounded by so many Roman stories and for loving me in spite of it all, because I'm her father.

Thank you to Alba, for appearing in my life to illuminate me.

APPENDICES

HISTORICAL NOTE

SPOILER ALERT: Do not read before finishing the novel.

JULIUS CAESAR'S CHILDHOOD AND ADOLESCENCE IS considered to be something of a blind spot in his biography since precise information about his public and private life was only recorded as he rose to prominence. We know very little about the first twenty-three years of his life, the period that this novel is focused on.

We do know for certain, however, that Senator Dolabella was accused of corruption. We also know who acted as his defense attorneys, the date of the trial, the pertaining laws at the time, and we know who served as the prosecuting attorney: a young Gaius Julius Caesar. Additionally, we know the outcome of the trial, that Senator Dolabella was declared innocent and exonerated of all charges. But all records of the trial itself, transcripts of the speeches given by both sides, have been lost to history. This makes sense if you think about it from the Ancient Roman perspective. The Roman patricians who served as lawyers, like Cicero or Caesar himself, only published speeches from trials that they won. What sense did it make to publicize a defeat? Any defeat in Rome was seen as a failure, regardless of the corrupt conditions under which it occurred. Only time would show that, although Caesar lost this trial, it served an important purpose. It made the people of Rome see Julius Caesar as a new popular leader: fearless, intelligent, and audacious, a perfect substitute for his uncle Marius. And that's what this novel aims to demonstrate.

It surprises me, nevertheless, how little has been written about Caesar's early life, the time in which he served as a lawyer, a crucial period of formation for many young Roman aristocrats seeking to make a name for themselves through trials in the Roman halls of justice. Without a doubt, Julius Caesar was the most skilled in this means of garnering publicity for himself. But there is an important distinction to be made: many young aristocrats tried to build their reputations by taking on trials that would assure an easy victory. Caesar, on the other hand, dared to challenge a powerful defendant in a trial where the odds were stacked against him. He was bold enough to stand up against corruption and injustice. To be certain, Caesar aimed to benefit personally from the trial, but he chose to align himself with the Macedonians, the aggrieved parties, the weaker side in this legal battle. It would've been easy for him to join Dolabella's team, like his uncle Cotta, but he took the side that he felt more honorable regardless of the fact that it was risky, danger-ous, and doomed to failure. In time it would become clear that this defeat, as stated in the novel, was not actually a failure at all. It was an inflection point in the life of Julius Caesar and the history of Rome. From a moral perspective, it was a win. If the goal was to make a name for himself, this trial certainly did that, marking a be-fore and after in his political life.

Since no records of the trial's speeches have survived, I've at-tempted to reconstruct them with help from Alejandro Valiño, Pro-fessor of Roman Law at the University of Valencia. With his input, I was able to imagine these sections of the trial under the laws passed by Sulla, which would've been in effect in 77 B.C. Any error in the recreation of events is attributable to me alone.

To bring this trial to life, I also turned to what could be called "parallel texts": published trials for corruption from around that same time, such as Cicero's arguments in his prosecution of Verres. These served as inspiration when it came time to recreate the law-yers' speeches and their interrogation of witnesses.

I have aimed for accuracy in the timeline of the historical events narrated in this novel, but this was a tumultuous period in Ancient Rome, and the date listed for a rebellion, siege, battle, or urban brawl can vary by months or even years depending on the source. Specifically, I have stated that the siege of Mytilene, on the island of Lesbos, coincided with Sulla's death, when—depending on the source consulted—there could in fact have been months or even as much as a year between one event and the other. In any case, the incidences occurred more or less around the same time.

Additionally, all the historical events narrated in the different flashbacks centering on Aurelia, Marius, Cornelia, Sulla, or Labienus, did in fact take place, but little is known about Caesar's personal relationship with his wife Cornelia and his friend Labienus. So, once again, faced with a dearth of information, I have had to fill in the blanks to build a plot. There is broad consensus, however, that Caesar's mother, Aurelia, was a tremendously significant figure in her son's life and that Gaius Marius, one of the most important Roman leaders of all time, had a notable influence on his nephew Caesar. Many sources refer to Caesar's marriage to Cornelia as happy and passionate, and agree that his decision to disobey Sulla proved very dangerous for him. Lastly, Labienus was well-documented as being one of Caesar's closest friends, although the specific origin of that relationship is unclear. More is known about the later friendship between them, but that's a matter for another novel.

When it comes to the two most important war scenes narrated in *I Am Rome*, there are many sources documenting the Battle of Aquae Sextiae in which Marius defeated the Ambrones and the Teutons, and I have based my narration on this existing information. Little has survived, however, about how the siege of Mytilene unfolded. All we know is that it was the first relevant battle that Caesar took part in and that he must've done something noteworthy, since he was in fact awarded a civic crown for his actions. We also know that the top Roman leaders were Lucullus and Minucius Thermus, and it would seem that the Roman troops pretended to leave the island in order to lure the Mytilene troops out into the open. But the names of the leaders of Lesbos, and the details of how the siege ended in the taking of the city, remain unclear.

The novel concludes with Pompey positioned as an emerging leader of the conservative faction in Rome; Sertorius, Marius's right-hand man, at the head of the popular uprising in Hispania; and Caesar, needing to distance himself from a Rome controlled by hostile optimates. The mounting tension between Caesar and Pompey through their parallel ascents to power as they each gain allies and grow to become mortal enemies will lead to another epic, brutal confrontation. All these conflicts will play out in future chapters of this legendary tale. Soon.

GLOSSARY OF TERMS

accusator: Corresponds to the public prosecutor who brings charges against the accused person in a trial. There was one lead prosecutor for every trial, appointed by the tribunal during the *divinatio,* a preliminary hearing in which different lawyers could present themselves as the best candidate for prosecutor.

Aeolus: God of the wind.

as: Coin used as legal currency in the late third century B.C. throughout the Western Mediterranean region. The *as grave* was used to pay the Roman legions. It was equivalent to twelve Roman ounces in weight and was round in shape like the coins of Magna Graecia, the Greek-speaking coastal areas of southern Italy. During the Second Punic War it began to be forged in gold as well as bronze.

atriense: The highest-ranking and most trusted slave in a Roman *domus.* They acted as overseer, supervising the activities of the other slaves, and were afforded great autonomy.

Basilica Sempronia: One of the four basilicas in the period of the Roman Republic, constructed in 169 B.C. by Tiberius Sempronius Gracchus, father to the famed Gracchi brothers who both served as leaders of the popular political faction. Roman basilicas functioned as courthouses and had no religious connotations until much later, when Christians began gathering in these buildings. The Basilica Sempronia seems to have been built in the center of the Roman Forum on lands occupied previously by Scipio Africanus which Tiberius Sempronius Gracchus either inherited upon marrying Scipio's daughter Cornelia or acquired through purchase. In the year 54 B.C., Julius Caesar would construct his own Basilica Julia upon the ruins of the Basilica Sempronia, which was apparently destroyed in a fire that same year or slightly earlier.

buccellati: Crackers probably made of flour, salt, butter, and water that formed part of the habitual diet of the Roman legionaries sent to battle. They weighed next to nothing, took up little space, remained edible for long periods, and provided a lot of the calories that a Roman legionary needed.

buccinator: Trumpeter for the legions.

bulla: Amulet commonly worn by young boys in Rome. Thought to stave off evil spirits.

calon: Slave to a legionary. They did not normally participate in combat.

carcere: One of twelve compartments in the Great Hippodrome of Rome from which a chariot exited. There was one *carcere* for each of the chariots that competed in a race.

Castor: One of the two Dioscuri, along with his brother Pollux, sons of Zeus assimilated into the Roman religion. Their temple served as the archive for the order of the *equites* or Roman cavalrymen. The names of both gods were used as interjections.

cathedra: Chair without armrests and with a slightly curved back. Originally reserved only for women because they were considered too luxurious for men, but their usage soon extended to men as well. Later on they were used by judges in trial and by professors of classic rhetoric. From there the expression "to speak *ex cathedra.*"

Charon: God of hell who transported souls of the recently deceased down the Rivers Styx and Acheron. He charged his passengers for their final journey, from there the Roman custom of placing a coin in the mouth of the dead.

clarissimus vir: Term of respect used to address a Roman senator.

civic crown: One of the most important military decorations that a legionary or Roman officer could receive. It was granted in recognition of a heroic action in combat to anyone who saved the life of at least one legionary or officer.

cognomen: Third part of a Roman name, indicating the specific family that a person belonged to. The protagonist of *I Am Rome,* for example, had the *praenomen* Gaius, was part of the Julia *gens* or tribe, and within the different branches or families of this tribe, he was a Caesare. The *cognomen* often originated from a characteristic or anecdote related to some distinguished family member.

comissatio: Time spent around the table after a Roman banquet. This could go on for hours, often lasting all night.

Comitium: Tullus Hostilius enclosed a wide space to the north of the forum where the people could gather. To the north of this space, the Curia Hostilia was built for the Senate to meet. In general, the senators congregated in the Comitium before each session.

corruptio: Generic term equivalent to "corruption" that referred to a series of crimes ranging from misappropriation of public funds to a more moral type of corruption.

cubiculum; cubicula: Singular and plural form of the rooms of a Roman home, generally distributed around a central atrium.

cum manu: A Roman marriage in which the woman passed from her father's guardianship to live instead under her husband's complete guardianship.

Curia: Shortened form of the Curia Hostilia.

Curia Hostilia: The Senate building, constructed in the Comitium by order of Tullus Hostilius, for which the building bears his name. Although the Senate could meet in other locations, their sessions were generally held here. It was destroyed by fire in the year 52 B.C. and replaced by a larger construction, the Curia Julia, in honor of Caesar, which endured for the rest of the Roman Empire until another fire destroyed it during Carinus's reign. Diocletian later rebuilt and expanded it.

cursus honorum: Name given to an Ancient Roman politician's career as they ascended to different political and military positions, from an *aedile,* or magistrate, to *quaestor, censor, proconsul, consul,* or, in extenuating circumstances, dictator. These were all elected positions, although the true validity of the elections varied depending on the degree of social upheaval the Roman Republic was experiencing.

de iure: Literally "of law," or "according to the law."

deductio: Procession through the streets of Rome carried out to mark different important moments of civil life. It could be held to mourn a death, taking on a funerary tone, or to celebrate a young couple that had been recently wed, with a more festive quality.

devotio: Supreme sacrifice in which a general, officer, or soldier takes his own life on the battlefield to protect the honor of his army.

dies fasti: Days in which a wedding or other type of celebration were allowed to be held and new projects or journeys could begin, because, according to the Roman calendar, these days portended well and were appropriate for such occasions.

dies nefasti: Days in which, according to the complex Roman calendar, marriages, family celebrations, and public events could not be held and no new projects or journeys could be undertaken, for religious reasons or due to a negative portent.

divinatio: When more than one lawyer wanted to prosecute a given trial, a special hearing, called the *divinatio,* was held so that the tribunal could choose the lead prosecutor.

domus: Typical dwelling for the wealthier classes of Ancient Rome, normally composed of a vestibule or entryway that gave onto a large atrium with an *impluvium* pool in the center. The main rooms were distributed around the atrium with the *tablinum* at the back. The atrium also contained a small altar for offerings to the *lares* and *penates,* gods who guarded the home. The more extravagant *domuses* had a second peristyle atrium behind the first, generally landscaped and surrounded by porticoes.

fasces: A bundle or sheaf of sticks tied together with an ax hanging from it. They were carried by the *lictores,* or guards that accompanied certain important Roman magistrates and politicians. The ax could be used to decapitate criminals, making it a symbol of the power over life and death held by the Roman magistrates as well as, to a certain point, the vestals, who were also escorted by a *lictor* carrying a fasces. This symbol was made into an insignia adopted by Mussolini in the twentieth century as representative of his regime's power in Italy and from there the word "Fascism" is derived.

favete linguis: Latin expression that means "hold your tongue." It was used by Roman court clerks to demand silence during a trial and was also used during ritual sacrifices, just before the selected animal was killed, to keep the beast from panicking.

februa: Small strips of leather that the Luperci used to playfully slap young Roman women under the belief that said ritual would grant them fertility.

flamen Dialis: The high priest of Jupiter, one of the most important priests of the Roman church. Caesar was named *flamen Dialis* when the populares controlled Rome, but Sulla later stripped him of said post. It would seem that the charge remained vacant for years, due to the many restrictions it implied for the private life of the person who occupied this position.

Forum Boarium: The cattle market, situated beside the Tiber River, at the end of the Clivus Victoriae road.

Fossa Mariana: Canal that Gaius Marius ordered to be dug at the mouth of the Rhone River to assure provision of supplies by sea to his camp in southern Gaul, where he trained his troops in expectation of a confrontation with the Teutons and other barbarians that threatened to invade Italy.

gens: The specific family or tribe within a Roman clan that shared the same *nomen*.

gladius: Double-edged sword of Iberian origin that the Roman legions adopted in the period of the Second Punic War.

glans plumbea: Small projectiles launched by Roman slingsmen, oval or spherical in shape, causing great injury among the enemies due to the enormous speed they could reach as they flew through the air in their descent.

gradus deiectio: Demotion or loss of official rank.

Hades: The king of the dead. Also, general name for the underworld.

Hercules: Equivalent to Heracles in Greek, illegitimate son of Zeus, conceived through his deception of Queen Alcmene. Hercules, through assimilation, was the son of Jupiter and Alcmene. His name was used as an interjection.

homo novus: The name given to a man who was the first in his family to reach the office of consul. Sometimes, the expression was extended to the first man in his family to become a senator.

Hymenaeus: The Roman god of marital relations. His name was used as an exclamation of congratulations for a newlywed bride and groom.

ignominia missio: Dishonorable discharge from the Roman army for reasons of cowardice or for having disobeyed orders of a superior during combat.

imperator: Roman general with command over one or more legions. Normally a consul was *imperator* of a consular army of two legions.

imperium: Originally the embodiment of Jupiter's divine power invested in consuls as they exercised the political and military might of the Republic during their mandate. This *imperium* implied the command of a consular army composed of two complete legions as well as auxiliary troops.

impluvium: Small pool or pond in the center of a Roman atrium that collected rainwater to be used for domestic purposes.

in aeternum: For all of eternity, lasting forever.

in extremis: Latin expression meaning "as a last resort." In some contexts it can be seen as synonymous with *in articulo mortis,* but not in this novel.

inquisitio: In the context of a trial in Ancient Rome, the tribunal granted this the period of time to the lawyers for both the defense and the prosecution so that they could gather evidence and witnesses. From this word stem the terms "investigation," and "inquisition," although this last word holds some negative connotations that it does not have in the case of Roman law.

insulae: Apartment buildings. Their construction, often without any oversight, produced low quality buildings that could easily collapse or catch fire, often leading to large-scale disaster.

iudices: Judges of a Roman tribunal. The number of *iudices* varied depending on the time and the laws in effect. It's difficult to be certain, but, very possibly, in the year 77 B.C. the judges on a tribunal would have numbered fifty-two. The makeup of the tribunal varied depending on the time period as well. It was a source of great political conflict when the more conservative senators ruled that a tribunal could only be comprised of senators, effectively doing away with judicial impartiality.

Jupiter Optimus Maximus: The supreme god, assimilated from the Greek god Zeus. His *flamen,* the *Dialis,* was the most important priest. Originally, Jupiter was Latin more than Roman, but once adopted by the Romans he was considered to be a protector of the city, for which every military triumph was dedicated to his honor.

lares: The gods that watch over the family home.

Laudes Herculis: Poem written by Caesar, probably in his youth, hailing Hercules's feats. Caesar's great nephew and heir, Emperor Augustus, later blocked publication of the text as he considered it to be lacking in merit and did not want it to interfere with his plan to deify his great uncle.

lectus genialis: Marriage bed designated and prepared for a newly-wed couple, adorned in the manner described in the novel.

legati: Delegates, representatives, or ambassadors, with different levels of authority throughout the long history of Rome. During the period of the Republic a military *legatus* commanded a legion and answered in turn to a *consul* or *proconsul.* During the Empire, the military *legati* reported directly to the emperor.

lemures: Spirits of people who have not been buried according to sacred Roman rites or tortured souls who must be placated so that they will not attack or harm the living.

lictor: Legionary of the Roman consular army who served as bodyguard to the supreme leader of the legion: the consul. A consul had the right to be escorted by twelve *lictores,* and a dictator, by twenty-four. Other magistrates could also be escorted by *lictores* depending on their rank or importance, such as the *flamen Dialis,* who was always preceded by one *lictor.*

ludus latrunculorum: Literally, "the game of thieves," this was a board game played with pawns similar to checkers or chess. The Roman army distributed their troops in combat like the pieces on a chessboard. In this way, they had several lines of soldiers who could take turns fighting on the front line, synchronized in such a way that the enemy could not break through the line of Roman attack.

Lupercalia: Festivities held with the double objective of protecting Roman territory and promoting fertility. The *luperci* ran through the streets with their *febura* to "whip" young Roman women under the belief that this ritual would encourage fertility.

luperci: Persons belonging to a religious brotherhood charged with a series of rituals to promote fertility in Ancient Rome.

magnis itineribus: Forced marches in which the legions were required to advance as quickly as possible if, for example, they had to intercept an enemy with great urgency.

Mars: God of war and of planting. The legions were consecrated to him every year in the month of March, when they prepared for a new campaign. A lamb was traditionally sacrificed to Mars on this occasion.

medicus: Doctor, a common professional figure in Rome from the third century B.C. onward. Some Romans, such as Cato the Elder, disliked the profession, due to its Greek origin, at a time in which Rome was distrusting of foreign influences. For him, the *pater familias* should care for the health of those under his charge. Eventually doctors, originally of Greek origin and later others formed in Rome, were regularly consulted for everything concerning health. The Roman legions incorporated doctors into their ranks to treat injuries in the *valetudinarium,* or field hospitals.

mile: The Romans measured distance in miles but a Roman mile was equal to a thousand paces, with each one measuring approximately five feet, although there is some debate over the exact value of these units of Roman measurement.

Neptune: In his origins, the god of fresh water. Later, through assimilation of the Greek god Poseidon, he became the god of salt water and the sea as well.

nomen: Also called *nomen gentile* or *nomen gentilicium,* indicated the *gens* or tribe to which a person belonged. The protagonist of this novel belonged to the Julia tribe, from there his *nomen* Julius.

oppugnatio repentina: Attack without stopping. When this order was given, the legions rushed on an enemy army, camp, or city without slowing their advance. This was intended to create the element of surprise, since it was more common for days to go by before a major battle after two enemy armies met face-to-face.

optimas, optimates: Singular and plural forms; literally meaning "the best of the best," an arrogant form of self-description used by the more conservative faction of the Roman Senate. They were considered conservatives in the sense that they wanted to preserve the privileges of the senatorial class over the other social classes of Rome and the *socii,* or allied peoples, as well as the inhabitants of the provinces. During the later years of the Roman Republic, the optimates had brutal clashes with the populares, the opposing political faction, who were more willing to expand the rights of other social classes beyond the senatorial patricians. As the novel reflects, these clashes led to violence and even civil war on more than one occasion.

optio, optiones: Singular and plural forms of the name given to the official directly below centurion in the hierarchy of the Roman army. An *optio* had the distinction of *duplicatus,* meaning they received a double salary and were exempt from some of the particularly grueling tasks in the military camp.

palla: Mantle worn by Roman women over their tunics when leaving the house.

pater familias: Head of the family for religious celebrations and to all legal effects.

patres conscripti: The fathers of the country; traditional form of referring to senators, derived from the ancient *patres et conscripti.*

peculatus: The crime of unduly appropriating public funds.

petitio: In the context of a trial, this is the initial phase in which one citizen could ask another to represent them as their lawyer. In the case detailed in this book, the Macedonians had to find a Roman citizen willing to bring charges against Dolabella given that they, as non-Romans, were not legally allowed to accuse him directly.

pilum, pila: Singular and plural of the wooden shaft up to a meter and a half long tipped with an iron rod of similar length. In the times recorded by the historian Polybius and, probably, the period in which this novel is set, the iron was incrusted into the shaft up to half of its length and fastened with strong rivets. Later on, the *pila* would evolve to substitute one of the rivets for a peg that would break off when it penetrated an enemy's shield, leaving the wooden handle hanging from the inserted iron so that the enemy would likely have to discard their defensive armor. In the times of Caesar, a similar effect was achieved with an iron tip that was impossible to remove from a shield. The weight of the pilum varied between 1.5 and 2.5 pounds and the legionaries could throw them an average distance of 27 yards, although expert throwers could launch them as far as 43 yards. In their rapid descent, they could penetrate up to 3 centimeters of wood or even a metal shield.

Pollux: One of the two Greek Dioscuri, along with his brother Castor, assimilated into the Roman religion. Their temple, called the Temple of Castor or Castor and Pollux, served as the archive for the *equites,* or equestrian order of Roman cavalrymen. The names of both gods were used frequently as interjections in the period in which this novel is set.

pomerium: Literally meaning "beyond the wall" or "outside the wall." In Ancient Rome it made reference to the sacred heart of the city, where, among other things, it was prohibited to carry weapons, a custom that was often ignored during the tumultuous times of the Roman Republic and Empire. The *pomerium* was established by King Servius Tullius and remained unaltered until Sulla expanded it during his dictatorship. It would seem that a line of boundary stones within the city marked the border of this sacred inner core.

populares: Certain members of the Senate and other representatives or magistrates, such as the plebeian tribune, who pushed for a redistribution of the lands controlled by the oligarchical optimates in the Senate so that the Roman people, and their allies outside of Rome, to some extent, could enjoy these rights. The populares were also in favor of an expansion of the right to vote and Roman citizenship, among other things. The origins of the populares' demands can be traced back to the end of the Second Punic War and the Gracchi brothers, grandsons of Scipio Africanus, both plebeian tribunes. Various plebeian tribunes and other popular leaders would continue to make these demands including Gaius Marius, uncle of Julius Caesar, and then Cinna, as supreme leaders of the popular faction.

Porta Collina: One of the ancient entrances to Rome through the Servian Wall, site of a brutal battle between Sulla's troops and the Samnites, in rebellion against Rome.

praecones: Clerks who assisted magistrates or judges in different judicial proceedings, from the call to elections, vote counts, and trials. In the novel, the *praecones* assist the president of the tribunal in the trial against Dolabella.

praenomen: A person's given name, which was followed by their *nomen*, or tribal name, and their *cognomen*, or family name. In the case of the protagonist of *I Am Rome*, the *praenomen* is Gaius. Compared to the vast array of names that we have to choose from today, the scant variety offered by the Roman system is shocking: there was a very small list of *praenomen* to choose from. Added to this fact, each *gens* or tribe tended to use only a small pool of names as well, making it very common for members of a given family to share the same *praenomen, nomen,* and *cognomen,* creating confusion among historians as well as readers of works such as this novel. I've tried to mitigate confusion by referring to the main characters as Caesar Sr. and Caesar Jr. when I felt it would aid clarity. The most common *praenomia* of the Julia family were Julius, Sextus, and Lucius.

praetorium: Tent reserved for the general in command of a Roman army. It was set up in the center of the camp, between the *quaestorium* and the forum.

prima actio: In a Roman trial, when there was a lot of evidence and many witnesses, the tribunal could break the trial into more than one session. The *prima actio* would be the first session of the trial.

primus pilus: The first centurion of a legion, generally a veteran soldier who was greatly trusted by the tribunes and the consul or proconsul in command of the legions.

privatus: Literally "private," used in the Roman Republic as a contrast to "public." As a noun it implied that a person was a private citizen without any elected civic or military role. Occasionally, if there was a military crisis, a private citizen could be granted *imperium,* effective military command over one or more legions, even though they were only a *privatus.* The Senate or the Assembly could designate a *privatus* with military *imperium,* but, since such an appointment was so rare, it almost always caused political controversy and conflict.

proquaestor: Like the *quaestor,* this person was in charge of supplies, provisions, and logistics for an army, but only for a specified period that varied depending on what the senate decreed.

pugio: Roman knife or dagger of about twenty-four centimeters long by six centimeters wide at its base. It had a central core that made it thicker in the middle, making it a very resistant weapon, capable of penetrating chain mail.

Pythia: Priestesses of the Oracle of Delphi in Greece who were believed to be able to predict the future. Initially the Pythia were supposed to be virgins but, after the rape of a priestess, it was decided that they should be women of a certain age who, nevertheless, dressed as virgins. The fame of their predictions spread widely throughout the ancient world and there were as many as three Pythia at a time during the height of their popularity, when the priestesses were asked to answer questions posed to the oracle from all over Greece and beyond.

quaestio perpetua: Special tribunal focused only on cases related to specific crimes, such as the misappropriation of funds and other matters related to corruption, as we saw in this novel. These specialized tribunals or *quaestiones perpetuae* were created as a way to avoid the *iudicium populi,* notoriously biased since, if the public admired a person, they would be unwilling to grant merit to even well-founded accusations. For this reason, it became increasingly more common for specialized tribunals to try very popular senators. This, however, gave way to other abuses of power as a popular senator would face tribunals of more conservative senators, clearly biased against them. To solve this issue, the Assembly of the Roman People passed a law in the year 149 B.C. stating that all cases of misappropriation of funds or abuse of power by governors of different provinces should be tried by a permanent commission of senators and *equites,* members of the equestrian class, in an attempt to create a more objective tribunal. Sulla later reformed these laws so that all tribunals were conformed only of senators, thus assuring *de facto* immunity for the senatorial class, given that senators never charged another senator accused by the Assembly of the Roman People, the people in general, or, as in the case in the novel, by foreigners.

quaestor: During the period of the Republic, this was the person in charge of supplies and provisions for the troops of the Roman legions; they managed expenses, among other administrative tasks.

quadrireme: Military ship with four rows of oars. A variation on the trireme.

quindecimviri sacris faciundis: Also called "*quindecimviri*" in the novel. Priests, generally appointed for life, whose functions included consulting sacred prophetic texts to help interpret events or predict future outcomes. These priests often consulted these books at the Senate's request.

reiectio: In the context of a trial in Ancient Rome, the lawyers, on both sides, had the right to recuse one or more judges of the tribunal. In this preliminary session of the trial, the lawyers argued their reasons for said recusals, including a judge's personal, familial, or business ties to the accused that might make it difficult for them to remain impartial. The number of total recusals that a lawyer could ask for during a *reiectio* is unclear.

repetundis: Corruption. Specific tribunals were established to try crimes of this category with the aim of reducing corruption across the different governmental institutions of Rome.

reus: The accused person in a trial in Ancient Rome. This did not imply that the person was incarcerated, only accused and facing a judicial trial.

sacrilegium: The plundering or destruction of a sacred temple. Considered a heinous crime.

salarium: Regular payment received by legionaries; initially paid partially or totally in salt, from where it takes its name. Salt was very important in antiquity not only for its taste, but also as a means of conserving food. Over time, the *salarium* was paid exclusively in money.

sarisa: Long lance between four and seven meters long utilized by the infantry troops of the Hellenic armies. It was introduced by Phillip II of Macedonia, father of Alexander the Great, and used subsequently by Alexander himself and his generals after his premature death. It would be employed as a common weapon by different Hellenic kingdoms for a long time.

scortum: Whore, prostitute.

secunda actio: In a Roman trial, when there were many witnesses and a lot of evidence to be presented, the tribunal could divide the trial into more than one session. This was the second session of the trial.

sella: The most simple of Roman seats, similar to a stool.

sella curulis: Like a *sella,* backless, but considered a luxurious seat reserved for those in power with curved legs made of ivory that could be folded easily for transport, since the seat went with the consul everywhere they traveled to fulfill their military and civil duties.

senatus consultum ultimum: Senate edict granting power to one of the consuls, or both, so that they could carry out a concrete action, such as arresting and, if necessary, executing someone deemed by the Senate to be an enemy of the state.

sine manu: A form of Roman matrimony considered freer than the *cum manu* because the wife did not have to sever all ties with her family.

socii: Allies of Rome; initially the Italic tribes who had established pacts with Rome. Over time, decisions that affected these allied people were made in Rome without consulting the *socii,* for which they demanded Roman citizenship in order to have a voice and a vote in all matters that concerned them. Their requests were rejected by the optimates and a large portion of the Roman people. Some popular leaders, however, were more willing to listen to the demands of the *socii.* The conflict reached a tipping point when one of these allied tribes, the Marsi, rebelled against Rome. The

Romans of Caesar's time called this "the war against the Marsi" and it was only later classified as a "social war."

socors: Noun equating to "help" or "assistance"; verb meaning "to give assistance." In the book, used as an adjective, it refers to someone inactive, who does not act because they are lacking in energy and vitality. In the specific context of *I Am Rome,* it would equate to calling someone a "coward."

solium: Austere wooden seat with a straight back.

spatha: A sword, slightly longer than a *gladius,* normally carried by officers of the legions or riders of the Roman cavalry.

spintriae: Coins or tokens depicting men and women engaged in different sexual acts. Possibly used by the legionaries in brothels across their immense empire so that they could make their wishes easily understood by proffering the coin indicating the sexual services they wished to receive.

sponsalia: Term that corresponds to "engagement," the pact or promise of marriage. In Rome, a ceremony was held in which the exact conditions of the marriage were agreed upon, such as the amount of dowry that would be provided for the bride and whether this would be paid by the *pater familias* in a *cum manu* or *sine manu* marriage.

status quo: Latin expression meaning "the current state or situation."

strategos: Originally, term referring to a magistrate of Ancient Athens. The term later evolved to mean a general or commander of the army of Ancient Greece. In the Hellenic kingdoms it was also used to indicate a military ruler and it is still used as a term for a military officer in modern-day Greece.

Suburra: Neighborhood in Ancient Rome where the more popular classes resided in a maze of narrow streets in stark contrast to the more noble neighborhoods. Curiously, the Julia family lived in the Suburra, a fact that helped Caesar connect with the people. In modern-day Rome the Suburra corresponds to the Monti neighborhood, where the Piazza della Suburra still exists today.

tabernae veteres: Stalls to the south of the forum, dedicated mainly, but not exclusively, to currency exchange.

tablinum: Room that gave on to the atrium, situated opposite from the entrance to the *domus.* This room was reserved for the *pater familias* and served as the homeowner's private office.

Temple of Aphrodite: An important temple in Macedonian Thessaloniki, equivalent to the Parthenon of this city. It was rediscovered in the year 2000 to great controversy when it came to light that the site had previously been used as a garbage dump. Some of the columns, statues, and other pieces can be viewed in the Museum of Modern Architecture of Thessaloniki.

terra sigillata: Ceramic tableware, normally decorated and of the highest quality, used to serve only the most important guests.

testudo: Typical battle formation employed by the Roman legions in which each military unit formed with their shields held either above, behind, or to the side, in such a way that the legionaries were protected on all flanks from possible projectiles as they advanced in combat.

toga viril: The *toga virilis* replaced the *toga praetexta* of childhood. This new toga was gifted to a young man during the Liberalia festival that introduced new adolescents into the adult world.

tonsor: Barber.

tribunus laticlavius: Military charge granted to young Roman citizens, normally of senatorial rank, so that they could gain military experience under the command of a *legatus.*

triclinium, triclinia: Singular and plural, divans that the Romans reclined on during mealtime, especially while eating dinner. It was common to have three around a table but more could be added as necessary for guests.

triplex acies: Typical battle formation for the Roman legions in which the cohorts distributed themselves along three lines of combat in such a way that they could take turns moving to the front line and thus prevent exhaustion of the troops as they fought.

trireme: Boat for military use like a galley ship. Its Roman name makes reference to the three lines of oars on each side of the boat that were used to propel it through the water. This type of vessel was used beginning in the seventh century B.C. in naval battles of the ancient world. Some historians believe that it was invented by the Egyptians, although others see the Corinthian *trireme* as the more likely precursor. Thucydides attributes its invention to Ameinocles. Armies of antiquity used these ships for the bulk of their fleets, although they added boats of greater size with more lines of oars such as the *quadriremes,* with four lines, or the quinqueremes, with five. Boats with six to ten lines of oars were described, such as those used as flagships in the naval battle of Actium between Octavian and Mark Anthony. Calígeno describes a true sea monster of forty lines built under the reign of Ptolemy IV Philopator (221–204 B.C.) but, if such a ship existed, it would have been more of a life-size toy than a practical vessel for use in a naval battle.

triumph: Parade that traveled through the streets to great fanfare in honor of a victorious general. To be considered worthy of such a commemoration, the victory for which the celebration was held had to have occurred during the general's term as consul or proconsul of a consular or proconsular army.

Tullianum: Underground prison in Ancient Rome dug beneath the forum, near the Senate building. It was extremely dark and filthy with horrific conditions for the prisoners incarcerated there.

tunic: Kind of slip or light shirt that Roman women used as an undergarment.

turmae: Term that described a small detachment of cavalry troops composed of three decury of ten riders each.

ubi tu Gaius, ego Gaia: Expression used during an Ancient Roman wedding ceremony. It meant: "Where you are Gaius, I am Gaia," originating from the prototypical Roman names Gaius and Gaia, used as generic terms for any person.

umbones: Large metal knobs usually situated in the center of the shields used by Roman soldiers to push back enemy troops.

valetudinarium: Field hospitals for the Roman legions. The Roman armies always designated a space to treat wounds incurred in combat and soldiers who fell ill due to the rigors of a military campaign.

vallum: Wooden fence built by legionaries to protect their camp. On occasion the *vallum* could be made of stone or embankments reinforced by trenches with traps for the enemies to fall into as they approached the camp. These pits were often filled with *lila* and *sudes,* stakes and lances that would impale anyone who fell in.

venatio: Hunting of wild animals for the entertainment of the Roman people in amphitheaters or circuses. The *venationes* held at the Flavian amphitheater, known today as the Coliseum, were particularly spectacular, as not only were wild animals let loose, but the animals' supposed habitats were also recreated, often meticulously. In the time of Caesar, these hunts took place in closed spaces as part of the entertainment that the city of Rome organized periodically.

Venus: Roman goddess of love, fertility, and beauty. Up to a certain point she can be seen as equivalent to the goddess Aphrodite from Greek mythology.

vestal: Priestess belonging to the order of the vestals, worshippers of the goddess Vesta. Originally there were only four but the number of vestals was later expanded to six and, later, to seven. They were chosen at the ages of six or ten from families in which both parents were alive. Their term as priestess lasted for thirty years and the vestals were free to marry afterwards if they desired. During their time as priestess, however, they were expected to remain celibate and safeguard the city's sacred flame. Any priestess who broke her vows would be buried alive but they otherwise enjoyed great social prestige to the point that they could pardon any person who had been condemned to death. They lived in a large mansion near the temple of Vesta and were also in charge of preparing the *mola salsa,* a sacred unguent used in many sacrifices.

vexillationes: Military units that were recruited temporarily or moved around from place to place as reinforcements for specific military actions or campaigns.

Via Apia: Roman road leading from the Porta Capena in Rome down through the south of Italy.

Via Egnatia: Long Roman road that connected the Adriatic Sea to Byzantium through the Roman provinces of Ilyria, Macedonia, and Thrace, on a route that traverses modern-day Albania,

Northern Macedonia, Greece, and Turkey. It was a road of great military and commercial importance.

Via Sacra: One of the main avenues of Ancient Rome that connected the Capitoline Hill to the Coliseum. Based on its orientation and the fact that it traverses the entirety of the forum it is very possible that it corresponded to the original ancient *decumanus,* the east-west street intersected by the north-south *cardo,* built as the starting point for all Roman cities. The Via Sacra was the road along which a victorious consul would parade in triumph after a successful military campaign.

violatio: The sexual violation of a woman or man.

viri potens: Term that categorized a young woman as capable, literally, of "able to bear a male"; used to indicate that she was mature enough to have sexual relations and become pregnant and therefore her hand could be given in marriage.

BIBLIOGRAPHY

ADKINS, LESLEY AND ADKINS, ROY A. *Introduction to the Romans: The History, Culture and Art of the Roman Empire.* Secaucus, 1991.

ALFARO, CARMEN. *El tejido en época romana.* Arco Libros, 1997.

ALVAREZ, PACO. *Somos romanos: descubre el romano que hay en ti.* EDAF, 2019.

ALVAREZ MARTÍNEZ, JOSÉ MARÍA, ET AL. *Guía del Museo Nacional de Arte Romano.* Ministerio de Cultura, 2008.

ANGELA, ALBERTO. *A Day in the Life of Ancient Rome: Daily Life, Mysteries, and Curiosities.* Translated by Gregory Conti. Europa Editions, 2009.

——*The Reach of Rome: A Journey Through the Lands of the Ancient Empire Following a Coin.* Translated by Gregory Conti. Rizzoli ex libris, 2013.

ANGLIM, SIMON; JESTICE, PHYLLIS G.; RICE, ROB S.; RUSCH, SCOTT M. AND SERRATI, JOHN. *Fighting Techniques of the Ancient World.* Greenhill Books, 2002.

APPIAN. *Roman History.* Translated by Brian Charles McGing. Harvard University Press, 2019.

ASIMOV, ISSAC. *The Near East: 10,000 Years of History.* Houghton Mifflin, 1968.

BARREIRO, RUBÍN V. *La Guerra en el mundo antiguo.* Almena, 2004.

BEARD, MARY. *Women and Power: A Manifesto.* London Review of Books, 2017.

——*SPQR: A History of Ancient Rome.* WW Norton, 2015.

BIESTY, STEPHEN AND SOLWAY, ANDREW. *Rome: In Spectacular Cross-Section.* Oxford University Press, 2004.

BOARDMAN, JOHN; GRIFFIN, JASPER AND MURRIA, OSWYN. *The Oxford History of the Roman World.* Oxford University Press, 2001.

BRAVO, GONZALO. *Historia de la Roma Antigua.* Alianza Editorial, 2001.

BUSSAGLI, MARCO. *Rome: Art and Architecture.* Ullmann Publishing, 2007.

CABRERO, JAVIER AND CORDENTE, FÉLIX. *Roma, el imperio que generó por igual genios y locos.* Edimat, 2008.

CANFORA, LUCIANO. *Julius Caesar: The Life and Times of the People's Dictator.* Translated by Stuart Midgley, Marian Hill, and Kevin Windle. University of California Press, 2007.

CANTOR, PAUL. A. *Shakespeare's Rome.* University of Chicago Press, 2017.

CARRERAS MONFORT, C. "Aprovisionamiento del soldado romano en campaña: la figura del praefectus vehiculorum," in *Habis,* no. 35, 2004.

CASCÓN, ANTONIO AND PICÓN, VICENTE (EDS). *Historia Augusta.* Akal, 1989.

CASSON, LIONEL. *Libraries in the Ancient World.* Yale University Press, 2002.

CASTELLÓ, GABRIEL. *Archienemigos de Roma.* Book Sapiens, 2015.

CASTILLO, E. "Ostia, el principal puerto de Roma," in *Historia-National Geographic* no. 107, 2012.

CHIC GARCÍA, GENARO. *El comercio y el Mediterráneo en la Antigüedad.* Akal, 2009.

CHRYSTAL, PAUL. *Women in Ancient Rome.* Amberley Publishing, 2013.

CICERO, MARCUS TULLIUS. *Cicero: The Verrine Orations I: Against Caecilius. Against Verres, Part I; Part II, Books 1-2.* Harvard University Press, 1928.

CILLIERS, L. AND RETIEF, F.P. "Poison, Poisoning and the Drug Trade in Ancient Rome." *Akroterion* Vol. 45, 2002. https://doi.org/10.7445/45-0-166

CLARKE, JOHN. *Roman Sex: 100 B.C. to A.D. 250.* Echo Point Books and Media, 2014.

CODOÑER, CARMEN (ED). *Historia de la literatura latina.* Cátedra, 1997.

——AND FERNÁNDEZ CORTE, CARLOS. *Roma y su imperio.* Anaya, 2004.

COMOTTI, GIOVANNI. *Music in Greek and Roman Culture (Ancient Society and History).* Translated by Rosaria V. Munson. John Hopkins University Press, 1991.

CONNOLLY, PETER. *Tiberius Claudius Maximus: The Cavalry Man.* Oxford University Press, 1988.

——*Tiberius Claudius Maximus: The Legionary.* Oxford University Press, 1988.

——*Ancient Rome.* Oxford University Press, 2001.

CORREAS, S. (ED). *Memoria de la Historia de cerca.* IX, 2006.

CRAWFORD, MICHAEL. *The Roman Republic.* Harvard University Press, 1993.

CRUSE, AUDREY. *Roman Medicine.* Stroud, 2006.

DANDO-COLLINS, STEPHEN. *Legions of Rome: The Definitive History of Every Imperial Roman Legion.* Thomas Dunne Books, 2012.

DESPERTAFERRO EDICIONES. *La legión Romana (I).* Despertaferro ediciones, 2013.

DUPUY, RICHARD ERNEST AND DUPUY, TREVOR N. *The Harper Encyclopedia of Military History from 3500 B.C. to the Present.* Harper Collins Publishing, 1933.

EDICIONES AKAL. *Historia año por año: La guía visual definitiva de los hechos históricos que han conformado el mundo.* Akal, 2012.

ELLIADE, MIRCEA AND COLLUIANO, IOAN P. *The Eliade Guide to World Religions.* Harper San Francisco, 1991.

ENRIQUE, CELIAR AND SEGARA, MENA. *La civilización romana. Cuadernos de estudio, 10. Serie Historia Universal.* Editorial Cincel and Kapelusz, 1979.

ESCARPA, ALEJANDRO. *Historia de la ciencia y de la técnica: tecnología romana.* Akal, 2000.

ESPINÓS, JOSEFA; MASIÁ, PASCUAL; SÁNCHEZ, DOLORES AND VILAR, MERCEDES. *Así vivían los romanos.* Anaya, 2003.

ESPULGA, XAVIER AND MIRÓ VINAIXA, MONICA. *Vida religiosa en la antigua Roma.* Editorial UOC, 2003.

FERNÁNDEZ ALGABA, MILAGROS. *Vivir en Emérita Augusta.* La Esfera de los Libros, 2009.

FERNÁNDEZ VEGA, PEDRO ANGEL. *La casa romana.* Akal, 2003.

FOX, ROBIN LANE. *The Classical World: An Epic History of Greece and Rome.* Penguin, 2006.

FREISENBRUCH, ANNELISE. *The First Ladies of Rome: The Women Behind the Caesars.* Vintage Books, 2011.

GARCÍA CAMPA, FRANCISCO. *Cayo Mario, el tercero fundador de Roma.* HRM ediciones, 2017.

GARCÍA GUAL, CARLOS. *Historia, novela y tragedia.* Alianza Editorial, 2006.

GARCÍA SÁNCHEZ, JORGE. *Viajes por el antiguo imperio romano.* Akal, 2000.

GARDNER, JANE F. *Roman Myths (the Legendary Past).* University of Texas Press, 1993.

GARGANTILLA, PEDRO. *Breve historia de la medicina: Del chamán a la gripe A.* Nowtilus, 2011.

GARLAN, YVON. *War in the Ancient World: A Social History.* WW Norton, 1976.

GASSET, CARMEN (ED). *El arte de comer en Roma: alimentos de hombres, manjares de dioses.* Fundación de Estudios Romanos, 2004.

GIAVOTTO, C. (ED). *Roma.* Electa Mondadori, 2006.

GOLDSWORTHY, ADRIAN. *In the Name of Rome: The Men Who Won the Roman Empire.* Yale University Press, 2003.

———*Caesar, Life of a Colossus.* Yale University Press, 2006.

GOLVIN, JEAN CLAUDE. *Ancient Cities Brought to Life.* Thalamus Publishing, 2007.

GÓMEZ PANTOJA, JOAQUÍN. *Historia Antigua (Grecia y Roma).* Ariel, 2003.

GONZÁLEZ SERRANO, PILAR. *Roma, la ciudad del Tíber.* Ediciones Evohé, 2015.

GONZÁLEZ TASCÓN, IGNACIO (ED). *Artifex: ingeniería romana en España.* Ministerio de Cultura, 2002.

GOODMAN, MARTIN. *The Roman World: 44 B.C.–A.D. 180.* Routledge, 2009.

GRANT, MICHAEL. *Atlas Akal de Historia Clásica del 1700 a.C. al 565 d.C.* Akal, 2009.

GRIMAL, PIERRE. *La vida en la Roma antigua.* Paidós, 1993.

———*The Civilization of Rome.* Simon and Schuster, 1963.

GUILLÉN, JOSÉ. *Urbs Roma. Vida y costumbres de los romanos. I. La vida privada.* Ediciones Síguenme, 1994.

———*Urbs Roma. Vida y costumbres de los romanos. II. La vida pública.* Ediciones Síguenme, 1994.

———*Urbs Roma. Vida y costumbres de los romanos. III. Religión y ejército.* Ediciones Síguenme, 1994.

HACQUARD, GEORGES. *Guía de la Roma antigua.* Centro de Lingüista Aplicada ATENEA, 2003.

HAMEY, L.A. AND HAMEY, J.A. *The Roman Engineers.* Cambridge University Press, 1981.

HAYWOOD, JOHN. *Great Empires and Discoveries.* Southwater, 2001.

HEMELRIJK, EMILY A. *Matrona Docta: Educated Women in the Roman Elite from Cornelia to Julia Domna.* Routledge, 1999.

HERRERO LLORENTE, VICTOR JOSE. *Diccionario de expresiones y frases latinas.* Gredos, 1992.

HOLLAND, TOM. *Rubicon: The Triumph and Tragedy of the Roman Republic.* Abacus, 2003.

HUBBARD, BEN. *Poison: The History of Potions, Powders and Muderous Practitioners.* Welbeck Publishing, 2020.

JAMES, SIMON. *Ancient Rome (Eyewitness).* Knopf Books for Young Readers, 1990.

JOHNSTON, HAROLD W. *The Private Life of the Romans.* ECM, 2018.

JONES, PETER. *Veni, vidi, vici. Everything You Ever Wanted to Know About the Romans But Were Afraid to Ask.* Atlantic Books, 2013.

KNAPP, ROBERT. *Invisible Romans: Prostitutes, Outlaws, Slaves, Gladiators: Ordinary Men and Women . . . the Romans that History Forgot.* Profile Books, 2011.

KUNZL, ERNST. *Ancient Rome.* Tessloff Publishing, 1998.

LACEY, MINNA AND DAVIDSON, SUSANA. *Gladiators.* Usborne, 2006.

LAES, CHRISTIAN. *Children in the Roman Empire: Outsiders Within.* Cambridge University Press, 2011.

LAGO, JOSÉ IGNACIO. *Las campañas de Julio César: el triunfo de las Aguilas.* Almena Ediciones, 2014.

LE BOHEC, YANN. *The Imperial Roman Army.* Routledge, 2000.

LEWIS, JON (ED). *The Mammoth Book of Eyewitness. Ancient Rome: The History of the Rise and Fall of the Roman Empire in the Words of Those Who Were There.* Carroll and Graf, 2006.

LIVY, TITUS. *The Early History of Rome: Books I-V of The History of Rome from Its Foundation.* Penguin Publishing Group, 2002.

MACAULAY, DAVID. *City: A Story of Roman Planning and Construction.* Houghton Mifflin Company, 1974.

MACDONALD, FIONA. *100 Things You Should Know about Ancient Rome.* Miles Kelly Publishing, 2004.

MAIER, JESSICA. *The Eternal City: A History of Rome in Maps.* The University of Chicago Press, 2020.

MALISSARD, ALAIN. *Los romanos y el agua: La cultura del agua en la Roma Antigua.* Herder, 2001.

———*Historia del mundo antiguo no. 55. Roma: artesano y comercio durante el Alto Imperio.* Akal, 1990.

———*Historia Universal. Edad Antigua, Roma.* Vicens Vives, 2004.

MANIX, DANIEL P. *The Way of the Gladiator.* I Books, 2001.

MARCO SIMÓN, FRANCISCO; PINA POLO, FRANCISCO AND REMESAL RODRÍGUEZ, JOSÉ (EDS). *Viajeros, peregrinos y aventureros en el mundo antiguo.* Publicacions i Edicions de la Universitat de Barcelona, 2010.

MARQUÉS, NÉSTOR. *Un año en la antigua Roma.* Espasa, 2018.

MARTÍN, REGIS F. *Los doce césares: Del mito a la realidad.* Aldebarán, 1998.

MATTESINI, SILVANO. *Gladiators.* Archeos, 2009.

MATYSZAK, PHILIP. *The Enemies of Rome: From Hannibal to Attila the Hun.* Thames and Hudson, 2009.

———*Legionary: The Roman Soldier's (Unofficial) Manual.* Thames and Hudson, 2009.

———*Ancient Rome on 5 Denarii a Day.* Thames and Hudson, 2008.

———24 Hours in Ancient Rome: A Day in the Life of the People Who Lived There. Michael O'Mara Books, 2017.

MCKEOWN, J.C. A Cabinet of Roman Curiosities: Strange Tales and Surprising Facts from the World's Greatest Empire. Oxford University Press, 2010.

MELANI, CHIARA; FONTANELLA, FRANCESCA AND CECCONI, GIOVANNI ALBERTO. Atlas ilustrado de la Antigua Roma: De los orígenes a la caída del Imperio. Susaeta, 2002.

MENA SEGARRA, ENRIQUE. La civilización romana. Cincel Kapelusz, 1982.

MONTANELLI, INDRO. Rome: The First Thousand Years. Collins, 1962.

NAVARRO, FRANCESC (ED). Historia Universal. Atlas Histórico. Salvat-El País, 2005.

NEIRA, LUZ (ED). Representaciones de mujeres en los mosaicos romanos y su impacto en el imaginario de estereotipos femeninos. Creaciones Vincent Gabrielle, 2011.

NICOLAUS OF DAMASCUS. The Life of Augustus and The Autobiography. Cambridge University Press, 2021.

NIETO, JOSÉ. Historia de Roma: Día a día en la Roma antigua. Libsa, 2006.

NOGALES BASARRATE, TRINIDAD. Espectaculos en Augusta Emérita. Ministerio de Educación, Cultura y Deporte, Museo Romano de Mérida, 2000.

NOSSOV, KONSTANTIN. Gladiator: Rome's Bloody Spectacle. Osprey Publishing, 2009.

NOVILLO LÓPEZ, MIGUEL ANGEL. Breve historia de Julio César. Nowtilus, 2011.

PAYNE, ROBERT. Ancient Rome. Horizon, 2005.

PÉREZ MÍNGUEZ, R. Los trabajos y los días de un ciudadano romano. Diputación Provincial, 2008.

PISA SÁNCHEZ, JORGE. Breve historia de Hispania. Nowtilus, 2009.

POLYBIUS. The Rise of the Roman Empire. Translated by Ian Scott-Kilvert. Penguin, 1979.

POMEROY, SARAH. Goddesses, Whores, Wives, and Slaves: Women in Classical Antiquity. Schocken, 1995.

POTTER, DAVID. Emperors of Rome: The Story of Imperial Rome from Julius Caesar to the Last Emperor. Quercus, 2011.

PLUTARCH. Lives, Volume VIII: Sertorius and Eumenes. Phocion and Cato the Younger. Translated by Bernadotte Perrin. Harvard University Press, 1919.

QUESADA SANZ, FERNANDO. Armas de Grecia y Roma. La Esfera de Almuzara, 2017.

RAMOS, JAVIER. Eso no estaba en mi libro de historia de Roma. Almuzara, 2017.

RIBAS, JOSÉ MARÍA AND SERRANO-VICENTE, MARTÍN. El derecho en Roma (segunda edición corregida y aumentada). Comares historia, 2012.

ROSTOVTZEFF, MICHAEL. The Social and Economic History of the Hellenistic World, Vol. 1. Oxford University Press, 1986.

———The Social and Economic History of the Hellenistic World, Vol. 2. Oxford University Press, 1986.

SAMPSON, GARETH C. Rome's Great Eastern War: Lucullus, Pompey and the Conquest of the East, 74–62 B.C. Pen and Sword Books, 2021.

SANTOS YANGUAS, NARCISO. *Textos para la historia Antigua de Roma.* Cátedra, 1980.

SCARRE, CHRISTOPHER. *The Penguin Historical Atlas of Ancient Rome.* Penguin, 1995.

SEGURA MURGUÍA, SANTIAGO. *El teatro en Grecia y Roma.* Zidor Consulting, 2001.

SMITH, WILLIAM. *A Dictionary of Greek and Roman Antiquities.* John Murray, 1875.

SUETONIUS. *The Twelve Caesars.* Penguin Classics, 2007.

SYME, RONALD. *The Roman Revolution.* Oxford University Press, 2002.

TONER, JERRY. *Popular Culture in Ancient Rome.* Polity, 2009.

VALENTÍ FIOL, EDUARDO. *Sintaxis latina.* Crítica, 2017.

VEYNE, PAUL. *Sexo y poder en Roma.* Paidós Orígenes, 2010.

WATTS, EDWARD J. *Mortal Republic: How Rome Fell into Tyranny.* Basic Books, 2018.

WILKES, JOHN. *The Roman Army (Cambridge Introduction to World History).* Cambridge University Press, 1973.

WISDOM, STEPHEN AND McBRIDE, ANGUS. *Gladiators: 100 BC–AD200.* Osprey Publishing, 2001.

STRUCTURE OF
THE NOVEL

THE TRIAL

CRIME: CORRUPTION

Accused: Senator Gnaeus Cornelius Dolabella
Prosecuting Attorney: Gaius Julius Caesar
Defense Attorneys: Hortensius and Aurelius Cotta
Location: Basilica Sempronia, Rome
Date: 77 B.C.

THE TRIAL I: *Petitio*

(77 B.C.)

THE TRIAL II: *Divinatio*

(77 B.C.)

THE TRIAL III: *Inquisitio*

(77 B.C.)

THE TRIAL IV: *Reiectio*

(77 B.C.)

Reus: DOLABELLA

(78 B.C.)

THE TRIAL V: *Prima Actio*

(77 B.C.)

THE TRIAL VI: *Secunda Actio*

(77 B.C.)

THE TRIAL VII: *Sententia*

(77 B.C.)

GAIUS JULIUS CAESAR

Childhood and Youth (Flashbacks)

Memoria Prima: AURELIA

(100 B.C.)

Memoria Secunda: GAIUS MARIUS

(91–88 B.C.)

Memoria in Memoria: AQUAE SEXTIAE

(105–102 B.C.)

Memoria Tertia: CORNELIA

(88–82 B.C.)

Memoria Quarta: SULLA

(82–81 B.C.)

Memoria Quinta: LABIENUS

(80–78 B.C.)

Dramatis personae

JULIUS CAESAR (GAIUS JULIUS CAESAR)
LAWYER AND MILITARY TRIBUNE

JULIUS CAESAR'S FAMILY

Aurelia: Julius Caesar's mother
Julius Caesar Sr.: Julius Caesar's father
Cornelia: Julius Caesar's wife
Cotta (Aurelius Cotta): Julius Caesar's maternal uncle
Julia Major: Julius Caesar's sister
Julia Minor: Julius Caesar's sister
Marcus Antonius Gnipho: Julius Caesar's tutor

OPTIMATE LEADERS AND OTHER SENATORS

Cicero (Marcus Tullius Cicero): lawyer and senator
Crassus (Marcus Licinius Crassus): young senator
Dolabella (Gnaeus Cornelius Dolabella): senator and governor
Lucullus (Lucius Licinius Lucullus): general and Eastern *proquaestor*
Metellus (Quintus Caecilius Metellus Pius): leader of the optimate party
Pompey (Gnaeus Pompeius Magnus): judge and senator
Sulla (Lucius Cornelius Sulla): dictator
Thermus (Minucius Thermus): propraetor at Lesbos

POPULIST LEADERS AND SENATORS

Cinna (Lucius Cornelius Cinna): populist leader,
senator, and consul, father of Cornelia
Fimbria (Gaius Flavius Fimbria): *legatus*
Flaccus (Valerius Flaccus): consul
Glaucia (Gaius Servilius Glaucia): plebeian tribune and praetor
Labienus (Titus Labienus): Caesar's close friend, military tribune
Marius (Gaius Marius): populist leader, seven-time consul,
Julius Caesar's paternal uncle
Saturninus (Lucius Appuleius Saturninus):
plebeian tribune
Sertorius (Quintus Sertorius): populist leader,
Gaius Marius's most trusted man
Rufus (Sulpicius Rufus): plebeian tribune

MACEDONIAN CITIZENS

Aeropus: Myrtale's father, Macedonian nobleman
Archelaus: young nobleman
Myrtale: young noblewoman, daughter of Aeropus
Orestes: elder nobleman
Perdiccas: young nobleman, betrothed to Myrtale

MILITARY LEADERS ON THE ISLAND OF LESBOS

Anaxagoras: satrap of Mytilene
Pittacus: second-in-command of Mytilene
Theophanes: local aristocratic leader of Mytilene

OTHER CHARACTERS

Annia: Cornelia's mother
Gaius Volcacius Tullus: centurion
Claudius Marcellus: high-ranking Roman officer
Cornelius Fagites: Roman centurion
Hortensius: lawyer
Marcus: Roman engineer
Metrobius: actor
Mithridates VI: King of Pontus, Rome's rival in the East
Mucia: spice merchant in Rome
Sextus: ship's captain
Sorex: actor
Valeria: Sulla's wife
Vetus: Roman engineer
Teutobod: king of the Teutons
Praecones: members of the serving class in Ancient Rome,
including court clerks, slaves, *atrienses,* legionaries,
Roman officers, Pontic officers, water clock adjusters,
among other anonymous Roman citizens

About the Author

———

SANTIAGO POSTEGUILLO is the bestselling author of historical novels in the Spanish language, with more than 4 million readers. His numerous novels set in the ancient world include the Planeta Prize–winning *I, Julia* (about Rome's most powerful empress) and his Scipio Africanus trilogy. He combines his writing with his work as a tenured professor of English language and literature at the Jaume I University in Castellón. Posteguillo holds a doctorate from the University of Valencia and has studied literature, linguistics, and translation at various universities in the United States and the United Kingdom.

About the Translator

———

FRANCES RIDDLE has translated numerous Spanish-language authors including Isabel Allende, Claudia Piñeiro, Leila Guerriero, María Fernanda Ampuero, and Sara Gallardo. Her translation of *Elena Knows* by Claudia Piñeiro was shortlisted for the International Booker Prize and the Reina Sofia Prize in 2022, and her translation of *Theatre of War* by Andrea Jeftanovic was granted an English PEN Award in 2020. Her work has appeared in journals such as *Granta*, *Electric Literature*, and *Southwest Review*, among others. Originally from Houston, Texas, she lives in Buenos Aires, Argentina.

About the Type

———

This book was set in Bulmer, a typeface designed in the late eighteenth century by the London type cutter William Martin (1757–1830). The typeface was created especially for the Shakespeare Press, directed by William Bulmer (1757–1830)—hence the font's name. Bulmer is considered to be a transitional typeface, containing characteristics of old-style and modern designs. It is recognized for its elegantly proportioned letters, with their long ascenders and descenders.